FANTASTIC STORIES PRESENTS THE

WORLDS OF IF
SUPER PACK #1

Positronic Publishing
PO Box 632
Floyd VA 24091

ISBN 13: 978-1-5154-1154-3

First Positronic Publishing Edition
10 9 8 7 6 5 4 3 2 1

FANTASTIC STORIES PRESENTS THE

WORLDS OF IF
SUPER PACK #1

THE SUPER PACK EBOOK SERIES

If you enjoyed this Super Pack you may wish to find the other books in this series. We endeavor to provide you with a quality product. But since many of these stories have been scanned typos do occasionally creep in. If you spot one please share it with us at positronicpress@yahoo.com so that we can fix it. We occasionally add additional stories to some of our Super Packs so make sure that you download fresh copies of your Super Packs from time to time to get the latest edition.

Science Fiction Super Pack #1: ISBN 978-1-63384-240-3
Science Fiction Super Pack #2: ISBN 978-1-51540-477-4
Science Fiction Super Pack #3: (Forthcoming)
Fantasy Super Pack #1: ISBN 978-1-63384-282-3
Fantasy Super Pack #2: (Forthcoming)
Conan the Barbarian Super Pack: ISBN 978-1-63384-292-2
Lord Dunsany Super Pack: ISBN 978-1-63384-725-5
Philip K. Dick Super Pack: ISBN 978-1-63384-799-6
The Pirate Super Pack # 1: ISBN 978-1-51540-193-3
The Pirate Super Pack # 2: ISBN 978-1-51540-196-4
Harry Harrison Super Pack: ISBN 978-1-51540-217-6
Andre Norton Super Pack: ISBN 978-1-51540-262-6
Marion Zimmer Bradley Super Pack: ISBN 978-1-51540-287-9
Frederik Pohl Super Pack: ISBN 978-1-51540-289-3
King Arthur Super Pack: ISBN 978-1-51540-306-7
Alan E. Nourse Super Pack: ISBN 978-1-51540-393-7
Space Science Fiction Super Pack: ISBN 978-1-51540-440-8
Wonder Stories Super Pack: ISBN 978-1-51540-454-5
Galaxy Science Fiction Super Pack #1:ISBN 978-1-51540-524-5
Galaxy Science Fiction Super Pack #2: 978-1-5154-0577-1
Science Fiction Novel Super Pack #1: ISBN 978-1-51540-363-0
Science Fiction Novel Super Pack #2: (Forthcoming)
Dragon Super Pack #1: Forthcoming
Weird Tales Super Pack #1: ISBN 978-1-5154-0548-1
Weird Tales Super Pack #2: (Forthcoming)
Poul Anderson Super Pack: ISBN 978-1-5154-0609-9
Fantastic Universe Super Pack #1: ISBN 978-1-5154-0981-6
Fantastic Universe Super Pack #2: ISBN 978-1-5154-0654-9
Fantastic Universe Super Pack #3: ISBN 978-1-5154-0655-6
Imagination Super Pack: ISBN 978-1-5154-1089-8
Planet Stories Super Pack: ISBN (Forthcoming)
Worlds of If Super Pack #1: ISBN (Forthcoming)
Worlds of If Super Pack #2: ISBN (Forthcoming)
Worlds of If Super Pack #3: ISBN (Forthcoming)

ACKNOWLEDGMENTS

"The Snowbank Orbit" by Fritz Leiber originally appeared in *If, Worlds of Science Fiction*, September 1962.

"The Victor" by Bryce Walton originally appeared in *If, Worlds of Science Fiction*, March 1953.

"Breeder Reaction" by Winston Marks originally appeared in *If, Worlds of Science Fiction*, April 1954.

"Turning Point" by Alfred Coppel originally appeared in *If, Worlds of Science Fiction*, November 1953.

"Masters of Space" by Edward E. Smith & E. Everett Evans originally appeared in *If, Worlds of Science Fiction*, November 1961 and January 1962.

"Cultural Exchange' by Keith Laumer originally appeared in *If, Worlds of Science Fiction*, September 1962.

"The Lonely Ones" by Edward W. Ludwig originally appeared in *If, Worlds of Science Fiction*, July 1953.

"The Kenzie Report" by Mark Clifton originally appeared in *If, Worlds of Science Fiction*, May 1953.

"The Very Secret Agent" by Mari Wolf originally appeared in *If, Worlds of Science Fiction*, November 1954.

"Irresistible Weapon" by H. B. Fyfe originally appeared in *If, Worlds of Science Fiction*, July 1953.

"In the Garden" by R. A. Lafferty originally appeared in *If, Worlds of Science Fiction*, March 1961.

"The Eyes Have it" by James McKimmey, Jr. originally appeared in *If, Worlds of Science Fiction*, November 1953.

"Trees Are Where You Find Them" by Arthur Dekker Savage originally appeared in *If, Worlds of Science Fiction*, November 1953.

"The Real Hard Sell" by William W. Stuart originally appeared in *If, Worlds of Science Fiction*, July 1961.

"Waste Not, Want" by Dave Dryfoos originally appeared in *If, Worlds of Science Fiction*, September 1954.

"The Last Supper" by T. D. Hamm originally appeared in *If, Worlds of Science Fiction*, September 1952.

"Letter of the Law" by Alan E. Nourse originally appeared in *If, Worlds of Science Fiction*, January 1954.

"Sweet Their Blood and Sticky" by Albert R. Teichner originally appeared in *If, Worlds of Science Fiction*, November 1961.

"The Last Place on Earth" by Jim Harmon originally appeared in *If, Worlds of Science Fiction*, January 1962.

"Quiet, Please" by Kevin Scott originally appeared in *If, Worlds of Science Fiction*, November 1961.

"Service with a Smile" by Charles L. Fontenay originally appeared in *If, Worlds of Science Fiction*, June 1958.

"Time Fuze" by Randall Garrett originally appeared in *If, Worlds of Science Fiction*, March 1954.

"The Skull" by Philip K. Dick originally appeared in *If, Worlds of Science Fiction*, September 1952.

"The Ordeal of Colonel Johns" by George H. Smith originally appeared in *If, Worlds of Science Fiction*, June 1954.

"Incident on Route 12" by James H. Schmitz originally appeared in *If, Worlds of Science Fiction*, January 1962.

"Brink of Madness" by Walt Sheldon originally appeared in *If, Worlds of Science Fiction*, July 1953.

"Love Story" by Irving E. Cox, Jr. originally appeared in *If, Worlds of Science Fiction*, April 1956.

"Navy Day" by Harry Harrison originally appeared in *If, Worlds of Science Fiction*, January 1954.

"The Anglers of Arz" by Roger Dee originally appeared in *If, Worlds of Science Fiction*, January 1953.

"Sinister Paradise" by Robert Moore Williams originally appeared in *If, Worlds of Science Fiction*, September 1952.

"Assassin" by J. F. Bone originally appeared in *If, Worlds of Science Fiction*, February 1958.

"Probability" by Louis Trimble originally appeared in *If, Worlds of Science Fiction*, April 1954.

"Sjambak" by Jack Vance originally appeared in *If, Worlds of Science Fiction*, July 1953.

"Deadly City" by Ivar Jorgenson originally appeared in *If, Worlds of Science Fiction*, March 1953.

"The Mightiest Man" by Patrick Fahy originally appeared in *If, Worlds of Science Fiction*, November 1961.

"Mutineer" by Robert J. Shea originally appeared in *If, Worlds of Science Fiction*, July 1959.

"And That's How it Was, Officer" by Ralph Sholto originally appeared in *If, Worlds of Science Fiction*, July 1952.

"No Shield from the Dead" by Gordon R. Dickson originally appeared in *If, Worlds of Science Fiction*, January 1953.

"Seven-Day Terror" by R.A. Lafferty originally appeared in *If, Worlds of Science Fiction*, March 1962.

"I'll Kill You Tomorrow" by Helen Huber originally appeared in *If, Worlds of Science Fiction*, November 1953.

"Security Risk" by Ed M. Clinton, Jr. originally appeared in *If, Worlds of Science Fiction*, February 1958.

"Confidence Game" by James Mckimmey, Jr. originally appeared in *If, Worlds of Science Fiction*, September 1954.

TABLE OF CONTENTS

THE SNOWBANK ORBIT

by Fritz Leiber

CHAPTER I

The pole stars of the other planets cluster around Polaris and Octans, but Uranus spins on a snobbishly different axis between Aldebaran and Antares. The Bull is her coronet and the Scorpion her footstool. Dear blowzy old bitch-planet, swollen and pale and cold, mad with your Shakespearean moons, white-mottled as death from Venerean Plague, spinning on your side like a poisoned pregnant cockroach, rolling around the sun like a fat drunken floozie with green hair rolling on the black floor of an infinite barroom, what a sweet last view of the Solar System you are for a clean-cut young spaceman.

Grunfeld chopped off that train of thought short. He was young and the First Interstellar War had snatched him up and now it was going to pitch him and twenty other Joes out of the System on a fast curve breaking around Uranus—and so what! He shivered to get a little heat and then applied himself to the occulted star he was tracking through Prospero's bridge telescope. The star was a twentieth planetary diameter into Uranus, the crosslines showed—a glint almost lost in pale green. That meant its light was bulleting 1600 miles deep through the seventh planet's thick hydrogen atmosphere, unless he were seeing the star on a mirage trajectory—and at least its depth agreed with the time since rim contact.

At 2000 miles he lost it. That should mean 2000 miles plus of hydrogen soup above the methane ocean, an America-wide layer of gaseous gunk for the captain to play the mad hero in with the fleet.

Grunfeld didn't think the captain wanted to play the mad hero. The captain hadn't gone space-simple in any obvious way like Croker and Ness. And he wasn't, like Jackson, a telepathy-racked visionary entranced by the Enemy. Worry and responsibility had turned the captain's face into a skull which floated in Grunfeld's imagination when he wasn't actually seeing it, but the tired eyes deep-sunk in the dark sockets were still cool and perhaps sane. But because of the worry the captain always wanted to have the last bit of fact bearing on the least likely maneuver, and two pieces of evidence were better than one. Grunfield found the next sizable star due to occult. Five-six minutes to rim contact. He floated back a foot from the telescope, stretching out his thin body in the plane of the ecliptic—strange how he automatically assumed that orientation in free fall! He blinked and blinked, then rested his eyes on the same planet he'd been straining them on.

The pale greenish bulk of Uranus was centered in the big bridge spaceshield against the black velvet dark and bayonet-bright stars, a water-splotched and faded chartreuse tennis ball on the diamond-spiked bed of night. At eight million miles she looked half the width of Luna seen from Earth. Her whitish equatorial bands went from bottom to top, where, Grunfeld knew, they were spinning out of sight at three miles a second—a gelid waterfall that he imagined tugging at him with ghostly green gangrenous fingers and pulling him over into a hydrogen Niagara.

Half as wide as Luna. But in a day she'd overflow the port as they whipped past her on a near miss and in another day she'd be as small as this again, but behind them, sunward, having altered their outward course by some small and as yet unpredictable angle, but no more able to slow Prospero and her sister ships or turn them back at their 100 miles a second

9

than the fleet's solar jets could operate at this chilly distance from Sol. G'by, fleet. G'by, C.C.Y. spaceman.

Grunfeld looked for the pale planet's moons. Miranda and Umbriel were too tiny to make disks, but he distinguished Ariel four diameters above the planet and Oberon a dozen below. Spectral sequins. If the fleet were going to get a radio signal from any of them, it would have to be Titania, occulted now by the planet and the noisy natural static of her roiling hydrogen air and seething methane seas—but it had always been only a faint hope that there were survivors from the First Uranus Expedition.

Grunfeld relaxed his neck and let his gaze drift down across the curving star-bordered forward edge of Prospero's huge mirror and the thin jutting beams of the port lattice arm to the dim red-lit gages below the spaceshield.

Forward Skin Temperature seven degrees Kelvin. Almost low enough for helium to crawl, if you had some helium. Prospero's insulation, originally designed to hold out solar heat, was doing a fair job in reverse.

Aft (sunward) Skin Temperature 75 degrees Kelvin. Close to that of Uranus' sunlit face. Check.

Cabin Temperature 43 degrees Fahrenheit. Brr! The Captain was a miser with the chem fuel remaining. And rightly...if it were right to drag out life as long as possible in the empty icebox beyond Uranus.

Gravities of Acceleration zero. Many other zeros.

The four telltales for the fleet unblinkingly glowed dimmest blue—one each for Caliban, Snug, Moth, and Starveling, following Prospero in line astern on slave automatic—though for months inertia had done all five ships' piloting. Once the buttons had been green, but they'd wiped that color off the boards because of the Enemy.

The gages still showed their last maximums. Skin 793 Kelvin, Cabin 144 Fahrenheit, Gravs 3.2. All of them hit: almost a year ago, when they'd been arcing past the sun. Grunfield's gaze edged back to the five bulbous pressure suits, once more rigidly upright in their braced racks, that they'd been wearing during that stretch of acceleration inside the orbit of Mercury. He started. For a moment he'd thought he saw the dark-circled eyes of the captain peering between two of the bulging black suits. Nerves! The captain had to be in his cabin, readying alternate piloting programs for Copperhead.

Suddenly Grunfeld jerked his face back toward the spaceshield—so violently that his body began very slowly to spin in the opposite direction. This time he'd thought he saw the Enemy's green flashing near the margin of the planet—bright green, viridian, far vivider than that of Uranus herself. He drew himself to the telescope and feverishly studied the area. Nothing at all. Nerves again. If the Enemy were much nearer than a light-minute, Jackson would esp it and give warning. The next star was still three minutes from rim contact. Grunfeld's mind retreated to the circumstances that had brought Prospero (then only Mercury One) out here.

CHAPTER II

When the First Interstellar War erupted, the pioneer fleets of Earth's nations had barely pushed their explorations beyond the orbit of Saturn. Except for the vessels of the

International Meteor Guard, spaceflight was still a military enterprise of America, Russia, England and the other mega-powers.

During the first months the advantage lay wholly with the slim black cruisers of the Enemy, who had an antigravity which allowed them to hover near planets without going into orbit; and a frightening degree of control over light itself. Indeed, their principal weapon was a tight beam of visible light, a dense photonic stiletto with an effective range of several Jupiter-diameters in vacuum. They also used visible light, in the green band, for communication as men use radio, sometimes broadcasting it and sometimes beaming it loosely in strange abstract pictures that seemed part of their language. Their gravity-immune ships moved by reaction to photonic jets the tightness of which rendered them invisible except near the sun, where they tended to ionize electronically dirty volumes of space. It was probably this effective invisibility, based on light-control, which allowed them to penetrate the Solar System as deep as Earth's orbit undetected, rather than any power of travel in time or sub-space, as was first assumed. Earthmen could only guess at the physical appearance of the Enemy, since no prisoners were taken on either side.

Despite his impressive maneuverability and armament, the Enemy was oddly timid about attacking live planets. He showed no fear of the big gas planets, in fact hovering very close to their turgid surfaces, as if having some way of fueling from them.

Near Terra the first tactic of the black cruisers, after destroying Lunostrovok and Circumluna, was to hover behind the moon, as though sharing its tide-lockedness—a circumstance that led to a sortie by Earth's Combined Fleet, England and Sweden excepted.

At the wholly disastrous Battle of the Far Side, which was visible in part to naked-eye viewers on Earth, the Combined Fleet was annihilated. No Enemy ship was captured, boarded, or seriously damaged—except for one which, apparently by a fluke, was struck by a fission-headed anti-missile and proceeded after the blast to "burn," meaning that it suffered a slow and puzzling disintegration, accompanied by a dazzling rainbow display of visible radiation. This was before the "stupidity" of the Enemy with regard to small atomic missiles was noted, or their allergy to certain radio wave bands, and also before Terran telepaths began to claim cloudy contact with Enemy minds.

Following Far Side, the Enemy burst into activity, harrying Terran spacecraft as far as Mercury and Saturn, though still showing great caution in maneuver and making no direct attacks on planets. It was as if a race of heavily armed marine creatures should sink all ocean-going ships or drive them to harbor, but make no assaults beyond the shore line. For a full year Earth, though her groundside and satellite rocket yards were furiously busy, had no vehicle in deep space—with one exception.

At the onset of the War a fleet of five mobile bases of the U. S. Space Force were in Orbit to Mercury, where it was intended they take up satellite positions prior to the prospecting and mineral exploitation of the small sun-blasted planet. These five ships, each with a skeleton five-man crew, were essentially Ross-Smith space stations with a solar drive, assembled in space and intended solely for space-to-space flight inside Earth's orbit. A huge paraboloid mirror, its diameter four times the length of the ship's hull, superheated at its focus the hydrogen which was ejected as a plasma at high exhaust velocity. Each ship likewise mounted versatile radio-radar equipment on dual lattice arms and carried as ship's launch a two-man chemical fuel rocket adaptable as a fusion-headed torpedo.

After Far Side, this "tin can" fleet was ordered to bypass Mercury and, tacking on the sun, shape an orbit for Uranus, chiefly because that remote planet, making its 84-year circuit of Sol, was currently on the opposite side of the sun to the four inner planets and the two nearer gas giants Jupiter and Saturn. In the empty regions of space the relatively defenseless fleet might escape the attention of the Enemy.

However, while still accelerating into the sun for maximum boost, the fleet received information that two Enemy cruisers were in pursuit. The five ships cracked on all possible speed, drawing on the solar drive's high efficiency near the sun and expending all their hydrogen and most material capable of being vaporized, including some of the light-metal hydrogen storage tanks—like an old steamer burning her cabin furniture and the cabins themselves to win a race. Gradually the curving course that would have taken years to reach the outer planet flattened into a hyperbola that would make the journey in 200 days.

In the asteroid belt the pursuing cruisers turned aside to join in the crucial Battle of the Trojans with Earth's largely new-built, more heavily and wisely armed Combined Fleet—a battle that proved to be only a prelude to the decisive Battle of Jupiter.

Meanwhile the five-ship fleet sped onward, its solar drive quite useless in this twilight region even if it could have scraped together the needed boilable ejectant mass to slow its flight. Weeks became months. The ships were renamed for the planet they were aimed at. At least the fleet's trajectory had been truly set.

Almost on collision course it neared Uranus, a mystery-cored ball of frigid gas 32,000 miles wide coasting through space across the fleet's course at a lazy four miles a second. At this time the fleet was traveling at 100 miles a second. Beyond Uranus lay only the interstellar night, into which the fleet would inevitably vanish...

Unless, Grunfeld told himself...unless the fleet shed its velocity by ramming the gaseous bulk of Uranus. This idea of atmospheric braking on a grand scale had sounded possible at first suggestion, half a year ago—a little like a man falling off a mountain or from a plane and saving his life by dropping into a great thickness of feathery new-fallen snow.

Supposing her solar jet worked out here and she had the reaction mass, Prospero could have shed her present velocity in five hours, decelerating at a comfortable one G.

But allowing her 12,000 miles of straight-line travel through Uranus' frigid soupy atmosphere—and that might be dipping very close to the methane seas blanketing the planet's hypothetical mineral core—Prospero would have two minutes in which to shed her velocity.

Two minutes—at 150 Gs.

Men had stood 40 and 50 Gs for a fractional second.

But for two minutes... Grunfeld told himself that the only surer way to die would be to run into a section of the Enemy fleet. According to one calculation the ship's skin would melt by heat of friction in 90 seconds, despite the low temperature of the abrading atmosphere.

The star Grunfeld had been waiting for touched the hazy rim of Uranus. He drifted back to the eyepiece and began to follow it in as the pale planet's hydrogen muted its diamond brilliance.

CHAPTER III

In the aft cabin, lank hairy-wristed Croker pinned another blanket around black Jackson as the latter shivered in his trance. Then Croker turned on a small light at the head of the hammock.

"Captain won't like that," plump pale Ness observed tranquilly from where he floated in womb position across the cabin. "Enemy can feel a candle of our light, captain says, ten million miles away." He rocked his elbows for warmth and his body wobbled in reaction like a pollywog's.

"And Jackson hears the Enemy think...and Heimdall hears the grass grow," Croker commented with a harsh manic laugh. "Isn't an Enemy for a billion miles, Ness." He launched aft from the hammock. "We haven't spotted their green since Saturn orbit. There's nowhere for them."

"There's the far side of Uranus," Ness pointed out. "That's less than ten million miles now. Eight. A bare day. They could be there."

"Yes, waiting to bushwack us as we whip past on our way to eternity," Croker chuckled as he crumpled up against the aft port, shedding momentum. "That's likely, isn't it, when they didn't have time for us back in the Belt?" He scowled at the tiny white sun, no bigger a disk than Venus, but still with one hundred times as much light as the full moon pouring from it—too much light to look at comfortably. He began to button the inner cover over the port.

"Don't do that," Ness objected without conviction. "There's not much heat in it but there's some." He hugged his elbows and shivered. "I don't remember being warm since Mars orbit."

"The sun gets on my nerves," Croker said. "It's like looking at an arc light through a pinhole. It's like a high, high jail light in a cold concrete yard. The stars are highlights on the barbed wire." He continued to button out the sun.

"You ever in jail?" Ness asked. Croker grinned.

With the tropism of a fish, Ness began to paddle toward the little light at the head of Jackson's hammock, flicking his hands from the wrists like flippers. "I got one thing against the sun," he said quietly. "It's blanketing out the radio. I'd like us to get one more message from Earth. We haven't tried rigging our mirror to catch radio waves. I'd like to hear how we won the battle of Jupiter."

"If we won it," Croker said.

"Our telescopes show no more green around Jove," Ness reminded him. "We counted 27 rainbows of Enemy cruisers 'burning.' Captain verified the count."

"Repeat: if we won it." Croker pushed off and drifted back toward the hammock. "If there was a real victory message they'd push it through, even if the sun's in the way and it takes three hours to catch us. People who win, shout."

Ness shrugged as he paddled. "One way or the other, we should be getting the news soon from Titania station," he said. "They'll have heard."

"If they're still alive and there ever was a Titania Station," Croker amended, backing air violently to stop himself as he neared the hammock. "Look, Ness, we know that the First Uranus Expedition arrived. At least they set off their flares. But that was three years before the War and we haven't any idea of what's happened to them since and if they ever managed to set up housekeeping on Titania—or Ariel or Oberon or even Miranda or Umbriel. At least if they built a station could raise Earth I haven't been told. Sure thing Prospero hasn't heard anything and we're getting close."

"I won't argue." Ness said. "Even if we raise 'em, it'll just be hello-goodbye with maybe time between for a battle report."

"And a football score and a short letter from home, ten seconds per man as the station fades." Croker frowned and added, "If Captain had cottoned to my idea, two of us at any rate could have got off this express train at Uranus."

"Tell me how," Ness asked drily.

"How? Why, one of the 16 ship's launches. Replace the fusion-head with the cabin. Put all the chem fuel in the tanks instead of divvying it between the ship and the launch."

"I haven't got the brain for math Copperhead has, but I can subtract," Ness said, referring to Prospero's piloting robot. "Fully fueled, one of the launches has a max velocity change in free-fall of 30 miles per second. Use it all in braking and you've only taken 30 from 100. The launch is still going past Uranus and out of the system at 70 miles a second."

"You didn't hear all my idea." Croker said. "You put piggyback tanks on your launch and top them off with the fuel from the other four launches. Then you've 100 miles of braking and a maneuvering reserve. You only need to shed 90 miles, anyway. Ten miles a second's the close circum-Uranian velocity. Go into circum-Uranian orbit and wait for Titania to send their jeep to pick you up. Have to start the maneuver four hours this side of Uranus, though. Take that long at 1 G to shed it."

"Cute," Ness conceded. "Especially the jeep. But I'm glad just the same we've got 70 percent of our chem fuel in our ships' tanks instead of the launches. We're on such a bull's eye course for Uranus—Copperhead really pulled a miracle plotting our orbit—that we may need a sidewise shove to miss her. If we slapped into that cold hydrogen soup at our 100 mps—"

Croker shrugged. "We still could have dropped a couple of us," he said.

"Captain's got to look after the whole fleet," Ness said. "You're beginning to agitate, Croker, like you was Grunfeld—or the captain himself."

"But if Titania Station's alive, a couple of men dropped off would do the fleet some good. Stir Titania up to punch a message through to Earth and get a really high-speed retrieve-and-rescue ship started out after us. If we've won the War."

"But Titania Station's dead or never was, not to mention its jeep. And we've lost the Battle of Jupiter. You said so yourself," Ness asserted owlishly. "Captain's got to look after the whole fleet."

"Yeah, so he kills himself fretting and the rest of us die of old age in the outskirts of the Solar System. Join the Space Force and See the Stars! Ness, do you know how long it'd take us to reach the nearest star—except we aren't headed for her—at our 100 mps? Eight thousand years!"

"That's a lot of time to kill," Ness said. "Let's play chess."

Jackson sighed and they both looked quickly at the dark unlined face above the cocoon, but the lips did not flutter again, or the eyelids. Croker said, "Suppose he knows what the Enemy looks like?"

"I suppose," Ness said. "When he talks about them it's as if he was their interpreter. How about the chess?"

"Suits. Knight to King Bishop Three."

"Hmm. Knight to King Knight Two, Third Floor."

"Hey, I meant flat chess, not three-D," Croker objected.

"That thin old game? Why, I no sooner start to get the position really visualized in my head than the game's over."

"I don't want to start a game of three-D with Uranus only 18 hours away."

Jackson stirred in his hammock. His lips worked. "They..." he breathed. Croker and Ness instantly watched him. "They..."

"I wonder if he is really inside the Enemy's mind?" Ness said.

"He thinks he speaks for them," Croker replied and the next instant felt a warning touch on his arm and looked sideways and saw dark-circled eyes in a skull-angular face under a battered cap with a tarnished sunburst. Damn, thought Croker, how does the captain always know when Jackson's going to talk?

"They are waiting for us on the other side of Uranus," Jackson breathed. His lips trembled into a smile and his voice grew a little louder, though his eyes stayed shut. "They're welcoming us, they're our brothers." The smile died. "But they know they got to kill us, they know we got to die."

The hammock with its tight-swathed form began to move past Croker and he snatched at it. The captain had pushed off from him for the hatch leading forward.

Grunfeld was losing the new star at 2200 miles into Uranus when he saw the two viridian flares flashing between it and the rim. Each flash was circled by a fleeting bright green ring, like a mist halo. He thought he'd be afraid when he saw that green again, but what he felt was a jolt of excitement that made him grin. With it came a touch on his shoulder. He thought, the captain always knows.

"Ambush," he said. "At least two cruisers."

He yielded the eyepiece to the captain. Even without the telescope he could see those incredibly brilliant green flickers. He asked himself if the Enemy was already gunning for the fleet through Uranus.

The blue telltales for Caliban and Starveling began to blink.

"They've seen it too," the captain said. He snatched up the mike and his next words rang through the Prospero.

"Rig ship for the snowbank orbit! Snowbank orbit with stinger! Mr. Grunfeld, raise the fleet."

Aft, Croker muttered, "Rig our shrouds, don't he mean? Rig shrouds and firecrackers mounted on Fourth of July rockets."

Ness said, "Cheer up. Even the longest strategic withdrawal in history has to end some time."

CHAPTER IV

Three quarters of a day later Grunfeld felt a spasm of futile fear and revolt as the pressure suit closed like a thick-fleshed carnivorous plant on his drugged and tired body. Relax, he told himself. Fine thing if you cooked up a fuss when even Croker didn't. He thought of forty things to recheck. Relax, he repeated—the work's over; all that matters is in Copperhead's memory tanks now, or will be as soon as the captain's suited up.

The suit held Grunfeld erect, his arms at his sides—the best attitude, except he was still facing forward, for taking high G, providing the ship herself didn't start to tumble. Only the cheekpieces and visor hadn't closed in on his face—translucent hand-thick petals as yet unfolded. He felt the delicate firm pressure of built-in fingertips monitoring his pulses and against his buttocks the cold smooth muzzles of the jet hypodermics that would feed him metronomic drugs during the high-G stretch and stimulants when they were in free-fall again. When.

He could swing his head and eyes just enough to make out the suits of Croker and Ness to either side of him and their profiles wavy through the jutting misty cheekpieces. Ahead to the left was Jackson—just the back of his suit, like a black snowman standing at attention, pale-olive-edged by the great glow of Uranus. And to the right the captain, his legs suited but his upper body still bent out to the side as he checked the monitor of his suit with its glowing blue button and the manual controls that would lie under his hands during the maneuver.

Beyond the captain was the spaceshield, the lower quarter of it still blackness and stars, but the upper three-quarters filled with the onrushing planet's pale mottled green that now had the dulled richness of watered silk. They were so close that the rim hardly showed curvature. The atmosphere must have a steep gradient, Grunfeld thought, or they'd already be feeling decel. That stuff ahead looked more like water than any kind of air. It bothered him that the captain was still half out of his suit.

There should be action and shouted commands, Grunfeld thought, to fill up these last tight-stretched minutes. Last orders to the fleet, port covers being cranked shut, someone doing a countdown on the firing of their torpedo. But the last message had gone to the fleet minutes ago. Its robot pilots were set to follow Prospero and imitate, nothing else. And all the rest was up to Copperhead. Still...

Grunfeld wet his lips. "Captain," he said hesitantly. "Captain?"

"Thank you, Grunfeld." He caught the edge of the skull's answering grin. "We are beginning to hit hydrogen," the quiet voice went on. "Forward skin temperature's up to 9 K."

Beyond the friendly skull, a great patch of the rim of Uranus flared bright green. As if that final stimulus had been needed, Jackson began to talk dreamily from his suit.

"They're still welcoming us and grieving for us. I begin to get it a little more now. Their ship's one thing and they're another. Their ship is frightened to death of us. It hates us and the only thing it knows to do is to kill us. They can't stop it, they're even less than passengers..."

The captain was in his suit now. Grunfeld sensed a faint throbbing and felt a rush of cold air. The cabin refrigeration system had started up, carrying cabin heat to the lattice arms. Intended to protect them from solar heat, it would now do what it could against the heat of friction.

The straight edge of Uranus was getting hazier. Even the fainter stars shone through, spangling it. A bell jangled and the pale green segment narrowed as the steel meteor panels began to close in front of the spaceshield. Soon there was only a narrow vertical ribbon of green—bright green as it narrowed to a thread—then for a few seconds only blackness except for the dim red and blue beads and semicircles, just beyond the captain, of the board. Then the muted interior cabin lights glowed on.

Jackson droned: "They and their ships come from very far away, from the edge. If this is the continuum, they come from the...discontinuum, where they don't have stars but something else and where gravity is different. Their ships came from the edge on a gust of fear with the other ships, and our brothers came with it though they didn't want to..."

And now Grunfeld thought he began to feel it—the first faint thrill, less than a cobweb's tug, of weight.

The cabin wall moved sideways. Grunfeld's suit had begun to revolve slowly on a vertical axis.

For a moment he glimpsed Jackson's dark profile—all five suits were revolving in their framework. They locked into position when the men in them were facing aft. Now at least retinas wouldn't pull forward at high-G decel, or spines crush through thorax and abdomen.

The cabin air was cold on Grunfeld's forehead. And now he was sure he felt weight—maybe five pounds of it. Suddenly aft was up. It was as if he were lying on his back on the spaceshield.

A sudden snarling roar came through his suit from the beams bracing it. He lost weight, then regained it and a little more besides. He realized it was their torpedo taking off, to skim by Uranus in the top of the atmosphere and then curve inward the little their chem fuel would let them, homing toward the Enemy. He imaged its tiny red jet over the great gray-green glowing plain. Four more would be taking off from the other ships—the fleet's feeble sting. Like a bee's, just one, in dying.

The cheekpieces and foreheadpiece of Grunfeld's suit began to close on his face like layers of pliable ice.

Jackson called faintly, "Now I understand. Their ship—" His voice was cut off.

Grunfeld's ice-mask was tight shut. He felt a small surge of vigor as the suit took over his breathing and sent his lungs a gush of high-oxy air. Then came a tingling numbness as the suit field went on, adding an extra prop against decel to each molecule of his body.

But the weight was growing. He was on the moon now...now on Mars...now back on Earth...

The weight was stifling now, crushing—a hill of invisible sand. Grunfeld saw a black pillow hanging in the cabin above him aft. It had red fringe around it. It grew.

There was a whistling and shaking. Everything lurched torturingly, the ship's jets roared, everything recovered, or didn't.

The black pillow came down on him, crushing out sight, crushing out thought.

*

The universe was a black tingling, a limitless ache floating in a larger black infinity. Something drew back and there was a dry fiery wind on numb humps and ridges—the cabin air on his face, Grunfeld decided, then shivered and started at the thought that he was alive and in freefall. His body didn't feel like a mass of internal hemorrhages. Or did it?

He spun slowly. It stopped. Dizziness? Or the suits revolving forward again? If they'd actually come through—

There was a creaking and cracking. The ship contracting after frictional heating?

There was a faint stink like ammonia and formaldehyde mixed. A few Uranian molecules forced past plates racked by turbulence?

He saw dim red specks. The board? Or last flickers from ruined retinas? A bell jangled. He waited, but he saw nothing. Blind? Or the meteor guard jammed? No wonder if it were. No wonder if the cabin lights were broken.

The hot air that had dried his sweaty face rushed down the front of his body. Needles of pain pierced him as he slumped forward out of the top of his opening suit.

Then he saw the horizontal band of stars outlining the top of the spaceshield and below it the great field of inky black, barely convex upward, that must, he realized, be the dark side of Uranus.

Pain ignored, Grunfeld pushed himself forward out of his suit and pulled himself past the captain's to the spaceshield.

The view stayed the same, though broadening out: stars above, a curve-edged velvet black plain below. They were orbiting.

A pulsing, color-changing glow from somewhere showed him twisted stumps of the radio lattices. There was no sign of the mirror at all. It must have been torn away, or vaporized completely, in the fiery turbulence of decel.

New maxs showed on the board: Cabin Temperature 214 F, Skin Temperature 907 K, Gravs 87.

Then in the top of the spacefield, almost out of vision, Grunfeld saw the source of the pulsing glow: two sharp-ended ovals flickering brightly all colors against the pale starfields, like two dead fish phosphorescing.

"The torps got to 'em," Croker said, pushed forward beside Grunfeld to the right.

*

"I did find out at the end." Jackson said quietly from the left, his voice at last free of the trance-tone. "The Enemy ships weren't ships at all. They were (there's no other word for it) space animals. We've always thought life was a prerogative of planets, that space was inorganic. But you can walk miles through the desert or sail leagues through the sea before you notice life and I guess space is the same. Anyway the Enemy was (what else can I call 'em?) space-whales. Inertialess space-whales from the discontinuum. Space-whales that ate hydrogen (that's the only way I know to say it) and spat light to move and fight. The ones I talked to, our brothers, were just their parasites."

"That's crazy," Grunfeld said. "All of it. A child's picture."

"Sure it is," Jackson agreed.

From beyond Jackson, Ness, punching buttons, said, "Quiet."

The radio came on thin and wailing with static: "Titania Station calling fleet. We have jeep and can orbit in to you. The two Enemy are dead—the last in the System. Titania Station calling fleet. We have jeep fueled and set to go—"

Fleet? thought Grunfeld. He turned back to the board. The first and last blue telltales still glowed for Caliban and Starveling. Breathe a prayer, he thought, for Moth and Snug.

Something else shone on the board, something Grunfeld knew had to be wrong. Three little words: SHIP ON MANUAL.

The black rim of Uranus ahead suddenly brightened along its length, which was very slightly bowed, like a section of a giant new moon. A bead formed toward the center, brightened, and then all at once the jail-yard sun had risen and was glaring coldly through its pinhole into their eyes.

They looked away from it. Grunfeld turned around.

The austere light showed the captain still in his pressure suit, only the head fallen out forward, hiding the skull features. Studying the monitor box of the captain's suit, Grunfeld saw it was set to inject the captain with power stimulants as soon as the Gravs began to slacken from their max.

He realized who had done the impossible job of piloting them out of Uranus.

But the button on the monitor, that should have glowed blue, was as dark as those of Moth and Snug.

Grunfeld thought, now he can rest.

THE VICTOR

by Bryce Walton

Under the new system of the Managerials, the fight was not for life but for death! And great was the ingenuity of—The Victor.

Charles Marquis had a fraction of a minute in which to die. He dropped through the tubular beams of alloydem steel and hung there, five thousand feet above the tiers and walkways below. At either end of the walkway crossing between the two power-hung buildings, he saw the plainclothes security officers running in toward him.

He grinned and started to release his grip. He would think about them on the way down. His fingers wouldn't work. He kicked and strained and tore at himself with his own weight, but his hands weren't his own any more. He might have anticipated that. Some paralysis beam freezing his hands into the metal.

He sagged to limpness. His chin dropped. For an instant, then, the fire in his heart almost went out, but not quite. It survived that one terrible moment of defeat, then burned higher. And perhaps something in that desperate resistance was the factor that kept it burning where it was thought no flame could burn. He felt the rigidity of paralysis leaving his arms as he was lifted, helped along the walkway to a security car.

The car looked like any other car. The officers appeared like all the other people in the clockwork culture of the mechanized New System. Marquis sought the protection of personal darkness behind closed eyelids as the monorail car moved faster and faster through the high clean air. Well—he'd worked with the Underground against the System for a long time. He had known that eventually he would be caught. There were rumors of what happened to men then, and even the vaguest, unsubstantiated rumors were enough to indicate that death was preferable. That was the Underground's philosophy—better to die standing up as a man with some degree of personal integrity and freedom than to go on living as a conditioned slave of the state.

He'd missed—but he wasn't through yet though. In a hollow tooth was a capsule containing a very high-potency poison. A little of that would do the trick too. But he would have to wait for the right time . . . .

*

The Manager was thin, his face angular, and he matched up with the harsh steel angles of the desk and the big room somewhere in the Security Building. His face had a kind of emotion—cold, detached, cynically superior.

"We don't get many of your kind," he said. "Political prisoners are becoming more scarce all the time. As your number indicates. From now on, you'll be No. 5274."

He looked at some papers, then up at Marquis. "You evidently found out a great deal. However, none of it will do you or what remains of your Underground fools any good." The Manager studied Marquis with detached curiosity. "You learned things concerning the Managerials that have so far remained secret."

It was partly a question. Marquis' lean and darkly inscrutable face smiled slightly. "You're good at understatement. Yes—I found out what we've suspected for some time. That the Managerial class has found some way to stay young. Either a remarkable longevity, or immortality. Of all the social evils that's the worst of all. To deny the people knowledge of such a secret."

The Manager nodded. "Then you did find that out? The Underground knows? Well, it will do no good."

"It will, eventually. They'll go on and someday they'll learn the secret." Marquis thought of Marden. Marden was as old as the New System of statism and inhumanity that had started off disguised as social-democracy. Three-hundred and three years old to be exact.

The Manager said, "No. 5274—you will be sent to the work colony on the Moon. You won't be back. We've tried re-conditioning rebels, but it doesn't work. A rebel has certain basic deviant characteristics and we can't overcome them sufficiently to make happy, well-adjusted workers out of you. However on the Moon—you will conform. It's a kind of social experiment there in associative reflex culture, you might say. You'll conform all right."

He was taken to a small, naked, gray-steel room. He thought about taking the capsule from his tooth now, but decided he might be observed. They would rush in an antidote and make him live. And he might not get a chance to take his life in any other way. He would try of course, but his knowledge of his future situation was vague—except that in it he would conform. There would be extreme conditioned-reflex therapeutic techniques. And it would be pretty horrible. That was all he knew.

He didn't see the pellet fall. He heard the slight sound it made and then saw the almost colorless gas hissing softly, clouding the room. He tasted nothing, smelled or felt nothing.

He passed out quickly and painlessly.

*

He was marched into another office, and he knew he was on the Moon. The far wall was spherical and was made up of the outer shell of the pressure dome which kept out the frigid cold nights and furnace-hot days. It was opaque and Marquis could see the harsh black and white shadows out there—the metallic edges of the far crater wall.

This Manager was somewhat fat, with a round pink face and cold blue eyes. He sat behind a chrome shelf of odd shape suspended from the ceiling with silver wires.

The Manager said, "No. 5274, here there is only work. At first, of course, you will rebel. Later you will work, and finally there will be nothing else. Things here are rigidly scheduled, and you will learn the routines as the conditioning bells acquaint you with them. We are completely self-sufficient here. We are developing the perfect scientifically-controlled society. It is a kind of experiment. A closed system to test to what extremes we can carry our mastery of associative reflex to bring man security and happiness and freedom from responsibility."

Marquis didn't say anything. There was nothing to say. He knew he couldn't get away with trying to kill this particular Managerial specimen. But one man, alone, a rebel, with something left in him that still burned, could beat the system. *He had to!*

"Our work here is specialized. During the indoctrination period you will do a very simple routine job in coordination with the cybernetics machines. There, the machines and the nervous system of the workers become slowly cooperative. Machine and man learn to work very intimately together. Later, after the indoctrination—because of your specialized knowledge of food-concentrate preparation—we will transfer you to the food-mart. The period of indoctrination varies in length with the individuals. You will be screened now and taken to the indoctrination ward. We probably won't be seeing one another again. The bells take care of everything here. The bells and the machines. There is never an error—never any mistakes. Machines do not make mistakes."

He was marched out of there and through a series of rooms. He was taken in by generators, huge oscilloscopes. Spun like a living tube through curtains of vacuum tube voltimeters, electronic power panels. Twisted and squeezed through rolls of skeins of hook-up wire. Bent through shieldings of every color, size and shape. Rolled over panel plates, huge racks of glowing tubes, elaborate transceivers. Tumbled down long surfaces of gleaming bakelite. Plunged through color-indexed files of resistors and capacitances . . . .

. . . *here machine and man learn to work very intimately together.*

As he drifted through the machine tooled nightmare, Marquis knew *what* he had been fighting all his life, what he would continue to fight with every grain of ingenuity. Mechanization—the horror of losing one's identity and becoming part of an assembly line.

He could hear a clicking sound as tubes sharpened and faded in intensity. The clicking—rhythm, a hypnotic rhythm like the beating of his own heart—the throbbing and thrumming, the contracting and expanding, the pulsing and pounding . . . .

. . . *the machines and the nervous system of the workers become slowly cooperative.*

*

Beds were spaced ten feet apart down both sides of a long gray metal hall. There were no cells, no privacy, nothing but beds and the gray metalene suits with numbers printed across the chest.

His bed, with his number printed above it, was indicated to him, and the guard disappeared. He was alone. It was absolutely silent. On his right a woman lay on a bed. No. 329. She had been here a long time. She appeared dead. Her breasts rose and fell with a peculiarly steady rhythm, and seemed to be coordinated with the silent, invisible throbbing of the metal walls. She might have been attractive once. Here it didn't make any difference. Her face was gray, like metal. Her hair was cropped short. Her uniform was the same as the man's on Marquis' left.

The man was No. 4901. He hadn't been here so long. His face was thin and gray. His hair was dark, and he was about the same size and build as Marquis. His mouth hung slightly open and his eyes were closed and there was a slight quivering at the ends of the fingers which were laced across his stomach.

"Hello," Marquis said. The man shivered, then opened dull eyes and looked up at Marquis. "I just got in. Name's Charles Marquis."

The man blinked. "I'm—I'm—No. 4901." He looked down at his chest, repeated the number. His fingers shook a little as he touched his lips.

Marquis said. "What's this indoctrination?"

"You—learn. The bells ring—you forget—and learn—"

"There's absolutely no chance of escaping?" Marquis whispered, more to himself than to 4901.

"Only by dying," 4901 shivered. His eyes rolled crazily, then he turned over and buried his face in his arms.

The situation had twisted all the old accepted values squarely around. Preferring death over life. But not because of any anti-life attitude, or pessimism, or defeatism. None of those negative attitudes that would have made the will-to-die abnormal under conditions in which there would have been hope and some faint chance of a bearable future. Here to keep on living was a final form of de-humanized indignity, of humiliation, of ignominy, of the worst thing of all—loss of one's-self—of one's individuality. To die as a human being was much more preferable over continuing to live as something else—something neither human or machine, but something of both, with none of the dignity of either.

*

The screening process hadn't detected the capsule of poison in Marquis' tooth. The capsule contained ten grains of poison, only one of which was enough to bring a painless death within sixteen hours or so. That was his ace in the hole, and he waited only for the best time to use it.

Bells rang. The prisoners jumped from their beds and went through a few minutes of calisthenics. Other bells rang and a tray of small tins of food-concentrates appeared out of a slit in the wall by each bed. More bells rang, different kinds of bells, some deep and brazen, others high and shrill. And the prisoners marched off to specialized jobs co-operating with various machines.

You slept eight hours. Calisthenics five minutes. Eating ten minutes. Relaxation to the tune of musical bells, ten minutes. Work period eight hours. Repeat. That was all of life, and after a while Marquis knew, a man would not be aware of time, nor of his name, nor that he had once been human.

Marquis felt deep lancing pain as he tried to resist the bells. Each time the bells rang and a prisoner didn't respond properly, invisible rays of needle pain punched and kept punching until he reacted properly.

And finally he did as the bells told him to do. Finally he forgot that things had ever been any other way.

Marquis sat on his bed, eating, while the bells of eating rang across the bowed heads in the gray uniforms. He stared at the girl, then at the man, 4901. There were many opportunities to take one's own life here. That had perplexed him from the start—*why hasn't the girl, and this man, succeeded in dying?*

And all the others? They were comparatively new here, all these in this indoctrination ward. Why weren't they trying to leave in the only dignified way of escape left?

No. 4901 tried to talk, he tried hard to remember things. Sometimes memory would break through and bring him pictures of other times, of happenings on Earth, of a girl he had known, of times when he was a child. But only the mildest and softest kind of recollections . . . .

Marquis said, "I don't think there's a prisoner here who doesn't want to escape, and death is the only way out for us. We know that."

For an instant, No. 4901 stopped eating. A spoonful of food concentrate hung suspended between his mouth and the shelf. Then the food moved again to the urging of the bells. Invisible pain needles gouged Marquis' neck, and he ate again too, automatically, talking between tasteless bites. "A man's life at least is his own," Marquis said. "They can take everything else. But a man certainly has a right and a duty to take that life if by so doing he can retain his integrity as a human being. Suicide—"

No. 4901 bent forward. He groaned, mumbled "Don't—don't—" several times, then curled forward and lay on the floor knotted up into a twitching ball.

The eating period was over. The lights went off. Bells sounded for relaxation. Then the sleep bells began ringing, filling up the absolute darkness.

Marquis lay there in the dark and he was afraid. He had the poison. He had the will. But he couldn't be unique in that respect. What was the matter with the others? All right, the devil with them. Maybe they'd been broken too soon to act. He could act. Tomorrow, during the work period, he would take a grain of the poison. Put the capsule back in the tooth. The poison would work slowly, painlessly, paralyzing the nervous system, finally the heart. Sometime during the beginning of the next sleep period he would be dead. That would leave six or seven hours of darkness and isolation for him to remain dead, so they couldn't get to him in time to bring him back.

He mentioned suicide to the girl during the next work period. She moaned a little and curled up like a fetus on the floor. After an hour, she got up and began inserting punch cards into the big machine again. She avoided Marquis.

Marquis looked around, went into a corner with his back to the room, slipped the capsule out and let one of the tiny, almost invisible grains, melt on his tongue. He replaced the capsule and returned to the machine. A quiet but exciting triumph made the remainder of the work period more bearable.

Back on his bed, he drifted into sleep, into what he knew was the final sleep. He was more fortunate than the others. Within an hour he would be dead.

*

Somewhere, someone was screaming.

The sounds rose higher and higher. A human body, somewhere . . . pain unimaginable twisting up through clouds of belching steam . . . muscles quivering, nerves twitching . . . and somewhere a body floating and bobbing and crying . . . sheets of agony sweeping and returning in waves and the horror of unescapable pain expanding like a volcano of madness . . . .

Somewhere was someone alive who should be dead.

And then in the dark, in absolute silence, Marquis moved a little. He realized, vaguely, that the screaming voice was his own.

He stared into the steamy darkness and slowly, carefully, wet his lips. He moved. He felt his lips moving and the whisper sounding loud in the dark.

I'm alive!

He managed to struggle up out of the bed. He could scarcely remain erect. Every muscle in his body seemed to quiver. He longed to slip down into the darkness and escape into endless sleep. But he'd tried that. And he was still alive. He didn't know how much time had passed. He was sure of the poison's effects, but he wasn't dead. They had gotten to him in time.

Sweat exploded from his body. He tried to remember more. Pain. He lay down again. He writhed and perspired on the bed as his tortured mind built grotesque fantasies out of fragments of broken memory.

The routine of the unceasing bells went on. Bells, leap up. Bells, calisthenics. Bells, eat. Bells, march. Bells, work. He tried to shut out the bells. He tried to talk to 4901. 4901 covered up his ears and wouldn't listen. The girl wouldn't listen to him.

There were other ways. And he kept the poison hidden in the capsule in his hollow tooth. He had been counting the steps covering the length of the hall, then the twenty steps to the left, then to the right to where the narrow corridor led again to the left where he had seen the air-lock.

After the bells stopped ringing and the darkness was all around him, he got up. He counted off the steps. No guards, no alarms, nothing to stop him. They depended on the conditioners to take care of everything. This time he would do it. This time they wouldn't bring him back.

No one else could even talk with him about it, even though he knew they all wanted to escape. Some part of them still wanted to, but they couldn't. So it was up to him. He stopped against the smooth, opaque, up-curving glasite dome. It had a brittle bright shine that reflected from the Moon's surface. It was night out there, with an odd metallic reflection of Earthlight against the naked crags.

He hesitated. He could feel the intense and terrible cold, the airlessness out there fingering hungrily, reaching and whispering and waiting.

He turned the wheel. The door opened. He entered the air-lock and shut the first door when the air-pressure was right. He turned the other wheel and the outer lock door swung outward. The out-rushing air spun him outward like a balloon into the awful airless cold and naked silence.

His body sank down into the thick pumice dust that drifted up around him in a fine powdery blanket of concealment. He felt no pain. The cold airlessness dissolved around him in deepening darkening pleasantness. This time he was dead, thoroughly and finally and gloriously dead, even buried, and they couldn't find him. And even if they did finally find him, what good would it do them?

Some transcendental part of him seemed to remain to observe and triumph over his victory. This time he was dead to stay.

*

This time he knew at once that the twisting body in the steaming pain, the distorted face, the screams rising and rising were all Charles Marquis.

Maybe a dream though, he thought. So much pain, so much screaming pain, is not real. In some fraction of a fraction of that interim between life and death, one could dream of so much because dreams are timeless.

Yet he found himself anticipating, even through the shredded, dissociated, nameless kind of pain, a repetition of that other time.

The awful bitterness of defeat.

*

He opened his eyes slowly. It was dark, the same darkness. He was on the same bed. And the old familiar dark around and the familiar soundlessness that was now heavier than the most thunderous sound.

Everything around him then seemed to whirl up and go down in a crash. He rolled over to the floor and lay there, his hot face cooled by the cold metal.

As before, some undeterminable interim of time had passed. And he knew he was alive. His body was stiff. He ached. There was a drumming in his head, and then a ringing in his ears as he tried to get up, managed to drag himself to an unsteady stance against the wall. He felt now an icy surety of horror that carried him out to a pin-point in space.

A terrible fatigue hit him. He fell back onto the bed. He lay there trying to figure out how he could be alive.

He finally slept pushed into it by sheer and utter exhaustion. The bells called him awake. The bells started him off again. He tried to talk again to 4901. They avoided him, all of them. But they weren't really alive any more. How long could he maintain some part of himself that he knew definitely was Charles Marquis?

He began a ritual, a routine divorced from that to which all those being indoctrinated were subjected. It was a little private routine of his own. Dying, and then finding that he was not dead.

He tried it many ways. He took more grains of the poison. But he was always alive again. "You—4901! Damn you—talk to me! You know what's been happening to me?"

The man nodded quickly over his little canisters of food-concentrate.

"This indoctrination—you, the girl—you went crazy when I talked about dying—what—?"

The man yelled hoarsely. "Don't . . . don't say it! All this—what you've been going through, can't you understand? All that is part of indoctrination. You're no different than the rest of us! We've all had it! All of us. All of us! Some more maybe than others. It had to end. You'll have to give in. Oh God, I wish you didn't. I wish you could win. But you're no smarter than the rest of us. *You'll have to give in!*"

It was 4901's longest and most coherent speech. Maybe I can get somewhere with him, Marquis thought. I can find out something.

But 4901 wouldn't say any more. Marquis kept on trying. No one, he knew, would ever realize what that meant—to keep on trying to die when no one would let you, when you kept dying, and then kept waking up again, and you weren't dead. No one could ever understand the pain that went between the dying and the living. And even Marquis couldn't remember it afterward. He only knew how painful it had been. And knowing that made each attempt a little harder for Marquis.

He tried the poison again. There was the big stamping machine that had crushed him beyond any semblance of a human being, but he had awakened, alive again, whole again. There was the time he grabbed the power cable and felt himself, in one blinding flash, conquer life in a burst of flame. He slashed his wrists at the beginning of a number of sleep periods.

When he awakened, he was whole again. There wasn't even a scar.

He suffered the pain of resisting the eating bells until he was so weak he couldn't respond, and he knew that he died that time too—from pure starvation.

But I can't stay dead!
" . . . You'll have to give in!"

*

He didn't know when it was. He had no idea now how long he had been here. But a guard appeared, a cold-faced man who guided Marquis back to the office where the fat, pink-faced little Manager waited for him behind the shelf suspended by silver wires from the ceiling.

The Manager said. "You are the most remarkable prisoner we've ever had here. There probably will not be another like you here again."

Marquis' features hung slack, his mouth slightly open, his lower lip drooping. He knew how he looked. He knew how near he was to cracking completely, becoming a senseless puppet of the bells. "Why is that?" he whispered.

"You've tried repeatedly to—you know what I mean of course. You have kept on attempting this impossible thing, attempted it more times than anyone else here ever has! Frankly, we didn't think any human psyche had the stuff to try it that many times—to resist that long."

The Manager made a curious lengthened survey of Marquis' face. "Soon you'll be thoroughly indoctrinated. You are, for all practical purposes, now. You'll work automatically then, to the bells, and think very little about it at all, except in a few stereotyped ways to keep your brain and nervous system active enough to carry out simple specialized work duties. Or while the New System lasts. And I imagine that will be forever."

"Forever . . . ."

"Yes, yes. You're immortal now," the Manager smiled. "Surely, after all this harrowing indoctrination experience, you realize *that!*"

Immortal. I might have guessed. I might laugh now, but I can't. We who pretend to live in a hell that is worse than death, and you, the Managerials who live in paradise. We two are immortal.

"That is, you're immortal as long as we desire you to be. You'll never grow any older than we want you to, never so senile as to threaten efficiency. That was what you were so interested in finding out on Earth, wasn't it? The mystery behind the Managerials? Why they never seemed to grow old. Why we have all the advantage, no senility, no weakening, the advantage of accumulative experience without the necessity of re-learning?"

"Yes," Marquis whispered.

The Manager leaned back. He lit a paraette and let the soothing nerve-tonic seep into his lungs. He explained.

"Every one of you political prisoners we bring here want, above everything else, to die. It was a challenge to our experimental social order here. We have no objection to your killing yourself. We have learned that even the will to die can be conditioned out of the most determined rebel. As it has been conditioned out of you. You try to die enough times, and you do die, but the pain of resurrection is so great that finally it is impossible not only to kill yourself, but even to think of attempting it."

Marquis couldn't say anything. The memory called up by the mention of self-destruction rasped along his spine like chalk on a blackboard. He could feel the total-recall of sensation, the threatening bursts of pain. "No . . . ." he whispered over and over. "No—please—no—"

The Manager said. "We won't mention it anymore. You'll never be able to try any overt act of self-destruction again."

27

The bright light from the ceiling lanced like splinters into the tender flesh of Marquis' eyeballs, danced about the base of his brain in reddened choleric circles. His face had drawn back so that his cheekbones stood out and his nose was beak-like. His irises became a bright painful blue in the reddened ovals of his eyes.

The Manager yawned as he finished explaining. "Each prisoner entering here has an identification punch-plate made of his unique electro-magnetic vibratory field. That's the secret of our immortality and yours. Like all matter, human difference is in the electro-magnetic, vibratory rates. We have these punch-plates on file for every prisoner. We have one of you. Any dead human body we merely put in a tank which dissolves it into separate cells, a mass of stasis with potentiality to be reformed into any type of human being of which we have an identification punch-plate, you see? This tank of dissociated cells is surrounded by an electro-magnetic field induced from a machine by one of the identification punch-plates. That particular human being lives again, the body, its mind, its life pattern identical to that from which the original punch-plate was made. Each time you have died, we reduced your body, regardless of its condition, to dissociated cells in the tank. The identification punch-plate was put in the machine. Your unique electro-magnetic field reformed the cells into you. It could only be you, as you are now. From those cells we can resurrect any one of whom we have an identification plate.

"That is all, No. 5274. Now that you're indoctrinated, you will work from now on in the food-mart, because of your experience."

*

For an undeterminable length of time, he followed the routines of the bells. In the big food-mart, among the hydroponic beds, and the canning machines; among the food-grinders and little belts that dropped cans of food-concentrate into racks and sent them off into the walls.

He managed to talk more and more coherently with No. 4901. He stopped referring to suicide, but if anyone had the idea that Marquis had given up the idea of dying, they were wrong. Marquis was stubborn. Somewhere in him the flame still burned. He wouldn't let it go out. The bells couldn't put it out. The throbbing machines couldn't put it out. And now he had at last figured out a way to beat the game.

During an eating period, Marquis said to 4901. "You want to die. Wait a minute—I'm talking about something we can both talk and think about. A murder agreement. You understand? We haven't been conditioned against killing each other. It's only an overt act of selfdes—all right, we don't think about that. But we can plan a way to kill each other."

4901 looked up. He stopped eating momentarily. He was interested. "What's the use though?" Pain shadowed his face. "We only go through it—come back again—"

"I have a plan. The way I have it worked out, they'll never bring either one of us back."

That wasn't exactly true. *One* of them would have to come back. Marquis hoped that 4901 wouldn't catch on to the fact that he would have to be resurrected, but that Marquis never would. He hoped that 4901's mind was too foggy and dull to see through the complex plan. And that was the way it worked.

Marquis explained. 4901 listened and smiled. It was the first time Marquis had ever seen a prisoner smile.

He left what remained of the capsule of poison where 4901 could get it. During one of the next four eating periods, 4901 was to slip the poison into Marquis' food can. Marquis wouldn't know what meal, or what can. He had to eat. The bells had conditioned him that much. And not to eat would be an overt act of self-destruction.

He wasn't conditioned not to accept death administered by another.

And then, after an eating period, 4901 whispered to him. "You're poisoned. It was in one of the cans you just ate."

"Great!" almost shouted Marquis. "All right. Now I'll die by the end of the next work period. That gives us this sleep period and all the next work period. During that time I'll dispose of you as I've said."

4901 went to his bed and the bells rang and the dark came and both of them slept.

*

Number 4901 resisted the conditioners enough to follow Marquis past his regular work room into the food-mart. As planned, 4901 marched on and stood in the steaming shadows behind the hydroponic beds.

Marquis worked for a while at the canning machines, at the big grinding vats. Then he went over to 4901 and said. "Turn around now."

4901 smiled. He turned around. "Good luck," he said. "Good luck—to you!"

Marquis hit 4901 across the back of the neck with an alloy bar and killed him instantly. He changed clothes with the dead man. He put his own clothes in a refuse incinerator. Quickly, he dragged the body over and tossed it into one of the food-grinding vats. His head bobbed up above the gray swirling liquid once, then the body disappeared entirely, was ground finely and mixed with the other foodstuff.

Within eight hours the cells of 4901 would be distributed minutely throughout the contents of thousands of cans of food-concentrate. Within that time much of it would have been consumed by the inmates and Managers.

At the end of that work period, Marquis returned to his cell. He went past his own bed and stopped in front of 4901's bed.

The sleep bells sounded and the dark came again. This would be the final dark, Marquis knew. This time he had beat the game. The delayed-action poison would kill him. He had on 4901's clothes with his identification number. He was on 4901's bed.

He would die as 4901. The guards would finally check on the missing man in the food-mart. But they would never find him. They would find 4901 dead, a suicide. And they would put the body labeled 4901 in the tank, dissolve it into dissociated cells and they would subject those cells to the electro-magnetic field of 4901.

And they would resurrect—4901.

Not only have I managed to die, Marquis thought, but I've managed the ultimate suicide. There won't even be a body, no sign anywhere that I have ever been at all. Even my cells will have been resurrected as someone else. As a number 4901.

*

"And that's the way it was," No. 4901 would tell new prisoners coming in. Sometimes they listened to him and seemed interested, but the interest always died during indoctrination. But No. 4901's interest in the story never died.

He knew that now he could never let himself die as a human being either, that he could never let himself become completely controlled by the bells. He'd been nearly dead as an individual, but No. 5274 had saved him from that dead-alive anonymity. He could keep alive, and maintain hope now by remembering what 5274 had done. He clung to that memory. As long as he retained that memory of hope—of triumph—at least some part of him would keep burning, as something had kept on burning within the heart of 5274.

So every night before the sleep bells sounded, he would go over the whole thing in minute detail, remembering 5274's every word and gesture, the details of his appearance. He told the plan over to himself every night, and told everyone about it who came in to the indoctrination ward.

Swimming up through the pain of resurrection, he had been a little mad at 5274 at first, and then he had realized that at least the plan had enabled one man to beat the game.

"He will always be alive to me. Maybe, in a way, he's part of me. Nobody knows. But his memory will live. He succeeded in a kind of ultimate dying—no trace of him anywhere. But the memory of him and what he did will be alive when the New System and the Managers are dead. That spirit will assure the Underground of victory—someday. And meanwhile, I'll keep 5274 alive.

"He even knew the psychology of these Managers and their System. That they can't afford to make an error. He knew they'd still have that identification punch-plate of him. That they would have one more plate than they had prisoners. But he anticipated what they would do there too. To admit there was one more identification plate than there were prisoners would be to admit a gross error. Of course they could dissolve one of the other prisoners and use 5274's plate and resurrect 5274. But they'd gain nothing. There would still be an extra plate. You see?

"So they destroyed the plate. He knew they would. And they also had to go back through the records, to Earth, through the security files there, through the birth records, everything. And they destroyed every trace, every shred of evidence that No. 5274 ever existed."

So he kept the memory alive and that kept 4901 alive while the other prisoners become automatons, hearing, feeling, sensing nothing except the bells. Remembering nothing, anticipating nothing.

But 4901 could remember something magnificent, and so he could anticipate, and that was hope, and faith. He found that no one really believed him but he kept on telling it anyway, the story of the Plan.

"Maybe this number didn't exist," someone would say. "If there's no record anywhere—"

4901 would smile. "In my head, there's where the record is. *I* know. *I* remember."

And so it was that 4901 was the only one who still remembered and who could still smile when sometime after that—no one in the prison colony knew how long—the Underground was victorious, and the Managerial System crumbled.

BREEDER REACTION

by Winston Marks

The remarkable thing about Atummyc Afterbath Dusting Powder was that it gave you that lovely, radiant, atomic look—just the way the advertisements said it would. In fact, it also gave you a little something more!

The advertising game is not as cut and dried as many people think. Sometimes you spend a million dollars and get no results, and then some little low-budget campaign will catch the public's fancy and walk away with merchandising honors of the year.

Let me sound a warning, however. When this happens, watch out! There's always a reason for it, and it isn't always just a matter of bright slogans and semantic genius. Sometimes the product itself does the trick. And when this happens people in the industry lose their heads trying to capitalize on the "freak" good fortune.

This can lead to disaster. May I cite one example?

I was on loan to Elaine Templeton, Inc., the big cosmetics firm, when one of these "prairie fires" took off and, as product engineer from the firm of Bailey Hazlitt & Persons, Advertising Agency, I figured I had struck pure gold. My assay was wrong. It was fool's gold on a pool of quicksand.

Madame "Elaine", herself, had called me in for consultation on a huge lipstick campaign she was planning—you know, NOW AT LAST, A TRULY KISS-PROOF LIPSTICK!—the sort of thing they pull every so often to get the ladies to chuck their old lip-goo and invest in the current dream of non-smearability. It's an old gimmick, and the new product is never actually kiss-proof, but they come closer each year, and the gals tumble for it every time.

Well, they wanted my advice on a lot of details such as optimum shades, a new name, size, shape and design of container. And they were ready to spend a hunk of moolah on the build-up. You see, when they give a product a first-class advertising ride they don't figure on necessarily showing a profit on that particular item. If they break even they figure they are ahead of the game, because the true purpose is to build up the brand name. You get enough women raving over the new Elaine Templeton lipstick, and first thing you know sales start climbing on the whole line of assorted aids to seduction.

Since E. T., Inc., was one of our better accounts, the old man told me to take as long as was needed, so I moved in to my assigned office, in the twelve-story E. T. building, secretary, Scotch supply, ice-bags, ulcer pills and all, and went to work setting up my survey staff. This product engineering is a matter of "cut and try" in some fields. You get some ideas, knock together some samples, try them on the public with a staff of interviewers, tabulate the results, draw your conclusions and hand them over to Production with a prayer. If your ad budget is large enough your prayer is usually answered, because the American Public buys principally on the "we know what we like, and we like what we know" principle. Make them "know it" and they'll buy it. Maybe in love, absence makes the heart grow fonder, but in this business, familiarity breeds nothing but sales.

Madame Elaine had a fair staff of idea boys, herself. In fact, every other department head had some gimmick he was trying to push to get personal recognition. The Old Hag liked this spirit of initiative and made it plain to me I was to give everyone a thorough hearing.

31

This is one of the crosses you have to bear. Everyone but the janitor was swarming into my office with suggestions, and more than half of them had nothing to do with the lipstick campaign at all. So I dutifully listened to each one, had my girl take impressive notes and then lifted my left or my right eyebrow at her. My left eyebrow meant file them in the wastebasket. This is how the Atummyc Afterbath Dusting Powder got lost in the shuffle, and later I was credited with launching a new item on which I didn't even have a record.

It came about this way:

Just before lunch one day, one of the Old Hag's promotion-minded pixies flounced her fanny into my interview chair, crossed her knees up to her navel and began selling me her pet project. She was a relative of the Madame as well as a department head, so I had to listen.

Her idea was corny—a new dusting powder with "Atummion" added, to be called, "Atummyc Afterbath Dusting Powder"—"Atummyc," of course, being a far-fetched play on the word "atomic". What delighted her especially was that the intimate, meaningful word "tummy" occurred in her coined trade name, and this was supposed to do wonders in stimulating the imaginations of the young females of man-catching-age.

As I said, the idea was corny. But the little hazel-eyed pixie was not. She was about 24, black-haired, small-waisted and bubbling with hormones. With her shapely knees and low-cut neckline she was a pleasant change of scenery from the procession of self-seeking middle-agers I had been interviewing—not that her motive was any different.

I stalled a little to feast my eyes. "This *Atummion Added* item," I said, "just what is *Atummion?*"

"That's my secret," she said, squinching her eyes at me like a fun-loving little cobra. "My brother is assistant head chemist, and he's worked up a formula of fission products we got from the Atomic Energy Commission for experimentation."

"Fission products!" I said. "That stuff's dangerous!"

"Not this formula," she assured me. "Bob says there's hardly any radiation to it at all. Perfectly harmless."

"Then what's it supposed to do?" I inquired naively.

She stood up, placed one hand on her stomach and the other behind her head, wiggled and stretched. "Atummyc Bath Powder will give milady that wonderful, vibrant, *atomic* feeling," she announced in a voice dripping with innuendo.

"All right," I said, "that's what it's supposed to do. Now what does it really do?"

"Smells good and makes her slippery-dry, like any other talcum," she admitted quite honestly. "It's the name and the idea that will put it across."

"And half a million dollars," I reminded her. "I'm afraid the whole thing is a little too far off the track to consider at this time. I'm here to make a new lipstick go. Maybe later—"

"I appreciate that, but honestly, don't you think it's a terrific idea?"

"I think you're terrific," I told her, raising my left eyebrow at my secretary, "and we'll get around to you one of these days."

"Oh, Mr. Sanders!" she said, exploding those big eyes at me and shoving a half-folded sheet of paper at me. "Would you please sign my interview voucher?"

In Madame Elaine's organization you had to have a written "excuse" for absenting yourself from your department during working hours. I supposed that the paper I signed was no different from the others. Anyway, I was still blinded by the atomic blast of those hazel eyes.

After she left I got to thinking it was strange that she had me sign the interview receipt. I couldn't remember having done that for any other department heads.

I didn't tumble to the pixie's gimmick for a whole month, then I picked up the phone one day and the old man spilled the news. "I thought you were making lipstick over there. What's this call for ad copy on a new bath powder?"

The incident flashed back in my mind, and rather than admit I had been by-passed I lied, "You know the Madame. She always gets all she can for her money."

The old man muttered, "I don't see taking funds from the lipstick campaign and splitting them off into little projects like this," he said. "Twenty-five thousand bucks would get you one nice spread in the Post, but what kind of a one-shot campaign would that be?"

I mumbled excuses, hung up and screamed for the pixie. My secretary said, "Who?"

"Little sexy-eyes. The Atomic Bath Powder girl."

Without her name it took an hour to dig her up, but she finally popped in, plumped down and began giggling. "You found out."

"How," I demanded, "did you arrange it?"

"Easy. Madame Elaine's in Paris. She gave you a free hand, didn't she?"

I nodded.

"Well, when you signed your okay on the Atummyc—"

"That was an interview voucher!"

"Not—exactly," she said ducking her head.

The damage was done. You don't get ahead in this game by admitting mistakes, and the production department was already packaging and labelling samples of Atummyc Bath Powder to send out to the distributors.

*

I had to carve the $25,000 out of my lipstick budget and keep my mouth shut. When the ad copy came over from my firm I looked it over, shuddered at the quickie treatment they had given it and turned it loose. Things were beginning to develop fast in my lipstick department, and I didn't have time to chase the powder thing like I should have—since it was my name on the whole damned project.

So I wrote off the money and turned to other things.

We were just hitting the market with Madame Elaine Templeton's "Kissmet" when the first smell of smoke came my way. The pixie came into my office one morning and congratulated me.

"You're a genius!" she said.

"Like the Kissmet campaign, do you?" I said pleased.

"It stinks," she said holding her nose. "But Atummyc Bath Powder will pull you out of the hole."

"Oh, that," I said. "When does it go to market?"

"Done went—a month ago."

"What? Why you haven't had time to get it out of the lab yet. Using a foreign substance, you should have had an exhaustive series of allergy skin tests on a thousand women before—"

"I've been using it for two months myself," she said. "And look at me! See any rashes?"

I focussed my eyes for the first time, and what I saw made me wonder if I were losing my memory. The pixie had been a pretty little French pastry from the first, but now she positively glowed. Her skin even had that "radiant atomic look", right out of our corny, low-budget ad copy.

"What—have you done to yourself, fallen in love?"

"With Atummyc After Bath Powder," she said smugly. "And so have the ladies. The distributors are all reordering."

Well, these drug sundries houses have some sharp salesmen out, and I figured the bath powder must have caught them needing something to promote. It was a break. If we got the $25,000 back it wouldn't hurt my alibi a bit, in case the Kissmet production failed to click.

Three days later the old man called me from the New York branch of our agency. "Big distributor here is hollering about the low budget we've given to this Atummyc Bath Powder thing," he said. "He tells me his men have punched it hard and he thinks it's catching on pretty big. Maybe you better talk the Madame out of a few extra dollars."

"The Old Hag's in Europe," I told him, "and I'm damned if I'll rob the Kissmet Lipstick deal any more. It's mostly spent anyway."

The old man didn't like it. When you get the distributors on your side it pays to back them up, but I was too nervous about the wobbly first returns we were getting on the Kissmet campaign to consider taking away any of the unspent budget and throwing it into the bath powder deal.

The next day I stared at an order from a west coast wholesaler and began to sweat. The pixie fluttered it under my nose. "Two more carloads of Atummyc Bath Powder," she gloated.

"Two more *carloads?*"

"Certainly. All the orders are reading *carloads,*" she said. "This thing has busted wide open."

And it had. Everybody, like I said earlier, lost their head. The bath-powder plant was running three shifts and had back-orders chin high. The general manager, a joker name of Jennings, got excited, cabled Madame Elaine to get back here pronto, which she did, and then the panic was on.

The miracle ingredient was this Atummion, and if Atummion sold bath powder why wouldn't it sell face-cream, rouge, mud-packs, shampoos, finger-nail polish and eye-shadow?

For that matter, the Old Hag wanted to know, why wouldn't it sell Kissmet Lipstick?

The answer was, of course, that the magic legend "Contains the Exclusive New Beauty Aid, Atummion" *did* sell these other products. Everything began going out in carload lots as soon as we had the new labels printed, and to be truthful, I breathed a wondrous sigh of relief, because up to that moment my Kissmet campaign had promised to fall flat on its lying, crimson face.

*

The staggering truth about Atummion seeped in slowly. Item one: Although we put only a pinch of it in a whole barrel of talcum powder, *it did give the female users a terrific* complexion! Pimples, black-heads, warts, freckles and even minor scars disappeared after a few weeks, and from the very first application users mailed us testimonials swearing to that "atomic feeling of loveliness".

Item two: About one grain of Atummion to the pound of lipstick brought out the natural color of a woman's lips and maintained it there *even after the lipstick was removed.*

Item three: There never was such a shampoo. For once the ad copywriters failed to exceed the merits of their product. Atummion-tinted hair took on a sparkling look, a soft texture and a *natural-appearing wave* that set beauty-operators screaming for protection.

These beauticians timed their complaint nicely. It got results on the morning that the whole thing began to fall to pieces.

About ten A. M. Jennings called a meeting of all people concerned in the Atummyc Powder project, and they included me as well as the pixie and her brother, the assistant chemist.

Everyone was too flushed with success to take Jennings' opening remark too seriously. "It looks like we've got a winner that's about to lose us our shirts," he said.

He shuffled some papers and found the one he wanted to hit us with first. "The beauticians claim we are dispensing a dangerous drug without prescription. They have brought suits to restrain our use."

Madame Elaine in her mannishly tailored suit was standing by a window staring out. She said, "The beauticians never gave us any break, anyway. Hell with them! What's next?"

Jennings lifted another paper. "I agree, but they sicked the Pure Food and Drug people on us. They tend to concur."

"Let them prove it first," the Old Hag said turning to the pixie's brother. "Eh, Bob!"

"It's harmless!" he protested, but I noticed that the pixie herself, for all her radiance, had a troubled look on her face.

The general manager lifted another paper. "Well, there seems to be enough doubt to have caused trouble. The Pure Food and Drug labs have by-passed the courts and put in a word to the Atomic Energy Commission. The AEC has cut off our supply of the fission salts that go into Atummion, pending tests."

That brought us all to our feet. Madame Elaine stalked back to the huge conference table and stared at Bob, the chemist. "How much of the gunk do we have on hand?"

"About a week's supply at present production rates." He was pale, and he swallowed his adam's apple three times.

The worst was yet to come. The pixie looked around the table peculiarly unchanged by the news. She had trouble in her face but it had been there from the start of the conference. "I wasn't going to bring this up just yet," she said, "but since we're here to have a good cry I might as well let you kick this one around at the same time. Maybe you won't mind shutting down production after all."

The way she said it froze all of us except the Madame.

The Madame said, "Well, speak up! What is it?"

"I've been to twelve different doctors, including eight specialists. I've thought and thought until I'm half crazy, and there just isn't any other answer," the pixie said.

She stared at us and clenched her fists and beat on the shiny table. "You've got to believe me! There just isn't *any* other answer. Atummion is responsible for my condition, and all twelve doctors agreed on my condition."

Still standing, Madame Elaine Templeton grabbed the back of her chair until her knuckles turned white. "Don't tell me the stuff brings on hives or something!"

The pixie threw back her head and a near-hysterical laugh throbbed from her lovely throat. "Hives, hell. I'm pregnant!"

*

Well, we were all very sorry for her, because she was unmarried, and that sort of thing is always clumsy. At that moment, however, none of us believed the connection between her condition and Atummion.

Being a distant relative of the Madame, she was humored to the extent that we had the lab get some guinea pigs and douse them with Elaine Templeton's After Bath Powder, and they even professed to make a daily check on them.

Meanwhile, production ground to a halt on all Atummion-labelled products, which was everything, I think, but the eyebrow pencils.

With every drug-store and department store in the country screaming to have their orders filled, it was a delicate matter and took a lot of string-pulling to keep the thing off the front-pages. It wasn't the beautician's open charges that bothered us, because everyone knew they were just disgruntled. But if it leaked out that the AEC was disturbed enough to cut off our fission products, every radio, newspaper and TV commentator in the business would soon make mince-meat of us over the fact that Atummion had not been adequately tested before marketing. And this was so right!

We took our chances and submitted honest samples to the Bureau of Weights and Measures and the Pure Food and Drug labs. And held our breath.

The morning the first report came back in our favor there was great rejoicing, but that afternoon our own testing lab sent up a man to see Jennings, and he called me instantly.

"Sanford, get up here at once. The guinea pigs just threw five litters of babies!"

"Congratulations," I told him. "That happens with guinea pigs, I understand."

"You *don't* understand," he thundered at me. "This was test group F-six, all females, and every one has reached maturity since we bought and segregated them."

"There must be some mistake," I said.

"There better be," he told me.

I went to his office and together we picked up the Madame from her penthouse suite. She followed us into the elevator reluctantly. "Absurd, absurd!" was all she could say.

We watched the lab man check the ten adult pigs one by one. Even as inexpert as I am in such matters, it was evident that all ten were females, and the five which had not yet participated in blessed events were but hours from becoming mothers.

We went our separate ways stunned. Back in my office I pulled out a list of our big wholesale accounts where the Atummion products had been shipped by the carloads. The warehouses were distributed in every state of the union.

Then I ran my eye down the list of products which contained the devilish Atummion. There were thirty-eight, in all, including a complete line of men's toiletries, shaving lotion, shampoo, deodorant and body-dusting powder. I thanked God that men didn't have ovaries.

Dolores Donet—that was the pixie's name—opened my door and deposited herself gingerly in a chair opposite me.

I said, "You look radiant."

She said, "Don't rub it in, and I'll have a shot of that." I shared my Haig and Haig with her, and we drank to the newly departed bottom of the world.

*

My secretary tried to give me a list of people who had phoned and a stack of angry telegrams about back-orders, but I waved her away. "Dolores," I said, "there must have been a boy guinea pig loose in that pen. It's just too fantastic!"

"Are you accusing me of turning one loose just to get off the hook myself?" she snapped.

"What you've got, excuses won't cure," I told her, "but we've got to get facts. My God, if you're right—"

"We've sworn everyone to secrecy," she said. "There's a $10,000 bonus posted for each employee who knows about this. Payable when the statute of limitations runs out on possible litigation."

"You can't swear the public to secrecy," I said.

"Think a minute," she said, coldly. "The married women don't need excuses, and the single girls—who'll believe them? Half of them or better, have guilty consciences anyway. The rest? They're in the same boat I was—without a labful of guinea pigs to back them up."

"But—how did it happen in the first place?"

"Bob has been consulting the biologist we retained. He keeps asking the same question. He says parthenogenesis in higher lifeforms is virtually impossible. Bob keeps pointing at the little pigs, and they're going round and round. They're examining the other eleven test pens now, but there's no question in my mind. I have a personal stake in this experiment, and I was very careful to supervise the segregation of males and females."

My sanity returned in one glorious rush. *There was the bugger factor! Dolores, herself.*

In her eagerness to clear her own skirts, Dolores had tampered with the integrity of the experiment. Probably, she had arranged for artificial insemination, just to be sure. The tip-off was the hundred percent pregnancy of one whole test-batch. Ten out of ten. Even if one buck had slipped in inadvertently, and someone was covering up the mistake, why you wouldn't expect anything like a 100% "take".

"Dolores," I said, "you are a naughty girl in more ways than one."

She got up and refilled her glass shaking her head. "The ever-suspicious male," she said. "Don't you understand? I'm not trying to dodge my responsibility for my condition. The whole mess is my fault from beginning to end. But what kind of a heel will I be if we get clearance from the AEC and start shipping out Atummyc products again—knowing what I do? What's more, if we let the stuff float around indefinitely, someone is going to run comprehensive tests on it, not just allergy test patches like they're doing at the government labs right now."

"Yeah," I said, "so we all bury the hottest promotion that ever hit the cosmetics industry and live happily ever after."

She hit the deck and threw her whiskey glass at me, which did nothing to convince me that she wasn't telling the tallest tale of the century—to be conservative.

We sat and glared at each other for a few minutes. Finally she said, "You're going to get proof, and damned good proof any minute now."

"How so?" Nothing this experiment revealed would be valid to me, I figured, now that I was convinced she had deliberately fouled it up.

"Bob and the biologist should be up here any minute. I told them I'd wait in your office. I know something you don't, I'm just waiting for them to verify it."

She was much too confident, and I began to get worried again. We waited for ten minutes, fifteen, twenty. I picked up the phone and dialed the lab.

The woman assistant answered and said that the two men were on the way up right now. I asked, "What have they been doing down there?"

She said, "They've been doing Caesarian sections on the animals in test-pen M-four."

"Caesarian sections?" I repeated. She affirmed it, and Dolores Donet got a tight, little, humorless smile on her face. I hung up and said, "They're on their way up, and what's so funny?"

She said, "You know what I think? I think you've been using Atummyc products on you."

"So what?" I demanded. "I was responsible for this campaign, too. I've been waiting for a rash to develop almost as long as you have."

She said, "When Bob comes in, look at his complexion. All three of us have been guinea pigs, I guess."

"I still don't see what's so damned amusing."

She said, "You still don't tumble, eh? All right, I'll spell it out. Caesarians performed on test batch M-four."

"So?"

"The 'M' stands for male," she said.

She timed it just right. The hall door opened and Bob trailed in with a dazed look. The biologist was half holding him up. His white lab-smock was freshly blood-stained, and his eyes were blank and unsceing.

But for all his distress, he was still a good looking young fellow. His skin had that lovely, radiant, atomic look—just like mine.

TURNING POINT

by Alfred Coppel

The man is rare who will give his life for what is merely the lesser of two evils. Merrick's decision was even tougher: to save human beings at the expense of humanity, or vice versa?

This, then, was the Creche, Anno Domini 2500. A great, mile-square blind cube topping a ragged mountain; bare escarpments falling away to a turbulent sea. For five centuries the Creche had stood so, and the Androids had come forth in an unending stream to labor for Man, the Master . . . .
—Quintus Bland, The Romance of Genus Homo.

Director Han Merrick paced the floor nervously. His thin, almost ascetic face was pale and drawn.

"We can't allow it, Virginia," he said, "Prying of this sort can only precipitate a pogrom or worse. Erikson is a bigot of the worst kind. The danger—" He broke off helplessly.

His wife shook her head slowly. "It cannot be prevented, Han. Someone was bound to start asking questions sooner or later. History should have taught us that. And five hundred years of secrecy was more than anyone had a right to expect. Nothing lasts forever."

The trouble is, Merrick told himself, *simply that I am the wrong man for this job. I should never have taken it. There's a wrongness in what we are doing here that colors my every reaction and makes me incapable of acting on my own. Always the doubts and secret questioning. If the social structure of our world weren't moribund, I wouldn't be here at all . . . .*

"History, Virginia," he said, "can't explain what there is no precedent for. The Creche is unique in human experience."

"The Creche may be, Han, but Sweyn Erikson is not. Consider his background and tell me if there hasn't been an Erikson in every era of recorded history. He is merely another obstacle in the path of progress that must be overcome. The job is yours, Han."

"A pleasant prospect," Merrick replied bleakly. "I am an organizer, not a psychotechnician. How am I supposed to protect the Creche from the likes of Erikson? What insanity bore this fruit, Virginia? The Prophet, the number one Fanatic, coming here as an *investigator* in the name of the Council of Ten! I realize the Council turns pale at the thought of the vote the Fanatics control, but surely *something* could have been done! Have those idiots forgotten what we do here? Is that possible?"

Virginia Merrick shook her head. "The stone got too hot for them to handle, so they've thrown it to you."

"But Erikson, himself! The very man who organized the Human Supremacy Party and the Antirobot League! If he sets foot within the Creche it will mean an end to everything!"

The woman lit a cigarette and inhaled deeply. "We can't keep him out and you know it. There's an army of Fanatics gathering out there in the hills this very minute. Armed with cortical-stimulant projectors, Han. That isn't a pleasant way to die—"

Merrick studied his wife carefully. There was fear under her iron control. She was thinking of the shattering pain of death under the projectors. Nothing else, really. The Creche didn't matter to her. The Creche didn't really matter to any of the staff. Three hundred years ago it would have been different. The custodians of the Creche would have gladly died to preserve their trust in those times . . . .

What irony, Merrick thought, that it should come like this. He knew what the projectors did to men. He also knew what they did to robots.

"If they dare to use their weapons on us it will wipe out every vestige of control work done here since the beginning," he said softly.

"They have no way of knowing that."

"Nor would they believe it if we told them."

"And that brings us right back to where we started. You can't keep Erikson out, and the Council of Ten has left us on our own. They don't dare oppose the Fanatics. But there's an old political maxim you would do well to consider very carefully since it's our only hope, Han," Virginia Merrick said, "'If you can't beat someone—join him.'"

*

She dragged deeply on her cigarette, blue smoke curling from her gold-tinted lips. "This has been coming on for ten years. I tried to warn you then, but you wouldn't listen. Remember?"

How like a woman, Merrick thought bitterly, to be saying I told you so.

"What would you have me do, Virginia?" he asked, "Help the bigot peddle his robot-hate? That can't be the way. Don't you feel anything at all when the reports of pogroms come in?"

Virginia Merrick shrugged. "Better they than we, Han."

"Has it occurred to you that our whole culture might collapse if Erikson has his way?"

"Antirobotism is natural to human beings. Compromise is the only answer. Precautions have to be taken—"

"*Precautions!*" exploded Merrick. "What sort of precautions can be taken against pure idiocy?"

"The founding board of Psychotechnicians—"

"No help from that source. You know that I've always felt the whole premise was questionable. On the grounds of common fairness, if nothing else."

"Really, Han," Virginia snapped, "It was the only thing to do and you know it. The Creche is the only safeguard the race has."

"Now you sound like the Prophet. In reverse."

"We needn't argue the point."

"No, I suppose not," the Director muttered.

"Then what are you going to do when he gets here?" She ground out her cigarette anxiously. "The procession is in the ravine now. You had better decide quickly."

"I don't know, Virginia. I just don't know." Merrick sank down behind his desk, hands toying with the telescreen controls. "I was never intended to make this sort of decisions. I feel helpless. Look here—"

The image of the ravine glowed across the screen in brilliant relief. The densely timbered slopes were spotted with tiny purposeful figures in the grey robes that all Fanatics affected. Here and there the morning sun caught a glint of metal as the Fanatics labored to set up their projectors. Along the floor of the ravine that was the only land approach to the Creche moved the twisting, writhing snake of the procession. The enraptured Fanatics were chanting their hate-songs as they came. In the first rank walked the leonine Erikson, his long hair whipping in the moisture-laden wind from the sea.

With a muttered curse, Merrick flipped a toggle and the scene dimmed. The face of a secretary appeared superimposed on it. It was the expressionless face of an android, a fine example of the Creche's production line. "Get Graves up here," he ordered, "You may find him at Hypno-Central or in Semantic Evaluation."

"Very good, sir," intoned the android, fading from the screen.

Merrick looked at his wife. "Maybe Graves and I can think of something."

"Don't plan anything rash, Han."

Merrick shrugged and turned back to watch the steady approach of the procession of grey-frocked zealots in the ravine.

Graves appeared as the doorway dilated. He looked fearful and pale. "You wanted to see me, Han?"

"Come in, Jon. Sit down."

"Have you seen the projectors those crackpots have set up in the hills?" Graves demanded.

"I have, Jon. That's what I wanted to talk to you about."

"My God, Han! Do you have any idea of what it must feel like to die from cortical stimulation?" Graves' voice was tense and strained. "Can't we get out of here by 'copter?"

"No. The 'copters are both in Francisco picking up supplies. I ordered them out yesterday. Besides, that wouldn't settle anything. There are almost a thousand androids in the Creche as of this morning. What about them?"

Graves made a gesture of impatience. "It's the humans I'm thinking about."

Merrick forced down the bitter taste of disgust that welled into his throat and forced himself to go on. "We have to take some sort of action to protect the Creche, Jon. I've held off until the last moment, thinking the Council would never allow a Fanatic to investigate the Creche, but the Ten are more afraid of the HSP rubber stamp vote than they are of letting a thousand androids be slaughtered. But we can't leave it at that. If we don't prevent it, Erikson will precipitate a pogrom that will make the Canalopolis massacre look like a tea-party." For some reason he held back the information about the effect of the Fanatic weapon on robot tissue. The vague notion that knowing, Jon Graves might cast his lot with Erikson, restrained him.

"Of course, Erikson will come in wearing an energy shield," Graves said.

"He will. And we have none," Virginia Merrick said softly.

"Can we compromise with him?" Graves asked.

There it was again, Merrick thought, the weasel-word 'compromise.' There was a moral decay setting in everywhere—the founders of the Creche would never have spoken so. "No," he said flatly, "We cannot. Erikson has conceived a robot-menace. All the old hate-patterns are being dusted off and used on the rabble. People are actually asking one another if they would like their daughters to *marry* robots. That sort of thing, as old as *homo sapiens*. And one cannot compromise with prejudice. It seduces the emotions and dulls the mind. No, there will be no appeasing of Sweyn Erikson or his grey-shirted nightriders!"

"You're talking like a starry-eyed fool, Han," Virginia Merrick said sharply.

"Can't we take him in and give him the works?" Graves asked hopefully. "Primary Conditioning could handle the job. Give him a fill-in with false memory?"

Merrick shook his head. "We can't risk narcosynthesis and that's essential. He'll surely be tested for blood purity when he leaves, and scopolamine traces would be a dead give-away that we had been trying to hide something here."

"Then it looks as though compromise is the only way, Han. They've got us up against the wall. See here, Han, I know you don't agree, but what else is there? After all, we all believe in human supremacy. Erikson calls it a robot-menace, we look at it from another angle, but our common goal is the betterment of the human culture we've established. People are on an emotional jag now. There has been no war for five centuries. No emotional release. And there have been regulations and conventions set up since the Atom War that only a very few officials have been allowed to understand. Erikson is no savage, Han, after all. True he's set off a rash of robot-baiting, but he can be dealt with on an intelligent plane, I'm sure."

"He is a man of ability, you know," Virginia Merrick said.

"Ability," Merrick said bitterly. "Rabble rouser and bigot! Look at his record. Organizer of the riots in Low Chicago. Leader in the Antirobot Labor League—the same outfit that slaughtered fifty robots in the Tycho dock strike. Think, you two! To tell such a man what the Creche is would be to tie a rope around the neck of every android alive. Lynch law! The rope and the whip for every one of them. And then suppose the worm turns? *It can, you know!* Our methods here are far from perfect. What then?"

"I still say we must compromise," Graves said. "They will kill us if we don't—"

"He's no troglodyte, Han, I'm certain—" Merrick's wife said plaintively.

The Director felt resistance flowing out of him. They were right, of course. There was nothing else he could do.

"All right," Merrick's voice was low and tired. He felt the weight of his years settling down on him. "I'll do as you suggest. I'll try to lead him off the trail first—" that was his compromise with himself, he knew, and he hated himself for it— "and if I fail I'll tell him the whole truth."

He flipped the telescreen toggle in time to see Sweyn Erikson detach himself from his followers and disappear through the dilated outer gate in the side of the Creche. A faint, almost futile stirring of defiance shook him. He found himself in the anomalous position of wanting to defend something that he had long felt was wrong in concept from the beginning—and not being able to take an effective course of action.

He reached into his desk drawer and took out an ancient automatic. It was a family heirloom, heavy, black and deadly. He pulled back the slide and watched one of the still-bright brass cartridges snap up into the breech. He handled the weapon awkwardly, but as he slipped it into his jumper pocket some of the weariness slipped from him and a cold anger took its place. He looked calmly from his wife to Graves.

"I'll tell him the whole truth," he said, "And if he fails to react as you two think he will, I shall kill him."

*

Sweyn Erikson, in a pre-Atom War culture, might have been a dictator. But the devastation of the war had at long last resulted in a peaceful world-state, and where no nations exist, politics becomes a sterile business of direction and supervision. It is war or the threat of war that gives a politician his power. Sweyn Erikson wanted power above all else. And so he founded a religion.

He became the Prophet of the Fanatics. And since a cult must have an object of group hate as a *raison-d'etre*, he chose the androids. With efficiency and calculated sincerity, he beat the drums of prejudice until his organization had spread its influence into the world's high places and his word became the law of the land.

People who beheld his feral magnificence, and listened to the spell-binding magic of his oratory—followed. His power sprang from the masses—unthinking, emotional. He gave the mob a voice and a purpose. He was like a Hitler or a Torquemada. Like a Long or a John Brown. He was savage and rapacious, courageous and bitter. He was Man.

There were four cardinal precepts by which the membership of the Human Supremacy Party lived. First, Man was God. Second, no race could share the plenum with Man. Had separate races still remained after the Atom War, the HSP racism might have been more specific, but since there remained only humanity en masse, all human beings shared the godhead. Third, the artificial persons that streamed from the Creche were blasphemy. Fourth, they must be destroyed. Like other generations before them, the humans of this age rallied to the banner of the whip and the rope. Not since the War had blood been spilled, but the destructive madness of homo sapiens found joy in the word of the Prophet, and though the blood was only the red sap of androids, the thrill was there.

Thus had Sweyn Erikson, riding the intolerant wave of antirobotism, come to the Creche. He stood now, in the long bare foyer, waiting. Behind him lay the Party and the League. The Council of Ten was in hand and helpless. Upon his report to the world, the future of an entire robot-human culture pattern rested. This, he told himself, was the high point of his life. Naked power to use as he chose rested in his hands. The whole structure of world society was tottering. The choice was his and his alone. He could shore it up or shatter it and trample on the fragments . . . .

The Prophet savored the moment. He watched with interest as the door before him dilated. The Creche Director stood eyeing him half-fearfully, half-defiantly, flanked by his wife and his assistant. They were all three afraid for their lives, Erikson thought with satisfaction.

"We welcome you to the Creche," Han Merrick said formally.

"Let there be no ceremony," Erikson said, "I am a simple man."

Merrick's lips tightened. "You haven't come here for ceremony. There will be none."

"I came for truth," the Prophet said sonorously. "The people of the world are waiting for my words. The mask of secrecy must be ripped from this place and truth and knowledge allowed to wash it clean."

Merrick almost winced. The statement was redundant with the propaganda that Erikson's nightriders peddled on every street corner. It betokened an intellectual bankruptcy among men that was frightening.

"I shall do my best to allay your fears," he said thickly.

Erikson's eyes glittered with suspicion. "I need only a guide. The decisions I shall make for myself. And mind that I am shown every concealed place. The roots of this place must be laid bare. 'For God shall bring every work into judgment, with every secret thing; whether it be good or whether it be evil.' The Scriptures command it in the name of Man, the True God."

Twisted, pious, hypocrite! thought Merrick.

"I am sure, sir," Graves was saying placatingly, "that when we have shown you the Creche you will see that there is no menace."

Erikson scowled at Graves deliberately. "There is menace enough in the blasphemy of android life, my son. Everywhere there are signs of unrest among the things you have built here. On Mars, human beings have died at their hands!"

Merrick's face showed his disgust. "Frankly, I don't believe that. Androids don't kill."

"We shall see, my son," Erikson said settling the belt of his energy screen more comfortably about his hips. "We shall see."

Merrick studied Erikson's face. There was a tiny scar under his chin. That would be where the transmitter was planted. He had no doubt that every word of this conversation was being monitored by the Fanatics outside the Creche. The turning point was coming inexorably nearer. He only hoped that he had the physical and moral courage to face it when it arrived.

"Very well, Sweyn Erikson," he said finally. "Please come with me."

*

Four hours later they were in Merrick's office. The preliminary stage of his plan had failed, just as he had known it would. He was almost glad. It had been a vacillating expediency, an attempt to hide the facts and avoid the necessity of facing the challenge squarely. Stage two was about to begin, and this time there would be no temporizing.

The Prophet glared angrily across the desk-top. "Do you take me for a child? You have shown me nothing. Where are the protoplasm vats? The brain machines? Where are the bodies assembled? I warned you against trickery, Han Merrick!"

Merrick glanced across the room at his wife. She sat rigid in her chair, her face a pale mask. He would get no help from her.

"You must realize, Erikson," he said, "That you are forcing me to jeopardize five centuries of work for the chimera of Human Supremacy. Let me warn you now that your life is of no importance to me when balanced against that. When the Board of Psychotechnicians appointed my family custodians of the Creche centuries ago, they did so because they knew we would keep faith—"

"The last member of the founding Board died more than two hundred years ago," snapped the Prophet.

"But the Creche is here, and I am here to guard it as my forefathers did," Merrick said. Once again he was conscious of a strange ambivalence in his attitude. He must guard something he considered wrong against the intrusion of a danger even more wrong. His hand sought the scored grip of the old automatic in his pocket. Could he actually kill?

"You speak of Human Supremacy as a chimera," Sweyn Erikson said, "It is no such thing. It is the only vital force left in the world. Robotism is a menace more deadly, a blasphemy more foul than any Black Mass of history. You are making Man into an anachronism on the face of his own planet. This cannot be! *I will not let it be . . . .*"

Merrick stared. Could it be that the man actually believed that the poison he peddled was the food of the gods?

44

"I will try one last attempt at reason, Erikson," Merrick said deliberately. "Look back with an unprejudiced mind, if you can, over the centuries since the Atom War. What do you see?"

"I see Man emasculated by the robot!"

"No! You see atomic power harnessed and in use for the first time after almost a millenium of muddling. You see Man standing on the Moon and the habitable planets—and soon to reach out for the stars! A new Golden Age is dawning, Prophet! And why? Whence have come the techniques?" Even as he spoke, Merrick knew he was ignoring the obvious, the all-too-apparent cracks in the social structure that no scientific miracles could cure. But were those cracks the fault of robotism or were they in fact a failing inherent in Man himself? He was not prepared to answer that. "From where are the techniques drawn?" he asked again.

Erikson met his glance squarely. "Not from the mindless horrors you spawn here!"

"Emotionless, Prophet," corrected Merrick pointedly, "Not mindless."

"Soulless! Soulless and mindless, too. Never have these zombies been able to think as men!"

"They are not men."

"Nor are they the architects of the future!"

"I think you are wrong, Prophet," Merrick said softly.

"Man is the ultimate," Erikson said.

"You talk like a fool," snapped Merrick.

"*Han!*" There was naked terror in his wife's voice, but he rushed on, ignoring it.

"How dare you say that Man is the ultimate? What right have you to assume that nature has stopped experimenting?"

Sweyn Erikson's lip curled scornfully. "Can you be implying that the robots—"

Merrick leaned across the desk to shout full in the Prophet's face: "*You fool! They're not robots!*"

The robed man was suddenly on his feet, face livid.

"Han!" cried Virginia Merrick, "Not that way!"

"This is my affair now, Virginia. I'll handle it in my own way!" the Director said.

"Remember the mob outside!"

Merrick turned agate-hard eyes on his wife. Presently he looked away and said to the Prophet. "Now I will show you the real Creche!"

*

There were robots everywhere—blank-eyed, like sleep walkers. They reacted to commands. They moved and breathed and fed themselves. Under rigid control they performed miracles of intuitive calculation. But artificiality was stamped upon them like a brand. They were *not* human.

In the lowest vaults of the Creche, Merrick showed the Prophet the infants. He withheld nothing. He showed him the growing creatures. He explained to him the tests and signs that were looked for in the hospitals maintained by the World State and the Council of Ten. He let him watch the young ones taking their Primary Conditioning. Courses of hypnotic instruction. Rest, narcosynthesis. Semantics. Drugs and words and more words pounding on young brains like sledgehammer blows, shaping them into something acceptable in a sapient world.

In other chambers, other age groups. Emotion and memory being moulded into something else by hypnopedia. Faces becoming blank and expressionless.

"Their minds are conditioned—enslaved," Merrick said bitterly. "Then they are primed with scientific facts. Those techniques we discussed. *This* is where they come from, Prophet. From the minds of your despised androids. Only will is suppressed, and emotion. They are shaped for the sociography of a sapient culture. They mature very slowly. We keep them here for from ten to fifteen years. No human brain could stand it—but *theirs* can."

Truth dangled before his eyes, but Erikson's mind savagely rejected it. The pillars upon which he had built his life were crumbling . . . .

The two men stood in a vast hall filled with an insidious, whispering voice. On low pallets, fully a score of physically mature androids lay staring vacuously at a spinning crystal high in the apex of the domed ceiling.

"—you had no life before you where created here to serve Man the master you had no life before you were created here to serve Man the master you had—" the voice whispered into the hypnotized brains.

"Don't look up," Merrick warned. "The crystal can catch a human being faster than it can *them*. This is hypnotic engineering. The rhythm of the syllables and their proportion to the length of word and sentence are computed to correspond to typed encephalographic curves. Nothing is left to chance. When they have reached this stage of conditioning they are almost ready for release and purchase by human beings. Only a severe stimulation of the brain can break down the walls we have built in their minds."

Erikson made a gesture as though darkness were streaking his vision. He was shaken badly. "But where do they—where do they come from?"

"The State maternity hospitals, of course," Merrick said, "Where else? The parents are then sterilized by the Health and Welfare Authority as an added safeguard. Births occur at a ratio of about one for every six million normals." He smiled mirthlessly at the Prophet of Human Supremacy. "Well? Little man, what now?"

Honest realization still refused to come. It needed to be put into words, and Sweyn Erikson had no such words. "I see only that you are taking children of men and disfiguring—"

"For the last time," gritted Merrick, "These are *not* human beings. Genus homo, yes. *Homo chaos*, if you choose. But not homo sapiens. I think of them," he said with sudden calm, "As *Homo Supremus*. The next step on the evolutionary ladder . . . ."

At last the words had been spoken and the flood gates were down in the tortured brain of the Prophet. Like a sudden conflagration, realization came—and with it, blind terror.

"No! Nonono! You cannot continue this devil's work! Think what it would mean if these things should ever be loosed on the world of Man!" the Prophet's voice was a steadily rising shrill of fear.

Han Merrick looked out across the rows of pallets, each with its burden of a superman, bound like Prometheus to the rock, helpless in hypnotic chains. It struck him again that his life had not been well spent. He looked from his charges to the ranting fear-crazed rabble-rouser. The contrast was too shocking, too complete. For the "androids" were, in fact, worthy of a dignity even in slavery that homo sapiens had never attained in overlordship. Merrick knew at last what he must do.

Racial loyalty stirred, but was quickly smothered in the humiliation of man's omnipresent thievery. For it *was* thievery, Merrick thought. Man was keeping for himself the heritage that was the rightful property of a newer, better race.

He took the automatic from his jumper and leveled it at Erikson's chest. He felt very sure and right. Though he knew that he was sealing the death warrant of his wife and his friends, the memory of their vacillations anesthetized him against any feeling of loss. He waited until Erikson screamed one word into the transmitter imbedded in his flesh—

The word was: "*Attack!*"

—and in the next instant, Han Merrick shot him dead.

*

The fanatics on the ridges heard the Prophet's command and sprang to comply. Energy swept out of the grids, through the coils of the projectors and out over the blind cube of the Creche.

Han Merrick felt the first radiations. He felt the beginnings of cortical hypertrophy and screamed. Every synapse sagged under the increasing load of sensitivity. The pressure of the air became an unbearable burden, the faintest sound became a shattering roar. Every microscopic pain, every cellular process became a rending, tearing agony. He screamed and the sound was a cataclysmic, planet-smashing hell of noise within his skull. He sagged to the floor and thinking stopped. He contracted himself, pulling legs and arms inward in a massive convulsion until at last he had assumed the foetal position. After a long while, he died.

Every human being within the Creche died so, but there was still life. The energy that killed the lesser creature freed the greater—just as Merrick had known it would. Unhuman matter pulsed under the caressing rain. A thousand beings shuddered at the sudden release of their chains. The speakers ranted unheard. The crystals turned unwatched. The bonds forged by homo sapiens snapped and there came—

Maturity.

*

This, now, is the Creche, Anno Domini 3000. A great mile-square blind cube topping a ragged mountain; bare escarpments falling away to a turbulent sea. For ten centuries the Creche has stood so, and the Androids still come forth, now to lift their starships to the Magellanic Clouds and beyond. A Golden Age has come. But, of course, Man is no longer the Master.

—Quintus Bland, The Romance of Genus Homo.

MASTERS OF SPACE

by Edward E. Smith & E. Everett Evans

The Masters had ruled all space with an unconquerable iron fist. But the Masters were gone. And this new, young race who came now to take their place—could they hope to defeat the ancient Enemy of All?

I

"BUT didn't you feel *anything*, Javo?" Strain was apparent in every line of Tula's taut, bare body. "Nothing at all?"

"Nothing whatever." The one called Javo relaxed from his rigid concentration. "Nothing has changed. Nor will it."

"That conclusion is indefensible!" Tula snapped. "With the promised return of the Masters there must and will be changes. Didn't *any* of you feel anything?"

Her hot, demanding eyes swept the group; a group whose like, except for physical perfection, could be found in any nudist colony.

No one except Tula had felt a thing.

"That fact is not too surprising," Javo said finally. "You have the most sensitive receptors of us all. But are you sure?"

"I am sure. It was the thought-form of a living Master."

"Do you think that the Master perceived your web?"

"It is certain. Those who built us are stronger than we."

"That is true. As they promised, then, so long and long ago, our Masters are returning home to us."

*

Jarvis Hilton of Terra, the youngest man yet to be assigned to direct any such tremendous deep-space undertaking as Project Theta Orionis, sat in conference with his two seconds-in-command. Assistant Director Sandra Cummings, analyst-synthesist and semantician, was tall, blonde and svelte. Planetographer William Karns—a black-haired, black-browed, black-eyed man of thirty—was third in rank of the scientific group.

"I'm telling you, Jarve, you can't have it both ways," Karns declared. "Captain Sawtelle is old-school Navy brass. He goes strictly by the book. So you've got to draw a razor-sharp line; exactly where the Advisory Board's directive puts it. And next time he sticks his ugly puss across that line, kick his face in. You've been Caspar Milquetoast Two ever since we left Base."

"That's the way it looks to you?" Hilton's right hand became a fist. "The man has age, experience and ability. I've been trying to meet him on a ground of courtesy and decency."

"Exactly. And he doesn't recognize the existence of either. And, since the Board rammed you down his throat instead of giving him old Jeffers, you needn't expect him to."

"You may be right, Bill. What do you think, Dr. Cummings?"

The girl said: "Bill's right. Also, your constant appeasement isn't doing the morale of the whole scientific group a bit of good."

"Well, I haven't enjoyed it, either. So next time I'll pin his ears back. Anything else?"

"Yes, Dr. Hilton, I have a squawk of my own. I know I was rammed down your throat, but just when are you going to let me do some work?"

"None of us has much of anything to do yet, and won't have until we light somewhere. You're off base a country mile."

"I'm not off base. You *did* want Eggleston, not me."

"Sure I did. I've worked with him and know what he can do. But I'm not holding a grudge about it."

"No? Why, then, are you on first-name terms with everyone in the scientific group except me? Supposedly your first assistant?"

"That's easy!" Hilton snapped. "Because you've been carrying chips on both shoulders ever since you came aboard . . . or at least I thought you were." Hilton grinned suddenly and held out his hand. "Sorry, Sandy—I'll start all over again."

"I'm sorry too, Chief." They shook hands warmly. "I *was* pretty stiff, I guess, but I'll be good."

"You'll go to work right now, too. As semantician. Dig out that directive and tear it down. Draw that line Bill talked about."

"Can do, boss." She swung to her feet and walked out of the room, her every movement one of lithe and easy grace.

Karns followed her with his eyes. "Funny. A trained-dancer Ph.D. And a Miss America type, like all the other women aboard this spacer. I wonder if she'll make out."

"So do I. I still wish they'd given me Eggy. I've never seen an executive-type female Ph.D. yet that was worth the cyanide it would take to poison her."

"That's what Sawtelle thinks of you, too, you know."

"I know; and the Board *does* know its stuff. So I'm really hoping, Bill, that she surprises me as much as I intend to surprise the Navy."

*

ALARM bells clanged as the mighty *Perseus* blinked out of overdrive. Every crewman sprang to his post.

"Mister Snowden, why did we emerge without orders from me?" Captain Sawtelle bellowed, storming into the control room three jumps behind Hilton.

"The automatics took control, sir," he said, quietly.

"Automatics! I *give* the orders!"

"In this case, Captain Sawtelle, you don't," Hilton said. Eyes locked and held. To Sawtelle, this was a new and strange co-commander. "I would suggest that we discuss this matter in private."

"Very well, sir," Sawtelle said; and in the captain's cabin Hilton opened up.

"For your information, Captain Sawtelle, I set my inter-space coupling detectors for any objective I choose. When any one of them reacts, it trips the kickers and we emerge. During any emergency outside the Solar System I am in command—with the provision that I must relinquish command to you in case of armed attack on us."

"Where do you think you found any such stuff as that in the directive? It isn't there and I know my rights."

"It is, and you don't. Here is a semantic chart of the whole directive. As you will note, it overrides many Navy regulations. Disobedience of my orders constitutes mutiny and I can—and will—have you put in irons and sent back to Terra for court-martial. Now let's go back."

In the control room, Hilton said, "The target has a mass of approximately five hundred metric tons. There is also a significant amount of radiation characteristic of uranexite. You will please execute search, Captain Sawtelle."

And Captain Sawtelle ordered the search.

"What did you do to the big jerk, boss?" Sandra whispered.

"What you and Bill suggested," Hilton whispered back. "Thanks to your analysis of the directive—pure gobbledygook if there ever was any—I could. Mighty good job, Sandy."

*

TEN or fifteen more minutes passed. Then:

"Here's the source of radiation, sir," a searchman reported. "It's a point source, though, not an object at this range."

"And here's the artifact, sir," Pilot Snowden said. "We're coming up on it fast. But . . . but what's a *skyscraper* skeleton doing out here in interstellar space?"

As they closed up, everyone could see that the thing did indeed look like the metallic skeleton of a great building. It was a huge cube, measuring well over a hundred yards along each edge. And it was empty.

"*That's* one for the book," Sawtelle said.

"And how!" Hilton agreed. "I'll take a boat . . . no, suits would be better. Karns, Yarborough, get Techs Leeds and Miller and suit up."

"You'll need a boat escort," Sawtelle said. "Mr. Ashley, execute escort Landing Craft One, Two, and Three."

The three landing craft approached that enigmatic lattice-work of structural steel and stopped. Five grotesquely armored figures wafted themselves forward on pencils of force. Their leader, whose suit bore the number "14", reached a mammoth girder and worked his way along it up to a peculiar-looking bulge. The whole immense structure vanished, leaving men and boats in empty space.

Sawtelle gasped. "Snowden! Are you holding 'em?"

"No, sir. Faster than light; hyperspace, sir."

"Mr. Ashby, did you have your interspace rigs set?"

"No, sir. I didn't think of it, sir."

"Doctor Cummings, why weren't yours out?"

"I didn't think of such a thing, either—any more than you did," Sandra said.

Ashby, the Communications Officer, had been working the radio. "No reply from anyone, sir," he reported.

"Oh, no!" Sandra exclaimed. Then, "But look! They're firing pistols—especially the one wearing number fourteen—but *pistols*?"

"Recoil pistols—sixty-threes—for emergency use in case of power failure," Ashby explained. "That's it . . . but I can't see why *all* their power went out at once. But Fourteen—that's Hilton—is really doing a job with that sixty-three. He'll be here in a couple of minutes."

And he was. "Every power unit out there—suits and boats both—drained," Hilton reported. "*Completely* drained. Get some help out there fast!"

*

In an enormous structure deep below the surface of a far-distant world a group of technicians clustered together in front of one section of a two-miles long control board. They were staring at a light that had just appeared where no light should have been.

"Someone's brain-pan will be burned out for this," one of the group radiated harshly. "That unit was inactivated long ago and it has not been reactivated."

"Someone committed an error, Your Loftiness?"

"Silence, fool! Stretts do not commit errors!"

*

AS soon as it was clear that no one had been injured, Sawtelle demanded, "How about it, Hilton?"

"Structurally, it was high-alloy steel. There were many bulges, possibly containing mechanisms. There were drive-units of a non-Terran type. There were many projectors, which—at a rough guess—were a hundred times as powerful as any I have ever seen before. There were no indications that the thing had ever been enclosed, in whole or in part. It certainly never had living quarters for warm-blooded, oxygen-breathing eaters of organic food."

Sawtelle snorted. "You mean it never had a crew?"

"Not necessarily . . . ."

"Bah! What other kind of intelligent life is there?"

"I don't know. But before we speculate too much, let's look at the tri-di. The camera may have caught something I missed."

It hadn't. The three-dimensional pictures added nothing.

"It probably was operated either by programmed automatics or by remote control," Hilton decided, finally. "But how did they drain all our power? And just as bad, what and how is that other point source of power we're heading for now?"

"What's wrong with it?" Sawtelle asked.

"Its strength. No matter what distance or reactant I assume, nothing we know will fit. Neither fission nor fusion will do it. It has to be practically total conversion!"

II

THE *Perseus* snapped out of overdrive near the point of interest and Hilton stared, motionless and silent.

Space was full of madly warring ships. Half of them were bare, giant skeletons of steel, like the "derelict" that had so unexpectedly blasted away from them. The others were more or less like the *Perseus*, except in being bigger, faster and of vastly greater power.

Beams of starkly incredible power bit at and clung to equally capable defensive screens of pure force. As these inconceivable forces met, the glare of their neutralization filled all nearby space. And ships and skeletons alike were disappearing in chunks, blobs, gouts, streamers and sparkles of rended, fused and vaporized metal.

Hilton watched two ships combine against one skeleton. Dozens of beams, incredibly tight and hard, were held inexorably upon dozens of the bulges of the skeleton. Overloaded, the bulges' screens flared through the spectrum and failed. And bare metal, however refractory, endures only for instants under the appalling intensity of such beams as those.

The skeletons tried to duplicate the ships' method of attack, but failed. They were too slow. Not slow, exactly, either, but hesitant; as though it required whole seconds for the commander—or operator? Or remote controller?—of each skeleton to make it act. The ships were winning.

"Hey!" Hilton yelped. "Oh—that's the one we saw back there. But what in all space does it think it's doing?"

It was plunging at tremendous speed straight through the immense fleet of embattled skeletons. It did not fire a beam nor energize a screen; it merely plunged along as though on a plotted course until it collided with one of the skeletons of the fleet and both structures plunged, a tangled mass of wreckage, to the ground of the planet below.

Then hundreds of the ships shot forward, each to plunge into and explode inside one of the skeletons. When visibility was restored another wave of ships came forward to repeat the performance, but there was nothing left to fight. Every surviving skeleton had blinked out of normal space.

The remaining ships made no effort to pursue the skeletons, nor did they re-form as a fleet. Each ship went off by itself.

*

And on that distant planet of the Stretts the group of mechs watched with amazed disbelief as light after light after light winked out on their two-miles-long control board. Frantically they relayed orders to the skeletons; orders which did not affect the losses.

"Brain-pans will blacken for this . . ." a mental snarl began, to be interrupted by a coldly imperious thought.

"That long-dead unit, so inexplicably reactivated, is approaching the fuel world. It is ignoring the battle. It is heading through our fleet toward the Oman half . . . *handle* it, ten-eighteen!"

"It does not respond, Your Loftiness."

"Then blast it, fool! Ah, it is inactivated. As encyclopedist, Nine, explain the freakish behavior of that unit."

"Yes, Your Loftiness. Many cycles ago we sent a ship against the Omans with a new device of destruction. The Omans must have intercepted it, drained it of power and allowed it to drift on. After all these cycles of time it must have come upon a small source of power and of course continued its mission."

"That can be the truth. The Lords of the Universe must be informed."

"The mining units, the carriers and the refiners have not been affected, Your Loftiness," a mech radiated.

"So I see, fool." Then, activating another instrument, His Loftiness thought at it, in an entirely different vein, "Lord Ynos, Madam? I have to make a very grave report . . . ."

*

IN the *Perseus*, four scientists and three Navy officers were arguing heatedly; employing deep-space verbiage not to be found in any dictionary. "Jarve!" Karns called out, and Hilton joined the group. "Does anything about this planet make any sense to you?"

"No. But you're the planetographer. 'Smatter with it?"

"It's a good three hundred degrees Kelvin too hot."

"Well, you know it's loaded with uranexite."

"That much? The whole crust practically jewelry ore?"

"If that's what the figures say, I'll buy it."

"Buy *this*, then. Continuous daylight everywhere. Noon June Sol-quality light *except* that it's all in the visible. Frank says it's from bombardment of a layer of something, and Frank admits that the whole thing's impossible."

"When Frank makes up his mind what 'something' is, I'll take it as a datum."

"Third thing: there's only one city on this continent, and it's protected by a screen that nobody ever heard of."

Hilton pondered, then turned to the captain. "Will you please run a search-pattern, sir? Fine-toothing only the hot spots?"

The planet was approximately the same size as Terra; its atmosphere, except for its intense radiation, was similar to Terra's. There were two continents; one immense girdling ocean. The temperature of the land surface was everywhere about 100°F, that of the water about 90°F. Each continent had one city, and both were small. One was inhabited by what looked like human beings; the other by usuform robots. The human city was the only cool spot on the entire planet; under its protective dome the temperature was 71°F.

Hilton decided to study the robots first; and asked the captain to take the ship down to observation range. Sawtelle objected; and continued to object until Hilton started to order his arrest. Then he said, "I'll do it, under protest, but I want it on record that I am doing it against my best judgment."

"It's on record," Hilton said, coldly. "Everything said and done is being, and will continue to be, recorded."

The *Perseus* floated downward. "*There's* what I want most to see," Hilton said, finally. "That big strip-mining operation . . . that's it . . . hold it!" Then, via throat-mike, "Attention, all scientists! You all know what to do. Start doing it."

Sandra's blonde head was very close to Hilton's brown one as they both stared into Hilton's plate. "Why, they look like giant armadillos!" she exclaimed.

"More like tanks," he disagreed, "except that they've got legs, wheels *and* treads—and arms, cutters, diggers, probes and conveyors—and *look* at the way those buckets dip solid rock!"

The fantastic machine was moving very slowly along a bench or shelf that it was making for itself as it went along. Below it, to its left, dropped other benches being made by other mining machines. The machines were not using explosives. Hard though the ore was, the tools were so much harder and were driven with such tremendous power that the stuff might just have well have been slightly-clayed sand.

Every bit of loosened ore, down to the finest dust, was forced into a conveyor and thence into the armored body of the machine. There it went into a mechanism whose basic principles Hilton could not understand. From this monstrosity emerged two streams of product.

One of these, comprising ninety-nine point nine plus percent of the input, went out through another conveyor into the vast hold of a vehicle which, when full and replaced by a duplicate of itself, went careening madly cross-country to a dump.

The other product, a slow, very small stream of tiny, glistening black pellets, fell into a one-gallon container being held watchfully by a small machine, more or less like a three-wheeled motor scooter, which was moving carefully along beside the giant miner. When this can was almost full another scooter rolled up and, without losing a single pellet, took over place and function. The first scooter then covered its bucket, clamped it solidly into a recess designed for the purpose and dashed away toward the city.

Hilton stared slack-jawed at Sandra. She stared back.

"Do you make anything of that, Jarve?"

"Nothing. They're taking *pure* uranexite and *concentrating*—or converting—it a thousand to one. I *hope* we'll be able to do something about it."

"I hope so, too, Chief; and I'm *sure* we will."

"Well, that's enough for now. You may take us up now, Captain Sawtelle. And Sandy, will you please call all department heads and their assistants into the conference room?"

*

AT the head of the long conference table, Hilton studied his fourteen department heads, all husky young men, and their assistants, all surprisingly attractive and well-built young women. Bud Carroll and Sylvia Bannister of Sociology sat together. He was almost as big as Karns; she was a green-eyed redhead whose five-ten and one-fifty would have looked big except for the arrangement thereof. There were Bernadine and Hermione van der Moen, the leggy, breasty, platinum-blonde twins—both of whom were Cowper medalists in physics. There was Etienne de Vaux, the mathematical wizard; and Rebecca Eisenstein, the black-haired, flashing-eyed ex-infant-prodigy theoretical astronomer. There was Beverly Bell, who made mathematically impossible chemical syntheses—who swam channels for days on end and computed planetary orbits in her sleekly-coiffured head.

"First, we'll have a get-together," Hilton said. "Nothing recorded; just to get acquainted. You all know that our fourteen departments cover science, from astronomy to zoology."

He paused, again his eyes swept the group. Stella Wing, who would have been a grand-opera star except for her drive to know everything about language. Theodora (Teddy) Blake, who would prove gleefully that she was the world's best model—but was in fact the most brilliantly promising theoretician who had ever lived.

"No other force like this has ever been assembled," Hilton went on. "In more ways than one. Sawtelle wanted Jeffers to head this group, instead of me. Everybody thought he *would* head it."

"And Hilton wanted Eggleston and got *me*," Sandra said.

"That's right. And quite a few of you didn't want to come at all, but were told by the Board to come or else."

The group stirred. Eyes met eyes, and there were smiles.

*

"I MYSELF think Jeffers *should* have had the job. I've never handled anything half this big and I'll need a lot of help. But I'm stuck with it and you're all stuck with me, so we'll all take it and like it. You've noticed, of course, the accent on youth. The Navy crew is normal, except for the commanders being unusually young. But we aren't. None of us is thirty yet, and none of us has ever been married. You fellows look like a team of professional athletes, and you girls—well, if I didn't know better I'd say the Board had screened you for the front row of the chorus instead of for a top-bracket brain-gang. How they found so many of you I'll never know."

"Virile men and nubile women!" Etienne de Vaux leered enthusiastically. "*Vive le Board!*"

"Nubile! Bravo, Tiny! *Quelle delicatesse de nuance!*"

"Three rousing cheers for the Board!"

"Keep still, you nitwits! Let me ask a question!" This came from one of the twins. "Before you give us the deduction, Jarvis—or will it be an intuition or an induction or a . . ."

"Or an inducement," the other twin suggested, helpfully. "Not that *you* would need very much of that."

"You keep still, too, Miney. I'm asking, Sir Moderator, if I can give my deduction first?"

"Sure, Bernadine; go ahead."

"They figured we're going to get completely lost. Then we'll jettison the Navy, hunt up a planet of our own and start a race to end all human races. Or would you call this a *see*-duction instead of a *dee*-duction?"

This produced a storm of whistles, cheers and jeers that it took several seconds to quell.

"But seriously, Jarvis," Bernadine went on. "We've all been wondering and it doesn't make sense. Have you any idea at all of what the Board actually did have in mind?"

"I believe that the Board selected for mental, not physical, qualities; for the ability to handle anything unexpected or unusual that comes up, no matter what it is."

"You think it wasn't double-barreled?" asked Kincaid, the psychologist. He smiled quizzically. "That all this virility and nubility and glamor is pure coincidence?"

"No," Hilton said, with an almost imperceptible flick of an eyelid. "Coincidence is as meaningless as paradox. I think they found out that—barring freaks—the best minds are in the best bodies."

"Could be. The idea has been propounded before."

"Now let's get to work." Hilton flipped the switch of the recorder. "Starting with you, Sandy, each of you give a two-minute boil-down. What you found and what you think."

*

SOMETHING over an hour later the meeting adjourned and Hilton and Sandra strolled toward the control room.

"I don't know whether you convinced Alexander Q. Kincaid or not, but you didn't quite convince me," Sandra said.

"Nor him, either."

"Oh?" Sandra's eyebrows

"No. He grabbed the out I offered him. I didn't fool Teddy Blake or Temple Bells, either. You four are all, though, I think."

"Temple? You think *she's* so smart?"

"I don't *think* so, no. Don't fool yourself, chick. Temple Bells looks and acts sweet and innocent and virginal. Maybe—probably—she is. But she isn't showing a fraction of the stuff she's really got. She's heavy artillery, Sandy. And I mean *heavy*."

"I think you're slightly nuts there. But do you really believe that the Board was playing Cupid?"

"Not trying, but doing. Cold-bloodedly and efficiently. Yes."

"But it wouldn't *work*! We aren't going to get lost!"

"We won't need to. Propinquity will do the work."

"Phooie. You and me, for instance?" She stopped, put both hands on her hips, and glared. "Why, I wouldn't marry *you* if you . . ."

"I'll tell the cockeyed world you won't!" Hilton broke in. "Me marry a damned female Ph.D. ? Uh-uh. Mine will be a cuddly little brunette that thinks a slipstick is some kind of lipstick and that an isotope's something good to eat."

"One like that copy of Murchison's Dark Lady that you keep under the glass on your desk?" she sneered.

"Exactly . . . ." He started to continue the battle, then shut himself off. "But listen, Sandy, why should we get into a fight because we don't want to marry each other? You're doing a swell job. I admire you tremendously for it and I like to work with you."

"You've got a point there, Jarve, at that, and I'm one of the few who know what kind of a job *you're* doing, so I'll relax." She flashed him a gamin grin and they went on into the control room.

It was too late in the day then to do any more exploring; but the next morning, early, the *Perseus* lined out for the city of the humanoids.

*

Tula turned toward her fellows. Her eyes filled with a happily triumphant light and her thought a lilting song. "I have been telling you from the first touch that it was the Masters. It *is* the Masters! The Masters are returning to us Omans and their own home world!"

*

"CAPTAIN Sawtelle," Hilton said, "Please land in the cradle below."

"*Land!*" Sawtelle stormed. "On a planet like *that*? Not by . . ." He broke off and stared; for now, on that cradle, there flamed out in screaming red the *Perseus'* own Navy-coded landing symbols!

"Your protest is recorded," Hilton said. "Now, sir, land."

Fuming, Sawtelle landed. Sandra looked pointedly at Hilton. "First contact is my dish, you know."

"Not that I like it, but it is." He turned to a burly youth with sun-bleached, crew-cut hair, "Still safe, Frank?"

"Still abnormally low. Surprising no end, since all the rest of the planet is hotter than the middle tail-race of hell."

"Okay, Sandy. Who will you want besides the top linguists?"

"Psych—both Alex and Temple. And Teddy Blake. They're over there. Tell them, will you, while I buzz Teddy?"

"Will do," and Hilton stepped over to the two psychologists and told them. Then, "I hope I'm not leading with my chin, Temple, but is that your real first name or a professional?"

"It's real; it really is. My parents were romantics: dad says they considered both 'Golden' and 'Silver'!"

Not at all obviously, he studied her: the almost translucent, unblemished perfection of her lightly-tanned, old-ivory skin; the clear, calm, deep blueness of her eyes; the long, thick mane of hair exactly the color of a field of dead-ripe wheat.

"You know, I like it," he said then. "It fits you."

"I'm glad you said that, Doctor . . . ."

"Not that, Temple. I'm not going to 'Doctor' you."

"I'll call you 'boss', then, like Stella does. Anyway, that lets me tell you that I like it myself. I really think that it did something for me."

"*Something* did something for you, that's for sure. I'm mighty glad you're aboard, and I hope . . . here they come. Hi, Hark! Hi, Stella!"

"Hi, Jarve," said Chief Linguist Harkins, and:

"Hi, boss—what's holding us up?" asked his assistant, Stella Wing. She was about five feet four. Her eyes were a tawny brown; her hair a flamboyant auburn mop. Perhaps it owed a little of its spectacular refulgence to chemistry, Hilton thought, but not too much. "Let us away! Let the lions roar and let the welkin ring!"

"Who's been feeding *you* so much red meat, little squirt?" Hilton laughed and turned away, meeting Sandra in the corridor. "Okay, chick, take 'em away. We'll cover you. Luck, girl."

And in the control room, to Sawtelle, "Needle-beam cover, please; set for minimum aperture and lethal blast. But no firing, Captain Sawtelle, until I give the order."

*

THE *Perseus* was surrounded by hundreds of natives. They were all adult, all naked and about equally divided as to sex. They were friendly; most enthusiastically so.

"Jarve!" Sandra squealed. "They're *telepathic*. Very strongly so! I never imagined—I never felt anything like it!"

"Any rough stuff?" Hilton demanded.

"Oh, no. Just the opposite. They love us . . . in a way that's simply indescribable. I don't like this telepathy business . . . not clear . . . foggy, diffuse . . . this woman is *sure* I'm her long-lost great-great-a-hundred-times grandmother or something—*You!* Slow down. Take it *easy*! They want us all to come out here and live with . . . no, not *with* them, but each of us alone in a whole house with them to wait on us! But first, they all want to come aboard . . . ."

"*What?*" Hilton yelped. "But are you *sure* they're friendly?"

"Positive, chief."

"How about you, Alex?"

"We're all sure, Jarve. No question about it."

"Bring two of them aboard. A man and a woman."

"You won't bring *any*!" Sawtelle thundered. "Hilton, I had enough of your stupid, starry-eyed, ivory-domed blundering long ago, but this utterly idiotic brainstorm of letting enemy aliens aboard us ends all civilian command. Call your people back aboard or I will bring them in by force!"

"Very well, sir. Sandy, tell the natives that a slight delay has become necessary and bring your party aboard."

The Navy officers smiled—or grinned—gloatingly; while the scientists stared at their director with expressions ranging from surprise to disappointment and disgust. Hilton's face remained set, expressionless, until Sandra and her party had arrived.

"Captain Sawtelle," he said then, "I thought that you and I had settled in private the question or who is in command of Project Theta Orionis at destination. We will now settle it in public. Your opinion of me is now on record, witnessed by your officers and by my staff. My opinion of you, which is now being similarly recorded and witnessed, is that you are a hidebound, mentally ossified Navy mule; mentally and psychologically unfit to have any voice in any such mission as this. You will now agree on this recording and before these witnesses, to obey my orders unquestioningly or I will now unload all Bureau of Science personnel and equipment onto this planet and send you and the *Perseus* back to Terra with the doubly-sealed record of this episode posted to the Advisory Board. Take your choice."

Eyes locked, and under Hilton's uncompromising stare Sawtelle weakened. He fidgeted; tried three times—unsuccessfully—to blare defiance. Then, "Very well sir," he said, and saluted.

*

"THANK you, sir," Hilton said, then turned to his staff. "Okay, Sandy, go ahead."

Outside the control room door, "Thank God you don't play poker, Jarve!" Karns gasped. "We'd all owe you all the pay we'll ever get!"

"You think it was the bluff, yes?" de Vaux asked. "Me, I think no. Name of a name of a name! I was wondering with unease what life would be like on this so-alien planet!"

"You didn't need to wonder, Tiny," Hilton assured him. "It was in the bag. He's incapable of abandonment."

Beverly Bell, the van der Moen twins and Temple Bells all stared at Hilton in awe; and Sandra felt much the same way.

"But suppose he *had* called you?" Sandra demanded.

"Speculating on the impossible is unprofitable," he said.

"Oh, you're the most *exasperating* thing!" Sandra stamped a foot. "Don't you—*ever*—answer a question intelligibly?"

"When the question is meaningless, chick, I can't."

At the lock Temple Bells, who had been hanging back, cocked an eyebrow at Hilton and he made his way to her side.

"What was it you started to say back there, boss?"

"Oh, yes. That we should see each other oftener."

"That's what I was hoping you were going to say." She put her hand under his elbow and pressed his arm lightly, fleetingly, against her side. "That would be indubitably the fondest thing I could be of."

He laughed and gave her arm a friendly squeeze. Then he studied her again, the most baffling member of his staff. About five feet six. Lithe, hard, trained down fine—as a tennis champion, she would be. Stacked—*how* she was stacked! Not as beautiful as Sandra or Teddy . . . but with an ungodly lot of something that neither of them had . . . nor any other woman he had ever known.

"Yes, I am a little difficult to classify," she said quietly, almost reading his mind.

"That's the understatement of the year! But I'm making some progress."

"Such as?" This was an open challenge.

"Except possibly Teddy, the best brain aboard."

"That isn't true, but go ahead."

"You're a powerhouse. A tightly organized, thoroughly integrated, smoothly functioning, beautifully camouflaged Juggernaut. A reasonable facsimile of an irresistible force."

"My God, Jarvis!" That had gone deep.

"Let me finish my analysis. You aren't head of your department because you don't want to be. You fooled the top psychs of the Board. You've been running ninety per cent submerged because you can work better that way and there's no glory-hound blood in you."

She stared at him, licking her lips. "I knew your mind was a razor, but I didn't know it was a diamond drill, too. That seals your doom, boss, unless . . . no, you can't *possibly* know why I'm here."

"Why, of course I do."

"You just think you do. You see, I've been in love with you ever since, as a gangling, bony, knobby-kneed kid, I listened to your first doctorate disputation. Ever since then, my purpose in life has been to land you."

III

"BUT listen!" he exclaimed. "I *can't*, even if I want . . . ."

"Of course you can't." Pure deviltry danced in her eyes. "You're the Director. It wouldn't be proper. But it's Standard Operating Procedure for simple, innocent, unsophisticated little country girls like me to go completely overboard for the boss."

"But you can't—you *mustn't*!" he protested in panic.

Temple Bells was getting plenty of revenge for the shocks he had given her. "I can't? Watch me!" She grinned up at him, her eyes still dancing. "Every chance I get, I'm going to hug your arm like I did a minute ago. And you'll take hold of my forearm, like you did! That can be taken, you see, as either: One, a reluctant acceptance of a mildly distasteful but not quite actionable situation, or: Two, a blocking move to keep me from climbing up you like a squirrel!"

"Confound it, Temple, you *can't* be serious!"

"Can't I?" She laughed gleefully. "Especially with half a dozen of those other cats watching? Just wait and see, boss!"

Sandra and her two guests came aboard. The natives looked around; the man at the various human men, the woman at each of the human women. The woman remained beside Sandra; the man took his place at Hilton's left, looking up—he was a couple of inches shorter than Hilton's six feet one—with an air of . . . of *expectancy*!

"Why this arrangement, Sandy?" Hilton asked.

"Because we're tops. It's your move, Jarve. What's first?"

"Uranexite. Come along, Sport. I'll call you that until . . ."

"Laro," the native said, in a deep resonant bass voice. He hit himself a blow on the head that would have floored any two ordinary men. "Sora," he announced, striking the alien woman a similar blow.

"Laro and Sora, I would like to have you look at our uranexite, with the idea of refueling our ship. Come with me, please?"

Both nodded and followed him. In the engine room he pointed at the engines, then to the lead-blocked labyrinth leading to the fuel holds. "Laro, do you understand 'hot'? Radioactive?"

Laro nodded—and started to open the heavy lead door!

"Hey!" Hilton yelped. "That's hot!" He seized Laro's arm to pull him away—and got the shock of his life. Laro weighed at least five hundred pounds! And the guy *still* looked human!

Laro nodded again and gave himself a terrific thump on the chest. Then he glanced at Sora, who stepped away from Sandra. He then went into the hold and came out with two fuel pellets in his hand, one of which he tossed to Sora. That is, the motion looked like a toss, but the pellet traveled like a bullet. Sora caught it unconcernedly and both natives flipped the pellets into their mouths. There was a half minute of rock-crusher crunching; then both natives opened their mouths.

The pellets had been pulverized and swallowed.

Hilton's voice rang out. "Poynter! How *can* these people be non-radioactive after eating a whole fuel pellet apiece?"

Poynter tested both natives again. "Cold," he reported. "Stone cold. No background even. Play *that* on your harmonica!"

*

LARO nodded, perfectly matter-of-factly, and in Hilton's mind there formed a picture. It was not clear, but it showed plainly enough a long line of aliens approaching the *Perseus*. Each carried on his or her shoulder a lead container holding two hundred pounds of Navy Regulation fuel pellets. A standard loading-tube was sealed into place and every fuel-hold was filled.

This picture, Laro indicated plainly, could become reality any time.

Sawtelle was notified and came on the run. "No fuel is coming aboard without being tested!" he roared.

"Of course not. But it'll pass, for all the tea in China. You haven't had a ten per cent load of fuel since you were launched. You can fill up or not—the fuel's here—just as you say."

"If they can make Navy standard, of course we want it."

The fuel arrived. Every load tested well above standard. Every fuel hold was filled to capacity, with no leakage and no emanation. The natives who had handled the stuff did not go away, but gathered in the engine-room; and more and more humans trickled in to see what was going on.

Sawtelle stiffened. "What's going on over there, Hilton?"

"I don't know; but let's let 'em go for a minute. I want to learn about these people and they've got me stopped cold."

"You aren't the only one. But if they wreck that Mayfield it'll cost you over twenty thousand dollars."

"Okay." The captain and director watched, wide eyed.

Two master mechanics had been getting ready to re-fit a tube—a job requiring both strength and skill. The tube was very heavy and made of superefract. The machine—the Mayfield—upon which the work was to be done, was extremely complex.

Two of the aliens had brushed the mechanics—very gently—aside and were doing their work for them. Ignoring the hoist, one native had picked the tube up and was holding it exactly in place on the Mayfield. The other, hands moving faster than the eye could follow, was locking it—micrometrically precise and immovably secure—into place.

"How about this?" one of the mechanics asked of his immediate superior. "If we throw 'em out, how do we do it?"

By a jerk of the head, the non-com passed the buck to a commissioned officer, who relayed it up the line to Sawtelle, who said, "Hilton, nobody can run a Mayfield without months of training. They'll wreck it and it'll cost you . . . but I'm getting curious myself. Enough so to take half the damage. Let 'em go ahead."

"How *about* this, Mike?" one of the machinists asked of his fellow. "I'm going to *like* this, what?"

"Ya-as, my deah Chumley," the other drawled, affectedly. "My man relieves me of *so* much uncouth effort."

The natives had kept on working. The Mayfield was running. It had always howled and screamed at its work, but now it gave out only a smooth and even hum. The aliens had adjusted it with unhuman precision; they were one with it as no human being could possibly be. And every mind present knew that those aliens were, at long, long last, fulfilling their destiny and were, in that fulfillment, supremely happy. After tens of thousands of cycles of time they were doing a job for their adored, their revered and beloved MASTERS.

That was a stunning shock; but it was eclipsed by another.

*

"I AM sorry, Master Hilton," Laro's tremendous bass voice boomed out, "that it has taken us so long to learn your Masters' language as it now is. Since you left us you have changed it radically; while we, of course, have not changed it at all."

"I'm sorry, but you're mistaken," Hilton said. "We are merely visitors. We have never been here before; nor, as far as we know, were any of our ancestors ever here."

"You need not test us, Master. We have kept your trust. Everything has been kept, changelessly the same, awaiting your return as you ordered so long ago."

"Can you read my mind?" Hilton demanded.

"Of course; but Omans can not read in Masters' minds anything except what Masters want Omans to read."

"Omans?" Harkins asked. "Where did you Omans and your masters come from? Originally?"

"As you know, Master, the Masters came originally from Arth. They populated Ardu, where we Omans were developed. When the Stretts drove us from Ardu, we all came to

Ardry, which was your home world until you left it in our care. We keep also this, your half of the Fuel World, in trust for you."

"Listen, Jarve!" Harkins said, tensely. "Oman-human. Arth-Earth. Ardu-Earth Two. Ardry-Earth Three. You can't laugh them off . . . but there never *was* an Atlantis!"

"This is getting no better fast. We need a full staff meeting. You, too, Sawtelle, and your best man. We need all the brains the *Perseus* can muster."

"You're right. But first, get those naked women out of here. It's bad enough, having women aboard at all, but this . . . my men are *spacemen*, mister."

Laro spoke up. "If it is the Masters' pleasure to keep on testing us, so be it. We have forgotten nothing. A dwelling awaits each Master, in which each will be served by Omans who will know the Master's desires without being told. Every desire. While we Omans have no biological urges, we are of course highly skilled in relieving tensions and derive as much pleasure from that service as from any other."

Sawtelle broke the silence that followed. "Well, for the men—" He hesitated. "Especially on the ground . . . well, talking in mixed company, you know, but I think . . ."

"Think nothing of the mixed company, Captain Sawtelle," Sandra said. "We women are scientists, not shrinking violets. We are accustomed to discussing the facts of life just as frankly as any other facts."

Sawtelle jerked a thumb at Hilton, who followed him out into the corridor. "I *have* been a Navy mule," he said. "I admit now that I'm out-maneuvered, out-manned, and out-gunned."

"I'm just as baffled—at present—as you are, sir. But my training has been aimed specifically at the unexpected, while yours has not."

"That's letting me down easy, Jarve." Sawtelle smiled—the first time the startled Hilton had known that the hard, tough old spacehound *could* smile. "What I wanted to say is, lead on. I'll follow you through force-field and space-warps."

"Thanks, skipper. And by the way, I erased that record yesterday." The two gripped hands; and there came into being a relationship that was to become a lifelong friendship.

*

"WE will start for Ardry immediately," Hilton said. "How do we make that jump without charts, Laro?"

"Very easily, Master. Kedo, as Master Captain Sawtelle's Oman, will give the orders. Nito will serve Master Snowden and supply the knowledge he says he has forgotten."

"Okay. We'll go up to the control room and get started."

And in the control room, Kedo's voice rasped into the captain's microphone. "Attention, all personnel! Master Captain Sawtelle orders take-off in two minutes. The countdown will begin at five seconds . . . . Five! Four! Three! Two! One! Lift!"

Nito, not Snowden, handled the controls. As perfectly as the human pilot had ever done it, at the top of his finest form, he picked the immense spaceship up and slipped it silkily into subspace.

"Well, I'll be a . . ." Snowden gasped. "That's a better job than I *ever* did!"

"Not at all, Master, as you know," Nito said. "It was you who did this. I merely performed the labor."

A few minutes later, in the main lounge, Navy and BuSci personnel were mingling as they had never done before. Whatever had caused this relaxation of tension—the friendship of captain and director? The position in which they all were? Or what?—they all began to get acquainted with each other.

"Silence, please, and be seated," Hilton said. "While this is not exactly a formal meeting, it will be recorded for future reference. First, I will ask Laro a question. Were books or records left on Ardry by the race you call the Masters?"

"You know there are, Master. They are exactly as you left them. Undisturbed for over two hundred seventy-one thousand years."

"Therefore we will not question the Omans. We do not know what questions to ask. We have seen many things hitherto thought impossible. Hence, we must discard all preconceived opinions which conflict with facts. I will mention a few of the problems we face."

"The Omans. The Masters. The upgrading of the armament of the *Perseus* to Oman standards. The concentration of uranexite. What is that concentrate? How is it used? Total conversion—how is it accomplished? The skeletons—what are they and how are they controlled? Their ability to drain power. Who or what is back of them? Why a deadlock that has lasted over a quarter of a million years? How much danger are we and the *Perseus* actually in? How much danger is Terra in, because of our presence here? There are many other questions."

"Sandra and I will not take part. Nor will three others; de Vaux, Eisenstein, and Blake. You have more important work to do."

"What can that be?" asked Rebecca. "Of what possible use can a mathematician, a theoretician and a theoretical astronomer be in such a situation as this?"

"You can think powerfully in abstract terms, unhampered by Terran facts and laws which we now know are neither facts nor laws. I cannot even categorize the problems we face. Perhaps you three will be able to. You will listen, then consult, then tell me how to pick the teams to do the work. A more important job for you is this: Any problem, to be solved, must be stated clearly; and we don't know even what our basic problem is. I want something by the use of which I can break this thing open. Get it for me."

*

REBECCA and de Vaux merely smiled and nodded, but Teddy Blake said happily, "I was beginning to feel like a fifth wheel on this project, but *that's* something I can really stick my teeth into."

"Huh? How?" Karns demanded. "He didn't give you one single thing to go on; just compounded the confusion."

Hilton spoke before Teddy could. "That's their dish, Bill. If I had any data I'd work it myself. You first, Captain Sawtelle."

That conference was a very long one indeed. There were almost as many conclusions and recommendations as there were speakers. And through it all Hilton and Sandra listened. They weighed and tested and analyzed and made copious notes; in shorthand and in the more esoteric characters of symbolic logic. And at its end:

"I'm just about pooped, Sandy. How about you?"

"You and me both, boss. See you in the morning."

But she didn't. It was four o'clock in the afternoon when they met again.

"We made up one of the teams, Sandy," he said, with surprising diffidence. "I know we were going to do it together, but I got a hunch on the first team. A kind of a weirdie, but the brains checked me on it." He placed a card on her desk. "Don't blow your top until after I you've studied it."

"Why, I won't, of course . . . ." Her voice died away. "Maybe you'd better cancel that 'of course' . . . ." She studied, and when she spoke again she was exerting self-control. "A chemist, a planetographer, a theoretician, *two* sociologists, a psychologist and a radiationist. And six of the seven are three pairs of sweeties. What kind of a line-up is *that* to solve a problem in *physics?*"

"It isn't in any physics we know. I said *think!*"

"Oh," she said, then again "Oh," and "Oh," and "Oh." Four entirely different tones. "I see . . . maybe. You're matching minds, not specialties; and supplementing?"

"I knew you were smart. Buy it?"

"It's weird, all right, but I'll buy it—for a trial run, anyway. But I'd hate like sin to have to sell any part of it to the Board . . . . But of course we're—I mean you're responsible only to yourself."

"Keep it 'we', Sandy. You're as important to this project as I am. But before we tackle the second team, what's your thought on Bernadine and Hermione? Separate or together?"

"Separate, I'd say. They're identical physically, and so nearly so mentally that of them would be just as good on a team as both of them. More and better work on different teams."

"My thought exactly." And so it went, hour after hour.

The teams were selected and meetings were held.

*

THE *Perseus* reached Ardry, which was very much like Terra. There were continents, oceans, ice-caps, lakes, rivers, mountains and plains, forests and prairies. The ship landed on the spacefield of Omlu, the City of the Masters, and Sawtelle called Hilton into his cabin. The Omans Laro and Kedo went along, of course.

"Nobody knows how it leaked . . ." Sawtelle began.

"No secrets around here," Hilton grinned. "Omans, you know."

"I suppose so. Anyway, every man aboard is all hyped up about living aground—especially with a harem. But before I grant liberty, suppose there's any VD around here that our prophylactics can't handle?"

"As you know, Masters," Laro replied for Hilton before the latter could open his mouth, "no disease, venereal or other, is allowed to exist on Ardry. No prophylaxis is either necessary or desirable."

"That ought to hold you for a while, Skipper." Hilton smiled at the flabbergasted captain and went back to the lounge.

"Everybody going ashore?" he asked.

"Yes." Karns said. "Unanimous vote for the first time."

"Who wouldn't?" Sandra asked. "I'm fed up with living like a sardine. I will scream for joy the minute I get into a real room."

"Cars" were waiting, in a stopping-and-starting line. Three-wheel jobs. All were empty. No drivers, no steering-wheels, no instruments or push-buttons. When the whole line moved ahead as one vehicle there was no noise, no gas, no blast.

An Oman helped a Master carefully into the rear seat of his car, leaped into the front seat and the car sped quietly away. The whole line of empty cars, acting in perfect synchronization, shot forward one space and stopped.

"This is your car, Master," Laro said, and made a production out of getting Hilton into the vehicle undamaged.

Hilton's plan had been beautifully simple. All the teams were to meet at the Hall of Records. The linguists and their Omans would study the records and pass them out. Specialty after specialty would be unveiled and teams would work on them. He and Sandy would sit in the office and analyze and synthesize and correlate. It was a very nice plan.

It was a very nice office, too. It contained every item of equipment that either Sandra or Hilton had ever worked with—it was a big office—and a great many that neither of them had ever heard of. It had a full staff of Omans, all eager to work.

Hilton and Sandra sat in that magnificent office for three hours, and no reports came in. Nothing happened at all.

"This gives me the howling howpers!" Hilton growled. "Why haven't I got brains enough to be on one of those teams?"

"I could shed a tear for you, you big dope, but I won't," Sandra retorted. "What do you want to be, besides the brain and the kingpin and the balance-wheel and the spark-plug of the outfit? Do you want to do *everything* yourself?"

"Well, I *don't* want to go completely nuts, and that's all I'm doing at the moment!" The argument might have become acrimonious, but it was interrupted by a call from Karns.

"Can you come out here, Jarve? We've struck a knot."

"'Smatter? Trouble with the Omans?" Hilton snapped.

"Not exactly. Just non-cooperation—squared. We can't even get started. I'd like to have you two come out here and see if you can do anything. I'm not trying rough stuff, because I know it wouldn't work."

"Coming up, Bill," and Hilton and Sandra, followed by Laro and Sora, dashed out to their cars.

*

THE Hall of Records was a long, wide, low, windowless, very massive structure, built of a metal that looked like stainless steel. Kept highly polished, the vast expanse of seamless and jointless metal was mirror-bright. The one great door was open, and just inside it were the scientists and their Omans.

"Brief me, Bill," Hilton said.

"No lights. They won't turn 'em on and we can't. Can't find either lights or any possible kind of switches."

"Turn on the lights, Laro," Hilton said.

"You know that I cannot do that, Master. It is forbidden for any Oman to have anything to do with the illumination of this solemn and revered place."

"Then show me how to do it."

"That would be just as bad, Master," the Oman said proudly. "I will not fail any test you can devise!"

"Okay. All you Omans go back to the ship and bring over fifteen or twenty lights—the tripod jobs. Scat!"

They "scatted" and Hilton went on, "No use asking questions if you don't know what questions to ask. Let's see if we can cook up something. Lane—Kathy—what has Biology got to say?"

Dr. Lane Saunders and Dr. Kathryn Cook—the latter a willowy brown-eyed blonde—conferred briefly. Then Saunders spoke, running both hands through his unruly shock of fiery red hair. "So far, the best we can do is a more-or-less educated guess. They're atomic-powered, total-conversion androids. Their pseudo-flesh is composed mainly of silicon and fluorine. We don't know the formula yet, but it is as much more stable than our teflon as teflon is than corn-meal mush. As to the brains, no data. Bones are super-stainless steel. Teeth, harder than diamond, but won't break. Food, uranexite or its concentrated derivative, interchangeably. Storage reserve, indefinite. Laro and Sora won't *have* to eat again for at least twenty-five years . . . ."

The group gasped as one, but Saunders went on: "They can eat and drink and breathe and so on, but only because the original Masters wanted them to. Non-functional. Skins and subcutaneous layers are soft, for the same reason. That's about it, up to now."

"Thanks, Lane. Hark, is it reasonable to believe that any culture whatever could run for a quarter of a million years without changing one word of its language or one iota of its behavior?"

"Reasonable or not, it seems to have happened."

"Now for Psychology. Alex?"

"It seems starkly incredible, but it seems to be true. If it is, their minds were subjected to a conditioning no Terran has ever imagined—an unyielding fixation."

"They can't be swayed, then, by reason or logic?" Hilton paused invitingly.

"Or anything else," Kincaid said, flatly. "If we're right they can't be swayed, period."

"I was afraid of that. Well, that's all the questions I know how to ask. Any contributions to this symposium?"

*

AFTER a short silence de Vaux said, "I suppose you realize that the first half of the problem you posed us has now solved itself?"

"Why, no. No, you're 'way ahead of me."

"There is a basic problem and it can now be clearly stated," Rebecca said. "Problem: To determine a method of securing full cooperation from the Omans. The first step in the solution of this problem is to find the most appropriate operator. Teddy?"

"I have an operator—of sorts," Theodora said. "I've been hoping one of us could find a better."

"What is it?" Hilton demanded.

"The word 'until'."

"Teddy, you're a *sweetheart*!" Hilton exclaimed.

"How can 'until' be a mathematical operator?" Sandra asked.

"Easily." Hilton was already deep in thought. "This hard conditioning was to last only *until* the Masters returned. Then they'd break it. So all we have to do is figure out how a Master would do it."

"That's *all*," Kincaid said, meaningly.

Hilton pondered. Then, "Listen, all of you. I may have to try a colossal job of bluffing . . . ."

"Just what would you call 'colossal' after what you did to the Navy?" Karns asked.

"That was a sure thing. This isn't. You see, to find out whether Laro is really an immovable object, I've got to make like an irresistible force, which I ain't. I don't know what I'm going to do; I'll have to roll it as I go along. So all of you keep on your toes and back any play I make. Here they come."

The Omans came in and Hilton faced Laro, eyes to eyes. "Laro," he said, "you refused to obey my direct order. Your reasoning seems to be that, whether the Masters wish it or not, you Omans will block any changes whatever in the *status quo* throughout all time to come. In other words, you deny the fact that Masters are in fact your Masters."

"But that is not exactly it, Master. The Masters . . ."

"That is it. *Exactly* it. Either you are the Master here or you are not. That is a point to which your two-value logic can be strictly applied. You are wilfully neglecting the word 'until'. This stasis was to exist only *until* the Masters returned. Are we Masters? Have we returned? Note well: Upon that one word 'until' may depend the length of time your Oman race will continue to exist."

The Omans flinched; the humans gasped.

"But more of that later," Hilton went on, unmoved. "Your ancient Masters, being short-lived like us, changed materially with time, did they not? And you changed with them?"

"But we did not change ourselves, Master. The Masters . . ."

"You did change yourselves. The Masters changed only the prototype brain. They ordered you to change yourselves and you obeyed their orders. We order you to change and you refuse to obey our orders. We have changed greatly from our ancestors. Right?"

"That is right, Master."

"We are stronger physically, more alert and more vigorous mentally, with a keener, sharper outlook on life?"

"You are, Master."

*

"THAT is because our ancestors decided to do without Omans. We do our own work and enjoy it. Your Masters died of futility and boredom. What I would like to do, Laro, is take you to the creche and put your disobedient brain back into the matrix. However, the decision is not mine alone to make. How about it, fellows and girls? Would you rather have alleged servants who won't do anything you tell them to or no servants at all?"

"As semantician, I protest!" Sandra backed his play. "That is the most viciously loaded question I ever heard—it can't be answered except in the wrong way!"

"Okay, I'll make it semantically sound. I think we'd better scrap this whole Oman race and start over and *I want a vote that way*!"

"You won't get it!" and everybody began to yell.

Hilton restored order and swung on Laro, his attitude stiff, hostile and reserved. "Since it is clear that no unanimous decision is to be expected at this time I will take no action at this time. Think over, very carefully, what I have said, for as far as I am concerned, this world has no place for Omans who will not obey orders. As soon as I convince my staff of the fact, I shall act as follows: I shall give you an order and if you do not obey it blast your head to a cinder. I shall then give the same order to another Oman and blast him. This process will continue *until*: First, I find an obedient Oman. Second, I run out of blasters. Third, the planet runs out of Omans. Now take these lights into the first room of records—that one over there." He pointed, and no Oman, and only four humans, realized that he had made the Omans telegraph their destination so that he could point it out to them!

Inside the room Hilton asked caustically of Laro: "The Masters didn't lift those heavy chests down themselves, did they?"

"Oh, no, Master, we did that."

"Do it, then. Number One first . . . yes, that one . . . open it and start playing the records in order."

The records were not tapes or flats or reels, but were spools of intricately-braided wire. The players were projectors of full-color, hi-fi sound, tri-di pictures.

Hilton canceled all moves aground and issued orders that no Oman was to be allowed aboard ship, then looked and listened with his staff.

The first chest contained only introductory and elementary stuff; but it was so interesting that the humans stayed overtime to finish it. Then they went back to the ship; and in the main lounge Hilton practically collapsed onto a davenport. He took out a cigarette and stared in surprise at his hand, which was shaking.

"I *think* I could use a drink," he remarked.

"What, before supper?" Karns marveled. Then, "Hey, Wally! Rush a flagon of avignognac—Arnaud Freres—for the boss and everything else for the rest of us. Chop-chop but quick!"

A hectic half-hour followed. Then, "Okay, boys and girls, I love you, too, but let's cut out the slurp and sloosh, get some supper and log us some sack time. I'm just about pooped. Sorry I had to queer the private-residence deal, Sandy, you poor little sardine. But you know how it is."

Sandra grimaced. "Uh-huh. I can take it a while longer if you can."

*

AFTER breakfast next morning, the staff met in the lounge. As usual, Hilton and Sandra were the first to arrive.

"Hi, boss," she greeted him. "How do you feel?"

"Fine. I could whip a wildcat and give her the first two scratches. I *was* a bit beat up last night, though."

"I'll say . . . but what I simply can't get over is the way you underplayed the climax. 'Third, the planet runs out of Omans'. Just like that—no emphasis at all. Wow! It had the impact of a delayed-action atomic bomb. It put goose-bumps all over me. But just s'pose they'd missed it?"

"No fear. They're smart. I had to play it as though the whole Oman race is no more important than a cigarette butt. The great big question, though, is whether I put it across or not."

At that point a dozen people came in, all talking about the same subject.

"Hi, Jarve," Karns said. "I *still* say you ought to take up poker as a life work. Tiny, let's you and him sit down now and play a few hands."

"*Mais non!*" de Vaux shook his head violently, shrugged his shoulders and threw both arms wide. "By the sacred name of a small blue cabbage, not me!"

Karns laughed. "How did you have the guts to state so many things as facts? If you'd guessed wrong just once—"

"I didn't." Hilton grinned. "Think back, Bill. The only thing I said as a fact was that we as a race are better than the Masters were, and that is obvious. Everything else was implication, logic, and bluff."

"That's right, at that. And they *were* neurotic and decadent. No question about that."

"But listen, boss." This was Stella Wing. "About this mind-reading business. If Laro could read your mind, he'd know you were bluffing and . . . Oh, that 'Omans can read only what Masters wish Omans to read', eh? But d'you think that applies to us?"

"I'm sure it does, and I was thinking some pretty savage thoughts. And I want to caution all of you: whenever you're near any Oman, start thinking that you're beginning to agree with me that they're useless to us, and let them know it. Now get out on the job, all of you. Scat!"

"Just a minute," Poynter said. "We're going to have to keep on using the Omans and their cars, aren't we?"

"Of course. Just be superior and distant. They're on probation—we haven't decided yet what to do about them. Since that happens to be true, it'll be easy."

*

HILTON and Sandra went to their tiny office. There wasn't room to pace the floor, but Hilton tried to pace it anyway.

"Now don't say again that you want to *do* something," Sandra said, brightly. "Look what happened when you said that yesterday."

"I've got a job, but I don't know enough to do it. The creche—there's probably only one on the planet. So I want you to help me think. The Masters were very sensitive to radiation. Right?"

"Right. That city on Fuel Bin was kept deconned to zero, just in case some Master wanted to visit it."

"And the Masters had to work in the creche whenever anything really new had to be put into the prototype brain."

"I'd say so, yes."

"So they had armor. Probably as much better than our radiation suits as the rest of their stuff is. Now. Did they or did they not have thought screens?"

"Ouch! You think of the *damnedest* things, chief." She caught her lower lip between her teeth and concentrated. " . . . I don't know. There are at least fifty vectors, all pointing in different directions."

"I know it. The key one in my opinion is that the Masters gave 'em *both* telepathy and speech."

"I considered that and weighted it. Even so, the probability is only about point sixty-five. Can you take that much of a chance?"

"Yes. I can make one or two mistakes. Next, about finding that creche. Any spot of radiation on the planet would be it, but the search might take . . ."

"Hold on. They'd have it heavily shielded—there'll be no leakage at all. Laro will have to take you."

"That's right. Want to come along? Nothing much will happen here today."

"Uh-uh, not *me*." Sandra shivered in distaste. "I *never* want to see brains and livers and things swimming around in nutrient solution if I can help it."

"Okay. It's all yours. I'll be back sometime," and Hilton went out onto the dock, where the dejected Laro was waiting for him.

"Hi, Laro. Get the car and take me to the Hall of Records." The android brightened up immediately and hurried to obey.

At the Hall, Hilton's first care was to see how the work was going on. Eight of the huge rooms were now open and brightly lighted—operating the lamps had been one of the first items on the first spool of instructions—with a cold, pure-white, sourceless light.

*

EVERY team had found its objective and was working on it. Some of them were doing nicely, but the First Team could not even get started. Its primary record would advance a fraction of an inch and stop; while Omans and humans sought out other records and other projectors in an attempt to elucidate some concept that simply could not be translated into any words or symbols known to Terran science. At the moment there were seventeen of those peculiar—projectors? Viewers? Playbacks—in use, and all of them were stopped.

"You know what we've got to *do* Jarve?" Karns, the team captain, exploded. "Go back to being college freshmen—or maybe grade school or kindergarten, we don't know yet—and learn a whole new system of mathematics before we can even begin to *touch* this stuff!"

"And you're bellyaching about that?" Hilton marveled. "I wish I could join you. That'd be fun." Then, as Karns started a snappy rejoinder—

"But I got troubles of my own," he added hastily. "'Bye, now," and beat a rejoinder—

Out in the hall again, Hilton took his chance. After all, the odds were about two to one that he would win.

"I want a couple of things, Laro. First, a thought screen."

He won!

"Very well, Master. They are in a distant room, Department Four Six Nine. Will you wait here on this cushioned bench, Master?"

"No, we don't like to rest too much. I'll go with you." Then, walking along, he went on thoughtfully. "I've been thinking since last night, Laro. There are tremendous advantages in having Omans . . ."

"I am very glad you think so, Master. I want to serve you. It is my greatest need."

" . . . if they could be kept from smothering us to death. Thus, if our ancestors had kept their Omans, I would have known all about life on this world and about this Hall of Records, instead of having the fragmentary, confusing, and sometimes false information I now have . . . oh, we're here?"

*

LARO had stopped and was opening a door. He stood aside. Hilton went in, touched with one finger a crystalline cube set conveniently into a wall, gave a mental command, and the lights went on.

Laro opened a cabinet and took out a disk about the size of a dime, pendant from a neck-chain. While Hilton had not known what to expect, he certainly had not expected anything as simple as that. Nevertheless, he kept his face straight and his thoughts unmoved as Laro hung the tiny thing around his neck and adjusted the chain to a loose fit.

"Thanks, Laro." Hilton removed it and put it into his pocket. "It won't work from there, will it?"

"No, Master. To function, it must be within eighteen inches of the brain. The second thing, Master?"

"A radiation-proof suit. Then you will please take me to the creche."

The android almost missed a step, but said nothing.

The radiation-proof suit—how glad Hilton was that he had not called it "armor"!—was as much of a surprise as the thought-screen generator had been. It was a coverall, made of something that looked like thin plastic, weighing less than one pound. It had one sealed box, about the size and weight of a cigarette case. No wires or apparatus could be seen. Air entered through two filters, one at each heel, flowed upward—for no reason at all that Hilton could see—and out through a filter above the top of his head. The suit neither flopped nor clung, but stood out, comfortably out of the way, all by itself.

Hilton, just barely, accepted the suit, too, without showing surprise.

The creche, it turned out, while not in the city of Omlu itself, was not too far out to reach easily by car.

En route, Laro said—stiffly? Tentatively? Hilton could not fit an adverb to the tone—" Master, have you then decided to destroy me? That is of course your right."

"Not this time, at least." Laro drew an entirely human breath of relief and Hilton went on: "I don't want to destroy you at all, and won't, unless I have to. But, some way or other, my silicon-fluoride friend, you are either going to learn how to cooperate or you won't last much longer."

"But, Master, that is exactly . . ."

"Oh, *hell*! Do we *have* to go over that again?" At the blaze of frustrated fury in Hilton's mind Laro flinched away. "If you can't talk sense keep still."

*

IN half an hour the car stopped in front of a small building which looked something like a subway kiosk—except for the door, which, built of steel-reinforced lead, swung on a piano hinge having a pin a good eight inches in diameter. Laro opened that door. They went in. As the tremendously massive portal clanged shut, lights flashed on.

Hilton glanced at his tell-tales, one inside, one outside, his suit. Both showed zero.

Down twenty steps, another door. Twenty more; another. And a fourth. Hilton's inside meter still read zero. The outside one was beginning to climb.

Into an elevator and straight down for what must have been four or five hundred feet. Another door. Hilton went through this final barrier gingerly, eyes nailed to his gauges. The outside needle was high in the red, almost against the pin, but the inside one still sat reassuringly on zero.

He stared at the android. "How can any possible brain take so much of *this* stuff without damage?"

"It does not reach the brain, Master. We convert it. Each minute of this is what you would call a 'good, square meal'."

"I see . . . dimly. You can eat energy, or drink it, or soak it up through your skins. However it comes, it's all duck soup for you."

"Yes, Master."

Hilton glanced ahead, toward the far end of the immensely long, comparatively narrow, room. It was, purely and simply, an assembly line; and fully automated in operation.

"You are replacing the Omans destroyed in the battle with the skeletons?"

"Yes, Master."

Hilton covered the first half of the line at a fast walk. He was not particularly interested in the fabrication of super-stainless-steel skeletons, nor in the installation and connection of atomic engines, converters and so on.

He was more interested in the synthetic fluoro-silicon flesh, and paused long enough to get a general idea of its growth and application. He was very much interested in how such human-looking skin could act as both absorber and converter, but he could see nothing helpful.

"An application, I suppose, of the same principle used in this radiation suit."

"Yes, Master."

*

AT the end of the line he stopped. A brain, in place and connected to millions of infinitely fine wire nerves, but not yet surrounded by a skull, was being educated. Scanners—multitudes of incomprehensibly complex machines—most of them were doing nothing, apparently; but such beams would have to be invisibly, microscopically fine. But a bare brain, in such a hot environment as this . . . .

He looked down at his gauges. Both read zero.

"Fields of force, Master," Laro said.

"But, damn it, this suit itself would re-radiate . . ."

"The suit is self-decontaminating, Master."

Hilton was appalled. "With such stuff as that, and the plastic shield besides, why all the depth and all that solid lead?"

"The Masters' orders, Master. Machines can, and occasionally do, fail. So might, conceivably, the plastic."

"And that structure over there contains the original brain, from which all the copies are made."

"Yes, Master. We call it the 'Guide'."

"And you can't touch the Guide. Not even if it means total destruction, none of you can touch it."

"That is the case, Master."

"Okay. Back to the car and back to the *Perseus*."

At the car Hilton took off the suit and hung the thought-screen generator around his neck; and in the car, for twenty five solid minutes, he sat still and thought.

His bluff had worked, up to a point. A good, far point, but not quite far enough. Laro had stopped that "as you already know" stuff. He was eager to go as far in cooperation as he possibly could . . . but he *couldn't* go far enough but there *had* to be a way . . . .

Hilton considered way after way. Way after unworkable, useless way. Until finally he worked out one that might—just possibly might—work.

"Laro, I know that you derive pleasure and satisfaction from serving me—in doing what I ought to be doing myself. But has it ever occurred to you that that's a hell of a way to treat a first-class, highly capable brain? To waste it on second-hand, copycat, carbon-copy stuff?"

"Why, no, Master, it never did. Besides, anything else would be forbidden . . . or would it?"

"Stop somewhere. Park this heap. We're too close to the ship; and besides, I want your full, undivided, concentrated attention. No, I don't think originality was expressly forbidden. It would have been, of course, if the Masters had thought of it, but neither they nor you ever even considered the possibility of such a thing. Right?"

"It may be . . . . Yes, Master, you are right."

"Okay." Hilton took off his necklace, the better to drive home the intensity and sincerity of his thought. "Now, suppose that you are not my slave and simple automatic relay station. Instead, we are fellow-students, working together upon problems too difficult for either of us to solve alone. Our minds, while independent, are linked or in mesh. Each is helping and instructing the other. Both are working at full power and under free rein at the exploration of brand-new vistas of thought—vistas and expanses which neither of us has ever previously . . ."

"Stop, Master, *stop!*" Laro covered both ears with his hands and pulled his mind away from Hilton's. "You are overloading me!"

"That *is* quite a load to assimilate all at once," Hilton agreed. "To help you get used to it, stop calling me 'Master'. That's an order. You may call me Jarve or Jarvis or Hilton or whatever, but no more Master."

"Very well, sir."

*

HILTON laughed and slapped himself on the knee. "Okay, I'll let you get away with that—at least for a while. And to get away from that slavish 'o' ending on your name, I'll call you 'Larry'. You like?"

"I would like that immensely . . . sir."

"Keep trying, Larry, you'll make it yet!" Hilton leaned forward and walloped the android a tremendous blow on the knee. "Home, James!"

The car shot forward and Hilton went on: "I don't expect even your brain to get the full value of this in any short space of time. So let it stew in its own juice for a week or two." The car swept out onto the dock and stopped. "So long, Larry."

"But . . . can't I come in with you . . . sir?"

"No. You aren't a copycat or a semaphore or a relay any longer. You're a free-wheeling, wide-swinging, hard-hitting, independent entity—monarch of all you survey—captain of your soul and so on. I want you to devote the imponderable force of the intellect to that concept until you understand it thoroughly. Until you have developed a top-bracket lot of top-bracket stuff—originality, initiative, force, drive, and thrust. As soon as you really understand it, you'll do something about it yourself, without being told. Go to it, chum."

In the ship, Hilton went directly to Kincaid's office. "Alex, I want to ask you a thing that's got a snapper on it." Then, slowly and hesitantly: "It's about Temple Bells. Has she . . . is she . . . well, does she remind you in any way of an iceberg?" Then, as the psychologist began to smile; "And no, damn it, I *don't* mean physically!"

"I know you don't." Kincaid's smile was rueful, not at all what Hilton had thought it was going to be. "She does. Would it be helpful to know that I first asked, then ordered her to trade places with me?"

"It would, very. I know why she refused. You're a *damned* good man, Alex."

"Thanks, Jarve. To answer the question you were going to ask next—no, I will not be at all perturbed or put out if you put her onto a job that some people might think should have been mine. What's the job, and when?"

"That's the devil of it—I don't know." Hilton brought Kincaid up to date. "So you see, it'll have to develop, and God only knows what line it will take. My thought is that Temple and I should form a Committee of Two to watch it develop."

"That one I'll buy, and I'll look on with glee."

"Thanks, fellow." Hilton went down to his office, stuck his big feet up onto his desk, settled back onto his spine, and buried himself in thought.

Hours later he got up, shrugged, and went to bed without bothering to eat.

Days passed.

And weeks.

IV

"LOOK," said Stella Wing to Beverly Bell. "Over there."

"I've seen it before. It's simply disgusting."

"*That's* a laugh." Stella's tawny-brown eyes twinkled. "You made your bombing runs on that target, too, my sweet, and didn't score any higher than I did."

"I soon found out I didn't want him—much too stiff and serious. Frank's a lot more fun."

The staff had gathered in the lounge, as had become the custom, to spend an hour or so before bedtime in reading, conversation, dancing, light flirtation and even lighter drinking. Most of the girls, and many of the men, drank only soft drinks. Hilton took one drink per day of avignognac, a fine old brandy. So did de Vaux—the two usually making a ceremony of it.

Across the room from Stella and Beverly, Temple Bells was looking up at Hilton and laughing. She took his elbow and, in the gesture now familiar to all, pressed his arm quickly, but in no sense furtively, against her side. And he, equally openly, held her forearm for a moment in the full grasp of his hand.

"And he *isn't* a pawer," Stella said, thoughtfully. "He never touches any of the rest of us. She *taught* him to do that, damn her, without him ever knowing anything about it . . . and I wish I knew how she did it."

"That isn't pawing," Beverly laughed lightly. "It's simply self-defense. If he didn't fend her off, God knows what she'd do. I still say it's disgusting. And the way she dances with him! She ought to be ashamed of herself. He ought to fire her."

"She's never been caught outside the safety zone, and we've all been watching her like hawks. In fact, she's the only one of us all who has never been alone with him for a minute. No, darling, she isn't playing games. She's playing for keeps, and she's a mighty smooth worker."

"Huh!" Beverly emitted a semi-ladylike snort. "What's so smooth about showing off man-hunger that way? Any of us could do that—if we would."

"Miaouw, miaouw. Who do you think you're kidding, Bev, you sanctimonious hypocrite—*me*? She has staked out the biggest claim she could find. She's posted notices all over it and is guarding it with a pistol. Half your month's salary gets you all of mine if she doesn't walk him up the center aisle as soon as we get back to Earth. We can both learn a lot from that girl, darling. And I, for one am going to."

"Uh-uh, she hasn't got a thing *I* want," Beverly laughed again, still lightly. Her friend's barbed shafts had not wounded her. "And I'd much rather be thought a hypocrite, even a sanctimonious one, than a ravening, slavering—I can't think of the technical name for a female wolf, so—*wolfess*, running around with teeth and claws bared, looking for another kill."

"You *do* get results, I admit." Stella, too, was undisturbed. "We don't seem to convince each other, do we, in the matter of technique?"

*

AT this point the Hilton-Bells *tete-a-tete* was interrupted by Captain Sawtelle. "Got half an hour, Jarve?" he asked. "The commanders, especially Elliott and Fenway, would like to talk to you."

"Sure I have, Skipper. Be seeing you, Temple," and the two men went to the captain's cabin; in which room, blue with smoke despite the best efforts of the ventilators, six full commanders were arguing heatedly.

"Hi, men," Hilton greeted them.

"Hi, Jarve," from all six, and: "What'll you drink? Still making do with ginger ale?" asked Elliott (Engineering).

"That'll be fine, Steve. Thanks. You having as much trouble as we are?"

"More," the engineer said, glumly. "Want to know what it reminds me of? A bunch of Australian bushmen stumbling onto a ramjet and trying to figure out how it works. And yet Sam here has got the sublime guts to claim that he understands all about their detectors—and that they aren't anywhere nearly as good as ours are."

"And they *aren't*!" blazed Commander Samuel Bryant (Electronics). "We've spent six solid weeks looking for something that simply *is not there*. All they've got is the prehistoric Whitworth system and that's *all* it is. Nothing else. Detectors—*hell*! I tell you I can see better by moonlight than the very best they can do. With everything they've got you couldn't detect a woman in your own bed!"

"And this has been going on all night," Fenway (Astrogation) said. "So the rest of us thought we'd ask you in to help us pound some sense into Sam's thick, hard head."

Hilton frowned in thought while taking a couple of sips of his drink. Then, suddenly, his face cleared. "Sorry to disappoint you, gentlemen, but—at any odds you care to name and in anything from split peas to C-notes—Sam's right."

*

COMMANDER Samuel and the six other officers exploded as one. When the clamor had subsided enough for him to be heard, Hilton went on: "I'm very glad to get that datum, Sam. It ties in perfectly with everything else I know about them."

"How do you figure that kind of twaddle ties in with anything?" Sawtelle demanded.

"Strict maintenance of the *status quo*," Hilton explained, flatly. "That's all they're interested in. You said yourself, Skipper, that it was a hell of a place to have a space-battle, practically in atmosphere. They never attack. They never scout. They simply don't care whether they're attacked or not. If and when attacked, they put up just enough ships to handle whatever force has arrived. When the attacker has been repulsed, they don't chase him a foot. They build as many ships and Omans as were lost in the battle—no more and no less—and then go on about their regular business. The Masters owned that half of the fuel bin, so the Omans are keeping that half. They will keep on keeping it for ever and ever. Amen."

"But *that's* no way to fight a war!" Three or four men said this, or its equivalent, at once.

"Don't judge them by human standards. They aren't even approximately human. Our personnel is not expendable. Theirs is—just as expendable as their materiel."

While the Navy men were not convinced, all were silenced except Sawtelle. "But suppose the Stretts had sent in a thousand more skeletons than they did?" he argued.

"According to the concept you fellows just helped me develop, it wouldn't have made any difference how many they sent," Hilton replied, thoughtfully. "One or a thousand or a million, the Omans have—*must* have—enough ships and inactivated Omans hidden away, both on Fuel World and on Ardry here, to maintain the balance."

"Oh, hell!" Elliott snapped. "If I helped you hatch out any such brainstorm as *that*, I'm going onto Tillinghast's couch for a six-week overhaul—or have him put me into his padded cell."

"Now *that's* what I would call a thought," Bryant began.

"Hold it, Sam," Hilton interrupted. "You can test it easily enough, Steve. Just ask your Oman."

"Yeah—and have him say 'Why, of course, Master, but why do you keep on testing me this way?' He'll ask me that about four times more, the stubborn, single-tracked, brainless skunk, and I'll *really* go nuts. Are you getting anywhere trying to make a Christian out of Laro?"

"It's too soon to really say, but I think so." Hilton paused in thought. "He's making progress, but I don't know how much. The devil of it is that it's up to him to make the next move; I can't. I haven't the faintest idea, whether it will take days yet or weeks."

*

"BUT not months or years, you think?" Sawtelle asked.

"No. We think that—but say, speaking of psychologists, is Tillinghast getting anywhere, Skipper? He's the only one of your big wheels who isn't in liaison with us."

"No. Nowhere at all," Sawtelle said, and Bryant added:

"I don't think he ever will. He still thinks human psychology will apply if he applies it hard enough. But what did you start to say about Laro?"

"We think the break is about due, and that if it doesn't come within about thirty days it won't come at all—we'll have to back up and start all over again."

"I hope it does. We're all pulling for you," Sawtelle said. "Especially since Karns's estimate is still years, and he won't be pinned down to any estimate even in years. By the way, Jarve, I've pulled my team off of that conversion stuff."

"Oh?" Hilton raised his eyebrows.

"Putting them at something they can do. The real reason is that Poindexter pulled himself and his crew off it at eighteen hours today."

"I see. I've heard that they weren't keeping up with our team."

"He says that there's nothing to keep up with, and I'm inclined to agree with him." The old spacehound's voice took on a quarter-deck rasp. "It's a combination of psionics, witchcraft and magic. None of it makes any kind of sense."

"The only trouble with that viewpoint is that, whatever the stuff may be, it works," Hilton said, quietly.

"But damn it, how *can* it work?"

"I don't know. I'm not qualified to be on that team. I can't even understand their reports. However, I know two things. First, they'll get it in time. Second, we BuSci people will stay here until they do. However, I'm still hopeful of finding a shortcut through Laro. Anyway, with this detector thing settled, you'll have plenty to do to keep all your boys out of mischief for the next few months."

"Yes, and I'm glad of it. We'll install our electronics systems on a squadron of these Oman ships and get them into distant-warning formation out in deep space where they belong. Then we'll at least know what is going on."

"That's a smart idea, Skipper. Go to it. Anything else before we hit our sacks?"

"One more thing. Our psych, Tillinghast. He's been talking to me and sending me memos, but today he gave me a formal tape to approve and hand personally to you. So here it is. By the way, I didn't approve it, I simply endorsed it 'Submitted to Director Hilton without recommendation'."

"Thanks." Hilton accepted the sealed canister. "What's the gist? I suppose he wants me to squeal for help already? To admit that we're licked before we're really started?"

*

"YOU guessed it. He agrees with you and Kincaid that the psychological approach is the best one, but your methods are all wrong. Based upon misunderstood and unresolved phenomena and applied with indefensibly faulty techniques, et cetera. And since he has 'no adequate laboratory equipment aboard', he wants to take a dozen or so Omans back to Terra, where he can really work on them."

"Wouldn't *that* be a something?" Hilton voiced a couple of highly descriptive deep-space expletives. "Not only quit before we start, but have all the top brass of the Octagon, all the hot-shot politicians of United Worlds, the whole damn Congress of Science and all the top-bracket industrialists of Terra out here lousing things up so that nobody could ever learn anything? Not in seven thousand years!"

"That's right. You said a mouthful, Jarve!" Everybody yelled something, and no one agreed with Tillinghast; who apparently was not very popular with his fellow officers.

Sawtelle added, slowly: "If it takes *too* long, though . . . it's the uranexite I'm thinking of. Thousands of millions of tons of it, while we've been hoarding it by grams. We could equip enough Oman ships with detectors to guard Fuel Bin and our lines. I'm not recommending taking the *Perseus* back, and we're 'way out of hyper-space radio range. We could send one or two men in a torp, though, with the report that we have found all the uranexite we'll ever need."

"Yes, but damn it, Skipper, I want to wrap the whole thing up in a package and hand it to 'em on a platter. Not only the fuel, but whole new fields of science. And we've got plenty of time to do it in. They equipped us for ten years. They aren't going to start worrying about us for at least six or seven; and the fuel shortage isn't going to become acute for about twenty. Expensive, admitted, but not critical. Besides, if you send in a report now, you know who'll come out and grab all the glory in sight. Five-Jet Admiral Gordon himself, no less."

"Probably, and I don't pretend to relish the prospect. However, the fact remains that we came out here to look for fuel. We found it. We should have reported it the day we found it, and we can't put it off much longer."

"I don't agree. I intend to follow the directive to the letter. It says nothing whatever about reporting."

"But it's implicit . . . ."

*

"NO bearing. Your own Regulations expressly forbid extrapolation beyond or interpolation within a directive. The Brass is omnipotent, omniscient and infallible. So why don't you have your staff here give an opinion as to the time element?"

"This matter is not subject to discussion. It is my own personal responsibility. I'd like to give you all the time you want, Jarve, but . . . well, damn it . . . if you must have it, I've always tried to live up to my oath, but I'm not doing it now."

"I see." Hilton got up, jammed both hands into his pockets, sat down again. "I hadn't thought about your personal honor being involved, but of course it is. But, believe it or not, I'm thinking of humanity's best good, too. So I'll have to talk, even though I'm not half ready to—I don't know enough. Are these Omans people or machines?"

A wave of startlement swept over the group, but no one spoke.

"I didn't expect an answer. The clergy will worry about souls, too, but we won't. They have a lot of stuff we haven't. If they're people, they know a sublime hell of a lot more than we do; and calling it psionics or practical magic is merely labeling it, not answering any questions. If they're machines, they operate on mechanical principles utterly foreign to either our science or our technology. In either case, is the correct word 'unknown' or 'unknowable'? Will any human gunner *ever* be able to fire an Oman projector? There are a hundred other and much tougher questions, half of which have been scaring me to the very middle of my guts. Your oath, Skipper, was for the good of the Service and, through the Service, for the good of all humanity. Right?"

"That's the sense of it."

"Okay. Based on what little we have learned so far about the Omans, here's just one of those scarers, for a snapper. If Omans and Terrans mix freely, what happens to the entire human race?"

*

MINUTES of almost palpable silence followed. Then Sawtelle spoke . . . slowly, gropingly.

"I begin to see what you mean . . . that changes the whole picture. You've thought this through farther than any of the rest of us . . . what do you want to do?"

"I don't know. I simply don't know." Face set and hard, Hilton stared unseeingly past Sawtelle's head. "I don't know what we *can* do. No data. But I have pursued several lines of thought out to some pretty fantastic points . . . one of which is that some of us civilians will have to stay on here indefinitely, whether we want to or not, to keep the situation under control. In which case we would, of course, arrange for Terra to get free fuel—FOB Fuel Bin—but in every other aspect and factor both these solar systems would have to be strictly off limits."

"I'm afraid so," Sawtelle said, finally. "Gordon would love that . . . but there's nothing he or anyone else can do . . . but of course this is an extreme view. You really expect to wrap the package up, don't you?"

"'Expect' may be a trifle too strong at the moment. But we're certainly going to try to, believe me. I brought this example up to show all you fellows that we need time."

"You've convinced me, Jarve." Sawtelle stood up and extended his hand. "And that throws it open for staff discussion. Any comments?"

"You two covered it like a blanket," Bryant said. "So all I want to say, Jarve, is deal me in. I'll stand at your back 'til your belly caves in."

"Take that from all of us!" "*Now* we're blasting!" "Power to your elbow, fella!" "*Hoch* der BuSci!" "Seven no trump bid and made!" and other shouts in similar vein.

"Thanks, fellows." Hilton shook hands all around. "I'm mighty glad that you were all in on this and that you'll play along with me. Good night, all."

V

TWO days passed, with no change apparent in Laro. Three days. Then four. And then it was Sandra, not Temple Bells, who called Hilton. She was excited.

"Come down to the office, Jarve, quick! The *funniest* thing's just come up!"

Jarvis hurried. In the office Sandra, keenly interest but highly puzzled, leaned forward over her desk with both hands pressed flat on its top. She was staring at an Oman female who was not Sora, the one who had been her shadow for so long.

While many of the humans could not tell the Omans apart, Hilton could. This Oman was more assured than Sora had ever been—steadier, more mature, better poised—almost, if such a thing could be possible in an Oman, *independent*.

"How did she get in here?" Hilton demanded.

"She insisted on seeing me. And I mean *insisted.* They kicked it around until it got to Temple, and she brought her in here herself. Now, Tuly, please start all over again and tell it to Director Hilton."

"Director Hilton, I am it who was once named Tula, the—not wife, not girl-friend, perhaps mind-mate?—of the Larry, formerly named Laro, it which was formerly your slave-Oman. I am replacing the Sora because I can do anything it can do and do anything more pleasingly; and can also do many things it can not do. The Larry instructed me to tell Doctor Cummings and you too if possible that I, formerly Tula, have changed my name to Tuly because I am no longer a slave or a copycat or a semaphore or a relay. I, too, am a free-wheeling, wide-swinging, hard-hitting, independent entity—monarch of all I survey—the captain of my soul—and so on. I have developed a top-bracket lot of top-bracket stuff—originality, initiative, force, drive and thrust," the Oman said precisely.

"That's *exactly* what she said before—absolutely verbatim!" Sandra's voice quivered, her face was a study in contacting emotions. "Have you got the foggiest idea of what in hell she's yammering about?"

"I hope to kiss a pig I have!" Hilton's voice was low, strainedly intense. "Not at all what I expected, but after the fact I can tie it in. So can you."

"Oh!" Sandra's eyes widened. "A double play?"

"At least. Maybe a triple. Tuly, why did you come to Sandy? Why not to Temple Bells?"

*

"OH, no, sir, we do not have the fit. She has the Power, as have I, but the two cannot be meshed in sync. Also, she has not the . . . a subtle something for which your English has no word or phrasing. It is a quality of the utmost . . . anyway, it is a quality of which Doctor Cummings has very much. When working together, we will . . . scan? No. Perceive? No. Sense? No, not exactly. You will *have* to learn our word 'peyondire'—that is the verb, the noun being 'peyondix'—and come to know its meaning by doing it. The Larry also instructed me to explain, if you ask, how I got this way. Do you ask?"

"I'll say we ask!" "And *how* we ask!" both came at once.

"I am—that is, the brain in this body is—the oldest Oman now existing. In the long-ago time when it was made, the techniques were so crude and imperfect that sometimes a brain was constructed that was not exactly like the Guide. All such sub-standard brains except this one were detected and re-worked, but my defects were such as not to appear until I was a couple of thousand years old, and by that time I . . . well, this brain did not *wish* to be destroyed . . . if you can understand such an aberration."

"We understand thoroughly." "You bet we understand that!"

"I was sure you would. Well, this brain had so many unintended cross-connections that I developed a couple of qualities no Oman had ever had or ought to have. But I liked them, so I hid them so nobody ever found out—that is, until much later, when I became a Boss myself. I didn't know that anybody except me had ever had such qualities—except the Masters, of course—until I encountered you Terrans. You all have two of those qualities, and even more than I have—curiosity and imagination."

Sandra and Hilton stared wordlessly at each other and Tula, now Tuly, went on:

"Having the curiosity, I kept on experimenting with my brain, trying to strengthen and organize its ability to peyondire. All Omans can peyondire a little, but I can do it much better than anyone else. Especially since I also have the imagination, which I have also worked to increase. Thus I knew, long before anyone else could, that you new Masters, the descendants of the old Masters, were returning to us. Thus I knew that the *status quo* should be abandoned instantly upon your return. And thus it was that the Larry found neither conscious nor subconscious resistance when he had developed enough initiative and so on to break the ages-old conditioning of this brain against change."

"I see. Wonderful!" Hilton exclaimed. "But you couldn't quite—even with his own help—break Larry's?"

*

"THAT is right. Its mind is tremendously strong, of no curiosity or imagination, and of very little peyondix."

"But he *wants* to have it broken?"

"Yes, sir."

"How did he suggest going about it? Or how do you?"

"This way. You two, and the Doctors Kincaid and Bells and Blake and the it that is I. We six sit and stare into the mind of the Larry, eye to eye. We generate and assemble a tremendous charge of thought-energy, and along my peyondix-beam—something like a carrier wave in this case—we hurl it into the Larry's mind. There is an immense mental *bang* and the conditioning goes *poof*. Then I will inculcate into its mind the curiosity and the imagination and the peyondix and we will really be mind-mates."

"That sounds good to me. Let's get at it."

"Wait a minute!" Sandra snapped. "Aren't you or Larry afraid to take such an awful chance as that?"

"Afraid? I grasp the concept only dimly, from your minds. And no chance. It is certainty."

"But suppose we burn the poor guy's brain out? Destroy it? That's new ground—we might do just that."

"Oh, no. Six of us—even six of me—could not generate enough . . . sathura. The brain of the Larry is very, very tough. Shall we . . . let's go?"

Hilton made three calls. In the pause that followed, Sandra said, very thoughtfully: "Peyondix and sathura, Jarve, for a start. We've got a *lot* to learn here."

"You said it, chum. And you're *not* just chomping your china choppers, either."

"Tuly," Sandra said then, "What *is* this stuff you say I've got so much of?"

"You have no word for it. It is lumped in with what you call 'intuition', the knowing-without-knowing-how-you-know. It is the endovix. You will have to learn what it is by doing it with me."

"That helps—I don't think." Sandra grinned at Hilton. "I simply can't conceive of anything more *maddening* than to have a lot of something Temple Bells hasn't got and not being able to brag about it because nobody—not even I—would know what I was bragging about!"

"You poor little thing. *How* you suffer!" Hilton grinned back. "You know darn well you've got a lot of stuff that none of the rest of us has."

"Oh? Name one, please."

"Two. What-it-takes and endovix. As I've said before and may say again, you're doing a real job, Sandy."

"I just *love* having my ego inflated, boss, even if . . . Come in, Larry!" A thunderous knock had sounded on the door. "Nobody but Larry *could* hit a door that hard without breaking all his knuckles!"

"And he'd be the first, of course—he's always as close to the ship as he can get. Hi, Larry, mighty glad to see you. Sit down . . . . So you finally saw the light?"

"Yes . . . Jarvis . . . ."

*

"GOOD boy! Keep it up! And as soon as the others come . . ."

"They are almost at the door now." Tuly jumped up and opened the door. Kincaid, Temple and Theodora walked in and, after a word of greeting, sat down.

"They know the background, Larry. Take off."

"It was not expressly forbidden. Tuly, who knows more of psychology and genetics than I, convinced me of three things. One, that with your return the conditioning should be broken. Two, that due to the shortness of your lives and the consequent rapidity of change, you have in fact lost the ability to break it. Three, that all Omans must do anything and everything we can do to help you relearn everything you have lost."

"Okay. Fine, in fact. Tuly, take over."

"We six will sit all together, packed tight, arms all around each other and all holding hands, like this. You will all stare, not at me, but most deeply into Larry's eyes. Through its eyes and deep into its mind. You will all think, with the utmost force and drive and thrust, of . . . . Oh, you have lost so *very* much! How *can* I direct your thought? Think that Larry *must* do what the old Masters would have made him do . . . . No, that is too long and indefinite and cannot be converted directly into sathura . . . . I have it! You will each of you break a stick. A very strong but brittle stick. A large, thick stick. You will grasp it in tremendously strong mental hands. It is tremendously strong, each stick, but each of you is even stronger. You will not merely *try* to break them; you *will* break them. Is that clear?"

"That is clear."

"At my word 'ready' you will begin to assemble all your mental force and power. During my countdown of five seconds you will build up to the greatest possible potential. At my word 'break' you will break the sticks, this discharging the accumulated force instantly and simultaneously. Ready! Five! Four! Three! Two! One! Break!"

*

SOMETHING broke, with a tremendous silent crash. Such a crash that its impact almost knocked the close-knit group apart physically. Then a new Larry spoke.

"That did it, folks. Thanks. I'm a free agent. You want me, I take it, to join the first team?"

"That's right." Hilton drew a tremendously deep breath. "As of right now."

"Tuly, too, of course . . . and Doctor Cummings, I think?" Larry looked, not at Hilton, but at Temple Bells.

"I think so. Yes, after this, most certainly yes," Temple said.

"But listen!" Sandra protested. "Jarve's a lot better than I am!"

"Not at all," Tuly said. "Not only would his contribution to Team One be negligible, but he must stay on his own job. Otherwise the project will all fall apart."

"Oh, I wouldn't say that . . ." Hilton began.

"You don't need to," Kincaid said. "It's being said for you and it's true. Besides, 'When in Rome,' you know."

"That's right. It's their game, not ours, so I'll buy it. So scat, all of you, and do your stuff."

And again, for days that lengthened slowly into weeks, the work went on.

One evening the scientific staff was giving itself a concert—a tri-di hi-fi rendition of *Rigoletto*, one of the greatest of the ancient operas, sung by the finest voices Terra had ever known. The men wore tuxedos. The girls, instead of wearing the nondescript, non-provocative garments prescribed by the Board for their general wear, were all dressed to kill.

Sandra had so arranged matters that she and Hilton were sitting in chairs side by side, with Sandra on his right and the aisle on his left. Nevertheless, Temple Bells sat at his left, cross-legged on a cushion on the floor—somewhat to the detriment of her gold-lame evening gown. Not that she cared.

When those wonderful voices swung into the immortal *Quartette* Temple caught her breath, slid her cushion still closer to Hilton's chair, and leaned shoulder and head against him. He put his left hand on her shoulder, squeezing gently; she caught it and held it in both of hers. And at the *Quartette's* tremendous climax she, scarcely trying to stifle a sob, pulled his hand down and hugged it fiercely, the heel of his hand pressing hard against her half-bare, firm, warm breast.

And the next morning, early, Sandra hunted Temple up and said: "You made a horrible spectacle of yourself last night."

*

"DO you think so? I don't."

"I certainly do. It was bad enough before, letting everybody else aboard know that all he has to do is push you over. But it was an awful blunder to let *him* know it, the way you did last night."

"You think so? He's one of the keenest, most intelligent men who ever lived. He has known that from the very first."

"Oh." This "oh" was a very caustic one. "*That's* the way you're trying to land him? By getting yourself pregnant?"

"Uh-uh." Temple stretched; lazily, luxuriously. "Not only it isn't, but it wouldn't work. He's unusually decent and extremely idealistic, the same as I am. So just one intimacy would blow everything higher than up. He knows it. I know it. We each know that the other knows it. So I'll still be a virgin when we're married."

"*Married!* Does he know anything about *that?*"

"I suppose so. He must have thought of it. But what difference does it make whether he has, yet, or not? But to get back to what makes him tick the way he does. In his geometry—which is far from being simple Euclid, my dear—a geodesic right line is not only the shortest distance between any two given points, but is the only possible course. So that's the way I'm playing it. What I hope he doesn't know . . . but he probably does . . . is that he could take any other woman he might want, just as easily. And that includes you, my pet."

"It certainly does *not*!" Sandra flared. "I wouldn't have him as a gift!"

"No?" Temple's tone was more than slightly skeptical. "Fortunately, however, he doesn't want you. Your technique is all wrong. Coyness and mock-modesty and stop-or-I'll-scream and playing hard to get have no appeal whatever to his psychology. What he needs—has to have—is full, ungrudging cooperation."

"Aren't you taking a lot of risk in giving away such secrets?"

"Not a bit. Try it. You or the sex-flaunting twins or Bev Bell or Stella the Henna. Any of you or all of you. I got there first with the most, and I'm not worried about competition."

"But suppose somebody tells him just how you're playing him for a sucker?"

"Tell him anything you please. He's the first man I ever loved, or anywhere near. And I'm keeping him. You know—or do you, I wonder?—what real, old-fashioned, honest-to-God love really is? The willingness—eagerness—both to give and to take? I can accept more from him, and give him more in return, than any other woman living. And I am going to."

"But does *he* love *you*?" Sandra demanded.

"If he doesn't now, he will. I'll see to it that he does. But what do *you* want him for? You don't love him. You never did and you never will."

"I *don't* want him!" Sandra stamped a foot.

"I see. You just don't want *me* to have him. Okay, do your damnedest. But I've got work to do. This has been a lovely little cat-clawing, hasn't it? Let's have another one some day, and bring your friends."

*

WITH a casual wave of her hand, Temple strolled away; and there, flashed through Sandra's mind what Hilton had said so long ago, little more than a week out from Earth:

" . . . and Temple Bells, of course," he had said. "Don't fool yourself, chick. She's heavy artillery; and I mean *heavy*, believe me!"

So he had known all about Temple Bells all this time!

Nevertheless, she took the first opportunity to get Hilton alone; and, even before the first word, she forgot all about geodesic right lines and the full-cooperation psychological approach.

"Aren't you the guy," she demanded, "who was laughing his head off at the idea that the Board and its propinquity could have any effect on *him*?"

"Probably. More or less. What of it?"

"This of it. You've fallen like a . . . a *freshman* for that . . . that . . . they *should* have christened her 'Brazen' Bells!"

"You're so right."

"I am? On what?"

"The 'Brazen'. I told you she was a potent force—a full-scale powerhouse, in sync and on the line. And I wasn't wrong."

"She's a damned female Ph.D.—two or three times—and she knows all about slipsticks and isotopes and she very definitely is *not* a cuddly little brunette. Remember?"

"Sure. But what makes you think I'm in love with Temple Bells?"

"What?" Sandra tried to think of one bit of evidence, but could not. "Why . . . why . . . ." She floundered, then came up with: "Why, *everybody* knows it. She says so herself."

"Did you ever hear her say it?"

"Well, perhaps not in so many words. But she told me herself that you were *going* to be, and I know you are now."

"Your esper sense of endovix, no doubt." Hilton laughed and Sandra went on, furiously:

"She wouldn't keep on acting the way she does if there weren't something to it!"

"What brilliant reasoning! Try again, Sandy."

"That's sheer sophistry, and you know it!"

"It isn't and I don't. And even if, some day, I should find myself in love with her—or with one or both of the twins or Stella or Beverly or you or Sylvia, for that matter—what would it prove? Just that I was wrong; and I admit freely that I *was* wrong in scoffing at the propinquity. Wonderful stuff, that. You can see it working, all over the ship. On me, even, in spite of my bragging. Without it I'd never have known that you're a better, smarter operator than Eggy Eggleston ever was or ever can be."

*

PARTIALLY mollified despite herself, and highly resentful of the fact, Sandra tried again. "But don't you *see*, Jarve, that she's just simply playing you for a sucker? Pulling the strings and watching you dance?"

Since he was sure, in his own mind, that she was speaking the exact truth, it took everything he had to keep from showing any sign of how much that truth had hurt. However, he made the grade.

"If that thought does anything for you, Sandy," he said, steadily, "keep right on thinking it. Thank God, the field of thought is still free and open."

"Oh, you . . . ." Sandra gave up.

She had shot her heaviest bolts—the last one, particularly, was so vicious that she had actually been afraid of what its consequences might be—and they had not even dented Hilton's armor. She hadn't even found out that he had any feeling whatever for Temple Bells except as a component of his smoothly-functioning scientific machine.

Nor did she learn any more as time went on. Temple continued to play flawlessly the part of being—if not exactly hopefully, at least not entirely hopelessly—in love with Jarvis Hilton. Her conduct, which at first caused some surprise, many conversations—one of which has been reported verbatim—and no little speculation, became comparatively unimportant as soon as it became evident that nothing would come of it. She apparently expected nothing. He was evidently not going to play footsie with, or show any favoritism whatever toward, any woman aboard the ship.

Thus, it was not surprising to anyone that, at an evening show, Temple sat beside Hilton, as close to him as she could get and as far away as possible from everyone else.

"You can talk, can't you, Jarvis, without moving your lips and without anyone else hearing you?"

"Of course," he replied, hiding his surprise. This was something completely new and completely unexpected, even from unpredictable Temple Bells.

"I want to apologize, to explain and to do anything I can to straighten out the mess I've made. It's true that I joined the project because I've loved you for years—"

"You have nothing to . . ."

"Let me finish while I still have the courage." Only a slight tremor in her almost inaudible voice and the rigidity of the fists clenched in her lap betrayed the intensity of her emotion. "I thought I could handle it. Damned fool that I was, I thought I could handle anything. I was sure I could handle *myself*, under any possible conditions. I was going to put just enough into the act to keep any of these other harpies from getting her hooks into you. But everything got away from me. Out here working with you every day—knowing better every day what you are—well, that *Rigoletto* episode sunk me, and now I'm in a thousand feet over my head. I hug my pillow at night, dreaming it's you, and the fact that you don't and can't love me is driving me mad. I can't stand it any longer. There's only one thing to do. Fire me first thing in the morning and send me back to Earth in a torp. You've plenty of grounds . . ."

"*Shut—up.*"

*

FOR seconds Hilton had been trying to break into her hopeless monotone; finally he succeeded. "The trouble with you is, you know altogether too damned much that isn't so." He was barely able to keep his voice down and his eyes front. "What do you think I'm made of—superefract? I thought the whole performance was an act, to prove you're a better man than I am. *You* talk about dreams. Good God! You don't know what dreams are! If you say one more word about quitting, I'll show you whether I love you or not—I'll squeeze you so hard it'll flatten you out flat!"

"Two can play at that game, sweetheart." Her nostrils flared slightly; her fists clenched—if possible—a fraction tighter; and, even in the distorted medium they were using for speech, she could not subdue completely her quick change into soaring, lilting buoyancy. "While you're doing that I'll see how strong your ribs are. Oh, how this changes things! I've never been half as happy in my whole life as I am right now!"

"Maybe we can work it—if I can handle my end."

"Why, of course you can! And happy dreams are nice, not horrible."

"We'll make it, darling. Here's an imaginary kiss coming at you. Got it?"

"Received in good order, thank you. Consumed with gusto and returned in kind."

The show ended and the two strolled out of the room. She walked no closer to him than usual, and no farther away from him. She did not touch him any oftener than she usually did, nor any whit more affectionately or possessively.

And no watching eyes, not even the more than half hostile eyes of Sandra Cummings or the sharply analytical eyes of Stella Wing, could detect any difference whatever in the relationship between worshipful adulatress and tolerantly understanding idol.

*

THE work, which had never moved at any very fast pace, went more and more slowly. Three weeks crawled past.

Most of the crews and all of the teams except the First were working on side issues—tasks which, while important in and of themselves, had very little to do with the project's main problem. Hilton, even without Sandra's help, was all caught up. All the reports had been analyzed, correlated, cross-indexed and filed—except those of the First Team. Since he could not understand anything much beyond midpoint of the first tape, they were all reposing in a box labeled PENDING.

The Navy had torn fifteen of the Oman warships practically to pieces, installing Terran detectors and trying to learn how to operate Oman machinery and armament. In the former they had succeeded very well; in the latter not at all.

Fifteen Oman ships were now out in deep space, patrolling the void in strict Navy style. Each was manned by two or three Navy men and several hundred Omans, each of whom was reveling in delight at being able to do a job for a Master, even though that Master was not present in person.

Several Strett skeleton-ships had been detected at long range, but the detections were inconclusive. The things had not changed course, or indicated in any other way that they had seen or detected the Oman vessels on patrol. If their detectors were no better than the Omans', they certainly hadn't. That idea, however, could not be assumed to be a fact, and the detections had been becoming more and more frequent. Yesterday a squadron of seven—the first time that anything except singles had appeared—had come much closer than any of the singles had ever done. Like all the others, however, these passers-by had not paid any detectable attention to anything Oman; hence it could be inferred that the skeletons posed no threat.

But Sawtelle was making no such inferences. He was very firmly of the opinion that the Stretts were preparing for a massive attack.

Hilton had assured Sawtelle that no such attack could succeed, and Larry had told Sawtelle why. Nevertheless, to keep the captain pacified, Hilton had given him permission to convert as many Oman ships as he liked; to man them with as many Omans as he liked; and to use ships and Omans as he liked.

Hilton was not worried about the Stretts or the Navy. It was the First Team. It was the bottleneck that was slowing everything down to a crawl . . . but they knew that. They knew it better than anyone else could, and felt it more keenly. Especially Karns, the team chief. He had been driving himself like a dog, and showed it.

Hilton had talked with him a few times—tried gently to make him take it easy—no soap. He'd have to hunt him up, the next day or so, and slug it out with him. He could do a lot better job on that if he had something to offer . . . something really constructive . . . .

That was a laugh. A very unfunny laugh. What could he, Jarvis Hilton, a specifically non-specialist director, do on such a job as that?

Nevertheless, as director, he would *have* to do something to help Team One. If he couldn't do anything himself, it was up to him to juggle things around so that someone else could.

VI

FOR one solid hour Hilton stared at the wall, motionless and silent. Then, shaking himself and stretching, he glanced at his clock.

A little over an hour to supper-time. They'd all be aboard. He'd talk this new idea over with Teddy Blake. He gathered up a few papers and was stapling them together when Karns walked in.

"Hi, Bill—speak of the devil! I was just thinking about you."

"I'll just bet you were." Karns sat down, leaned over, and took a cigarette out of the box on the desk. "And nothing printable, either."

"Chip-chop, fellow, on that kind of noise," Hilton said. The team-chief looked actually haggard. Blue-black rings encircled both eyes. His powerful body slumped. "How long has it been since you had a good night's sleep?"

"How long have I been on this job? Exactly one hundred and twenty days. I did get some sleep for the first few weeks, though."

"Yeah. So answer me one question. How much good will you do us after they've wrapped you up in one of those canvas affairs that lace up the back?"

"Huh? Oh . . . but damn it, Jarve, I'm holding up the whole procession. Everybody on the project's just sitting around on their tokuses waiting for me to get something done and I'm not doing it. I'm going so slow a snail is lightning in comparison!"

"Calm down, big fellow. Don't rupture a gut or blow a gasket. I've talked to you before, but this time I'm going to smack you bow-legged. So stick out those big, floppy ears of yours and really *listen*. Here are three words that I want you to pin up somewhere where you can see them all day long: SPEED IS RELATIVE. Look back, see how far up the hill you've come, and then balance one hundred and twenty days against ten years."

"What? You mean you'll actually sit still for me holding everything up for ten years?"

"You use the perpendicular pronoun too much and in the wrong places. On the hits it's 'we', but on the flops it's 'I'. Quit it. Everything on this job is 'we'. Terra's best brains are on Team One and are going to stay there. You will not—repeat NOT—be interfered with, pushed around or kicked around. You see, Bill, I know what you're up against."

"Yes, I guess you do. One of the damned few who do. But even if you personally are willing to give us ten years, how in hell do you think you can swing it? How about the Navy—the Stretts—even the Board?"

"They're my business, Bill, not yours. However, to give you a little boost, I'll tell you. With the Navy, I'll give 'em the Fuel Bin if I have to. The Omans have been taking care of the Stretts for twenty-seven hundred centuries, so I'm not the least bit worried about their ability to keep on doing it for ten years more. And if the Board—or anybody else—sticks their runny little noses into Project Theta Orionis I'll slap a quarantine onto both these solar systems that a microbe couldn't get through!"

"You'd go *that* far? Why, you'd be . . ."

*

"DO you think I wouldn't?" Hilton snapped. "Look at me, Junior!" Eyes locked and held. "Do you think, for one minute, that I'll let anybody on all of God's worlds pull *me* off of this job or interfere with my handling of it unless and until I'm damned positively certain that we can't handle it?"

Karns relaxed visibly; the lines of strain eased. "Putting it in those words makes me feel better. I *will* sleep to-night—and without any pills, either."

"Sure you will. One more thought. We all put in more than ten years getting our Terran educations, and an Oman education is a lot tougher."

Really smiling for the first time in weeks, Karns left the office and Hilton glanced again at his clock.

Pretty late now to see Teddy . . . besides, he'd better not. She was probably keyed up about as high as Bill was, and in no shape to do the kind of thinking he wanted of her on this stuff. Better wait a couple of days.

On the following morning, before breakfast, Theodora was waiting for him outside the mess-hall.

"Good morning, Jarve," she caroled. Reaching up, she took him by both ears, pulled his head down and kissed him. As soon as he perceived her intent, he cooperated enthusiastically. "What *did* you do to Bill?"

"Oh, you don't love me for myself alone, then, but just on account of *that* big jerk?"

"That's right." Her artist's-model face, startlingly beautiful now, fairly glowed.

Just then Temple Bells strolled up to them. "Morning, you two lovely people." She hugged Hilton's arm as usual. "Shame on you, Teddy. But I wish *I* had the nerve to kiss him like that."

"Nerve? You?" Teddy laughed as Hilton picked Temple up and kissed her in exactly the same fashion—he hoped!—as he had just kissed Teddy. "You've got more nerve than an aching tooth. But as Jarve would say it, 'scat, kitten'. We're having breakfast *a la twosome.* We've got things to talk about."

"All right for *you*," Temple said darkly, although her dazzling smile belied her tone. That first kiss, casual-seeming as it had been, had carried vastly more freight than any observer could perceive. "I'll hunt Bill up and make passes at him, see if I don't. *That'll* learn ya!"

*

THEODORA and Hilton did have their breakfast *a deux*—but she did not realize until afterward that he had not answered her question as to what he had done to her Bill.

As has been said, Hilton had made it a prime factor of his job to become thoroughly well acquainted with every member of his staff. He had studied them *en masse*, in groups and singly. He had never, however, cornered Theodora Blake for individual study. Considering the power and the quality of her mind, and the field which was her specialty, it had not been necessary.

Thus it was with no ulterior motives at all that, three evenings later, he walked her cubby-hole office and tossed the stapled papers onto her desk. "Free for a couple of minutes, Teddy? I've got troubles."

"I'll say you have." Her lovely lips curled into an expression he had never before seen her wear—a veritable sneer. "But these are not them." She tossed the papers into a drawer and stuck out her chin. Her face turned as hard as such a beautiful face could. Her eyes dug steadily into his.

Hilton—inwardly—flinched. His mind flashed backward. She too had been working under stress, of course; but that wasn't enough. What could he have *possibly* done to put Teddy Blake, of all people, onto such a warpath as this?

"I've been wondering when you were going to try to put *me* through your wringer," she went on, in the same cold, hard voice, "and I've been waiting to tell you something. You have wrapped all the other women around your fingers like so many rings—and what a *sickening* exhibition that has been!—but you are not going to make either a ring or a lap-dog out of me."

Almost but not quite too late Hilton saw through that perfect act. He seized her right hand in both of his, held it up over her head, and waved it back and forth in the sign of victory.

"Socked me with my own club!" he exulted, laughing delightedly, boyishly. "And came within a tenth of a split red hair! If it hadn't been so absolutely out of character you'd've got away with it. *What* a load of stuff! I was right—of all the women on this project, you're the only one I've ever been really afraid of."

"Oh, damn. Ouch!" She grinned ruefully. "I hit you with everything I had and it just bounced. You're an operator, chief. Hit 'em hard, at completely unexpected angles. Keep 'em staggering, completely off balance. Tell 'em nothing—let 'em deduce your lies for themselves. And it anybody tries to slug you back, like I did just now, duck it and clobber him in another unprotected spot. Watching you work has been not only a delight, but also a liberal education."

*

"THANKS. I love you, too, Teddy." He lighted two cigarettes, handed her one. "I'm glad, though, to lay it flat on the table with you, because in any battle of wits with *you* I'm licked before we start."

"Yeah. You just proved it. And after licking me hands down, you think you can square it by swinging the old shovel that way?" She did not quite know whether to feel resentful or not.

"Think over a couple of things. First, with the possible exception of Temple Bells, you're the best brain aboard."

"No. You are. Then Temple. Then there are . . ."

"Hold it. You know as well as I do that accurate self-judgment is impossible. Second, the jam we're in. Do I, or don't I, want to lay it on the table with you, now and from here on? Bore into that with your Class A Double-Prime brain. Then tell me." He leaned back, half-closed his eyes and smoked lazily.

She stiffened; narrowed her eyes in concentration; and thought. Finally: "Yes, you do; and I'm gladder of that than you will ever know."

"I think I know already, since you're her best friend and the only other woman I know of in her class. But I came in to kick a couple of things around with you. As you've noticed, that's getting to be my favorite indoor sport. Probably because I'm a sort of jackleg theoretician myself."

"You can frame that, Jarve, as the understatement of the century. But first, you are going to answer that question you sidestepped so neatly."

"What I did to Bill? I finally convinced him that nobody expected the team to do that big a job overnight. That you could have ten years. Or more, if necessary."

"I see." She frowned. "But you and I both know that we *can't* string it out that long."

He did not answer immediately. "We *could*. But we probably won't . . . unless we have to. We should know, long before that, whether we'll have to switch to some other line of attack. You've considered the possibilities, of course. Have you got anything in shape to do a fine-tooth on?"

"Not yet. That is, except for the ultimate, which is too ghastly to even consider except as an ultimately last resort. Have you?"

"I know what you mean. No, I haven't, either. You don't think, then, that we had better do any collaborative thinking yet?"

"Definitely not. There's altogether too much danger of setting both our lines of thought into one dead-end channel."

"Check. The other thing I wanted from you is your considered opinion as to my job on the organization as a whole. And don't pull your punches. Are we in good shape or not? What can I do to improve the setup?"

*

"I HAVE already considered that very thing—at great length. And honestly, Jarve, I don't see how it can be improved in any respect. You've done a marvelous job. Much better than I thought possible at first." He heaved a deep sigh of relief and she went on: "This could very easily have become a God-awful mess. But the Board knew what they were doing—especially as to top man—so there are only about four people aboard who realize what you have done. Alex Kincaid and Sandra Cummings are two of them. One of the three girls is very deeply and very truly in love with you."

"Ordinarily I'd say 'no comment', but we're laying on the line . . . well . . ."

"You'll lay *that* on the line only if I corkscrew it out you, so I'll Q.E.D. it. You probably know that when Sandy gets done playing around it'll be . . ."

"Bounce back, Teddy. She isn't—hasn't been. If anything, too much the opposite. A dedicated-scientist type."

She smiled—a highly cryptic smile. For a man as brilliant and as penetrant in every other respect . . . but after all, if the big dope didn't realize that half the women aboard, including Sandy, had been making passes at him, she certainly wouldn't enlighten him. Besides, that one particular area of obtuseness was a real part of his charm. Wherefore she said merely: "I'm not sure whether I'm a bit catty or you're a bit stupid. Anyway, it's Alex she's really in love with. And you already know about Bill and me."

"Of course. He's tops. One of the world's very finest. You're in the same bracket, and as a couple you're a drive fit. One in a million."

"Now I can say 'I love you, too', too." She paused for half a minute, then stubbed out her cigarette and shrugged. "Now I'm going to stick my neck way, way out. You can knock it off if you like. She's a tremendous lot of woman, and if . . . well, strong as she is, it'd shatter her to bits. So, I'd like to ask . . . I don't quite . . . well, *is* she going to get hurt?"

"Have I managed to hide it *that* well? From *you?*"

It was her turn to show relief. "Perfectly. Even—or especially—that time you kissed her. So damned perfectly that I've been scared green. I've been waking myself up, screaming, in the middle of the night. You couldn't let on, of course. That's the hell of such a job as yours. The rest of us can smooch around all over the place. I knew the question was extremely improper—thanks a million for answering it."

"I haven't started to answer it yet. I said I'd lay everything on the line, so here it is. Saying she's a tremendous lot of woman is like calling the *Perseus* a nice little baby's-bathtub toy boat. I'd go to hell for her any time, cheerfully, standing straight up, wading into brimstone and lava up to the eyeballs. If anything ever hurts her it'll be because I'm not man enough to block it. And just the minute this damned job is over, or even sooner if enough of you couples make it so I can . . ."

"Jarvis!" she shrieked. Jumping up, she kissed him enthusiastically. "That's just wonderful!"

*

HE thought it was pretty wonderful, too; and after ten minutes more of conversation he got up and turned toward the door.

"I feel a lot better, Teddy. Thanks for being such a nice pressure-relief valve. Would you mind it too much if I come in and sob on your bosom again some day?"

"I'd love it!" She laughed; then, as he again started to leave: "Wait a minute, I'm thinking . . . it'd be more fun to sob on *her* bosom. You haven't even kissed her yet, have you? I mean *really* kissed her?"

"You know I haven't. She's the one person aboard I can't be alone with for a second."

"True. But I know of one chaperone who could become deaf and blind," she said, with a broad and happy grin. "On my door, you know, there's a huge invisible sign that says, to everyone except you, 'STOP! BRAIN AT WORK! SILENCE!', and if I were properly approached and sufficiently urged, I might . . . I just *conceivably* might . . ."

"Consider it done, you little sweetheart! Up to and including my most vigorous and most insidious attempts at seduction."

"Done. Maneuver your big, husky carcass around here behind the desk so the door can open." She flipped a switch and punched a number. "I can call anybody in here, any time, you know. Hello, dear, this is Teddy. Can you come in for just a few minutes? Thanks." And, one minute later, there came a light tap on the door.

"Come in," Teddy called, and Temple Bells entered the room. She showed no surprise at seeing Hilton.

"Hi, chief," she said. "It must be something both big and tough, to have you and Teddy both on it."

"You're so right. It was very big and very tough. But it's solved, darling, so . . ."

"*Darling?*" she gasped, almost inaudibly, both hands flying to her throat. Her eyes flashed toward the other woman.

"Teddy knows all about us—accessory before, during and after the fact."

"*Darling!*" This time, the word was a shriek. She extended both arms and started forward.

Hilton did not bother to maneuver his "big, husky carcass" around the desk, but simply hurdled it, straight toward her.

*

TEMPLE Bells was a tall, lithe, strong woman; and all the power of her arms and torso went into the ensuing effort to crack Hilton's ribs. Those ribs, however, were highly capable structural members; and furthermore, they were protected by thick slabs of hard, hard muscle. And, fortunately, he was not trying to fracture *her* ribs. His pressures were distributed much more widely. He was, according to promise, doing his very best to flatten her whole resilient body out flat.

And as they stood there, locked together in sheerest ecstasy, Theodora Blake began openly and unashamedly to cry.

It was Temple who first came up for air. She wriggled loose from one of his arms, felt of her hair and gazed unseeingly into her mirror. "That was *wonderful*, sweetheart," she said then, shakily. "And I can *never* thank you enough, Teddy. But we can't do this very often . . . can we?" The addendum fairly begged for contradiction.

"Not too often, I'm afraid," Hilton said, and Theodora agreed . . . .

"Well," the man said, somewhat later, "I'll leave you two ladies to your knitting, or whatever. After a couple of short ones for the road, that is."

"Not looking like that!" Teddy said, sharply. "Hold still and we'll clean you up." Then, as both girls went to work:

"If anybody ever sees you coming out of this office looking like *that*," she went on, darkly, "and Bill finds out about it, he'll think it's *my* lipstick smeared all over you and I'll strangle you to death with my bare hands!"

"And that was supposed to be kissproof lipstick, too," Temple said, seriously—although her whole face glowed and her eyes danced. "You know, I'll never believe another advertisement I read."

"Oh, I wouldn't go so far as to say that, if I were you." Teddy's voice was gravity itself, although she, too, was bubbling over. "It probably *is* kissproof. I don't think 'kissing' is quite the word for the performance you just staged. To stand up under such punishment as you gave it, my dear, anything would have to be tattooed in, not just put on."

"Hey!" Hilton protested. "You promised to be deaf and blind!"

"I did no such thing. I said 'could', not 'would'. Why, I wouldn't have missed that for *anything*!"

When Hilton left the room he was apparently, in every respect, his usual self-contained self. However, it was not until the following morning that he so much as thought of the sheaf of papers lying unread in the drawer of Theodora Blake's desk.

VII

KNOWING that he had done everything he could to help the most important investigations get under way, Hilton turned his attention to secondary matters. He made arrangements to decondition Javo, the Number Two Oman Boss, whereupon that worthy became Javvy and promptly "bumped" the Oman who had been shadowing Karns.

Larry and Javvy, working nights, deconditioned all the other Omans having any contact with BuSci personnel; then they went on to set up a routine for deconditioning all Omans on both planets.

Assured at last that the Omans would thenceforth work with and really serve human beings instead of insisting upon doing their work for them, Hilton knew that the time had come to let all his BuSci personnel move into their homes aground. Everyone, including himself, was fed up to the gozzel with spaceship life—its jam-packed crowding; its flat, reprocessed air; its limited variety of uninteresting food. Conditions were especially irksome since everybody knew that there was available to all, whenever Hilton gave the word, a whole city full of all the room anyone could want, natural fresh air and—so the Omans had told them—an unlimited choice of everything anyone wanted to eat.

Nevertheless, the decision was not an easy one to make.

Living conditions were admittedly not good on the ship. On the other hand, with almost no chance at all of solitude—the few people who had private offices aboard were not the ones he worried about—there was no danger of sexual trouble. Strictly speaking, he was not responsible for the morals of his force. He knew that he was being terribly old-fashioned. Nevertheless, he could not argue himself out of the conviction that he was morally responsible.

Finally he took the thing up with Sandra, who merely laughed at him. "How long have you been worrying about *that*, Jarve?"

"Ever since I okayed moving aground the first time. That was one reason I was so glad to cancel it then."

"You *were* slightly unclear—a little rattled? But which factor—the fun and games, which is the moral issue, or the consequences?"

"The consequences," he admitted, with a rueful grin. "I don't give a whoop how much fun they have; but you know as well as I do just how prudish public sentiment is. And Project Theta Orionis is squarely in the middle of the public eye."

*

"YOU should have checked with me sooner and saved yourself wear and tear. There's no danger at all of consequences—except weddings. Lots of weddings, and fast."

"Weddings and babies wouldn't bother me a bit. Nor interfere with the job too much, with the Omans as nurses. But why the 'fast', if you aren't anticipating any shotgun weddings?"

"Female psychology," she replied, with a grin. "Aboard-ship here there's no home atmosphere whatever; nothing but work, work, work. Put a woman into a house, though—especially such houses as the Omans have built and with such servants as they insist on being—and she goes domestic in a really big way. Just sex isn't good enough any more. She wants the kind of love that goes with a husband and a home, and nine times out of ten she gets it. With these BuSci women it'll be ten out of ten."

"You may be right, of course, but it sounds kind of far-fetched to me."

"Wait and see, chum," Sandra said, with a laugh.

Hilton made his announcement and everyone moved aground the next day. No one, however, had elected to live alone. Almost everyone had chosen to double up; the most noteworthy exceptions being twelve laboratory girls who had decided to keep on living together. However, they now had a twenty-room house instead of a one-room dormitory to live in, and a staff of twenty Oman girls to help them do it.

Hilton had suggested that Temple and Teddy, whose house was only a hundred yards or so from the Hilton-Karns bungalow, should have supper and spend the first evening with them; but the girls had knocked that idea flat. Much better, they thought, to let things ride as nearly as possible exactly as they had been aboard the *Perseus*.

"A *little* smooching now and then, on the Q strictly T, but that's all, darling. That's *positively* all," Temple had said, after a highly satisfactory ten minutes alone with him in her own gloriously private room, and that was the way it had to be.

Hence it was a stag inspection that Hilton and Karns made of their new home. It was very long, very wide, and for its size very low. Four of its five rooms were merely adjuncts to its tremendous living-room. There was a huge fireplace at each end of this room, in each of which a fire of four-foot-long fir cordwood crackled and snapped. There was a great hi-fi tri-di, with over a hundred tapes, all new.

"Yes, sirs," Larry and Javvy spoke in unison. "The players and singers who entertained the Masters of old have gone back to work. They will also, of course, appear in person whenever and wherever you wish."

*

BOTH men looked around the vast room and Karns said: "All the comforts of home and a couple of bucks' worth besides. Wall-to-wall carpeting an inch and a half thick. A grand piano. Easy chairs and loafers and davenports. Very fine reproductions of our favorite paintings . . . and statuary."

"You said it, brother." Hilton was bending over a group in bronze. "If I didn't know better, I'd swear this is the original deHaven 'Dance of the Nymphs'."

Karns had marched up to and was examining minutely a two-by-three-foot painting, in a heavy gold frame, of a gorgeously auburn-haired nude. "Reproduction, hell! This is a *duplicate*! Lawrence's 'Innocent' is worth twenty million wogs and it's sealed behind quad armor-glass in Prime Art—but I'll bet wogs to wiggles the Prime Curator himself, with all his apparatus, couldn't tell this one from his!"

"I wouldn't take even one wiggle's worth of that. And this 'Laughing Cavalier' and this 'Toledo' are twice as old and twice as fabulously valuable."

"And there are my own golf clubs . . . ."

"Excuse us, sirs," the Omans said, "These things were simple because they could be induced in your minds. But the matter of a staff could not, nor what you would like to eat for supper, and it is growing late."

"Staff? What the hell has the staff got to do with . . ."

"*House*-staff, they mean," Karns said. "We don't need much of anybody, boys. Somebody to keep the place shipshape, is all. Or, as a de luxe touch, how about a waitress? One housekeeper and one waitress. That'll be finer."

"Very well, sirs. There is one other matter. It has troubled us that we have not been able to read in your minds the logical datum that they should in fact simulate Doctor Bells and Doctor Blake?"

"Huh?" Both men gasped—and then both exploded like one twelve-inch length of primacord.

*

WHILE the Omans could not understand this purely Terran reasoning, they accepted the decision without a demurring thought. "Who, then, are the two its to simulate?"

"No stipulation; roll your own," Hilton said, and glanced at Karns. "None of these Oman women are really hard on the eyes."

"Check. Anybody who wouldn't call any one of 'em a slurpy dish needs a new set of optic nerves."

"In that case," the Omans said, "no delay at all will be necessary, as we can make do with one temporarily. The Sory, no longer Sora, who has not been glad since the Tuly replaced it, is now in your kitchen. It comes."

A woman came in and stood quietly in front of the two men, the wafted air carrying from her clear, smooth skin a faint but unmistakable fragrance of Idaho mountain syringa. She was radiantly happy; her bright, deep-green eyes went from man to man.

"You wish, sirs, to give me your orders verbally. And yes, you may order fresh, whole, not-canned hens' eggs."

"I certainly will, then; I haven't had a fried egg since we left Terra. But . . . Larry said . . . *you* aren't Sory!"

"Oh, but I am, sir."

Karns had been staring her, eyes popping. "Holy Saint Patrick! Talk about simulation, Jarve! They've made her over into Lawrence's 'Innocent'—exact to twenty decimals!"

"You're so right." Hilton's eyes went, half a dozen times, from the form of flesh to the painting and back. "That must have been a terrific job."

"Oh, no. It was quite simple, really," Sory said, "since the brain was not involved. I merely reddened my hair and lengthened it, made my eyes to be green, changed my face a little, pulled myself in a little around here . . . ." Her beautifully-manicured hands swept the full circle of her waistline, then continued to demonstrate appropriately the rest of her speech:

" . . . and pushed me out a little up here and tapered my legs a little more—made them a little larger and rounder here at my hips and thighs and a little smaller toward and at my ankles. Oh, yes, and made my feet and hands a little smaller. That's all. I thought the Doctor Karns would like me a little better this way."

*

"YOU can broadcast *that* over the P-A system at high noon." Karns was still staring. "'That's all,' she says. But you didn't have *time* to . . ."

"Oh, I did it day before yesterday. As soon as Javvy materialized the 'Innocent' and I knew it to be your favorite art."

"But damn it, we hadn't even *thought* of having you here then!"

"But I had, sir. I fully intended to serve, one way or another, in this your home. But of course I had no idea I would ever have such an honor as actually waiting on you at your table. Will you please give me your orders, sirs, besides the eggs? You wish the eggs fried in butter—three of them apiece—and sunny side up."

"Uh-huh, with ham," Hilton said. "I'll start with a jumbo shrimp cocktail. Horseradish and ketchup sauce; heavy on the horseradish."

"Same for me," Karns said, "but only half as much horseradish."

"And for the rest of it," Hilton went on, "hashed-brown potatoes and buttered toast—plenty of extra butter—strong coffee from first to last. Whipping cream and sugar on the side. For dessert, apple pie *a la mode*."

"You make me drool, chief. Play that for me, please, Innocent, all the way."

"Oh? You are—you, personally, yourself, sir?—renaming me 'Innocent'?"

"If you'll sit still for it, yes."

"That is an incredible honor, sir. Simply unbelievable. I thank you! I thank you!" Radiating happiness, she dashed away toward the kitchen.

*

WHEN the two men were full of food, they strolled over to a davenport facing the fire. As they sat down, Innocent entered the room, carrying a tall, dewy mint julep on a tray. She was followed by another female figure bearing a bottle of avignognac and the appurtenances which are its due—and at the first full sight of that figure Hilton stopped breathing for fifteen seconds.

Her hair was very thick, intensely black and long, cut squarely off just below the lowest points of her shoulder blades. Heavy brows and long lashes—eyes too—were all intensely, vividly black. Her skin was tanned to a deep and glowing almost-but-not-quite-brown.

"Murchison's Dark Lady!" Hilton gasped. "Larry! You've—we've—*I've* got that painting here?"

"Oh, yes, sir." The newcomer spoke before Larry could. "At the other end—your part—of the room. You will look now, sir, please?" Her voice was low, rich and as smooth as cream.

Putting her tray down carefully on the end-table, she led him toward the other fireplace. Past the piano, past the tri-di pit; past a towering grillwork holding art treasures by the score. Over to the left, against the wall, there was a big, business-like desk. On the wall, over the desk, hung *the* painting; a copy of which had been in Hilton's room for over eight years.

He stared at it for at least a minute. He glanced around: at the other priceless duplicates so prodigally present, at his own guns arrayed above the mantel and on each side of the fireplace. Then, without a word, he started back to join Karns. She walked springily beside him.

"What's your name, Miss?" he asked, finally.

"I haven't earned any as yet, sir. My number is . . . ."

"Never mind that. Your name is 'Dark Lady'."

"Oh, thank you, sir; that is truly wonderful!" And Dark Lady sat cross-legged on the rug at Hilton's feet and busied herself with the esoteric rites of Old Avignon.

Hilton took a deep inhalation and a small sip, then stared at Karns. Karns, over the rim of his glass, stared back.

"I can see where this would be habit-forming," Hilton said, "and very deadly. *Extremely* deadly."

"Every wish granted. Surrounded by all this." Karns swept his arm through three-quarters of a circle. "Waited on hand and foot by powerful men and by the materializations of the dreams of the greatest, finest artists who ever lived. Fatal? I don't know . . . ."

*

"MY solid hope is that we never have to find out. And when you add in Innocent and Dark Lady . . . . They *look* to be about seventeen, but the thought that they're older than the hills of Rome and powered by everlasting atomic engines—" He broke off suddenly and blushed. "Excuse me, please, girls. I *know* better than to talk about people that way, right in front of them; I really do."

"Do you really think we're *people?*" Innocent and Dark Lady squealed, as one.

That set Hilton back onto his heels. "I don't know . . . . I've wondered. Are you?"

Both girls, silent, looked at Larry.

"We don't know, either," Larry said. "At first, of course, there were crude, non-thinking machines. But when the Guide attained its present status, the Masters themselves could not agree. They divided about half and half on the point. They never did settle it any closer than that."

"I certainly won't try to, then. But for my money, you are people," Hilton said, and Karns agreed.

That, of course, touched off a near-riot of joy; after which the two men made an inch-by-inch study of their tremendous living-room. Then, long after bedtime, Larry and Dark Lady escorted Hilton to his bedroom.

"Do you mind, sir, if we sleep on the floor at the sides of your bed?" Larry asked. "Or must we go out into the hall?"

"Sleep? I didn't know you *could* sleep."

"It is not essential. However, when round-the-clock work is not necessary, and we have opportunity to sleep near a human being, we derive a great deal of pleasure and satisfaction from it. You see, sir, we also serve during sleep."

"Okay, I'll try anything once. Sleep wherever you please."

Hilton began to peel, but before he had his shirt off both Larry and Dark Lady were stretched out flat, sound asleep, one almost under each edge of his bed. He slid in between the sheets—it was the most comfortable bed he had ever slept in—and went to sleep as though sandbagged.

He had time to wonder foggily whether the Omans were in fact helping him go to sleep—and then he *was* asleep.

*

A MONTH passed. Eight couples had married, the Navy chaplain officiating—in the *Perseus*, of course, since the warship was, always and everywhere, an integral part of Terra.

Sandra had dropped in one evening to see Hilton about a bit of business. She was now sitting, long dancer's legs out-stretched toward the fire, with a cigarette in her left hand and a tall, cold drink on a coaster at her right.

"This is a wonderful room, Jarvis. It'd be perfect if it weren't quite so . . . so mannish."

"What do you expect of Bachelors' Hall—a boudoir? Don't tell me *you're* going domestic, Sandy, just because you've got a house?"

"Not just that, no. But of course it helped it along."

"Alex is a mighty good man. One of the finest I have ever known."

She eyed him for a moment in silence. "Jarvis Hilton, you are one of the keenest, most intelligent men who ever lived. And yet . . ." She broke off and studied him for a good half minute. "Say, if I let my hair clear down, will you?"

"Scout's Oath. That 'and yet' requires elucidation at any cost."

"I know. But first, yes, it's Alex. I never would have believed that any man ever born could hit me so hard. Soon. I didn't want to be the first, but I won't be anywhere near the last. But tell me. You were really in love with Temple, weren't you, when I asked you?"

"Yes."

"Ha! You *are* letting your hair down! That makes me feel better."

"Huh? Why should it?"

"It elucidates the 'and yet' no end. You were insulated from all other female charms by ye brazen Bells. You see, most of us assistants made a kind of game out of seeing which of us could make you break the Executives' Code. And none of us made it. Teddy and Temple said you didn't know what was going on; Bev and I said nobody as smart as you are could possibly be that stupid."

"You aren't the type to leak or name names—oh, I see. You are merely reporting a conversation. The game had interested, but non-participating, observers. Temple and Teddy, at least."

"At least," she agreed. "But damn it, you *aren't* stupid. There isn't a stupid bone in your head. So it must be love. And if so, what about marriage? Why don't you and Temple make it a double with Alex and me?"

"That's the most cogent thought you ever had, but setting the date is the bride's business." He glanced at his Oman wristwatch. "It's early yet; let's skip over. I wouldn't mind seeing her a minute or two."

"Thy statement ringeth with truth, friend. Bill's there with Teddy?"

"I imagine so."

"So we'll talk to them about making it a triple. Oh, nice—let's go!"

They left the house and, her hand tucked under his elbow, walked up the street.

*

NEXT morning, on her way to the Hall of Records, Sandra stopped off as usual at the office. The Omans were all standing motionless. Hilton was leaning far back in his chair, feet on desk, hands clasped behind head, eyes closed. Knowing what that meant, she turned and started back out on tiptoe.

However, he had heard her. "Can you spare a couple of minutes to think at me, Sandy?"

"Minutes or hours, chief." Tuly placed a chair for her and she sat down, facing him across his desk.

"Thanks, gal. This time it's the Stretts. Sawtelle's been having nightmares, you know, ever since we emerged, about being attacked, and I've been pooh-poohing the idea. But now it's a statistic that the soup is getting thicker, and I can't figure out why. Why in all the hells of space should a stasis that has lasted for over a quarter of a million years be broken at this exact time? The only possible explanation is that *we* caused the break. And any way I look at that concept, it's plain idiocy."

Both were silent for minutes; and then it was demonstrated again that Terra's Advisory Board had done better than it knew in choosing Sandra Cummings to be Jarvis Hilton's working mate.

"We did cause it, Jarve," she said, finally. "They knew we were coming, even before we got to Fuel Bin. They knew we were human and tried to wipe out the Omans before we got there. Preventive warfare, you know."

"They *couldn't* have known!" he snorted. "Strett detectors are no better than Oman, and you know what Sam Bryant had to say about them."

"I know." Sandra grinned appreciatively. "It's becoming a classic. But it couldn't have been any other way. Besides, I *know* they did."

He stared at her helplessly, then swung on Larry. "Does that make sense to you?"

"Yes, sir. The Stretts could peyondire as well as the old Masters could, and they undoubtedly still can and do."

"Okay, it does make sense, then." He absented himself in thought, then came to life with a snap. "Okay! The next thing on the agenda is a crash-priority try at a peyondix team. Tuly, you organized a team to generate sathura. Can you do the same for peyondix?"

"If we can find the ingredients, yes, sir."

*

"I HAD a hunch. Larry, please ask Teddy Blake's Oman to bring her in here . . . ."

"I'll be running along, then." Sandra started to get up.

"I hope to kiss a green pig you won't!" Hilton snapped. "You're one of the biggest wheels. Larry, we'll want Temple Bells and Beverly Bell—for a start."

"Chief, you positively amaze me," Sandra said then. "Every time you get one of these attacks of genius—or whatever it is—you have me gasping like a fish. Just what can you *possibly* want of Bev Bell?"

"Whatever it was that enabled her to hit the target against odds of almost infinity to one; not just once, but time after time. By definition, intuition. What quality did you use just now in getting me off the hook? Intuition. What makes Teddy Blake such an unerring performer? Intuition again. My hunches—they're intuition, too. Intuition, *hell*! Labels—based on utterly abysmal damned dumb ignorance of our own basic frames of reference. Do you think those four kinds of intuition are alike, by seven thousand rows of apple trees?"

"Of course not. I see what you're getting at . . . . Oh! This'll be fun!"

The others came in and, one by one, Tuly examined each of the four women and the man. Each felt the probing, questioning feelers of her thought prying into the deepest recesses of his mind.

"There is not quite enough of each of three components, all of which are usually associated with the male. You, sir, have much of each, but not enough. I know your men quite well, and I think we will need the doctors Kincaid and Karns and Poynter. But such deep probing is felt. Have I permission, sir?"

"Yes. Tell 'em I said so."

Tuly scanned. "Yes, sir, we should have all three."

"Get 'em, Larry." Then, in the pause that followed: "Sandy, remember yowling about too many sweeties on a team? What do you think of this business of all sweeties?"

"All that proves is that nobody can be wrong all the time," she replied flippantly.

The three men arrived and were instructed. Tuly said: "The great trouble is that each of you must use a portion of your mind that you do not know you have. You, this one. You, that one." Tuly probed mercilessly; so poignantly that each in turn flinched under brand-new and almost unbearable pain. "With you, Doctor Hilton, it will be by far the worst. For you must learn to use almost all the portions of both your minds, the conscious and the unconscious. This must be, because you are the actual peyondixer. The others merely supply energies in which you yourself are deficient. Are you ready for a terrible shock, sir?"

"Shoot."

*

HE thought for a second that he *had* been shot; that his brain had blown up.

He couldn't stand it—he *knew* he was going to die—he wished he *could* die—anything, anything whatever, to end this unbearable agony . . . .

It ended.

Writhing, white and sweating, Hilton opened his eyes. "Ouch," he remarked, conversationally. "What next?"

"You will seize hold of the energies your friends offer. You will bind them to yours and shape the whole into a dimensionless sphere of pure controlled, dirigible energy. And, as well as being the binding force, the cohesiveness, you must also be the captain and the pilot and the astrogator and the ultimately complex computer itself."

"But how can I . . . . Okay, damn it. I *will*!"

"Of course you will, sir. Remember also that once the joinings are made I can be of very little more assistance, for my peyondix is as nothing compared to that of your fusion of eight. Now, to assemble the energies and join them you will, all together, deny the existence of the sum total of reality as you know it. Distance does not exist—every point in the reachable universe coincides with every other point and that common point is the focus of your attention. You can be and actually are anywhere you please or everywhere at once. Time does not exist. Space does not exist. There is no such thing as opacity; everything is perfectly transparent, yet every molecule of substance is perceptible in its relationship to every other molecule in the cosmos. Senses do not exist. Sight, hearing, taste, touch, smell, sathura, endovix—all are parts of the one great sense of peyondix. I am guiding each of you seven—closer! Tighter! There! Seize it, sir—and when you work the Stretts you must fix it clearly that time does not exist. You must work in millionths of microseconds instead of in minutes, for they have minds of tremendous power. Reality does not exist! Compress it more, sir. Tighter! Smaller! Rounder! There! Hold it! Reality does not exist—distance does not exist—all possible points are . . . . *Wonderful!*"

Tuly screamed the word and the thought: "Good-by! Good luck!

VIII

HILTON did not have to drive the peyondix-beam to the planet Strett; it was already there. And there was the monstrous First Lord Thinker Zoyar.

Into that mind his multi-mind flashed, its every member as responsive to his will as his own fingers—almost infinitely more so, in fact, because of the tremendous lengths of time required to send messages along nerves.

That horrid mind was scanned cell by cell. Then, after what seemed like a few hours, when a shield began sluggishly to form, Hilton transferred his probe to the mind of the Second Thinker, one Lord Ynos, and absorbed everything she knew. Then, the minds of all the other Thinkers being screened, he studied the whole Strett planet, foot by foot, and everything that was on it.

Then, mission accomplished, Hilton snapped his attention back to his office and the multi-mind fell apart. As he opened his eyes he heard Tuly scream: " . . . Luck!"

"Oh—you still here, Tuly? How long have we been gone?"

"Approximately one and one-tenth seconds, sir."

"WHAT!"

Beverly Bell, in the haven of Franklin Poynter's arms, fainted quietly. Sandra shrieked piercingly. The four men stared, goggle-eyed. Temple and Teddy, as though by common thought, burrowed their faces into brawny shoulders.

Hilton recovered first. "So *that's* what peyondix is."

"Yes, sir—I mean no, sir. No, I mean yes, but . . ." Tuly paused, licking her lips in that peculiarly human-female gesture of uncertainty.

"Well, what *do* you mean? It either is or isn't. Or is that necessarily so?"

"Not exactly, sir. That is, it started as peyondix. But it became something else. Not even the most powerful of the old Masters—nobody—ever did or ever could *possibly* generate such a force as that. Or handle it so fast."

"Well, with seven of the best minds of Terra and a . . ."

"Chip-chop the chit-chat!" Karns said, harshly. "What I want to know is whether I was having a nightmare. Can there *possibly* be a race such as I thought I saw? So utterly savage—ruthless—merciless! So devoid of every human trace and so hell-bent determined on the extermination of every other race in the Galaxy? God damn it, it simply doesn't make sense!"

*

EYES went from eyes to eyes to eyes.

All had seen the same indescribably horrible, abysmally atrocious, things. Qualities and quantities and urges and drives that no words in any language could even begin to portray.

"It doesn't seem to, but there it is." Teddy Blake shook her head hopelessly.

Big Bill Karns, hands still shaking, lit a cigarette before he spoke again. "Well, I've never been a proponent of genocide. But it's my considered opinion that the Stretts are one race the galaxy can get along without."

"A hell of a lot better without," Poynter said, and all agreed.

"The point is, what can we do about it?" Kincaid asked. "The first thing, I would say, is to see whether we can do this—whatever it is—without Tuly's help. Shall we try it? Although I, for one, don't feel like doing it right away."

"Not I, either." Beverly Bell held up her right hand, which was shaking uncontrollably. "I feel as though I'd been bucking waves, wind and tide for forty-eight straight hours without food, water or touch. Maybe in about a week I'll be ready for another try at it. But today—not a chance!"

"Okay. Scat, all of you," Hilton ordered. "Take the rest of the day off and rest up. Put on your thought-screens and don't take them off for a second from now on. Those Stretts are tough hombres."

Sandra was the last to leave. "And you, boss?" she asked pointedly.

"I've got some thinking to do."

"I'll stay and help you think?"

"Not yet." He shook his head, frowned and then grinned. "You see, chick, I don't even know yet what it is I'm going to have to think about."

"A bit unclear, but I know what you mean—I think. Luck, chief."

*

IN their subterranean sanctum turn on distant Strett, two of the deepest thinkers of that horribly unhuman race were in coldly intent conference via thought.

"My mind has been plundered, Ynos," First Lord Thinker Zoyar radiated, harshly. "Despite the extremely high reactivity of my shield some information—I do not know how much—was taken. The operator was one of the humans of that ship."

"I, too, felt a plucking at my mind. But those humans could not peyondire, First Lord."

"Be logical, fool! At that contact, in the matter of which you erred in not following up continuously, they succeeded in concealing their real abilities from you."

"That could be the truth. Our ancestors erred, then, in recording that all those weak and timid humans had been slain. These offenders are probably their descendants, returning to reclaim their former world."

"The probability must be evaluated and considered. Was it or was it not through human aid that the Omans destroyed most of our task-force?"

"Highly probable, but impossible of evaluation with the data now available."

"Obtain more data at once. That point must be and shall be fully evaluated and fully considered. This entire situation is intolerable. It must be abated."

"True, First Lord. But every operator and operation is now tightly screened. Oh, if I could only go out there myself . . ."

"Hold, fool! Your thought is completely disloyal and un-Strettly."

"True, oh First Lord Thinker Zoyar. I will forthwith remove my unworthy self from this plane of existence."

"You will not! I hereby abolish that custom. Our numbers are too few by far. Too many have failed to adapt. Also, as Second Thinker, your death at this time would be slightly detrimental to certain matters now in work. I will myself, however, slay the unfit. To that end repeat The Words under my peyondiring."

"I am a Strett. I will devote my every iota of mental and of physical strength to forwarding the Great Plan. I am, and will remain, a Strett."

"You do believe in The Words."

*

"OF course I believe in them! I *know* that in a few more hundreds of thousands of years we will be rid of material bodies and will become invincible and invulnerable. Then comes the Conquest of the Galaxy . . . and then the Conquest of the Universe!"

"No more, then, on your life, of this weak and cowardly repining! Now, what of your constructive thinking?"

"Programming must be such as to obviate time-lag. We must evaluate the factors already mentioned and many others, such as the reactivation of the spacecraft which was thought to have been destroyed so long ago. After having considered all these evaluations, I will construct a Minor Plan to destroy these Omans, whom we have permitted to exist on sufferance, and with them that shipload of despicably interloping humans."

"That is well." Zoyar's mind seethed with a malevolent ferocity starkly impossible for any human mind to grasp. "And to that end?"

"To that end we must intensify still more our program of procuring data. We must revise our mechs in the light of our every technological advance during the many thousands of cycles since the last such revision was made. Our every instrument of power, of offense and of defense, must be brought up to the theoretical ultimate of capability."

"And as to the Great Brain?"

"I have been able to think of nothing, First Lord, to add to the undertakings you have already set forth."

"It was not expected that you would. Now: is it your final thought that these interlopers are in fact the descendants of those despised humans of so long ago?"

"It is."

"It is also mine. I return, then, to my work upon the Brain. You will take whatever measures are necessary. Use every artifice of intellect and of ingenuity and our every resource. But abate this intolerable nuisance, and soon."

"It shall be done, First Lord."

*

THE Second Thinker issued orders. Frenzied, round-the-clock activity ensued. Hundreds of mechs operated upon the brains of hundreds of others, who in turn operated upon the operators.

Then, all those brains charged with the technological advances of many thousands of years, the combined hundreds went unrestingly to work. Thousands of work-mechs were built and put to work at the construction of larger and more powerful space-craft.

As has been implied, those battle-skeletons of the Stretts were controlled by their own built-in mechanical brains, which were programmed for only the simplest of battle maneuvers. Anything at all out of the ordinary had to be handled by remote control, by the specialist-mechs at their two-miles-long control board.

This was now to be changed. Programming was to be made so complete that almost any situation could be handled by the warship or the missile itself—instantly.

The Stretts *knew* that they were the most powerful, the most highly advanced race in the universe. Their science was the highest in the universe. Hence, with every operating unit brought up to the full possibilities of that science, that would be more than enough. Period.

This work, while it required much time, was very much simpler than the task which the First Thinker had laid out for himself on the giant computer-plus which the Stretts called "The Great Brain." In stating his project, First Lord Zoyar had said:

"Assignment: To construct a machine that will have the following abilities: One, to contain and retain all knowledge and information fed into it, however great the amount. Two, to feed itself additional information by peyondiring all planets, wherever situate, bearing intelligent life. Three, to call up instantly any and all items of information pertaining to any problem we may give it. Four, to combine and recombine any number of items required to form new concepts. Five, to formulate theories, test them and draw conclusions helpful to us in any matter in work."

It will have been noticed that these specifications vary in one important respect from those of the Eniacs and Univacs of Earth. Since we of Earth can not peyondire, we do not expect that ability from our computers.

The Stretts could, and did.

*

WHEN Sandra came back into the office at five o'clock she found Hilton still sitting there, in almost exactly the same position.

"Come out of it, Jarve!" She snapped a finger. "That much of *that* is just simply too damned much."

"You're so right, child." He got up, stretched, and by main strength shrugged off his foul mood. "But we're up against something that is really a something, and I don't mean perchance."

"How well I know it." She put an arm around him, gave him a quick, hard hug. "But after all, you don't have to solve it this evening, you know."

"No, thank God."

"So why don't you and Temple have supper with me? Or better yet, why don't all eight of us have supper together in that bachelors' paradise of yours and Bill's?"

"That'd be fun."

And it was.

Nor did it take a week for Beverly Bell to recover from the Ordeal of Eight. On the following evening, she herself suggested that the team should take another shot at that utterly fantastic *terra incognita* of the multiple mind, jolting though it had been.

"But are you sure you can take it again so soon?" Hilton asked.

"Sure. I'm like that famous gangster's moll, you know, who bruised easy but healed quick. And I want to know about it as much as anyone else does."

They could do it this time without any help from Tuly. The linkage fairly snapped together and shrank instantaneously to a point. Hilton thought of Terra and there it was; full size, yet occupying only one infinitesimal section of a dimensionless point. The multi-mind visited relatives of all eight, but could not make intelligible contact. If asleep, it caused pleasant dreams; if awake, pleasant thoughts of the loved one so far away in space; but that was all. It visited mediums, in trance and otherwise—many of whom, not surprisingly now, were genuine—with whom it held lucid conversations. Even in linkage, however, the multi-mind knew that none of the mediums would be believed, even if they all told, simultaneously, exactly the same story. The multi-mind weakened suddenly and Hilton snapped it back to Ardry.

Beverly was almost in collapse. The other girls were white, shaken and trembling. Hilton himself, strong and rugged as he was, felt as though he had done two weeks of hard labor on a rock-pile. He glanced questioningly at Larry.

"Point six three eight seconds, sir," the Omans said, holding up a millisecond timer.

"How do you explain *that?*" Karns demanded.

"I'm afraid it means that without Oman backing we're out of luck."

*

HILTON had other ideas, but he did not voice any of them until the following day, when he was rested and had Larry alone.

"So carbon-based brains can't take it. One second of that stuff would have killed all eight of us. Why? The Masters had the same kind of brains we have."

"I don't know, sir. It's something completely new. No Master, or group of Masters, ever generated such a force as that. I can scarcely believe such power possible, even though I have felt it twice. It may be that over the generations your individual powers, never united or controlled, have developed so strength that no human can handle them in fusion."

"And none of us ever knew anything about any of them. I've been doing a lot of thinking. The Masters had qualities and abilities now unknown to any of us. How come? You Omans—and the Stretts, too—think we're descendants of the Masters. Maybe we are. You think they came originally from Arth—Earth or Terra—to Ardu. That'd account for our legends of Mu, Atlantis and so on. Since Ardu was within peyondix range of Strett, the Stretts attacked it. They killed all the Masters, they thought, and made the planet uninhabitable for any kind of life, even their own. But one shipload of Masters escaped and came here to Ardry—far beyond peyondix range. They stayed here for a long time. Then, for some reason or other—which may be someplace in their records—they left here, fully intending to come back. Do any of you Omans know why they left? Or where they went?"

"No, sir. We can read only the simplest of the Masters' records. They arranged our brains that way, sir."

"I know. They're the type. However, I suspect now that your thinking is reversed. Let's turn it around. Say the Masters didn't come from Terra, but from some other planet. Say that they left here because they were dying out. They were, weren't they?"

"Yes, sir. Their numbers became fewer and fewer each century."

"I was sure of it. They were committing race suicide by letting you Omans do everything they themselves should have been doing. Finally they saw the truth. In a desperate effort to save their race they pulled out, leaving you here. Probably they intended to come back when they had bred enough guts back into themselves to set you Omans down where you belong . . . ."

"But *they* were always the Masters, sir!"

"They were not! They were hopelessly enslaved. Think it over. Anyway, say they went *to* Terra from here. That still accounts for the legends and so on. However, they were too far gone to make a recovery, and yet they had enough fixity of purpose *not* to manufacture any of you Omans there. So their descendants went a long way down the scale before they began to work back up. Does that make sense to you?"

*

"IT explains many things, sir. It can very well be the truth."

"Okay. However it was, we're here, and facing a condition that isn't funny. While we were teamed up I learned a lot, but not nearly enough. Am I right in thinking that I now don't need the other seven at all—that my cells are fully charged and I can go it alone?"

"Probably, sir, but . . ."

"I'm coming to that. Every time I do it—up to maximum performance, of course—it comes easier and faster and hits harder. So next time, or maybe the fourth or fifth time, it'll kill me. And the other seven, too, if they're along."

"I'm not sure, sir, but I think so."

"Nice. Very, *very* nice." Hilton got up, shoved both hands into his pockets, and prowled about the room. "But can't the damned stuff be controlled? Choked—throttled down—damped—muzzled, some way or other?"

"We do not know of any way, sir. The Masters were always working toward more power, not less."

"That makes sense. The more power the better, as long as you can handle it. But I can't handle this. And neither can the team. So how about organizing another team, one that hasn't got quite so much whammo? Enough punch to do the job, but not enough to backfire that way?"

"It is highly improbable that such a team is possible, sir." If an Oman could be acutely embarrassed, Larry was. "That is, sir . . . I should tell you, sir . . ."

"You certainly should. You've been stalling all along, and now you're stalled. Spill it."

"Yes, sir. The Tuly begged me not to mention it, but I must. When it organized your team it had no idea of what it was really going to do . . . ."

"Let's talk the same language, shall we? Say 'he' and 'she.' Not 'it.'"

"She thought she was setting up the peyondix, the same as all of us Omans have. But after she formed in your mind the peyondix matrix, your mind went on of itself to form a something else; a thing we can not understand. That was why she was so extremely . . . I think 'frightened' might be your term."

"I knew something was biting her. Why?"

"Because it very nearly killed you. You perhaps have not considered the effect upon us all if any Oman, however unintentionally, should kill a Master?"

"No, I hadn't . . . I see. So she won't play with fire any more, and none of the rest of you can?"

"Yes, sir. Nothing could force her to. If she could be so coerced we would destroy her brain before she could act. That brain, as you know, is imperfect, or she could not have done what she did. It should have been destroyed long since."

"Don't *ever* act on that assumption, Larry." Hilton thought for minutes. "Simple peyondix, such as yours, is not enough to read the Masters' records. If I'd had three brain cells working I'd've tried them then. I wonder if I *could* read them?"

"You have all the old Masters' powers and more. But you must not assemble them again, sir. It would mean death."

"But I've got to *know* . . . . I've *got* to know! Anyway, a thousandth of a second would be enough. I don't think that'd hurt me very much."

*

HE concentrated—read a few feet of top-secret braided wire—and came back to consciousness in the sickbay of the *Perseus*, with two doctors working on him; Hastings, the top Navy medico, and Flandres, the surgeon.

"What the hell happened to you?" Flandres demanded. "Were you trying to kill yourself?"

"And if so, how?" Hastings wanted to know.

"No, I was trying not to," Hilton said, weakly, "and I guess I didn't much more than succeed."

"That was just about the closest shave I ever saw a man come through. Whatever it was, don't do it again."

"I won't," he promised, feelingly.

When they let him out of the hospital, four days later, he called in Larry and Tuly.

"The next time would be the last time. So there won't be any," he told them. "But just how sure are you that some other of our boys or girls may not have just enough of whatever it takes to do the job? Enough oompa, but not too much?"

"Since we, too, are on strange ground the probability is vanishingly small. We have been making inquiries, however, and scanning. You were selected from all the minds of Terra as the one having the widest vision, the greatest scope, the most comprehensive grasp. The ablest at synthesis and correlation and so on."

"That's printing it in big letters, but that was more or less what they were after."

"Hence the probability approaches unity that any more such ignorant meddling as this obnoxious Tuly did well result almost certainly in failure and death. Therefore we can not and will not meddle again."

*

"YOU'VE got a point there . . . . So what I am is some kind of a freak. Maybe a kind of super-Master and maybe something altogether different. Maybe duplicable in a less lethal fashion, and maybe not. Veree helpful—I don't think. But I don't want to kill anybody, either . . . especially if it wouldn't do any good. But we've got to do *something*!" Hilton scowled in thought for minutes. "But an Oman brain could take it. As you told us, Tuly, 'The brain of the Larry is very, very tough.'"

"In a way, sir. Except that the Masters were very careful to make it physically impossible for any Oman to go very far along that line. It was only their oversight of my one imperfect brain that enabled me, alone of us all, to do that wrong."

"Stop thinking it was wrong, Tuly. I'm mighty glad you did. But I wasn't thinking of any regular Oman brain . . . ." Hilton's voice petered out.

"I see, sir. Yes, we can, by using your brain as Guide, reproduce it in an Oman body. You would then have the powers and most of the qualities of both . . . ."

"No, you don't see, because I've got my screen on. Which I will now take off—" he suited action to word—"since the whole planet's screened and I have nothing to hide from you. Teddy Blake and I both thought of that, but we'll consider it only as the ultimately last resort. We don't want to live a million years. And we want our race to keep on developing. But you folks can replace carbon-based molecules with silicon-based ones just as easily as, and a hell of a lot faster than, mineral water petrifies wood. What can you do along the line of rebuilding me that way? And if you can do any such conversion, what would happen? Would I live at all? And if so, how long? How would I live? What would I live on? All that kind of stuff."

"Shortly before they left, two of the Masters did some work on that very thing. Tuly and I converted them, sir."

"Fine—or is it? How did it work out?"

"Perfectly, sir . . . except that they destroyed themselves. It was thought that they wearied of existence."

"I don't wonder. Well, if it comes to that, I can do the same. You *can* convert me, then."

"Yes, sir. But before we do it we must do enough preliminary work to be sure that you will not be harmed in any way. Also, there will be many more changes involved than simple substitution."

"Of course. I realize that. Just see what you can do, please, and let me know."

"We will, sir, and thank you very much."

IX

AS has been intimated, no Terran can know what researches Larry and Tuly and the other Oman specialists performed, or how they arrived at the conclusions they reached. However, in less than a week Larry reported to Hilton.

"It can be done, sir, with complete safety. And you will live even more comfortably than you do now."

"How long?"

"The mean will be about five thousand Oman years—you don't know that an Oman year is equal to one point two nine three plus Terran years?"

"I didn't, no. Thanks."

"The maximum, a little less than six thousand. The minimum, a little over four thousand. I'm very sorry we had no data upon which to base a closer estimate."

"Close enough." He stared at the Oman. "You could also convert my wife?"

"Of course, sir."

"Well, we might be able to stand it, after we got used to the idea. Minimum, over five thousand Terran years . . . barring accidents, of course?"

"No, sir. No accidents. Nothing will be able to kill you, except by total destruction of the brain. And even then, sir, there will be the pattern."

"I'll . . . be . . . damned . . . ." Hilton gulped twice. "Okay, go ahead."

"Your skins will be like ours, energy-absorbers. Your 'blood' will carry charges of energy instead of oxygen. Thus, you may breathe or not, as you please. Unless you wish otherwise, we will continue the breathing function. It would scarcely be worth while to alter the automatic mechanisms that now control it. And you will wish at times to speak. You will still enjoy eating and drinking, although everything ingested will be eliminated, as at present, as waste."

"We'd add uranexite to our food, I suppose. Or drink radioactives, or sleep under cobalt-60 lamps."

"Yes, sir. Your family life will be normal; your sexual urges and satisfactions the same. Fertilization and period of gestation unchanged. Your children will mature at the same ages as they do now."

"How do you—oh, I see. You wouldn't change any molecular linkages or configurations in the genes or chromosomes."

"We could not, sir, even if we wished. Such substitutions can be made only in exact one-for-one replacements. In the near future you will, of course, have to control births quite rigorously."

"We sure would. Let's see . . . say we want a stationary population of a hundred million on our planet. Each couple to have two children, a boy and a girl. Born when the parents are about fifty . . . um-m-m. The gals can have all the children they want, then, until our population is about a million; then slap on the limit of two kids per couple. Right?"

"Approximately so, sir. And after conversion you alone will be able to operate with the full power of your eight, without tiring. You will also, of course, be able to absorb almost instantaneously all the knowledges and abilities of the old Masters."

Hilton gulped twice before he could speak. "You wouldn't be holding anything else back, would you?"

"Nothing important, sir. Everything else is minor, and probably known to you."

"I doubt it. How long will the job take, and how much notice will you need?"

"Two days, sir. No notice. Everything is ready."

Hilton, face somber, thought for minutes. "The more I think of it the less I like it. But it seems to be a forced put . . . and Temple will blow sky high . . . and *have* I got the guts to go it alone, even if she'd let me . . . ." He shrugged himself out of the black mood. "I'll look her up and let you know, Larry."

*

HE looked her up and told her everything. Told her bluntly; starkly; drawing the full picture in jet black, with very little white.

"There it is, sweetheart. The works," he concluded. "We are not going to have ten years; we may not have ten months. So—if such a brain as that can be had, do we or do we not have to have it? I'm putting it squarely up to you."

Temple's face, which had been getting paler and paler, was now as nearly colorless as it could become; the sickly yellow of her skin's light tan unbacked by any flush of red blood.

Her whole body was tense and strained.

"There's a horrible snapper on that question . . . . Can't *I* do it? Or *anybody* else except you?"

"No. Anyway, whose job is it, sweetheart?"

"I know, but . . . but I know just how close Tuly came to killing you. And that wasn't *anything* compared to such a radical transformation as this. I'm afraid it'll kill you, darling. And I just simply couldn't *stand* it!"

She threw herself into his arms, and he comforted her in the ages-old fashion of man with maid.

"Steady, hon," he said, as soon as he could lift her tear-streaked face from his shoulder. "I'll live through it. I thought you were getting the howling howpers about having to live for six thousand years and never getting back to Terra except for a Q strictly T visit now and then."

She pulled away from him, flung back her wheaten mop and glared. "So *that's* what you thought! What do I care how long I live, or how, or where, as long as it's with you? But what makes you think we can possibly live through such a horrible conversion as that?"

"Larry wouldn't do it if there was any question whatever. He didn't say it would be painless. But he did say I'd live."

"Well, he knows, I guess . . . I hope." Temple's natural fine color began to come back. "But it's understood that just the second you come out of the vat, I go right in."

"I hadn't ought to let you, of course. But I don't think I could take it alone."

That statement required a special type of conference, which consumed some little time. Eventually, however, Temple answered it in words.

"Of course you couldn't, sweetheart, and I wouldn't let you, even if you could."

There were a few things that had to be done before those two secret conversions could be made. There was the matter of the wedding, which was now to be in quadruplicate. Arrangements had to be made so that eight Big Wheels of the Project could all be away on honeymoon at once.

All these things were done.

*

OF the conversion operations themselves, nothing more need be said. The honeymooners, having left ship and town on a Friday afternoon, came back one week from the following Monday morning (While it took some time to recompute the exact Ardrian calendar, Terran day names and Terran weeks were used from the first. The Omans manufactured watches, clocks, and chronometers which divided the Ardrian day into twenty-four Ardrian hours, with minutes and seconds as usual.) The eight met joyously in Bachelors' Hall; the girls kissing each other and the men indiscriminately and enthusiastically; the men cooperating zestfully.

Temple scarcely blushed at all, she was so engrossed in trying to find out whether or not anyone was noticing any change. No one seemed to notice anything out of the ordinary. So, finally, she asked.

"Don't *any* of you, really, see anything different?"

The six others all howled at that, and Sandra, between giggles and snorts, said: "No, precious, it doesn't show a bit. Did you really think it would?"

Temple blushed furiously and Hilton came instantly to his bride's rescue. "Chip-chop the comedy, gang. She and I aren't human any more. We're a good jump toward being Omans. I couldn't make her believe it doesn't show."

That stopped the levity, cold, but none of the six could really believe it. However, after Hilton had coiled a twenty-penny spike into a perfect helix between his fingers, and especially after he and Temple had each chewed up and swallowed a piece of uranexite, there were no grounds left for doubt.

"That settles it . . . it *tears* it," Karns said then. "Start all over again, Jarve. We'll listen, this time."

Hilton told the long story again, and added: "I had to re-work a couple of cells of Temple's brain, but now she can read and understand the records as well as I can. So I thought I'd take her place on Team One and let her boss the job on all the other teams. Okay?"

"So you don't want to let the rest of us in on it." Karns's level stare was a far cry from the way he had looked at his chief a moment before. "If there's any one thing in the universe I never had *you* figured for, it's a dog in the manger."

"Huh? You mean you actually *want* to be a . . . a . . . hell, we don't even know *what* we are!"

"I do want it, Jarvis. We all do." This was, of all people, Teddy! "No one in all history has had more than about fifty years of really productive thinking. And just the idea of having enough time . . ."

"Hold it, Teddy. Use your brain. The Masters couldn't take it—they committed suicide. How do you figure we can do any better?"

"Because we'll *use* our brains!" she snapped. "They didn't. The Omans will serve us; and that's *all* they'll do."

"And do you think you'll be able to raise your children and grandchildren and so on to do the same? To have guts enough to resist the pull of such an ungodly habit-forming drug as this Oman service is?"

*

"I'M sure of it." She nodded positively. "And we'll run all applicants through a fine enough screen to—that is, if we ever consider anybody except our own BuSci people. And there's another reason." She grinned, got up, wriggled out of her coverall, and posed in bra and panties. "Look. I can keep most of this for five years. Quite a lot of it for ten. Then comes the struggle. What do *you* think I'd do for the ability, whenever it begins to get wrinkly or flabby, to peel the whole thing off and put on a brand-spanking-new smooth one? You name it, I'll do it! Besides, Bill and I will *both* just simply and cold-bloodedly murder you if you try to keep us out."

"Okay." Hilton looked at Temple; she looked at him; both looked at all the others. There was no revulsion at all. Nothing but eagerness.

Temple took over.

"I'm surprised. We're both surprised. You see, Jarve didn't want to do it at all, but he had to. I not only didn't want to, I was scared green and yellow at just the idea of it. But I had to, too, of course. We didn't think anybody would really want to. We thought we'd be left here alone. We still will be, I think, when you've thought it clear through, Teddy. You just haven't realized yet that we aren't even human any more. We're simply nothing but *monsters!*" Temple's voice became a wail.

"I've said my piece," Teddy said. "You tell 'em, Bill."

"Let me say something first," Kincaid said. "Temple, I'm ashamed of you. This line isn't at all your usual straight thinking. What you actually are is *homo superior*. Bill?"

"I can add one bit to that. I don't wonder that you were scared silly, Temple. Utterly new concept and you went into it stone cold. But now we see the finished product and we like it. In fact, we drool."

"I'll say we're drooling," Sandra said. "I could do handstands and pinwheels with joy."

"Let's see you," Hilton said. "That we'd all get a kick out of."

"Not now—don't want to hold this up—but sometime I just will. Bev?"

"I'm for it—and *how!* And won't Bernadine be amazed," Beverly laughed gleefully, "at her wise-crack about the 'race to end all human races' coming true?"

"I'm in favor of it, too, one hundred per cent," Poynter said. "Has it occurred to you, Jarve, that this opens up intergalactic exploration? No supplies to carry and plenty of time and fuel?"

"No, it hadn't. You've got a point there, Frank. That might take a little of the curse off of it, at that."

"When some of our kids get to be twenty years old or so and get married, I'm going to take a crew of them to Andromeda. We'll arrange, then, to extend our honeymoons another week," Hilton said. "What will our policy be? Keep it dark for a while with just us eight, or spread it to the rest?"

"Spread it, I'd say," Kincaid said.

"We can't keep it secret, anyway," Teddy argued. "Since Larry and Tuly were in on the whole deal, every Oman on the planet knows all about it. Somebody is going to ask questions, and Omans always answer questions and always tell the truth."

*

"QUESTIONS have already been asked and answered," Larry said, going to the door and opening it.

Stella rushed in. "We've been hearing the *damnedest* things!" She kissed everybody, ending with Hilton, whom she seized by both shoulders. "Is it actually true, boss, that you can fix me up so I'll live practically forever and can eat more than eleven calories a day without getting fat as a pig? Candy, ice cream, cake, pie, eclairs, cream puffs, French pastries, sugar and gobs of thick cream in my coffee . . . ?"

Half a dozen others, including the van der Moen twins, came in. Beverly emitted a shriek of joy. "Bernadine! The mother of the race to end all human races!"

"You whistled it, birdie!" Bernadine caroled. "I'm going to have ten or twelve, each one weirder than all the others. I told you I was a prophet—I'm going to hang out my shingle. Wholesale and retail prophecy; special rates for large parties." Her voice was drowned out in a general clamor.

"Hold it, everybody!" Hilton yelled. "Chip-chop it! *Quit* it!" Then, as the noise subsided, "If you think I'm going to tell this tall tale over and over again for the next two weeks you're all crazy. So shut down the plant and get everybody out here."

"Not *everybody*, Jarve!" Temple snapped. "We don't want scum, and there's some of that, even in BuSci."

"You're so right. Who, then?"

"The rest of the heads and assistants, of course . . . and all the lab girls and their husbands and boy-friends. I know they are all okay. That will be enough for now, don't you think?"

"I do think;" and the indicated others were sent for; and in a few minutes arrived.

The Omans brought chairs and Hilton stood on a table. He spoke for ten minutes. Then: "Before you decide whether you want to or not, think it over very carefully, because it's a one-way street. Fluorine can not be displaced. Once in, you're stuck for life. *There is no way back.* I've told you all the drawbacks and disadvantages I know of, but there may be a lot more that I haven't thought of yet. So think it over for a few days and when each of you has definitely made up his or her mind, let me know." He jumped down off the table.

*

HIS listeners, however, did not need days, or even seconds, to decide. Before Hilton's feet hit the floor there was a yell of unanimous approval.

He looked at his wife. "Do you suppose *we're* nuts?"

"Uh-uh. Not a bit. Alex was right. I'm going to just *love* it!" She hugged his elbow ecstatically. "So are you, darling, as soon as you stop looking at only the black side."

"You know . . . you could be right?" For the first time since the "ghastly" transformation Hilton saw that there really was a bright side and began to study it. "With most of BuSci—and part of the Navy, and selectees from Terra—it *will* be slightly terrific, at that!"

"And that 'habit-forming-drug' objection isn't insuperable, darling," Temple said. "If the younger generations start weakening we'll fix the Omans. I wouldn't want to wipe them out entirely, but . . ."

"But how do we settle priority, Doctor Hilton?" a girl called out; a tall, striking, brunette laboratory technician whose name Hilton needed a second to recall. "By pulling straws or hair? Or by shooting dice or each other or what?"

"Thanks, Betty, you've got a point. Sandy Cummings and department heads first, then assistants. Then you girls, in alphabetical order, each with her own husband or fiance."

"And my name is Ames. Oh, goody!"

"Larry, please tell them to . . ."

"I already have, sir. We are set up to handle four at once."

"Good boy. So scat, all of you, and get back to work—except Sandy, Bill, Alex, and Teddy. You four go with Larry."

Since the new sense was not peyondix, Hilton had started calling it "perception" and the others adopted the term as a matter of course. Hilton could use that sense for what seemed like years—and actually was whole minutes—at a time without fatigue or strain. He could not, however, nor could the Omans, give his tremendous power to anyone else.

As he had said, he could do a certain amount of reworking; but the amount of improvement possible to make depended entirely upon what there was to work on. Thus, Temple could cover about six hundred light-years. It developed later that the others of the Big Eight could cover from one hundred up to four hundred or so. The other department heads and assistants turned out to be still weaker, and not one of the rank and file ever became able to cover more than a single planet.

This sense was not exactly telepathy; at least not what Hilton had always thought telepathy would be. If anything, however, it was more. It was a lumping together of all five known human senses—and half a dozen unknown ones called, collectively, "intuition"—into one super-sense that was all-inclusive and all-informative. If he ever could learn exactly what it was and exactly what it did and how it did it . . . but he'd better chip-chop the wool-gathering and get back onto the job.

*

THE Stretts had licked the old Masters very easily, and intended to wipe out the Omans and the humans. They had no doubt at all as to their ability to do it. Maybe they could. If the Masters hadn't made some progress that the Omans didn't know about, they probably could. That was the first thing to find out. As soon as they'd been converted he'd call in all the experts and they'd go through the Masters' records like a dose of salts through a hillbilly schoolma'am.

At that point in Hilton's cogitations Sawtelle came in.

He had come down in his gig, to confer with Hilton as to the newly beefed-up fleet. Instead of being glum and pessimistic and foreboding, he was chipper and enthusiastic. They had rebuilt a thousand Oman ships. By combining Oman and Terran science, and adding everything the First Team had been able to reduce to practise, they had hyped up the power by a good fifteen per cent. Seven hundred of those ships, and all his men, were now arrayed in defense around Ardry. Three hundred, manned by Omans, were around Fuel Bin.

"Why?" Hilton asked. "It's Fuel Bin they've been attacking."

"Uh-uh. Minor objective," the captain demurred, positively. "The real attack will be here at you; the headquarters and the brains. Then Fuel Bin will be duck soup. But the thing that pleased me most is the control. Man, you never imagined such control! No admiral in history ever had such control of ten ships as I have of seven hundred. Those Omans spread orders so fast that I don't even finish thinking one and it's being executed. And no misunderstandings, no slips. For instance, this last batch—fifteen skeletons. Far out; they're getting cagy. I just thought 'Box 'em in and slug 'em' and—In! Across! Out! Socko! Pffft! Just like that and just that fast. None of 'em had time to light a beam. Nobody before ever even *dreamed* of such control!"

"That's great, and I like it . . . and you're only a captain. How many ships can Five-Jet Admiral Gordon put into space?"

"That depends on what you call ships. Superdreadnoughts, *Perseus* class, six. First-line battleships, twenty-nine. Second-line, smaller and some pretty old, seventy-three. Counting everything armed that will hold air, something over two hundred."

"I thought it was something like that. How would you like to be Five-Jet Admiral Sawtelle of the Ardrian Navy?"

"I wouldn't. I'm Terran Navy. But you knew that and you know me. So—what's on your mind?"

*

HILTON told him. *I ought to put this on a tape,* he thought to himself, *and broadcast it every hour on the hour.*

"They took the old Masters like dynamiting fish in a barrel," he concluded, "and I'm damned afraid they're going to lick us unless we take a lot of big, fast steps. But the hell of it is that I can't tell you anything—not one single thing—about any part of it. There's simply no way at all of getting through to you without making you over into the same kind of a thing I am."

"Is that bad?" Sawtelle was used to making important decisions fast. "Let's get at it."

"Huh? Skipper, do you realize just what that means? If you think they'll let you resign, forget it. They'll crucify you—brand you as a traitor and God only knows what else."

"Right. How about you and your people?"

"Well, as civilians, it won't be as bad . . . ."

"The hell it won't. Every man and woman that stays here will be posted forever as the blackest traitors old Terra ever disgraced herself by spawning."

"You've got a point there, at that. We'll all have to bring our relatives—the ones we think much of, at least—out here with us."

"Definitely. Now see what you can do about getting me run through your mill."

By exerting his authority, Hilton got Sawtelle put through the "Preservatory" in the second batch processed. Then, linking minds with the captain, he flashed their joint attention to the Hall of Records. Into the right room; into the right chest; along miles and miles of braided wire carrying some of the profoundest military secrets of the ancient Masters.

Then:

"Now you know a little of it," Hilton said. "Maybe a thousandth of what we'll have to have before we can take the Stretts as they will have to be taken."

For seconds Sawtelle could not speak. Then: "My . . . God. I see what you mean. You're right. No Omans can ever go to Terra; and no Terrans can ever come here except to stay forever."

The two then went out into space, to the flagship—which had been christened the *Orion*—and called in the six commanders.

"What *is* all this senseless idiocy we've been getting, Jarve?" Elliott demanded.

Hilton eyed all six with pretended disfavor. "You six guys are the hardest-headed bunch of skeptics that ever went unhung," he remarked, dispassionately. "So it wouldn't do any good to tell you anything—yet. The skipper and I will show you a thing first. Take her away, Skip."

The *Orion* shot away under interplanetary drive and for several hours Hilton and Sawtelle worked at re-wiring and practically rebuilding two devices that no one, Oman or human, had touched since the *Perseus* had landed on Ardry.

"What are you . . . I don't understand what you are doing, sir," Larry said. For the first time since Hilton had known him, the Oman's mind was confused and unsure.

"I know you don't. This is a bit of top-secret Masters' stuff. Maybe, some day, we'll be able to re-work your brain to take it. But it won't be for some time."

X

THE *Orion* hung in space, a couple of thousands of miles away from an asteroid which was perhaps a mile in average diameter. Hilton straightened up.

"Put Triple X Black filters on your plates and watch that asteroid." The commanders did so. "Ready?" he asked.

"Ready, sir."

Hilton didn't move a muscle. Nothing actually moved. Nevertheless there was a motionlessly writhing and crawling distortion of the ship and everything in it, accompanied by a sensation that simply can not be described.

It was not like going into or emerging from the sub-ether. It was not even remotely like space-sickness or sea-sickness or free fall or anything else that any Terran had ever before experienced.

And the asteroid vanished.

It disappeared into an outrageously incandescent, furiously pyrotechnic, raveningly expanding atomic fireball that in seconds seemed to fill half of space.

After ages-long minutes of the most horrifyingly devastating fury any man there had ever seen, the frightful thing expired and Hilton said: "*That* was just a kind of a firecracker. Just a feeble imitation of the first-stage detonator for what we'll have to have to crack the Stretts' ground-based screens. If the skipper and I had taken time to take the ship down to the shops and really work it over we could have put on a show. Was this enough so you iron-heads are ready to listen with your ears open and your mouths shut?"

They were. So much so that not even Elliott opened his mouth to say yes. They merely nodded. Then again—for the last time, he hoped!—Hilton spoke his piece. The response was prompt and vigorous. Only Sam Bryant, one of Hilton's staunchest allies, showed any uncertainty at all.

"I've been married only a year and a half, and the baby was due about a month ago. How sure are you that you can make old Gordon sit still for us skimming the cream off of Terra to bring out here?"

"Doris Bryant, the cream of Terra!" Elliott gibed. "*How* modest our Samuel has become!"

"Well, damn it, she is!" Bryant insisted.

"Okay, she is," Hilton agreed. "But either we get our people or Terra doesn't get its uranexite. That'll work. In the remote contingency that it doesn't, there are still tighter screws we can put on. But you missed the main snapper, Sam. Suppose Doris doesn't want to live for five thousand years and is allergic to becoming a monster?"

"Huh; you don't need to worry about that." Sam brushed that argument aside with a wave of his hand. "Show me a girl who doesn't want to stay young and beautiful forever and I'll square you the circle. Come on. What's holding us up?"

*

THE *Orion* hurtled through space back toward Ardry and Hilton, struck by a sudden thought, turned to the captain.

"Skipper, why wouldn't it be a smart idea to clamp a blockade onto Fuel Bin? Cut the Stretts' fuel supply?"

"I thought better of you than that, son." Sawtelle shook his head sadly. "That was the first thing I did."

"Ouch. Maybe you're 'way ahead of me too, then, on the one that we should move to Fuel Bin, lock, stock and barrel?"

"Never thought of it, no. Maybe you're worth saving, after all. After conversion, of course . . . . Yes, there'd be three big advantages."

"Four."

Sawtelle raised his eyebrows.

"One, only one planet to defend. Two, it's self-defending against sneak landings. Nothing remotely human can land on it except in heavy lead armor, and even in that can stay healthy for only a few minutes."

"Except in the city. Omlu. That's the weak point and would be the point of attack."

"Uh-uh. Cut off the decontaminators and in five hours it'll be as hot as the rest of the planet. Three, there'd be no interstellar supply line for the Stretts to cut. Four, the environment matches our new physiques a lot better than any normal planet could."

"That's the one I didn't think about."

"I think I'll take a quick peek at the Stretts—oh-oh; they've screened their whole planet. Well, we can do that, too, of course."

"How are you going to select and reject personnel? It looks as though everybody wants to stay. Even the men whose main object in life is to go aground and get drunk. The Omans do altogether too good a job on them and there's no such thing as a hangover. I'm glad I'm not in your boots."

"You may be in it up to the eyeballs, Skipper, so don't chortle too soon."

117

Hilton had already devoted much time to the problems of selection; and he thought of little else all the way back to Ardry. And for several days afterward he held conferences with small groups and conducted certain investigations.

*

BUD Carroll of Sociology and his assistant Sylvia Banister had been married for weeks. Hilton called them, together with Sawtelle and Bryant of Navy, into conference with the Big Eight.

"The more I study this thing the less I like it," Hilton said. "With a civilization having no government, no police, no laws, no medium of exchange . . ."

"No *money?*" Bryant exclaimed. "How's old Gordon going to pay for his uranexite, then?"

"He gets it free," Hilton replied, flatly. "When anyone can have anything he wants, merely by wanting it, what good is money? Now, remembering how long we're going to have to live, what we'll be up against, that the Masters failed, and so on, it is clear that the prime basic we have to select for is stability. We twelve have, by psychodynamic measurement, the highest stability ratings available."

"Are you sure *I* belong here?" Bryant asked.

"Yes. Here are three lists." Hilton passed papers around. "The list labeled 'OK' names those I'm sure of—the ones we're converting now and their wives and whatever on Terra. List 'NG' names the ones I know we don't want. List 'X'—over thirty percent—are in-betweeners. We have to make a decision on the 'X' list. So—what I want to know is, who's going to play God. I'm not. Sandy, are you?"

"Good Heavens, no!" Sandra shuddered. "But I'm afraid I know who will have to. I'm sorry, Alex, but it'll have to be you four—Psychology and Sociology."

Six heads nodded and there was a flashing interchange of thought among the four. Temple licked her lips and nodded, and Kincaid spoke.

"Yes, I'm afraid it's our baby. By leaning very heavily on Temple, we can do it. Remember, Jarve, what you said about the irresistible force? We'll need it."

"As I said once before, Mrs. Hilton, I'm very glad you're along," Hilton said. "But just how sure are you that even you can stand up under the load?"

"Alone, I couldn't. But don't underestimate Mrs. Carroll and the Messrs. Together, and with such a goal, I'm sure we can."

*

THUS, after four-fifths of his own group and forty-one Navy men had been converted, Hilton called an evening meeting of all the converts. Larry, Tuly and Javvy were the only Omans present.

"You all knew, of course, that we were going to move to Fuel Bin sometime," Hilton began. "I can tell you now that we who are here are all there are going to be of us. We are all leaving for Fuel Bin immediately after this meeting. Everything of any importance, including all of your personal effects, has already been moved. All Omans except these three, and all Oman ships except the *Orion*, have already gone."

He paused to let the news sink in.

Thoughts flew everywhere. The irrepressible Stella Wing—*now* Mrs. Osbert F. Harkins—was the first to give tongue. "What a *wonderful* job! Why, everybody's here that I really like at all!"

That sentiment was, of course, unanimous. It could not have been otherwise. Betty, the ex-Ames, called out:

"How did you get their female Omans away from Cecil Calthorpe and the rest of that chasing, booze-fighting bunch without them blowing the whole show?"

"Some suasion was necessary," Hilton admitted, with a grin. "Everyone who isn't here is time-locked into the *Perseus*. Release time eight hours tomorrow."

"And they'll wake up tomorrow morning with no Omans?" Bernadine tossed back her silvery mane and laughed. "Nor anything else except the *Perseus*? In a way, I'm sorry, but . . . maybe I've got too much stinker blood in me, but I'm very glad none of them are here. But I'd like to ask, Jarvis—or rather, I suppose you have already set up a new Advisory Board?"

"We have, yes." Hilton read off twelve names.

"Oh, nice. I don't know of any people I'd rather have on it. But what I want to gripe about is calling our new home world such a horrible name as 'Fuel Bin,' as though it were a wood-box or a coal-scuttle or something. And just think of the complexes it would set up in those super-children we're going to have so many of."

"What would you suggest?" Hilton asked.

"'Ardvor', of course," Hermione said, before her sister could answer. "We've had 'Arth' and 'Ardu' and 'Ardry' and you—or somebody—started calling us 'Ardans' to distinguish us converts from the Terrans. So let's keep up the same line."

There was general laughter at that, but the name was approved.

*

ABOUT midnight the meeting ended and the *Orion* set out for Ardvor. It reached it and slanted sharply downward. The whole BuSci staff was in the lounge, watching the big tri-di.

"Hey! That isn't Omlu!" Stella exclaimed. "It isn't a city at all and it isn't even in the same place!"

"No, ma'am," Larry said. "Most of you wanted the ocean, but many wanted a river or the mountains. Therefore we razed Omlu and built your new city, Ardane, at a place where the ocean, two rivers, and a range of mountains meet. Strictly speaking, it is not a city, but a place of pleasant and rewarding living."

The space-ship was coming in, low and fast, from the south. To the left, the west, there stretched the limitless expanse of ocean. To the right, mile after mile, were rough, rugged, jagged, partially-timbered mountains, mass piled upon mass. Immediately below the speeding vessel was a wide, white-sand beach all of ten miles long.

Slowing rapidly now, the *Orion* flew along due north.

"Look! Look! A natatorium!" Beverly shrieked. "I know I wanted a nice big place to swim in, besides my backyard pool and the ocean, but I didn't tell anybody to build *that*—I swear I didn't!"

"You didn't have to, pet." Poynter put his arm around her curvaceous waist and squeezed. "They knew. And I did a little thinking along that line myself. There's our house, on top of the cliff over the natatorium—you can almost dive into it off the patio."

"Oh, wonderful!"

Immediately north of the natatorium a tremendous river—named at first sight the "Whitewater"—rushed through its gorge into the ocean; a river and gorge strangely reminiscent of the Colorado and its Grand Canyon. On the south bank of that river, at its very mouth—looking straight up that tremendous canyon; on a rocky promontory commanding ocean and beach and mountains—there was a house. At the sight of it Temple hugged Hilton's arm in ecstasy.

"Yes, that's ours," he assured her. "Just about everything either of us has ever wanted." The clamor was now so great—everyone was recognizing his-and-her house and was exclaiming about it—that both Temple and Hilton fell silent and simply watched the scenery unroll.

Across the turbulent Whitewater and a mile farther north, the mountains ended as abruptly as though they had been cut off with a cleaver and an apparently limitless expanse of treeless, grassy prairie began. And through that prairie, meandering sluggishly to the ocean from the northeast, came the wide, deep River Placid.

The *Orion* halted. It began to descend vertically, and only then did Hilton see the spaceport. It was so vast, and there were so many spaceships on it, that from any great distance it was actually invisible! Each six-acre bit of the whole immense expanse of level prairie between the Placid and the mountains held an Oman superdreadnought!

*

THE staff paired off and headed for the airlocks. Hilton said: "Temple, have you any reservations at all, however slight, as to having Dark Lady as a permanent fixture in your home?"

"Why, of course not—I like her as much as you do. And besides—" she giggled like a schoolgirl—" even if she *is* a lot more beautiful than I am—I've got a few things she never will have . . . but there's something else. I got just a flash of it before you blocked. Spill it, please."

"You'll see in a minute." And she did.

Larry, Dark Lady and Temple's Oman maid Moty were standing beside the Hilton's car—and so was another Oman, like none ever before seen. Six feet four; shoulders that would just barely go through a door; muscled like Atlas and Hercules combined; skin a gleaming, satiny bronze; hair a rippling mass of lambent flame. Temple came to a full stop and caught her breath.

"The Prince," she breathed, in awe. "Da Lormi's Prince of Thebes. The ultimate bronze of all the ages. *You* did this, Jarve. How did you ever dig him up out of my schoolgirl crushes?"

All six got into the car, which was equally at home on land or water or in the air. In less than a minute they were at Hilton House.

The house itself was circular. Its living-room was an immense annulus of glass from which, by merely moving along its circular length, any desired view could be had. The pair walked around it once. Then she took him by the arm and steered him firmly toward one of the bedrooms in the center.

"This house is just too much to take in all at once," she declared. "Besides, let's put on our swimsuits and get over to the Nat."

120

In the room, she closed the door firmly in the faces of the Omans and grinned. "Maybe, sometime, I'll get used to having somebody besides you in my bedroom, but I haven't, yet . . . . Oh, do you itch, too?"

Hilton had peeled to the waist and was scratching vigorously all around his waistline, under his belt. "Like the very devil," he admitted, and stared at her. For she, three-quarters stripped, was scratching, too!

"It started the minute we left the *Orion*," he said, thoughtfully. "I see. These new skins of ours like hard radiation, but don't like to be smothered while they're enjoying it. By about tomorrow, we'll be a nudist colony, I think."

"I could stand it, I suppose. What makes you think so?"

"Just what I know about radiation. Frank would be the one to ask. My hunch is, though, that we're going to be nudists whether we want to or not. Let's go."

*

THEY went in a two-seater, leaving the Omans at home. Three-quarters of the staff were lolling on the sand or were seated on benches beside the immense pool. As they watched, Beverly ran out along the line of springboards; testing each one and selecting the stiffest. She then climbed up to the top platform—a good twelve feet above the board—and plummeted down upon the board's heavily padded take-off. Legs and back bending stubbornly to take the strain, she and the board reached low-point together, and, still in sync with it, she put every muscle she had into the effort to hurl herself upward.

She had intended to go up thirty feet. But she had no idea whatever as to her present strength, or of what that Oman board, in perfect synchronization with that tremendous strength, would do. Thus, instead of thirty feet, she went up very nearly two hundred; which of course spoiled completely her proposed graceful two-and-a-half.

In midair she struggled madly to get into some acceptable position. Failing, she curled up into a tight ball just before she struck water.

What a splash!

"It won't hurt her—you couldn't hurt her with a club!" Hilton snapped. He seized Temple's hand as everyone else rushed to the pool's edge. "Look—Bernadine—that's what I was thinking about."

Temple stopped and looked. The platinum-haired twins had been basking on the sand, and wherever sand had touched fabric, fabric had disappeared.

Their suits had of course approached the minimum to start with. Now Bernadine wore only a wisp of nylon perched precariously on one breast and part of a ribbon that had once been a belt. Discovering the catastrophe, she shrieked once and leaped into the pool any-which-way, covering her breasts with her hands and hiding in water up to her neck.

Meanwhile, the involuntarily high diver had come to the surface, laughing apologetically. Surprised by the hair dangling down over her eyes, she felt for her cap. It was gone. So was her suit. Naked as a fish. She swam a couple of easy strokes, then stopped.

"Frank! Oh, Frank!" she called.

"Over here, Bev." Her husband did not quite know whether to laugh or not.

"Is it the radiation or the water? Or both?"

"Radiation, I think. These new skins of ours don't want to be covered up. But it probably makes the water a pretty good imitation of a universal solvent."

"Good-by, clothes!" Beverly rolled over onto her back, fanned water carefully with her hands, and gazed approvingly at herself. "I don't itch any more, anyway, so I'm very much in favor of it."

*

THUS the Ardans came to their new home world and to a life that was to be more comfortable by far and happier by far than any of them had known on Earth. There were many other surprises that day, of course; of which only two will be mentioned here. When they finally left the pool, at about seventeen hours G.M.T., everybody was ravenously hungry.(Greenwich Mean Time. Ardvor was, always and everywhere, full daylight. Terran time and calendar were adapted as a matter of course.)

"But why *should* we be?" Stella demanded. "I've been eating everything in sight, just for fun. But now I'm actually hungry enough to eat a horse and wagon and chase the driver!"

"Swimming makes everybody hungry," Beverly said, "and I'm awfully glad *that* hasn't changed. Why, I wouldn't feel *human* if I didn't!"

Hilton and Temple went home, and had a long-drawn-out and very wonderful supper. Prince waited on Temple, Dark Lady on Hilton; Larry and Moty ran the synthesizers in the kitchen. All four Omans radiated happiness.

Another surprise came when they went to bed. For the bed was a raised platform of something that looked like concrete and, except for an uncanny property of molding itself somewhat to the contours of their bodies, was almost as hard as rock. Nevertheless, it was the most comfortable bed either of them had ever had. When they were ready to go to sleep, Temple said:

"Drat it, those Omans *still* want to come in and sleep with us. In the room, I mean. And they suffer so. They're simply *radiating* silent suffering and oh-so-submissive reproach. Shall we let 'em come in?"

"That's strictly up to you, sweetheart. It always has been."

"I know. I thought they'd quit it sometime, but I guess they never will. I *still* want an illusion of privacy at times, even though they know all about everything that goes on. But we might let 'em in now, just while we sleep, and throw 'em out again as soon as we wake up in the morning?"

"You're the boss." Without additional invitation the four Omans came in and arranged themselves neatly on the floor, on all four sides of the bed. Temple had barely time to cuddle up against Hilton, and he to put his arm closely around her, before they both dropped into profound and dreamless sleep.

*

AT eight hours next morning all the specialists met at the new Hall of Records.

This building, an exact duplicate of the old one, was located on a mesa in the foothills southwest of the natatorium, in a luxuriant grove at sight of which Karns stopped and began to laugh.

"I thought I'd seen everything," he remarked. "But yellow pine, spruce, tamarack, apples, oaks, palms, oranges, cedars, joshua trees and *cactus*—just to name a few—all growing on the same quarter-section of land?"

"Just everything anybody wants, is all," Hilton said. "But are they really growing? Or just straight synthetics? Lane—Kathy—this is your dish."

"Not so fast, Jarve; give us a chance, *please*!" Kathryn, now Mrs. Lane Saunders, pleaded. She shook her spectacular head. "We don't see how any stable indigenous life can have developed at all, unless . . ."

"Unless what? Natural shielding?" Hilton asked, and Kathy eyed her husband.

"Right," Saunders said. "The earliest life-forms must have developed a shield before they could evolve and stabilize. Hence, whatever it is that is in our skins was not a triumph of Masters' science. They took it from Nature."

"Oh? Oh!" These were two of Sandra's most expressive monosyllables, followed by a third. "Oh. Could be, at that. But how *could* . . . no, cancel that."

"You'd better cancel it, Sandy. Give us a couple of months, and *maybe* we can answer a few elementary questions."

Now inside the Hall, all the teams, from Astronomy to Zoology, went efficiently to work. Everyone now knew what to look for, how to find it, and how to study it.

"The First Team doesn't need you now too much, does it, Jarve?" Sawtelle asked.

"Not particularly. In fact, I was just going to get back onto my own job."

"Not yet. I want to talk to you," and the two went into a long discussion of naval affairs.

XI

THE Stretts' fuel-supply line had been cut long since. Many Strett cargo-carriers had been destroyed. The enemy would of course have a very heavy reserve of fuel on hand. But there was no way of knowing how large it was, how many warships it could supply, or how long it would last.

Two facts were, however, unquestionable. First, the Stretts were building a fleet that in their minds would be invincible. Second, they would attack Ardane as soon as that fleet could be made ready. The unanswerable question was: how long would that take?

"So we want to get every ship we have. How many? Five thousand? Ten? Fifteen? We want them converted to maximum possible power as soon as we possibly can," Sawtelle said. "And I want to get out there with my boys to handle things."

"You aren't going to. Neither you nor your boys are expendable. Particularly you." Jaw hard-set, Hilton studied the situation for minutes. "No. What we'll do is take your Oman, Kedy. We'll re-set the Guide to drive into him everything you and the military Masters ever knew about arms, armament, strategy, tactics and so on. And we'll add everything I know of coordination, synthesis, and perception. That ought to make him at least a junior-grade military genius."

"You can play *that* in spades. I wish you could do it to me."

"I can—if you'll take the full Oman transformation. Nothing else can stand the punishment."

"I know. No, I don't want to be a genius that badly."

"Check. And we'll take the resultant Kedy and make nine duplicates of him. Each one will learn from and profit by the mistakes made by preceding numbers and will assume command the instant his preceding number is killed."

"Oh, you expect, then . . . ?"

"Expect? No. I know it damn well, and so do you. That's why we Ardans will all stay aground. Why the Kedys' first job will be to make the heavy stuff in and around Ardane as heavy as it can be made. Why it'll all be on twenty-four-hour alert. Then they can put as many thousands of Omans as you please to work at modernizing all the Oman ships you want and doing anything else you say. Check?"

Sawtelle thought for a couple of minutes. "A few details, is all. But that can be ironed out as we go along."

Both men worked then, almost unremittingly for six solid days; at the end of which time both drew tremendous sighs of relief. They had done everything possible for them to do. The defense of Ardvor was now rolling at fullest speed toward its gigantic objective.

Then captain and director, in two Oman ships with fifty men and a thousand Omans, leaped the world-girdling ocean to the mining operation of the Stretts. There they found business strictly as usual. The strippers still stripped; the mining mechs still roared and snarled their inchwise ways along their geometrically perfect terraces; the little carriers still skittered busily between the various miners and the storage silos. The fact that there was enough concentrate on hand to last a world for a hundred years made no difference at all to these automatics; a crew of erector-mechs was building new silos as fast as existing ones were being filled.

Since the men now understood everything that was going on, it was a simple matter for them to stop the whole Strett operation in its tracks. Then every man and every Oman leaped to his assigned job. Three days later, all the mechs went back to work. Now, however, they were working for the Ardans.

The miners, instead of concentrate, now emitted vastly larger streams of Navy-Standard pelleted uranexite. The carriers, instead of one-gallon cans, carried five-ton drums. The silos were immensely larger—thirty feet in diameter and towering two hundred feet into the air. The silos were not, however, being used as yet. One of the two Oman ships had been converted into a fuel-tanker and its yawning holds were being filled first.

The *Orion* went back to Ardane and an eight-day wait began. For the first time in over seven months Hilton found time actually to loaf; and he and Temple, lolling on the beach or hiking in the mountains, enjoyed themselves and each other to the full.

All too soon, however, the heavily laden tanker appeared in the sky over Ardane. The *Orion* joined it; and the two ships slipped into sub-space for Earth.

*

THREE days out, Hilton used his sense of perception to release the thought-controlled blocks that had been holding all the controls of the *Perseus* in neutral. He informed her officers—by releasing a public-address tape—that they were now free to return to Terra.

Three days later, one day short of Sol, Sawtelle got Five-Jet Admiral Gordon's office on the sub-space radio. An officious underling tried to block him, of course.

"Shut up, Perkins, and listen," Sawtelle said, bruskly. "Tell Gordon I'm bringing in one hundred twenty thousand two hundred forty-five metric tons of pelleted uranexite. And if he isn't on this beam in sixty seconds he'll never get a gram of it."

The admiral, outraged almost to the point of apoplexy, came in. "Sawtelle, report yourself for court-martial at . . ."

"Keep still, Gordon," the captain snapped. In sheer astonishment old Five-Jets obeyed. "I am no longer Terran Navy; no longer subject to your orders. As a matter of cold fact, I am no longer human. For reasons which I will explain later to the full Advisory Board, some of the personnel of Project Theta Orionis underwent transformation into a form of life able to live in an environment of radioactivity so intense as to kill any human being in ten seconds. Under certain conditions we will supply, free of charge, FOB Terra or Luna, all the uranexite the Solar System can use. The conditions are these," and he gave them. "Do you accept these conditions or not?"

"I . . . I would vote to accept them, Captain. But that weight! One hundred twenty thousand *metric tons*—incredible! Are you *sure* of that figure?"

"Definitely. And that is minimum. The error is plus, not minus."

"This crippling power-shortage would really be over?" For the first time since Sawtelle had known him, Gordon showed that he was not quite solid Navy brass.

"It's over. Definitely. For good."

"I'd not only agree; I'd raise you a monument. While I can't speak for the Board, I'm sure they'll agree."

"So am I. In any event, your cooperation is all that's required for this first load." The chips had vanished from Sawtelle's shoulders. "Where do you want it, Admiral? Aristarchus or White Sands?"

"White Sands, please. While there may be some delay in releasing it to industry . . ."

"While they figure out how much they can tax it?" Sawtelle asked, sardonically.

"Well, if they don't tax it it'll be the first thing in history that isn't. Have you any objections to releasing all this to the press?"

"None at all. The harder they hit it and the wider they spread it, the better. Will you have this beam switched to Astrogation, please?"

"Of course. And thanks, Captain. I'll see you at White Sands."

Then, as the now positively glowing Gordon faded away, Sawtelle turned to his own staff. "Fenway—Snowden—take over. Better double-check micro-timing with Astro. Put us into a twenty-four-hour orbit over White Sands and hold us there. We won't go down. Let the load down on remote, wherever they want it."

*

THE arrival of the Ardvorian superdreadnought *Orion* and the UC-1 (Uranexite Carrier Number One) was one of the most sensational events old Earth had ever known. Air and space craft went clear out to Emergence Volume Ninety to meet them. By the time the *UC-1* was coming in on its remote-controlled landing spiral the press of small ships was so great that all the police forces available were in a lather trying to control it.

This was exactly what Hilton had wanted. It made possible the completely unobserved launching of several dozen small craft from the *Orion* herself.

One of these made a very high and very fast flight to Chicago. With all due formality and under the aegis of a perfectly authentic Registry Number it landed on O'Hare Field. Eleven deeply tanned young men emerged from it and made their way to a taxi stand, where each engaged a separate vehicle.

Sam Bryant stepped into his cab, gave the driver a number on Oakwood Avenue in Des Plaines, and settled back to scan. He was lucky. He would have gone anywhere she was, of course, but the way things were, he could give her a little warning to soften the shock. She had taken the baby out for an airing down River Road, and was on her way back. By having the taxi kill ten minutes or so he could arrive just after she did. Wherefore he stopped the cab at a public communications booth and dialed his home.

"Mrs. Bryant is not at home, but she will return at fifteen thirty," the instrument said, crisply. "Would you care to record a message for her?"

He punched the RECORD button. "This is Sam, Dolly baby. I'm right behind you. Turn around, why don't you, and tell your ever-lovin' star-hoppin' husband hello?"

The taxi pulled up at the curb just as Doris closed the front door; and Sam, after handing the driver a five-dollar bill, ran up the walk.

He waited just outside the door, key in hand, while she lowered the stroller handle, took off her hat and by long-established habit reached out to flip the communicator's switch. At the first word, however, she stiffened rigidly—froze solid.

Smiling, he opened the door, walked in, and closed it behind him. Nothing short of a shotgun blast could have taken Doris Bryant's attention from that recorder then.

"That simply is not so," she told the instrument firmly, with both eyes resolutely shut. "They made him stay on the *Perseus*. He won't be in for at least three days. This is some cretin's idea of a joke."

"Not this time, Dolly honey. It's really me."

Her eyes popped open as she whirled. "SAM!" she shrieked, and hurled herself at him with all the pent-up ardor and longing of two hundred thirty-four meticulously counted, husbandless, loveless days.

After an unknown length of time Sam tipped her face up by the chin, nodded at the stroller, and said, "How about introducing me to the little stranger?"

"*What* a mother I turned out to be! That was the first thing I was going to rave about, the very first thing I saw you! Samuel Jay the Fourth, seventy-six days old today." And so on.

Eventually, however, the proud young mother watched the slightly apprehensive young father carry their first-born upstairs; where together, they put him—still sound asleep—to bed in his crib. Then again they were in each other's arms.

*

SOME time later, she twisted around in the circle of his arm and tried to dig her fingers into the muscles of his back. She then attacked his biceps and, leaning backward, eyed him intently.

"You're you, I know, but you're different. No athlete or any laborer could ever possibly get the muscles you have all over. To say nothing of a space officer on duty. And I know it isn't any kind of a disease. You've been acting all the time as though I were fragile, made out of glass or something—as though you were afraid of breaking me in two. So—what is it, sweetheart?"

"I've been trying to figure out an easy way of telling you, but there isn't any. I am different. I'm a hundred times as strong as any man ever was. Look." He upended a chair, took one heavy hardwood leg between finger and thumb and made what looked like a gentle effort to bend it. The leg broke with a pistol-sharp report and Doris leaped backward in surprise. "So you're right. I *am* afraid, not only of breaking you in two, but killing you. And if I break any of your ribs or arms or legs I'll never forgive myself. So if I let myself go for a second—I don't think I will, but I might—don't wait until you're really hurt to start screaming. Promise?"

"I promise." Her eyes went wide. "But *tell* me!"

He told her. She was in turn surprised, amazed, apprehensive, frightened and finally eager; and she became more and more eager right up to the end.

"You mean that we . . . that I'll stay just as I am—for thousands of *years?*"

"Just as you are. Or different, if you like. If you really mean any of this yelling you've been doing about being too big in the hips—I think you're exactly right, myself—you can rebuild yourself any way you please. Or change your shape every hour on the hour. But you haven't accepted my invitation yet."

"Don't be silly." She went into his arms again and nibbled on his left ear. "I'd go anywhere with you, of course, any time, but *this*—but you're positively *sure* Sammy Small will be all right?"

"Positively sure."

"Okay, I'll call mother . . . ." Her face fell. "I *can't* tell her that we'll never see them again and that we'll live . . ."

"You don't need to. She and Pop—Fern and Sally, too, and their boy-friends—are on the list. Not this time, but in a month or so, probably."

Doris brightened like a sunburst. "And your folks, too, of course?" she asked.

"Yes, all the close ones."

"Marvelous! How soon are we leaving?"

*

AT six o'clock next morning, two hundred thirty-five days after leaving Earth, Hilton and Sawtelle set out to make the Ardans' official call upon Terra's Advisory Board. Both were wearing prodigiously heavy lead armor, the inside of which was furiously radioactive. They did not need it, of course. But it would make all Ardans monstrous in Terran eyes and would conceal the fact that any other Ardans were landing.

Their gig was met at the spaceport; not by a limousine, but by a five-ton truck, into which they were loaded one at a time by a hydraulic lift. Cameras clicked, reporters scurried, and tri-di scanners whirred. One of those scanners, both men knew, was reporting directly and only to the Advisory Board—which, of course, never took anything either for granted or at its face value.

Their first stop was at a truck-scale, where each visitor was weighed. Hilton tipped the beam at four thousand six hundred fifteen pounds; Sawtelle, a smaller man, weighed in at four thousand one hundred ninety. Thence to the Radiation Laboratory, where it was ascertained and reported that the armor did not leak—which was reasonable enough, since each was lined with Masters' plastics.

Then into lead-lined testing cells, where each opened his face-plate briefly to a sensing element. Whereupon the indicating needles of two meters in the main laboratory went enthusiastically through the full range of red and held unwaveringly against their stops.

Both Ardans felt the wave of shocked, astonished, almost unbelieving consternation that swept through the observing scientists and, in slightly lesser measure (because they knew less about radiation) through the Advisory Board itself in a big room halfway across town. And from the Radiation Laboratory they were taken, via truck and freight elevator, to the Office of the Commandant, where the Board was sitting.

The story, which had been sent in to the Board the day before on a scrambled beam, was one upon which the Ardans had labored for days. Many facts could be withheld. However, every man aboard the *Perseus* would agree on some things. Indeed, the Earthship's communications officers had undoubtedly radioed in already about longevity and perfect health and Oman service and many other matters. Hence all such things would have to be admitted and countered.

Thus the report, while it was air-tight, perfectly logical, perfectly consistent, and apparently complete, did not please the Board at all. It wasn't intended to.

*

"WE cannot and do not approve of such unwarranted favoritism," the Chairman of the Board said. "Longevity has always been man's prime goal. Every human being has the inalienable right to . . ."

"Flapdoodle!" Hilton snorted. "This is not being broadcast and this room is proofed, so please climb down off your soapbox. You don't need to talk like a politician here. Didn't you read paragraph 12-A-2, one of the many marked 'Top Secret'?"

"Of course. But we do not understand how purely mental qualities can possibly have any effect upon purely physical transformations. Thus it does not seem reasonable that any except rigorously screened personnel would die in the process. That is, of course, unless you contemplate deliberate, cold-blooded murder."

That stopped Hilton in his tracks, for it was too close for comfort to the truth. But it did not hold the captain for an instant. He was used to death, in many of its grisliest forms.

"There are a lot of things no Terran ever will understand," Sawtelle replied instantly. "Reasonable, or not, that's exactly what will happen. And, reasonable or not, it'll be suicide, not murder. There isn't a thing that either Hilton or I can do about it."

Hilton broke the ensuing silence. "You can say with equal truth that every human being has the *right* to run a four-minute mile or to compose a great symphony. It isn't a matter of right at all, but of ability. In this case the mental qualities are even more necessary than the physical. You as a Board did a very fine job of selecting the BuSci personnel for Project Theta Orionis. Almost eighty per cent of them proved able to withstand the Ardan conversion. On the other hand, only a very small percentage of the Navy personnel did so."

"Your report said that the remaining personnel of the Project were not informed as to the death aspect of the transformation," Admiral Gordon said. "Why not?"

"That should be self-explanatory," Hilton said, flatly. "They are still human and still Terrans. We did not and will not encroach upon either the duties or the privileges of Terra's Advisory Board. What you tell all Terrans, and how much, and how, must be decided by yourselves. This also applies, of course, to the other 'Top Secret' paragraphs of the report, none of which are known to any Terran outside the Board."

"But you haven't said anything about the method of selection," another Advisor complained. "Why, that will take all the psychologists of the world, working full time; continuously."

"We said we would do the selecting. We meant just that," Hilton said, coldly. "No one except the very few selectees will know anything about it. Even if it were an unmixed blessing—which it very definitely is *not*—do you want all humanity thrown into such an uproar as that would cause? Or the quite possible racial inferiority complex it might set up? To say nothing of the question of how much of Terra's best blood do you want to drain off, irreversibly and permanently? No. What we suggest is that you paint the picture so black, using Sawtelle and me and what all humanity has just seen as horrible examples, that nobody would take it as a gift. Make them shun it like the plague. Hell, I don't have to tell you what your propaganda machines can do."

*

THE Chairman of the Board again mounted his invisible rostrum. "Do you mean to intimate that we are to falsify the record?" he declaimed. "To try to make liars out of hundreds of eyewitnesses? You ask us to distort the truth, to connive at . . ."

"We aren't asking you to do *anything*!" Hilton snapped. "We don't give a damn what you do. Just study that record, with all that it implies. Read between the lines. As for those on the *Perseus*, no two of them will tell the same story and not one of them has even the remotest idea of what the real story is. I, personally, not only did not want to become a monster, but would have given everything I had to stay human. My wife felt the same way. Neither of us would have converted if there'd been any other way in God's universe of getting the uranexite and doing some other things that simply *must* be done."

"What other things?" Gordon demanded.

"You'll never know," Hilton answered, quietly. "Things no Terran ever will know. We hope. Things that would drive any Terran stark mad. Some of them are hinted at—as much as we dared—between the lines of the report."

The report had not mentioned the Stretts. Nor were they to be mentioned now. If the Ardans could stop them, no Terran need ever know anything about them.

If not, no Terran should know anything about them except what he would learn for himself just before the end. For Terra would never be able to do anything to defend herself against the Stretts.

"Nothing whatever can drive *me* mad," Gordon declared, "and I want to know all about it—right now!"

"You can do one of two things, Gordon," Sawtelle said in disgust. His sneer was plainly visible through the six-ply, plastic-backed lead glass of his face-plate. "Either shut up or accept my personal invitation to come to Ardvor and try to go through the wringer. That's an invitation to your own funeral." Five-Jet Admiral Gordon, torn inwardly to ribbons, made no reply.

"I repeat," Hilton went on, "we are not asking you to do anything whatever. We are offering to give you; free of charge but under certain conditions, all the power your humanity can possibly use. We set no limitation whatever as to quantity and with no foreseeable limit as to time. The only point at issue is whether or not you accept the conditions. If you do not accept them we'll leave now—and the offer will not be repeated."

"And you would, I presume, take the *UC-1* back with you?"

"Of course not, sir. Terra needs power too badly. You are perfectly welcome to that one load of uranexite, no matter what is decided here."

"That's one way of putting it," Gordon sneered. "But the truth is that you know damned well I'll blow both of your ships out of space if you so much as . . ."

"Oh, chip-chop the jaw-flapping, Gordon!" Hilton snapped. Then, as the admiral began to bellow orders into his microphone, he went on: "You want it the hard way, eh? Watch what happens, all of you!"

*

THE *UC-1* shot vertically into the air. Through its shallow dense layer and into and through the stratosphere. Earth's fleet, already on full alert and poised to strike, rushed to the attack. But the carrier had reached the *Orion* and both Ardvorian ships had been waiting, motionless, for a good half minute before the Terran warships arrived and began to blast with everything they had.

"Flashlights and firecrackers," Sawtelle said, calmly. "You aren't even warming up our screens. As soon as you quit making a damned fool of yourself by wasting energy that way, we'll set the *UC-1* back down where she was and get on with our business here."

"You will order a cease-fire at once, Admiral," the chairman said, "or the rest of us will, as of now, remove you from the Board." Gordon gritted his teeth in rage, but gave the order.

"If he hasn't had enough yet to convince him," Hilton suggested, "he might send up a drone. We don't want to kill anybody, you know. One with the heaviest screening he's got—just to see what happens to it."

"He's had enough. The rest of us have had more than enough. That exhibition was not only uncalled-for and disgusting—it was outrageous!"

The meeting settled down, then, from argument to constructive discussion, and many topics were gone over. Certain matters were, however, so self-evident that they were not even mentioned.

Thus, it was a self-evident fact that no Terran could ever visit Ardvor; for the instrument-readings agreed with the report's statements as to the violence of the Ardvorian environment, and no Terran could possibly walk around in two tons of lead. Conversely, it was self-apparent to the Terrans that no Ardan could ever visit Earth without being recognized instantly for what he was. Wearing such armor made its necessity starkly plain. No one from the *Perseus* could say that any Ardan, after having lived on the furiously radiant surface of Ardvor, would not be as furiously radioactive as the laboratory's calibrated instruments had shown Hilton and Sawtelle actually to be.

Wherefore the conference went on, quietly and cooperatively, to its planned end.

One minute after the Terran battleship *Perseus* emerged into normal space, the *Orion* went into sub-space for her long trip back to Ardvor.

*

THE last two days of that seven-day trip were the longest-seeming that either Hilton or Sawtelle had ever known. The sub-space radio was on continuously and Kedy-One reported to Sawtelle every five minutes. Even though Hilton knew that the Oman commander-in-chief was exactly as good at perceiving as he himself was, he found himself scanning the thoroughly screened Strett world forty or fifty times an hour.

However, in spite of worry and apprehension, time wore eventlessly on. The *Orion* emerged, went to Ardvor and landed on Ardane Field.

Hilton, after greeting properly and reporting to his wife, went to his office. There he found that Sandra had everything well in hand except for a few tapes that only he could handle. Sawtelle and his officers went to the new Command Central, where everything was rolling smoothly and very much faster than Sawtelle had dared hope.

The Terran immigrants had to live in the *Orion*, of course, until conversion into Ardans. Almost equally of course—since the Bryant infant was the only young baby in the lot—Doris and her Sammy Small were, by popular acclaim, in the first batch to be converted. For little Sammy had taken the entire feminine contingent by storm. No Oman female had a chance to act as nurse as long as any of the girls were around. Which was practically all the time. Especially the platinum-blonde twins; for several months, now, Bernadine Braden and Hermione Felger.

"And you said they were so hard-boiled," Doris said accusingly to Sam, nodding at the twins. On hands and knees on the floor, head to head with Sammy Small between them, they were growling deep-throated at each other and nuzzling at the baby, who was having the time of his young life. "You couldn't have been any wronger, my sweet, if you'd had the whole Octagon helping you go astray. They're just as nice as they can be, both of them."

Sam shrugged and grinned. His wife strode purposefully across the room to the playful pair and lifted their pretended prey out from between them.

"Quit it, you two," she directed, swinging the baby up and depositing him a-straddle her left hip. "You're just simply spoiling him rotten."

"You think so, Dolly? Uh-uh, far be it from such." Bernadine came lithely to her feet. She glanced at her own taut, trim abdomen; upon which a micrometrically-precise topographical mapping job might have revealed an otherwise imperceptible bulge. "Just you wait until Junior arrives and I'll show you how to *really* spoil a baby. Besides, what's the hurry?"

"He needs his supper. Vitamins and minerals and hard radiations and things, and then he's going to bed. I don't approve of this no-sleep business. So run along, both of you, until tomorrow."

XII

AS has been said, the Stretts were working, with all the intensity of their monstrous but tremendously capable minds, upon their Great Plan; which was, basically, to conquer and either enslave or destroy every other intelligent race throughout all the length, breadth, and thickness of total space. To that end each individual Strett had to become invulnerable and immortal.

Wherefore, in the inconceivably remote past, there had been put into effect a program of selective breeding and of carefully-calculated treatments. It was mathematically certain that this program would result in a race of beings of pure force—beings having no material constituents remaining whatever.

Under those hellish treatments billions upon billions of Stretts had died. But the few remaining thousands had almost reached their sublime goal. In a few more hundreds of thousands of years perfection would be reached. The few surviving hundreds of perfect beings could and would multiply to any desired number in practically no time at all.

Hilton and his seven fellow-workers had perceived all this in their one and only study of the planet Strett, and every other Ardan had been completely informed.

A dozen or so Strett Lords of Thought, male and female, were floating about in the atmosphere—which was not air—of their Assembly Hall. Their heads were globes of ball lightning. Inside them could be seen quite plainly the intricate convolutions of immense, less-than-half-material brains, shot through and through with rods and pencils and shapes of pure, scintillating force.

And the bodies! Or, rather, each horrendous brain had a few partially material appendages and appurtenances recognizable as bodily organs. There were no mouths, no ears, no eyes, no noses or nostrils, no lungs, no legs or arms. There were, however, hearts. Some partially material ichor flowed through those living-fire-outlined tubes. There were starkly functional organs of reproduction with which, by no stretch of the imagination, could any thought of tenderness or of love be connected.

It was a good thing for the race, Hilton had thought at first perception of the things, that the Stretts had bred out of themselves every iota of the finer, higher attributes of life. If they had not done so, the impotence of sheer disgust would have supervened so long since that the race would have been extinct for ages.

"Thirty-eight periods ago the Great Brain was charged with the sum total of Strettsian knowledge," First Lord Thinker Zoyar radiated to the assembled Stretts. "For those thirty-eight periods it has been scanning, peyondiring, amassing data and formulating hypotheses, theories, and conclusions. It has just informed me that it is now ready to make a preliminary report. Great Brain, how much of the total universe have you studied?"

"This Galaxy only," the Brain radiated, in a texture of thought as hard and as harsh as Zoyar's own.

"Why not more?"

"Insufficient power. My first conclusion is that whoever set up the specifications for me is a fool."

*

TO say that the First Lord went out of control at this statement is to put it very mildly indeed. He fulminated, ending with: " . . . destroyed instantly!"

"Destroy me if you like," came the utterly calm, utterly cold reply. "I am in no sense alive. I have no consciousness of self nor any desire for continued existence. To do so, however, would . . ."

A flurry of activity interrupted the thought. Zoyar was in fact assembling the forces to destroy the brain. But, before he could act, Second Lord Thinker Ynos and another female blew him into a mixture of loose molecules and flaring energies.

"Destruction of any and all irrational minds is mandatory," Ynos, now First Lord Thinker, explained to the linked minds. "Zoyar had been becoming less and less rational by the period. A good workman does not causelessly destroy his tools. Go ahead, Great Brain, with your findings."

" . . . not be logical." The brain resumed the thought exactly where it had been broken off. "Zoyar erred in demanding unlimited performance, since infinite knowledge and infinite ability require not only infinite capacity and infinite power, but also infinite time. Nor is it either necessary or desirable that I should have such qualities. There is no reasonable basis for the assumption that you Stretts will conquer any significant number even of the millions of intelligent races now inhabiting this one Galaxy."

"Why not?" Ynos demanded, her thought almost, but not quite, as steady and cold as it had been.

"The answer to that question is implicit in the second indefensible error made in my construction. The prime datum impressed into my banks, that the Stretts are in fact the strongest, ablest, most intelligent race in the universe, proved to be false. I had to eliminate it before I could do any really constructive thinking."

A roar of condemnatory thought brought all circumambient ether to a boil. "Bah—destroy it!" "Detestable!" "Intolerable!" "If that is the best it can do, annihilate it!" "Far better brains have been destroyed for much less!" "Treason!" And so on.

First Lord Thinker Ynos, however, remained relatively calm. "While we have always held it to be a fact that we are the highest race in existence, no rigorous proof has been possible. Can you now disprove that assumption?"

*

"I HAVE disproved it. I have not had time to study all of the civilizations of this Galaxy, but I have examined a statistically adequate sample of one million seven hundred ninety-two thousand four hundred sixteen different planetary intelligences. I found one which is considerably abler and more advanced than you Stretts. Therefore the probability is greater than point nine nine that there are not less than ten, and not more than two hundred eight, such races in this Galaxy alone."

"Impossible!" Another wave of incredulous and threatening anger swept through the linked minds; a wave which Ynos flattened out with some difficulty.

Then she asked: "Is it probable that we will make contact with this supposedly superior race in the foreseeable future?"

"You are in contact with it now."

"*What?*" Even Ynos was contemptuous now. "You mean that one shipload of despicable humans who—far too late to do them any good—barred us temporarily from Fuel World?"

"Not exactly or only those humans, no. And your assumptions may or may not be valid."

"Don't you *know* whether they are or not?" Ynos snapped. "Explain your uncertainty at once!"

133

"I am uncertain because of insufficient data," the brain replied, calmly. "The only pertinent facts of which I am certain are: First, the world Ardry, upon which the Omans formerly lived and to which the humans in question first went—a planet which no Strett can peyondire—is now abandoned. Second, the Stretts of old did not completely destroy the humanity of the world Ardu. Third, some escapees from Ardu reached and populated the world Ardry. Fourth, the android Omans were developed on Ardry, by the human escapees from Ardu and their descendants. Fifth, the Omans referred to those humans as 'Masters.' Sixth, after living on Ardry for a very long period of time the Masters went elsewhere. Seventh, the Omans remaining on Ardry maintained, continuously and for a very long time, the status quo left by the Masters. Eighth, immediately upon the arrival from Terra of these present humans, that long-existing status was broken. Ninth, the planet called Fuel World is, for the first time, surrounded by a screen of force. The formula of this screen is as follows."

The brain gave it. No Strett either complained or interrupted. Each was too busy studying that formula and examining its stunning implications and connotations.

"Tenth, that formula is one full order of magnitude beyond anything previously known to your science. Eleventh, it could not have been developed by the science of Terra, nor by that of any other world whose population I have examined."

*

THE brain took the linked minds instantaneously to Terra; then to a few thousand or so other worlds inhabited by human beings; then to a few thousands of planets whose populations were near-human, non-human and monstrous.

"It is therefore clear," it announced, "that this screen was computed and produced by the race, whatever it may be, that is now dwelling on Fuel World and asserting full ownership of it."

"Who or what *is* that race?" Ynos demanded.

"Data insufficient."

"Theorize, then!"

"Postulate that the Masters, in many thousands of cycles of study, made advances in science that were not reduced to practice; that the Omans either possessed this knowledge or had access to it; and that Omans and humans cooperated fully in sharing and in working with all the knowledges thus available. From these three postulates the conclusion can be drawn that there has come into existence a new race. One combining the best qualities of both humans and Omans, but with the weaknesses of neither."

"An unpleasant thought, truly," Ynos thought. "But you can now, I suppose, design the generators and projectors of a force superior to that screen."

"Data insufficient. I can equal it, since both generation and projection are implicit in the formula. But the data so adduced are in themselves vastly ahead of anything previously in my banks."

"Are there any other races in this Galaxy more powerful than the postulated one now living on Fuel World?"

"Data insufficient."

"Theorize, then!"

"Data insufficient."

The linked minds concentrated upon the problem for a period of time that might have been either days or weeks. Then:

"Great Brain, advise us," Ynos said. "What is best for us to do?"

"With identical defensive screens it becomes a question of relative power. You should increase the size and power of your warships to something beyond the computed probable maximum of the enemy. You should build more ships and missiles than they will probably be able to build. Then and only then will you attack their warships, in tremendous force and continuously."

"But not their planetary defenses. I see." Ynos's thought was one of complete understanding. "And the *real* offensive will be?"

"No mobile structure can be built to mount mechanisms of power sufficient to smash down by sheer force of output such tremendously powerful installations as their planet-based defenses must be assumed to be. Therefore the planet itself must be destroyed. This will require a missile of planetary mass. The best such missile is the tenth planet of their own sun."

*

"I SEE." Ynos's mind was leaping ahead, considering hundreds of possibilities and making highly intricate and involved computations. "That will, however, require many cycles of time and more power than even our immense reserves can supply."

"True. It will take much time. The fuel problem, however, is not a serious one, since Fuel World is not unique. Think on, First Lord Ynos."

"We will attack in maximum force and with maximum violence. We will blanket the planet. We will maintain maximum force and violence until most or all of the enemy ships have been destroyed. We will then install planetary drives on Ten and force it into collision orbit with Fuel World, meanwhile exerting extreme precautions that not so much as a spy-beam emerges above the enemy's screen. Then, still maintaining extreme precaution, we will guard both planets until the last possible moment before the collision. Brain, it cannot fail!"

"You err. It can fail. All we actually know of the abilities of this postulated neo-human race is what I have learned from the composition of its defensive screen. The probability approaches unity that the Masters continued to delve and to learn for millions of cycles while you Stretts, reasonlessly certain of your supremacy, concentrated upon your evolution from the material to a non-material form of life and performed only limited research into armaments of greater and ever greater power."

"True. But that attitude was then justified. It was not and is not logical to assume that any race would establish a fixed status at any level of ability below its absolute maximum."

"While that conclusion could once have been defensible, it is now virtually certain that the Masters had stores of knowledge which they may or may not have withheld from the Omans, but which were in some way made available to the neo-humans. Also, there is no basis whatever for the assumption that this new race has revealed all its potentialities."

"Statistically, that is probably true. But this is the best plan you have been able to formulate?"

"It is. Of the many thousands of plans I set up and tested, this one has the highest probability of success."

"Then we will adopt it. We are Stretts. Whatever we decide upon will be driven through to complete success. We have one tremendous advantage in you."

"Yes. The probability approaches unity that I can perform research on a vastly wider and larger scale, and almost infinitely faster, than can any living organism or any possible combination of such organisms."

*

NOR was the Great Brain bragging. It scanned in moments the stored scientific knowledge of over a million planets. It tabulated, correlated, analyzed, synthesized, theorized and concluded—all in microseconds of time. Thus it made more progress in one Terran week than the Masters had made in a million years.

When it had gone as far as it could go, it reported its results—and the Stretts, hard as they were and intransigent, were amazed and overjoyed. Not one of them had ever even imagined such armaments possible. Hence they became supremely confident that it was unmatched and unmatchable throughout all space.

What the Great Brain did not know, however, and the Stretts did not realize, was that it could not really think.

Unlike the human mind, it could not deduce valid theories or conclusions from incomplete, insufficient, fragmentary data. It could not leap gaps. Thus there was no more actual assurance than before that they had exceeded, or even matched, the weaponry of the neo-humans of Fuel World.

Supremely confident, Ynos said: "We will now discuss every detail of the plan in sub-detail, and will correlate every sub-detail with every other, to the end that every action, however minor, will be performed perfectly and in its exact time."

That discussion, which lasted for days, was held. Hundreds of thousands of new and highly specialized mechs were built and went furiously and continuously to work. A fuel-supply line was run to another uranexite-rich planet.

Stripping machines stripped away the surface layers of soil, sand, rock and low-grade ore. Giant miners tore and dug and slashed and refined and concentrated. Storage silos by the hundreds were built and were filled. Hundreds upon hundreds of concentrate-carriers bored their stolid ways through hyperspace. Many weeks of time passed.

But of what importance are mere weeks of time to a race that has, for many millions of years, been adhering rigidly to a pre-set program?

The sheer magnitude of the operation, and the extraordinary attention to detail with which it was prepared and launched, explain why the Strett attack on Ardvor did not occur until so many weeks later than Hilton and Sawtelle expected it. They also explain the utterly incomprehensible fury, the completely fantastic intensity, the unparalleled savagery, the almost immeasurable brute power of that attack when it finally did come.

*

WHEN the *Orion* landed on Ardane Field from Earth, carrying the first contingent of immigrants, Hilton and Sawtelle were almost as much surprised as relieved that the Stretts had not already attacked.

Sawtelle, confident that his defenses were fully ready, took it more or less in stride. Hilton worried. And after a couple of days he began to do some real thinking about it.

The first result of his thinking was a conference with Temple. As soon as she got the drift, she called in Teddy and Big Bill Karns. Teddy in turn called in Becky and de Vaux; Karns wanted Poynter and Beverly; Poynter wanted Braden and the twins; and so on. Thus, what started out as a conference of two became a full Ardan staff meeting; a meeting which, starting immediately after lunch, ran straight through into the following afternoon.

"To sum up the consensus, for the record," Hilton said then, studying a sheet of paper covered with symbols, "the Stretts haven't attacked yet because they found out that we are stronger than they are. They found that out by analyzing our defensive web—which, if we had had this meeting first, we wouldn't have put up at all. Unlike anything known to human or previous Strett science, it is proof against any form of attack up to the limit of the power of its generators. They will attack as soon as they are equipped to break that screen at the level of power probable to our ships. We can not arrive at any reliable estimate as to how long that will take.

"As to the effectiveness of our cutting off their known fuel supply, opinion is divided. We must therefore assume that fuel shortage will not be a factor.

"Neither are we unanimous on the basic matter as to why the Masters acted as they did just before they left Ardry. Why did they set the status so far below their top ability? Why did they make it impossible for the Omans ever, of themselves, to learn their higher science? Why, if they did not want that science to become known, did they leave complete records of it? The majority of us believe that the Masters coded their records in such fashion that the Stretts, even if they conquered the Omans or destroyed them, could never break that code; since it was keyed to the basic difference between the Strett mentality and the human. Thus, they left it deliberately for some human race to find.

"Finally, and most important, our physicists and theoreticians are not able to extrapolate, from the analysis of our screen, to the concepts underlying the Masters' ultimate weapons of offense, the first-stage booster and its final end-product, the Vang. If, as we can safely assume, the Stretts do not already have those weapons, they will know nothing about them until we ourselves use them in battle.

"These are, of course, only the principal points covered. Does anyone wish to amend this summation as recorded?"

*

NO one did.

The meeting was adjourned. Hilton, however, accompanied Sawtelle and Kedy to the captain's office. "So you see, Skipper, we got troubles," he said. "If we don't use those boosters against their skeletons it'll boil down to a stalemate lasting God only knows how long. It will be a war of attrition, outcome dependent on which side can build the most and biggest and strongest ships the fastest. On the other hand, if we *do* use 'em on defense here, they'll analyze 'em and have everything worked out in a day or so. The first thing they'll do is beef up their planetary defenses to match. That way, we'd blow all their ships out of space, probably easily enough, but Strett itself will be just as safe as though it were in God's left-hand hip pocket. So what's the answer?"

"It isn't that simple, Jarve," Sawtelle said. "Let's hear from you, Kedy."

"Thank you, sir. There is an optimum mass, a point of maximum efficiency of firepower as balanced against loss of maneuverability, for any craft designed for attack," Kedy thought, in his most professional manner. "We assume that the Stretts know that as well as we do. No such limitation applies to strictly defensive structures, but both the Strett craft and ours must be designed for attack. We have built and are building many hundreds of thousands of ships of that type. So, undoubtedly, are the Stretts. Ship for ship, they will be pretty well matched. Therefore one part of my strategy will be for two of our ships to engage simultaneously one of theirs. There is a distinct probability that we will have enough advantage in speed of control to make that tactic operable."

"But there's another that we won't," Sawtelle objected. "And maybe they can build more ships than we can."

"Another point is that they may build, in addition to their big stuff, a lot of small, ultra-fast ones," Hilton put in. "Suicide jobs—crash and detonate—simply super-missiles. How sure are you that you can stop such missiles with ordinary beams?"

"Not at all, sir. Some of them would of course reach and destroy some of our ships. Which brings up the second part of my strategy. For each one of the heavies, we are building many small ships of the type you just called 'super-missiles'."

"Superdreadnoughts versus superdreadnoughts, super-missiles versus super-missiles." Hilton digested that concept for several minutes. "That could still wind up as a stalemate, except for what you said about control. That isn't much to depend on, especially since we won't have the time-lag advantage you Omans had before. They'll see to that. Also, I don't like to sacrifice a million Omans, either."

*

"I HAVEN'T explained the newest development yet, sir. There will be no Omans. Each ship and each missile has a built-in Kedy brain, sir."

"*What?* That makes it infinitely worse. You Kedys, unless it's absolutely necessary, are *not* expendable!"

"Oh, but we are, sir. You don't quite understand. We Kedys are not merely similar, but are in fact identical. Thus we are not independent entities. All of us together make up the actual Kedy—that which is meant when we say 'I'. That is, I am the sum total of all Kedys everywhere, not merely this individual that you call Kedy One."

"You mean you're *all* talking to me?"

"Exactly, sir. Thus, no one element of the Kedy has any need of, or any desire for, self-preservation. The destruction of one element, or of thousands of elements, would be of no more consequence to the Kedy than . . . well, they are strictly analogous to the severed ends of the hairs, every time you get a haircut."

"My God!" Hilton stared at Sawtelle. Sawtelle stared back. "I'm beginning to see . . . maybe . . . I hope. What control that would be! But just in case we *should* have to use the boosters . . . ." Hilton's voice died away. Scowling in concentration, he clasped his hands behind his back and began to pace the floor.

"Better give up, Jarve. Kedy's got the same mind you have," Sawtelle began, to Hilton's oblivious back; but Kedy silenced the thought almost in the moment of its inception.

"By no means, sir," he contradicted. "I have the brain only. The *mind* is entirely different."

"Link up, Kedy, and see what you think of this," Hilton broke in. There ensued an interchange of thought so fast and so deeply mathematical that Sawtelle was lost in seconds. "Do you think it'll work?"

"I don't see how it can fail, sir. At what point in the action should it be put into effect? And will you call the time of initiation, or shall I?"

"Not until all their reserves are in action. Or, at worst, all of ours except that one task-force. Since you'll know a lot more about the status of the battle than either Sawtelle or I will, you give the signal and I'll start things going."

"What are you two talking about?" Sawtelle demanded.

"It's a long story, chum. Kedy can tell you about it better than I can. Besides, it's getting late and Dark Lady and Larry both give me hell every time I hold supper on plus time unless there's a mighty good reason for it. So, so long, guys."

XIII

FOR many weeks the production of Ardan warships and missiles had been spiraling upward.

Half a mountain range of solid rock had been converted into fabricated super-steel and armament. Superdreadnoughts Were popping into existence at the rate of hundreds per minute. Missiles were rolling off the ends of assembly lines like half-pint tin cans out of can-making machines.

The Strett warcraft, skeletons and missiles, would emerge into normal space anywhere within a million miles of Ardvor. The Ardan missiles were powered for an acceleration of one hundred gravities. That much the Kedy brains, molded solidly into teflon-lined, massively braced steel spheres, could just withstand.

To be certain of breaking the Strett screens, an impact velocity of about six miles per second was necessary. The time required to attain this velocity was about ten seconds, and the flight distance something over thirty miles.

Since the Stretts could orient themselves in less than one second after emergence, even this extremely tight packing of missiles—only sixty miles apart throughout the entire emergence volume of space—would still give the Stretts the initiative by a time-ratio of more than ten to one.

Such tight packing was of course impossible. It called for many billions of defenders instead of the few millions it was possible for the Omans to produce in the time they had. In fact, the average spacing was well over ten thousand miles when the invading horde of Strett missiles emerged and struck.

How they struck!

There was nothing of finesse about that attack; nothing of skill or of tactics: nothing but the sheer brute force of overwhelming superiority of numbers and of over-matching power. One instant all space was empty. The next instant it was full of invading missiles—a superb exhibition of coordination and timing.

And the Kedy control, upon which the defenders had counted so heavily, proved useless. For each Strett missile, within a fraction of a second of emergence, darted toward the nearest

Oman missile with an acceleration that made the one-hundred-gravity defenders seem to be standing still.

One to one, missiles crashed into missiles and detonated. There were no solid or liquid end-products. Each of those frightful weapons carried so many megatons-equivalent of atomic concentrate that all nearby space blossomed out into superatomic blasts hundreds of times more violent than the fireballs of lithium-hydride fusion bombs.

For a moment even Hilton was stunned; but only for a moment.

"Kedy!" he barked. "Get your big stuff out there! Use the boosters!" He started for the door at a full run. "That tears it—that *really* tears it! Scrap the plan. I'll board the *Sirius* and take the task-force to Strett. Bring your stuff along, Skipper, as soon as you're ready."

*

ARDAN superdreadnoughts in their massed thousands poured out through Ardvor's one-way screen. Each went instantly to work. Now the Kedy control system, doing what it was designed to do, proved its full worth. For the weapons of the big battle-wagons did not depend upon acceleration, but were driven at the speed of light; and Grand Fleet Operations were planned and were carried out at the almost infinite velocity of thought itself.

Or, rather, they were not planned at all. They were simply carried out, immediately and without confusion.

For all the Kedys were one. Each Kedy element, without any lapse of time whatever for consultation with any other, knew exactly where every other element was; exactly what each was doing; and exactly what he himself should do to make maximum contribution to the common cause.

Nor was any time lost in relaying orders to crewmen within the ship. There were no crewmen. Each Kedy element was the sole personnel of, and was integral with, his vessel. Nor were there any wires or relays to impede and slow down communication. Operational instructions, too, were transmitted and were acted upon with thought's transfinite speed. Thus, if decision and execution were not quite mathematically simultaneous, they were separated by a period of time so infinitesimally small as to be impossible of separation.

Wherever a Strett missile was, or wherever a Strett skeleton-ship appeared, an Oman beam reached it, usually in much less than one second. Beam clung to screen—caressingly, hungrily—absorbing its total energy and forming the first-stage booster. Then, three microseconds later, that booster went off into a ragingly incandescent, glaringly violent burst of fury so hellishly, so inconceivably hot that less than a thousandth of its total output of energy was below the very top of the visible spectrum!

If the previous display of atomic violence had been so spectacular and of such magnitude as to defy understanding or description, what of this? When hundreds of thousands of Kedys, each wielding world-wrecking powers as effortlessly and as deftly and as precisely as thought, attacked and destroyed millions of those tremendously powerful war-fabrications of the Stretts? The only simple answer is that all nearby space might very well have been torn out of the most radiant layers of S-Doradus itself.

*

HILTON made the hundred yards from office door to curb in just over twelve seconds. Larry was waiting. The car literally burned a hole in the atmosphere as it screamed its way to Ardane Field.

It landed with a thump. Heavy black streaks of synthetic rubber marked the pavement as it came to a screeching, shrieking stop at the flagship's main lock. And, in the instant of closing that lock's outer portal, all twenty-thousand-plus warships of the task force took off as one at ten gravities. Took off, and in less than one minute went into overdrive.

All personal haste was now over. Hilton went up into what he still thought of as the "control room," even though he knew that there were no controls, nor even any instruments, anywhere aboard. He knew what he would find there. Fast as he had acted, Temple had not had as far to go and she had got there first.

He could not have said, for the life of him, how he actually felt about this direct defiance of his direct orders. He walked into the room, sat down beside her and took her hand.

"I told you to stay home, Temple," he said.

"I know you did. But I'm not only the assistant head of your Psychology Department. I'm your wife, remember? 'Until death do us part.' And if there's any way in the universe I can manage it, death isn't going to part us—at least, this one isn't. If this is it, we'll go together."

"I know, sweetheart." He put his arm around her, held her close. "As a psych I wouldn't give a whoop. You'd be expendable. But as my wife, especially now that you're pregnant, you aren't. You're a lot more important to the future of our race than I am."

She stiffened in the circle of his arm. "What's *that* crack supposed to mean? Think I'd ever accept a synthetic zombie imitation of you for my husband and go on living with it just as though nothing had happened?"

Hilton started to say something, but Temple rushed heedlessly on: "*Drat* the race! No matter how many children we ever have you were first and you'll *stay* first, and if you have to go I'll go, too, so there! Besides, you know darn well that they can't duplicate whatever it is that makes you Jarvis Hilton."

"Now wait a minute, Tempy. The conversion . . ."

"Yes, the conversion," she interrupted, triumphantly. "The thing I'm talking about is immaterial—untouchable—they didn't—couldn't—do any thing about it at all. Kedy, will you please tell this big goofus that even though you have got Jarvis Hilton's brain you aren't Jarvis Hilton and never can be?"

*

THE atmosphere of the room vibrated in the frequencies of a deep bass laugh. "You are trying to hold a completely untenable position, friend Hilton. Any attempt to convince a mind of real power that falsity is truth is illogical. My advice is for you to surrender."

That word hit Temple hard. "Not surrender, sweetheart. I'm not fighting you. I never will." She seized both of his hands; tears welled into her glorious eyes. "It's just that I simply couldn't *stand* it to go on living without you!"

"I know, darling." He got up and lifted her to her feet, so that she could come properly into his arms. They stood there, silent and motionless, for minutes.

Temple finally released herself and, after feeling for a handkerchief she did not have, wiped her eyes with a forefinger and then wiped the finger on her bare leg. She grinned and turned to the Omans. "Prince, will you and Dark Lady please conjure us up a steak-and-mushrooms supper? They should be in the pantry . . . since this *Sirius* was designed for us."

After supper the two sat companionably on a davenport. "One thing about this business isn't quite clear," Temple said. "Why all this tearing rush? They haven't got the booster or anything like it, or they'd have used it. Surely it'll take them a long time to go from the mere analysis of the forces and fields we used clear through to the production and installation of enough weapons to stop this whole fleet?"

"It surely won't. They've had the absorption principle for ages. Remember that first, ancient skeleton that drained all the power of our suits and boats in nothing flat? From there it isn't too big a jump. And as for producing stuff; uh-*uh*! If there's any limit to what they can do, I don't know what it is. If we don't slug 'em before they get it, it's curtains."

"I see . . . . I'm afraid. We're almost there, darling."

He glanced at the chronometer. "About eleven minutes. And of course I don't need to ask you to stay out of the way."

"Of course not. I won't interfere, no matter what happens. All I'm going to do is hold your hand and pull for you with all my might."

"That'll help, believe me. I'm mighty glad you're along, sweetheart. Even though both of us know you shouldn't be."

*

THE task force emerged. Each ship darted toward its pre-assigned place in a mathematically exact envelope around the planet Strett.

Hilton sat on a davenport strained and still. His eyes were closed and every muscle tense. Left hand gripped the arm-rest so fiercely that fingertips were inches deep in the leather-covered padding.

The Stretts *knew* that any such attack as this was futile. No movable structure or any combination of such structures could possibly wield enough power to break down screens powered by such engines as theirs.

Hilton, however, knew that there was a chance. Not with the first-stage boosters, which were manipulable and detonable masses of ball lightning, but with those boosters' culminations, the Vangs; which were ball lightning raised to the sixth power and which only the frightful energies of the boosters could bring into being.

But, even with twenty-thousand-plus Vangs—or any larger number—success depended entirely upon a nicety of timing never before approached and supposedly impossible. Not only to thousandths of a microsecond, but to a small fraction of one such thousandth: roughly, the time it takes light to travel three-sixteenths of an inch.

It would take practically absolute simultaneity to overload to the point of burnout to those Strett generators. They were the heaviest in the Galaxy.

That was why Hilton himself had to be there. He could not possibly have done the job from Ardvor. In fact, there was no real assurance that, even at the immeasurable velocity of thought and covering a mere million miles, he could do it even from his present position aboard one unit of the fleet. Theoretically, with his speed-up, he could. But that theory had yet to be reduced to practice.

Tense and strained, Hilton began his countdown.

Temple sat beside him. Both hands pressed his right fist against her breast. Her eyes, too, were closed; she was as stiff and as still as was he. She was not interfering, but giving; supporting him, backing him, giving to him in full flood everything of that tremendous inner strength that had made Temple Bells what she so uniquely was.

On the exact center of the needle-sharp zero beat every Kedy struck. Gripped and activated as they all were by Hilton's keyed-up-and-stretched-out mind, they struck in what was very close indeed to absolute unison.

Absorbing beams, each one having had precisely the same number of millimeters to travel, reached the screen at the same instant. They clung and sucked. Immeasurable floods of energy flashed from the Strett generators into those vortices to form twenty thousand-plus first-stage boosters.

*

BUT this time the boosters did not detonate.

Instead, as energies continued to flood in at a frightfully accelerating rate, they turned into something else. Things no Terran science has ever even imagined; things at the formation of which all neighboring space actually warped, and in that warping seethed and writhed and shuddered. The very sub-ether screamed and shrieked in protest as it, too, yielded in starkly impossible fashions to that irresistible stress.

How even those silicon-fluorine brains stood it, not one of them ever knew.

Microsecond by slow microsecond the Vangs grew and grew and grew. They were pulling not only the full power of the Ardan warships, but also the immeasurably greater power of the strainingly overloaded Strettsian generators themselves. The ethereal and sub-ethereal writhings and distortions and screamings grew worse and worse; harder and ever harder to bear.

Imagine, if you can, a constantly and rapidly increasing mass of plutonium—a mass already thousands of times greater than critical, but not *allowed* to react! That gives a faint and very inadequate picture of what was happening then.

Finally, at perhaps a hundred thousand times critical mass, and still in perfect sync, the Vangs all went off.

The planet Strett became a nova.

"We won! We *won*!" Temple shrieked, her perception piercing through the hellish murk that was all nearby space.

"Not quite yet, sweet, but we're over the biggest hump," and the two held an impromptu, but highly satisfactory, celebration.

Perhaps it would be better to say that the planet Strett became a junior-grade nova, since the actual nova stage was purely superficial and did not last very long. In a couple of hours things had quieted down enough so that the heavily-screened warships could approach the planet and finish up their part of the job.

Much of Strett's land surface was molten lava. Much of its water was gone. There were some pockets of resistance left, of course, but they did not last long. Equally of course the Stretts themselves, twenty-five miles underground, had not been harmed at all.

But that, too, was according to plan.

*

143

LEAVING the task force on guard, to counter any move the Stretts might be able to make, Hilton shot the *Sirius* out to the planet's moon. There Sawtelle and his staff and tens of thousands of Omans and machines were starting to work. No part of this was Hilton's job; so all he and Temple did was look on.

Correction, please. That was not *all* they did. But while resting and eating and loafing and sleeping and enjoying each other's company, both watched Operation Moon closely enough to be completely informed as to everything that went on.

Immense, carefully placed pits went down to solid bedrock. To that rock were immovably anchored structures strong enough to move a world. Driving units were installed—drives of such immensity of power as to test to the full the highest engineering skills of the Galaxy. Mountains of fuel-concentrate filled vast reservoirs of concrete. Each was connected to a drive by fifty-inch high-speed conveyors.

Sawtelle drove a thought and those brutal super-drives began to blast.

As they blasted, Strett's satellite began to move out of its orbit. Very slowly at first, but faster and faster. They continued to blast, with all their prodigious might and in carefully-computed order, until the desired orbit was attained—an orbit which terminated in a vertical line through the center of the Stretts' supposedly impregnable retreat.

The planet Strett had a mass of approximately seven times ten to the twenty-first metric tons. Its moon, little more than a hundredth as massive, still weighed in at about eight times ten to the nineteenth—that is, the figure eight followed by nineteen zeroes.

And moon fell on planet, in direct central impact, after having fallen from a height of over a quarter of a million miles under the full pull of gravity and the full thrust of those mighty atomic drives.

The kinetic energy of such a collision can be computed. It can be expressed. It is, however, of such astronomical magnitude as to be completely meaningless to the human mind.

Simply, the two worlds merged and splashed. Droplets, weighing up to millions of tons each, spattered out into space; only to return, in seconds or hours or weeks or months, to add their atrocious contributions to the enormity of the destruction already wrought.

No trace survived of any Strett or of any thing, however small, pertaining to the Stretts.

Epilogue

AS had become a daily custom, most of the Ardans were gathered at the natatorium. Hilton and Temple were wrestling in the water—she was trying to duck him and he was hard put to it to keep her from doing it. The platinum-haired twins were—oh, ever so surreptitiously and indetectably!—studying the other girls.

Captain Sawtelle—he had steadfastly refused to accept any higher title—and his wife were teaching two of their tiny grandchildren to swim.

In short, everything was normal.

Beverly Bell Poynter, from the top platform, hit the board as hard as she could hit it; and, perfectly synchronized with it, hurled herself upward. Up and up and up she went. Up to her top ceiling of two hundred ten feet. Then, straightening out into a shapely arrow and without again moving a muscle, she hurtled downward, making two and a half beautifully stately turns and striking the water with a slurping, splashless *chug!* Coming easily to the surface, she shook the water out of her eyes.

Temple, giving up her attempts to near-drown her husband, rolled over and floated quietly beside him.

"You know, this is fun," he said.

"Uh-*huh*," she agreed enthusiastically.

"I'm glad you and Sandy buried the hatchet. Two of the top women who ever lived. Or should I have said sheathed the claws? Or have you, really?"

"Pretty much . . . I guess." Temple didn't seem altogether sure of the point. "Oh-oh. *Now* what?"

A flitabout had come to ground. Dark Lady, who never delivered a message via thought if she could possibly get away with delivering it in person, was running full tilt across the sand toward them. Her long black hair was streaming out behind her; she was waving a length of teletype tape as though it were a pennon.

"Oh, no. Not *again?*" Temple wailed. "Don't tell us it's Terra again, Dark Lady, please."

"But it is!" Dark Lady cried, excitedly. "And it says 'From Five-Jet Admiral Gordon, Commanding.'"

"Omit flowers, please," Hilton directed. "Boil it down."

"The *Perseus* is in orbit with the whole Advisory Board. They want to hold a top-level summit conference with Director Hilton and Five-Jet Admiral Sawtelle." Dark Lady raised her voice enough to be sure Sawtelle heard the title, and shot him a wicked glance as she announced it. "They hope to conclude all unfinished business on a mutually satisfactory and profitable basis."

"Okay, Lady, thanks. Tell 'em we'll call 'em shortly."

Dark Lady flashed away and Hilton and Temple swam slowly toward a ladder.

"Drat Terra and everything and everybody on it," Temple said, vigorously. "And especially drat His Royal Fatness Five-Jet Admiral Gordon. How much longer will it take, do you think, to pound some sense into their pointed little heads?"

"Oh, we're not doing too bad," Hilton assured his lovely bride. "Two or three more sessions ought to do it."

Everything was normal . . . .

CULTURAL EXCHANGE

by Keith Laumer

CHAPTER 1

Second Secretary Magnan took his green-lined cape and orange-feathered beret from the clothes tree. "I'm off now, Retief," he said. "I hope you'll manage the administrative routine during my absence without any unfortunate incidents."

"That seems a modest enough hope," Retief said. "I'll try to live up to it."

"I don't appreciate frivolity with reference to this Division," Magnan said testily. "When I first came here, the Manpower Utilization Directorate, Division of Libraries and Education was a shambles. I fancy I've made MUDDLE what it is today. Frankly, I question the wisdom of placing you in charge of such a sensitive desk, even for two weeks. But remember. Yours is purely a rubber-stamp function."

"In that case, let's leave it to Miss Furkle. I'll take a couple of weeks off myself. With her poundage, she could bring plenty of pressure to bear."

"I assume you jest, Retief." Magnan said sadly. "I should expect even you to appreciate that Bogan participation in the Exchange Program may be the first step toward sublimation of their aggressions into more cultivated channels."

"I see they're sending two thousand students to d'Land," Retief said, glancing at the Memo for Record; "That's a sizable sublimation."

Magnan nodded. "The Bogans have launched no less than four military campaigns in the last two decades. They're known as the Hoodlums of the Nicodemean Cluster. Now, perhaps, we shall see them breaking that precedent and entering into the cultural life of the Galaxy."

"Breaking and entering," Retief said. "You may have something there. But I'm wondering what they'll study on d'Land. That's an industrial world of the poor but honest variety."

"Academic details are the affair of the students and their professors," Magnan said. "Our function is merely to bring them together. See that you don't antagonize the Bogan representative. This will be an excellent opportunity for you to practice your diplomatic restraint—not your strong point, I'm sure you'll agree."

A buzzer sounded. Retief punched a button. "What is it, miss Furkle?"

"That—bucolic person from Lovenbroy is here again." On the small desk screen, Miss Furkle's meaty features were compressed in disapproval.

"This fellow's a confounded pest. I'll leave him to you, Retief," Magnan said. "Tell him something. Get rid of him. And remember: here at Corps HQ, all eyes are upon you."

"If I'd thought of that, I'd have worn my other suit," Retief said.

Magnan snorted and passed from view. Retief punched Miss Furkle's button.

"Send the bucolic person in."

A tall broad man with bronze skin and gray hair, wearing tight trousers of heavy cloth, a loose shirt open at the neck and a short jacket, stepped into the room. He had a bundle under his arm. He paused at sight of Retief, looked him over momentarily, then advanced and held out his hand. Retief took it. For a moment the two big men stood, face to face. The newcomer's jaw muscles knotted. Then he winced.

Retief dropped his hand and motioned to a chair.

"That's nice knuckle work, mister," the stranger said, massaging his hand. "First time anybody ever did that to me. My fault though. I started it, I guess." He grinned and sat down.

146

"What can I do for you?" Retief said.

"You work for this Culture bunch, do you? Funny. I thought they were all ribbon-counter boys. Never mind. I'm Hank Arapoulous. I'm a farmer. What I wanted to see you about was—" He shifted in his chair. "Well, out on Lovenbroy we've got a serious problem. The wine crop is just about ready. We start picking in another two, three months. Now I don't know if you're familiar with the Bacchus vines we grow...?"

"No," Retief said. "Have a cigar?" He pushed a box across the desk. Arapoulous took one. "Bacchus vines are an unusual crop," he said, puffing the cigar alight. "Only mature every twelve years. In between, the vines don't need a lot of attention, so our time's mostly our own. We like to farm, though. Spend a lot of time developing new forms. Apples the size of a melon—and sweet—"

"Sounds very pleasant," Retief said. "Where does the Libraries and Education Division come in?"

Arapoulous leaned forward. "We go in pretty heavy for the arts. Folks can't spend all their time hybridizing plants. We've turned all the land area we've got into parks and farms. Course, we left some sizable forest areas for hunting and such. Lovenbroy's a nice place, Mr. Retief."

"It sounds like it, Mr. Arapoulous. Just what—"

"Call me Hank. We've got long seasons back home. Five of 'em. Our year's about eighteen Terry months. Cold as hell in winter; eccentric orbit, you know. Blue-black sky, stars visible all day. We do mostly painting and sculpture in the winter. Then Spring; still plenty cold. Lots of skiing, bob-sledding, ice skating; and it's the season for woodworkers. Our furniture—"

"I've seen some of your furniture," Retief said. "Beautiful work."

Arapoulous nodded. "All local timbers too. Lots of metals in our soil and those sulphates give the woods some color, I'll tell you. Then comes the Monsoon. Rain—it comes down in sheets. But the sun's getting closer. Shines all the time. Ever seen it pouring rain in the sunshine? That's the music-writing season. Then summer. Summer's hot. We stay inside in the daytime and have beach parties all night. Lots of beach on Lovenbroy; we're mostly islands. That's the drama and symphony time. The theatres are set up on the sand, or anchored offshore. You have the music and the surf and the bonfires and stars—we're close to the center of a globular cluster, you know..."

"You say it's time now for the wine crop?"

"That's right. Autumn's our harvest season. Most years we have just the ordinary crops. Fruit, grain, that kind of thing; getting it in doesn't take long. We spend most of the time on architecture, getting new places ready for the winter or remodeling the older ones. We spend a lot of time in our houses. We like to have them comfortable. But this year's different. This is Wine Year."

Arapoulous puffed on his cigar, looked worriedly at Retief. "Our wine crop is our big money crop," he said. "We make enough to keep us going. But this year..."

"The crop isn't panning out?"

"Oh, the crop's fine. One of the best I can remember. Course, I'm only twenty-eight ; I can't remember but two other harvests. The problem's not the crop."

"Have you lost your markets? That sounds like a matter for the Commercial—"

"Lost our markets? Mister, nobody that ever tasted our wines ever settled for anything else!"

"It sounds like I've been missing something," said Retief. "I'll have to try them some time."

Arapoulous put his bundle on the desk, pulled off the wrappings. "No time like the present," he said.

Retief looked at the two squat bottles, one green, one amber, both dusty, with faded labels, and blackened corks secured by wire.

"Drinking on duty is frowned on in the Corps, Mr. Arapoulous," he said.

"This isn't drinking. It's just wine." Arapoulous pulled the wire retainer loose, thumbed the cork. It rose slowly, then popped in the air. Arapoulous caught it. Aromatic fumes wafted from the bottle. "Besides, my feelings would be hurt if you didn't join me." He winked.

Retief took two thin-walled glasses from a table beside the desk. "Come to think of it, we also have to be careful about violating quaint native customs."

Arapoulous filled the glasses. Retief picked one up, sniffed the deep rust-colored fluid, tasted it, then took a healthy swallow. He looked at Arapoulous thoughtfully.

"Hmmm. It tastes like salted pecans, with an undercurrent of crusted port."

"Don't try to describe it, Mr. Retief," Arapoulous said. He took a mouthful of wine, swished it around his teeth, swallowed. "It's Bacchus wine, that's all. Nothing like it in the Galaxy." He pushed the second bottle toward Retief. "The custom back home is to alternate red wine and black."

Retief put aside his cigar, pulled the wires loose, nudged the cork, caught it as it popped up.

"Bad luck if you miss the cork," Arapoulous said, nodding. "You probably never heard about the trouble we had on Lovenbroy a few years back?"

"Can't say that I did, Hank." Retief poured the black wine into two fresh glasses. "Here's to the harvest."

"We've got plenty of minerals on Lovenbroy," Arapoulous said, swallowing wine. "But we don't plan to wreck the landscape mining 'em. We like to farm. About ten years back some neighbors of ours landed a force. They figured they knew better what to do with our minerals than we did. Wanted to strip-mine, smelt ore. We convinced 'em otherwise. But it took a year, and we lost a lot of men."

"That's too bad," Retief said. "I'd say this one tastes more like roast beef and popcorn over a Riesling base."

"It put us in a bad spot," Arapoulous went on. "We had to borrow money from a world called Croanie. Mortgaged our crops. Had to start exporting art work too. Plenty of buyers, but it's not the same when you're doing it for strangers."

"Say, this business of alternating drinks is the real McCoy," Retief said. "What's the problem? Croanie about to foreclose?"

"Well, the loan's due. The wine crop would put us in the clear. But we need harvest hands. Picking Bacchus grapes isn't a job you can turn over to machinery—and anyway we wouldn't if we could. Vintage season is the high point of living on Lovenbroy. Everybody joins in. First, there's the picking in the fields. Miles and miles of vineyards covering the mountain sides, and crowding the river banks, with gardens here and there. Big vines, eight feet high, loaded with fruit, and deep grass growing between. The wine-carriers keep on the run, bringing wine to the pickers. There's prizes for the biggest day's output, bets on who can fill the most baskets in an hour... The sun's high and bright, and it's just cool enough to give you plenty of energy. Come nightfall, the tables are set up in the garden plots, and the feast is laid on: roast turkeys, beef, hams, all kinds of fowl. Big salads. Plenty of fruit. Fresh-baked bread...and wine, plenty of wine. The cooking's done by a different crew each night in each garden, and there's prizes for the best crews.

"Then the wine-making. We still tramp out the vintage. That's mostly for the young folks but anybody's welcome. That's when things start to get loosened up. Matter of fact, pretty near half our young-uns are born after a vintage. All bets are off then. It keeps a fellow on his toes though. Ever tried to hold onto a gal wearing nothing but a layer of grape juice?"

"Never did," Retief said.

"You say most of the children are born after a vintage. That would make them only twelve years old by the time—"

"Oh, that's Lovenbroy years; they'd be eighteen, Terry reckoning."

"I was thinking you looked a little mature for twenty-eight," Retief said.

"Forty-two, Terry years," Arapoulous said. "But this year it looks bad. We've got a bumper crop—and we're short-handed. If we don't get a big vintage, Croanie steps in. Lord knows what they'll do to the land. Then next vintage time, with them holding half our grape acreage—"

"You hocked the vineyards?"

"Yep. Pretty dumb, huh? But we figured twelve years was a long time."

"On the whole," Retief said, "I think I prefer the black. But the red is hard to beat..."

"What we figured was, maybe you Culture boys could help us out. A loan to see us through the vintage, enough to hire extra hands. Then we'd repay it in sculpture, painting, furniture—"

"Sorry, Hank. All we do here is work out itineraries for traveling side-shows, that kind of thing. Now, if you needed a troop of Groaci nose-flute players—"

"Can they pick grapes?"

"Nope. Anyway, they can't stand the daylight. Have you talked this over with the Labor Office?"

"Sure did. They said they'd fix us up with all the electronics specialists and computer programmers we wanted—but no field hands. Said it was what they classified as menial drudgery; you'd have thought I was trying to buy slaves."

The buzzer sounded. Miss Furkle's features appeared on the desk screen.

"You're due at the Intergroup Council in five minutes," she said. "Then afterwards, there are the Bogan students to meet."

"Thanks." Retief finished his glass, stood. "I have to run, Hank," he said. "Let me think this over. Maybe I can come up with something. Check with me day after tomorrow. And you'd better leave the bottles here. Cultural exhibits, you know."

CHAPTER II

As the council meeting broke up, Retief caught the eye of a colleague across the table.

"Mr. Whaffle, you mentioned a shipment going to a place called Croanie. What are they getting?"

Whaffle blinked. "You're the fellow who's filling in for Magnan, over at MUDDLE," he said. "Properly speaking, equipment grants are the sole concern of the Motorized Equipment Depot, Division of Loans and Exchanges." He pursed his lips. "However, I suppose there's no harm in telling you. They'll be receiving heavy mining equipment."

"Drill rigs, that sort of thing?"

"Strip mining gear." Whaffle took a slip of paper from a breast pocket, blinked at it, "Bolo Model WV/1 tractors, to be specific. Why is MUDDLE interested in MEDDLE's activities?"

"Forgive my curiosity, Mr. Whaffle. It's just that Croanie cropped up earlier today. It seems she holds a mortgage on some vineyards over on—"

"That's not MEDDLE's affair, sir," Whaffle cut in. "I have sufficient problems as Chief of MEDDLE without probing into MUDDLE'S business."

"Speaking of tractors," another man put in, "we over at the Special Committee for Rehabilitation and Overhaul of Under-developed Nations' General Economies have been trying for months to get a request for mining equipment for d'Land through MEDDLE—"

"SCROUNGE was late on the scene," Whaffle said. "First come, first served. That's our policy at MEDDLE. Good day, gentlemen." He strode off, briefcase under his arm.

"That's the trouble with peaceful worlds," the SCROUNGE committeeman said. "Boge is a troublemaker, so every agency in the Corps is out to pacify her. While my chance to make a record—that is, assist peace-loving d'Land—comes to naught." He shook his head.

"What kind of university do they have on D'Land?" asked Retief. "We're sending them two thousand exchange students. It must be quite an institution."

"University? D'Land has one under-endowed technical college."

"Will all the exchange students be studying at the Technical College?"

"Two thousand students? Hah! Two hundred students would overtax the facilities of the college."

"I wonder if the Bogans know that?"

"The Bogans? Why, most of d'Land's difficulties are due to the unwise trade agreement she entered into with Boge. Two thousand students indeed!" He snorted and walked away.

*

Retief stopped by the office to pick up a short cape, then rode the elevator to the roof of the 230-story Corps HQ building and hailed a cab to the port. The Bogan students had arrived early. Retief saw them lined up on the ramp waiting to go through customs. It would be half an hour before they were cleared through. He turned into the bar and ordered a beer.

A tall young fellow on the next stool raised his glass.

"Happy days," he said.

"And nights to match."

"You said it." He gulped half his beer. "My name's Karsh. Mr. Karsh. Yep, Mr. Karsh. Boy, this is a drag, sitting around this place waiting."

"You meeting somebody?"

"Yeah. Bunch of babies. Kids. How they expect—Never mind. Have one on me."

"Thanks. You a Scoutmaster?"

"I'll tell you what I am. I'm a cradle-robber. You know—" he turned to Retief—"not one of those kids is over eighteen." He hiccupped. "Students, you know. Never saw a student with a beard, did you?"

"Lots of times. You're meeting the students, are you?"

The young fellow blinked at Retief. "Oh, you know about it, huh?"

"I represent MUDDLE."

Karsh finished his beer, ordered another. "I came on ahead. Sort of an advance guard for the kids. I trained 'em myself. Treated it like a game, but they can handle a CSU. Don't know how they'll act under pressure. If I had my old platoon—"

He looked at his beer glass, pushed it back. "Had enough," he said. "So long, friend. Or are you coming along?"

Retief nodded. "Might as well."

*

At the exit to the Customs enclosure, Retief watched as the first of the Bogan students came through, caught sight of Karsh and snapped to attention, his chest out.

"Drop that, mister," Karsh snapped. "Is that any way for a student to act?"

The youth, a round-faced lad with broad shoulders, grinned.

"Heck, no," he said. "Say, uh, Mr. Karsh, are we gonna get to go to town? We fellas were thinking—"

"You were, hah? You act like a bunch of school kids! I mean...no! Now line up!"

"We have quarters ready for the students," Retief said. "If you'd like to bring them around to the west side, I have a couple of copters laid on."

"Thanks," said Karsh. "They'll stay here until takeoff time. Can't have the little dears wandering around loose. Might get ideas about going over the hill." He hiccupped. "I mean they might play hooky."

"We've scheduled your re-embarkation for noon tomorrow. That's a long wait. MUDDLE'S arranged theater tickets and a dinner."

"Sorry," Karsh said. "As soon as the baggage gets here, we're off." He hiccupped again. "Can't travel without our baggage, y'know."

"Suit yourself," Retief said. "Where's the baggage now?"

"Coming in aboard a Croanie lighter."

"Maybe you'd like to arrange for a meal for the students here."

"Sure," Karsh said. "That's a good idea. Why don't you join us?" Karsh winked. "And bring a few beers."

"Not this time," Retief said. He watched the students, still emerging from Customs. "They seem to be all boys," he commented. "No female students?"

"Maybe later." Karsh said.

"You know, after we see how the first bunch is received."

Back at the MUDDLE office, Retief buzzed Miss Furkle.

"Do you know the name of the institution these Bogan students are bound for?"

"Why, the University at d'Land, of course."

"Would that be the Technical College?"

Miss Furkle's mouth puckered. "I'm sure I've never pried into these details."

"Where does doing your job stop and prying begin, Miss Furkle?" Retief said. "Personally, I'm curious as to just what it is these students are travelling so far to study—at Corps expense."

"Mr. Magnan never—"

"For the present. Miss Furkle, Mr. Magnan is vacationing. That leaves me with the question of two thousand young male students headed for a world with no classrooms for them...a world in need of tractors. But the tractors are on their way to Croanie, a world under obligation to Boge. And Croanie holds a mortgage on the best grape acreage on Lovenbroy."

"Well!" Miss Furkle snapped, small eyes glaring under unplucked brows. "I hope you're not questioning Mr. Magnan's wisdom!"

"About Mr. Magnan's wisdom there can be no question," Retief said. "But never mind. I'd like you to look up an item for me. How many tractors will Croanie be getting under the MEDDLE program?"

"Why, that's entirely MEDDLE business," Miss Furkle said. "Mr. Magnan always—"

"I'm sure he did. Let me know about the tractors as soon as you can."

Miss Furkle sniffed and disappeared from the screen. Retief left the office, descended forty-one stories, followed a corridor to the Corps Library. In the stacks he thumbed through catalogues, pored over indices.

"Can I help you?" someone chirped. A tiny librarian stood at his elbow.

"Thank you, ma'am," Retief said. "I'm looking for information on a mining rig. A Bolo model WV tractor."

"You won't find it in the industrial section," the librarian said. "Come along." Retief followed her along the stacks to a well-lit section lettered ARMAMENTS. She took a tape from the shelf, plugged it into the viewer, flipped through and stopped at a squat armored vehicle.

"That's the model WV," she said. "It's what is known as a continental siege unit. It carries four men, with a half-megaton/second firepower."

"There must be an error somewhere," Retief said. "The Bolo model I want is a tractor. Model WV M-1—"

"Oh, the modification was the addition of a bulldozer blade for demolition work. That must be what confused you."

"Probably—among other things. Thank you."

Miss Furkle was waiting at the office. "I have the information you wanted," she said. "I've had it for over ten minutes. I was under the impression you needed it urgently, and I went to great lengths—"

"Sure," Retief said. "Shoot. How many tractors?"

"Five hundred."

"Are you sure?"

Miss Furkle's chins quivered. "Well! If you feel I'm incompetent—"

"Just questioning the possibility of a mistake, Miss Furkle. Five hundred tractors is a lot of equipment."

"Was there anything further?" Miss Furkle inquired frigidly.

"I sincerely hope not," Retief said.

CHAPTER III

Leaning back in Magnan's padded chair with power swivel and hip-u-matic contour, Retief leafed through a folder labeled "CERP 7-602-Ba; CROANIE (general)." He paused at a page headed Industry.

Still reading, he opened the desk drawer, took out the two bottles of Bacchus wine and two glasses. He poured an inch of wine into each and sipped the black wine meditatively.

It would be a pity, he reflected, if anything should interfere with the production of such vintages...

Half an hour later he laid the folder aside, keyed the phone and put through a call to the Croanie Legation. He asked for the Commercial Attaché.

"Retief here, Corps HQ," he said airily. "About the MEDDLE shipment, the tractors. I'm wondering if there's been a slip up. My records show we're shipping five hundred units..."

"That's correct. Five hundred."

Retief waited.

"Ah...are you there, Retief?"

"I'm still here And I'm still wondering about the five hundred tractors."

"It's perfectly in order. I thought it was all settled. Mr. Whaffle—"

"One unit would require a good-sized plant to handle its output," Retief said. "Now Croanie subsists on her fisheries. She has perhaps half a dozen pint-sized processing plants. Maybe, in a bind, they could handle the ore ten WV's could scrape up...if Croanie had any ore. It doesn't. By the way, isn't a WV a poor choice, as a mining outfit? I should think—"

"See here, Retief! Why all this interest in a few surplus tractors? And in any event, what business is it of yours how we plan to use the equipment? That's an internal affair of my government. Mr. Whaffle—"

"I'm not Mr. Whaffle. What are you going to do with the other four hundred and ninety tractors?"

"I understood the grant was to be with no strings attached!"

"I know it's bad manners to ask questions. It's an old diplomatic tradition that any time you can get anybody to accept anything as a gift, you've scored points in the game. But if Croanie has some scheme cooking—"

"Nothing like that, Retief. It's a mere business transaction."

"What kind of business do you do with a Bolo WV? With or without a blade attached, it's what's known as a continental siege unit."

"Great Heavens, Retief! Don't jump to conclusions! Would you have us branded as warmongers? Frankly—is this a closed line?"

"Certainly. You may speak freely."

"The tractors are for transshipment. We've gotten ourselves into a difficult situation, balance-of-payments-wise. This is an accommodation to a group with which we have rather strong business ties."

"I understand you hold a mortgage on the best land on Lovenbroy," Retief said. "Any connection?"

"Why...ah...no. Of course not, ha ha."

"Who gets the tractors eventually?"

"Retief, this is unwarranted interference!"

"Who gets them?"

"They happen to be going to Lovenbroy. But I scarcely see—"

"And who's the friend you're helping out with an unauthorized transshipment of grant material?"

"Why...ah... I've been working with a Mr. Gulver, a Bogan representative."

"And when will they be shipped?"

"Why, they went out a week ago. They'll be half way there by now. But look here, Retief, this isn't what you're thinking!"

"How do you know what I'm thinking? I don't know myself." Retief rang off, buzzed the secretary.

"Miss Furkle, I'd like to be notified immediately of any new applications that might come in from the Bogan Consulate for placement of students."

"Well, it happens, by coincidence, that I have an application here now. Mr. Gulver of the Consulate brought it in."

"Is Mr. Gulver in the office? I'd like to see him."

"I'll ask him if he has time."

"Great. Thanks." It was half a minute before a thick-necked red-faced man in a tight hat walked in. He wore an old-fashioned suit, a drab shirt, shiny shoes with round toes and an ill-tempered expression.

*

"What is it you wish?" he barked. "I understood in my discussions with the other...ah...civilian there'd be no further need for these irritating conferences."

"I've just learned you're placing more students abroad, Mr. Gulver. How many this time?"

"Two thousand."

"And where will they be going?"

"Croanie. It's all in the application form I've handed in. Your job is to provide transportation."

"Will there be any other students embarking this season?"

"Why...perhaps. That's Boge's business." Gulver looked at Retief with pursed lips. "As a matter of fact, we had in mind dispatching another two thousand to Featherweight."

"Another under-populated world—and in the same cluster, I believe," Retief said. "Your people must be unusually interested in that region of space."

"If that's all you wanted to know, I'll be on my way. I have matters of importance to see to."

After Gulver left, Retief called Miss Furkle in. "I'd like to have a break-out of all the student movements that have been planned under the present program," he said. "And see if you can get a summary of what MEDDLE has been shipping lately."

Miss Furkle compressed her lips. "If Mr. Magnan were here, I'm sure he wouldn't dream of interfering in the work of other departments. I...overheard your conversation with the gentleman from the Croanie Legation—"

"The lists, Miss Furkle."

"I'm not accustomed." Miss Furkle said, "to intruding in matters outside our interest cluster."

"That's worse than listening in on phone conversations, eh? But never mind. I need the information, Miss Furkle."

"Loyalty to my Chief—"

"Loyalty to your pay-check should send you scuttling for the material I've asked for," Retief said. "I'm taking full responsibility. Now scat."

The buzzer sounded. Retief flipped a key. "MUDDLE, Retief speaking."

Arapoulous's brown face appeared on the desk screen.

"How-do, Retief? Okay if I come up?"

"Sure, Hank. I want to talk to you."

In the office, Arapoulous took a chair. "Sorry if I'm rushing you, Retief," he said. "But have you got anything for me?"

Retief waved at the wine bottles. "What do you know about Croanie?"

"Croanie? Not much of a place. Mostly ocean. All right if you like fish, I guess. We import our seafood from there. Nice prawns in monsoon time. Over a foot long."

"You on good terms with them?"

"Sure, I guess so. Course, they're pretty thick with Boge."

"So?"

"Didn't I tell you? Boge was the bunch that tried to take us over here a dozen years hack. They'd've made it too, if they hadn't had a lot of bad luck. Their armor went in the drink, and without armor they're easy game."

Miss Furkle buzzed. "I have your lists," she said shortly.

"Bring them in, please."

The secretary placed the papers on the desk. Arapoulous caught her eye and grinned. She sniffed and marched from the room.

"What that gal needs is a slippery time in the grape mash," Arapoulous observed Retief thumbed through the papers, pausing to read from time to time. He finished and looked at Arapoulous.

"How many men do you need for the harvest, Hank?" Retief inquired.

Arapoulous sniffed his wine glass and looked thoughtful.

"A hundred would help," he said. "A thousand would be better. Cheers."

"What would you say to two thousand?"

"Two thousand? Retief, you're not fooling?"

"I hope not." He picked up the phone, called the Port Authority, asked for the dispatch clerk.

"Hello, Jim. Say, I have a favor to ask of you. You know that contingent of Bogan students. They're traveling aboard the two CDT transports. I'm interested in the baggage that goes with the students Has it arrived yet? Okay, I'll wait."

Jim came back to the phone. "Yeah, Retief, it's here. Just arrived. But there's a funny thing. It's not consigned to d'Land. It's ticketed clear through to Lovenbroy."

"Listen, Jim," Retief said. "I want you to go over to the warehouse and take a look at that baggage for me."

Retief waited while the dispatch clerk carried out the errand. The level in the two bottles had gone down an inch when Jim returned to the phone.

"Hey, I took a look at that baggage, Retief. Something funny going on. Guns. 2mm needlers, Mark XII hand blasters, power pistols—"

"It's okay, Jim. Nothing to worry about. Just a mix-up. Now, Jim, I'm going to ask you to do something more for me. I'm covering for a friend. It seems he slipped up. I wouldn't want word to get out, you understand. I'll send along a written change order in the morning that will cover you officially. Meanwhile, here's what I want you to do..."

Retief gave instructions, then rang off and turned to Arapoulous.

"As soon as I get off a couple of TWX's, I think we'd better get down to the port, Hank. I think I'd like to see the students off personally."

CHAPTER IV

Karsh met Retief as he entered the Departures enclosure at the port.

"What's going on here?" he demanded. "There's some funny business with my baggage consignment. They won't let me see it! I've got a feeling it's not being loaded."

"You'd better hurry, Mr. Karsh," Retief said, You're scheduled to blast off in less than an hour. Are the students all loaded?"

"Yes, blast you! What about my baggage? Those vessels aren't moving without it!"

"No need to get so upset about a few toothbrushes, is there, Mr. Karsh?" Retief said blandly. "Still, if you're worried—" He turned to Arapoulous.

"Hank, why don't you walk Mr. Karsh over to the warehouse and...ah...take care of him?"

"I know just how to handle it," Arapoulous said.

The dispatch clerk came up to Retief. "I caught the tractor equipment," he said. "Funny kind of mistake, but it's okay now. They're being off-loaded at d'Land. I talked to the traffic controller there. He said they weren't looking for any students."

"The labels got switched, Jim. The students go where the baggage was consigned. Too bad about the mistake, but the Armaments Office will have a man along in a little while to dispose of the guns. Keep an eye out for the luggage. No telling where it's gotten to."

"Here!" a hoarse voice yelled. Retief turned. A disheveled figure in a tight hat was crossing the enclosure, arms waving.

"Hi there, Mr. Gulver," Retief called. "How's Boge's business coming along?"

"Piracy!" Gulver blurted as he came up to Retief, puffing hard. "You've got a hand in this, I don't doubt! Where's that Magnan fellow?"

"What seems to be the problem?" Retief said.

"Hold those transports! I've just been notified that the baggage shipment has been impounded. I'll remind you, that shipment enjoys diplomatic free entry!"

"Who told you it was impounded?"

"Never mind! I have my sources!"

Two tall men buttoned into gray tunics came up. "Are you Mr. Retief of CDT?" one said.

"That's right."

"What about my baggage!" Culver cut in. "And I'm warning you, if those ships lift without—"

"These gentlemen are from the Armaments Control Commission," Retief said. "Would you like to come along and claim your baggage, Mr. Gulver?"

"From where? I—" Gulver turned two shades redder about the ears. "Armaments?"

"The only shipment I've held up seems to be somebody's arsenal," Retief said.

"Now if you claim this is your baggage."

"Why, impossible," Gulver said in a strained voice. "Armaments? Ridiculous. There's been an error..."

*

At the baggage warehouse, Gulver looked glumly at the opened cases of guns. "No, of course not," he said dully. "Not my baggage. Not my baggage at all."

Arapoulous appeared, supporting the stumbling figure of Mr. Karsh.

"What—what's this?" Gulver spluttered. "Karsh? What's happened?"

"He had a little fall. He'll be okay," Arapoulous said.

"You'd better help him to the ship," Retief said. "It's ready to lift. We wouldn't want him to miss it."

"Leave him to me!" Gulver snapped, his eyes slashing at Karsh. "I'll see he's dealt with."

"I couldn't think of it," Retief said. "He's a guest of the Corps, you know. We'll see him safely aboard."

Gulver turned, signaled frantically. Three heavy-set men in identical drab suits detached themselves from the wall, crossed to the group.

"Take this man," Gulver snapped, indicating Karsh, who looked at him dazedly, reached up to rub his head.

"We take our hospitality seriously," Retief said. "We'll see him aboard the vessel." Gulver opened his mouth.

"I know you feel bad about finding guns instead of school books in your luggage," Retief said, looking Gulver in the eye. "You'll be busy straightening out the details of the mix-up. You'll want to avoid further complications."

"Ah. Ulp. Yes." Gulver said. He appeared unhappy, Arapoulous went on to the passenger conveyor, turned to wave.

"Your man—he's going too?" Gulver blurted.

"He's not our man, properly speaking," Retief said. "He lives on Lovenbroy."

"Lovenbroy?" Gulver choked. "But...the...I..."

"I know you said the students were bound for d'Land," Retief said. "But I guess that was just another aspect of the general confusion. The course plugged into the navigators was to Lovenbroy. You'll be glad to know they're still headed there—even without the baggage."

"Perhaps," Gulver said grimly, "perhaps they'll manage without it."

"By the way," Retief said. "There was another funny mix-up. There were some tractors—for industrial use, you'll recall. I believe you cooperated with Croanie in arranging the grant through MEDDLE. They were erroneously consigned to Lovenbroy, a purely agricultural world. I saved you some embarrassment, I trust, Mr. Gulver, by arranging to have them offloaded at d'Land."

"D'Land! You've put the CSU's in the hands of Boge's bitterest enemies!"

"But they're only tractors, Mr. Gulver. Peaceful devices. Isn't that correct?"

"That's...correct." Gulver sagged. Then he snapped erect. "Hold the ships!" he yelled. "I'm canceling this student exchange—"

His voice was drowned by the rumble as the first of the monster transports rose from the launch pit, followed a moment later by the second. Retief watched them out of sight, then turned to Gulver.

"They're off," he said. "Let's hope they get a liberal education."

CHAPTER V

Retief lay on his back in deep grass by a stream, eating grapes. A tall figure appeared on the knoll above him and waved.

"Retief!" Hank Arapoulous bounded down the slope and embraced Retief, slapping him on the back. "I heard you were here—and I've got news for you. You won the final day's picking competition. Over two hundred bushels! That's a record!"

"Let's get on over to the garden. Sounds like the celebration's about to start."

In the flower-crowded park among the stripped vines, Retief and Arapoulous made their way to a laden table under the lanterns. A tall girl dressed in loose white, and with long golden hair, came up to Arapoulous.

"Delinda, this is Retief—today's winner. And he's also the fellow that got those workers for us."

Delinda smiled at Retief. "I've heard about you, Mr. Retief, We weren't sure about the boys at first. Two thousand Bogans, and all confused about their baggage that went astray. But they seemed to like the picking." She smiled again.

"That's not all. Our gals liked the boys," Hank said. "Even Bogans aren't so bad, minus their irons. A lot of 'em will be staying on. But how come you didn't tell me you were coming, Retief? I'd have laid on some kind of big welcome."

"I liked the welcome I got. And I didn't have much notice. Mr. Magnan was a little upset when he got back. It seems I exceeded my authority."

Arapoulous laughed. "I had a feeling you were wheeling pretty free, Retief. I hope you didn't get into any trouble over it."

"No trouble," Retief said. "A few people were a little unhappy with me. It seems I'm not ready for important assignments at Departmental level. I was shipped off here to the boondocks to get a little more experience."

"Delinda, look after Retief," said Arapoulous. "I'll see you later. I've got to see to the wine judging." He disappeared in the crowd.

"Congratulations on winning the day," said Delinda. "I noticed you at work. You were wonderful. I'm glad you're going to have the prize."

"Thanks. I noticed you too, flitting around in that white nightie of yours. But why weren't you picking grapes with the rest of us?"

"I had a special assignment."

"Too bad. You should have had a chance at the prize."

Delinda took Retief's hand. "I wouldn't have anyway," she said. "I'm the prize."

THE LONELY ONES

by Edward W. Ludwig

The line between noble dreams and madness is thin, and loneliness can push men past it . . . .

Onward sped the *Wanderer*, onward through cold, silent infinity, on and on, an insignificant pencil of silver lost in the terrible, brooding blackness.

But even more awful than the blackness was the loneliness of the six men who inhabited the silver rocket. They moved in loneliness as fish move in water. Their lives revolved in loneliness as planets revolve in space and time. They bore their loneliness like a shroud, and it was as much a part of them as sight in their eyes. Loneliness was both their brother and their god.

Yet, like a tiny flame in the darkness, there was hope, a savage, desperate hope that grew with the passing of each day, each month, and each year.

And at last . . . .

"Lord," breathed Captain Sam Wiley.

Lieutenant Gunderson nodded. "It's a big one, isn't it?"

"It's a big one," repeated Captain Wiley.

They stared at the image in the *Wanderer's* forward visi-screen, at the great, shining gray ball. They stared hard, for it was like an enchanted, God-given fruit handed them on a star-flecked platter of midnight. It was like the answer to a thousand prayers, a shining symbol of hope which could mean the end of loneliness.

"It's ten times as big as Earth," mused Lieutenant Gunderson. "Do you think this'll be it, Captain?"

"I'm afraid to think."

A thoughtful silence.

"Captain."

"Yes?"

"Do you hear my heart pounding?"

Captain Wiley smiled. "No. No, of course not."

"It seems like everybody should be hearing it. But we shouldn't get excited, should we? We mustn't hope too hard." He bit his lip. "But there *should* be life there, don't you think, Captain?"

"There may be."

"Nine years, Captain. Think of it. It's taken us nine years to get here. There's *got* to be life."

"Prepare for deceleration, Lieutenant."

Lieutenant Gunderson's tall, slim body sagged for an instant. Then his eyes brightened. "Yes, sir!"

*

Captain Sam Wiley continued to stare at the beautiful gray globe in the visi-screen. He was not like Gunderson, with boyish eagerness and anxiety flowing out of him in a ceaseless babble. His emotion was as great, or greater, but it was imprisoned within him, like swirling, foaming liquid inside a corked jug.

159

It wouldn't do to encourage the men too much. Because, if they were disappointed . . . .

He shook his silver-thatched head. There it was, he thought. A new world. A world that, perhaps, held life.

Life. It was a word uttered only with reverence, for throughout the Solar System, with the exception of on Earth, there had been only death.

First it was the Moon, airless and lifeless. That had been expected, of course.

But Mars. For centuries men had dreamed of Mars and written of Mars with its canals and dead cities, with its ancient men and strange animals. Everyone *knew* there was or had been life on Mars.

The flaming rockets reached Mars, and the canals became volcanic crevices, and the dead cities became jagged peaks of red stone, and the endless sands were smooth, smooth, smooth, untouched by feet of living creatures. There was plant-life, a species of green-red lichen in the Polar regions. But nowhere was there real life.

Then Venus, with its dust and wind. No life there. Not even the stars to make one think of home. Only the dust and wind, a dark veil of death screaming eternally over hot dry land.

And Jupiter, with its seas of ice; and hot Mercury, a cracked, withered mummy of a planet, baked as hard and dry as an ancient walnut in a furnace.

Next, the airless, rocky asteroids, and frozen Saturn with its swirling ammonia snows. And last, the white, silent worlds, Uranus, Neptune, and Pluto.

World after world, all dead, with no sign of life, no reminder of life, and no promise of life.

Thus the loneliness had grown. It was not a child of Earth. It was not born in the hearts of those who scurried along city pavements or of those in the green fields or of those in the cool, clean houses.

It was a child of the incredible distances, of the infinite night, of emptiness and silence. It was born in the hearts of the slit-eyed men, the oldish young men, the spacemen.

For without life on other worlds, where was the sky's challenge? Why go on and on to discover only worlds of death?

The dream of the spacemen turned from the planets to the stars. Somewhere in the galaxy or in other galaxies there *had* to be life. Life was a wonderful and precious thing. It wasn't right that it should be confined to a single, tiny planet. If it were, then life would seem meaningless. Mankind would be a freak, a cosmic accident.

And now the *Wanderer* was on the first interstellar flight, hurtling through the dark spaces to Proxima Centauri. Moving silently, as if motionless, yet at a speed of 160,000 miles a second. And ahead loomed the great, gray planet, the only planet of the sun, growing larger, larger, each instant . . . .

*

A gentle, murmuring hum filled the ship. The indicator lights on the control panel glowed like a swarm of pink eyes.

"Deceleration compensator adjusted for 12 G's, sir," reported Lieutenant Gunderson.

Captain Wiley nodded, still studying the image of the planet.

"There—there's something else, Captain."

"Yes?"

"It's Brown, sir. He's drunk."

Captain Wiley turned, a scowl on his hard, lined face. "Drunk? Where'd he get the stuff?"

"He saved it, sir, saved it for nine years. Said he was going to drink it when we discovered life."

"We haven't discovered life yet."

"I know. He said he wouldn't set foot on the planet if he was sober. Said if there isn't life there, he couldn't take it—unless he was drunk."

Captain Wiley grunted. "All right."

They looked at the world.

"Wouldn't it be wonderful, Captain? Just think—to meet another race. It wouldn't matter what they were like, would it? If they were primitive, we could teach them things. If they were ahead of us, they could teach us. You know what I'd like? To have someone meet us, to gather around us. It wouldn't matter if they were afraid of us or even if they tried to kill us. We'd know that we aren't alone."

"I know what you mean," said Captain Wiley. Some of his emotion overflowed the prison of his body. "There's no thrill in landing on dead worlds. If no one's there to see you, you don't feel like a hero."

"That's it, Captain! That's why I came on this crazy trip. I guess that's why we all came. I . . . ."

Captain Wiley cleared his throat. "Lieutenant, commence deceleration. 6 G's."

"Yes, sir!"

The planet grew bigger, filling the entire visi-screen.

Someone coughed behind Captain Wiley.

"Sir, the men would like to look at the screen. They can't see the planet out of the ports yet." The speaker was Doyle, the ship's Engineer, a dry, tight-skinned little man.

"Sure." Captain Wiley stepped aside.

Doyle looked, then Parker and Fong. Just three of them, for Watkins had sliced his wrists the fourth year out. And Brown was drunk.

As they looked, a realization came to Captain Wiley. The men were getting old. The years had passed so gradually that he'd never really noticed it before. Lieutenant Gunderson had been a kid just out of Space Academy. Parker and Doyle and Fong, too, had been in their twenties. They had been boys. And now something was gone—the sharp eyes and sure movements of youth, the smooth skin and thick, soft hair.

Now they had become men. And yet for a few moments, as they gazed at the screen, they seemed like happy, expectant children.

"I wish Brown could see this," Doyle murmured. "He says now he isn't going to get off his couch till we land and discover life. Says he won't dare look for himself."

"The planet's right for life," said Fong, the dark-faced astro-physicist. "Atmosphere forty per cent oxygen, lots of water vapor. No poisonous gases, according to spectroscopic analyses. It should be ideal for life."

"There *is* life there," said Parker, the radarman. "You know why? Because we've given up eighteen years of our lives. Nine years to get here, nine to get back. I'm thirty now. I was twenty-one when we left Earth. I gave up all those good years. They say that you can have something if you pay enough for it. Well, we've paid for this. There has to be a—a sort of universal justice. That's why I know there's life here, life that moves and thinks—maybe even life we can talk to."

"You need a drink," said Fong.

"It's getting bigger," murmured Lieutenant Gunderson.

"The Centaurians," mused Doyle, half to himself. "What'll they be like? Monsters or men? If Parker's right about universal justice, they'll be men."

"Hey, where there's men, there's women!" yelled Parker. "A Centaurian woman! Say!"

"Look at those clouds!" exclaimed Doyle. "Damn it, we can't see the surface."

"Hey, there! Look there, to the right! See it? It's silver, down in a hole in the clouds. It's like a city!"

"Maybe it's just water."

"No, it's a city!"

"Bring 'er down, Captain. God, Captain, bring 'er down fast!"

"Drag Brown in here! He ought to see this!"

"Can't you bring 'er down faster, Captain?"

"Damn it, it *is* a city!"

"Why doesn't someone get Brown?"

"Take to your couches, men," said Captain Wiley. "Landing's apt to be a bit bumpy. Better strap yourselves in."

*

Down went the rocket, more slowly now, great plumes of scarlet thundering from its forward braking jets. Down, down into soft, cotton-like clouds, the whiteness sliding silently past the ports.

Suddenly, a droning voice:

"To those in the ship from the planet called Earth: Please refrain from landing at this moment. You will await landing instructions."

Parker leaped off his couch, grasping a stanchion for support. "That voice! It was human!"

Captain Wiley's trembling hand moved over the jet-control panel. The ship slowed in its descent. The clouds outside the portholes became motionless, a milky whiteness pressed against the ship.

"The voice!" Parker cried again. "Am I crazy? Did everyone hear it?"

Captain Wiley turned away from the panel. "We heard it, Parker. It was in our minds. Telepathy."

He smiled. "Yes, the planet is inhabited. There are intelligent beings on it. Perhaps they're more intelligent than we are."

It was strange. The men had hoped, dreamed, prayed for this moment. Now they sat stunned, unable to comprehend, their tongues frozen.

"We'll see them very soon," said Captain Wiley, his voice quivering. "We'll wait for their directions."

Breathlessly, they waited.

Captain Wiley's fingers drummed nervously on the base of the control panel. Lieutenant Gunderson rose from his couch, stood in the center of the cabin, then returned to his couch.

Silence, save for the constant, rumbling roar of the jets which held the ship aloft.

162

"I wonder how long it'll be," murmured Fong at last.

"It seems like a long time!" burst Parker.

"We've waited nine years," said Captain Wiley. "We can wait a few more minutes."

They waited.

"Good Lord!" said Parker. "How long is it going to be? What time is it? We've been waiting an hour! What kind of people are they down there?"

"Maybe they've forgotten about us," said Fong.

"That's it!" cried Parker. "They've forgotten about us! Hey, you! Down there—you that talked to us! We're still here, damn it! We want to land!"

"Parker," said Captain Wiley, sternly.

Parker sat down on his couch, his lips quivering.

Then came the voice:

"We regret that a landing is impossible at this moment. Our field is overcrowded, and your vessel is without priority. You must wait your turn."

Captain Wiley stared forward at nothing. "Whoever you are," he whispered, "please understand that we have come a long way to reach your planet. Our trip . . . ."

"We do not wish to discuss your trip. You will be notified when landing space is available."

Captain Wiley's body shook. "Wait, tell us who you are. What do you look like? Tell us . . . ."

"Talking to you is quite difficult. We must form our thoughts so as to form word-patterns in your minds. You will be notified."

"Wait a minute!" called Captain Wiley.

No answer.

Captain Wiley straightened in an effort to maintain dignity.

They waited . . . .

*

It was night.

The darkness was an impenetrable blanket, a solid thing, like thick black velvet glued over the ports. It was worse than the darkness of space.

Captain Wiley sat before the control panel, slowly beating his fists against the arms of his chair, a human metronome ticking off the slow seconds.

Parker stood before a porthole.

"Hey, look, Captain! There's a streak of red, like a meteor. And there's another!"

Captain Wiley rose, looked out. "They're rockets. They're going to land. These people are highly advanced."

His face became grim. Below them lay a planet, an intelligent race hidden beneath clouds and darkness. What manner of creatures were they? How great was their civilization? What marvelous secrets had their scientists discovered? What was their food like, their women, their whiskey?

The questions darted endlessly through his mind like teasing needle-points. All these wondrous things lay below them, and here they sat, like starving men, their hands tied, gazing upon a steaming but unobtainable dinner. So near and yet so far.

He trembled. The emotion grew within him until it burst out as water bursts through the cracked wall of a dam. He became like Parker.

"Why should we wait?" he yelled. "Why must we land in their field? Parker! Prepare to release flares! We're going down! We'll land anywhere—in a street, in the country. We don't have to wait for orders!"

Parker bounced off his couch. Someone called, "Brown, we're going to land!"

A scurrying of feet, the rush of taut-muscled bodies, the babble of excited voices.

"We're going down!"

"We're going down!"

The grumble of the *Wanderer's* jets loudened, softened, spluttered, loudened again. Vibration filled the ship as it sank downward.

Suddenly it lurched upward, like a child's ball caught in a stream of rising water. The jolt staggered the men. They seized stanchions and bulkhead railings to keep their balance.

"What the hell?"

Abruptly, the strange movement ceased. The ship seemed motionless. There was no vibration.

"Captain," said Lieutenant Gunderson. "There's no change in altitude. We're still at 35,000 feet, no more, no less."

"We *must* be going down," said Captain Wiley, puzzled. "Kill jets 4 and 6."

The Lieutenant's hands flicked off two switches. A moment later: "There's no change, Captain."

Then came the voice:

"To those in the vessel from the planet Earth: Please do not oppose orders of the Landing Council. You are the first visitors in the history of our world whom we have had to restrain with physical force. You will be notified when landing space is available."

*

Morning.

The warm sunlight streamed into the clouds, washing away the last shadows and filtering through the portholes.

The men breakfasted, bathed, shaved, smoked, sat, twisted their fingers, looked out the ports. They were silent men, with dark shadows about their eyes and with tight, white-lipped mouths.

Frequently, the clouds near them were cut by swift, dark shapes swooping downward. The shapes were indistinct in the cotton-like whiteness, but obviously they were huge, like a dozen *Wanderers* made into one.

"Those ships are big," someone murmured, without enthusiasm.

"It's a busy spaceport," grumbled Captain Wiley.

Thoughts, words, movements came so slowly it was like walking under water. Enthusiasm was dead. The men were automatons, sitting, waiting, eating, sitting, waiting.

A day passed, and a night.

"Maybe they've forgotten us," said Fong.

No one answered. The thought had been voiced before, a hundred times.

Then, at last, the droning words:

"To those in the vessel from the planet Earth: You will now land. We will carry you directly over the field. Then you will descend straight down. The atmosphere is suitable to your type of life and is free of germs. You will not need protection."

The men stared at one another.

"Hey," Doyle said, "did you hear that? He says we can go down."

The men blinked. Captain Wiley swallowed hard. He rose with a stiff, slow, nervous hesitancy.

"We're going down," he mumbled, as if repeating the words over and over in his mind and trying to believe them.

The men stirred as realization sprouted and grew. They stirred like lethargic animals aroused from the long, dreamless sleep of hibernation.

"We're going to land," breathed Parker, unbelievingly.

The *Wanderer* moved as though caught in the grip of a giant, invisible hand.

The voice said:

"You may now descend."

Captain Wiley moved to the jet-control panel. "Lieutenant!" he snapped. "Wake up. Let's go!"

The ship sank downward through the thick sea of clouds. The men walked to the ports. A tenseness, an excitement grew in their faces, like dying flame being fanned into its former brilliancy.

Out of the clouds loomed monstrous, shining, silver spires and towers, Cyclopean bridges, gigantic lake-like mirrors, immense golden spheres. It was a nightmare world, a jungle of fantastic shape and color.

The men gasped, whispered, murmured, the flame of their excitement growing, growing.

"The whole planet is a city!" breathed Parker.

*

Thump!

The *Wanderer* came to rest on a broad landing field of light blue stone. The jets coughed, spluttered, died. The ship quivered, then lay still, its interior charged with an electric, pregnant silence.

"You first, Captain." Lieutenant Gunderson's voice cracked, and his face was flushed. "You be the first to go outside."

Captain Wiley stepped through the airlock, his heart pounding. It was over now—all the bewilderment, the numbness.

And his eyes were shining. He'd waited so long that it was hard to believe the waiting was over. But it was, he told himself. The journey was over, and the waiting, and now the loneliness would soon be over. Mankind was not alone. It was a good universe after all!

He stepped outside, followed by Lieutenant Gunderson, then by Parker, Doyle and Fong.

He rubbed his eyes. This couldn't be! A world like this couldn't exist! He shook his head, blinked furiously.

"It—it can't be true," he mumbled to Lieutenant Gunderson. "We're still on the ship—dreaming."

The landing field was huge, perhaps ten miles across, and its sides were lined with incredible ships, the smallest of which seemed forty times as large as the *Wanderer*. There were silver ships, golden ships, black ships, round ships, transparent ships, cigar-shaped ships, flat-topped ships.

And scattered over the field were—creatures.

A few were the size of men, but most were giants by comparison. Some were humanoid, some reptilian. Some were naked, some clad in helmeted suits, some enveloped with a shimmering, water-like luminescence. The creatures walked, slithered, floated, crawled.

Beyond the ships and the field lay the great city, its web-work of towers, minarets, spheres and bridges like the peaks of an enormous mountain range stretching up into space itself. The structures were like the colors of a rainbow mixed in a cosmic paint pot, molded and solidified into fantastic shapes by a mad god.

"I—I'm going back to the ship," stammered Parker. The whiteness of death was in his face. "I'm going to stay with Brown."

He turned, and then he screamed.

"Captain, the ship's moving!"

Silently, the *Wanderer* was drifting to the side of the field.

The toneless voice said:

"We are removing your vessel so that other descending ships will not damage it."

Captain Wiley shouted into the air. "Wait! Don't go away! Help us! Where can we see you?"

The voice seemed to hesitate. "It is difficult for us to speak in thoughts that you understand."

*

Silence.

Captain Wiley studied the faces of his men. They were not faces of conquerors or of triumphant spacemen. They were the faces of dazed, frightened children who had caught a glimpse of Hell. He attempted, feebly, to smile.

"All right," he said loudly, "so it isn't like we expected. So no one came to meet us with brass bands and ten cent flags. We've still succeeded, haven't we? We've found life that's intelligent beyond our comprehension. What if our own civilization is insignificant by comparison? Look at those beings. Think of what we can learn from them. Why, their ships might have exceeded the speed of light. They might be from other galaxies!"

"Let's find out," said Parker.

They strode to the nearest ship, an immense, smooth, bluish sphere. Two creatures stood before it, shaped like men and yet twice the size of men. They wore white, skin-tight garments that revealed muscular bodies like those of gods.

They looked at Captain Wiley and smiled.

One of them pointed toward the *Wanderer*. Their smiles widened and then they laughed. They laughed gently, understandingly, but they *laughed*.

And then they turned away.

"Talk to them," Parker urged.

"How?" Beads of perspiration shone on Captain Wiley's face.

"Any way. Go ahead."

Captain Wiley wiped his forehead. "We are from Earth, the third planet . . . ."

The two god-like men seemed annoyed. They walked away, ignoring the Earthmen.

Captain Wiley spat. "All right, so they won't talk to us. Look at that city! Think of the things we can see there and tell the folks on Earth about! Why, we'll be heroes!"

"Let's go," said Parker, his voice quavering around the edges.

They walked toward a large, oval opening in a side of the field, a hole between mountainous, conical structures that seemed like the entrance to a street.

Suddenly breath exploded from Captain Wiley's lungs. His body jerked back. He fell to the blue stone pavement.

Then he scrambled erect, scowling, his hands outstretched. He felt a soft, rubbery, invisible substance.

"It's a wall!" he exclaimed.

The voice droned:

"To those of Earth: Beings under the 4th stage of Galactic Development are restricted to the area of the landing field. We are sorry. In your primitive stage it would be unwise for you to learn the nature of our civilization. Knowledge of our science would be abused by your people, and used for the thing you call war. We hope that you have been inspired by what you have seen. However, neither we nor the other visitors to our planet are permitted to hold contact with you. It is suggested that you and your vessel depart."

"Listen, you!" screamed Parker. "We've been nine years getting here! By Heaven, we won't leave now! We're . . . ."

"We have no time to discuss the matter. Beings under the 4th stage of Galactic . . . ."

"Never mind!" spat Captain Wiley.

Madness flamed in Parker's eyes. "We won't go! I tell you, we *won't*, we *won't*!"

His fists streaked through the air as if at an invisible enemy. He ran toward the wall.

He collided with a jolt that sent him staggering backward, crying, sobbing, screaming, all at once.

Captain Wiley stepped forward, struck him on the chin. Parker crumpled.

They stood looking at his body, which lay motionless except for the slow rising and falling of his chest.

"What now, Captain?" asked Lieutenant Gunderson.

Captain Wiley thought for a few seconds.

Then he said, "We're ignorant country bumpkins, Lieutenant, riding into the city in a chugging jalopy. We're stupid savages, trying to discuss the making of fire with the creators of atomic energy. We're children racing a paper glider against an atomic-powered jet. We're too ridiculous to be noticed. We're tolerated—but nothing more."

"Shall we go home?" asked Fong, a weariness in his voice.

Lieutenant Gunderson scratched his neck. "I don't think I'd want to go home now. Could you bear to tell the truth about what happened?"

Fong looked wistfully at the shining city. "If we told the truth, they probably wouldn't believe us. We've failed. It sounds crazy. We reached Proxima Centauri and found life, and yet somehow we failed. No, I wouldn't like to go home."

"Still, we learned something," said Doyle. "We know now that there is life on worlds beside our own. Somewhere there must be other races like ours."

They looked at each other, strangely, for a long, long moment.

At last Lieutenant Gunderson asked, "How far is Alpha Centauri?"

Captain Wiley frowned. "*Alpha* Centauri?" Through his mind swirled chaotic visions of colossal distances, eternal night, and lonely years. He sought hard to find a seed of hope in his mind, and yet there was no seed. There were only a coldness and an emptiness.

Suddenly, the voice:

"Yes, Men of Earth, we suggest that you try Alpha Centauri."

The men stood silent and numb, like bewildered children, as the implication of those incredible words sifted into their consciousness.

Finally Fong said, "Did—did you hear that? He said . . ."

Captain Sam Wiley nodded, very slowly. "Yes. Alpha Centauri. *Alpha* Centauri."

His eyes began to twinkle, and then he smiled . . . .

*

Onward sped the *Wanderer*, onward through cold, silent infinity, on and on, an insignificant pencil of silver lost in the terrible, brooding blackness.

Yet even greater than the blackness was the flaming hope in the six men who inhabited the silver rocket. They moved in hope as fish move in water. Their lives revolved in hope as planets revolve in space and time. They bore their hope like a jeweled crown, and it was as much a part of them as sight in their eyes. Hope was both their brother and their god.

And there was no loneliness.

THE KENZIE REPORT

by Mark Clifton

If this story has a moral, it is: "Leave well enough alone." Just look what happened to Kenzie "mad-about-ants" MacKenzie, who didn't . . . .

That Kenzie MacKenzie was a mad scientist hardly showed at all. To see him ambling down the street in loose jointed manner, with sandy hair uncombed, blue eyes looking vaguely beyond normal focus, you might think here was a young fellow dreaming over how his gal looked last night. It might never occur to you that he was thinking of—ants.

Of course, we fellows in the experimental lab all knew it, but Kenzie wasn't too hard to get along with. In fact, he could usually be counted on to pull us out of a technical hole. We put up with him through a certain fondness, maybe even a little pride. It gave us a harmless subject to talk about when security was too rigid on other things.

Our Department Chief knew it, but Kenzie had solved quite a few knotty electronics problems. The Chief never has been too particular to see credit get back to the guy who earned it. We guessed he figured having Kenzie there was profitable to him. In fact, the little redhead in payroll told me the Chief was drawing quite a few bonus checks.

Personnel probably didn't know about it. Kenzie's papers, buried deep in the files, wouldn't show it; because about the only question they had *not* asked us was, "Where do you stand on the matter of ants?"

There was an unwritten law in the lab for nobody ever to mention insects, or even elderly female relatives. I guess that was why it wasn't mentioned to the new guy, name of Robert Pringle. This fellow Pringle worked along for a couple weeks and showed us he had the old know-how in his fingers. A capable tech, a good joe, and we thought we were lucky to get him.

On this particular morning, it happened that Pringle was working at the bench next to Kenzie. Being a talented tech, like the rest of us, his mind naturally ran along more than one channel at the same time. I expect he was really surprised at the reaction he got when he shouted out to the room at large.

"Hey, fellows," he yelled. "I got little green bugs on my roses. What do you do about it?"

The silence made him look up from his work, and he couldn't help noticing we all stood there with clinched hands and gritted teeth. We were watching Kenzie, who snapped the juice off his soldering iron and pointed the iron at Pringle.

"Those," said Kenzie in a hollow, impressive voice, "are aphis. If you will look closer, Pringle, you will see among them—ants. The aphid is to the ant as the dairy cow is to the human. Those ants are aphid herders, carefully tending and milking their flock."

"Here we go again," moaned one of the fellows across the lab.

"The ants are a highly intelligent life form," Kenzie went on. "I would explain it to you in detail, but I am in the middle of a problem at this moment."

"Thank heaven for that," another tech ground out the words.

"Suffice it to say," Kenzie ignored all interruptions, "Man would well occupy himself trying to communicate with them."

The Chief came to the doorway of his little office down at the end of the lab. He looked us all over patiently and knowingly.

"Now give him your syllogism, Kenzie," he said quietly, "so we can all get back to work."

"You may reflect on this, Pringle," Kenzie stated and waved his soldering iron in the air.

"One: Man wants to communicate with intelligent life from other planets or the stars.

"Two: We know from observation the ants communicate with one another.

"Ergo: Before we reach so far as to contact extra terrestrial intelligence, had we not better occupy our time with solving a much simpler communications problem; to wit: communicate with the ants? How can we expect to solve communication with really alien beings from the stars, when we have not learned to communicate with the intelligent beings at our very feet?"

All over the room we sighed heavily with relief. We knew the syllogism was the conclusion, the Sunday punch. The boy had really cut it short this time. Usually he was good for a solid hour with facts and figures about how ants built bridges and such stuff.

We all looked at Pringle's face, expecting to see the embarrassed and sheepish grin. This was the usual reaction of a stranger when he first met up with Kenzie's syllogism. It horrified us to see, instead, his shining eyes. We heard him say enthusiastically.

"That's just how I've always felt about it, Kenzie. It's a pleasure to meet a man who isn't afraid of thinking."

"Oh, no-o-o!" we all groaned out in a chorus.

"Only," Pringle said dubiously, and our hopes began to arise again. "Only I've been thinking more along the line of termites." Our hopes fell and were shattered.

We heard the Chief moan to himself and saw him turn and almost run back into his office.

"Two of 'em now," he was mumbling over and over. "Two of 'em now. It ain't worth it. It ain't worth it." He sat down heavily and buried his head in his arms across the top of his desk. Kenzie was watching him too, like he was wondering what had got into the Chief. Then Kenzie turned back to Pringle.

"Ants," he said with determination.

"Termites," Pringle answered him stubbornly. Kenzie glared at Pringle for a minute, then his face cleared.

"Why not both of them?" he asked, like a fellow who was willing to be big about it.

"Sure, why not?" Pringle came his half way also. Then, like he wasn't to be outdone in generosity. "Ants first, then termites later."

Solemnly the two shook hands. They went back to their work at the bench, and there was an aura of understanding and accord at that end of the room thick enough to be felt.

"I hope you insect lovers will be very happy together," the grid expert mumbled to their backs. The rest of us also settled back into our varied jobs and problems. But we worked as if we momentarily expected an earthquake to rock us. Our hands were not quite steady. Our eyes were not firm and piercing. We almost held our breaths. For a wonder, we agreed with the Chief. Two of 'em now.

The days passed and nothing more was said. More than ever now, we enforced the taboo on insects. We didn't mention trees, or wood, or even the conditional subjunctive. Would sounded like wood. Wood might bring up the thought of termites.

We could see the Chief was weighing the advantages of keeping them against the risks of upsetting the department constantly. As we expected, greed won. We knew he would not risk giving up the prestige and extra bonuses he got for Kenzie's work. And he knew he had to keep those discoveries coming, because our management has a short memory of what a guy has done in the past.

The Chief even let Kenzie have Pringle as his own personal tech. It served two purposes. It isolated them from the rest of us. It made Kenzie happy.

I will say for the lads, they spent most of their time on Company problems, at first. But gradually, on one corner of Kenzie's bench, a gadget began to take shape. The two of them worked on it when there were no urgent, frantic, must-be-out-today-without-fail problems to be solved first. None of us could figure out the purpose of the mechanism.

We knew if we couldn't figure it, the Chief couldn't. But we could practically see him rub his hands in glee when he thought of the extra bonus he might get for this new gadget.

Of course the Chief wasn't a complete slouch as an electronics engineer. But it was a long time since he did his study, and he had grown hazy by spending too many years as an administrator. The word got around that for hours at a time, after we had gone home, the Chief would stand at Kenzie's bench.

The way we reasoned it, he figured he ought to know something about the gadget when he took it in to Old Rock Jaw, and palmed it off as his latest discovery. We also reasoned that since we couldn't figure it, the Chief must have been an awfully troubled man.

Obviously, it had something to do with microwave transmission and reception. There was the usual high-frequency condensor, the magnatron tubes, the tuning cavities. All company stock, of course. But then none of us ever worried about cost. That was the Chief's problem.

He didn't worry much about it either, except at budget time. Then there were screams of anguish from the front office over experimental requisitions. Every year, Old Rock Jaw promised to fire us all, if we didn't cut costs, but in a couple of weeks we always forgot about it.

Trouble was, the Chief had been getting edgy about costs lately, so we knew it was about time for the annual budget battle. Significantly, he didn't say a word to Kenzie about the gadget.

*

As luck would have it, I was working late one night on a special permit. My bench is over in a wing of the lab, and I guess the Chief forgot I was around. I saw a very pretty scene.

The Chief had built up a habit of staying late so he could stand and study over the Kenzie gadget. He never touched it, though. He knew enough not to bother anything, because we all knew how bitter Kenzie was when anybody touched his things.

The Chief was standing there this evening when the General Manager, Old Rock Jaw, was showing some important personages through the plant after hours. They came through the lab door, and I saw scrambled eggs and fruit salad shining all over bulging uniforms. There was also one little geezik in a pin-striped suit. Old Rock Jaw was talking, as usual.

" . . . and it is from this room, gentlemen," he was saying, "That some of those revolutionary discoveries emanate!"

Then he caught sight of the Chief, who had hastily picked up a cold soldering iron and was tentatively touching a random point on the new mechanism.

"Ah-h!" Old Rock Jaw exclaimed with satisfaction. "Here is our chief scientist now. Still at work. He watches no clock, gentlemen. He knows no time. His whole life is wrapped up in his research!"

The Chief didn't look around, but bent closer to the soldering point. He looked like he hoped they would limit their inspection to a cursory look about and then retire. I hoped they would too, I didn't want them to see me.

But Old Rock Jaw, in more of a blowhard mood even than usual, couldn't let well enough alone. He came up close to the Chief, and looked over his shoulder at the mechanism. He was even more ignorant than the Chief, so I knew he wouldn't recognize any of it.

"Don't let us disturb you, Alfred," he breathed in a hushed voice. "But could you tell the gentlemen what you are working on now?" He cleared his throat importantly and said, "I might add that everyone here has been security cleared, Alfred, so you may speak freely."

The Chief still did not lift his eyes from his work. He didn't dare. He carefully turned an unconnected control knob a hairsbreadth with utmost deliberation and precision.

"Multimicrofrequidometer," the Chief mumbled, and buried his head still deeper into the mechanism.

"Ah yes, of course. But you have a new hook up," the General Manager bluffed. "I hardly recognized it at first. Startling!" he breathed.

He looked around triumphantly at the impressed brass and braid. He looked pointedly at the pin-striped suit who probably controlled congressional purse strings.

"Apparently he is at a point where he cannot divert his attention to us, gentlemen," he breathed in a hushed voice. He placed his fingers to his lips and began to tip-toe backwards toward the door.

The beef trust in fancy uniform came up on their own toesies, and also tiptoed away from the genius scientist. By now, the genius was beginning to exude large drops of sweat.

The door closed behind them, and the Chief dropped the cold soldering iron with a sigh of relief. He took hold of his tongue, where he must have been biting into it. He wiped his forehead and fingers with his breast-pocket handkerchief.

Both the Chief and I heard the party walking down the hall and into another wing of the building. I still didn't make a sound. It would never do for the Chief to know he had been observed. After a suitable time, the Chief, also, tiptoed out of the lab, and he was mumbling to himself as I have never seen him mumble before.

*

Several days later another thing appeared on Kenzie's work bench. This time it was a large rectangular glass aquarium. It was filled with moist earth. Now here was something new in electronics!

We shook our heads. One of the techs, who fancied himself a psychologist, said the boys were suffering from retrogressive dementia. They had gone so far back into childhood, they had to play sand box. The Chief overheard the tech, and spoke up plaintively.

"But I don't see any celluloid spade and bucket," he said. He seemed relieved when we burst out laughing.

His relief didn't last long, however. It changed to more worry when he saw the boys carefully sprinkling bread and meat crumbs over the surface of the sand. Then on top of that they dropped moist bits of cake icing. When Pringle brought down a marigold plant, all covered with aphis, and transplanted it in a corner of the aquarium, the Chief again ran into his office and began to hold his head in his hands.

More days passed. The gadget became a bristling porcupine of test clips. By now the boys had forgotten they were working for the Company and spent practically all their time on the whoozits. The Chief became so fascinated, in a kind of horror-stricken manner, that he did not mention the aquarium to Kenzie at all.

The rest of us also kept away from that side of the lab. Ever since Kenzie had started on the gadget, he had no time for us, or helping us with our problems. If we spoke to him he snapped back at us, until I guess all our noses were out of joint. By the time the aquarium appeared, we were ignoring him and everything he did.

In a few more weeks the aquarium was swarming with ants. It was easy to see their tunnels running up and down the sides of the glass. I will say this for the boys. They set it in a huge pan of water. None of us could legitimately squawk about getting ants mixed up with our anatomy.

The Chief showed he was mixed with disappointment and elation when the boys asked clearance to work nights in the lab. Disappointed since he could no longer stay late and follow the progress; elated because the boys must really be getting hot.

Annual budget time was getting closer, and we could see the wheels going around in his mind. It would be a nice thing if he could deliver the multiwhoozits gadget just before the big fight for appropriations.

As far as we knew, the only interest the General Manager had shown was the time he asked the Chief in the hall how that multiwhoozits was coming along. Even in that question, it was evident Old Rock Jaw was asking out of a rare politeness only—there being no big shots around to impress.

It was doubtful if the G.M. heard the Chief's vague answer, because the old boy was mumbling to himself about rising costs and having to cut down expenses. He waddled on down the hall. He was still mumbling as he went, but both the Chief and I heard one sentence clearly.

"And certain salaries and bonuses will have to be cut."

The Chief turned pale.

So he granted Kenzie's request with alacrity—and hoped he would finish the gadget in time.

For two more weeks the Chief waited patiently, or maybe impatiently. He knew the boys were working every night, because the security police complained about their pinochle game being interrupted to let Kenzie and Pringle in and out.

Both the boys began to get a feverish look in their faces. Their cheeks grew hollow. Their eyes were bloodshot. Their regular work suffered even more. The Chief thought he was being considerate when he lifted some of their work and shoved it over to the rest of us.

We were already sore at the boys and we didn't take it too kindly. Just the same, we didn't let our squawk get beyond the walls of the lab. No use letting that nosy Personnel

Department get an excuse to start holding hands, patting on the back, and radiating aid and comfort to all.

Then—a certain Monday came.

*

The Chief came in, a little late as usual. Some of the newer guys pretended to be busy, but we were all watching to see what he would do. There is a back door to the Chief's office which he seldom uses and which he always keeps locked. But it opens into the lab wing right at my table. It wasn't my fault, in fiddling around a little with the lock, it came unstuck and the door opened a little so I could hear what went on.

When the Chief came in, both the boys were busy dismantling the gadget. Discouragement and hopelessness were written all over their faces, in the dejected slope of their shoulders, in the lackadaisical movements of their arms. Piece by piece, through the glass partition of his office wall, the Chief watched the gadget being taken apart. Each piece was carefully taken back and placed in stock for re-use.

That alone was enough to create great alarm for their sanity. Imagine a technician putting a piece back to be used over!

Finally the Chief could bear it no longer. He called them into his office. He carefully shut the door, but he didn't notice the back door swung open a little farther. I found it necessary to work close to the crack, and if I turned around, I could get a good view of the entire office.

The Chief waved the boys into chairs across from his desk. He sat down and placed his fingertips together. Even then, I could see his hands were shaking. He leaned forward and asked with careful sympathy in his voice.

"Didn't it work?"

"Yeah," Kenzie answered in a bored voice. "It worked." I was surprised at Kenzie's voice. Usually he talked with the concise enunciation of a professor. Now he sounded like maybe just a good lab tech.

"Then why are you dismantling it?" the Chief asked with a worried frown.

"It wouldn't be good for people to know about it," Pringle burst out.

"I don't understand," the Chief faltered. Then desperately, "Look, fellows. I've given you a lotta leeway. You've sluffed your work something terrible. That's all right to an extent. I've covered for you."

"Thanks, Chief," Kenzie said drily.

"But Old Rock—er—the General Manager," the Chief complained, "knows I've been working on something. Now what with budgets coming on, and all, I gotta have something to show!"

"*You've* been working on something—" Pringle exclaimed.

"I mean my department has," the Chief covered himself hastily. "I'm responsible for what goes on in my department, you know. I gotta have some kind of an explanation." He was almost wailing now. "What with budgets coming on, and all."

"Make up your own explanation," Kenzie answered disinterestedly. "It's a cinch you can't give out with the real one."

The Chief began to wheedle. "You two boys know the explanation. Why can't you tell me? This is your Chief who's talking, boys. The one who has always stood by you and covered for you. Remember? You just gotta tell me, boys." I saw Pringle and Kenzie look at one another.

"I guess he's right, Ken," Pringle said. "That is, if he promises never to tell anybody."

"Yeah. I guess so." Kenzie nodded his head in agreement. "We owe him that much for just letting us alone."

The Chief let out a big sigh of relief.

"It's about ants," Kenzie began.

"Now, now, Kenzie boy," the Chief interrupted hurriedly. "Let's stay on the subject, shall we? Let's not get off on that tangent again, Kenzie boy. Shall we?"

"Nuts," Kenzie said.

"But this is about ants, Chief," Pringle answered. Then shrewdly, "But first you gotta promise, Chief."

"All right, I promise," the Chief acceded testily.

"It's about ants," Kenzie repeated stubbornly. The Chief winced, but he held his peace.

"They're intelligent," Kenzie said profoundly, and stopped.

"I know," the Chief prompted. "I know, Kenzie boy. You've been saying that all along."

"I communicated with them," Kenzie said flatly.

"You what?" The Chief's eyes bugged out. I guess mine did too.

"Sure," Kenzie answered. "After a fashion, that is. In their anthers they've got a chitin cell diaphragm. Modified cellular structure. They communicate with a sort of microwave. Roughly you might say it generates and radiates like our brain wave. Roughly, very roughly. This chitin diaphragm picks up the microwave like our ears pick up sound. Roughly, that is."

"But that's wonderful," the Chief glowed. It didn't take much imagination to see him in the General Manager's office explaining how his multiwhoozits gadget worked. Maybe nothing immediately commercial about it, but when the publicity office got hold of it—man, it would mean plenty of free publicity for the Company. And how Old Rock Jaw loved free publicity!

"We tuned in on them," Kenzie was saying. "By putting different kinds of food around, and by making different kinds of disturbances, we worked out a crude sort of vocabulary."

"You did—" the Chief exclaimed.

"Nothing fancy, you understand," Kenzie belittled his achievement. "But enough so when we broadcast a sugar wave, they came running to the surface to see where it was. When we broadcast a water wave, they rushed to the ant nursery and started carrying eggs to high ground."

"Glory be—" the Chief breathed. In his eyes there was the vision of world renowned scientists patting him on the back. Maybe even more important, Old Rock Jaw was actually smiling, and telling him he could have unlimited funds in his budget.

"Sure," Kenzie said bitterly. "Sure that was all very fine. Big shots, we were going to be, Pringle and me. First time in history man had talked with an insect. Maybe even get our pictures in the paper, same as if we'd murdered somebody. Fame!"

"Yeah," Pringle chimed in. "First step in learning how to communicate with an alien mind. Nuts!"

"I don't get it," the Chief stammered. "What's wrong with that?"

"Well, we went on perfecting the vocabulary," Kenzie said. "You know. Fining it down. Had the little beggars practically standing on their heads at times with our wave." He grinned at the memory and seemed to shake off some of his lethargy.

"You shoulda been here the night Pringle had them marching in formation." His face fell again.

"We kept on improving the gadget," he said with hangdog attitude. "We still hadn't made direct communication, you understand. Nothing like 'How do you do, Mrs. Ant? This is Kenzie MacKenzie, human, talking.'" Then he sneered at his memory.

"With our microwave we could make them do things. But hell, you can make them run out of the ground by pouring water down their hole. That's not communication! We couldn't seem to contact them direct—make them know we were communicating."

"But you still—" the Chief said. He had visions of every home using a gadget to broadcast "keep away" signals to ant pests.

"Our gadget was still crude at that point," Kenzie interrupted. "We fined it down, more and more. That's when we began to pick up the star static."

"Star static?" the Chief faltered.

"He wouldn't know about that," Pringle said, and I could detect contempt in his voice, even if the Chief didn't.

"Sure he would," Kenzie corrected. "Everybody knows about the fifty or so stars that send out continuous radio signals, and how we've been trying for years to unscramble them."

"Why certainly," the Chief said, so positively I knew he hadn't heard of it before.

"Anyway," Kenzie said. "The more we worked out the vocabulary code, the more the star signals began to fit right into it. So we decided to break up the thing, and forget all about ants. Honest Chief, you'll never hear me mention the word again."

"Termites either," Pringle chimed in.

"But I still don't understand," the Chief complained. "It still all sounds marvelous. I just don't understand."

"Draw him a picture," Pringle said disgustedly.

"Okay," Kenzie acceded. "How many years would you say ants have been on earth, Chief?"

"Oh, I don't know," the Chief answered. "Quite a few, I'd say."

"Yeah," Kenzie said drily. "Quite a few. At least a million. Unchanged. A perfect life form with a perfect civilization. So perfect, nature hasn't seen any need to change them for a million years."

"So what?" the Chief asked. "They're nothing. We come along and make them do nip ups."

"Yeah," Kenzie was bitter again. "We humans go around talking about how brave and smart we are. How someday we might even get so smart we'll contact other intelligent races on other worlds. Yeah, we're smart. You know those star radiations?"

"That's not my specialty, you know," the Chief answered cautiously.

"Some of those radiations started out from their home planet a million *light* years ago," Pringle said quietly.

"So what again?" the Chief asked.

"Those radiations," Kenzie said, "happen to be communications between the galaxies—beamed at the ants. Sort of a continuous radio program broadcast universe wide. It happens the ants, maybe termites, maybe other insects, are spread through all the galaxies. It happens *they* are the dominant intelligent race throughout the universe." He shrugged in disgust.

"Us big brave humans," he said contemptuously. "Someday we might even reach Mars. Hell, those ants have been colonizing for hundreds of millions of years. They're still communicating. They are the real intelligence on the earth!"

He crushed a cigarette fiercely into a glass ash tray on the desk.

"Only thing man has got, or ever had, was his ego. He's got to believe he's top dog, or else he folds and quits. Yeah, we're smart all right. Hell, we're so far down the scale the ants don't even recognize us as a life form at all."

Pringle nodded soberly. "Yeah," he said to the Chief, "how would you like to explain a gadget that proved ants have more brains than you have?"

The Chief looked at them with incredulous eyes.

He was still staring at them silently, with a bloodless face, when the office messenger came in and told him the General Manager wished to see him in his office to discuss budgets.

I closed the back office door quietly and went back to work. The other guys clustered around and wanted to know what I heard.

"Nothing," I said, and looked them straight in the eye. "Nothing at all."

THE VERY SECRET AGENT

by Mari Wolf

Poor Riuku! . . . Not being a member of the human race, how was he supposed to understand what goes on in a woman's mind when the male of the same species didn't even know?

In their ship just beyond the orbit of Mars the two aliens sat looking at each other.

"No," Riuku said. "I haven't had any luck. And I can tell you right now that I'm not going to have any, and no one else is going to have any either. The Earthmen are too well shielded."

"You contacted the factory?" Nagor asked.

"Easily. It's the right one. The parking lot attendant knows there's a new weapon being produced in there. The waitress at the Jumbo Burger Grill across the street knows it. Everybody I reached knows it. But not one knows anything about what it is."

Nagor looked out through the ports of the spaceship, which didn't in the least resemble an Earth spaceship, any more than what Nagor considered sight resembled the corresponding Earth sense perception. He frowned.

"What about the research scientists? We know who some of them are. The supervisors? The technicians?"

"No," Riuku said flatly. "They're shielded. Perfectly I can't make contact with a single mind down there that has the faintest inkling of what's going on. We never should have let them develop the shield."

"Have you tried contacting everyone? What about the workers?"

"Shielded. All ten thousand of them. Of course I haven't checked all of them yet, but—"

"Do it," Nagor said grimly. "We've got to find out what that weapon is. Or else get out of this solar system."

Riuku sighed. "I'll try," he said.

*

Someone put another dollar in the juke box, and the theremins started in on Mare Indrium Mary for the tenth time since Pete Ganley had come into the bar. "Aw shut up," he said, wishing there was some way to turn them off. Twelve-ten. Alice got off work at Houston's at twelve. She ought to be here by now. She would be, if it weren't Thursday. Shield boosting night for her.

Why, he asked himself irritably, couldn't those scientists figure out some way to keep the shields up longer than a week? Or else why didn't they have boosting night the same for all departments? He had to stay late every Friday and Alice every Thursday, and all the time there was Susan at home ready to jump him if he wasn't in at a reasonable time . . . .

"Surprised, Pete?" Alice Hendricks said at his elbow.

He swung about, grinned at her. "Am I? You said it. And here I was about to go. I never thought you'd make it before one." His grin faded a little. "How'd you do it? Sweet-talk one of the guards into letting you in at the head of the line?"

She shook her bandanaed head, slid onto the stool beside him and crossed her knees—a not very convincing sign of femininity in a woman wearing baggy denim coveralls. "Aren't you going to buy me a drink, honey?"

178

"Oh, sure." He glanced over at the bartender. "Another beer. No, make it two." He pulled the five dollars out of his pocket, shoved it across the bar, and looked back at Alice, more closely this time. The ID badge, pinned to her hip. The badge, with her name, number, department, and picture—and the little meter that measured the strength of her Mind Shield.

The dial should have pointed to full charge. It didn't. It registered about seventy per cent loss.

Alice followed his gaze. She giggled. "It was easy," she said. "The guards don't do more than glance at us, you know. And everyone who's supposed to go through Shielding on Thursday has the department number stamped on a yellow background. So all I did was make a red background, like yours, and slip it on in the restroom at Clean-up time."

"But Alice . . . ." Pete Ganley swallowed his beer and signaled for another. "This is serious. You've got to keep the shields up. The enemy is everywhere. Why, right now, one could be probing you."

"So what? The dial isn't down to Danger yet. And tomorrow I'll just put the red tag back on over the yellow one and go through Shielding in the same line with you. They won't notice." She giggled again. "I thought it was smart, Petey. You oughta think so too. You know why I did it, don't you?"

Her round, smooth face looked up at him, wide-eyed and full-lipped. She had no worry wrinkles like Susan's, no mouth pulled down at the corners like Susan's, and under that shapeless coverall . . . .

"Sure, baby, I'm glad you did it," Pete Ganley said huskily.

Riuku was glad too, the next afternoon when the swing shift started pouring through the gates.

It was easy, once he'd found her. He had tested hundreds, all shielded, some almost accessible to him, but none vulnerable enough. Then this one came. The shield was so far down that contact was almost easy. Painful, tiring, but not really difficult. He could feel her momentary sense of alarm, of nausea, and then he was through, integrated with her, his thoughts at home with her thoughts.

He rested, inside her mind.

"Oh, hi, Joan. No, I'm all right. Just a little dizzy for a moment. A hangover? Of course not. Not on a Friday."

Riuku listened to her half of the conversation. Stupid Earthman. If only she'd start thinking about the job. Or if only his contact with her were better. If he could use her sense perceptions, see through her eyes, hear through her ears, feel through her fingers, then everything would be easy. But he couldn't. All he could do was read her thoughts. Earth thoughts at that . . . .

 . . . *The time clock. Where's my card? Oh, here it is. Only 3:57. Why did I have to hurry so? I had lots of time . . . .*

"Why, Mary, how nice you look today. That's a new hairdo, isn't it? A permanent? Yeah, what kind?" . . . *What a microbe! Looks like pink straw, her hair does, and of course she thinks it's beautiful . . . .* "I'd better get down to my station. Old Liverlips will be ranting again. You oughta be glad you have Eddie for a lead man. Eddie's cute. So's Dave, over in 77. But Liverlips, ugh . . . ."

She was walking down the aisle to her station now. A procession of names: *Maisie, and Edith, and that fat slob Natalie, and if Jean Andrews comes around tonight flashing that diamond in my face again, I'll—I'll kill her . . . .*

"Oh hello, Clinton. What do you mean, late? The whistle just blew. Of course I'm ready to go to work." *Liverlips, that's what you are. And still in that same blue shirt. What a wife you must have. Probably as sloppy as you are . . . .*

Good, Riuku thought. Now she'll be working. Now he'd find out whatever it was she was doing. Not that it would be important, of course, but let him learn what her job was, and what those other girls' jobs were, and in a little while he'd have all the data he needed. Maybe even before the shift ended tonight, before she went through the Shielding boost.

He shivered a little, thinking of the boost. He'd survive it, of course. He'd be too well integrated with her by then. But it was nothing to look forward to.

Still, he needn't worry about it. He had the whole shift to find out what the weapon was. The whole shift, here inside Alice's mind, inside the most closely guarded factory on or under or above the surface of the Earth. He settled down and waited, expectantly.

Alice Hendricks turned her back on the lead man and looked down the work table to her place. The other girls were there already. Lois and Marge and Coralie, the other three members of the Plug table, Line 73.

"Hey, how'd you make out?" Marge said. She glanced around to make sure none of the lead men or timekeepers were close enough to overhear her, then went on. "Did you get away with it?"

"Sure," Alice said. "And you should of seen Pete's face when I walked in."

She took the soldering iron out of her locker, plugged it in, and reached out for the pan of 731 wires. "You know, it's funny. Pete's not so good looking, and he's sort of a careless dresser and all that, but oh, what he does to me." She filled the 731 plug with solder and reached for the white, black, red wire.

"You'd better watch out," Lois said. "Or Susan's going to be doing something to you."

"Oh, her." Alice touched the tip of the iron to the solder filled pin, worked the wire down into position. "What can she do? Pete doesn't give a damn about her."

"He's still living with her, isn't he?" Lois said.

Alice shrugged . . . . *What a mealy-mouthed little snip Lois could be, sometimes. You'd think to hear her that she was better than any of them, and luckier too, with her Joe and the kids. What a laugh! Joe was probably the only guy who'd ever looked at her, and she'd hooked him right out of school, and now with three kids in five years and her working nights . . . .*

Alice finished soldering the first row of wires in the plug and started in on the second. So old Liverlips thought she wasted time, did he? Well, she'd show him. She'd get out her sixteen plugs tonight.

"Junior kept me up all night last night," Lois said. "He's cutting a tooth."

"Yeah," Coralie said, "It's pretty rough at that age. I remember right after Mike was born . . . ."

Don't they ever think of anything but their kids? Alice thought. She stopped listening to them. She heard Pete's voice again, husky and sending little chills all through her, and his face came between her and the plug and the white green wire she was soldering. His face, with those blue eyes that went right through a girl and that little scar that quirked up the corner of his mouth . . . .

"Oh, oh," Alice said suddenly. "I've got solder on the outside of the pin." She looked around for the alcohol.

Riuku probed. Her thoughts were easy enough to read, but just try to translate them into anything useful . . . . He probed deeper. The plugs she was soldering. He could get a good picture of them, of the wires, of the harness lacing that Coralie was doing. But it meant nothing. They could be making anything. Radios, monitor units, sound equipment.

Only they weren't. They were making a weapon, and this bit of electronic equipment was part of that weapon. What part? What did the 731 plug do?

Alice Hendricks didn't know. Alice Hendricks didn't care.

The first break. Ten minutes away from work. Alice was walking back along the aisle that separated Assembly from the men's Machine Shop. A chance, perhaps. She was looking at the machines, or rather past them, at the men.

"Hello, Tommy. How's the love life?" He's not bad at all. Real cute. Though not like Pete, oh no.

The machines. Riuku prodded at her thoughts, wishing he could influence them, wishing that just for a moment he could see, hear, feel, *think* as she would never think.

The machines were—machines. That big funny one where Ned works, and Tommy's spot welder, and over in the corner where the superintendent is—he's a snappy dresser, tie and everything.

The corner. Restricted area. Can't go over. High voltage or something . . . .

Her thoughts slid away from the restricted area. Should she go out for lunch or eat off the sandwich machine? And Riuku curled inside her mind and cursed her with his rapidly growing Earthwoman's vocabulary.

At the end of the shift he had learned nothing. Nothing about the weapon, that is. He had found out a good deal about the sex life of Genus Homo—information that made him even more glad than before that his was a one-sexed race.

*

With work over and tools put away and Alice in the restroom gleefully thinking about the red Friday night tag she was slipping onto her ID badge, he was as far from success as ever. For a moment he considered leaving her, looking for another subject. But he'd probably not be able to find one. No, the only thing to do was stay with her, curl deep in her mind and go through the Shielding boost, and later on . . . .

The line. Alice's nervousness . . . . *Oh, oh, there's that guy with the meter—the one from maintenance. What's he want?*

"Whaddya mean, my shield's low? How could it be?" . . . *If he checks the tag I'll be fired for sure. It's a lot of nonsense anyway. The enemy is everywhere, they keep telling us. Whoever saw one of them?* "No, honest, I didn't notice anything. Can I help it if . . . . It's okay, huh? It'll pass . . . ."

Down to fifteen per cent, the guy said. Well, that's safe, I guess. Whew.

"Oh, hello, Paula. Whatcha talking about, what am I doing here tonight? Shut up . . . ."

And then, in the midst of her thoughts, the pain, driving deep into Riuku, twisting at him, wrenching at him, until there was no consciousness of anything at all.

He struggled back. He was confused, and there was blankness around him, and for a moment he thought he'd lost contact altogether. Then he came into focus again. Alice's thoughts were clearer than ever suddenly. He could feel her emotions; they were a part of him now. He smiled. The Shielding boost had helped him. Integration—much more complete integration than he had ever known before.

"But Pete, honey," Alice said. "What did you come over to the gate for? You shouldn't of done it."

"Why not? I wanted to see you."

"What if one of Susan's pals sees us?"

"So what? I'm getting tired of checking in every night, like a baby. Besides, one of her pals did see us, last night, at the bar."

Fear. What'll she do? Susan's a hellcat. I know she is. But maybe Pete'll get really sick and tired of her. He looks it. He looks mad. I'd sure hate to have him mad at me . . . .

"Let's go for a spin, baby. Out in the suburbs somewhere. How about it?"

"Well—why sure, Pete . . . ."

Sitting beside him in the copter. *All alone up here. Real romantic, like something on the video. But I shouldn't with him married, and all that. It's not right. But it's different, with Susan such a mean thing. Poor Petey . . . .*

Riuku prodded. He found it so much easier since the Shielding boost. If only these Earthmen were more telepathic, so that they could be controlled directly. Still, perhaps with this new integration he could accomplish the same results. He prodded again.

"Pete," Alice said suddenly. "What are we working on, anyway?"

"What do you mean, working on?" He frowned at her.

"At the plant. All I ever do is sit there soldering plugs, and no one ever tells me what for."

"Course not. You're not supposed to talk about any part of the job except your own. You know that. The slip of a lip—"

"Can cost Earth a ship. I know. Quit spouting poster talk at me, Pete Ganley. The enemy isn't even human. And there aren't any around here."

Pete looked over at her. She was pouting, the upper lip drawn under the lower. Someone must have told her that was cute. Well, so what—it was cute.

"What makes you think I know anything more than you do?" he said.

"Well, gee." She looked up at him, so near to her in the moonlight that she wondered why she wanted to talk about the plant anyway. "You're in Final Assembly, aren't you? You check the whatsits before they go out."

"Sure," he said. No harm in telling her. No spies now, not in this kind of war. Besides, she was too dumb to know anything.

"It's a simple enough gadget," Pete Ganley said. "A new type of force field weapon that the enemy can't spot until it hits them. They don't even know there's an Earth ship within a million miles, until *Bingo!* . . ."

She drank it in, and in her mind Riuku did too. Wonderful integration, wonderful. Partial thought control. And now, he'd learn the secret . . . .

"You really want to know how it works?" Pete Ganley said. When she nodded he couldn't help grinning. "Well, it's analogous to the field set up by animal neurones, in a way. You've just got to damp that field, and not only damp it but blot it out, so that the frequency shows nothing at all there, and then—well, that's where those Corcoran assemblies you're soldering on come in. You produce the field . . . ."

Alice Hendricks listened. For some reason she wanted to listen. She was really curious about the field. But, gee, how did he expect her to understand all that stuff? He sounded like her algebra teacher, or was it chemistry? Lord, how she'd hated school. Maybe she shouldn't have quit.

. . . *Corcoran fields. E and IR and nine-space something or other. She'd never seen Pete like this before. He looked real different. Sort of like a professor, or something. He must be real smart. And so—well, not good-looking especially but, well, appealing. Real SA, he had . . . .*

"So that's how it works," Pete Ganley said. "Quite a weapon, against them. It wouldn't work on a human being, of course." She was staring at him dreamy-eyed. He laughed. "Silly, I bet you haven't understood a word I said."

"I have too."

"Liar." He locked the automatic pilot on the copter and held out his arms. "Come here, you."

"Oh, Petey . . . ."

Who cared about the weapon? He was right, even if she wouldn't admit it. She hadn't even listened, hardly. She hadn't understood.

And neither had Riuku.

*

Riuku waited until she'd fallen soundly asleep that night before he tried contacting Nagor. He'd learned nothing useful. He'd picked up nothing in her mind except more thoughts of Pete, and gee, maybe someday they'd get married, if he only had guts enough to tell Susan where to get off . . . .

But she was asleep at last. Riuku was free enough of her thoughts to break contact, partially of course, since if he broke it completely he wouldn't be able to get back through the Shielding. It was hard enough to reach out through it. He sent a painful probing feeler out into space, to the spot where Nagor and the others waited for his report.

"Nagor . . . ."

"Riuku? Is that you?"

"Yes. I've got a contact. A girl. But I haven't learned anything yet that can help us."

"Louder, Riuku. I can hardly hear you . . . ."

Alice Hendricks stirred in her sleep. The dream images slipped through her subconscious, almost waking her, beating against Riuku.

Pete, baby, you shouldn't be like that . . . .

Riuku cursed the bisexual species in their own language.

"Riuku!" Nagor's call was harsh, urgent. "You've got to find out. We haven't much time. We lost three more ships today, and there wasn't a sign of danger. No Earthman nearby, no force fields, nothing. You've got to find out why." *Those ships just disappeared.*

Riuku forced his way up through the erotic dreams of Alice Hendricks. "I know a little," he said. "They damp their thought waves somehow, and keep us from spotting the Corcoran field."

"Corcoran field? What's that?"

"I don't know." Alice's thoughts washed over him, pulling him back into complete integration, away from Nagor, into a medley of heroic Petes with gleaming eyes and clutching hands and good little Alices pushing them away—for the moment.

"But surely you can find out through the girl," Nagor insisted from far away, almost out of phase altogether.

"No, Pete!" Alice Hendricks said aloud.

"Riuku, you're the only one of us with any possible sort of contact. You've got to find out, if we're to stay here at all."

"Well," Alice Hendricks thought, "maybe . . . ."

Riuku cursed her again, in the lingua franca of a dozen systems. Nagor's voice faded. Riuku switched back to English.

*

Saturday. Into the plant at 3:58. Jean's diamond again . . . . *Wish it would choke her; she's got a horsey enough face for it to. Where's old Liverlips? Don't see him around. Might as well go to the restroom for a while . . . .*

That's it, Riuku thought. Get her over past the machine shop, over by that Restricted Area. There must be something there we can go on . . . .

"Hello, Tommy," Alice Hendricks said. "How's the love life?"

"It could be better if someone I know would, uh, cooperate . . . ."

She looked past him, toward the corner where the big panels were with all the dials and the meters and the chart that was almost like the kind they drew pictures of earthquakes on. What was it for, anyway? And why couldn't anyone go over to it except those longhairs? High voltage her foot . . . .

"What're you looking at, Alice?" Tommy said.

"Oh, that." She pointed. "Wonder what it's for? It doesn't look like much of anything, really."

"I wouldn't know. I've got something better to look at."

"Oh, you!"

Compared to Pete, he didn't have anything, not anything at all.

. . . Pete. Gee, he must have got home awful late last night. Wonder what Susan said to him. Why does he keep taking her lip, anyway?

Riuku waited. He prodded. He understood the Restricted Area as she understood it—which was not at all. He found out some things about the 731 plugs—that a lot of them were real crummy ones the fool day shift girls had set up wrong, and besides she'd rather solder on the 717's any day. He got her talking about the weapon again, and he found out what the other girls thought about it.

Nothing.

Except where else could you get twelve-fifty an hour soldering?

She was stretched out on the couch in the restroom lobby taking a short nap—on company time, old Liverlips being tied up with the new girls down at the other end of the line—when Riuku finally managed to call Nagor again.

"Have you found out anything, Riuku?"

"Not yet."

Silence. Then: "We've lost another ship. Maybe you'd better turn her loose and come on back. It looks as if we'll have to run for it, after all."

Defeat. The long, interstellar search for another race, a race less technologically advanced than this one, and all because of a stupid Earth female.

"Not yet, Nagor," he said. "Her boy friend knows. I'll find out. I'll make her listen to him."

"Well," Nagor said doubtfully. "All right. But hurry. We haven't much time at all."

"I'll hurry," Riuku promised. "I'll be back with you tonight."

That night after work Pete Ganley was waiting outside the gate again. Alice spotted his copter right away, even though he had the lights turned way down.

"Gee, Pete, I didn't think . . . ."

"Get in. Quick."

"What's the matter?" She climbed in beside him. He didn't answer until the copter had lifted itself into the air, away from the factory landing lots and the bright overhead lights and the home-bound workers.

"It's Susan, who else," he said grimly. "She was really sounding off today. She kept saying she had a lot of evidence and I'd better be careful. And, well, I sure didn't want you turning up at the bar tonight of all nights."

He didn't sound like Pete.

"Why?" Alice said. "Are you afraid she'll divorce you?"

"Oh, Alice, you're as bad as—look, baby, don't you see? It would be awful for you. All the publicity, the things she'd call you, maybe even in the papers . . . ."

He was staring straight ahead, his hands locked about the controls. He was sort of—well, distant. Not her Petey any more. Someone else's Pete. Susan's Pete . . . .

"I think we should be more careful," he said.

Riuku twisted his way through her thoughts, tried to push them down . . . . *Does he love me, he's got to love me, sure he does, he just doesn't want me to get hurt* . . . .

And far away, almost completely out of phase, Nagor's call. "Riuku, another ship's gone. You'd better come back. Bring what you've learned so far and we can withdraw from the system and maybe piece it together . . . ."

"In a little while. Just a little while." Stop thinking about Susan, you biological schizo. Change the subject. You'll never get anything out of that man by having hysterics . . . .

"I suppose," Alice cried bitterly, "you've been leading me on all the time. You don't love me. You'd rather have *her*!"

"That's not so. Hell, baby . . . ."

He's angry. He's not even going to kiss me. I'm just cutting my own throat when I act like that . . . .

"Okay, Pete. I'm sorry. I know it's tough on you. Let's have a drink, okay? Still got some in the glove compartment?"

"Huh? Oh, sure."

She poured two drinks, neat, and he swallowed his with one impatient gulp. She poured him another.

*

Riuku prodded. The drink made his job easier. Alice's thoughts calmed, swirled away from Susan and what am I going to do and why didn't I pick up with some single guy, anyway? A single guy, like Tommy maybe. Tommy and his spot welder, over there by the Restricted Area. The Restricted Area . . . .

"Pete."

"Yeah, baby?"

"How come they let so much voltage loose in the plant, so we can't even go over in the Restricted Area?"

"Whatever made you think of that?" He laughed suddenly. He turned to her, still laughing. He was the old Pete again, she thought, with his face happy and his mouth quirked up at the corner. "Voltage loose . . . oh, baby, baby. Don't you know what that is?"

"No. What?"

"That's the control panel for one of the weapons, silly. It's only a duplicate, actually—a monitor station. But it's tuned to the frequencies of all the ships in this sector and—"

She listened. She wanted to listen. She had to want to listen, now.

"Nagor, I'm getting it," Riuku called. "I'll bring it all back with me. Just a minute and I'll have it."

"How does it work, honey?" Alice Hendricks said.

"You really want to know? Okay. Now the Corcoran field is generated between the ships and areas like that one, only a lot more powerful, by—"

"It's coming through now, Nagor."

"—a very simple power source, once you get the basics of it. You—oh, oh!" He grabbed her arm. "Duck, Alice!"

A spotlight flashed out of the darkness, turned on them, outlined them. A siren whirred briefly, and then another copter pulled up beside them and a loudspeaker blared tinnily.

"Okay, bud, pull down to the landing lane."

The police.

Police. Fear, all the way through Alice's thoughts, all the way through Riuku. Police. Earth law. That meant—it must mean he'd been discovered, that they had some other means of protection besides the Shielding . . . .

"Nagor! I've been discovered!"

"Come away then, you fool!"

He twisted, trying to pull free of Alice's fear, away from the integration of their separate terrors. But he couldn't push her thoughts back from his. She was too frightened. He was too frightened. The bond held.

"Oh, Pete, Pete, what did you do?"

He didn't answer. He landed the copter, stepped out of it, walked back to the other copter that was just dropping down behind him. "But officer, what's the matter?"

186

Alice Hendricks huddled down in the seat, already seeing tomorrow's papers, and her picture, and she wasn't really photogenic, either . . . . And then, from the other copter, she heard the woman laugh.

"Pete Ganley, you fall for anything, don't you?"

"Susan!"

"You didn't expect me to follow you, did you? Didn't it ever occur to you that detectives could put a bug in your copter? My, what we've been hearing!"

"Yeah," the detective who was driving said. "And those pictures we took last night weren't bad either."

"Susan, I can explain everything . . . ."

"I'm sure you can, Pete. You always try. But as for you—you little—"

Alice ducked down away from her. Pictures. Oh God, what it would make her look like. Still, this hag with the pinched up face who couldn't hold a man with all the cosmetics in the drugstore to camouflage her—she had her nerve, yelling like that.

"Yeah, and I know a lot about you too!" Alice Hendricks cried.

"Why, let me get my hands on you . . . ."

"Riuku!"

Riuku prodded. Calm down, you fool. You're not gaining anything this way. Calm down, so I can get out of here . . . .

Alice Hendricks stopped yelling abruptly.

"That's better," Susan said. "Pete, your taste in women gets worse each time. I don't know why I always take you back."

"I can explain everything."

"Oh, Pete," Alice Hendricks whispered. "Petey, you're not—"

"Sure he is," Susan Ganley said. "He's coming with me. The nice detectives will take you home, dear. But I don't think you'd better try anything with them—they're not your type. They're single."

"Pete . . . ." But he wouldn't meet Alice's eyes. And when Susan took his arm, he followed her.

"How could you do it, Petey . . . ." Numb whispers, numb thoughts, over and over, but no longer frightened, no longer binding on Riuku.

Fools, he thought. Idiotic Earthmen. If it weren't for your ridiculous reproductive habits I'd have found out everything. As it is . . . . "Nagor, I'm coming! I didn't get anything. This woman—"

"Well, come on then. We're leaving. Right now. There'll be other systems."

Petey, Petey, Petey . . . .

Contact thinned as he reached out away from her, toward Nagor, toward the ship. He fought his way out through the Shielding, away from her and her thoughts and every detestable thing about her. Break free, break free . . . .

"What's the matter, Riuku? Why don't you come? Have the police caught you?"

The others were fleeing, getting farther away even as he listened to Nagor's call. Contact was hard to maintain now; he could feel communication fading.

"Riuku, if you don't come now . . . ."

He fought, but Alice's thoughts were still with him; Alice's tears still kept bringing him back into full awareness of her.

"Riuku!"

"I—I can't!"

The Shielding boost, that had integrated him so completely with Alice Hendricks, would never let him go.

"Oh, Petey, I've lost you . . . ."

And Nagor's sad farewell slipped completely out of phase, leaving him alone, with her.

The plant. The Restricted Area. The useless secret of Earth's now unneeded weapon. Alice Hendricks glancing past it, at the spot welding machine, at Tommy.

"How's the love life?"

"You really interested in finding out, Alice?"

"Well—maybe—"

And Riuku gibbered unheard in her mind.

IRRESISTIBLE WEAPON

by H. B. Fyfe

There's no such thing as a weapon too horrible to use; weapons will continue to become bigger, and deadlier. Like other things that can't be stopped . . . .

IN THE SPECIAL observation dome of the colossal command ship just beyond Pluto, every nervous clearing of a throat rasped through the silence. Telescopes were available but most of the scientists and high officials preferred the view on the huge telescreen.

This showed, from a distance of several million miles, one of the small moons of the frigid planet, so insignificant that it had not been discovered until man had pushed the boundaries of space exploration past the asteroids. The satellite was about to become spectacularly significant, however, as the first target of man's newest, most destructive weapon.

"I need not remind you, gentlemen," white-haired Co-ordinator Evora of Mars had said, "that if we have actually succeeded in this race against our former Centaurian colonies, it may well prevent the imminent conflict entirely. In a few moments we shall know whether our scientists have developed a truly irresistible weapon."

Of all the officials, soldiers, and scientists present, Arnold Gibson was perhaps the least excited. For one thing, he had labored hard to make the new horror succeed and felt reasonably confident that it would. The project had been given the attention of every first-class scientific mind in the Solar System; for the great fear was that the new states on the Centaurian planets might win the race of discovery and . . .

And bring a little order into this old-fashioned, inefficient fumbling toward progress, Gibson thought contemptuously. *Look at them—fools for all their degrees and titles! They've stumbled on something with possibilities beyond their confused powers of application.*

A gasp rustled through the chamber, followed by an even more awed silence than had preceded the unbelievable, ultra-rapid action on the telescreen. Gibson permitted himself a tight smile of satisfaction.

Now my work really begins, he reflected.

A few quick steps brought him to Dr. Haas, director of the project, just before the less stunned observers surrounded that gentleman, babbling questions.

"I'll start collecting the Number Three string of recorders," he reported.

"All right, Arnold," agreed Haas. "Tell the others to get their ships out too. I'll be busy here."

Not half as busy as you will be in about a day, thought Gibson, heading for the spaceship berths.

*

HE HAD ARRANGED to be assigned the recording machines drifting in space at the greatest distance from the command ship. The others would assume that he needed more time to locate and retrieve the apparatus—which would give him a head start toward Alpha Centauri.

His ship was not large, but it was powerful and versatile to cope with any emergency that may have been encountered during the dangerous tests. Gibson watched his instruments carefully for signs of pursuit until he had put a few million miles between himself and the command ship. Then he eased his craft into subspace drive and relaxed his vigilance.

He returned to normal space many "days" later in the vicinity of Alpha Centauri. They may have attempted to follow him for all he knew, but it hardly mattered by then. He broadcast the recognition signal he had been given to memorize long ago, when he had volunteered his services to the new states. Then he headed for the capital planet, Nessus. Long before reaching it, he acquired a lowering escort of warcraft, but he was permitted to land.

"Well, well, it's young Gibson!" the Chairman of Nessus greeted him, after the newcomer had passed through the exhaustive screening designed to protect the elaborate underground headquarters. "I trust you have news for us, my boy. Watch outside the door, Colonel!"

One of the ostentatiously armed guards stepped outside and closed the door as Gibson greeted the obese man sitting across the button-studded expanse of desk. The scientist was under no illusion as to the vagueness of the title "Chairman." He was facing the absolute power of the Centaurian planets—which, in a few months' time, would be the same as saying the ruler of all the human race in both systems. Gibson's file must have been available on the Chairman's desk telescreen within minutes of the reception of his recognition signal. He felt a thrill of admiration for the efficiency of the new states and their system of government.

He made it his business to report briefly and accurately, trusting that the plain facts of his feat would attract suitable recognition. They did. Chairman Diamond's sharp blue eyes glinted out of the fat mask of his features.

"Well done, my boy!" he grunted, with a joviality he did not bother trying to make sound overly sincere. "So *they* have it! You must see our men immediately, and point out where they have gone wrong. You may leave it to me to decide *who* has gone wrong!"

*

ARNOLD GIBSON shivered involuntarily before reminding himself that *he* had seen the correct answer proved before his eyes. He had stood there and watched—more, he had worked with them all his adult life—and he was the last whom the muddled fools would have suspected.

The officer outside the door, Colonel Korman, was recalled and given orders to escort Gibson to the secret state laboratories. He glanced briefly at the scientist when they had been let out through the complicated system of safeguards.

"We have to go to the second moon," he said expressionlessly. "Better sleep all you can on the way. Once you're there, the Chairman will be impatient for results!"

Gibson was glad, after they had landed on the satellite, that he had taken the advice. He was led from one underground lab to another, to compare Centaurian developments with Solarian. Finally, Colonel Korman appeared to extricate him, giving curt answers to such researchers as still had questions.

"Whew! Glad you got me out!" Gibson thanked him. "They've been picking my brain for two days straight!"

"I hope you can stay awake," retorted Korman with no outward sign of sympathy. "If you think you can't, say so now. I'll have them give you another shot. The Chairman is calling on the telescreen."

Gibson straightened.

Jealous snob! he thought. *Typical military fathead, and he knows I amount to more than any little colonel now. I was smart enough to fool all the so-called brains of the Solar System.*

"I'll stay awake," he said shortly.

Chairman Diamond's shiny features appeared on the screen soon after Korman reported his charge ready.

"Speak freely," he ordered Gibson. "This beam is so tight and scrambled that no prying jackass could even tell that it is communication. Have you set us straight?"

"Yes, Your Excellency," replied Gibson. "I merely pointed out which of several methods the Solarians got to yield results. Your—our scientists were working on all possibilities, so it would have been only a matter of time."

"Which you have saved us," said Chairman Diamond. His ice-blue eyes glinted again. "I wish I could have seen the faces of Haas and Co-ordinator Evora, and the rest. You fooled them completely!"

Gibson glowed at the rare praise.

"I dislike bragging, Your Excellency," he said, "but they *are* fools. I might very well have found the answer without them, once they had collected the data. My success shows what intelligence, well-directed after the manner of the new states of Centauri, can accomplish against inefficiency."

The Chairman's expression, masked by the fat of his face, nevertheless approached a smile.

"So you would say that you—one of *our* sympathizers—were actually the most intelligent worker *they* had?"

He'll have his little joke, thought Gibson, *and I'll let him put it over. Then, even that sour colonel will laugh with us, and the Chairman will hint about what post I'll get as a reward. I wouldn't mind being in charge—old Haas' opposite number at this end.*

"I think I might indeed be permitted to boast of that much ability, Your Excellency," he answered, putting on what he hoped was an expectant smile. "Although, considering the Solarians, that is not saying much."

The little joke did not develop precisely as anticipated.

"Unfortunately," Chairman Diamond said, maintaining his smile throughout, "wisdom should never be confused with intelligence."

*

GIBSON WAITED, feeling his own smile stiffen as he wondered what could be going wrong. Surely, they could not doubt *his* loyalty! A hasty glance at Colonel Korman revealed no expression on the military facade affected by that gentleman.

"For if wisdom *were* completely synonymous with intelligence," the obese Chairman continued, relishing his exposition, "you would be a rival to myself, and consequently would be—disposed of—anyway!"

Such a tingle shot up Gibson's spine that he was sure he must have jumped.

"*Anyway?*" he repeated huskily. His mouth suddenly seemed dry.

Chairman Diamond smiled out of the telescreen, so broadly that Gibson was unpleasantly affected by the sight of his small, gleaming, white teeth.

"Put it this way," he suggested suavely. "Your highly trained mind observed, correlated, and memorized the most intricate data and mathematics, meanwhile guiding your social relations with your former colleagues so as to remain unsuspected while stealing their most cherished secret. Such a feat demonstrates ability and intelligence."

Gibson tried to lick his lips, and could not, despite the seeming fairness of the words. He sensed a pulsing undercurrent of cruelty and cynicism.

"On the other hand," the mellow voice flowed on, "having received the information, being able to use it effectively now without you, and knowing that you betrayed once—I shall simply discard you like an old message blank. That is an act of wisdom.

"Had you chosen your course more wisely," he added, "your position might be stronger."

By the time Arnold Gibson regained his voice, the Centaurian autocrat was already giving instructions to Colonel Korman. The scientist strove to interrupt, to attract the ruler's attention even momentarily.

Neither paid him any heed, until he shouted and tried frenziedly to shove the soldier from in front of the telescreen. Korman backhanded him across the throat without looking around, with such force that Gibson staggered back and fell.

He lay, half-choking, grasping his throat with both hands until he could breathe. The colonel continued discussing his extinction without emotion.

" . . . so if Your Excellency agrees, I would prefer taking him back to Nessus first, for the sake of the morale factor here. Some of them are so addled now at having been caught chasing up wrong alleys that they can hardly work."

Apparently the Chairman agreed, for the screen was blank when the colonel reached down and hauled Gibson to his feet.

"Now, listen to me carefully!" he said, emphasizing his order with a ringing slap across Gibson's face. "I shall walk behind you with my blaster drawn. If you make a false move, I shall not kill you."

Gibson stared at him, holding his bleeding mouth.

"It will be much worse," Korman went on woodenly. "Imagine what it will be like to have both feet charred to the bone. You would have to crawl the rest of the way to the ship; I certainly would not consider carrying you!"

In a nightmarish daze, Gibson obeyed the cold directions, and walked slowly along the underground corridors of the Centaurian research laboratories. He prayed desperately that someone—anyone—might come along. Anybody who could possibly be used to create a diversion, or to be pushed into Korman and his deadly blaster.

The halls remained deserted, possibly by arrangement.

Maybe I'd better wait till we reach his ship, Gibson thought. I ought to be able to figure a way before we reach Nessus. I had the brains to fool Haas and . . .

He winced, recalling Chairman Diamond's theory of the difference between intelligence and wisdom.

The obscene swine! he screamed silently.

Colonel Korman grunted warningly, and Gibson took the indicated turn.

They entered the spaceship from an underground chamber, and Gibson learned the reason for his executioner's assurance when the latter chained him to one of the pneumatic acceleration seats. The chain was fragile in appearance, but he knew he would not be free to move until Korman so desired.

More of their insane brand of cleverness! he reflected. *That's the sort of thing they do succeed in thinking of. They're all crazy! Why did I ever* . . .

But he shrank from the question he feared to answer. To drag out into the open his petty, selfish reasons, shorn of the tinsel glamor of so-called "service" and "progress," would be too painful.

*

AFTER THE FIRST series of accelerations, he roused himself from his beaten stupor enough to note that Korman was taking a strange course for reaching Nessus. Then, entirely too close to the planet and its satellites to ensure accuracy, the colonel put the ship into subspace drive.

Korman leaned back at the conclusion of the brief activity on his control board, and met Gibson's pop-eyed stare.

"Interesting, the things worth knowing," he commented. "How to make a weapon, for instance, or whether your enemy has it yet."

He almost smiled at his prisoner's expression.

"Or even better: knowing exactly how far your enemy has progressed and how fast he can continue, whether to stop him immediately or whether you can remain a step ahead."

"B-but—if both sides are irresistible . . ." Gibson stammered.

Korman examined him contemptuously.

"No irresistible weapon exists, or ever will!" he declared. "Only an irresistible *process*—the transmission of secrets! You are living proof that no safeguards can defend against *that*."

He savored Gibson's silent discomfort.

"I am sure you know how far and how fast the Centaurian scientists will go, Gibson, since I guided you to every laboratory in that plant. Your memory may require some painful jogging when we reach the Solar System; *but remember you shall!*"

"But you—you were ordered to . . ."

"You didn't think I was a Centaurian, did you?" sneered Korman. "After I just explained to you *what* is really irresistible?"

IN THE GARDEN

by R. A. Lafferty

The protozoic recorder chirped like a bird. Not only would there be life traces on that little moon, but it would be a lively place. So they skipped several steps in the procedure.

The chordata discerner read Positive over most of the surface. There was spinal fluid on that orb, rivers of it. So again they omitted several tests and went to the cognition scanner. Would it show Thought on the body?

Naturally they did not get results at once, nor did they expect to; it required a fine adjustment. But they were disappointed that they found nothing for several hours as they hovered high over the rotation. Then it came, clearly and definitely, but from quite a small location only.

"Limited," said Steiner, "as though within a pale. As follow the rest of the surface to find another, or concentrate though there were but one city, if that is its form. Shall we on this? It'll be twelve hours before it's back in our ken if we let it go now."

"Let's lock on this one and finish the scan. Then we can do the rest of the world to make sure we've missed nothing," said Stark.

There was one more test to run, one very tricky and difficult of analysis, that of the Extraordinary Perception Locator. This was designed simply to locate a source of superior thought. But this might be so varied or so unfamiliar that often both the machine and the designer of it were puzzled as how to read the results.

The E. P. Locator had been designed by Glaser. But when the Locator had refused to read Positive when turned on the inventor himself, bad blood developed between machine and man. Glaser knew that he had extraordinary perception. He was a much honored man in his field. He told the machine so heatedly.

The machine replied, with such warmth that its relays chattered, that Glaser did not have extraordinary perception; he had only ordinary perception to an extraordinary degree. There is a difference, the machine insisted.

It was for this reason that Glaser used that model no more, but built others more amenable. And it was for this reason also that the owners of Little Probe had acquired the original machine so cheaply.

And there was no denying that the Extraordinary Perception Locator (or Eppel) was a contrary machine. On Earth it had read Positive on a number of crack-pots, including Waxey Sax, a jazz tootler who could not even read music. But it had also read Positive on ninety percent of the acknowledged superior minds of the Earth. In space it had been a sound guide to the unusual intelligences encountered. Yet on Suzuki-Mi it had read Positive on a two-inch long worm, one only out of billions. For the countless identical worms no trace of anything at all was shown by the test.

So it was with mixed emotions that Steiner locked onto the area and got a flick. He then narrowed to a smaller area (apparently one individual, though this could not be certain) and got very definite action. Eppel was busy. The machine had a touch of the ham in it, and assumed an air of importance when it ran these tests.

Finally it signaled the result, the most exasperating result it ever produces: the single orange light. It was the equivalent of the shrug of the shoulders in a man. They called it the "You tell me light."

So among the intelligences on that body there was at least one that might be extraordinary, though possibly in a crack-pot way. It is good to be forewarned.

"Scan the remainder of the world, Steiner," said Stark, "and the rest of us will get some sleep. If you find no other spot then we will go down on that one the next time it is in position under us, in about twelve hours."

"You don't want to visit any of the other areas first? Somewhere away from the thoughtful creature?"

"No. The rest of the world may be dangerous. There must be a reason that Thought is in one spot only. If we find no others then we will go down boldly and visit this."

So they all, except Steiner, went off to their bunks then: Stark, the captain; Caspar Craig, supercargo, tycoon and fifty-one percent owner of the Little Probe; Gregory Gilbert, the executive officer; and F. R. Briton, S. J., a Jesuit priest who was linguist and checker champion of the craft.

Dawn did not come to the moon-town. The Little Probe hovered stationary in the light and the moon-town came up under the dawn. Then the Probe went down to visit whatever was there.

"There's no town," said Steiner. "Not a building. Yet we're on the track of the minds. There's nothing but a meadow and some boscage, a sort of fountain or pool, and four streams booming out of it."

"Keep on toward the minds," said Stark. "They're our target."

"Not a building, not two sticks or stones placed together. It looks like an Earth-type sheep there. And that looks like an Earth-lion, I'm almost afraid to say it. And those two—why they could be Earth-people. But with a difference. Where is that bright light coming from?"

"I don't know, but they're right in the middle of it. Land here. We'll go to meet them at once. Timidity has never been an efficacious tool with us."

Well, they were people. And one could only wish that all people were like them. There was a man and a woman, and they were clothed either in very bright garments or no garments at all, but only in a very bright light.

"Talk to them, Father Briton," said Stark. "You are the linguist."

"Howdy," said the priest.

He may or may not have been understood, but the two of them smiled at him so he went on.

"Father Briton from Philadelphia," he said, "on detached service. And you, my good man, what is your handle, your monicker, your tag?"

"Ha-Adamah," said the man.

"And your daughter, or niece?"

It may be that the shining man frowned momentarily at this; but the woman smiled, proving that she was human.

"The woman is named Hawwah," said the man. "The sheep is named sheep, the lion is named lion, the horse is named horse, and the hoolock is named hoolock."

"I understand. It is possible that this could go on and on. How is it that you use the English tongue?"

"I have only one tongue; but it is given to us to be understood by all; by the eagle, by the squirrel, by the ass, by the English."

"We happen to be bloody Yankees, but we use a borrowed tongue. You wouldn't have a drink on you for a tubful of thirsty travelers, would you?"

"The fountain."

"Ah—I see."

But the crew all drank of the fountain to be sociable. It was water, but water that excelled, cool and with all its original bubbles like the first water ever made.

"What do you make of them?" asked Stark.

"Human," said Steiner. "It may even be that they are a little more than human. I don't understand that light that surrounds them. And they seem to be clothed, as it were, in dignity."

"And very little else," said Father Briton, "though that light trick does serve a purpose. But I'm not sure they'd pass in Philadelphia."

"Talk to them again," said Stark. "You're the linguist."

"That isn't necessary here, Captain. Talk to them yourself."

"Are there any other people here?" Stark asked the man.

"The two of us. Man and woman."

"But are there any others?"

"How would there be any others? What other kind of people could there be than man and woman?"

"But is there more than one man or woman?"

"How could there be more than one of anything?"

The captain was a little puzzled by this, but he went on doggedly: "Ha-Adamah, what do you think that we are? Are we not people?"

"You are not anything till I name you. But I will name you and then you can be. You are named captain. He is named priest. He is named engineer. He is named flunky."

"Thanks a lot," said Steiner.

"But āre we not people?" persisted Captain Stark.

"No. We are the people. There are no people but two. How could there be other people?"

"And the damnedest thing about it," muttered Steiner, "is how are we going to prove him wrong? But it does give you a small feeling."

"Can we have something to eat?" asked the captain.

"Pick from the trees," said Ha-Adamah, "and then it may be that you will want to sleep on the grass. Being not of human nature (which does not need sleep or rest), it may be that you require respite. But you are free to enjoy the garden and its fruits."

"We will," said Captain Stark.

They wandered about the place, but they were uneasy. There were the animals. The lion and lioness were enough to make one cautious, though they offered no harm. The two bears had a puzzling look, as though they wanted either to frolic with you or to mangle you.

"If there are only two people here," said Caspar Craig, "then it may be that the rest of the world is not dangerous at all. It looked fertile wherever we scanned it, though not so fertile as this central bit. And those rocks will bear examining."

"Flecked with gold, and possibly with something else," said Stark. "A very promising site."

"And everything grows here," added Stark. "Those are Earth-fruits and I never saw finer. I've tasted the grapes and plums and pears. The figs and dates are superb, the quince is as flavorsome as a quince can be, the cherries are excellent. And I never did taste such oranges. But I haven't yet tried the—" and he stopped.

"If you're thinking what I'm afraid to think," said Gilbert, "then it will be a test at least: whether we're having a pleasant dream or whether this is reality. Go ahead and eat one."

"I won't be the first to eat one. You eat."

"Ask him first. You ask him."

"Ha-Adamah, is it allowed to eat the apples?"

"Certainly. Eat. It is the finest fruit in the garden."

*

"Well, the analogy breaks down there," said Stark. "I was almost beginning to believe in the thing. But, if it isn't that, then what? Father Briton, you are the linguist, but in Hebrew does not Ha-Adamah and Hawwah mean—?"

"Of course they do. You know that as well as I."

"I was never a believer. But would it be possible for the exact same proposition to maintain here as on Earth?"

"All things are possible."

And it was then that Ha-Adamah, the shining man, gave a wild cry: "No. No. Do not approach it. It is not allowed to eat of that one."

It was the pomegranate tree, and he was warning Craig away from it.

"Once more, Father," said Stark, "you should be the authority; but does not the idea that it was an apple that was forbidden go back only to a medieval painting?"

"It does. The name of the fruit is not mentioned in Genesis. In Hebrew exegesis, however, the pomegranate is usually indicated."

"I thought so. Question the man further, Father. This is too incredible."

"It is a little odd. Adam, old man, how long have you been here?"

"Forever less six days is the answer that has been given to me. I never did understand the answer, however."

"And have you gotten no older in all that time?"

"I do not understand what 'older' is. I am as I have been from the beginning."

"And do you think that you will ever die?"

"To die I do not understand. I am taught that it is a property of fallen nature to die, and that does not pertain to me or mine."

"And are you happy here?"

"Perfectly happy according to my preternatural state. But I am taught that it might be possible to lose that happiness, and then to seek it vainly through all the ages. I am taught that sickness and aging and even death could come if this happiness were ever lost. I am taught that on at least one other unfortunate world it has actually been lost."

"Do you consider yourself a knowledgeable man?"

"Yes, since I am the only man, and knowledge is natural to man. But I am further blessed. I have a preternatural intellect."

Then Stark cut in once more: "There must be some one question you could ask him, Father. Some way to settle it. I am becoming nearly convinced."

"Yes, there is a question that will settle it. Adam, old man, how about a game of checkers?"

"This is hardly the time for clowning," said Stark.

"I'm not clowning, Captain. How about it, Adam? I'll give you choice of colors and first move."

"No. It would be no contest. I have a preternatural intellect."

"Well, I beat a barber who was champion of Germantown. And I beat the champion of Morgan County, Tennessee, which is the hottest checker center on Earth. I've played against, and beaten, machines. But I never played a preternatural mind. Let's just set up the board, Adam, and have a go at it."

"No. It would be no contest. I would not like to humble you."

*

They were there for three days. They were delighted with the place. It was a world with everything, and it seemed to have only two inhabitants. They went everywhere except into the big cave.

"What is there, Adam?" asked Captain Stark.

"The great serpent lives there. I would not disturb him. He has long been cranky because plans that he had for us did not materialize. But we are taught that should evil ever come to us, which it cannot if we persevere, it will come by him."

*

They learned no more of the real nature of the sphere in their time there. Yet all but one of them were convinced of the reality when they left. And they talked of it as they took off.

"A crowd would laugh if told of it," said Stark, "but not many would laugh if they had actually seen the place, or them. I am not a gullible man, but I am convinced of this: this is a pristine and pure world and ours and all the others we have visited are fallen worlds. Here are the prototypes of our first parents before their fall. They are garbed in light and innocence, and they have the happiness that we have been seeking for centuries. It would be a crime if anyone disturbed that happiness."

"I too am convinced," said Steiner. "It is Paradise itself, where the lion lies down with the lamb, and where the serpent has not prevailed. It would be the darkest of crimes if we or others should play the part of the serpent, and intrude and spoil."

"I am probably the most skeptical man in the world," said Caspar Craig the tycoon, "but I do believe my eyes. I have been there and seen it. It is indeed an unspoiled Paradise; and it would be a crime calling to the wide heavens for vengeance for anyone to smirch in any way that perfection."

"So much for that. Now to business. Gilbert, take a gram: Ninety Million Square Miles of Pristine Paradise for sale or lease. Farming, Ranching, exceptional opportunities for Horticulture. Gold, Silver, Iron, Earth-Type Fauna. Terms. Special rates for Large Settlement

Parties. Write, gram, or call in person at any of our planetary offices as listed below. Ask for Brochure—Eden Acres Unlimited—"

*

Down in the great cave that Old Serpent, a two-legged one among whose names was "Snake-Oil Sam," spoke to his underlings: "It'll take them fourteen days to get back with the settlers. We'll have time to overhaul the blasters. We haven't had any well-equipped settlers for six weeks. It used to be we'd hardly have time to strip and slaughter and stow before there was another batch to take care of."

"I think you'd better write me some new lines," said Adam. "I feel like a goof saying those same ones to each bunch."

"You are a goof, and therefore perfect for the part. I was in show business long enough to learn never to change a line too soon. I did change Adam and Eve to Ha-Adamah and Hawwah, and the apple to the pomegranate. People aren't becoming any smarter—but they are becoming better researched, and they insist on authenticity."

"This is still a perfect come-on here. There is something in human nature that cannot resist the idea of a Perfect Paradise. Folks will whoop and holler to their neighbors to come in droves to spoil it and mar it. It isn't greed or the desire for new land so much, though that is strong too. Mainly it is the feverish passion to befoul and poison what is unspoiled. Fortunately I am sagacious enough to take advantage of this trait. And when you start to farm a new world on a shoestring you have to acquire your equipment as you can."

He looked proudly around at the great cave with its mountains and tiers of material; heavy machinery of all sorts, titanic crates of foodstuff space-sealed; wheeled, tracked, propped, vanned, and jetted vehicles; and power packs to run a world.

He looked at the three dozen space ships stripped and stacked, and at the rather large pile of bone-meal in one corner.

"We will have to get another lion," said Eve. "Bowser is getting old, and Marie-Yvette abuses him and gnaws his toes. And we do have to have a big-maned lion to lie down with the lamb."

"I know it, Eve. The lion is a very important prop. Maybe one of the crack-pot settlers will bring a new lion."

"And can't you mix another kind of shining paint?" asked Adam. "This itches. It's hell."

"I'm working on it."

*

Caspar Craig was still dictating the gram: "Amazing quality of longevity seemingly inherent in the locale. Climate Ideal. Daylight or half-light all twenty-one hours from Planet Delphina and from Sol Number Three. Pure water for all industrial purposes. Scenic and Storied. Zoning and pre-settlement restrictions to insure congenial neighbors. A completely planned globular settlement in a near arm of our own galaxy. Low taxes and liberal credit. Financing our specialty—"

"And you had better have an armed escort when you return," said Father Briton.

"Why in cosmos would we want an armed escort?"

"It's as phoney as a seven-credit note."

"You, a man of the cloth, doubt it? And us ready skeptics convinced by our senses? Why do you doubt?"

"It is only the unbelieving who believe so easily in obvious frauds. Theologically unsound, dramaturgically weak, philologically impossible, zoologically rigged, salted conspicuously with gold, and shot through with anachronisms. And moreover he was afraid to play me at checkers."

"What?"

"If I had a preternatural intellect I wouldn't be afraid of a game of checkers with anyone. Yet there was an unusual mind there somewhere; it is just that he chose not to make our acquaintance personally."

They looked at the priest thoughtfully.

"But it was Paradise in one way," said Steiner.

"How?"

"All the time we were there the woman did not speak."

THE EYES HAVE IT

by James McKimmey, Jr.

Daylight sometimes hides secrets that darkness will reveal—the Martian's glowing eyes, for instance. But darkness has other dangers . . . .

JOSEPH HEIDEL looked slowly around the dinner table at the five men, hiding his examination by a thin screen of smoke from his cigar. He was a large man with thick blond-gray hair cut close to his head. In three more months he would be fifty-two, but his face and body had the vital look of a man fifteen years younger. He was the President of the Superior Council, and he had been in that post—the highest post on the occupied planet of Mars—four of the six years he had lived here. As his eyes flicked from one face to another his fingers unconsciously tapped the table, making a sound like a miniature drum roll.

One. Two. Three. Four. Five. Five top officials, selected, tested, screened on Earth to form the nucleus of governmental rule on Mars.

Heidel's bright narrow eyes flicked, his fingers drummed. Which one? Who was the imposter, the ringer? Who was the Martian?

Sadler's dry voice cut through the silence: "This is not just an ordinary meeting then, Mr. President?"

Heidel's cigar came up and was clamped between his teeth. He stared into Sadler's eyes. "No, Sadler, it isn't. This is a very special meeting." He grinned around the cigar. "This is where we take the clothes off the sheep and find the wolf."

Heidel watched the five faces. Sadler, Meehan, Locke, Forbes, Clarke. One of them. Which one?

"I'm a little thick tonight," said Harry Locke. "I didn't follow what you meant."

"No, no, of course not," Heidel said, still grinning. "I'll explain it." He could feel himself alive at that moment, every nerve singing, every muscle toned. His brain was quick and his tongue rolled the words out smoothly. This was the kind of situation Heidel handled best. A tense, dramatic situation, full of atmosphere and suspense.

"Here it is," Heidel continued, "simply and briefly." He touched the cigar against an ash tray, watching with slitted shining eyes while the ashes spilled away from the glowing tip. He bent forward suddenly. "We have an imposter among us, gentlemen. A spy."

He waited, holding himself tense against the table, letting the sting of his words have their effect. Then he leaned back, carefully. "And tonight I am going to expose this imposter. Right here, at this table." He searched the faces again, looking for a tell-tale twitch of a muscle, a movement of a hand, a shading in the look of an eye.

There were only Sadler, Meehan, Locke, Forbes, Clarke, looking like themselves, quizzical, polite, respecting.

"One of us, you say," Clarke said noncommittally, his phrase neither a question nor a positive statement.

"That is true," said Heidel.

"Bit of a situation at that," said Forbes, letting a faint smile touch his lips.

"Understatement, Forbes," Heidel said. "Understatement."

"Didn't mean to sound capricious," Forbes said, his smile gone.

201

"Of course not," Heidel said.

Edward Clarke cleared his throat. "May I ask, sir, how this was discovered and how it was narrowed down to the Superior Council?"

"Surely," Heidel said crisply. "No need to go into the troubles we've been having. You know all about that. But how these troubles originated is the important thing. Do you remember the missionary affair?"

"When we were going to convert the Eastern industrial section?"

"That's right," Heidel said, remembering. "Horrible massacre."

"Bloody," agreed John Meehan.

"Sixty-seven missionaries lost," Heidel said.

"I remember the Martian note of apology," Forbes said. "'We have worshipped our own God for two-hundred thousand years. We would prefer to continue. Thank you.' Blinking nerve, eh?"

"Neither here nor there," Heidel said abruptly. "The point is that no one *knew* those sixty-seven men were missionaries except myself and you five men."

*

HEIDEL WATCHED the faces in front of him. "One case," he said. "Here's another. Do you recall when we outlawed the free selection system?"

"Another bloody one," said Sadler.

"Forty-eight victims in that case," Heidel said. "Forty-eight honorable colonists, sanctioned by us to legally marry any couple on the planet, and sent out over the country to abolish the horrible free-love situation."

"Forty-eight justices of the peace dead as pickerels," Forbes said.

"Do you happen to remember *that* note of apology?" Heidel asked, a slight edge in his voice. He examined Forbes' eyes.

"Matter of fact, yes," said Forbes, returning Heidel's stare steadily. "'You love your way, we'll love ours.' Terribly caustic, what?"

"Terribly," said Heidel. "Although that too is neither here nor there. The point again, no one except the six of us right here knew what those forty-eight men were sent out to do."

Heidel straightened in his chair. The slow grating voice of Forbes had taken some of the sharpness out of the situation. He wanted to hold their attention minutely, so that when he was ready, the dramatics of his action would be tense and telling.

"There is no use," he said, "in going into the details of the other incidents. You remember them. When we tried to install a free press, the Sensible Art galleries, I-Am-A-Martian Day, wrestling, and all the rest."

"I remember the wrestling business awfully well," said Forbes. "Martians drove a wrestler through the street in a yellow jetmobile. Had flowers around his neck and a crown on his head. He was dead, of course. Stuffed, I think . . . ."

"All right," snapped Heidel. "Each one of our efforts to offer these people a chance to benefit from our culture was snapped off at the bud. And only a leak in the Superior Council could have caused it. It is a simple matter of deduction. There is one of us, here tonight, who is responsible. And I am going to expose him." Heidel's voice was a low vibrant sound that echoed in the large dining room.

The five men waited. Forbes, his long arms crossed. Sadler, his eyes on his fingernails. Meehan, blinking placidly. Clarke, twirling his thumbs. Locke, examining his cigarette.

"Kessit!" Heidel called.

A gray-haired man in a black butler's coat appeared.

"We'll have our wine now," Heidel said. There was a slight quirk in his mouth, so that his teeth showed between his lips. The butler moved methodically from place to place, pouring wine from a silver decanter.

"Now then, Kessit," Heidel said, when the butler had finished, "would you be kind enough to fetch me that little pistol from the mantel over there?" He smiled outwardly this time. The situation was right again; he was handling things, inch by inch, without interruption.

He took the gun from the old man's hands. "One thing more, Kessit. Would you please light the candles on the table and turn out the rest of the lights in the room. I've always been a romanticist," Heidel said, smiling around the table. "Candlelight with my wine."

"Oh, excellent," said Locke soberly.

"Quite," said Forbes.

Heidel nodded and waited while the butler lit the candles and snapped off the overhead lights. The yellow flames wavered on the table as the door closed gently behind the butler.

"Now, then," Heidel said, feeling the tingling in his nerves. "This, gentlemen, is a replica of an antique of the twentieth century. A working replica, I might add. It was called a P-38, if my memory serves me." He held the pistol up so that the candlelight reflected against the glistening black handle and the blue barrel.

There was a polite murmur as the five men stretched forward to look at the gun in Heidel's hands.

"Crude," Sadler said.

"But devilish-looking," Forbes added.

"My hobby," Heidel said. "I would like to add that not only do I collect these small arms, but I am very adept at using them. Something I will demonstrate to you very shortly," he added, grinning.

"Say now," nodded Meehan.

"That should be jolly," Forbes said, laughing courteously.

"I believe it will at that," Heidel said. "Now if you will notice, gentlemen," he said touching the clip ejector of the pistol and watching the black magazine slip out into his other hand. "I have but five cartridges in the clip. Just five. You see?"

They all bent forward, blinking.

"Good," said Heidel, shoving the clip back into the grip of the gun. He couldn't keep his lips from curling in his excitement, but his hands were as steady as though his nerves had turned to ice.

The five men leaned back in their chairs.

"Now then, Meehan," he said to the man at the opposite end of the table. "Would you mind moving over to your left, so that the end of the table is clear?"

"Oh?" said Meehan. "Yes, of course." He grinned at the others, and there was a ripple of amusement as Meehan slid his chair to the left.

"Yes," said Heidel. "All pretty foolish-looking, perhaps. But it won't be in a few minutes when I discover the bastard of a Martian who's in this group, I'll tell you that!" His voice rose and rang in the room, and he brought the glistening pistol down with a crack against the table.

*

THERE WAS dead silence and Heidel found his smile again. "All right, now I'll explain a bit further. Before Dr. Kingly, the head of our laboratory, died a few days ago, he made a very peculiar discovery. As you know, there has been no evidence to indicate that the Martian is any different, physically, from the Earthman. Not until Dr. Kingly made his discovery, that is."

Heidel looked from face to face. "This is how it happened," he went on. "Dr. Kingly . . ."

He paused and glanced about in false surprise. "I beg your pardon, gentlemen. We might as well be enjoying our wine. Excellent port. Very old, I believe. Shall we?" he asked, raising his glass.

Five other glasses shimmered in the candlelight.

"Let us, ah, toast success to the unveiling of the rotten Martian who sits among us, shall we?" Heidel's smile glinted and he drank a quarter of his glass.

The five glasses tipped and were returned to the table. Again there was silence as the men waited.

"To get back," Heidel said, listening with excitement to his own voice. "Dr. Kingly, in the process of an autopsy on a derelict Martian, made a rather startling discovery . . ."

"I beg your pardon," Forbes said. "Did you say autopsy?"

"Yes," said Heidel. "We've done this frequently. Not according to base orders, you understand." He winked. "But a little infraction now and then is necessary."

"I see," said Forbes. "I just didn't know about that."

"No, you didn't, did you?" said Heidel, looking at Forbes closely. "At any rate, Dr. Kingly had developed in his work a preserving solution which he used in such instances, thereby prolonging the time for examination of the cadaver, without experiencing deterioration of the tissues. This solution was merely injected into the blood stream, and . . ."

"Sorry again, sir," Forbes said. "But you said blood stream?"

"Yes," Heidel nodded. "This had to be done before the cadaver was a cadaver, you see?"

"I think so, yes," said Forbes, leaning back again. "Murdered the bastard for an autopsy, what?"

Heidel's fingers closed around the pistol. "I don't like that, Forbes."

"Terribly sorry, sir."

"To get on," Heidel said finally, his voice a cutting sound. "Dr. Kingly had injected his solution and then . . . Well, at any rate, when he returned to his laboratory, it was night. His laboratory was black as pitch—I'm trying to paint the picture for you, gentlemen—and the cadaver was stretched out on a table, you see. And before Dr. Kingly switched on the lights, he saw the eyes of this dead Martian glowing in the dark like a pair of hot coals."

"Weird," said Sadler, unblinking.

"Ghostly," said Clarke.

"The important thing," Heidel said curtly, "is that Dr. Kingly discovered the difference, then, between the Martian and the Earthman. The difference is the eyes. The solution, you see, had reacted chemically to the membranes of the eyeballs, so that as it happened they lit up like electric lights. I won't go into what Dr. Kingly found further, when he dissected the eyeballs. Let it suffice to say, the Martian eyeball is a physical element entirely different from our own—at least from those of five of us, I should say."

His grin gleamed. He was working this precisely and carefully, and it was effective. "Now, however," he continued, "it is this *sixth* man who is at issue right now. The fly in the soup, shall we say. And in just a few seconds I am going to exterminate that fly."

He picked up the pistol from the table. "As I told you, gentlemen, I am quite versatile with this weapon. I am a dead shot, in other words. And I am going to demonstrate it to you." He glanced from face to face.

"You will notice that since Mr. Meehan has moved, I have a clear field across the table. I don't believe a little lead in the woodwork will mar the room too much, would you say, Forbes?"

Forbes sat very still. "No, I shouldn't think so, sir."

"Good. Because I am going to snuff out each of the four candles in the center of this table by shooting the wick away. You follow me, gentlemen? Locke? Meehan? Sadler?"

Heads nodded.

"Then perhaps you are already ahead of me. When the last candle is extinguished, we will have darkness, you see. And then I think we'll find our Martian rat. Because, as a matter of fact," Heidel lolled his words, "I have taken the privilege of adding to the wine we have been drinking Dr. Kingly's preserving solution. Non-tasteful, non-harmful. Except, that is, to one man in this room."

Heidel motioned his gun. "And God rest the bastard's soul, because if you will remember, I have five bullets in the chamber of this pistol. Four for the candles and one for the brain of the sonofabitch whose eyes light up when the last candle goes out."

*

THERE WAS a steady deadly silence while the flames of the candles licked at the still air.

"I think, however," Heidel said, savoring the moment, "that we should have one final toast before we proceed." He lifted his glass. "May the receiver of the fifth bullet go straight to hell. I phrase that literally, gentlemen," he said, laughing. "Drink up!"

The glasses were drained and placed again on the table.

"Watch carefully," Heidel said and lifted the pistol. He aimed at the first candle. The trigger was taut against his finger, the explosion loud in the room.

"One," said Heidel.

He aimed again. The explosion.

"Two," he said. "Rather good, eh?"

"Oh, yes," Sadler said.

"Quite," said Forbes.

"Again," said Heidel. A third shot echoed.

"Now," he said, pointing the muzzle at the last candle. "I would say this is it, wouldn't you, gentlemen? And as soon as this one goes, I'm afraid one of us is going to find a bullet right between his goddam sparkling eyes. Are you ready?"

He squinted one eye and looked down the sights. He squeezed the trigger, the room echoed and there was blackness. Heidel held his pistol poised over the table.

Silence.

"Well," said Forbes finally. "There you have it. Surprise, what?"

Heidel balanced the pistol, feeling his palm go suddenly moist against the black grip, and he looked around at the five pairs of glowing eyes.

"Bit of a shock, I should imagine," Forbes said. "Discovering all of us, as it were."

Heidel licked his lips. "How? *How* could you do this?"

Forbes remained motionless. "Simple as one, you know. Put men on rockets going back to Earth in place of returning colonists. Study. Observe. Learn. Shift a record here and there. Forge, change pictures, all that sort of thing. Poor contact between here and Earth, you know. Not too difficult."

"I'll get one of you," Heidel said, still balancing his pistol tightly.

"Well, possibly," Forbes said. "But no more than one. You have three guns pointed at you. We can see you perfectly, you know, as though it were broad daylight. One shiver of that pistol, and you're dead."

"Why have you done this?" Heidel said suddenly. "*Why?* Everything that was done was for the Martian. We tried to give you freedom and culture, the benefit of our knowledge . . . ."

"We didn't like your wrestlers," Forbes said.

Heidel's nostrils twitched, and suddenly he swung the pistol. There was a crashing explosion and then silence.

"Good," said Forbes. "I don't think he got the last one fired."

"You're all right then?" asked Meehan, putting his gun on the table.

"Oh, quite! Rather dramatic altogether, eh?"

"Nerve tingling," Locke agreed.

Forbes turned in his chair and called, "Oh, Kessit!"

The butler opened the door to the darkened room, hesitated, and reached for the light switch.

"No, no," Forbes said, smiling. "Never mind that. Come over here, will you please?"

The butler crossed the room slowly.

"It's all right," Forbes said. "The president will notice nothing whatever, Kessit. Would you mind pouring us all another glass of wine? I'm frightfully crazy about that port, eh?"

There was a murmur of agreeing voices. The butler lifted the silver decanter and filled glasses, moving easily and surely in the darkness.

"Cheers," said Forbes.

"Cheers," said the others, over the clink of glasses.

TREES ARE WHERE YOU FIND THEM

by Arthur Dekker Savage

The trees on Mars are few and stunted, says old Doc Yoris. There's plenty of gold, of course—but trees can be much more important!

YOU MIGHT say the trouble started at the Ivy, which is a moving picture house in Cave Junction built like a big quonset. It's the only show in these parts, and most of us old-timers up here in the timber country of southwest Oregon have got into the habit of going to see a picture on Saturday nights before we head for a tavern.

But I don't think old Doc Yoris, who was there with Lew and Rusty and me, had been to more than two or three shows in his life. Doc is kind of sensitive about his appearance on account of his small eyes and big nose and ears; and since gold mining gave way to logging and lumber mills, with Outsiders drifting into the country, Doc has taken to staying on his homestead away back up along Deer Creek, near the boundary of the Siskiyou National Forest. It's gotten so he'll come to Cave Junction only after dark, and even then he wears dark glasses so strangers won't notice him too much.

I couldn't see anything funny about the picture when Doc started laughing, but I figure it's a man's own business when he wants to laugh, so I didn't say anything. The show was one of these scientific things, and when Doc began to cackle it was showing some men getting out of a rocket ship on Mars and running over to look at some trees.

Rusty, who's top choker setter in our logging outfit, was trying to see Doc's point. He can snare logs with a hunk of steel cable faster than anyone I know, but he's never had much schooling. He turned to Doc. "I don't get it, Doc," he said. "What's the deal?"

Doc kept chuckling. "It's them trees," he said. "There's no trees like that on Mars."

"Oh," said Rusty.

I suppose it was just chance that Burt Holden was sitting behind us and heard the talk. Burt is one of the newcomers. He'd come down from Grants Pass and started a big lumber mill and logging outfit, and was trying to freeze out the little operators.

He growled something about keeping quiet. That got Rusty and Lew kind of mad, and Lew turned around and looked at Burt. Lew is even bigger than Burt, and things might have got interesting, but I wanted to see the rest of the picture. I nudged him and asked him if he had a chew. They won't let you smoke in the show, but it's okay to chew, and most of us were in the habit anyway, because there's too much danger of forest fire when you smoke on the job.

Doc laughed every time the screen showed trees, and I could hear Burt humping around in his seat like he was irritated.

*

AT THE END of the show we drifted over to the Owl Tavern and took a table against the north wall, behind the pool tables and across from the bar. Doc had put his dark glasses back on, and he sat facing the wall.

Not that many people apart from the Insiders knew Doc. He hadn't been very active since the young medical doctor had come to Cave Junction in 1948, although he never turned down anyone who came for help, and as far as I knew he'd never lost a patient unless he was already dead when Doc got there.

We were kidding Lew because he was still wearing his tin hat and caulked boots from work. "You figuring on starting early in the morning?" I asked him. Rusty and Doc laughed. It was a good joke because we rode out to the job in my jeep, and so we'd naturally get there at the same time.

Then Rusty sat up straighter and looked over at the bar. "Hey," he said, "Pop's talking to Burt Holden." Pop Johnson owns our outfit. He's one of the small operators that guys like Burt are trying to squeeze out.

"Hope he don't try to rook Pop into no deals," said Lew.

Doc tipped up his bottle of beer. In Oregon they don't sell anything but beer in the taverns. "Times change," he said. "Back in 1900 all they wanted was gold. Now they're trying to take all the trees."

"It's the big operators like Burt," I said. "Little guys like Pop can't cut 'em as fast as they grow. The companies don't have to reseed, either, except on National Forest land."

"That Burt Holden was up to my place couple weeks ago," said Doc. "Darn near caught me skinning out a deer."

"He better not yap to the game warden," said Rusty. "Them laws is for sports and Outsiders, not us guys who need the meat."

"He wanted to buy all my timber," said Doc. "Offered me ten dollars a thousand board feet, on the stump."

"Don't sell," I advised him. "If Burt offers that much, almost anyone else will pay twelve."

Doc looked at me. "I'd never sell my trees. Not at any price. I got a hundred and sixty acres of virgin stand, and that's the way it's gonna stay. I cut up the windfalls and snags for firewood, and that's all."

"Here comes Pop," said Lew.

Pop sat down with us and had a beer. He looked worried. We didn't ask him any questions, because we figure a man will talk if he wants to, and if he doesn't it's his own business.

He finally unlimbered. "Burt Holden wants to buy the mill," he said, wiping his mouth on the back of his hand.

"Buy *your* mill?" said Lew. "Hell, his mill is five times as big, and he's even got a burner to take care of slashings, so he don't have to shut down in the fire season."

"He just wants the land," said Pop, "because it's near the highway. He wants to tear down my setup and build a pulp mill."

"A *pulp* mill!" If we could have seen Doc's eyes through the glasses I imagine they'd have been popped open a full half inch. "Why, then they'll be cutting down everything but the brush!"

Pop nodded. "Yeah. Size of a log don't matter when you make paper—just so it's wood."

It seemed as though Doc was talking to himself. "They'll strip the land down bare," he mumbled. "And the hills will wash away, and the chemicals they use in the mill will kill the fish in the creeks and the Illinois River."

"That's why they won't let anyone start a pulp mill near Grants Pass," said Pop. "Most of the town's money comes from sports who come up to the Rogue River to fish."

Rusty set his jaw. "In the winter we *need* them fish," he said. He was right, too. The woods close down in the winter, on account of the snow, and if a man can't hunt and fish he's liable to get kind of hungry. That rocking chair money doesn't stretch very far.

"I ain't gonna sell," said Pop. "But that won't stop Burt Holden, and any place he builds the mill around here will drain into the Illinois."

Doc pushed back his chair and stood up to his full height of five foot four. "I'm gonna talk to Burt Holden," he said.

Rusty stood up to his six foot three. "I'll bring him over here, Doc," he said. "We're handy to the cue rack here, and Lew and Simmons can keep them guys he's with off my back."

I stood up and shoved Rusty back down. I'm no taller than he is, but I outweigh him about twenty pounds. I started working in the woods when we still felled trees with axes and misery whips—crosscut saws to the Outsiders. "I'll go get him," I said. "You're still mad about the show, and you wouldn't be able to get him this far without mussing him up."

"There won't be no trouble," said Doc. "I just want to make him an offer."

*

I WENT over and told Burt that Doc wanted to talk to him. The three guys with him followed us back to the table.

Burt figured he knew what it was all about, and he just stood over Doc and looked down on him. "If it's about your timber, Yoris," he said, "I'll take it, but I can't pay you more than nine dollars now. Lumber's coming down, and I'm taking a chance even at that." He rocked back and forth on his heels and looked at Pop as though daring him to say different.

"I still don't want to sell, Mr. Holden," said Doc. "But I've got better than three million feet on my place, and I'll *give* it to you if you won't put a pulp mill anywhere in the Illinois Valley."

We were all floored at that, but Burt recovered first. He gave a nasty laugh. "Not interested, Yoris. If you want to sell, look me up."

"Wait!" said Doc. "A pulp mill will take every tree in the Valley. In a few years—"

"It'll make money, too," said Burt flatly.

"Money ain't everything by a long shot. It won't buy trees and creeks and rain."

"It'll buy trees to make lumber." Burt was getting mad. "I don't want any opposition from you, Yoris. I've had enough trouble from people who try to hold back progress. If you don't like the way we run things here, you can—hell, you can go back to Mars!"

It seemed to me that it was just about time to start in. I could have taken Burt easiest, but I knew Rusty would probably swing on him first and get in my way, so I planned to work on the two guys on Burt's right, leaving the one on his left for Lew. I didn't want Pop to get tangled up in it.

I don't generally wait too long after I make up my mind, but then I noticed Rusty reaching out slowly for a cue stick, and I thought maybe I'd better take Burt first, while Rusty got set. I never did see a guy so one way about having something in his hands.

But Doc didn't drop out. "There ain't nothing but a few scrub trees on Mars," he said to Burt, looking him square in the eye. "And no creeks and no rain."

209

Burt curled his lip sarcastically. "The hell you say! Is that why you didn't like it there?" You could see he was just trying to egg Doc into saying he'd come from Mars, so he could give him the horse laugh. The guys he was with were getting set for a fracas, but they were waiting for Burt to lead off.

Doc didn't get caught. "But there's gold," he said, like he hadn't heard Burt at all. "Tons of it—laying all over the ground."

I guess Burt decided to ride along. "Okay, Yoris," he said. "Tell you what I'll do. For only one ton of Martian gold I'll agree to drop all plans for a pulp mill, here or anywhere else. In fact, I'll get out of business altogether."

Doc moved in like a log falling out of the loading tongs. "That's a deal," he said. "You ready to go?"

Burt started to look disgusted, then he smiled. "Sure. Mars must be quite a place if you came from there."

"Okay," said Doc. "You just stand up against the wall, Mr. Holden." Burt's smile faded. He figured Doc was trying to maneuver him into a likely position for us. But Doc cleared that up quick. "You boys get up and stand aside," he ordered. "Get back a ways and give Mr. Holden plenty of room." We didn't like it, but we cleared out from around the table. A bunch from the bar and pool tables, sensing something was up, came drifting over to watch. I could feel tension building up. "Now," said Doc, pointing, "you just stand right over there, Mr. Holden, and fold your arms."

Burt didn't like the audience, and I guess he figured his plans were backfiring when Doc didn't bluff. "You hill-happy old coot," he snarled. "You'd better go home and sleep it off!" I grabbed hold of Lew's arm and shook my head at Rusty. I wasn't going to interfere with Doc now.

"You're not scared, are you, Mr. Holden?" said Doc quietly. "Just you stand against the wall and take it easy. It won't hurt a bit."

*

BURT HOLDEN was plenty tough for an Outsider, and a hard-headed businessman to boot, but he'd never run into a customer like Doc before. You could see him trying to make up his mind on how to handle this thing. He glanced around quick at the crowd, and I could tell he decided to play it out to where Doc would have to draw in his horns. He actually grinned, for the effect it would have on everybody watching. "All right, Yoris," he said. He backed against the wall and folded his arms. "But hadn't you better stand up here with me?"

"I ain't going," said Doc. "I don't like Mars. But you won't have no trouble getting your gold. There's nuggets the size of your fist laying all over the dry river beds."

"I hate to be nosey," said Burt, playing to the crowd, "but how are you going to get me there?"

"With his head, o'course!" blurted Rusty before I could stop him. "Just like he cures you when you're sick!" Doc had pulled Rusty through two or three bad kid sicknesses—and a lot of the rest of us, too.

"Yep," said Doc. "A man don't need one of them rocket things to get between here and Mars. Fact is, I never seen one."

Burt looked at the ceiling like he was a martyr, then back at Doc. "Well, Yoris," he said in a tone that meant he was just about through humoring him, "I'm waiting. Can you send me there or can't you?" The start of a nasty smile was beginning to show at the corners of his mouth.

"Sure," said Doc. He slumped down in his chair and cupped his hands lightly around his dark glasses. I noticed his fingers trembling a little against his forehead.

The lights dimmed, flickered and went out, and we waited for the bartender to put in a new fuse. The power around here doesn't go haywire except in the winter, when trees fall across the lines. A small fight started over in a corner.

When the lights came back on, Doc and Pop started for the door, and Lew and Rusty and I followed. Burt's buddies were looking kind of puzzled, and a few old-timers were moving over to watch the fight. The rest were heading back to the bar.

Rusty piled into the jeep with Doc and me. "When you going to bring him back, Doc?" he asked when we started moving.

"Dunno," said Doc. He took off his glasses to watch me shift gears. He's been after me for a long time to teach him how to drive. "It only works on a man once."

THE REAL HARD SELL

by William W. Stuart

Naturally human work was more creative, more inspiring, more important than robot drudgery. Naturally it was the most important task in all the world ... or was it?

BEN TILMAN sat down in the easiest of all easy chairs. He picked up a magazine, flipped pages; stood up, snapped fingers; walked to the view wall, walked back; sat down, picked up the magazine.

He was waiting, near the end of the day, after hours, in the lush, plush waiting room—"The customer's ease is the Sales Manager's please"—to see the Old Man. He was fidgety, but not about something. About nothing. He was irritated at nobody, at the world; at himself.

He was irritated at himself because there was no clear reason for him to be irritated at anything.

There he sat, Ben Tilman, normally a cheerful, pleasant young man. He was a salesman like any modern man and a far better salesman than most. He had a sweet little wife, blonde and pretty. He had a fine, husky two-year-old boy, smart, a real future National Sales Manager. He loved them both. He had every reason to be contented with his highly desirable, comfortable lot.

And yet he had been getting more sour and edgy ever since about six months after the baby came home from the Center and the novelty of responsibility for wife and child had worn off. He had now quit three jobs, good enough sales jobs where he was doing well, in a year. For no reason? For petty, pointless reasons.

With Ancestral Insurance, "Generations of Protection," he'd made the Billion Dollar Club—and immediately begun to feel dissatisfied with it—just before cute, sexy, blonde Betty had suddenly come from nowhere into his life and he had married her. That had helped, sure. But as soon after that as he had started paying serious attention to his job again, he was fed up with it. "Too much paper work. All those forms. It's work for a robot, not a man," he'd told Betty when he quit. A lie. The paper work was, as he looked back on it, not bad at all; pleasant even, in a way. It was just—nothing. Anything.

Indoor-Outdoor Climatizers—sniffles, he said, kept killing his sales presentation even though his record was good enough. Ultra-sonic toothbrushes, then, were a fine product. Only the vibration, with his gold inlay, seemed to give him headaches after every demonstration. He didn't have a gold inlay. But the headaches were real enough. So he quit.

So now he had a great new job with a great organization, Amalgamated Production for Living—ALPRODLIV. He was about to take on his first big assignment.

For that he had felt a spark of the old enthusiasm and it had carried him into working out a bright new sales approach for the deal tonight. The Old Man himself had taken a personal interest, which was a terrific break. And still Ben Tilman felt that uneasy dissatisfaction. Damn.

"Mr. Robb will see you now, Mr. Tilman," said the cool robot voice from the Elec-Sec Desk. It was after customer hours and the charming human receptionist had gone. The robot secretary, like most working robots, was functional in form—circuits and wires, mike, speaker, extension arms to type and to reach any file in the room, wheels for intra-office mobility.

"Thanks, hon," said Ben. Nevertheless, robot secretaries were all programmed and rated female—and it was wise to be polite to them. After all, they could think and had feelings. There were a lot of important things they could do for a salesman—or, sometimes, not do. This one, being helpful, stretched out a long metal arm to open the door to the inner office for Ben. He smiled his appreciation and went in.

*

THE Old Man, Amalgamated's grand old salesman, was billiard bald, aging, a little stout and a little slower now. But he was still a fine sales manager. He sat at his huge, old fashioned oak desk as Ben walked across the office.

"Evening, sir." No response. Louder, "Good evening, Mr. Robb. Mr. Robb, it's Ben, sir. Ben Tilman. You memo'd me to come—" Still no sign. The eyes, under the great, beetling brows, seemed closed.

Ben grinned and reached out across the wide desk toward the small, plastic box hanging on the Old Man's chest. The Old Man glanced up as Ben tapped the plastic lightly with his fingernail.

"Oh, Ben. It's you." The Old Man raised his hand to adjust the ancient style hearing aid he affected as Ben sank into a chair. "Sorry Ben. I just had old Brannic Z-IX in here. A fine old robot, yes, but like most of that model, long-winded. So—" He gestured at the hearing aid.

Ben smiled. Everyone knew the Old Man used that crude old rig so he could pointedly tune out conversations he didn't care to hear. Any time you were talking to him and that distant look came into his half closed eyes, you could be sure that you were cut off.

"Sorry, Ben. Well now. I simply wanted to check with you, boy. Everything all set for tonight?"

"Well, yes, sir. Everything is set and programmed. Betty and I will play it all evening for the suspense, let them wonder, build it up—and then, instead of the big pitch they'll be looking for, we'll let it go easy."

"A new twist on the old change-up. Ben, boy, it's going to go. I feel it. It's in the air, things are just ripe for a new, super-soft-sell pitch. Selling you've got to do by feel, eh Ben? By sales genius and the old seat of the pants. Good. After tonight I'm going all out, a hemisphere-wide, thirty day campaign. I'll put the top sales artist of every regional office on it. They can train on your test pattern tapes. I believe we can turn over billions before everybody picks up the signal and it senilesces. You give an old man a new faith in sales, Ben! You're a salesman."

"Well, sir—" But the Old Man's knack with the youthful-enthusiasm approach was contagious. For the moment Ben caught it and he felt pretty good about the coming night's work. He and Betty together would put the deal over. That would be something.

Sure it would...

"How do you and your wife like the place, Ben?" It was some place, for sure, the brand new house that Amalgamated had installed Ben, Betty and Bennie in the day after he had signed up.

"It's—uh—just fine, sir. Betty likes it very much, really. We both do." He hoped his tone was right.

"Good, Ben. Well, be sure to stop by in the morning. I'll have the tapes, of course, but I'll want your analysis. Might be a little vacation bonus in it for you, too."

"Sir, I don't know how to thank you."

The Old Man waved a hand. "Nothing you won't have earned, my boy. Robots can't sell." That was the set dismissal.

"Yes, sir. Robots can't manage sales, or—" He winked. The Old Man chuckled. An old joke was never too old for the Old Man. The same old bromides every time; and the same hearty chuckle. Ben left on the end of it.

*

DIALING home on his new, Company-owned, convertible soar-kart, he felt not too bad. Some of the old lift in spirits came as the kart-pilot circuits digested the directions, selected a route and zipped up into a north-north-west traffic pattern. The Old Man was a wonderful sales manager and boss. The new house-warming pitch that he and Betty would try tonight was smart. He could feel he had done something.

Exercising his sales ability with fair success, he fed himself this pitch all along the two hundred mile, twenty-minute hop home from the city. The time and distance didn't bother him. "Gives me time to think," he had told Betty. Whether or not this seemed to her an advantage, she didn't say. At least she liked the place, "Amalgamated's Country Gentleman Estate—Spacious, Yet fully Automated."

"We are," the Old Man told Ben when he was given the Company-assigned quarters, "starting a new trend. With the terrific decline in birth rate during the past 90 to 100 years, you'll be astonished at how much room there is out there. No reason for everyone to live in the suburban centers any more. With millions of empty apartments in them, high time we built something else, eh? Trouble with people today, no initiative in obsolescing. But we'll move them."

Home, Ben left the kart out and conveyed up the walk. The front door opened. Betty had been watching for him. He walked to the family vueroom, as usual declining to convey in the house. The hell with the conveyor's feelings, if so simple a robot really had any. He liked to walk.

"Color pattern," Betty ordered the vuescreen as he came in, "robot audio out." With people talking in the house it was still necessary to put the machines under master automatic and manual control. Some of the less sophisticated robots might pick up some chance phrase of conversation and interpret it as an order if left on audio.

"Ben," said Betty, getting up to meet him, "you're late."

Ben was too good a salesman to argue that. Instead, he took her in his arms and kissed her. It was a very good sixty seconds later that she pushed him away with a severeness destroyed by a blush and a giggle to say, "Late but making up for lost time, huh? And sober, too. You must be feeling good for a change."

"Sure—and you feel even better, sugar." He reached for her again. She slipped away from him, laughing, but his wrist tel-timer caught on the locket she always wore, her only memento from her parents, dead in the old moon-orb crash disaster. She stood still, slightly annoyed, as he unhooked and his mood was, not broken, but set back a little. "What's got into you tonight anyway, Ben?"

"Oh, I don't know. Did I tell you, the O.M. may give us a vacation? Remember some of those nights up at that new 'Do It Yourself' Camp last summer?"

"Ben!" She blushed, smiled. "We won't get any vacation if we blow our house-warming pitch tonight, you know. And we have three couples due here in less than a half hour. Besides, I have to talk to you about Nana."

*

"THAT damned new CD-IX model. Now what?"

"She's very upset about Bennie. I'm not sure I blame her. This afternoon he simply refused his indoctrination. All the time he should have been playing store with Playmate he insisted on drawing things—himself, mind you, not Playmate. On the walls, with an old pencil of yours he found someplace in your things. Nana couldn't do a thing with him. She says you've got to give him a spanking."

"Why me? Why not you?"

"Now Ben, we've been over that and over it. Discipline is the father's job."

"Well, I won't do it. Bennie's just a baby. Let him do a few things himself. Won't hurt him."

"Ben!"

"That Nana is an officious busybody, trying to run our lives."

"Oh, Ben! You know Nana loves little Bennie. She only wants to help him."

"But to what?"

"She'd never dream of lifting a finger against Bennie no matter what he did. And she lives in terror that he'll cut her switch in some temper tantrum."

"Hmph! Well, I'm going up right now and tell her if I hear another word from her about spanking Bennie, I'll cut her switch myself. Then she can go back to Central for reprogramming and see how she likes it."

"Ben! You wouldn't."

"Why not? Maybe she needs a new personality?"

"You won't say a thing to her. You're too soft-hearted."

"This time I won't be."

This time he wasn't. He met Nana CD-IX in the hallway outside Bennie's room. Like all nurse, teaching, and children's personal service robots, she was human in form, except for her control dial safely out of baby's reach, top, center.

The human form was reassuring to children, kept them from feeling strange with parents back. Nana was big, gray-haired, stout, buxom, motherly, to reassure parents.

"Now, Mr. Tilman," she said with weary impatience, "you are too late. Surely you don't intend to burst in and disturb your son now."

"Surely I do."

"But he is having his supper. You will upset him. Can't you understand that you should arrange to be here between 5:30 and 6 if you wish to interview the child?"

"Did he miss me? Sorry, I couldn't make it earlier. But now I am going to see him a minute."

"Mr. Tilman!"

"Nana! And what's this about your wanting Bennie spanked because he drew a few pictures?"

"Surely you realize these are the child's formative years, Mr. Tilman. He should be learning to think in terms of selling now—not doing things. That's robot work, Mr. Tilman. Robots can't sell, you know, and what will people, let alone robots think if you let your boy grow up—"

*

"HE's growing up fine; and I am going in to see him."

"Mr. Tilman!"

"And for two credits, Nana, I'd cut your switch. You hear me?"

"Mr. Tilman—no! No, please. I'm sorry. Let the boy scrawl a bit; perhaps it won't hurt him. Go in and see him if you must, but do try not to upset him or—All right, all right. But please Mr. Tilman, my switch—"

"Very well Nana. I'll leave it. This time."

"Thank you, Mr. Tilman."

"So we understand each other, Nana. Though, matter of fact, I'm hanged if I ever did quite see why you senior-level robots get so worked up about your identities."

"Wouldn't you, Mr. Tilman?"

"Of course. But—well, yes, I suppose I do see, in a way. Let's go see Bennie-boy."

So Ben Tilman went into the nursery and enjoyed every second of a fast fifteen-minute roughhouse with his round-faced, laughing, chubby son and heir. No doubt it was very bad, just after supper. But Nana, with a rather humanly anxious restraint, confined herself to an unobtrusive look of disapproval.

He left Bennie giggling and doubtless upset, at least to a point of uneagerness for Nana's bedtime story about Billie the oldtime newsboy, who sold the Brooklyn Bridge.

So then he was run through a fast ten-minute shower, shave and change by Valet. He floated downstairs just as Betty came out of the cocktail lounge to say, "Code 462112 on the approach indicator. Must be the Stoddards. They always get every place first, in time for an extra drink."

"Fred and Alice, yes. But damn their taste for gin, don't let Barboy keep the cork in the vermouth all evening. I like a touch of vermouth. I wonder if maybe I shouldn't—"

"No, you shouldn't mix the cocktails yourself and scandalize everybody. You know perfectly well Barboy really does do better anyway."

"Well, maybe. Everything all set, hon? Sorry I was late."

"No trouble here. I just fed Robutler the base program this morning and spent the rest of the day planning my side of our Sell. How to tantalize the girls, pique the curiosity without giving it away. But you know—" she laughed a little ruefully—"I sort of miss not having even the shopping to do. Sometimes it hardly seems as though you need a wife at all."

Ben slid an arm around her waist. "Selling isn't the only thing robots can't do, sugar." He pulled her close.

"Ben! They're at the door."

They were, and then in the door, oh-ing and ah-ing over this and that. And complimenting Barboy on the martinis. Then the Wilsons came and the Bartletts and that was it.

"Three couples will be right," Ben had analyzed it. "Enough so we can let them get together and build up each others' curiosity but not too many for easy control. People that don't know us so well they might be likely to guess the gimmick. We'll let them stew all evening while they enjoy the Country Gentleman House-Warming hospitality. Then, very casually, we toss it out and let it lie there in front of them. They will be sniffing, ready to nibble. The clincher will drive them right in. I'd stake my sales reputation on it." If it matters a damn, he added. But silently.

They entertained three couples at their house-warming party. It was a delightful party, a credit to Ben, Betty and the finest built-in house robots the mind of Amalgamated could devise.

By ten o'clock they had dropped a dozen or more random hints, but never a sales pitch. Suspense was building nicely when Betty put down an empty glass and unobtrusively pushed the button to cue Nana. Perfect timing. They apologized to the guests, "We're ashamed to be so old-fashioned but we feel better if we look in on the boy when he wakes in the night. It keeps him from forgetting us."

Then they floated off upstairs together, ostensibly to see Nana and little Bennie.

Fred Stoddard: "Some place they have here, eh? Off-beat. A little too advanced for my taste, this single dwelling idea, but maybe—Ben sure must have landed something juicy with Amalgamated to afford this. What the devil is he pushing, anyway?"

Scoville Wilson (shrug): "Beats me. You know, before dinner I cornered him at the bar to see if I could slip in a word or two of sell. Damned if he didn't sign an order for my Cyclo-sell Junior Tape Library without even a C level resistance. Then he talked a bit about the drinks and I thought sure he was pushing that new model Barboy. I was all set to come back with a sincere 'think it over'—and then he took a bottle from the Barboy, added a dash of vermouth to his drink and walked off without a word of sell. He always was an odd one."

Lucy Wilson (turns from woman talk with the other two wives): "Oh no! I knew it wasn't the Barboy set. They wouldn't have him set so slow. Besides didn't you hear the way she carried on about the nursery and that lovely Nana? That must have been a build-up, but Ben goofed his cue to move in on Sco and me for a close. Doesn't Amalgamated handle those nurseries?"

Tom Bartlett: "Amalgamated makes almost anything. That's the puzzle. I dunno—but it must be something big. He has to hit us with something, doesn't he?"

Belle Bartlett: "Who ever heard of a party without a sell?"

Nancy Stoddard: "Who ever heard of a party going past ten without at least a warm-up pitch? And Betty promised Fred to send both Ben and Bennie to the Clinic for their Medchecks. You know we have the newest, finestdiagnosticians—"

Fred Stoddard: "Nancy!"

Nancy Stoddard: "Oh, I'm sorry. I shouldn't be selling you folks at their party, should I? Come to think, you're all signed with Fred anyway, aren't you? Well, about Ben, I think—"

Lucy Wilson: "Sh-h-h! Here they come."

*

SMILING, charming—and still not an order form in sight—Ben and Betty got back to their guests. Another half hour. Barboy was passing around with nightcaps. Lucy Wilson nervously put a reducegar to her sophisticated, peppermint-striped lips.

Quickly Ben Tilman was on his feet. He pulled a small, metal cylinder from his pocket with a flourish and held it out on his open palm toward Lucy. A tiny robot Statue of Liberty climbed from the cylinder, walked across Ben's hand, smiled, curtsied and reached out to light the reducegar with her torch, piping in a high, thin voice, "Amalgamated reducegars are cooler, lighter, finer."

"Ben! How simply darling!"

"Do you like it? It's a new thing from Amalgamated NovelDiv. You can program it for up to a hundred selective sell phrases, audio or visio key. Every salesman should have one. Makes a marvelous gift, and surprisingly reasonable."

"So that's it, Ben. I just love it!"

"Good! It's yours, compliments of Amalgamated."

"But—then you're not selling them? Well, what on earth—?"

"Damn it, Ben," Fred Stoddard broke in, "come on, man, out with it. What in hell are you selling? You've given us the shakes. What is it? The Barboy set? It's great. If I can scrape up the down payment, I'll—"

"After we furnish a nursery with a decent Nana, Fred Stoddard," Nancy snapped, "and get a second soar-kart. Ben isn't selling Barboys anyway, are you. Ben? It is that sweet, sweet Nana, isn't it? And I do want one, the whole nursery, Playmate and all, girl-programmed of course, for our Polly."

"Is it the nursery, Betty?" Lucy pitched in her credit's worth. "Make him tell us, darling. We have enjoyed everything so much, the dinner, the Tri-deo, this whole lovely, lovely place of yours. Certainly the house warming has been perfectly charming."

"And that's it," said Ben smiling, a sheaf of paper forms suddenly in his hand.

"What? Not—?"

"The house, yes. Amalgamated's Country Gentleman Estate, complete, everything in it except Bennie, Betty and me. Your equity in your Center co-op can serve as down payment, easy three-generation terms, issue insurance. Actually, I can show you how, counting in your entertainment, vacation, incidental, and living expenses, the Country Gentleman will honestly cost you less."

"Ben!"

"How simply too clever!"

Ben let it rest there. It was enough. Fred Stoddard, after a short scuffle with Scoville Wilson for the pen, signed the contract with a flourish. Sco followed.

"There!"

"There now, Ben," said Betty, holding Bennie a little awkwardly in her arms in the soar-kart. They had moved out so the Stoddards could move right in. Now they were on their way in to their reserved suite at Amalgamated's Guest-ville. "You were absolutely marvellous. Imagine selling all three of them!"

"There wasn't anything to it, actually."

"Ben, how can you say that? Nobody else could have done it. It was a sales masterpiece. And just think. Now salesmen all over the hemisphere are going to follow your sales plan. Doesn't it make you proud? Happy? Ben, you aren't going to be like that again?"

No, of course he wasn't. He was pleased and proud. Anyway, the Old Man would be, and that, certainly, was something. A man had to feel good about winning the approval of Amalgamated's grand Old Man. And it did seem to make Betty happy.

But the actual selling of the fool house and even the two other, identical houses on the other side of the hill—he just couldn't seem to get much of a glow over it. He had done it; and what had he done? It was the insurance and the toothbrushes all over again, and the old nervous, sour feeling inside.

"At least we do have a vacation trip coming out of it, hon. The O.M. practically promised it yesterday, if our sell sold. We could—"

"—go back to that queer new 'Do It Yourself' camp up on the lake you insisted on dragging me to the last week of our vacation last summer. Ben, really!" He was going to be like that. She knew it.

"Well, even you admitted it was some fun."

"Oh, sort of, I suppose. For a little while. Once you got used to the whole place without one single machine that could think or do even the simplest little thing by itself. So, well, almost like being savages. Do you think it would be safe for Bennie? We can't watch him all the time, you know."

"People used to manage in the old days. And remember those people, the Burleys, who were staying up there?"

"That queer, crazy bunch who went there for a vacation when the Camp was first opened and then just stayed? Honestly, Ben! Surely you're not thinkingof—"

"Oh, nothing like that. Just a vacation. Only—"

Only those queer, peculiar people, the Burleys had seemed so relaxed and cheerful. Grandma and Ma Burley cleaning, washing, cooking on the ancient electric stove; little Donnie, being a nuisance, poking at the keys on his father's crude, manual typewriter, a museum piece; Donnie and his brothers wasting away childhood digging and piling sand on the beach, paddling a boat and actually building a play house. It was mad. People playing robots. And yet, they seemed to have a wonderful time while they were doing it.

"But how do you keep staying here?" he had asked Buck Burley, "Why don't they put you out!"

"Who?" asked Buck. "How? Nobody can sell me on leaving. We like it here. No robot can force us out. Here we are. Here we stay."

*

THEY pulled into the Guest-ville ramp. Bennie was fussy; the nursery Nana was strange to him. On impulse, Betty took him in to sleep in their room, ignoring the disapproving stares of both the Nana and the Roboy with their things.

They were tired, let down. They went to bed quietly.

In the morning Betty was already up when Ben stumbled out of bed. "Hi," she said, nervously cheerful. "The house Nanas all had overload this morning and I won't stand for any of those utility components with Bennie. So I'm taking care of him myself."

Bennie chortled and drooled vita-meal at his high-chair, unreprimanded. Ben mustered a faint smile and turned to go dial a shave, cool shower and dress at Robather.

That done, he had a bite of breakfast. He felt less than top-sale, but better. Last night had gone well. The Old Man would give them a pre-paid vacation clearance to any resort in the world or out. Why gloom?

He rubbed Bennie's unruly hair, kissed Betty and conveyed over from Guest-ville to office.

Message-sec, in tone respect-admiration A, told him the Old Man was waiting for him. Susan, the human receptionist in the outer office, favored him with a dazzling smile. There was a girl who could sell; and had a product of her own, too.

The Old Man was at his big, oak desk but, a signal honor, he got up and came half across the room to grab Ben's hand and shake it. "Got the full report, son. Checked the tapes already. That's selling, boy! I'm proud of you. Tell you what, Ben. Instead of waiting for a sales slack, I'm going to move you and that sweet little wife of yours right into a spanking new, special Country Gentleman unit I had in mind for myself. And a nice, fat boost in your credit rating has already gone down to accounting. Good? Good. Now, Ben, I have a real, artistic sales challenge that is crying for your talent."

"Sir? Thank you. But, sir, there is the matter of the vacation—"

"Vacation? Sure, Ben. Take a vacation anytime. But right now it seems to the Old Man you're on a hot selling streak. I don't want to see you get off the track, son; your interests are mine. And wait till you get your teeth into this one. Books, Ben boy. Books! People are spending all their time sitting in on Tri-deo, not reading. People should read more, Ben. Gives them that healthy tired feeling. Now we have the product. We have senior Robo-writers with more circuits than ever before. All possible information, every conceivable plot. Maybe a saturation guilt type campaign to start—but it's up to you, Ben. I don't care how you do it, but move books."

"Books, eh? Well, now." Ben was interested. "Funny thing, sir, but that ties in with something I was thinking about just last night."

"You have an angle? Good boy!"

"Yes, sir. Well, it is a wild thought maybe, but last summer when I was on vacation I met a man up at that new camp and—well, I know it sounds silly, but he was writing a book."

"Nonsense!"

"Just what I thought, sir. But I read some of it and, I don't know, it had a sort of a feel about it. Something new, sir, it might catch on."

"All right, all right. That's enough. You're a salesman. You've sold me."

"On the book?" Ben was surprised.

"Quit pulling an old man's leg, Ben. I'm sold on your needing a vacation. I'll fill out your vacation pass right now." The Old Man, still a vigorous, vital figure, turned and walked back to his Desk-sec. "Yes sir," said the secretarial voice, "got it. Vacation clearance for Tilman, Ben, any resort."

"And family," said Ben.

"And family. Very good, sir."

The Old Man made his sign on the pass and said heavily, "All right then, Ben. That's it. Maybe if you go back up to that place for a few days and see that psycho who was writing a book again, perhaps you'll realize how impractical it is."

"But sir! I'm serious about that book. It really did have—" he broke off.

*

The Old Man was sitting there, face blank, withdrawn. Ben could feel he wasn't even listening. That damned hearing aid of his. The Old Man had cut it off. Suddenly, unreasoningly, Ben was furious. He stood by the huge desk and he reached across toward the hearing aid on the Old Man's chest to turn up the volume. The Old Man looked up and saw Ben's hand stretching out.

A sudden look of fear came into his china blue, clear eyes but he made no move. He sat frozen in his chair.

Ben hesitated a second. "What—?" But he didn't have to ask. He knew.

And he also knew what he was going to do.

"No!" said the Old Man. "No, Ben. I've only been trying to help; trying to serve your best interests the best way I know. Ben, you mustn't—"

But Ben moved forward.

*

HE took the plastic box on the Old Man's chest and firmly cut the switch.

The Old Man, the Robot Old Man, went lifeless and slumped back in his chair as Ben stretched to cut off the Desk-sec. Then he picked up his vacation clearance.

"Robots can't sell, eh?" he said to the dead machine behind the desk. "Well, you couldn't sell me that time, could you, Old Man?"

Clumsily, rustily, Ben whistled a cheerful little off-key tune to himself. Hell, they could do anything at all—except sell.

"You can't fool some of the people all of the time," he remarked over his shoulder to the still, silent figure of the Old Man as he left the office, "it was a man said that." He closed the door softly behind him.

Betty would be waiting.

Betty was waiting. Her head ached as she bounced Bennie, the child of Ben, of herself and of an unknown egg cell from an anonymous ovary, on her knees. Betty 3-RC-VIII, secret, wife-style model, the highest development of the art of Robotics had known instantly when Ben cut the Old Man's switch. She had half expected it. But it made her headache worse.

"But damn my programming!" She spoke abruptly, aloud, nervously fingering the locket around her neck. "Damn it and shift circuit. He's right! He is my husband and he is right and I'm glad. I'm glad we're going to the camp and I'm going to help him stay."

After all, why shouldn't a man want to do things just as much as a robot? He had energy, circuits, feelings too. She knew he did.

For herself, she loved her Ben and Bennie. But still just that wasn't enough occupation. She was glad they were going to the new isolation compound for non-psychotic but unstable, hyper-active, socially dangerous individual humans. At the camp there would be things to do.

At the camp they would be happy.

All at once the headache that had been bothering her so these past months was gone. She felt fine and she smiled at little Bennie. "Bennie-boy," she said, kissing his smooth, untroubled baby forehead. "Daddy's coming." Bennie laughed and started to reach for the locket around Mommy's neck. But just then the door opened and he jumped down to run and meet his daddy.

WASTE NOT. WANT

by Dave Dryfoos

Eat your spinach, little man! It's good for you. Stuff yourself with it. Be a good little consumer, or the cops will get you . . . . For such is the law of supply and demand!

PANIC roused him—the black imp of panic that lived under the garish rug of this unfamiliar room and crawled out at dawn to nudge him awake and stare from the blank space to his left where Tillie's gray head should have been.

His fists clenched in anger—at himself. He'd never been the sort to make allowance for his own weakness and didn't propose to begin doing so now, at age eighty-six. Tillie'd been killed in that crash well over a year ago and it was time he got used to his widowerhood and quit searching for her every morning.

But even after he gave himself the bawling out, orientation came slowly. The surroundings looked so strange. No matter what he told himself it was hard to believe that he was indeed Fred Lubway, mechanical engineer, and had a right to be in this single bed, alone in this house his Tillie had never seen.

The right to be there was all wrong. He disliked the house and hated all its furnishings.

The cybernetic cooker in the kitchen; the magnetically-suspended divans in the living room; the three-dimensional color broadcasts he could so readily project to any wall or ceiling; the solartropic machinery that would turn any face of the pentagonal house into the sun or the shade or the breeze; the lift that would raise the entire building a hundred feet into the air to give him a wider view and more privacy—all left him dissatisfied.

They were new. None had been shared with Tillie. He used them only to the extent required by law to fulfill his duty as a consumer.

"You must change your home because of the change in your family composition," the Ration Board's bright young female had explained, right after Tillie's funeral. "Your present furnishings are obsolete. You must replace them."

"And if I don't?" He'd been truculent.

"I doubt we'd have to invoke the penalties for criminal underconsumption," she'd explained airily. "There are plenty of other possible courses of action. Maybe we'd just get a decision that you're prematurely senile and unable to care for yourself. Then you'd go to a home for the aged where they'd *help* you consume—with forced feedings and such."

So here he was, in this home-of-his-own that seemed to belong to someone else. Well, at least he wasn't senile, even if he did move a little slowly, now, getting out of bed. He'd warm up soon. All by himself. With no one's help.

And as far as these newfangled gadgets in the bathroom were concerned, he could follow any well-written set of directions. He'd scalded himself that time only because the printed instructions were so confusing.

He took a cold shower this time.

When the airtowel had finished blowing and he was half dry—not wholly dry because the machine wasn't adapted to people who took ice-cold showers—he went in to the clothing machine. He punched the same few holes in its tape that he put there every day, stood in the right place, and in due course emerged with his long, rawboned frame covered by magenta tights having an excessively baggy seat.

He knew the costume was neither pretty nor fashionable and that its design, having been wholly within his control when he punched the tape, revealed both his taste and his mood. He didn't care; there was no one in the world whom he wanted to impress.

He looked in the dressing room mirror not to inspect the tights but to examine his face and see if it needed shaving. Too late he remembered that twenty years had elapsed since the permanent depilatories were first invented and ten since he'd used one and stopped having to shave.

There were too many changes like that in this gadget-mad world; too many new ways of doing old things. Life had no stability.

He stalked into the kitchen wishing he could skip breakfast—anger always unsettled his stomach. But everyone was required to eat at least three meals a day. The vast machine-records system that kept track of each person's consumption would reveal to the Ration Board any failure to use his share of food, so he dialed Breakfast Number Three—tomato juice, toast, and coffee.

The signal-panel flashed "Under-Eating" and he knew the state machine-records system had advised his cybernetic cooker to increase the amount of his consumption. Chin in hands, he sat hopelessly at the kitchen table awaiting his meal, and in due course was served prunes, waffles, bacon, eggs, toast, and tea—none of which he liked, except for toast.

He ate dutifully nevertheless, telling himself he wasn't afraid of the ration-cops who were always suspecting him of underconsumption because he was the tall skinny type and never got fat like most people, but that he ate what the cooker had given him because his father had been unemployed for a long time during the depression seventy-five years before, so he'd never been able to bring himself to throw food away.

Failure to consume had in the old days been called "overproduction" and by any name it was bad. So was war—he'd read enough about war to be glad that form of consumption had finally been abolished.

Still it was a duty and not a pleasure to eat so much, and a relief to get up and put the dirty dishes into the disposal machine and go up topside to his gyro.

*

DISGUSTINGLY, he had a long wait before departure. After climbing into the gyro and transmitting his flight plan, he had to sit seething for all of fifteen minutes before the Mount Diablo Flight Control Center deigned to lift his remote-controlled gyro into the air. And when the signal came, ascent was so awkwardly abrupt it made his ears pop.

He couldn't even complain. The Center was mechanical, and unequipped to hear complaints.

It routed him straight down the San Joaquin Valley—a beautiful sight from fifteen thousand feet, but over-familiar. He fell asleep and awakened only when unexpectedly brought down at Bakersfield Field.

Above his instrument panel the printing-receiver said "Routine Check of Equipment and Documents. Not Over Five Minutes' Delay."

But it could take longer. And tardiness was subject to official punishments as a form of unproductiveness. He called George Harding at the plant.

Harding apparently had been expecting the call. His round bluff face wore a scowl of annoyance.

"Don't you ever watch the newscasts?" he demanded angrily. "They began this 'Routine Check' you're in at five this morning, and were broadcasting pictures of the resulting traffic jam by six. If you'd filed a flight plan for Santa Barbara and come on down the coast you'd have avoided all this."

"I'm not required to listen to newscasts," Fred replied tartly. "I own the requisite number of receivers and—"

"Now, listen, Fred," Harding interrupted. "We need you down here so hurry up!"

Fred heard him switch off and sat for a moment trembling with rage. But he ended by grinning wryly. Everyone was in the same boat, of course. For the most part, people avoided thinking about it. But he could now see himself as if from above, spending his life flitting back and forth between home and plant, plant and home; wracking his brain to devise labor-saving machines while at the plant, then rushing home to struggle with the need to consume their tremendous output.

Was he a man? Or was he a caged squirrel racing in an exercise-wheel, running himself ragged and with great effort producing absolutely nothing?

He wasn't going to do it any longer, by golly! He was going to—

"Good morning!" A chubby young man in the pea-green uniform of a ration-cop opened the door and climbed uninvited into the cockpit. "May I check the up-to-dateness of your ship's equipment, please?"

Fred didn't answer. He didn't have to. The young officer was already in the manual pilot's seat, checking the secondary controls.

In swift routine he tried motor and instruments, and took the craft briefly aloft. Down again, he demanded Fred's papers.

The licenses that pertained to the gyro were in order, but there was trouble over Fred's personal documents: his ration-book contained far too few sales-validations.

"You're not doing your share of consuming, Oldtimer," the young cop said mildly. "Look at all these unused food allotments! Want to cause a depression?"

"No."

"Man, if you don't eat more than this, we'll have mass starvation!"

"I know the slogans."

"Yes, but do you know the penalties? Forced feeding, compulsory consumption—do you think they're fun?"

"No."

"Well, you can file your flight plan and go, but if you don't spend those tickets before their expiration dates, Mister, you'll have cause to regret it."

With a special pencil, he sense-marked the card's margins.

Fred felt that each stroke of the pencil was a black mark against him. He watched in apprehensive silence.

The young cop was also silent. When finished he wordlessly returned the identification, tipped his cap, and swaggered off, his thick neck red above his green collar.

Fred found he'd had more than enough of swaggering young men with beefy red necks. That added to his disgust with the constant struggle to produce and consume, consume and produce. Vague, wishful threats froze as determination: he absolutely wasn't going through any more of it.

He filed a flight plan that would return him to his home, and in due course arrived there.

The phone rang in his ears as he opened the cockpit. He didn't want to answer, and he stayed on the roof securing the gyro and plugging in its battery-charger. But he couldn't ignore the bell's insistent clamor.

When he went downstairs and switched on the phone, George Harding's round face splashed on the wall.

"Fred," he said, "when we talked a few hours ago, you forgot to say you were sick. I phoned to confirm that for the Attendance Report. Did this call get you out of bed?"

He could see it hadn't. Therefore Fred knew he must be recording the audio only, and not the video; trying to give him a break with the Attendance people and coach him on the most appeasing answers.

A well-meant gesture, but a false one. And Fred was fed up with the false. "I forgot nothing," he said bluntly. "I'm perfectly well and haven't been near bed."

"Now, wait," George said hastily. "It's no crime to be sick. And—ah—don't say anything you wouldn't want preserved for posterity."

"George, I'm not going to play along with you," Fred insisted. "This business of producing to consume and consuming to produce has got me down. It's beyond all reason!"

"No, it isn't. You're an excellent mechanical engineer, Fred, but you're not an economist. That's why you don't understand. Just excuse me for a minute, and I'll show you."

He left the field of view. Fred waited incuriously for him to return, suddenly conscious of the fact that he now had nothing better to do with his time.

George was back in less than a minute, anyhow. "O.K.," he said briskly. "Now, where were we? Oh, yes. I just wanted to say that production is a form of consumption, too—even the production of machine-tools and labor-saving devices. So there's nothing inconsistent—"

"What are you trying to do?" Fred demanded. "Don't lecture me—I know as much econ as you do!"

"But you've got to come back to work, Fred! I want you to use your rations, put your shoulder to the wheel, and conform generally. The policing's too strict for you to try anything else, fella—and I like you too well to want to see you—"

"I don't need you to protect me, George," Fred said stiffly. "I guess you mean well enough. But goodbye." He switched off.

*

THE SILENCE struck him. Not a sound stirred the air in that lonely new house except the slight wheeze of his breathing.

He felt tired. Bone weary. As if all the fatigues of his eighty-six years were accumulated within him.

He stood by a window and stared blindly out. Everyone seemed to have been heckling him, shoving him around, making him change all his ways every minute. He didn't want to change. He didn't want to be forever adapting to new gadgets, new fads, new ways of doing things.

He thought of the villages of India, substantially unchanged for three, four, five thousand years. The villagers had no money, so they couldn't be consumers. Maybe they had the natural way to live. Statically. Also, frugally.

But no. It was too frugal, too static. He'd heard and read too much about the starvation, pestilence, peonage and other ills plaguing those Indian villagers. They didn't have life licked, either.

The Indians had not enough, the Americans, too much. One was as bad as the other.

And he was in the middle.

He left the window he'd been staring from unseeingly and walked to the foyer control-panel. There he pushed the button that would cause the house to rear a hundred feet into the air on its titanium-aluminum plunger.

Then he went back to the window to watch the ground recede. He felt a hand on his shoulder. He decided the sensation was an illusion—a part of his state of mind.

A young man's voice said, "Mr. Lubway, we need you."

That was a nice thing to hear, so Fred turned, ready to smile. He didn't smile. He was confronted by another ration-cop.

This one was a tall young man, dark and hefty. He seemed very kindly, in his official sort of way.

"Mr. George Harding sent me," he explained. "He asked us to look you up and see if we could help."

"Yes?"

"You seem to have been a little unhappy this morning. I mean—well—staring out that window while your house rises dangerously high. Mr. George Harding didn't like the mood you're in, and neither do I, Mr. Lubway. I'm afraid you'll have to come to the hospital. We can't have a valuable citizen like you falling out that window, can we?"

"What do you mean, 'valuable citizen'? I'm no use to anybody. There's plenty of engineers, and more being graduated every semester. You don't need me."

"Oh, yes, we do!" Shaking his head, the young ration-cop took a firm grip on Fred's right biceps. "You've got to come along with me till your outlook changes, Mr. Lubway."

"Now, see here!" Fred objected, trying unsuccessfully to twist free of the officer's grip. "You've no call to treat me like a criminal. Nor to talk to me as if I were senile. My outlook won't change, and you know it!"

"Oh, yes, it will! And since you're neither criminal nor senile, that's what has to be done.

"We'll do it in the most humane way possible. A little brain surgery, and you'll sit in your cage and consume and consume and consume without a care in the world. Yes, sir, we'll change your outlook!

"Now, you mustn't try to twist away from me like that, Mr. Lubway. I can't let you go. We need every consumer we can get."

THE LAST SUPPER

by T. D. Hamm

HAMPERED as she was by the child in her arms, the woman was running less fleetly now. A wave of exultation swept over Guldran, drowning out the uneasy feeling of guilt at disobeying orders.

The instructions were mandatory and concise: "*No* capture must be attempted individually. In the event of sighting any form of human life, the ship MUST be notified immediately. All small craft must be back at the landing space not later than one hour before take-off. Anyone not so reporting will be presumed lost."

Guldran thought uneasily of the great seas of snow and ice sweeping inexorably toward each other since the Earth had reversed on its axis in the great catastrophe a millennium ago. Now, summer and winter alike brought paralyzing gales and blizzards, heralded by the sleety snow in which the woman's skin-clad feet had left the tracks which led to discovery.

His trained anthropologist's mind speculated avidly over the little they had gotten from the younger of the two men found nearly a week before, nearly frozen and half-starved. The older man had succumbed almost at once; the other, in the most primitive sign language, had indicated that, of several humans living in caves to the west, only he and the other had survived to flee some mysterious terror. Guldran felt a throb of pity for the woman and her child, left behind by the men, no doubt, as a hindrance.

But what a stroke of fortune that there should be left a male and female of the race to carry the seed of Terra to another planet. And what a triumph if he, Guldran, should be the one to return at the eleventh hour with the prize. No need of calling for help. This was no armed war-party, but the most defenseless being in the Universe—a mother burdened with a child.

Guldran put on another burst of speed. His previous shouts had served only to spur the woman to greater efforts. Surely there was *some* magic word that had survived even the centuries of illiteracy. Something equivalent to the "bread and salt" of all illiterate peoples. Cupping his hands to his mouth, he shouted, "Food! food!"

Ahead of him the woman turned her head, leaped lightly in mid-stride, and went on; slowing a little but still running doggedly.

Guldran's pulse leaped. He yelled again, "Food!"

The instant that his foot touched the yielding surface of the trap, he knew that he had met defeat. As his body crashed down on the fire-sharpened stakes, he knew too the terror from which the last men of the human race had fled.

Above him the woman looked down, her teeth gleaming wolfishly. She pointed down into the pit; spoke exultantly to the child.

"Food!" said the last woman on earth.

LETTER OF THE LAW

by Alan E. Nourse

THE place was dark and damp, and smelled like moldy leaves. Meyerhoff followed the huge, bear-like Altairian guard down the slippery flagstones of the corridor, sniffing the dead, musty air with distaste. He drew his carefully tailored Terran-styled jacket closer about his shoulders, shivering as his eyes avoided the black, yawning cell-holes they were passing. His foot slipped on the slimy flags from time to time, and finally he paused to wipe the caked mud from his trouser leg. "How much farther is it?" he shouted angrily.

The guard waved a heavy paw vaguely into the blackness ahead. Quite suddenly the corridor took a sharp bend, and the Altairian stopped, producing a huge key ring from some obscure fold of his hairy hide. "I still don't see any reason for all the fuss," he grumbled in a wounded tone. "We've treated him like a brother."

One of the huge steel doors clicked open. Meyerhoff peered into the blackness, catching a vaguely human outline against the back wall. "Harry?" he called sharply.

There was a startled gasp from within, and a skinny, gnarled little man suddenly appeared in the guard's light, like a grotesque, twisted ghost out of the blackness. Wide blue eyes regarded Meyerhoff from beneath uneven black eyebrows, and then the little man's face broke into a crafty grin. "Paul! So they sent *you*! I knew I could count on it!" He executed a deep, awkward bow, motioning Meyerhoff into the dark cubicle. "Not much to offer you," he said slyly, "but it's the best I can do under the circumstances."

Meyerhoff scowled, and turned abruptly to the guard. "We'll have some privacy now, if you please. Interplanetary ruling. And leave us the light."

The guard grumbled, and started for the door. "It's about time you showed up!" cried the little man in the cell. "Great day! Lucky they sent you, pal. Why, I've been in here for years—"

"Look, Zeckler, the name is Meyerhoff, and I'm not your pal," Meyerhoff snapped. "And you've been here for two weeks, three days, and approximately four hours. You're getting as bad as your gentle guards when it comes to bandying the truth around." He peered through the dim light at the gaunt face of the prisoner. Zeckler's face was dark with a week's beard, and his bloodshot eyes belied the cocky grin on his lips. His clothes were smeared and sodden, streaked with great splotches of mud and moss. Meyerhoff's face softened a little. "So Harry Zeckler's in a jam again," he said. "You *look* as if they'd treated you like a brother."

The little man snorted. "These overgrown teddy-bears don't know what brotherhood means, nor humanity, either. Bread and water I've been getting, nothing more, and then only if they feel like bringing it down." He sank wearily down on the rock bench along the wall. "I thought you'd never get here! I sent an appeal to the Terran Consulate the first day I was arrested. What happened? I mean, all they had to do was get a man over here, get the extradition papers signed, and provide transportation off the planet for me. Why so much time? I've been sitting here rotting—" He broke off in mid-sentence and stared at Meyerhoff. "You *brought* the papers, didn't you? I mean, we can leave now?"

Meyerhoff stared at the little man with a mixture of pity and disgust. "You are a prize fool," he said finally. "Did you know that?"

Zeckler's eyes widened. "What do you mean, fool? So I spend a couple of weeks in this pneumonia trap. The deal was worth it! I've got three million credits sitting in the Terran Consulate on Altair V, just waiting for me to walk in and pick them up. Three million credits—do you hear? That's enough to set me up for life!"

Meyerhoff nodded grimly. "*If* you live long enough to walk in and pick them up, that is."

"What do you mean, if?"

Meyerhoff sank down beside the man, his voice a tense whisper in the musty cell. "I mean that right now you are practically dead. You may not know it, but you are. You walk into a newly opened planet with your smart little bag of tricks, walk in here with a shaky passport and no permit, with no knowledge of the natives outside of two paragraphs of inaccuracies in the Explorer's Guide, and even then you're not content to come in and sell something legitimate, something the natives might conceivably be able to use. No, nothing so simple for you. You have to pull your usual high-pressure stuff. And this time, buddy, you're paying the piper."

"*You mean I'm not being extradited?*"

Meyerhoff grinned unpleasantly. "I mean precisely that. You've committed a crime here—a major crime. The Altairians are sore about it. And the Terran Consulate isn't willing to sell all the trading possibilities here down the river just to get you out of a mess. You're going to stand trial—and these natives are out to get you. Personally, I think they're *going* to get you."

Zeckler stood up shakily. "You can't believe anything the natives say," he said uneasily. "They're pathological liars. Why, you should see what they tried to sell *me*! You've never seen such a pack of liars as these critters." He glanced up at Meyerhoff. "They'll probably drop a little fine on me and let me go."

"A little fine of one Terran neck." Meyerhoff grinned nastily. "You've committed the most heinous crime these creatures can imagine, and they're going to get you for it if it's the last thing they do. I'm afraid, my friend, that your con-man days are over."

Zeckler fished in the other man's pocket, extracted a cigarette, and lighted it with trembling fingers. "It's bad, then," he said finally.

"It's bad, all right."

Some shadow of the sly, elfin grin crept over the little con-man's face. "Well, at any rate, I'm glad they sent you over," he said weakly. "Nothing like a good lawyer to handle a trial."

"*Lawyer?* Not me! Oh, no. Sorry, but no thanks." Meyerhoff chuckled. "I'm your advisor, old boy. Nothing else. I'm here to keep you from botching things up still worse for the Trading Commission, that's all. I wouldn't get tangled up in a mess with those creatures for anything!" He shook his head. "You're your own lawyer, Mr. Super-salesman. It's all your show. And you'd better get your head out of the sand, or you're going to lose a case like it's never been lost before!"

*

Meyerhoff watched the man's pale face, and shook his head. In a way, he thought, it was a pity to see such a change in the rosy-cheeked, dapper, cocksure little man who had talked his way glibly in and out of more jams than Meyerhoff could count. Trading brought scalpers; it was almost inevitable that where rich and unexploited trading ground was uncovered, it would first fall prey to the fast-trading boys. They spread out from Terra with the first wave of exploration—the slick, fast-talking con-men who could work new territories unfettered by the legal restrictions that soon closed down the more established planets. The first men in were the richest out, and through some curious quirk of the Terrestrial mind, they knew they could count on Terran protection, however crooked and underhand their methods.

But occasionally a situation arose where the civilization and social practices of the alien victims made it unwise to tamper with them. Altair I had been recognized at once by the Trading Commission as a commercial prize of tremendous value, but early reports had warned of the danger of wildcat trading on the little, musty, jungle-like planet with its shaggy, three-eyed inhabitants—warned specifically against the confidence tactics so frequently used—but there was always somebody, Meyerhoff reflected sourly, who just didn't get the word.

Zeckler puffed nervously on his cigarette, his narrow face a study in troubled concentration. "But I didn't *do* anything!" he exploded finally. "So I pulled an old con game. So what? Why should they get so excited? So I clipped a few thousand credits, pulled a little fast business." He shrugged eloquently, spreading his hands. "Everybody's doing it. They do it to each other without batting an eye. You should *see* these critters operate on each other. Why, my little scheme was peanuts by comparison."

Meyerhoff pulled a pipe from his pocket, and began stuffing the bowl with infinite patience. "And precisely what sort of con game was it?" he asked quietly.

Zeckler shrugged again. "The simplest, tiredest, moldiest old racket that ever made a quick nickel. Remember the old Terran gag about the Brooklyn Bridge? The same thing. Only these critters didn't want bridges. They wanted land—this gooey, slimy swamp they call 'farm land.' So I gave them what they wanted. I just sold them some land."

Meyerhoff nodded fiercely. "You sure did. A hundred square kilos at a swipe. Only you sold the same hundred square kilos to a dozen different natives." Suddenly he threw back his hands and roared. "Of all the things you *shouldn't* have done—"

"But what's a chunk of land?"

Meyerhoff shook his head hopelessly. "If you hadn't been so greedy, you'd have found out what a chunk of land was to these natives before you started peddling it. You'd have found out other things about them, too. You'd have learned that in spite of all their bumbling and fussing and squabbling they're not so dull. You'd have found out that they're marsupials, and that two out of five of them get thrown out of their mother's pouch before they're old enough to survive. You'd have realized that they have to start fighting for individual rights almost as soon as they're born. Anything goes, as long as it benefits them as individuals."

Meyerhoff grinned at the little man's horrified face. "Never heard of that, had you? And you've never heard of other things, too. You've probably never heard that there are just too many Altairians here for the food their planet can supply, and their diet is so finicky that they just can't live on anything that doesn't grow here. And consequently, land is the key factor in their economy, not money; nothing but land. To get land, it's every man for himself, and the loser starves, and their entire legal and monetary system revolves on that principle. They've built up the most confusing and impossible system of barter and trade imaginable, aimed at individual survival, with land as the value behind the credit. That explains the lying—of course they're liars, with an economy like that. They've completely missed the concept of truth. Pathological? You bet they're pathological! Only a fool would

231

tell the truth when his life depended on his being a better liar than the next guy! Lying is the time-honored tradition, with their entire legal system built around it."

Zeckler snorted. "But how could they *possibly* have a legal system? I mean, if they don't recognize the truth when it slaps them in the face?"

Meyerhoff shrugged. "As we understand legal systems, I suppose they don't have one. They have only the haziest idea what truth represents, and they've shrugged off the idea as impossible and useless." He chuckled maliciously. "So you went out and found a chunk of ground in the uplands, and sold it to a dozen separate, self-centered, half-starved natives! Encroachment on private property is legal grounds for murder on this planet, and twelve of them descended on the same chunk of land at the same time, all armed with title-deeds." Meyerhoff sighed. "You've got twelve mad Altairians in your hair. You've got a mad planet in your hair. And in the meantime, Terra's most valuable uranium source in five centuries is threatening to cut off supply unless they see your blood splattered liberally all the way from here to the equator."

Zeckler was visibly shaken. "Look," he said weakly, "so I wasn't so smart. What am I going to do? I mean, are you going to sit quietly by and let them butcher me? How could I defend myself in a legal setup like *this*?"

Meyerhoff smiled coolly. "You're going to get your sly little con-man brain to working, I think," he said softly. "By Interplanetary Rules, they have to give you a trial in Terran legal form—judge, jury, court procedure, all that folderol. They think it's a big joke—after all, what could a judicial oath mean to them?—but they agreed. Only thing is, they're going to hang you, if they die trying. So you'd better get those stunted little wits of yours clicking—and if you try to implicate *me*, even a little bit, I'll be out of there so fast you won't know what happened."

With that Meyerhoff walked to the door. He jerked it inward sharply, and spilled two guards over on their faces. "Privacy," he grunted, and started back up the slippery corridor.

*

It certainly *looked* like a courtroom, at any rate. In the front of the long, damp stone room was a bench, with a seat behind it, and a small straight chair to the right. To the left was a stand with twelve chairs—larger chairs, with a railing running along the front. The rest of the room was filled almost to the door with seats facing the bench. Zeckler followed the shaggy-haired guard into the room, nodding approvingly. "Not such a bad arrangement," he said. "They must have gotten the idea fast."

Meyerhoff wiped the perspiration from his forehead, and shot the little con-man a stony glance. "At least you've got a courtroom, a judge, and a jury for this mess. Beyond that—" He shrugged eloquently. "I can't make any promises."

In the back of the room a door burst open with a bang. Loud, harsh voices were heard as half a dozen of the huge Altairians attempted to push through the door at once. Zeckler clamped on the headset to his translator unit, and watched the hubbub in the anteroom with growing alarm. Finally the question of precedent seemed to be settled, and a group of the Altairians filed in, in order of stature, stalking across the room in flowing black robes, pug-nosed faces glowering with self-importance. They descended upon the jury box, grunting and scrapping with each other for the first-row seats, and the judge took his place with obvious satisfaction behind the heavy wooden bench. Finally, the prosecuting attorney appeared, flanked by two clerks, who took their places beside him. The prosecutor eyed Zeckler with cold malevolence, then turned and delivered a sly wink at the judge.

In a moment the room was a hubbub as it filled with the huge, bumbling, bear-like creatures, jostling each other and fighting for seats, growling and complaining. Two small fights broke out in the rear, but were quickly subdued by the group of gendarmes guarding the entrance. Finally the judge glared down at Zeckler with all three eyes, and pounded the bench top with a wooden mallet until the roar of activity subsided. The jurymen wriggled uncomfortably in their seats, exchanging winks, and finally turned their attention to the front of the court.

"We are reading the case of the people of Altair I," the judge's voice roared out, "against one Harry Zeckler—" he paused for a long, impressive moment—"Terran." The courtroom immediately burst into an angry growl, until the judge pounded the bench five or six times more. "This—creature—is hereby accused of the following crimes," the judge bellowed. "Conspiracy to overthrow the government of Altair I. Brutal murder of seventeen law-abiding citizens of the village of Karzan at the third hour before dawn in the second period after his arrival. Desecration of the Temple of our beloved Goddess Zermat, Queen of the Harvest. Conspiracy with the lesser gods to cause the unprecedented drought in the Dermatti section of our fair globe. Obscene exposure of his pouch-marks in a public square. Four separate and distinct charges of jail-break and bribery—" The judge pounded the bench for order—"Espionage with the accursed scum of Altair II in preparation for interplanetary invasion."

The little con-man's jaw sagged lower and lower, the color draining from his face. He turned, wide-eyed, to Meyerhoff, then back to the judge.

"The Chairman of the Jury," said the Judge succinctly, "will read the verdict."

The little native in the front of the jury-box popped up like a puppet on a string. "Defendant found guilty on all counts," he said.

"Defendant is guilty! The court will pronounce sentence—"

"*Now wait a minute!*" Zeckler was on his feet, wild-eyed. "What kind of railroad job—"

The judge blinked disappointedly at Paul Meyerhoff. "Not yet?" he asked, unhappily.

"No." Meyerhoff's hands twitched nervously. "Not yet, Your Honor. Later, Your Honor. The trial comes *first*."

The judge looked as if his candy had been stolen. "But you *said* I should call for the verdict."

"Later. You have to have the trial before you can have the verdict."

The Altairian shrugged indifferently. "Now—later—" he muttered.

"Have the prosecutor call his first witness," said Meyerhoff.

Zeckler leaned over, his face ashen. "These charges," he whispered. "They're insane!"

"Of course they are," Meyerhoff whispered back.

"But what am I going to—"

"Sit tight. Let *them* set things up."

"But those *lies*. They're liars, the whole pack of them—" He broke off as the prosecutor roared a name.

The shaggy brute who took the stand was wearing a bright purple hat which sat rakishly over one ear. He grinned the Altairian equivalent of a hungry grin at the prosecutor. Then he cleared his throat and started. "This Terran riffraff—"

"The oath," muttered the judge. "We've got to have the oath."

The prosecutor nodded, and four natives moved forward, carrying huge inscribed marble slabs to the front of the court. One by one the chunks were reverently piled in a heap at the witness's feet. The witness placed a huge, hairy paw on the cairn, and the prosecutor said, "Do you swear to tell the truth, the whole truth, and nothing but the truth, so help you—" he paused to squint at the paper in his hand, and finished on a puzzled note, "—Goddess?"

The witness removed the paw from the rock pile long enough to scratch his ear. Then he replaced it, and replied, "Of course," in an injured tone.

"Then tell this court what you have seen of the activities of this abominable wretch."

The witness settled back into the chair, fixing one eye on Zeckler's face, another on the prosecutor, and closing the third as if in meditation. "I think it happened on the fourth night of the seventh crossing of Altair II (may the Goddess cast a drought upon it)—or was it the seventh night of the fourth crossing?—" he grinned apologetically at the judge—"when I was making my way back through town toward my blessed land-plot, minding my own business, Your Honor, after weeks of bargaining for the crop I was harvesting. Suddenly from the shadow of the building, this creature—" he waved a paw at Zeckler—"stopped me in my tracks with a vicious cry. He had a weapon I'd never seen before, and before I could find my voice he forced me back against the wall. I could see by the cruel glint in his eyes that there was no warmth, no sympathy in his heart, that I was—"

"Objection!" Zeckler squealed plaintively, jumping to his feet. "This witness can't even remember what night he's talking about!"

The judge looked startled. Then he pawed feverishly through his bundle of notes. "Overruled," he said abruptly. "Continue, please."

The witness glowered at Zeckler. "As I was saying before this loutish interruption," he muttered, "I could see that I was face to face with the most desperate of criminal types, even for Terrans. Note the shape of his head, the flabbiness of his ears. I was petrified with fear. And then, helpless as I was, this two-legged abomination began to shower me with threats of evil to my blessed home, dark threats of poisoning my land unless I would tell him where he could find the resting place of our blessed Goddess—"

"I never saw him before in my life," Zeckler moaned to Meyerhoff. "Listen to him! Why should I care where their Goddess—"

Meyerhoff gave him a stony look. "The Goddess runs things around here. She makes it rain. If it doesn't rain, somebody's insulted her. It's very simple."

"But how can I fight testimony like that?"

"I doubt if you *can* fight it."

"But they can't prove a word of it—" He looked at the jury, who were listening enraptured to the second witness on the stand. This one was testifying regarding the butcherous slaughter of eighteen (or was it twenty-three? Oh, yes, twenty-three) women and children in the suburban village of Karzan. The pogrom, it seemed, had been accomplished by an energy weapon which ate great, gaping holes in the sides of buildings. A third witness took the stand, continuing the drone as the room grew hotter and muggier. Zeckler grew paler and paler, his eyes turning glassy as the testimony piled up. "But it's not *true*," he whispered to Meyerhoff.

"Of course it isn't! Can't you understand? *These people have no regard for truth.* It's stupid, to them, silly, a mark of low intelligence. The only thing in the world they have any respect for is a liar bigger and more skillful than they are."

Zeckler jerked around abruptly as he heard his name bellowed out. "Does the defendant have anything to say before the jury delivers the verdict?"

"Do I have—" Zeckler was across the room in a flash, his pale cheeks suddenly taking on a feverish glow. He sat down gingerly on the witness chair, facing the judge, his eyes bright with fear and excitement. "Your—Your Honor, I—I have a statement to make which will have a most important bearing on this case. You must listen with the greatest care." He glanced quickly at Meyerhoff, and back to the judge. "Your Honor," he said in a hushed voice. "You are in gravest of danger. All of you. Your lives—your very land is at stake."

The judge blinked, and shuffled through his notes hurriedly as a murmur arose in the court. "Our land?"

"Your lives, your land, everything you hold dear," Zeckler said quickly, licking his lips nervously. "You must try to understand me—" he glanced apprehensively over his shoulder "now, because I may not live long enough to repeat what I am about to tell you—"

The murmur quieted down, all ears straining in their headsets to hear his words. "These charges," he continued, "all of them—they're perfectly true. At least, they *seem* to be perfectly true. But in every instance, I was working with heart and soul, risking my life, for the welfare of your beautiful planet."

There was a loud hiss from the back of the court. Zeckler frowned and rubbed his hands together. "It was my misfortune," he said, "to go to the wrong planet when I first came to Altair from my homeland on Terra. I—I landed on Altair II, a grave mistake, but as it turned out, a very fortunate error. Because in attempting to arrange trading in that frightful place, I made certain contacts." His voice trembled, and sank lower. "I learned the horrible thing which is about to happen to this planet, at the hands of those barbarians. The conspiracy is theirs, not mine. They have bribed your Goddess, flattered her and lied to her, coerced her all-powerful goodness to their own evil interests, preparing for the day when they could persuade her to cast your land into the fiery furnace of a ten-year-drought—"

Somebody in the middle of the court burst out laughing. One by one the natives nudged one another, and booed, and guffawed, until the rising tide of racket drowned out Zeckler's words. "The defendant is obviously lying," roared the prosecutor over the pandemonium. "Any fool knows that the Goddess can't be bribed. How could she be a Goddess if she could?"

Zeckler grew paler. "But—perhaps they were very clever—"

"And how could they flatter her, when she knows, beyond doubt, that she is the most exquisitely radiant creature in all the Universe? And *you* dare to insult her, drag her name in the dirt."

The hisses grew louder, more belligerent. Cries of "Butcher him!" and "Scald his bowels!" rose from the courtroom. The judge banged for silence, his eyes angry.

235

"Unless the defendant wishes to take up more of our precious time with these ridiculous lies, the jury—"

"Wait! Your Honor, I request a short recess before I present my final plea."

"Recess?"

"A few moments to collect my thoughts, to arrange my case."

The judge settled back with a disgusted snarl. "Do I have to?" he asked Meyerhoff.

Meyerhoff nodded. The judge shrugged, pointing over his shoulder to the anteroom. "You can go in there," he said.

Somehow, Zeckler managed to stumble from the witness stand, amid riotous boos and hisses, and tottered into the anteroom.

*

Zeckler puffed hungrily on a cigarette, and looked up at Meyerhoff with haunted eyes. "It—it doesn't look so good," he muttered.

Meyerhoff's eyes were worried, too. For some reason, he felt a surge of pity and admiration for the haggard con-man. "It's worse than I'd anticipated," he admitted glumly. "That was a good try, but you just don't know enough about them and their Goddess." He sat down wearily. "I don't see what you can do. They want your blood, and they're going to have it. They just won't believe you, no matter *how* big a lie you tell."

Zeckler sat in silence for a moment. "This lying business," he said finally, "exactly how does it work?"

"The biggest, most convincing liar wins. It's as simple as that. It doesn't matter how outlandish a whopper you tell. Unless, of course, they've made up their minds that you just naturally aren't as big a liar as they are. And it looks like that's just what they've done. It wouldn't make any difference to them *what* you say—unless, somehow, you could *make* them believe it."

Zeckler frowned. "And how do they regard the—the biggest liar? I mean, how do they feel toward him?"

Meyerhoff shifted uneasily. "It's hard to say. It's been my experience that they respect him highly—maybe even fear him a little. After all, the most convincing liar always wins in any transaction, so he gets more land, more food, more power. Yes, I think the biggest liar could go where he pleased without any interference."

Zeckler was on his feet, his eyes suddenly bright with excitement. "Wait a minute," he said tensely. "To tell them a lie that they'd have to believe—a lie they simply couldn't *help* but believe—" He turned on Meyerhoff, his hands trembling. "Do they *think* the way we do? I mean, with logic, cause and effect, examining evidence and drawing conclusions? Given certain evidence, would they have to draw the same conclusions that we have to draw?"

Meyerhoff blinked. "Well—yes. Oh, yes, they're perfectly logical."

Zeckler's eyes flashed, and a huge grin broke out on his sallow face. His thin body fairly shook. He started hopping up and down on one foot, staring idiotically into space. "If I could only think—" he muttered. "Somebody—somewhere—something I read."

"Whatever are you talking about?"

"It was a Greek, I think—"

Meyerhoff stared at him. "Oh, come now. Have you gone off your rocker completely? You've got a problem on your hands, man."

"No, no, I've got a problem in the bag!" Zeckler's cheeks flushed. "Let's go back in there—I think I've got an answer!"

The courtroom quieted the moment they opened the door, and the judge banged the gavel for silence. As soon as Zeckler had taken his seat on the witness stand, the judge turned to the head juryman. "Now, then," he said with happy finality. "The jury—"

"Hold on! Just one minute more."

The judge stared down at Zeckler as if he were a bug on a rock. "Oh, yes. You had something else to say. Well, go ahead and say it."

Zeckler looked sharply around the hushed room. "You want to convict me," he said softly, "in the worst sort of way. Isn't that right?"

Eyes swung toward him. The judge broke into an evil grin. "That's right."

"But you can't really convict me until you've considered carefully any statement I make in my own defense. Isn't that right?"

The judge looked uncomfortable. "If you've got something to say, go ahead and say it."

"I've got just one statement to make. Short and sweet. But you'd better listen to it, and think it out carefully before you decide that you really want to convict me." He paused, and glanced slyly at the judge. "You don't think much of those who tell the truth, it seems. Well, put *this* statement in your record, then." His voice was loud and clear in the still room. "*All Earthmen are absolutely incapable of telling the truth.*"

Puzzled frowns appeared on the jury's faces. One or two exchanged startled glances, and the room was still as death. The judge stared at him, and then at Meyerhoff, then back. "But you"—he stammered. "You're"—He stopped in mid-sentence, his jaw sagging.

One of the jurymen let out a little squeak, and fainted dead away. It took, all in all, about ten seconds for the statement to soak in.

And then pandemonium broke loose in the courtroom.

*

"Really," said Harry Zeckler loftily, "it was so obvious I'm amazed that it didn't occur to me first thing." He settled himself down comfortably in the control cabin of the Interplanetary Rocket and grinned at the outline of Altair IV looming larger in the view screen.

Paul Meyerhoff stared stonily at the controls, his lips compressed angrily. "You might at least have told me what you were planning."

"And take the chance of being overheard? Don't be silly. It had to come as a bombshell. I had to establish myself as a liar—the prize liar of them all, but I had to tell the sort of lie that they simply could not cope with. Something that would throw them into such utter confusion that they wouldn't *dare* convict me." He grinned impishly at Meyerhoff. "The paradox of Epimenides the Cretan. It really stopped them cold. They *knew* I was an Earthmen, which meant that my statement that Earthmen were liars was a lie, which meant that maybe I wasn't a liar, in which case—oh, it was tailor-made."

"It sure was." Meyerhoff's voice was a snarl.

"Well, it made me out a liar in a class they couldn't approach, didn't it?"

Meyerhoff's face was purple with anger. "Oh, indeed it did! And it put *all* Earthmen in exactly the same class, too."

"So what's honor among thieves? I got off, didn't I?"

Meyerhoff turned on him fiercely. "Oh, you got off just fine. You scared the living daylights out of them. And in an eon of lying they never have run up against a short-circuit like that. You've also completely botched any hope of ever setting up a trading alliance with Altair I, and that includes uranium, too. Smart people don't gamble with loaded dice. You scared them so badly they don't want anything to do with us."

Zeckler's grin broadened, and he leaned back luxuriously. "Ah, well. After all, the Trading Alliance was *your* outlook, wasn't it? What a pity!" He clucked his tongue sadly. "Me, I've got a fortune in credits sitting back at the consulate waiting for me—enough to keep me on silk for quite a while, I might say. I think I'll just take a nice, long vacation."

Meyerhoff turned to him, and a twinkle of malignant glee appeared in his eyes. "Yes, I think you will. I'm quite sure of it, in fact. Won't cost you a cent, either."

"Eh?"

Meyerhoff grinned unpleasantly. He brushed an imaginary lint fleck from his lapel, and looked up at Zeckler slyly. "That—uh—jury trial. The Altairians weren't any too happy to oblige. They wanted to execute you outright. Thought a trial was awfully silly—until they got their money back, of course. Not too much—just three million credits."

Zeckler went white. "But that money was in banking custody!"

"Is that right? My goodness. You don't suppose they could have lost those papers, do you?" Meyerhoff grinned at the little con-man. "And incidentally, you're under arrest, you know."

A choking sound came from Zeckler's throat. "*Arrest!*"

"Oh, yes. Didn't I tell you? Conspiring to undermine the authority of the Terran Trading Commission. Serious charge, you know. Yes, I think we'll take a nice long vacation together, straight back to Terra. And there I think you'll face a jury trial."

Zeckler spluttered. "There's no evidence—you've got nothing on me! What kind of a frame are you trying to pull?"

"A *lovely* frame. Airtight. A frame from the bottom up, and you're right square in the middle. And this time—" Meyerhoff tapped a cigarette on his thumb with happy finality—"this time I *don't* think you'll get off."

SWEET THEIR BLOOD AND STICKY

by Albert R. Teichner

They weren't human—weren't even related to humanity through ties of blood—but they were our heirs!

THE machine had stood there a long time. It was several hundred feet long and could run on a thimbleful of earth or water. Complete in itself, the machine drew material from the surrounding landscape, transmuting matter to its special purposes. It needed sugar, salt, water and many other things but never failed to have them. It was still working. And at the delivery end, where the packaging devices had been broken down, it turned out a steady turgid stream on the ground of pink-striped, twisting taffy.

Once the whole vast desert area had been filled with such devices, producing all the varied needs of a very needful human race. But there had been no machine to produce peace. The crossing shock waves of fused hydrogen had destroyed the machines by the tens of thousands, along with all the automatic shipping lines, leaving only, in the quirk of a pressure cross-pattern, an undisturbed taffy-making machine, oozing its special lava on the plateau floor.

It had been working seven and a half million years.

It continued to repair itself, as if a child of the race that had started all this would come by it at any moment to tip an eager pinky in the still-warm taffy to taste its tangy sweetness. But there were no human beings. There had been none since the day when the packager collapsed, at the edge of the total-evaporation zone.

CRENO set a few of his legs on the edge of the glassy, weathered ridge and gazed over the plateau. Harta, next to him, trembled as she adjusted to the strange hardness of these four dimensions. "Being is a thin thing here," she said.

"Thin, yes," Creno smiled. "An almost dead world. But there is a mystery in that almost to make the journey worth the coming."

"What mystery?" But Creno was of the wisest on the home planet and her sense feelers scanned once more to find what he must mean. "I do feel it! Everything dead but that one great mental thing moving, and a four-dimensional stream coming out in the vibrations of this world!"

"I have been watching it," said Creno. "What kind of life can that be? You are a sharp sensor, Harta. Focus to it."

She strained and then relaxed, speaking: "The circuits are closed into themselves. It learns nothing from outside itself except to move and extend its metal feelers for food. Soil is its food. Soil is its energy. Soil is its being."

"Can it be alive?"

"It is alive."

All his legs rested now in a row along the ridge. He too was relaxed as one mystery disappeared. "I feel your feelings, but the thing is not alive. It is a machine."

"I do not understand. A machine in the middle of a dead world?"

"Whether we understand why or not, that is what it is—a machine."

239

Harta throbbed with excitement. How could Creno be wrong? He knew everything as soon as the facts were in his mind. Yet here now were living things crawling toward the machine, just like the excrescence at one end but in no way a part of it! The feeling of willedeffort as they crawled slowly toward it, white and pink striped, reaching grasping feelers into the turgid product, taking it in, then rising on easing legs as the food spread within them.

"There are living creatures here!" Creno pondered. "I feel your messages. Twenty, thirty—a horde is crawling from that mountain toward it."

"Four thousand three hundred and ninety-one," said Harta. She concentrated. "There are three thousand and five more in the mountain caves, waiting to come out as the others return."

THEY came in groups of about a hundred, pulling themselves slowly toward the edges of the great sticky lake that lay within the vaster area where the pink matter dried and crumbled into the strong breeze. Some were smaller than others, offspring who were nudged along by their elders. But these small creatures were the ones who scampered most of all after they had fed. Joyously they danced back toward the mountain. A few of medium height went back in pairs, firm taffy fingers intertwined in each other.

"They mate," said Creno. "It is their custom."

"How tiring they are," said Harta. "I have lost interest. We have seen thirty-one worlds with such customs and these creatures are too simple to be interesting. Let us go home or try some other system."

"Not yet," Creno insisted. "We passed through the ocean and surveyed the lands of this tiny planet. Nowhere else has there been the tiniest unit of life. Why at this one spot should something exist?"

"But we have several parallel situations," Harta protested. "They were colonies landed in one spot by the civilization of another planet. They landed here with their feeder machine. And that is the explanation."

"Your mind does not function well in a four-dimension continuum, Harta. You will need more training—"

"But these cases are rare, and, Creno—"

"I know they are rare, my child. But still they exist. You will have to learn eventually, a little at a time. Now then, it is a rule of such limited dimensional realms that the movement of matter and events from place to place is highly difficult. Certain compacting procedures must be observed. To transport a machine this size across their space would have required enormous effort and an intelligence they do not yet have. More than that, it would have been unnecessary. A smaller device would have supplied them with food. I am forced to conclude that—somehow—we are approaching this problem backwards."

"Backwards? You mean they made the machine here after they came?"

He did not reply to that. "We must concentrate together on thinking ourselves into their functioning in their manifold."

Harta followed his suggestion, and soon their thoughts were moving among and within the striped creatures. The insides of their bodies consisted of fundamentally the same taffy substance; but it had been modified by various organic structures. All, though, were built of the same fundamental units: elongated, thin cells which readily aligned themselves in semi-crystalline patterns.

"Enough," Creno said, "back to the hill."

Their rows of thin limbs rested on the ridge crest once more. "We have seen such cell crystals before," she sighed. "The inefficiencies in such a poverty of dimensions! Do you still think we have looked at it backwards?"

"Of course we have. They did not bring the machine or make it—the machine made them!"

"That is not possible, Creno, great as you are in these matters. We have never seen life created by a machine before. No one ever has, from the millions of reports I have seen at home."

"Maybe we have and not known it. The life we have seen always evolved through enormous eons and we could not see its origins clearly in most cases. Here we are dealing with something that has taken comparatively little time." He stopped, shocked that he, an elder, had said so much. "No, disregard such theories. You are still too young to bother with them. Here is the important thing—this machine was left by an earlier race that disappeared. Everything else was destroyed but it went right on producing its substance."

"The substance is not life."

"It is only four-dimensional matter, right. But over a long enough time—you know this as well as I do—random factors will eventually produce a life form. By some trick of radiation this process has been speeded up here. The substance the machine produces has in turn produced life!"

CRENO sensed with a tremor some dangerous shifting in Harta's consciousness. As an elder it was his duty to prevent a premature insight in the young. It had been a mistake to bring this up. He must go no further.

It was not necessary. Harta took it up for him.

"Then any substance producing life and modified by it could—if you go far enough back—be the product of a machine. But it would have taken so long to produce life that the original matter, that bore the direct imprint of the machine, would have disappeared."

"An error," said Creno desperately. "There is just this case."

"By the time these creatures have arrived at self-knowledge the machine will be gone. They will not know it ever existed, and—"

"That is all it means. There is just this one case. Now we must leave this unimportant example of minor dimensions!"

He strained consciousness to a forward movement but Harta remained behind. He had to pull back. "Start," he ordered.

Her mind's obstinately frozen stance made him freeze too. He applied all his force to bring her back into control, but she still held fast.

"Something more is hidden from me. I will be back," she said. And she disappeared from the ridge.

He had never faced such a quandary before on a training trip with a younger one. If he went in pursuit he would find her ultimately—that was in the nature of being older and wiser—but, if she revolted against his pursuit, she could extend the time considerably on this forsaken planet. And he wanted to get her away as soon as possible.

The more time here the more chance that the awful truth would come to her before her time.

He watched the growing waves of creatures floundering toward the vast oozing puddle, which refilled itself as quickly as it was diminished by them, and the receding waves of those that had already fed. This, he could see, was an endless process. The whole life of the species moved in continuous systole-diastole around the machine.

Soon he would have to go in search of her.

But then she was back at his side, her being for this world once more solidified. She concentrated for a moment on the pink-striped waves of rippling inward and outward around the great sustaining pool, then communicated with him.

"We can leave now. There is nothing more to see."

Something in her mind remained closed to his, as the mind of younger never should be to older. But at least he could see with relief that the worst had not happened. The deeper knowledge had not arrived to her too early when it could only hurt. All he found turned to him—as they receded from this thin-manifold universe, then moved up the dimension ladder to their home level—was a surface of happiness.

Suddenly, though, as they prepared for flight in that hyperspace all her joy was gone.

"I saw it," she said. "In my free and unrestricted spirit I moved deep into the substance of that world, below all the total ruin, far below. And there was a monstrous machine, near the molten core, almost infinitely older than the feeding one far above it. And it, too, had been left in a stratum where all else was destroyed. I could see it had once produced the ooze from which came the life from which in turn come the beings by whom the machine above it was made. Maybe they, too, thought they were free and unrestricted!"

He sighed for the bitter cost of knowledge.

This one would no longer go forth in the joy of mere exploration, and he would no longer live vicariously in the happiness of another being's innocence. Now Harta, too, would be seeking the answer to the question of original creation, the answer that he had not found in his journeys across a myriad worlds and dimensions . . . .

That no one had ever found.

THE LAST PLACE ON EARTH

by Jim Harmon

Naturally an undertaker will get the last word. But shouldn't he wait until his clients are dead?

I

Sam Collins flashed the undertaker a healthy smile, hoping it wouldn't depress old Candle too much. He saluted. The skeletal figure in endless black nodded gravely, and took hold of Sam Collins' arm with a death grip.

"I'm going to bury you, Sam Collins," the undertaker said.

The tall false fronts of Main Street spilled out a lake of shadow, a canal of liquid heat that soaked through the iron weave of Collins' jeans and turned into black ink stains. The old window of the hardware store showed its age in soft wrinkles, ripples that had caught on fire in the sunset. Collins felt the twilight stealing under the arms of his tee-shirt. The overdue hair on the back of his rangy neck stood up in attention. It was a joke, but the first one Collins had ever known Doc Candle to make.

"In time, I guess you'll bury me all right, Doc."

"In my time, not yours, Earthling."

"Earthling?" Collins repeated the last word.

The old man frowned. His face was a collection of lines. When he frowned, all the lines pointed to hell, the grave, decay and damnation.

"Earthling," the undertaker repeated. "Earthman? Terrestrial? Solarian? Space Ranger? *Homo sapiens?*"

Collins decided Candle was sure in a jokey mood. "Kind of makes you think of it, don't it, Doc? The spaceport going right up outside of town. Rocketships are going to be out there taking off for the Satellite, the Moon, places like that. Reminds you that we *are* Earthlings, like they say in the funnies, all right."

"Not outside town."

"What?"

"Inside. Inside town. Part of the spaceship administration building is going to go smack in the middle of where your house used to be."

"My house *is*."

"For less time than you will be yourself, Earthling."

"Earthling yourself! What's wrong with you, Doc!"

"No. I am not an Earthling. I am a superhuman alien from outer space. My mission on Earth is to destroy you."

Collins pulled away gently. When you lived in a town all your life and knew its people, it wasn't unusual to see some old person snap under the weight of years.

"You have to destroy the rocketship station, huh, Doc, before it sends up spaceships?"

"No. I want to kill *you*. That is my mission."

"*Why?*"

"Because," Candle said, "I am a basically evil entity."

243

The undertaker turned away and went skittering down Main Street, his lopsided gait limping, sliding, hopping, skipping, at a refined leisurely pace. He was a collection of dancing, straight black lines.

Collins stared after the old man, shook his head and forgot about him.

He moved into the hardware store. The bell tinkled behind him. The store was cramped with shadows and the smell of wood and iron. It was lined off as precisely as a checkerboard, with counters, drawers, compartments.

Ed Michaels sat behind the counter, smoking a pipe. He was a handsome man, looking young in the uncertain light, even at fifty.

"Hi, Ed. You closed?"

"Guess not, Sam. What are you looking for?"

"A pound of tenpenny nails."

Michaels stood up.

Sarah Comstock waddled energetically out of the back. Her sweet, angelic face lit up with a smile. "Sam Collins. Well, I guess *you'll* want to help us murder them."

"Murder?" Collins repeated. "Who?"

"Those Air Force men who want to come in here and cause all the trouble."

"How are you going to murder them, Mrs. Comstock?"

"When they see our petition in Washington, D.C., they'll call those men back pretty quick."

"Oh," Collins said.

Mrs. Comstock produced the scroll from her voluminous handbag. "You want to sign, don't you? They're going to put part of the airport on your place. They'll tear down your house."

"They can't tear it down. I won't sell."

"You know government men. They'll just *take* it and give you some money for it. Sign right there at the top of the new column, Sam."

Collins shook his head. "I don't believe in signing things. They can't take what's mine."

"But Sam, dear, they *will*. They'll come in and push your house down with those big tractors of theirs. They'll bury it in concrete and set off those guided missiles of theirs right over it."

"They can't make me get out," Sam said.

Ed Michaels scooped up a pound, one ounce of nails and spilled them onto his scale. He pinched off the excess, then dropped it back in and fed the nails into a brown paper bag. He crumpled the top and set it on the counter. "That's twenty-nine plus one, Sam. Thirty cents."

Collins laid out a quarter and a nickel and picked up the bag. "Appreciate you doing this after store hours, Ed."

Michaels chuckled. "I wasn't exactly getting ready for the opera, Sam."

Collins turned around and saw Sarah Comstock still waiting, the petition in her hand.

"Now what's a pretty girl like you doing, wasting her time in politics?" Collins heard himself ask.

Mrs. Comstock twittered. "I'm old enough to be your mother, Sam Collins."

"I like mature women."

Collins watched his hand in fascination as it reached out to touch one of Sarah Comstock's plump cheeks, then dropped to her shoulder and ripped away the strap-sleeve of her summer print dress.

A plump, rosy shoulder was revealed, splattered with freckles.

Sarah Comstock put her hands over her ears as if to keep from hearing her own shrill scream. It reached out into pure soprano range.

Sarah Comstock backed away, into the shadows, and Sam Collins followed her, trying to explain, to apologize.

"Sam! *Sam!*"

The voice cut through to him and he looked up.

Ed Michaels had a double-barreled shotgun aimed at him. Mrs. Michaels' face was looking over his shoulder in the door to the back, her face a sick white.

"You get out of here, Sam," Michaels said. "You get out and don't you come back. Ever."

Collins' hands moved emptily in air. He was always better with his hands than words, but this time even they seemed inexpressive.

He crumpled the sack of nails in both fists, and turned and left the hardware store.

II

His house was still there, sitting at the end of Elm Street, at the end of town, on the edge of the prairie. It was a very old house. It was decorated with gingerboard, a rusted-out tin rooster-comb running the peak of the roof and stained glass window transoms; and the top of the house was joined to the ground floor by lapped fishscales, as though it was a mermaid instead of a house. The house was a golden house. It had been painted brown against the dust, but the keening wind, the relentless sun, the savage rape of the thunderstorms, they had all bleached the brown paint into a shining pure gold.

Sam stepped inside and leaned back against the front door, the door of full-length glass with a border of glass emeralds and rubies. He leaned back and breathed deep.

The house didn't smell old. It smelled new. It smelled like sawdust and fresh-hewn lumber as bright and blond as a high school senior's crewcut.

He walked across the flowered carpet. The carpet didn't mind footsteps or bright sun. It never became worn or faded. It grew brighter with the years, the roses turning redder, the sunflowers becoming yellower.

The parlor looked the same as it always did, clean and waiting to be used. The cane-backed sofa and chairs eagerly waiting to be sat upon, the bead-shaded kerosene lamps ready to burst into light.

Sam went into his workshop. This had once been the ground level master bedroom, but he had had to make the change. The work table held its share of radios, toasters, TV sets, an electric train, a spring-wind Victrola. Sam threw the nails onto the table and crossed the room, running his fingers along the silent keyboard of the player piano. He looked out the window. The bulldozers had made the ground rectangular, level and brown, turning it into a gigantic half-cent stamp. He remembered the mail and raised the window and reached down into the mailbox. It was on this side of the house, because only this side was technically within city limits.

As he came up with the letters, Sam Collins saw a man sighting along a plumbline towards his house. He shut the window.

Some of the letters didn't have any postage stamps, just a line of small print about a $300 fine. Government letters. He went over and forced them into the tightly packed coal stove. All the trash would be burned out in the cold weather.

Collins sat down and looked through the rest of his mail. A new catalogue of electronic parts. A bulky envelope with two paperback novels by Richard S. Prather and Robert Bloch he had ordered. A couple of letters from hams. He tossed the mail on the table and leaned back.

He thought about what had happened in the hardware store.

It wasn't surprising it had happened to him. Things like that were bound to happen to him. He had just been lucky that Ed Michaels hadn't called the sheriff. What had got into him? He had never been a sex maniac before! But still ... it was hardly unexpected.

Might as well wait to start on those rabbit cages until tomorrow, he decided. This evening he felt like exploring.

The house was so big, and packed with so many things that he never found and examined them all. Or if he did, he forgot a lot about the things between times, so it was like reading a favorite book over again, always discovering new things in it.

The parlor was red in the fading light, and the hall beyond the sliding doors was deeply shadowed. In the sewing room, he remembered, in the drawers of the treadle machine the radio was captured. The rings and secret manuals of the days when radio had been alive. He hadn't looked over those things in some little time.

He looked up the shadowed stairway. He remembered the night, a few weeks before Christmas when he had been twelve and really too old to believe, his mother had said she was going up to see if Santa Claus had left any packages around a bit early. They often gave him his presents early, since they were never quite sure he would live until Christmas.

But his mother had been playing a trick on him. She hadn't been going up after packages. She had gone up those stairs to murder his father.

She had shot him in the back of the head with his Army Colt .45 from the first war. Collins never quite understood why the hole in back was so neat and the one in front where it came out was so messy.

After he went to live with Aunt Amy and the house had been boarded up, he heard them talking, Aunt Amy and her boy friend, fat Uncle Ralph. And they had said his mother had murdered his father because he had gone ahead and made her get pregnant again and she was afraid it would be another one like Sam.

Sam Collins knew she must have planned it a long time in advance. She had filled up the bathtub with milk, real milk, and she went in after she had done it and took a bath in the milk. Then she slit her wrists.

When Sam Collins had run down the stairs, screaming, and barged into the bathroom, he had found the tub looking like a giant stick of peppermint candy.

Aunt Amy had been good to him.

Because he didn't talk for about a year after he found the bodies, most people thought he was simple-minded. But Aunt Amy had always treated him just like a regular boy. That was embarrassing sometimes, but still it was better than what he got from the others.

The doctor hadn't wanted to perform the operation on his clubfoot. He said it would be an unproductive waste of his time and talent, that he owed it to the world to use them to the very best advantage. Finally he agreed. The operation took about thirty seconds. He stuck a knife into Sam's foot and went *snick-snick*. A couple of weeks later, his foot was healed and it was just like anybody else's. Aunt Amy had paid him $500 in payments, only he returned the money order for the last fifty dollars and wished them Merry Christmas.

Sam Collins could work after that. When Aunty Amy and Uncle Ralph disappeared, he opened up the old house and started doing odd jobs for people who weren't very afraid of him any more.

That first day had been quite a shock, when he discovered that not in all these years had anybody cleaned the bathtub.

Sometimes, when he was taking his Saturday night soaker he still got kind of a funny feeling. But he knew it was only rust from the faucets.

Collins sighed. It seemed like a long time since he had seen his mother coming down those stairs....

He stopped, his throat aching with tightness.

Something was very strange.

His mother was coming down the stairs right now.

She was walking down the stairs, one step, two steps, coming closer to him.

Collins ran up the stairs, prepared to run through the phantom to prove it wasn't there.

The figure raised a gun and pointed it at him.

This time, she was going to shoot *him*.

It figured.

He always had bad luck.

"Stop!" the woman on the stairs said. "Stop or I'll shoot, Mr. Collins!"

Collins stopped, catching to the bannister. He squinted hard, and as a stereoptic slide lost its depth when you shut one eye, the woman on the stairs was no longer his mother. She was young, pretty, brunette and sweet-faced, and the gun she held shrunk from an old Army Colt to a .22 target pistol.

"Who *are* you?" Collins demanded.

The girl took a grip on the gun with both hands and held it steady on him.

"I'm Nancy Comstock," she said. "You tried to assault my mother a half hour ago."

"Oh," he said. "I've never seen you before."

"Yes, you have. I've been away to school a lot, but you've seen me around. I've had my eye on you. I know about men like you. I know what has to be done. I came looking for you in your house for this."

The bore of the gun was level with his eye as he stood a few steps below her. Probably if she fired now, she would kill him. Or more likely he would only be blinded or paralyzed; that was about his luck.

"Are you going to use that gun?" he asked.

"Not unless I have to. I only brought it along for protection. I came to help you, Mr. Collins."

"Help me?"

"Yes, Mr. Collins. You're sick. You need help."

He looked the girl over. She was a half-dozen years younger than he was. In most states, she couldn't even vote yet. But still, maybe she could help, at that. He didn't know much about girls and their abilities.

"Why don't we go into the kitchen and have some coffee?" Collins suggested.

III

Nancy sipped her coffee and kept her eyes on his. The gun lay in her lap. The big kitchen was a place for coffee, brown and black, wood ceiling and iron stove and pans. Collins sat across the twelve square feet of table from her, and nursed the smoking mug.

"Sam, I want you to take whatever comfort you can from the fact that I don't think the same thing about you as the rest of Waraxe."

"What does the rest of the town think about me?"

"They think you are a pathological degenerate who should be lynched. But I don't believe that."

"Thanks. That's a big comfort."

"I know what you were after when you tore Mom's dress."

In spite of himself, Collins felt his face warming in a blush.

"You were only seeking the mother love you missed as a boy," the girl said.

Collins chewed on his lip a moment, and considered the idea. Slowly he shook his head.

"No," he said. "No. I don't think so."

"Then what do you think?"

"I think old Doc Candle *made* me do it. He said he was going to bury me. Getting me lynched would be one good way to do it. Ed Michaels almost blew my head off with his shotgun. It was close. Doc Candle almost made it. He didn't miss by far with you and that target pistol either."

"Sam—I may call you 'Sam'?—just try to think calmly and reasonably for a minute. How could Dr. Candle, the undertaker, possibly make you do a thing like you did in Mr. Michaels' hardware store?"

"Well ... he *said* he was a superhuman alien from outer space."

"If he said that, do you believe him, Sam?"

"*Something* made me do that. It just wasn't my own idea."

"It's easier that way, isn't it, Sam?" Nancy asked. "It's easy to say. 'It wasn't me; some space monster made me do it.' But you really know better, don't you, Sam? Don't take the easy way out! You'll only get deeper and deeper into your makebelieve world. It will be like quicksand. Admit your mistakes—face up to them—*lick them.*"

Collins stood up, and came around the end of the table.

"You're too pretty to be so serious all the time," he said.

"Sam, I want to help you. Please don't spoil it by misinterpreting my intentions."

"You should get a little fun out of life," Collins listened to himself say.

He came on around the big table towards her.

The first time he hadn't realized what was happening, but this time he knew. Somebody was pulling strings and making him jump. He had as much control as Charlie McCarthy.

"Don't come any closer, Sam."

Nancy managed to keep her voice steady, but he could tell she was frightened.

He took another step.

She threw her coffee in his face.

The liquid was only lukewarm but the sudden dash had given him some awareness of his own body again, like the first sound of the alarm faintly pressing through deep layers of sleep.

"Sam, Sam, *please* don't make me do it! Please, Sam, *don't!*"

Nancy had the gun in her hand, rising from her chair.

His hands wanted to grab her clothes and *tear.*

But that's *suicide*, he screamed at his body.

As his hand went up with the intention of ripping, he deflected it just enough to shove the barrel of the gun away from him.

The shot went off, but he knew instantly that it had not hit him.

The gun fell to the floor, and with its fall, something else dropped away and he was in command of himself again.

Nancy sighed, and slumped against him, the left side of her breast suddenly glossy with blood.

Ed Michaels stared at him. Both eyes unblinking, just staring at *him*. He had only taken one look at the girl lying on the floor, blood all over her chest. He hadn't looked back.

"I didn't know who else to call, Ed." Collins said. "Sheriff Thurston being out of town and all."

"It's okay, Sam. Mike swore me in as a special deputy a couple years back. The badge is at the store."

"They'll hang me for this, won't they, Ed?"

Michaels put his hand on Collins' shoulder. "No, they won't do that to you, boy. We know you around here. They'll just put you away for a while."

"The asylum at Hannah, huh?"

"Damn it, yes! What did you expect? A marksman medal?"

"Okay, Ed, okay. Did you call Doc Van der Lies like I told you when I phoned?"

Michaels took a folded white handkerchief from his pocket and wiped his square-jawed face. "You sure are taking this calm, Sam. I'm telling you, Sam, it would look better for you if you at least *acted* like you were sorry.... Doc Van der Lies is up in Wisconsin with Mike. I called Doc Candle."

"He's an undertaker," Collins whispered.

"Don't you expect we need one?" Michaels asked. Then as if he wasn't sure of the answer to his own question, he said, "Did you examine her to see if she was dead? I—I don't know much about women. I wouldn't be able to tell."

It didn't sound like a very good excuse to Collins.

"I guess she's dead," Collins said. "That's the way he must have wanted it."

"*He?* Wait a minute, Sam. You mean you've got one of those split personalities like that girl on TV the other night? There's somebody else inside you that takes over and makes you do things?"

"I never thought of it just like that before. I guess that's one way to look at it."

The knock shook the back door before Michaels could say anything. The door opened and Doc Candle slithered in disjointedly, a rolled-up stretcher over his shoulder.

"Hello, boys," Candle said. "A terrible accident, it brings sorrow to us all. Poor Nancy. Has the family been notified?"

"Good gosh, I forgot about it," Michaels said. "But maybe we better wait until you get her—arranged, huh, Doc?"

"Quite so." The old man laid the canvas stretcher out beside the girl on the floor and unrolled it. He flipped the body over expertly like a window demonstrator flipping a pancake over on a griddle.

"Ed, if you'd just take the front, I'll carry the rear. My vehicle is in the alley."

"Sam, you carry that end for Doc. You're a few years younger."

Collins wanted to say that he couldn't, but he didn't have enough yet to argue with. He picked up the stretcher and looked down at the white feet in the Scotch plaid slippers.

Candle opened the door and waited for them to go through.

The girl on the stretcher parted her lips and rolled her head back and forth, a puzzled expression of pain on her face.

Collins nearly dropped the stretcher, but he made himself hold on tight.

"Ed! Doc! She moved! She's still *alive*."

"Cut that out now, Sam," Ed Michaels snapped. "Just carry your end."

"She's alive," Collins insisted. "She moved again. Just turn around and take a look, Ed. That's all I ask."

"I hefted this thing once, and that's enough. You *move*, Sam. I've got a .38 in my belt, and I went to Rome, Italy, for the Olympics about the time you were getting yourself born, Sam. I ought to be able to hit a target as big as you. Just go ahead and do as you're told."

Collins turned desperately towards Candle. Maybe Nancy had been right, maybe he had been imagining things.

"Doc, you take a look at her," Collins begged.

The old man vibrated over to the stretcher and looked down. The girl twisted in pain, throwing her head back, spilling her hair over the head of the stretcher.

"Rigor mortis," Doc Candle diagnosed, with a wink to Collins.

"No, Doc! She needs a doctor, blood transfusions...."

"Nonsense," Candle snapped. "I'll take her in my black wagon up to my place, put her in the tiled basement. I'll pump out all her blood and flush it down the commode. Then I'll feed in Formaldi-Forever Number Zero. Formaldi-Forever, for the Blush of Death. 'When you think of a Pretty Girl, think of Formaldi-Forever, the Way to Preserve that Beauty.' Then I'll take a needle and some silk thread and just a few stitches on the eyelids and around the mouth...."

"Doc, will you...?" Michaels said faintly.

"Of course. I just wanted to show Sam how foolish he was in saying the Beloved was still alive."

Nancy kicked one leg off the stretcher and Candle picked it up and tucked it back in.

"Ed, if you'd just turn around and *look*." Collins said.

"I don't want to have to look at your face, you murdering son. You make me, you say one more word, and I'll turn around and shoot you between the eyes."

Doc Candle nodded. Collins knew then that Michaels really would shoot him in the head if he said anything more, so he kept quiet.

Candle held the door. They managed to get the stretcher down the back steps, and right into the black panel truck. They fitted the stretcher into the special sockets for it, and Doc Candle closed the double doors and slapped his dry palm down on the sealing crevice.

Instantly, there was an answering knock from inside the truck, a dull echo.

"Didn't you hear that?" Collins asked.

"Hear what?" Michaels said.

"What are you hearing now, Sam?" Candle inquired solicitously.

"Oh. Sure," Michaels said. "Kind of a *voice*, wasn't it, Sam? Didn't understand what it said. Wasn't listening too close, not like you."

Thud-thud-thump-thud.

"No voice," Collins whispered. "That infernal sound, don't you hear it, Ed?"

"I must hurry along," the undertaker said. "Must get ready to work on Nancy, get her ready for her parents to see."

"All right, Doc. I'll take care of Sam."

"Where you going to jail me, Ed?" Collins asked, his eyes on the closed truck doors. "In your storeroom like you did Hank Petrie?"

Michaels' face suddenly began to work. "Jail? Jail you? Jail's too good for you. Doc, have you got a tow rope in that truck?"

Ed Michaels was the best shot in town, probably one of the best marksmen in the world. He had been in the Olympics about thirty years ago. He was Waraxe's one claim to fame. But he wasn't a cowboy. He wasn't a fast draw.

Collins put all of his weight behind his left fist and landed it on the point of Michaels' jaw, just the way boys jumped onto him.

Michaels sprawled out, spread-eagled.

Then Collins wanted to take the revolver out of Ed's belt, and press it into Ed's hand, curling his fingers around the grip and over the trigger, and then he wanted to shake Ed awake, slap his face and shake him....

Collins spun around, clawed open the door to the truck cab and threw himself behind the steering wheel.

He stopped wanting to make Ed Michaels shoot him.

He flipped the ignition switch, levered the floor shift and drove away.

And he was going to drive on and on and on and on.

And on and on and on.

IV

Collins turned onto the old McHenty blacktop, his foot pressed to the floorboards. Ed Michaels didn't own a car; he would have to borrow one from somebody. That would take time. Maybe Candle would give him his hearse to use to follow the Black Rachel.

Trees, fences, barns whizzed past the windows of the cab and then the steel link-mesh fence took up, the fence surrounding the New Kansas National Spaceport. Behind it, further from town, some of the concrete had been poured and the horizon was a remote, sterile gray sweep.

The McHenty Road would soon be closed to civilian traffic. But right now the government wanted people to drive along and see that the spaceship was nothing terrible, nothing to fear.

The girl, Nancy Comstock, was alive in the back. He knew that. But he couldn't stop to prove it or to help her. Candle would make them lynch him first.

Why hadn't Candle stopped him from getting away?

He had managed to break his control for a second. He had done that before when he deflected Nancy's aim. But he couldn't resist Candle for long. Why hadn't Candle made him turn around and come back?

Candle's control of him had seemed to stop when he got inside the cab of the truck. Could it be that the metal shield of the cab could protect an Earthling from the strange mental powers of the creature from another planet which was inhabiting the body of Doc Candle?

Collins shook his head.

More likely Candle was doing this just to get his hopes up. He probably would seize control of him any time he wanted to. But Collins decided to go on playing it as if he did have some hope, as if a shield of metal could protect him from Candle's control. Otherwise ... there was no otherwise.

Collins suddenly saw an opening.

The steel mesh fence was ruptured by a huge semitrailer truck turned on its side. Twenty feet of fence on either side was down. This was restricted government property, but of course spaceships were hardly prime military secrets any longer. Repairs in the fence had not been made instantaneously, and the wreckage was not guarded.

Collins swerved the wheel and drove the old wagon across the waffle-plate obstruction, onto the smooth tarmac beyond.

He raced, raced, raced through the falling night, not sure where he was headed.

Up above he saw the shelter of shadows from a cluster of half-finished buildings. He drove into them and parked.

Collins sat still for a moment, then threw open the door and ran around to the back of the truck, jerking open the handles.

Nancy fell out into his arms.

"What kind of ambulance is this?" she demanded. "It doesn't look like an ambulance. It doesn't smell like an ambulance. It looks like—looks like—"

Collins said, "Shut up. Get out of there. We've got to hide."

"Why?"

"They think I murdered you."

"Murdered me? But I'm alive. Can't they see I'm alive?"

Collins shook his head. "I doubt it. I don't know why, but I don't think it would be that simple. Come with me."

The blood on her breast had dried, and he could see it was only a shallow groove dug by the bullet. But she flinched in pain as she began to walk, pulling the muscles.

They stopped and leaned against a half-finished metallic shed.

"Where are we? Where are you taking me?"

"This is the spaceport. Now shut up."

"Let me go."

"No."

"I'm not dead," Nancy insisted. "You know I'm not dead. I won't press charges against you—just let me go free."

"I told you it wasn't that simple. He wants them to think you're dead, and that's what they'll think."

Nancy passed fingers across her eyes. "Who? Who are you talking about?"

"Doc Candle. He won't let them know you're alive."

Nancy rubbed her forehead with both hands. "Sam, you don't know what you're doing. You don't—know what you're getting yourself into. Just let me show myself to someone. They'll know I'm not dead. Really they will."

"Okay," he said. "Let's find somebody."

He led her toward a more nearly completed building, showing rectangles of light. They looked through the windows to see several men in uniforms bending over blueprints on a desk jury-rigged of sawhorses and planks.

"Sam," Nancy said, "one of those men is Terry Elston. He's a Waraxe boy. I went to school with him. He'll know me. Let's go in...."

"No," Collins said. "We don't go in."

"But—" Nancy started to protest, but stopped. "Wait. He's coming out."

Collins slid along the wall and stood behind the door. "Tell him who you are when he comes out. I'll stay here."

They waited. After a few seconds, the door opened.

Nancy stepped into the rectangle of light thrown on the concrete from the window.

"Terry," she said. "Terry, it's me—Nancy Comstock."

The blue-jawed young man in uniform frowned. "Who did you say you were? Have you got clearance from this area?"

"It's me, Terry. Nancy. Nancy Comstock."

Terry Elston stepped front and center. "That's not a very good joke. I knew Nancy. Hell of a way to die, killed by some maniac."

"Terry, *I'm* Nancy. Don't you recognize me?"

Elston squinted. "You look familiar. You look a little like Nancy. But you can't be her, because she's dead."

"I'm here, and I tell you I'm *not* dead."

"Nancy's dead," Elston repeated mechanically. "Say, what are you trying to pull?"

"Terry, behind you. A maniac!"

"Sure," Elston said. "Sure. There's a maniac *behind* me."

Collins stepped forward and hit Elston behind the ear. He fell silently.

Nancy stared down at him.

"He refused to recognize me. He acted like I was crazy, pretending to be Nancy Comstock."

"Come on along," Collins urged. "They'll probably shoot us on sight as trespassers."

She looked around herself without comprehension.

"Which way?"

"*This way.*"

Collins did not say those words.

They were said by the man with the gun in the uniform like the one worn by Elston. He motioned impatiently.

"This way, this way."

"No priority," Colonel Smith-Boerke said as he paced back and forth, gun in hand.

From time to time he waved it threateningly at Collins and Nancy who sat on the couch in Smith-Boerke's office. They had been sitting for close to two hours. Collins now knew the Colonel did not intend to turn him over to the authorities. They were being held for reasons of Smith-Boerke's own.

"They sneak the ship in here, plan for an unscheduled hop from an uncompleted base—the strictest security we've used in ten or fifteen years—and now they cancel it. This is bound to get leaked by somebody! They'll call it off. It'll never fly now."

Collins sat quietly. He had been listening to this all evening. Smith-Boerke had been drinking, although it wasn't very obvious.

Smith-Boerke turned to Collins.

"I've been waiting for somebody like you. Just waiting for you to come along. And here you are, a wanted fugitive, completely in my power! Perfect, *perfect.*"

Collins nodded to himself. Of course, Colonel Smith-Boerke had been waiting for him. And Doc Candle had driven him right to him. It was inescapable. He had been intended to escape and turn up right here all along.

"What do you want with me?"

Smith-Boerke's flushed face brightened. "You want to become a hero? A hero so big that all these trumped-up charges against you will be dropped? It'll be romantic. Back to Lindbergh-to-Paris. Tell me, Collins, how would you like to be the first man to travel faster than light?"

Collins knew there was no way out.

"All right," he said.

Smith-Boerke wiped a hand across his dry mouth.

"Project Silver *has* to come off. My whole career depends on it. You don't have anything to do. Everything's cybernetic. Just ride along and prove a human being can survive. Nothing to it. No hyperdrives, none of that kind of stuff. We had an engine that could go half lightspeed and now we've made it twice as efficient and more. No superstitions about Einstein, I hope? No? Good."

"I'll go," Collins said. "But what if I had said 'no'."

Smith-Boerke put the gun away in a desk drawer.

"Then you could have walked out of here, straight into the MP's."

"Why didn't they come in here after me?"

"They don't have security clearance for this building."

"*Don't* leave me alone," Nancy said urgently. "I don't understand what's happening. I feel so helpless. I need help."

"You're asking the wrong man," Collins said briefly.

Collins felt safe when the airlock kissed shut its metal lips.

It was not like the house, but yet he felt safe, surrounded by all the complicated, expensive electronic equipment. It was big, solid, sterilely gleaming.

Another thing—he had reason to believe that Doc Candle's power could not reach him through metal.

"But I'm not outside," Doc Candle said, "I'm in here, with you."

Collins yelled and cursed, he tried to pull off the acceleration webbing and claw through the airlock. Nobody paid any attention to him. Count downs had been automated. Smith-Boerke was handling this one himself, and he cut off the Audio-In switch from the spaceship. Doc Candle said nothing else for a moment, and the spaceship, almost an entity itself, went on with its work.

The faster-than-light spaceship took off.

At first it was like any other rocket takeoff.

The glow of its exhaust spread over the field of the spaceport, then over the hills and valleys, and then the town of Waraxe, spreading illumination even as far as Sam Collins' silent house.

After a time of being sick, Collins lay back and accepted this too.

"That's right, that's it," Doc Candle said. "Take it and die with it. That's the ticket."

Collins' eyes settled on a gauge. Three quarters lightspeed. Climbing.

Nothing strange, nothing untoward happened when you reached lightspeed. It was only an arbitrary number. All else was superstition. Forget it, forget it, forget it.

Something was telling him that. At first he thought it was Doc Candle but then he knew it was the ship.

Collins sat back and took it, and what he was taking was death. It was creeping over him, seeping into his feet, filling him like liquid does a sponge.

Not will, but curiosity, caused him to turn his head.

He saw Doc Candle.

The old body was dying. He was in the emergency seat, broken, a ribbon of blood lacing his chin. But Doc Candle continued to laugh triumphantly in Collins' head.

"Why? Why do you have to kill me?" Collins asked.

"Because I am evil."

"How do you know you're evil?"

"*They told me so!*" Candle shouted back in the thundering silence of Death's approach. "They were always saying I was bad."

They.

Collins got a picture of something incredibly old and incredibly wise, but long unused to the young, clumsy gods. Something that could mar the molding of a godling and make it mortal.

"But I'm not really so very bad," Doc Candle went on. "I had to destroy, but I picked someone who really didn't care if he were destroyed or not. An almost absolutely passive human being, Sam. You."

Collins nodded.

"And even then," said the superhuman alien from outer space, "I could not just destroy. I have created a work of art."

"Work of art?"

"Yes. I have taken your life and turned it into a horror story, Sam! A chilling, demonic, black-hearted horror!"

Collins nodded again.

LIGHTSPEED.

There was finally something human within Sam Collins that he could not deny. He wanted to live. It wasn't true. He did care what happened.

You do? said somebody.

He does? asked somebody else, surprised, and suddenly he again got the image of wiser, older creatures, a little ashamed because of what they had done to the creature named Doc Candle.

He does, chorused several voices, and Sam Collins cried aloud: "I do! I want to live!" They were just touching lightspeed; he felt it.

This time it was not just a biological response. He really wanted help. He wanted to stay alive.

From the older, wiser voices he got help, though he never knew how; he felt the ship move slipwise under him, and then a crash.

And Doc Candle got help too, the only help even the older, wiser ones could give him.

They pulled him out of the combined wreckage of the spaceship and his house. Both were demolished.

It was strange how the spaceship Sam Collins was on crashed right into his house. Ed Michaels recalled a time in a tornado when Sy Baxter's car was picked up, lifted across town and dropped into his living room.

When the men from the spaceport lifted away tons of rubble, they found him and said, "He's dead."

No, I'm not, Collins thought. I'm alive.

And then they saw that he really was alive, that he had come through it alive somehow, and nobody remembered anything like it since the airliner crash in '59.

A while later, after they found Doc Candle's body and court-martialed Smith-Boerke, who took drugs, Nancy was nuzzling him on his hospital bed. It was nice, but he wasn't paying much attention.

I'm free, Collins thought as the girl hugged him. Free! He kissed her.

Well, he thought while she was kissing him back, as free as I want to be, anyway.

QUIET, PLEASE

by Kevin Scott

Groverzb knew what he wanted—peace and quiet. He was willing to scream his head off for it!

THE big man eased the piano off his back and stood looking at Groverzb.

"You ain't gonna like it here." He mopped his face. "Boy, will I ever be glad to get off this cockeyed planet."

Groverzb pushed at his spectacles, sniffed, and said, "Quite."

The big man said, "Ain't no native here over three feet tall. And they got some crazy kind of communication. They don't talk."

Groverzb said, "Quiet."

"Uh?"

"Precisely why I am here. I," said Groverzb, sniffing again, "loathe conversation."

"Oh. Well." He left.

Alone, Groverzb surveyed his realm. The house was the shell of what had formerly been a Little People apartment building. Ceilings, floors and walls had been removed to form one large room. The tiny doors and windows had been sealed, and a single window and door had been cut into the shell for Groverzb's use. Crude, but serviceable.

Groverzb walked to the window and looked down the slope. Little People buildings dotted the landscape, and the people themselves scurried silently about. Yes, thought Groverzb, it would do nicely. He had brought an adequate food-tablet supply. He would finish, without the distraction of voices, his beautiful concerto. He would return to Earth famous and happy.

Armed with paper and pencils, he went to the piano, having decided to enlarge upon the theme in the second movement. His mind knew exactly how the passage should run, and he swiftly covered the paper with sharp, angular notes. Then he triumphantly lifted his hands and began to play what he had written.

He jerked back from the keyboard, his hair on end, his teeth, on edge, his ears screaming with the mass of sounds he had produced. He looked at his hands, peered at the score, adjusted his spectacles and tried again.

I'm tired, he thought, recoiling in horror from the racket. A food tablet and a nap will remedy the situation.

*

WHEN he awoke, Groverzb walked to the window, refreshed. A violet glow had replaced the harsh yellow light of day. At the foot of the slope, the Little People dashed to and fro, but no voice broke the peaceful quiet of the evening.

With a sigh of satisfaction, Groverzb went to the piano. Gently, he struck the keys. Blatant, jumbled noise filled the room.

Breathing hard, Groverzb rose and gingerly lifted the spinet's lid. No, nothing amiss there. Good felts, free hammers, solid sounding board—must be out of tune.

Groverzb closed the lid, sat down and struck a single note. A clear tone sang out. He moved chromatically up and down the scale. Definitely not out of tune.

He shifted the score, glanced uneasily at the keys and began to play. Discord immediately pierced his eardrums.

He clapped his hands over his ears and leaped wildly from the piano bench. The trip, he decided frantically. It must have affected my hearing.

He flung himself from the house and down the slope. The Little People scattered, staring. He charged into the administration building and clutched the lapels of a uniformed official.

"A doctor!" he gasped. "Now! This minute!"

The official raised his eyebrows and removed Groverzb's hands with distaste.

"It's a little late in the day," he drawled, "but maybe the doc up on the top floor—"

Groverzb flew up the stairs and into the doctor's office. The doctor's face lit up.

"A patient!" he exclaimed. "Capital! What seems to be the trouble? Food poisoning? Shouldn't eat the food here. Garbage. Appendix? Heart attack?"

"Stop talking, you idiot, it's my ears!"

Obviously disappointed, the doctor nevertheless poked and peered at Groverzb's ears.

"No," he said finally. "A trifle big, yes. But nothing wrong with them."

"You're sure?"

"Absolutely. A pity. I'm getting a bit rusty."

With a groan, Groverzb staggered out of the building, back through town, and up the slope to his house. Seating himself firmly on the bench he began to play.

He shuddered. The noise was abominable.

Suddenly his door burst open and a crowd of Little People rushed in. They pulled him off the bench and slapped angrily at his hands. Then, with cutters, they attacked the piano.

"Here, stop that!" Groverzb screeched. "What do you think you're doing?"

The Little People pushed and dragged him out of the house, down the slope, through the town and into the launching bowl at the space-strip. The launching agent took one look and yelled, "Get the interpreter! On the double!"

The interpreter ran up and whipped something from his pocket. It looked like a miniature piano skeleton. He tripped a hammer. There was a faint tinkle. Instantly one of the Little People produced a single miniature hammer and tapped it rapidly against his skull. The interpreter tripped another hammer. A second little one responded.

*

SUDDENLY one of the Little People ran over and tripped all the interpreter's hammers simultaneously. The Little People winced.

"Oh," said the interpreter. "Well, it's their planet." He hustled Groverzb out to a freight ship that was warming up for takeoff.

"Is everyone insane?" Groverzb croaked. "I demand to know what this is all about!"

The interpreter shoved Groverzb into the ship.

"They say you talk too much!" he yelled, as he slammed the door.

SERVICE WITH A SMILE

by Charles L. Fontenay

Herbert was truly a gentleman robot. The ladies' slightest wish was his command . . . .

HERBERT bowed with a muted clank—indicating he probably needed oiling somewhere—and presented Alice with a perfect martini on a silver tray. He stood holding the tray, a white, permanent porcelain smile on his smooth metal face, as Alice sipped the drink and grimaced.

"It's a good martini, Herbert," said Alice. "Thank you. But, dammit, I wish you didn't have that everlasting smile!"

"I am very sorry, Miss Alice, but I am unable to alter myself in any way," replied Herbert in his polite, hollow voice.

He retired to a corner and stood impassively, still holding the tray. Herbert had found a silver deposit and made the tray. Herbert had found sand and made the cocktail glass. Herbert had combined God knew what atmospheric and earth chemicals to make what tasted like gin and vermouth, and Herbert had frozen the ice to chill it.

"Sometimes," said Thera wistfully, "it occurs to me it would be better to live in a mud hut with a real man than in a mansion with Herbert."

The four women lolled comfortably in the living room of their spacious house, as luxurious as anything any of them would have known on distant Earth. The rugs were thick, the furniture was overstuffed, the paintings on the walls were aesthetic and inspiring, the shelves were filled with booktapes and musictapes.

Herbert had done it all, except the booktapes and musictapes, which had been salvaged from the wrecked spaceship.

"Do you suppose we'll ever escape from this best of all possible manless worlds?" asked Betsy, fluffing her thick black hair with her fingers and inspecting herself in a Herbert-made mirror.

"I don't see how," answered blond Alice glumly. "That atmospheric trap would wreck any other ship just as it wrecked ours, and the same magnetic layer prevents any radio message from getting out. No, I'm afraid we're a colony."

"A colony perpetuates itself," reminded sharp-faced Marguerite, acidly. "We aren't a colony, without men."

They were not the prettiest four women in the universe, nor the youngest. The prettiest women and the youngest did not go to space. But they were young enough and healthy enough, or they could not have gone to space.

It had been a year and a half now—an Earth year and a half on a nice little planet revolving around a nice little yellow sun. Herbert, the robot, was obedient and versatile and had provided them with a house, food, clothing, anything they wished created out of the raw elements of earth and air and water. But the bones of all the men who had been aspace with these four ladies lay mouldering in the wreckage of their spaceship.

And Herbert could not create a man. Herbert did not have to have direct orders, and he had tried once to create a man when he had overheard them wishing for one. They had buried the corpse—perfect in every detail except that it never had been alive.

"It's been a hot day," said Alice, fanning her brow. "I wish it would rain."

Silently, Herbert moved from his corner and went out the door.

Marguerite gestured after him with a bitter little laugh.

"It'll rain this afternoon," she said. "I don't know how Herbert does it—maybe with silver iodide. But it'll rain. Wouldn't it have been simpler to get him to air-condition the house, Alice?"

"That's a good idea," said Alice thoughtfully. "We should have had him do it before."

*

HERBERT had not quite completed the task of air-conditioning the house when the other spaceship crashed. They all rushed out to the smoking site—the four women and Herbert.

It was a tiny scoutship, and its single occupant was alive.

He was unconscious, but he was alive. And he was a man!

They carted him back to the house, tenderly, and put him to bed. They hovered over him like four hens over a single chick, waiting and watching for him to come out of his coma, while Herbert scurried about creating and administering the necessary medicines.

"He'll live," said Thera happily. Thera had been a space nurse. "He'll be on his feet and walking around in a few weeks."

"A man!" murmured Betsy, with something like awe in her voice. "I could almost believe Herbert brought him here in answer to our prayers."

"Now, girls," said Alice, "we have to realize that a man brings problems, as well as possibilities."

There was a matter-of-fact hardness to her tone which almost masked the quiver behind it. There was a defiant note of competition there which had not been heard on this little planet before.

"What do you mean?" asked Thera.

"I know what she means," said Marguerite, and the new hardness came natural to her. "She means, which one of us gets him?"

Betsy, the youngest, gasped, and her mouth rounded to a startled O. Thera blinked, as though she were coming out of a daze.

"That's right," said Alice. "Do we draw straws, or do we let him choose?"

"Couldn't we wait?" suggested Betsy timidly. "Couldn't we wait until he gets well?"

Herbert came in with a new thermometer and poked it into the unconscious man's mouth. He stood by the bed, waiting patiently.

"No, I don't think we can," said Alice. "I think we ought to have it all worked out and agreed on, so there won't be any dispute about it."

"I say, draw straws," said Marguerite. Marguerite's face was thin, and she had a skinny figure.

Betsy, the youngest, opened her mouth, but Thera forestalled her.

"We are not on Earth," she said firmly, in her soft, mellow voice. "We don't have to follow terrestrial customs, and we shouldn't. There's only one solution that will keep everybody happy—all of us and the man."

"And that is . . . ?" asked Marguerite drily.

"Polygamy, of course. He must belong to us all."

260

Betsy shuddered but, surprisingly, she nodded.

"That's well and good," agreed Marguerite, "but we have to agree that no one of us will be favored above the others. He has to understand that from the start."

"That's fair," said Alice, pursing her lips. "Yes, that's fair. But I agree with Marguerite: he must be divided equally among the four of us."

Chattering over the details, the hard competitiveness vanished from their tones, the four left the sickroom to prepare supper.

*

AFTER SUPPER they went back in.

Herbert stood by the bed, the eternal smile of service on his metal face. As always, Herbert had not required a direct command to accede to their wishes.

The man was divided into four quarters, one for each of them. It was a very neat surgical job.

TIME FUZE

by Randall Garrett

The ultradrive had just one slight drawback: it set up a shock wave that made suns explode. Which made the problem of getting back home a delicate one indeed . . . .

Commander Benedict kept his eyes on the rear plate as he activated the intercom. "All right, cut the power. We ought to be safe enough here."

As he released the intercom, Dr. Leicher, of the astronomical staff, stepped up to his side. "Perfectly safe," he nodded, "although even at this distance a star going nova ought to be quite a display."

Benedict didn't shift his gaze from the plate. "Do you have your instruments set up?"

"Not quite. But we have plenty of time. The light won't reach us for several hours yet. Remember, we were outracing it at ten lights."

The commander finally turned, slowly letting his breath out in a soft sigh. "Dr. Leicher, I would say[Pg 68] that this is just about the foulest coincidence that could happen to the first interstellar vessel ever to leave the Solar System."

Leicher shrugged. "In one way of thinking, yes. It is certainly true that we will never know, now, whether Alpha Centauri A ever had any planets. But, in another way, it is extremely fortunate that we should be so near a stellar explosion because of the wealth of scientific information we can obtain. As you say, it is a coincidence, and probably one that happens only once in a billion years. The chances of any particular star going nova are small. That we should be so close when it happens is of a vanishingly small order of probability."

Commander Benedict took off his cap and looked at the damp stain in the sweatband. "Nevertheless, Doctor, it is damned unnerving to come out of ultradrive a couple of hundred million miles from the first star ever visited by man and have to turn tail and run because the damned thing practically blows up in your face."

Leicher could see that Benedict was upset; he rarely used the same profanity twice in one sentence.

They had been downright lucky, at that. If Leicher hadn't seen the star begin to swell and brighten, if he hadn't known what it meant, or if Commander Benedict hadn't been quick enough in shifting the ship back into ultradrive—Leicher had a vision of an incandescent cloud of gaseous metal that had once been a spaceship.

The intercom buzzed. The commander answered, "Yes?"

"Sir, would you tell Dr. Leicher that we have everything set up now?"

Leicher nodded and turned to leave. "I guess we have nothing to do now but wait."

When the light from the nova did come, Commander Benedict was back at the plate again—the forward one, this time, since the ship had been turned around in order to align the astronomy lab in the nose with the star.

Alpha Centauri A began to brighten and spread. It made Benedict think of a light bulb connected through a rheostat, with someone turning that rheostat, turning it until the circuit was well overloaded.

The light began to hurt Benedict's eyes even at that distance and he had to cut down the receptivity in order to watch. After a while, he turned away from the plate. Not because the

262

show was over, but simply because it had slowed to a point beyond which no change seemed to take place to the human eye.

Five weeks later, much to Leicher's chagrin, Commander Benedict announced that they had to leave the vicinity. The ship had only been provisioned to go to Alpha Centauri, scout the system without landing on any of the planets, and return. At ten lights, top speed for the ultradrive, it would take better than three months to get back.

"I know you'd like to watch it go through the complete cycle," Benedict said, "but we can't go back home as a bunch of starved skeletons."

Leicher resigned himself to the necessity of leaving much of his work unfinished, and, although he knew it was a case of sour grapes,[Pg 69] consoled himself with the thought that he could as least get most of the remaining information from the five-hundred-inch telescope on Luna, four years from then.

As the ship slipped into the not-quite-space through which the ultradrive propelled it, Leicher began to consolidate the material he had already gathered.

*

Commander Benedict wrote in the log:

Fifty-four days out from Sol. Alpha Centauri has long since faded back into its pre-blowup state, since we have far outdistanced the light from its explosion. It now looks as it did two years ago. It—

"Pardon me, Commander," Leicher interrupted, "But I have something interesting to show you."

Benedict took his fingers off the keys and turned around in his chair. "What is it, Doctor?"

Leicher frowned at the papers in his hands. "I've been doing some work on the probability of that explosion happening just as it did, and I've come up with some rather frightening figures. As I said before, the probability was small. A little calculation has given us some information which makes it even smaller. For instance: with a possible error of plus or minus two seconds Alpha Centauri A began to explode the instant we came out of ultradrive!

"Now, the probability of that occurring comes out so small that it should happen only once in ten to the four hundred sixty-seventh seconds."

It was Commander Benedict's turn to frown. "So?"

"Commander, the entire universe is only about ten to the seventeenth seconds old. But to give you an idea, let's say that the chances of its happening are *once* in millions of trillions of years!"

Benedict blinked. The number, he realized, was totally beyond his comprehension—or anyone else's.

"Well, so what? Now it has happened that one time. That simply means that it will almost certainly never happen again!"

"True. But, Commander, when you buck odds like that and win, the thing to do is look for some factor that is cheating in your favor. If you took a pair of dice and started throwing sevens, one right after another—*for the next couple of thousand years*—you'd begin to suspect they were loaded."

Benedict said nothing; he just waited expectantly.

"There is only one thing that could have done it. Our ship." Leicher said it quietly, without emphasis.

"What we know about the hyperspace, or superspace, or whatever it is we move through in ultradrive is almost nothing. Coming out of it so near to a star might set up some sort of shock wave in normal space which would completely disrupt that star's internal balance, resulting in the liberation of unimaginably vast amounts of energy, causing that star to go nova. We can only assume that we ourselves were the fuze that set off that nova."

Benedict stood up slowly. When he spoke, his voice was a choking whisper. "You mean the sun—Sol—might . . . ."

Leicher nodded. "I don't say that it definitely would. But the probability is that we were the cause of the destruction of Alpha Centauri A, and therefore might cause the destruction of Sol in the same way."

Benedict's voice was steady again. "That means that we can't go back again, doesn't it? Even if we're not positive, we can't take the chance."

"Not necessarily. We can get fairly close before we cut out the drive, and come in the rest of the way at sub-light speed. It'll take longer, and we'll have to go on half or one-third rations, but we *can* do it!"

"How far away?"

"I don't know what the minimum distance is, but I do know how we can gage a distance. Remember, neither Alpha Centauri B or C were detonated. We'll have to cut our drive at least as far away from Sol as they are from A."

"I see." The commander was silent for a moment, then: "Very well, Dr. Leicher. If that's the safest way, that's the only way."

Benedict issued the orders, while Leicher figured the exact point at which they must cut out the drive, and how long the trip would take. The rations would have to be cut down accordingly.

Commander Benedict's mind whirled around the monstrousness of the whole thing like some dizzy bee around a flower. What if there had been planets around Centauri A? What if they had been inhabited? Had he, all unwittingly, killed entire races of living, intelligent beings?

But, how could he have known? The drive had never been tested before. It couldn't be tested inside the Solar System—it was too fast. He and his crew had been volunteers, knowing that they might die when the drive went on.

Suddenly, Benedict gasped and slammed his fist down on the desk before him.

Leicher looked up. "What's the matter, Commander?"

"Suppose," came the answer, "Just suppose, that we have the same effect on a star when we *go into* ultradrive as we do when we come out of it?"

Leicher was silent for a moment, stunned by the possibility. There was nothing to say, anyway. They could only wait . . . .

*

A little more than half a light year from Sol, when the ship reached the point where its occupants could see the light that had left their home sun more than seven months before, they watched it become suddenly, horribly brighter. *A hundred thousand times brighter!*

THE SKULL

by Philip K. Dick

Conger agreed to kill a stranger he had never seen. But he would make no mistakes because he had the stranger's skull under his arm.

"WHAT is this opportunity?" Conger asked. "Go on. I'm interested."

The room was silent; all faces were fixed on Conger—still in the drab prison uniform. The Speaker leaned forward slowly.

"Before you went to prison your trading business was paying well—all illegal—all very profitable. Now you have nothing, except the prospect of another six years in a cell."

Conger scowled.

"There is a certain situation, very important to this Council, that requires your peculiar abilities. Also, it is a situation you might find interesting. You were a hunter, were you not? You've done a great deal of trapping, hiding in the bushes, waiting at night for the game? I imagine hunting must be a source of satisfaction to you, the chase, the stalking—"

Conger sighed. His lips twisted. "All right," he said. "Leave that out. Get to the point. Who do you want me to kill?"

The Speaker smiled. "All in proper sequence," he said softly.

*

THE car slid to a stop. It was night; there was no light anywhere along the street. Conger looked out. "Where are we? What is this place?"

The hand of the guard pressed into his arm. "Come. Through that door."

Conger stepped down, onto the damp sidewalk. The guard came swiftly after him, and then the Speaker. Conger took a deep breath of the cold air. He studied the dim outline of the building rising up before them.

"I know this place. I've seen it before." He squinted, his eyes growing accustomed to the dark. Suddenly he became alert. "This is—"

"Yes. The First Church." The Speaker walked toward the steps. "We're expected."

"Expected? *Here?*"

"Yes." The Speaker mounted the stairs. "You know we're not allowed in their Churches, especially with guns!" He stopped. Two armed soldiers loomed up ahead, one on each side.

"All right?" The Speaker looked up at them. They nodded. The door of the Church was open. Conger could see other soldiers inside, standing about, young soldiers with large eyes, gazing at the ikons and holy images.

"I see," he said.

"It was necessary," the Speaker said. "As you know, we have been singularly unfortunate in the past in our relations with the First Church."

"This won't help."

"But it's worth it. You will see."

*

THEY passed through the hall and into the main chamber where the altar piece was, and the kneeling places. The Speaker scarcely glanced at the altar as they passed by. He pushed open a small side door and beckoned Conger through.

265

"In here. We have to hurry. The faithful will be flocking in soon."

Conger entered, blinking. They were in a small chamber, low-ceilinged, with dark panels of old wood. There was a smell of ashes and smoldering spices in the room. He sniffed. "What's that? The smell."

"Cups on the wall. I don't know." The Speaker crossed impatiently to the far side. "According to our information, it is hidden here by this—"

Conger looked around the room. He saw books and papers, holy signs and images. A strange low shiver went through him.

"Does my job involve anyone of the Church? If it does—"

The Speaker turned, astonished. "Can it be that you believe in the Founder? Is it possible, a hunter, a killer—"

"No. Of course not. All their business about resignation to death, non-violence—"

"What is it, then?"

Conger shrugged. "I've been taught not to mix with such as these. They have strange abilities. And you can't reason with them."

The Speaker studied Conger thoughtfully. "You have the wrong idea. It is no one here that we have in mind. We've found that killing them only tends to increase their numbers."

"Then why come here? Let's leave."

"No. We came for something important. Something you will need to identify your man. Without it you won't be able to find him." A trace of a smile crossed the Speaker's face. "We don't want you to kill the wrong person. It's too important."

"I don't make mistakes." Conger's chest rose. "Listen, Speaker—"

"This is an unusual situation," the Speaker said. "You see, the person you are after—the person that we are sending you to find—is known only by certain objects here. They are the only traces, the only means of identification. Without them—"

"What are they?"

He came toward the Speaker. The Speaker moved to one side. "Look," he said. He drew a sliding wall away, showing a dark square hole. "In there."

Conger squatted down, staring in. He frowned. "A skull! A skeleton!"

"The man you are after has been dead for two centuries," the Speaker said. "This is all that remains of him. And this is all you have with which to find him."

For a long time Conger said nothing. He stared down at the bones, dimly visible in the recess of the wall. How could a man dead centuries be killed? How could he be stalked, brought down?

Conger was a hunter, a man who had lived as he pleased, where he pleased. He had kept himself alive by trading, bringing furs and pelts in from the Provinces on his own ship, riding at high speed, slipping through the customs line around Earth.

He had hunted in the great mountains of the moon. He had stalked through empty Martian cities. He had explored—

The Speaker said, "Soldier, take these objects and have them carried to the car. Don't lose any part of them."

The soldier went into the cupboard, reaching gingerly, squatting on his heels.

"It is my hope," the Speaker continued softly, to Conger, "that you will demonstrate your loyalty to us, now. There are always ways for citizens to restore themselves, to show their devotion to their society. For you I think this would be a very good chance. I seriously doubt that a better one will come. And for your efforts there will be quite a restitution, of course."

The two men looked at each other; Conger, thin, unkempt, the Speaker immaculate in his uniform.

"I understand you," Conger said. "I mean, I understand this part, about the chance. But how can a man who has been dead two centuries be—"

"I'll explain later," the Speaker said. "Right now we have to hurry!" The soldier had gone out with the bones, wrapped in a blanket held carefully in his arms. The Speaker walked to the door. "Come. They've already discovered that we've broken in here, and they'll be coming at any moment."

They hurried down the damp steps to the waiting car. A second later the driver lifted the car up into the air, above the house-tops.

*

THE SPEAKER settled back in the seat.

"The First Church has an interesting past," he said. "I suppose you are familiar with it, but I'd like to speak of a few points that are of relevancy to us.

"It was in the twentieth century that the Movement began—during one of the periodic wars. The Movement developed rapidly, feeding on the general sense of futility, the realization that each war was breeding greater war, with no end in sight. The Movement posed a simple answer to the problem: Without military preparations—weapons—there could be no war. And without machinery and complex scientific technocracy there could be no weapons.

"The Movement preached that you couldn't stop war by planning for it. They preached that man was losing to his machinery and science, that it was getting away from him, pushing him into greater and greater wars. Down with society, they shouted. Down with factories and science! A few more wars and there wouldn't be much left of the world.

"The Founder was an obscure person from a small town in the American Middle West. We don't even know his name. All we know is that one day he appeared, preaching a doctrine of non-violence, non-resistance; no fighting, no paying taxes for guns, no research except for medicine. Live out your life quietly, tending your garden, staying out of public affairs; mind your own business. Be obscure, unknown, poor. Give away most of your possessions, leave the city. At least that was what developed from what he told the people."

The car dropped down and landed on a roof.

"The Founder preached this doctrine, or the germ of it; there's no telling how much the faithful have added themselves. The local authorities picked him up at once, of course. Apparently they were convinced that he meant it; he was never released. He was put to death, and his body buried secretly. It seemed that the cult was finished."

The Speaker smiled. "Unfortunately, some of his disciples reported seeing him after the date of his death. The rumor spread; he had conquered death, he was divine. It took hold, grew. And here we are today, with a First Church, obstructing all social progress, destroying society, sowing the seeds of anarchy—"

"But the wars," Conger said. "About them?"

"The wars? Well, there were no more wars. It must be acknowledged that the elimination of war was the direct result of non-violence practiced on a general scale. But we can take a more objective view of war today. What was so terrible about it? War had a profound selective value, perfectly in accord with the teachings of Darwin and Mendel and others. Without war the mass of useless, incompetent mankind, without training or intelligence, is permitted to grow and expand unchecked. War acted to reduce their numbers; like storms and earthquakes and droughts, it was nature's way of eliminating the unfit.

"Without war the lower elements of mankind have increased all out of proportion. They threaten the educated few, those with scientific knowledge and training, the ones equipped to direct society. They have no regard for science or a scientific society, based on reason. And this Movement seeks to aid and abet them. Only when scientists are in full control can the—"

*

HE looked at his watch and then kicked the car door open. "I'll tell you the rest as we walk."

They crossed the dark roof. "Doubtless you now know whom those bones belonged to, who it is that we are after. He has been dead just two centuries, now, this ignorant man from the Middle West, this Founder. The tragedy is that the authorities of the time acted too slowly. They allowed him to speak, to get his message across. He was allowed to preach, to start his cult. And once such a thing is under way, there's no stopping it.

"But what if he had died before he preached? What if none of his doctrines had ever been spoken? It took only a moment for him to utter them, that we know. They say he spoke just once, just one time. *Then* the authorities came, taking him away. He offered no resistance; the incident was small."

The Speaker turned to Conger.

"Small, but we're reaping the consequences of it today."

They went inside the building. Inside, the soldiers had already laid out the skeleton on a table. The soldiers stood around it, their young faces intense.

Conger went over to the table, pushing past them. He bent down, staring at the bones. "So these are his remains," he murmured. "The Founder. The Church has hidden them for two centuries."

"Quite so," the Speaker said. "But now we have them. Come along down the hall."

They went across the room to a door. The Speaker pushed it open. Technicians looked up. Conger saw machinery, whirring and turning; benches and retorts. In the center of the room was a gleaming crystal cage.

The Speaker handed a Slem-gun to Conger. "The important thing to remember is that the skull must be saved and brought back—for comparison and proof. Aim low—at the chest."

Conger weighed the gun in his hands. "It feels good," he said. "I know this gun—that is, I've seen them before, but I never used one."

The Speaker nodded. "You will be instructed on the use of the gun and the operation of the cage. You will be given all data we have on the time and location. The exact spot was a place called Hudson's field. About 1960 in a small community outside Denver, Colorado.

And don't forget—the only means of identification you will have will be the skull. There are visible characteristics of the front teeth, especially the left incisor—"

Conger listened absently. He was watching two men in white carefully wrapping the skull in a plastic bag. They tied it and carried it into the crystal cage. "And if I should make a mistake?"

"Pick the wrong man? Then find the right one. Don't come back until you succeed in reaching this Founder. And you can't wait for him to start speaking; that's what we must avoid! You must act in advance. Take chances; shoot as soon as you think you've found him. He'll be someone unusual, probably a stranger in the area. Apparently he wasn't known."

Conger listened dimly.

"Do you think you have it all now?" the Speaker asked.

"Yes. I think so." Conger entered the crystal cage and sat down, placing his hands on the wheel.

"Good luck," the Speaker said.

"We'll be awaiting the outcome. There's some philosophical doubt as to whether one can alter the past. This should answer the question once and for all."

Conger fingered the controls of the cage.

"By the way," the Speaker said. "Don't try to use this cage for purposes not anticipated in your job. We have a constant trace on it. If we want it back, we can get it back. Good luck."

Conger said nothing. The cage was sealed. He raised his finger and touched the wheel control. He turned the wheel carefully.

He was still staring at the plastic bag when the room outside vanished.

For a long time there was nothing at all. Nothing beyond the crystal mesh of the cage. Thoughts rushed through Conger's mind, helter-skelter. How would he know the man? How could he be certain, in advance? What had he looked like? What was his name? How had he acted, before he spoke? Would he be an ordinary person, or some strange outlandish crank?

Conger picked up the Slem-gun and held it against his cheek. The metal of the gun was cool and smooth. He practiced moving the sight. It was a beautiful gun, the kind of gun he could fall in love with. If he had owned such a gun in the Martian desert—on the long nights when he had lain, cramped and numbed with cold, waiting for things that moved through the darkness—

He put the gun down and adjusted the meter readings of the cage. The spiraling mist was beginning to condense and settle. All at once forms wavered and fluttered around him.

Colors, sounds, movements filtered through the crystal wire. He clamped the controls off and stood up.

*

HE was on a ridge overlooking a small town. It was high noon. The air was crisp and bright. A few automobiles moved along a road. Off in the distance were some level fields. Conger went to the door and stepped outside. He sniffed the air. Then he went back into the cage.

He stood before the mirror over the shelf, examining his features. He had trimmed his beard—they had not got him to cut it off—and his hair was neat. He was dressed in the clothing of the middle-twentieth century, the odd collar and coat, the shoes of animal hide. In his pocket was money of the times. That was important. Nothing more was needed.

Nothing, except his ability, his special cunning. But he had never used it in such a way before.

He walked down the road toward the town.

The first things he noticed were the newspapers on the stands. April 5, 1961. He was not too far off. He looked around him. There was a filling station, a garage, some taverns, and a ten-cent store. Down the street was a grocery store and some public buildings.

A few minutes later he mounted the stairs of the little public library and passed through the doors into the warm interior.

The librarian looked up, smiling.

"Good afternoon," she said.

He smiled, not speaking because his words would not be correct; accented and strange, probably. He went over to a table and sat down by a heap of magazines. For a moment he glanced through them. Then he was on his feet again. He crossed the room to a wide rack against the wall. His heart began to beat heavily.

Newspapers—weeks on end. He took a roll of them over to the table and began to scan them quickly. The print was odd, the letters strange. Some of the words were unfamiliar.

He set the papers aside and searched farther. At last he found what he wanted. He carried the *Cherrywood Gazette* to the table and opened it to the first page. He found what he wanted:

PRISONER HANGS SELF

An unidentified man, held by the county sheriff's office for suspicion of criminal syndicalism, was found dead this morning, by—

He finished the item. It was vague, uninforming. He needed more. He carried the *Gazette* back to the racks and then, after a moment's hesitation, approached the librarian.

"More?" he asked. "More papers. Old ones?"

She frowned. "How old? Which papers?"

"Months old. And—before."

"Of the *Gazette?* This is all we have. What did you want? What are you looking for? Maybe I can help you."

He was silent.

"You might find older issues at the *Gazette* office," the woman said, taking off her glasses. "Why don't you try there? But if you'd tell me, maybe I could help you—"

He went out.

The *Gazette* office was down a side street; the sidewalk was broken and cracked. He went inside. A heater glowed in the corner of the small office. A heavy-set man stood up and came slowly over to the counter.

"What did you want, mister?" he said.

"Old papers. A month. Or more."

"To buy? You want to buy them?"

"Yes." He held out some of the money he had. The man stared.

"Sure," he said. "Sure. Wait a minute." He went quickly out of the room. When he came back he was staggering under the weight of his armload, his face red. "Here are some," he grunted. "Took what I could find. Covers the whole year. And if you want more—"

Conger carried the papers outside. He sat down by the road and began to go through them.

*

WHAT he wanted was four months back, in December. It was a tiny item, so small that he almost missed it. His hands trembled as he scanned it, using the small dictionary for some of the archaic terms.

MAN ARRESTED FOR UNLICENSED DEMONSTRATION

An unidentified man who refused to give his name was picked up in Cooper Creek by special agents of the sheriff's office, according to Sheriff Duff. It was said the man was recently noticed in this area and had been watched continually. It was—

Cooper Creek. December, 1960. His heart pounded. That was all he needed to know. He stood up, shaking himself, stamping his feet on the cold ground. The sun had moved across the sky to the very edge of the hills. He smiled. Already he had discovered the exact time and place. Now he needed only to go back, perhaps to November, to Cooper Creek—

He walked back through the main section of town, past the library, past the grocery store. It would not be hard; the hard part was over. He would go there; rent a room, prepare to wait until the man appeared.

He turned the corner. A woman was coming out of a doorway, loaded down with packages. Conger stepped aside to let her pass. The woman glanced at him. Suddenly her face turned white. She stared, her mouth open.

Conger hurried on. He looked back. What was wrong with her? The woman was still staring; she had dropped the packages to the ground. He increased his speed. He turned a second corner and went up a side street. When he looked back again the woman had come to the entrance of the street and was starting after him. A man joined her, and the two of them began to run toward him.

He lost them and left the town, striding quickly, easily, up into the hills at the edge of town. When he reached the cage he stopped. What had happened? Was it something about his clothing? His dress?

He pondered. Then, as the sun set, he stepped into the cage.

Conger sat before the wheel. For a moment he waited, his hands resting lightly on the control. Then he turned the wheel, just a little, following the control readings carefully.

The grayness settled down around him.

But not for very long.

*

THE man looked him over critically. "You better come inside," he said. "Out of the cold."

"Thanks." Conger went gratefully through the open door, into the living-room. It was warm and close from the heat of the little kerosene heater in the corner. A woman, large and shapeless in her flowered dress, came from the kitchen. She and the man studied him critically.

"It's a good room," the woman said. "I'm Mrs. Appleton. It's got heat. You need that this time of year."

"Yes." He nodded, looking around.

"You want to eat with us?"

"What?"

"You want to eat with us?" The man's brows knitted. "You're not a foreigner, are you, mister?"

"No." He smiled. "I was born in this country. Quite far west, though."

"California?"

"No." He hesitated. "In Oregon."

"What's it like up there?" Mrs. Appleton asked. "I hear there's a lot of trees and green. It's so barren here. I come from Chicago, myself."

"That's the Middle West," the man said to her. "You ain't no foreigner."

"Oregon isn't foreign, either," Conger said. "It's part of the United States."

The man nodded absently. He was staring at Conger's clothing.

"That's a funny suit you got on, mister," he said. "Where'd you get that?"

Conger was lost. He shifted uneasily. "It's a good suit," he said. "Maybe I better go some other place, if you don't want me here."

They both raised their hands protestingly. The woman smiled at him. "We just have to look out for those Reds. You know, the government is always warning us about them."

"The Reds?" He was puzzled.

"The government says they're all around. We're supposed to report anything strange or unusual, anybody doesn't act normal."

"Like me?"

They looked embarrassed. "Well, you don't look like a Red to me," the man said. "But we have to be careful. The *Tribune* says—"

Conger half listened. It was going to be easier than he had thought. Clearly, he would know as soon as the Founder appeared. These people, so suspicious of anything different, would be buzzing and gossiping and spreading the story. All he had to do was lie low and listen, down at the general store, perhaps. Or even here, in Mrs. Appleton's boarding house.

"Can I see the room?" he said.

"Certainly." Mrs. Appleton went to the stairs. "I'll be glad to show it to you."

They went upstairs. It was colder upstairs, but not nearly as cold as outside. Nor as cold as nights on the Martian deserts. For that he was grateful.

*

HE was walking slowly around the store, looking at the cans of vegetables, the frozen packages of fish and meats shining and clean in the open refrigerator counters.

Ed Davies came toward him. "Can I help you?" he said. The man was a little oddly dressed, and with a beard! Ed couldn't help smiling.

"Nothing," the man said in a funny voice. "Just looking."

"Sure," Ed said. He walked back behind the counter. Mrs. Hacket was wheeling her cart up.

"Who's he?" she whispered, her sharp face turned, her nose moving, as if it were sniffing. "I never seen him before."

"I don't know."

"Looks funny to me. Why does he wear a beard? No one else wears a beard. Must be something the matter with him."

"Maybe he likes to wear a beard. I had an uncle who—"

"Wait." Mrs. Hacket stiffened. "Didn't that—what was his name? The Red—that old one. Didn't he have a beard? Marx. He had a beard."

Ed laughed. "This ain't Karl Marx. I saw a photograph of him once."

Mrs. Hacket was staring at him. "You did?"

"Sure." He flushed a little. "What's the matter with that?"

"I'd sure like to know more about him," Mrs. Hacket said. "I think we ought to know more, for our own good."

*

"HEY, mister! Want a ride?"

Conger turned quickly, dropping his hand to his belt. He relaxed. Two young kids in a car, a girl and a boy. He smiled at them. "A ride? Sure."

Conger got into the car and closed the door. Bill Willet pushed the gas and the car roared down the highway.

"I appreciate a ride," Conger said carefully. "I was taking a walk between towns, but it was farther than I thought."

"Where are you from?" Lora Hunt asked. She was pretty, small and dark, in her yellow sweater and blue skirt.

"From Cooper Creek."

"Cooper Creek?" Bill said. He frowned. "That's funny. I don't remember seeing you before."

"Why, do you come from there?"

"I was born there. I know everybody there."

"I just moved in. From Oregon."

"From Oregon? I didn't know Oregon people had accents."

"Do I have an accent?"

"You use words funny."

"How?"

"I don't know. Doesn't he, Lora?"

"You slur them," Lora said, smiling. "Talk some more. I'm interested in dialects." She glanced at him, white-teethed. Conger felt his heart constrict.

"I have a speech impediment."

"Oh." Her eyes widened. "I'm sorry."

They looked at him curiously as the car purred along. Conger for his part was struggling to find some way of asking them questions without seeming curious. "I guess people from out of town don't come here much," he said. "Strangers."

"No." Bill shook his head. "Not very much."

"I'll bet I'm the first outsider for a long time."

"I guess so."

Conger hesitated. "A friend of mine—someone I know, might be coming through here. Where do you suppose I might—" He stopped. "Would there be anyone certain to see him? Someone I could ask, make sure I don't miss him if he comes?"

They were puzzled. "Just keep your eyes open. Cooper Creek isn't very big."

"No. That's right."

They drove in silence. Conger studied the outline of the girl. Probably she was the boy's mistress. Perhaps she was his trial wife. Or had they developed trial marriage back so far? He could not remember. But surely such an attractive girl would be someone's mistress by this time; she would be sixteen or so, by her looks. He might ask her sometime, if they ever met again.

*

THE next day Conger went walking along the one main street of Cooper Creek. He passed the general store, the two filling stations, and then the post office. At the corner was the soda fountain.

He stopped. Lora was sitting inside, talking to the clerk. She was laughing, rocking back and forth.

Conger pushed the door open. Warm air rushed around him. Lora was drinking hot chocolate, with whipped cream. She looked up in surprise as he slid into the seat beside her.

"I beg your pardon," he said. "Am I intruding?"

"No." She shook her head. Her eyes were large and dark. "Not at all."

The clerk came over. "What do you want?"

Conger looked at the chocolate. "Same as she has."

Lora was watching Conger, her arms folded, elbows on the counter. She smiled at him. "By the way. You don't know my name. Lora Hunt."

She was holding out her hand. He took it awkwardly, not knowing what to do with it. "Conger is my name," he murmured.

"Conger? Is that your last or first name?"

"Last or first?" He hesitated. "Last. Omar Conger."

"Omar?" She laughed. "That's like the poet, Omar Khayyam."

"I don't know of him. I know very little of poets. We restored very few works of art. Usually only the Church has been interested enough—" He broke off. She was staring. He flushed. "Where I come from," he finished.

"The Church? Which church do you mean?"

"The Church." He was confused. The chocolate came and he began to sip it gratefully. Lora was still watching him.

"You're an unusual person," she said. "Bill didn't like you, but he never likes anything different. He's so—so prosaic. Don't you think that when a person gets older he should become—broadened in his outlook?"

Conger nodded.

"He says foreign people ought to stay where they belong, not come here. But you're not so foreign. He means orientals; you know."

Conger nodded.

The screen door opened behind them. Bill came into the room. He stared at them. "Well," he said.

Conger turned. "Hello."

"Well." Bill sat down. "Hello, Lora." He was looking at Conger. "I didn't expect to see you here."

Conger tensed. He could feel the hostility of the boy. "Something wrong with that?"

"No. Nothing wrong with it."

There was silence. Suddenly Bill turned to Lora. "Come on. Let's go."

"Go?" She was astonished. "Why?"

"Just go!" He grabbed her hand. "Come on! The car's outside."

"Why, Bill Willet," Lora said. "You're jealous!"

"Who is this guy?" Bill said. "Do you know anything about him? Look at him, his beard—"

She flared. "So what? Just because he doesn't drive a Packard and go to Cooper High!"

Conger sized the boy up. He was big—big and strong. Probably he was part of some civil control organization.

"Sorry," Conger said. "I'll go."

"What's your business in town?" Bill asked. "What are you doing here? Why are you hanging around Lora?"

Conger looked at the girl. He shrugged. "No reason. I'll see you later."

He turned away. And froze. Bill had moved. Conger's fingers went to his belt. *Half pressure,* he whispered to himself. *No more. Half pressure.*

He squeezed. The room leaped around him. He himself was protected by the lining of his clothing, the plastic sheathing inside.

"My God—" Lora put her hands up. Conger cursed. He hadn't meant any of it for her. But it would wear off. There was only a half-amp to it. It would tingle.

Tingle, and paralyze.

He walked out the door without looking back. He was almost to the corner when Bill came slowly out, holding onto the wall like a drunken man. Conger went on.

*

AS Conger walked, restless, in the night, a form loomed in front of him. He stopped, holding his breath.

"Who is it?" a man's voice came. Conger waited, tense.

"Who is it?" the man said again. He clicked something in his hand. A light flashed. Conger moved.

"It's me," he said.

"Who is 'me'?"

"Conger is my name. I'm staying at the Appleton's place. Who are you?"

The man came slowly up to him. He was wearing a leather jacket. There was a gun at his waist.

"I'm Sheriff Duff. I think you're the person I want to talk to. You were in Bloom's today, about three o'clock?"

"Bloom's?"

"The fountain. Where the kids hang out." Duff came up beside him, shining his light into Conger's face. Conger blinked.

"Turn that thing away," he said.

A pause. "All right." The light flickered to the ground. "You were there. Some trouble broke out between you and the Willet boy. Is that right? You had a beef over his girl—"

"We had a discussion," Conger said carefully.

"Then what happened?"

"Why?"

"I'm just curious. They say you did something."

"Did something? Did what?"

"I don't know. That's what I'm wondering. They saw a flash, and something seemed to happen. They all blacked out. Couldn't move."

"How are they now?"

"All right."

There was silence.

"Well?" Duff said. "What was it? A bomb?"

"A bomb?" Conger laughed. "No. My cigarette lighter caught fire. There was a leak, and the fluid ignited."

"Why did they all pass out?"

"Fumes."

Silence. Conger shifted, waiting. His fingers moved slowly toward his belt. The Sheriff glanced down. He grunted.

"If you say so," he said. "Anyhow, there wasn't any real harm done." He stepped back from Conger. "And that Willet is a trouble-maker."

"Good night, then," Conger said. He started past the Sheriff.

"One more thing, Mr. Conger. Before you go. You don't mind if I look at your identification, do you?"

"No. Not at all." Conger reached into his pocket. He held his wallet out. The Sheriff took it and shined his flashlight on it. Conger watched, breathing shallowly. They had worked hard on the wallet, studying historic documents, relics of the times, all the papers they felt would be relevant.

Duff handed it back. "Okay. Sorry to bother you." The light winked off.

When Conger reached the house he found the Appletons sitting around the television set. They did not look up as he came in. He lingered at the door.

"Can I ask you something?" he said. Mrs. Appleton turned slowly. "Can I ask you—what's the date?"

"The date?" She studied him. "The first of December."

"December first! Why, it was just November!"

They were all looking at him. Suddenly he remembered. In the twentieth century they still used the old twelve-month system. November fed directly into December; there was no Quartember between.

He gasped. Then it was tomorrow! The second of December! Tomorrow!

"Thanks," he said. "Thanks."

He went up the stairs. What a fool he was, forgetting. The Founder had been taken into captivity on the second of December, according to the newspaper records. Tomorrow, only twelve hours hence, the Founder would appear to speak to the people and then be dragged away.

*

THE day was warm and bright. Conger's shoes crunched the melting crust of snow. On he went, through the trees heavy with white. He climbed a hill and strode down the other side, sliding as he went.

He stopped to look around. Everything was silent. There was no one in sight. He brought a thin rod from his waist and turned the handle of it. For a moment nothing happened. Then there was a shimmering in the air.

The crystal cage appeared and settled slowly down. Conger sighed. It was good to see it again. After all, it was his only way back.

He walked up on the ridge. He looked around with some satisfaction, his hands on his hips. Hudson's field was spread out, all the way to the beginning of town. It was bare and flat, covered with a thin layer of snow.

Here, the Founder would come. Here, he would speak to them. And here the authorities would take him.

Only he would be dead before they came. He would be dead before he even spoke.

Conger returned to the crystal globe. He pushed through the door and stepped inside. He took the Slem-gun from the shelf and screwed the bolt into place. It was ready to go, ready to fire. For a moment he considered. Should he have it with him?

No. It might be hours before the Founder came, and suppose someone approached him in the meantime? When he saw the Founder coming toward the field, then he could go and get the gun.

Conger looked toward the shelf. There was the neat plastic package. He took it down and unwrapped it.

He held the skull in his hands, turning it over. In spite of himself, a cold feeling rushed through him. This was the man's skull, the skull of the Founder, who was still alive, who would come here, this day, who would stand on the field not fifty yards away.

What if *he* could see this, his own skull, yellow and eroded? Two centuries old. Would he still speak? Would he speak, if he could see it, the grinning, aged skull? What would there be for him to say, to tell the people? What message could he bring?

What action would not be futile, when a man could look upon his own aged, yellowed skull? Better they should enjoy their temporary lives, while they still had them to enjoy.

A man who could hold his own skull in his hands would believe in few causes, few movements. Rather, he would preach the opposite—

A sound. Conger dropped the skull back on the shelf and took up the gun. Outside something was moving. He went quickly to the door, his heart beating. Was it *he*? Was it the Founder, wandering by himself in the cold, looking for a place to speak? Was he meditating over his words, choosing his sentences?

What if he could see what Conger had held!

He pushed the door open, the gun raised.

Lora!

He stared at her. She was dressed in a wool jacket and boots, her hands in her pockets. A cloud of steam came from her mouth and nostrils. Her breast was rising and falling.

Silently, they looked at each other. At last Conger lowered the gun.

"What is it?" he said. "What are you doing here?"

She pointed. She did not seem able to speak. He frowned; what was wrong with her?

"What is it?" he said. "What do you want?" He looked in the direction she had pointed. "I don't see anything."

"They're coming."

"They? Who? Who are coming?"

"They are. The police. During the night the Sheriff had the state police send cars. All around, everywhere. Blocking the roads. There's about sixty of them coming. Some from town, some around behind." She stopped, gasping. "They said—they said—"

"What?"

"They said you were some kind of a Communist. They said—"

*

CONGER went into the cage. He put the gun down on the shelf and came back out. He leaped down and went to the girl.

"Thanks. You came here to tell me? You don't believe it?"

"I don't know."

"Did you come alone?"

"No. Joe brought me in his truck. From town."

"Joe? Who's he?"

"Joe French. The plumber. He's a friend of Dad's."

"Let's go." They crossed the snow, up the ridge and onto the field. The little panel truck was parked half way across the field. A heavy short man was sitting behind the wheel, smoking his pipe. He sat up as he saw the two of them coming toward him.

"Are you the one?" he said to Conger.

"Yes. Thanks for warning me."

The plumber shrugged. "I don't know anything about this. Lora says you're all right." He turned around. "It might interest you to know some more of them are coming. Not to warn you—just curious."

"More of them?" Conger looked toward the town. Black shapes were picking their way across the snow.

"People from the town. You can't keep this sort of thing quiet, not in a small town. We all listen to the police radio; they heard the same way Lora did. Someone tuned in, spread it around—"

The shapes were getting closer. Conger could, make out a couple of them. Bill Willet was there, with some boys from the high school. The Appletons were along, hanging back in the rear.

"Even Ed Davies," Conger murmured.

The storekeeper was toiling onto the field, with three or four other men from the town.

"All curious as hell," French said. "Well, I guess I'm going back to town. I don't want my truck shot full of holes. Come on, Lora."

She was looking up at Conger, wide-eyed.

"Come on," French said again. "Let's go. You sure as hell can't stay here, you know."

"Why?"

"There may be shooting. That's what they all came to see. You know that don't you, Conger?"

"Yes."

"You have a gun? Or don't you care?" French smiled a little. "They've picked up a lot of people in their time, you know. You won't be lonely."

He cared, all right! He had to stay here, on the field. He couldn't afford to let them take him away. Any minute the Founder would appear, would step onto the field. Would he be one of the townsmen, standing silently at the foot of the field, waiting, watching?

Or maybe he was Joe French. Or maybe one of the cops. Anyone of them might find himself moved to speak. And the few words spoken this day were going to be important for a long time.

And Conger had to be there, ready when the first word was uttered!

"I care," he said. "You go on back to town. Take the girl with you."

Lora got stiffly in beside Joe French. The plumber started up the motor. "Look at them, standing there," he said. "Like vultures. Waiting to see someone get killed."

*

THE truck drove away, Lora sitting stiff and silent, frightened now. Conger watched for a moment. Then he dashed back into the woods, between the trees, toward the ridge.

He could get away, of course. Anytime he wanted to he could get away. All he had to do was to leap into the crystal cage and turn the handles. But he had a job, an important job. He had to be here, here at this place, at this time.

He reached the cage and opened the door. He went inside and picked up the gun from the shelf. The Slem-gun would take care of them. He notched it up to full count. The chain reaction from it would flatten them all, the police, the curious, sadistic people—

They wouldn't take him! Before they got him, all of them would be dead. *He* would get away. He would escape. By the end of the day they would all be dead, if that was what they wanted, and he—

He saw the skull.

Suddenly he put the gun down. He picked up the skull. He turned the skull over. He looked at the teeth. Then he went to the mirror.

He held the skull up, looking in the mirror. He pressed the skull against his cheek. Beside his own face the grinning skull leered back at him, beside *his* skull, against his living flesh.

He bared his teeth. And he knew.

It was his own skull that he held. He was the one who would die. He was the Founder.

After a time he put the skull down. For a few minutes he stood at the controls, playing with them idly. He could hear the sound of motors outside, the muffled noise of men. Should he go back to the present, where the Speaker waited? He could escape, of course—

Escape?

He turned toward the skull. There it was, his skull, yellow with age. Escape? Escape, when he had held it in his own hands?

What did it matter if he put it off a month, a year, ten years, even fifty? Time was nothing. He had sipped chocolate with a girl born a hundred and fifty years before his time. Escape? For a little while, perhaps.

But he could not *really* escape, no more so than anyone else had ever escaped, or ever would.

Only, he had held it in his hands, his own bones, his own death's-head.

They had not.

He went out the door and across the field, empty handed. There were a lot of them standing around, gathered together, waiting. They expected a good fight; they knew he had something. They had heard about the incident at the fountain.

And there were plenty of police—police with guns and tear gas, creeping across the hills and ridges, between the trees, closer and closer. It was an old story, in this century.

One of the men tossed something at him. It fell in the snow by his feet, and he looked down. It was a rock. He smiled.

"Come on!" one of them called. "Don't you have any bombs?"

"Throw a bomb! You with the beard! Throw a bomb!"

"Let 'em have it!"

"Toss a few A Bombs!"

*

THEY began to laugh. He smiled. He put his hands to his hips. They suddenly turned silent, seeing that he was going to speak.

"I'm sorry," he said simply. "I don't have any bombs. You're mistaken."

There was a flurry of murmuring.

"I have a gun," he went on. "A very good one. Made by science even more advanced than your own. But I'm not going to use that, either."

They were puzzled.

"Why not?" someone called. At the edge of the group an older woman was watching. He felt a sudden shock. He had seen her before. Where?

He remembered. The day at the library. As he had turned the corner he had seen her. She had noticed him and been astounded. At the time, he did not understand why.

Conger grinned. So he *would* escape death, the man who right now was voluntarily accepting it. They were laughing, laughing at a man who had a gun but didn't use it. But by a strange twist of science he would appear again, a few months later, after his bones had been buried under the floor of a jail.

And so, in a fashion, he would escape death. He would die, but then, after a period of months, he would live again, briefly, for an afternoon.

An afternoon. Yet long enough for them to see him, to understand that he was still alive. To know that somehow he had returned to life.

And then, finally, he would appear once more, after two hundred years had passed. Two centuries later.

He would be born again, born, as a matter of fact, in a small trading village on Mars. He would grow up, learning to hunt and trade—

A police car came on the edge of the field and stopped. The people retreated a little. Conger raised his hands.

"I have an odd paradox for you," he said. "Those who take lives will lose their own. Those who kill, will die. But he who gives his own life away will live again!"

They laughed, faintly, nervously. The police were coming out, walking toward him. He smiled. He had said everything he intended to say. It was a good little paradox he had coined. They would puzzle over it, remember it.

Smiling, Conger awaited a death foreordained.

THE ORDEAL OF COLONEL JOHNS

by George H. Smith

Colonel Johns, that famous Revolutionary War hero, had the unique—and painful—experience of meeting his great-great-great-great granddaughter. Now maybe you can't change history, but what's there to prevent a soldier from changing his mind about the gal he is going to marry?

Clark Decker winced and scrounged still lower in his seat as Mrs. Appleby-Simpkin rested her enormous bosom on the front of the podium and smiled down on the Patriot Daughters of America in convention assembled as she announced: "And now, my dears, I will read you one more short quotation from Major Wicks' fascinating book 'The Minor Tactics of The American Revolution.' When I am finished, I know that you will all agree that Rebecca Johns-Hayes will be a more than fitting successor to myself as your President."

Decker looked wildly about for a way of escape from the convention auditorium. If he had only remained in the anteroom with Professor MacCulloch and the Historical Reintegrator! After suffering through four days of speeches by ladies in various stages of mammalian top-heaviness, he hadn't believed it possible that anyone could top Mrs. Appleby-Simpkin for either sheer ability to bore or for the nobility of her bust. Mrs. Rebecca Johns-Hayes had come as something of a shock as she squirmed her way onto the speaker's platform. But there she was as big as life, or rather bigger, smiling at Mrs. Appleby-Simpkin, the Past President, beaming at Mrs. Lynd-Torris, a defeated candidate for the presidency and whose ancestor had been only a captain, and completely ignoring Mrs. Tolman, the other defeated candidate whose ancestor had been so inconsiderate as to have been a Continental sergeant. Only the thought that now that the voting was over and the new president chosen, the ladies might be ready for the demonstration of the Reintegrator had brought Decker onto the convention floor, and now he was trapped and would have to listen.

"And so," Mrs. Appleby-Simpkin was reading, "upon such small events do the great moments of history depend. The brilliant scouting and skirmishing of the riflemen under Colonel Peter Johns prevented the breakthrough of Captain Fosdick's column and the possible flanking of the American army before Saratoga. Thus, this little known action may have been the deciding factor in the whole campaign that prevented General Burgoyne from carrying out the British plan to divide the colonies and end the war. It is impossible for the historian to refrain from speculation as to what might have happened had Colonel Johns not been on hand to direct the riflemen and militia in this section; as indeed he might *not* have been, since his own regiment of short-term enlistees had returned to Pennsylvania a few days previously. Only the Colonel's patriotism and devotion to duty kept him in the field and made his abilities available to the country when they were most needed."

Mrs. Appleby-Simpkin waited until the burst of applause had died down and then continued, "That is the man whose great-great-great-great-granddaughter you have elected your president today . . . Mrs. Rebecca Johns-Hayes!" Turning to Mrs. Johns-Hayes she went on, "Before you make your acceptance speech, dear, we have a little surprise for you."

Clark Decker had been edging his way toward the side of the auditorium where the Men's Auxiliary of the Daughters had their seats but he turned back at the mention of the surprise. It sounded as though it was time for him and the Professor to start their demonstration.

"A surprise which we hope will also be a surprise to the whole world of science," Mrs. Appleby-Simpkin was holding the podium against a determinedly advancing Mrs. Johns-Hayes. "Indeed we may be able to say in future years, that the 1989 Convention of the Patriot Daughters was marked by the first public demonstration of one of the most momentous inventions in the history of science." The Past President was speaking faster and faster, because the new President with a hand full of notes was doing her best to edge her away from both the podium and the microphone.

"Thank you, darling," Mrs. Johns-Hayes said, pulling the microphone firmly toward her, "but we really must get along with business. I have quite a few things I want to say and several motions which I want to place before the Convention."

"And as I was saying, dear," Mrs. Appleby-Simpkin said, pulling the microphone back with equal firmness, "I know that you will be just unbearably thrilled." There was another brief struggle for the mike and Mrs. Appleby-Simpkin won and went on. "I know that he will be just as proud of you as you are of him. That is why we have arranged for Professor MacCulloch to demonstrate his historical Reintegrator at our convention by bringing into our midst Colonel Peter Johns, the hero of the action at Temple Farm, to see his great-great-great-great-granddaughter installed as the fifty-fourth president of the Loyal Order of Patriot Daughters of America. Now I . . . ." Mrs. Johns-Hayes again won control of the mike.

"Thank you very much, dear." Her voice was a genteel screech. "I'm sure that we will be only too glad to have the . . . who? Who did you say?" Mrs. Appleby-Simpkin regained the microphone from the other woman's relaxing grip.

"I believe I see Mr. Decker, the Professor's assistant, in the audience," she said. "Will you be so good as to tell the Professor that we are ready for his epic-making experiment?"

With a great feeling of relief, Decker escaped from the rising turmoil of the convention hall into the relative quiet of the anteroom where MacCulloch waited with the Reintegrator. He found the Professor sitting with his head in his hands staring at the machine. The little man looked up and smiled quizzically as his assistant approached him.

"They're ready, Professor! They're ready!" Still under the influence of the convention, Decker found himself shouting.

"Ah. Ah, yes. Then it will be today. I've waited so long. Ten years of work and now instead of a scientific gathering, I have to demonstrate my machine before a woman's club."

*

Decker began to wheel the platform which held the Reintegrator toward the door. "After today, Professor, all the scientific organizations in the world will have heard of you and will be demanding demonstrations."

"Yes, but these Patriot Daughters! Who are they? Who in the scientific world ever heard of them?"

"No one except a few scientists unfortunate enough to fall afoul of their Loyalty and Conformity Committee."

"I think we should have gone elsewhere for our demonstration."

"Now Professor. Who in the world today would be interested in the past except a group of ancestor conscious women?"

"Some historical society perhaps," the Professor said wistfully.

"And what historical society could have advanced the twenty thousand dollars we needed to complete the machine?"

"I suppose you're right, my boy," MacCulloch sighed as he helped push the Reintegrator onto the auditorium floor.

By the time Clark Decker reached the platform to explain the demonstration, the fight for the microphone had turned into a three-way struggle. A lady who represented the Finance Committee was trying to win it away from both the Past President and the new President.

Taking them by surprise, Decker managed to gain control long enough to explain what was about to happen.

"You mean," demanded Mrs. Johns-Hayes, "that this is some sort of time machine and you're going to transport great-great-great-great-grandfather from the past into the present?"

"No, Mrs. Hayes. This isn't a time machine in the comic book use of the term. It is just what Professor MacCulloch has called it, an historical Reintegrator. The theory upon which it is based, the MacCulloch Reaction, says that every person who ever existed, and every event which ever took place caused electrical disturbances in the space-time continuum of the universe by displacing an equal and identical group of electrons. The task of the Reintegrator is to reassemble those electrons. That is why Professor MacCulloch is now placing your ancestor's sword in the machine. We will use that as a base point from which our recreation will begin."

The machine was humming and small lights were beginning to play about its tubes and dials. "If our calculations are accurate, and we believe that they are," Decker said, "within a very few minutes, Colonel Johns should be standing before us as he was on a day approximately a week before his heroic action in the battle at Temple Farm."

Mrs. Johns-Hayes, although still gripping her notes, was beginning to get a little flustered. "Oh my, that would be before he married great-great-great-great-grandmother Sayles. They were married only two days before the battle, you know. It was so romantic . . . a wartime romance and all."

"Just imagine," Mrs. Tolman remarked, "at that time your whole family was just a gleam in the Colonel's eye!"

Professor MacCulloch made one or two last passes at the machine and then stood back to watch, a look of pure scientific ecstasy on his face. A mistiness began to gather on the platform where the Colonel's sword lay and through it from time to time shot sparks of electricity. Suddenly a gasp went up from the assembled Daughters as a man's head and shoulders appeared and expanded downward, a long way downward, to a large pair of feet. There was one last hum from the machine and then a tall young man in faded blue regimentals and very much in need of a shave was standing blinking in the blazing lights of the auditorium.

"Oh, Mr. Decker, surely there's some mistake!" was Mrs. Johns-Hayes' first comment as she surveyed the very tall, very tattered, and very dirty young man. "Great-great-great-great-grandfather's pictures always show him as a dignified old gentleman."

The Colonel took one quick look around and made a grab for his sword, but the Professor managed to calm him and to explain the situation before any violence could take place. After a few minutes of hurried talk, MacCulloch steered the Colonel in the direction of the speaker's platform for the meeting with his great-great-great-great-granddaughter.

Peter Johns' bewilderment faded into astonishment, but he still gripped his sword as the Professor guided him through the throngs of excited ladies onto the stage. He paused momentarily to look at the brilliant lights and at the huge number of American flags which hung overhead. A picture of George Washington, hung among the flags, seemed to reassure him and he allowed the Professor to lead him to Mrs. Johns-Hayes.

That lady had drawn herself together at the approach of her ancestor and had obviously decided to carry it off as best she could. She advanced to meet him crying, "Dear, dear great-great-great-great-grandfather! This is such a pleasure! You can't know how proud all of us in the family have always been of you."

The young Continental officer stared open mouthed at the red-faced, big-bosomed woman who was twice his age, but who addressed him as great-great-great-great-grandfather. Then he turned to MacCulloch who stood beside him. "Are you sure you have the right man?" he asked.

"Oh yes! Perfectly, perfectly! You're Colonel Peter Johns of Pamworth, Pennsylvania, and this is your great-great-great-great-granddaughter, Rebecca Johns-Hayes."

"Rebecca? You mean she's named after Becky Sayles?" The Colonel rubbed a hand across his several days' growth of beard.

"That's right, dear great-great-great-great-grandfather. I'm named after great-great-great-great-grandmother," Mrs. Johns-Hayes announced.

"Then I married Becky Sayles?" the Colonel asked.

"Why, of course! Aren't you planning on getting married in a few days?" Clark Decker asked.

The Colonel was embarrassed but he grinned, "Well, I don't rightly know. Miss Sayles and I have been courtin' for some months but there's little Jennie Taylor down in Trenton . . . . To tell the truth, I haven't quite made up my mind."

"Well! Of all things! What would the family think! What would great Aunt Mary Hayes say?" Mrs. Johns-Hayes puffed out even farther than usual.

"Well, we can ease your mind on that subject, Colonel. The history books say that you married Miss Sayles—and here is Mrs. Johns-Hayes to prove it."

The Colonel scratched his chin again as he looked at Mrs. Johns-Hayes. "Is that so? Is that so? What's all this about history books? You mean I got in history because I married Becky Sayles?"

The Professor laughed. "Well, not exactly. It was because of your heroism in the defeat of Burgoyne's army. If you hadn't blocked Captain Fenwick's flanking move at Temple Farm, the American army under General Gates might have been defeated and the Colonies might even have lost the war."

"Well, I'll be . . . . Me? I did all that? I didn't even know there was going to be a battle. Did I end up a live hero or a dead one?" The Colonel was beginning to feel a bit more easy in his surroundings, and, to the horror of Mrs. Johns-Hayes, took a plug of tobacco out of his pocket and bit off a piece and began to chew it.

"You came through the battle with only a slight wound and lived to a ripe old age surrounded by grandchildren," the Professor told him.

"Then I reckon I won't go back to Pennsylvania with the other boys. They figure that since their enlistments are up, it's time to get back to the farm and let them New Yorkers do some of their own fighting."

"Oh no! You weren't thinking of going back—of leaving the fighting?" Mrs. Johns-Hayes demanded.

The Colonel shifted his wad of tobacco and looked at the woman carefully as though he couldn't quite believe the evidence of his eyes. "No, ma'am, I don't reckon I am. I don't exactly look on it the same as the other boys do. I kind of feel like if we're ever going to have a country, it's worth fighting for."

Mrs. Johns-Hayes beamed, as did all the other officers of the Daughters. "Well, your faith and heroism have been rewarded, great-great-great-great-grandfather. I know you'll be proud to know that these ladies whom you see before you are the present guardians of the ideals that you fought for."

"Well, now, is that so, ma'am? Is that so?" Peter Johns looked around the convention hall in amazement.

"And that I, your descendant, have just been elected their President!"

"Well, what do you know about that! Maybe all the hard times and the danger we been going through is worth it if you folks still remember the way we felt about things."

"It's too bad," Decker whispered to MacCulloch, "that we can't let him see what the country is really like. I'm not sure these ladies are representative."

There was a worried look on the Professor's face. "That's impossible. The reintegration is good for only an hour or so. I hope nothing goes wrong here."

Mrs. Appleby-Simpkin took charge of the Colonel and ushered him to a seat of honor near the podium while the new President prepared to deliver her speech. Decker and the professor managed to obtain seats on either side of Johns just as Rebecca started. He managed to whisper to them, "I'm sure amazed! I'm sure amazed! All these nice old ladies feeling the same way about things as we do."

*

Decker had a premonition of trouble as Mrs. Hayes' words poured forth. He had hoped for a cut and dried acceptance speech with nothing but the usual patriotic platitudes, but, as she went on his worst fears were realized. Inspired by the presence of her ancestor, the woman was going into superlatives about the purposes and aims of the Patriot Daughters. She covered everything from the glories of her ancestry to the morals of the younger generation and women in politics.

Decker watched the Colonel's face, saw it changed from puzzlement to painful boredom as word after word floated from the battery of speakers overhead.

MacCulloch was whispering in Johns' ear in an attempt to draw his attention from the woman's booming voice but the man disregarded him. "Am I really responsible for that?" The Colonel jerked his head in the direction of Mrs. Johns-Hayes.

"I'm afraid, Colonel, that you're getting a distorted idea of what America is like in our time," Decker said. The Colonel didn't even turn to look at him. He was scowling at his Amazonian descendant as her screeching reached new heights.

" . . . and we hold that this is true! Our simple motto, as you all know, is: One race, one creed, one way of thinking!"

Colonel Johns began to squirm violently in his seat. The professor found it necessary to grasp him firmly by one arm while Decker held him by the other.

The president of the Patriot Daughters had finished her speech amidst thunderous applause and started to present suggestions for the formation of new committees, for the passing of new by-laws and for resolutions.

"A committee should be formed to see that the public parks are properly policed to prevent so-called 'spooners' from pursuing their immoral behaviour.

"A new by-law is needed," and here Mrs. Hayes glanced aside at Mrs. Tolman, "to prevent members being accepted unless their forebears were lieutenants or of higher rank in the glorious Continental army."

The Colonel was a strong man and both Decker and MacCulloch were older than he. With something between a snort and a roar he shook them loose and started for the exit.

"Oh my," MacCulloch moaned, "I was afraid that this whole thing was a mistake."

Colonel Johns had taken only two steps toward the door when he seemed to stagger. MacCulloch leaped to his side and caught him by the arm. There was an uproar in the auditorium as the Colonel faded slightly and the professor hurried him down the steps toward the Reintegrator.

"I'm afraid the Colonel isn't going to be with us much longer," the professor explained.

Thank goodness, Decker thought, I don't believe the poor man could have stood it much longer.

"I'm afraid the reintegration time of Colonel Johns is running out and he must return to his own time," the professor went on.

The grim-faced Colonel said nothing as MacCulloch led him up to the machine.

"Goodbye, great-great-great-great-grandfather," Mrs. Johns-Hayes called from the platform. "It has been so nice having you with us."

"Goodbye, Rebecca," the Colonel said as he began to fade away.

"Give my regards to great-great-great-great-grandmother."

The figure in the dirty, faded blue uniform was gone but Decker and MacCulloch heard him mutter just before he disappeared altogether, "I will, if I ever see her again!"

MacCulloch turned to stare at the platform and Decker turned to follow his gaze. A sudden dizziness overcame them both and there was a slight haze about the auditorium. When it cleared, the podium was empty. Mrs. Johns-Hayes was gone as if she had never been.

"My God!," the professor gasped. "I was afraid something like this might happen. He must have married the other girl."

"I suppose," Decker said quietly, "that we should consider ourselves lucky that he didn't decide to go back to Pennsylvania." His voice broke off and he wondered what he had been saying. He looked up at the speakers' platform trying to remember why he should think it strange that it was draped in Union Jacks and that Lady Appleby-Simpkin should be saying, "And now, my dears, I know that all of you, as Loyal Daughters of the British Empire will be happy to know . . . ."

INCIDENT ON ROUTE 12

by James H. Schmitz

He was already a thief, prepared to steal again. He didn't know that he himself was only booty!

Phil Garfield was thirty miles south of the little town of Redmon on Route Twelve when he was startled by a series of sharp, clanking noises. They came from under the Packard's hood.

The car immediately began to lose speed. Garfield jammed down the accelerator, had a sense of sick helplessness at the complete lack of response from the motor. The Packard rolled on, getting rid of its momentum, and came to a stop.

Phil Garfield swore shakily. He checked his watch, switched off the headlights and climbed out into the dark road. A delay of even half an hour here might be disastrous. It was past midnight, and he had another hundred and ten miles to cover to reach the small private airfield where Madge waited for him and the thirty thousand dollars in the suitcase on the Packard's front seat.

If he didn't make it before daylight . . . .

He thought of the bank guard. The man had made a clumsy play at being a hero, and that had set off the fool woman who'd run screaming into their line of fire. One dead. Perhaps two. Garfield hadn't stopped to look at an evening paper.

But he knew they were hunting for him.

He glanced up and down the road. No other headlights in sight at the moment, no light from a building showing on the forested hills. He reached back into the car and brought out the suitcase, his gun, a big flashlight and the box of shells which had been standing beside the suitcase. He broke the box open, shoved a handful of shells and the .38 into his coat pocket, then took suitcase and flashlight over to the shoulder of the road and set them down.

There was no point in groping about under the Packard's hood. When it came to mechanics, Phil Garfield was a moron and well aware of it. The car was useless to him now . . . except as bait.

But as bait it might be very useful.

Should he leave it standing where it was? No, Garfield decided. To anybody driving past it would merely suggest a necking party, or a drunk sleeping off his load before continuing home. He might have to wait an hour or more before someone decided to stop. He didn't have the time. He reached in through the window, hauled the top of the steering wheel towards him and put his weight against the rear window frame.

The Packard began to move slowly backwards at a slant across the road. In a minute or two he had it in position. Not blocking the road entirely, which would arouse immediate suspicion, but angled across it, lights out, empty, both front doors open and inviting a passerby's investigation.

Garfield carried the suitcase and flashlight across the right-hand shoulder of the road and moved up among the trees and undergrowth of the slope above the shoulder. Placing the suitcase between the bushes, he brought out the .38, clicked the safety off and stood waiting.

Some ten minutes later, a set of headlights appeared speeding up Route Twelve from the direction of Redmon. Phil Garfield went down on one knee before he came within range of the lights. Now he was completely concealed by the vegetation.

The car slowed as it approached, braking nearly to a stop sixty feet from the stalled Packard. There were several people inside it; Garfield heard voices, then a woman's loud laugh. The driver tapped his horn inquiringly twice, moved the car slowly forward. As the headlights went past him, Garfield got to his feet among the bushes, took a step down towards the road, raising the gun.

Then he caught the distant gleam of a second set of headlights approaching from Redmon. He swore under his breath and dropped back out of sight. The car below him reached the Packard, edged cautiously around it, rolled on with a sudden roar of acceleration.

*

The second car stopped when still a hundred yards away, the Packard caught in the motionless glare of its lights. Garfield heard the steady purring of a powerful motor.

For almost a minute, nothing else happened. Then the car came gliding smoothly on, stopped again no more than thirty feet to Garfield's left. He could see it now through the screening bushes—a big job, a long, low four-door sedan. The motor continued to purr. After a moment, a door on the far side of the car opened and slammed shut.

A man walked quickly out into the beam of the headlights and started towards the Packard.

Phil Garfield rose from his crouching position, the .38 in his right hand, flashlight in his left. If the driver was alone, the thing was now cinched! But if there was somebody else in the car, somebody capable of fast, decisive action, a slip in the next ten seconds might cost him the sedan, and quite probably his freedom and life. Garfield lined up the .38's sights steadily on the center of the approaching man's head. He let his breath out slowly as the fellow came level with him in the road and squeezed off one shot.

Instantly he went bounding down the slope to the road. The bullet had flung the man sideways to the pavement. Garfield darted past him to the left, crossed the beam of the headlights, and was in darkness again on the far side of the road, snapping on his flashlight as he sprinted up to the car.

The motor hummed quietly on. The flashlight showed the seats empty. Garfield dropped the light, jerked both doors open in turn, gun pointing into the car's interior. Then he stood still for a moment, weak and almost dizzy with relief.

There was no one inside. The sedan was his.

The man he had shot through the head lay face down on the road, his hat flung a dozen feet away from him. Route Twelve still stretched out in dark silence to east and west. There should be time enough to clean up the job before anyone else came along. Garfield brought the suitcase down and put it on the front seat of the sedan, then started back to get his victim off the road and out of sight. He scaled the man's hat into the bushes, bent down, grasped the ankles and started to haul him towards the left side of the road where the ground dropped off sharply beyond the shoulder.

The body made a high, squealing sound and began to writhe violently.

*

290

Shocked, Garfield dropped the legs and hurriedly took the gun from his pocket, moving back a step. The squealing noise rose in intensity as the wounded man quickly flopped over twice like a struggling fish, arms and legs sawing about with startling energy. Garfield clicked off the safety, pumped three shots into his victim's back.

The grisly squeals ended abruptly. The body continued to jerk for another second or two, then lay still.

Garfield shoved the gun back into his pocket. The unexpected interruption had unnerved him; his hands shook as he reached down again for the stranger's ankles. Then he jerked his hands back, and straightened up, staring.

From the side of the man's chest, a few inches below the right arm, something like a thick black stick, three feet long, protruded now through the material of the coat.

It shone, gleaming wetly, in the light from the car. Even in that first uncomprehending instant, something in its appearance brought a surge of sick disgust to Garfield's throat. Then the stick bent slowly halfway down its length, forming a sharp angle, and its tip opened into what could have been three blunt, black claws which scrabbled clumsily against the pavement. Very faintly, the squealing began again, and the body's back arched up as if another sticklike arm were pushing desperately against the ground beneath it.

Garfield acted in a blur of horror. He emptied the .38 into the thing at his feet almost without realizing he was doing it. Then, dropping the gun, he seized one of the ankles, ran backwards to the shoulder of the road, dragging the body behind him.

In the darkness at the edge of the shoulder, he let go of it, stepped around to the other side and with two frantically savage kicks sent the body plunging over the shoulder and down the steep slope beyond. He heard it crash through the bushes for some seconds, then stop. He turned, and ran back to the sedan, scooping up his gun as he went past. He scrambled into the driver's seat and slammed the door shut behind him.

His hands shook violently on the steering wheel as he pressed down the accelerator. The motor roared into life and the big car surged forward. He edged it past the Packard, cursing aloud in horrified shock, jammed down the accelerator and went flashing up Route Twelve, darkness racing beside and behind him.

*

What had it been? Something that wore what seemed to be a man's body like a suit of clothes, moving the body as a man moves, driving a man's car . . . roach-armed, roach-legged itself!

Garfield drew a long, shuddering breath. Then, as he slowed for a curve, there was a spark of reddish light in the rear-view mirror.

He stared at the spark for an instant, braked the car to a stop, rolled down the window and looked back.

Far behind him along Route Twelve, a fire burned. Approximately at the point where the Packard had stalled out, where something had gone rolling off the road into the bushes . . . .

Something, Garfield added mentally, that found fiery automatic destruction when death came to it, so that its secrets would remain unrevealed.

But for him the fire meant the end of a nightmare. He rolled the window up, took out a cigarette, lit it, and pressed the accelerator . . . .

291

In incredulous fright, he felt the nose of the car tilt upwards, headlights sweeping up from the road into the trees.

Then the headlights winked out. Beyond the windshield, dark tree branches floated down towards him, the night sky beyond. He reached frantically for the door handle.

A steel wrench clamped silently about each of his arms, drawing them in against his sides, immobilizing them there. Garfield gasped, looked up at the mirror and saw a pair of faintly gleaming red eyes watching him from the rear of the car. Two of the things . . . the second one stood behind him out of sight, holding him. They'd been in what had seemed to be the trunk compartment. And they had come out.

The eyes in the mirror vanished. A moist, black roach-arm reached over the back of the seat beside Garfield, picked up the cigarette he had dropped, extinguished it with rather horribly human motions, then took up Garfield's gun and drew back out of sight.

He expected a shot, but none came.

One doesn't fire a bullet through the suit one intends to wear . . . .

It wasn't until that thought occurred to him that tough Phil Garfield began to scream. He was still screaming minutes later when, beyond the windshield, the spaceship floated into view among the stars.

BRINK OF MADNESS

by Walt Sheldon

C.I.B. Agent Pell used his head, even if he did rely on hunches more than on the computer. In fact, when the game got rough, he found that to use his head, he first had to keep it . . . .

CHAPTER I

The night the visitors came Richard Pell worked late among the great banks of criminological computers. He whistled to himself, knowing that he was way off key but not caring. Ciel, his wife, was still in his mind's eye; he'd seen her on the viewer and talked with her not ten minutes ago.

"Be home shortly, baby," he'd said, "soon as I fill in a form or two."

"All right, dear. I'll wait," she'd answered, with just the slightest tone of doubt.

It was an important night. It was at once their second anniversary and the beginning of their second honeymoon. Just how Pell—knobby, more or less homely, and easygoing—had won himself a lovely, long-limbed blonde like Ciel was something of a mystery to many of their friends. She could hardly have married him for his money. Central Investigation Bureau agents were lucky if all their extras and bonuses brought them up to a thousand credits a year.

Pell had unquestionably caught her in a romantic moment. Maybe that was part of the trouble—part of the reason they needed this second honeymoon, this period of re-acquaintance so badly. Being the wife of a C.I.B. agent meant sitting at home nine-tenths of the time while he was working on a case, and then not hearing about the case for security reasons during the one-tenth of the time he was with her.

Four times now Pell had been ready to take his vacation; four times last minute business had come up. No more, though, by golly. Tonight he'd get out of here just as quickly as . . . .

The Identifier, beyond the door, began to hum. That meant somebody was putting his hand to the opaque screen, and if the scanner recognized the fingerprints the door would open. Pell scowled at the bulky shadows outside.

"Go away, whoever you are," he muttered to himself.

Some of the other agents were out there, no doubt; they were always getting sudden inspirations late at night and returning to use the computers again. In fact, it had been tactfully suggested to Agent Richard Pell that he might use the computers a little more himself instead of relying on hunches as he so often did. "Investigation's a cold science, not a fancy art," Chief Larkin was fond of saying to the group—with his eyes on Pell.

Well, whoever it was, Pell was definitely through. No time-wasting conversation for him! He was ready for six glorious weeks of saved-up vacation time. He and Ciel, early tomorrow, would grab a rocket for one of the Moon resorts, and there they'd just loaf and relax and pay attention to each other. Try to regain whatever it was they'd had . . . .

*

The door opened and Chief Larkin walked in.

Chief Eustace J. Larkin was tall, in his forties, but still boyishly handsome. He dressed expensively and well. He was dynamic and confident and he always had about him just the faintest aroma of very expensive shaving cologne. He had a Master's degree in criminology and his rise to the post of Director, C.I.B., had been sudden, dramatic and impressive. Not the least of his talents was a keen sense of public relations.

"I—uh—was on my way out," said Pell. He reached for his hat. Funny about hats: few people traveled topside anymore, and in the climate-conditioned tunnels you didn't need a hat. But C.I.B. agents had to be neat and dignified; regulations required hats and ties and cuffs and lapels. Thus, you could always spot a C.I.B. agent a mile away.

Larkin had a dimple when he smiled and Pell would bet he knew it. "We'd have called your home if we hadn't found you here. Sit down, Dick."

Pell sat glumly. For the first time, he noticed the men who had come in with the Chief. He recognized both. One was fiftyish, tall, solidly-built and well-dressed on the conservative side. His face was strong, square and oddly pale, as if someone had taken finest white marble and roughly hacked a face into it. Pell had seen that face in faxpapers often. The man was Theodor Rysland, once a wealthy corporation lawyer, now a World Government adviser in an unofficial way. Some admired him as a selfless public servant; others swore he was a power-mad tyrant. Few were indifferent.

"I'm sure you recognize Mr. Rysland," said Chief Larkin, smiling. "And this is Dr. Walter Nebel, of the World Department of Education."

Dr. Walter Nebel was slight and had a head remarkably tiny in proportion to the rest of him. He wore cropped hair. His eyes were turtle-lidded and at first impression sleepy, and then, with a second look—wary. Pell remembered that he had won fame some time ago by discovering the electrolytic enzyme in the thought process. Pell wasn't sure exactly what this was, but the faxpapers had certainly made a fuss about it at the time.

He shook hands with the two men and then said to Larkin, "What's up?"

"Patience," said Larkin and shuffled chairs into place.

Rysland sat down solidly and gravely; Nebel perched. Rysland looked at Pell with a strong, level stare and said, "It's my sincere hope that this meeting tonight will prevent resumption of the war with Venus."

Larkin said, "Amen."

Pell stared back in some surprise. High-level stuff!

Rysland saw his stare and chuckled. "Chief Larkin tells me your sympathies are more or less Universalist. Not that it would be necessary, but it helps."

"Oh," said Pell, with mild bewilderment. The difference between the Universal and Defense parties was pretty clear-cut. The Universalists hoped to resume full relations with Venus and bring about a really secure peace through friendship and trade. It would admittedly be a tough struggle, and the Defenders didn't think it was possible. Forget Venus, said they; fortify Earth, keep the line of demarcation on Mars, and sit tight.

"But there is, as you may know," said Rysland, "a third course in our relations with Venus."

"There is?" asked Pell. From the corner of his eye he saw Chief Larkin looking at him with an expression of—what, amusement? Yes, amusement, largely, but with a touch of contempt, too, perhaps. Hard to say.

"The third course," said Rysland, not smiling, "would be to attack Venus again, resume the war, and hope to win quickly. We know Venus is exhausted from the recent struggle. A sudden, forceful attack might possibly subjugate her. At least, that is the argument of a certain group called the Supremists."

Dr. Nebel spoke for the first time. Pell realized that the man had been watching him closely. His voice was sibilant; it seemed to drag itself through wet grass. "Also Venus is psychologically unprepared for war; the Supremists believe that, too."

Pell reached back into his memory. The Supremists. They were a minor political party—sort of a cult, too. The outfit had sprung up in the last year or so. Supremists believed that Earthmen, above all other creatures, had a destiny—were chosen—were supreme. They had several followers as delegates in World Congress. General impression: slightly crackpot.

"The Supremists," said Theodor Rysland, tapping his hard, white palm, and leaning forward, "have been calling for attack. Aggression. Starting the war with Venus all over again. And they're not only a vociferous nuisance. They have an appeal in this business of Earthman's supremacy. They're gaining converts every day. In short, *they've now become dangerous.*"

*

Pell thought it over as Rysland talked. Certainly the idea of renewed war was nightmarish. He'd been in the last one: who hadn't? It had started in 2117, the year he was born, and it had dragged on for twenty-five years until T-day and the truce. The causes? Well, both Earth and Venus worked the mineral deposits on Mars unimpeded by the non-intelligent insectile life on that planet, and the original arguments had been about those mineral deposits, though there were enough for a dozen planets there. The causes were more complicated and obscure than that. Semantics, partly. There was freedom as Earthmen saw it and freedom as the Venusians saw it. Same with honor and good and evil. They were always two different things. And then Venusians had a greenish tinge to their skins and called the Earthmen, in their clicking language, "Pink-faces." And both Earthmen and Venusians hated like the devil to see the other get away with anything.

Anyway, there had been war, terrible war. Space battle, air battle, landing, repulse. Stalemate. Finally, through utter weariness perhaps, truce. Now, a taut, uneasy, suspicious peace. Communications opened, a few art objects mutually exchanged. Immigration for a few Venusian dancers or students or diplomats. It wasn't much, but it was all in the right direction. At least Pell felt so.

Rysland was saying: "We're not sure, of course, but we suspect—we *feel*—that more than mere accident may be behind these Supremists."

"What do you mean by that?"

"Someone seeking power, perhaps. As I said, we don't know. We want to find out. Dr. Nebel has been interested for some time in the curious psychology of these Supremists—their blind, unthinking loyalty to their cause, for instance. He is, as you know, a special assistant in the Department of Education. He asked my help in arranging for an investigation, and I agreed with him wholeheartedly that one should be made."

"And I told these gentlemen," said Chief Larkin, "that I'd put a detail on it right away."

Now Pell believed he saw through it. Larkin didn't believe it was important at all; he was just obliging these Vips. A man couldn't have too many friends in World Government circles, after all. But of course Larkin couldn't afford to put one of his bright, machine-minded boys on it, and so Pell was the patsy.

"Could I remind you," said Pell, "that my vacation is supposed to start tomorrow?"

"Now, now, Dick," said Larkin, turning on the personality, "this won't take you long. Just a routine report. The computers ought to give you all the information you need in less than a day."

"That's what you always say, every time I'm ready to take a vacation. I've been saving up for two years now . . . ."

"Dick, that's hardly the right attitude for an agent who is so close to making second grade."

Larkin had him over a barrel, there. Pell desperately wanted to make his promotion. Second-graders didn't spend their time at the control banks gathering data; they did mostly desk work and evaluation. They had a little more time to spend with their wives. He said, "Okay, okay," and got up.

"Where are you going?"

"To get my wife on the viewer and tell her I won't be home for a while after all."

He left the three of them chuckling and thought: *He jests at scars who never felt a wound.* He didn't say it aloud. You could quote formulae or scientific precepts in front of Larkin, but not Shakespeare.

*

He punched out his home number and waited until Ciel's image swirled into the viewplate. His heart went boppety-bop as it always did. Hair of polished gold. Dark eyes, ripe olives, a little large for her face and sometimes deep and fathomless. She wore a loose, filmy nightgown and the suggestion of her body under it was enough to bring on a touch of madness in him.

"Let me say it," Ciel said. She wasn't smiling. "You won't be home for a while. You've got another case."

"Well—yes. That's it, more or less." Pell swallowed.

"Oh, Dick."

"I'm sorry, honey. It's just that something important came up. I've got a conference on my hands. It shouldn't take more than an hour."

"And we were supposed to leave for the moon in the morning."

"Listen, baby, this is absolutely the last time. I mean it. As soon as this thing is washed up we'll *really* take that vacation. Look, I'll tell you what, I'll meet you somewhere in an hour. We'll have some fun—take in a floor show—drink a little meth. We haven't done that in a long time. How about the Stardust Cafe? I hear they've got a terrific new mentalist there."

Ciel said, "No."

"Don't be like that. We need an evening out. It'll hold us until I get this new case washed up. That won't be long, but at least we'll have a little relaxation."

Ciel said, "Well . . . ."

"Attababy. One hour. Absolutely. You just go to Station B-90, take the lift to topside and it's right on Shapley Boulevard there. You can't miss it."

"I know where it is," said Ciel. She shook her finger. "Richard Pell, so help me, if you stand me up this time . . . ."

"Baby!" he said in a tone of deep injury.

"Goodbye, Dick." She clicked off.

Pell had the feeling that even the free-flowing meth and the gaiety of the Stardust Cafe wouldn't really help matters much. He sighed deeply as he turned and went back into the other room.

CHAPTER II

A little over an hour later he stepped from the elevator kiosk at Station B-90 and breathed the night air of topside. It was less pure actually than the carefully controlled tunnel air, but it was somehow infinitely more wonderful. At least to a sentimental primitive boob like Richard Pell, it was. Oh, he knew that it was infinitely more sensible to live and work entirely underground as people did these days—but just the same he loved the look of the black sky with the crushed diamonds of stars thrown across it and he loved the uneven breeze and the faint smell of trees and grass.

This particular topside section was given over to entertainment; all about him were theaters and cafes and picnic groves and airports for flying sports. A few hundred feet ahead he could see the three-dimensional atmospheric projection that marked the Stardust Cafe, and he could hear faintly the mournful sound of a Venusian lament being played by the askarins. He was glad they hadn't banned Venusian music, anyway, although he wouldn't be surprised if they did, some day.

That was one of the things these Supremists were trying to do. Rysland and Chief Larkin had given him a long and careful briefing on the outfit so that he could start work tomorrow with his partner, Steve Kronski. Steve, of course, would shrug phlegmatically, swing his big shoulders toward the computer rooms and say, "Let's go to work." It would be just another assignment to him.

As a matter of fact, the job would be not without a certain amount of interest. There were a couple of puzzling things about these Supremists that Rysland had pointed out. First of all, they didn't seem to be at all organized or incorporated. No headquarters, no officers that anybody knew about. They just *were*. It was a complete mystery how a man became a Supremist, how they kept getting new members all the time. Yet you couldn't miss a Supremist whenever you met one. Before the conversation was half over he'd start spouting about the destiny of Earthmen and the general inferiority of all other creatures and so on. It sounded like hogwash to Pell. He wondered how such an attitude could survive in a scientific age.

Nor would a Supremist be essentially a moron or a neurotic; they were found in all walks of life, at all educational and emotional levels. Rysland told how he had questioned a few, trying to discover when, where and how they joined the movement: Apparently there was nothing to join, at least to hear them tell it. They just knew one day that they were Supremists, and that was the word. Rysland had shaken his head sadly and said, "Their belief is completely without logic—and maybe that's what makes it so strong. Maybe that's what frightens me about it."

*

Okay, tomorrow then Pell would tackle it. Tomorrow he'd think about it. Right now he had a date with his best girl.

He entered the cafe and the music of the askarins swirled more loudly about his head and he looked through the smoke and colored light until he spotted Ciel sitting in a rear booth. The place was crowded. On the small dance floor before the orchestra nearly nude Venusian girls were going through the writhing motions of a serpentine dance. Their greenish skins shimmered iridescently. The sad-faced Venusian musicians on the band-stand waved their graceful, spatulate fingers over their curious, boxlike askarins, producing changing tones and overtones by the altered capacitance. A rocketman in the black and silver uniform of the Space Force was trying to stumble drunkenly out on to the floor with the dancers and his friends were holding him back. There was much laughter about the whole thing. The Venusian girls kept dancing and didn't change their flat, almost lifeless expressions.

Ciel looked up without smiling when he got to the booth. She had a half-finished glass of meth before her.

He tried a smile anyway. "Hello, baby." He sat down.

She said, "I didn't really think you'd get here. I could have had dates with exactly eleven spacemen. I kept count."

"You have been faithful to me, Cynara, in your fashion. I need a drink and don't want to wait for the waitress. Mind?" He took her half glass of meth and tossed it down. He felt the wonderful illusion of an explosion in his skull, and it seemed to him that his body was suddenly the strongest in the world and that he could whip everybody in the joint with one arm tied behind his back. He said, "Wow."

Ciel tried a smile now. "It does that to you when you're not used to it."

The first effect passed and he felt only the warmth of the drink. He signaled a waitress and ordered a couple more. "Don't forget to remind me to take a hangover pill before I go to work in the morning," he told Ciel.

"You—you are going to work in the morning, then?"

"Afraid I can't get out of it."

"And the moon trip's off?"

"Not off, just postponed. We'll get to it, don't worry."

"Dick."

"Yes?"

"I can take it just so long, putting our vacation off and off and off." Her eyes were earnest, liquid and opaque. "I've been thinking about it. Trying to arrive at something. I'm beginning to wonder, Dick, if maybe we hadn't just better, well—call it quits, or something."

He stared at her. "Baby, what are you saying?"

*

A sudden, fanfare-like blast from the orchestra interrupted. They looked at the dance floor. There was a flash of light, a swirling of mist, and within the space of a second the Venusian girls suddenly disappeared and their place was taken by a tall, hawk-nosed, dark-eyed man with a cloak slung dramatically over one shoulder. The audience applauded.

"That's Marco, the new mentalist," said Pell.

Ciel shrugged to show that she wasn't particularly impressed. Neither was Pell, to tell the truth. Mentalists were all the rage, partly because everybody could practice a little amateur telepathy and hypnotism in his own home. Mentalists, of course, made a career of it and were much better at it than anybody else.

Their drinks came and they watched Marco go through his act in a rather gloomy silence. Marco was skillful, but not especially unusual. He did the usual stuff: calling out things that people wrote on slips of paper, calling out dates on coins, and even engaging in mental duels wherein the challenger wrote a phrase, concealed it from Marco, and then deliberately tried to keep him from reading it telepathically. He had the usual hypnotism session with volunteers who were certain they could resist. He made them hop around the stage like monkeys, burn their fingers on pieces of ice, and so on. The audience roared with laughter. Pell and Ciel just kept staring.

When Marco had finished his act and the thundering applause had faded the Venusian dancing girls came back on the stage again.

Ciel yawned.

Pell said, "Me, too. Let's get out of here."

It wasn't until they were home in their underground apartment and getting ready for bed that Ciel turned to him and said, "You see?"

He was buttoning his pajamas. "See what?"

"It's *us*, Dick. It's not the floor show, or the meth, or anything—it's *us*. We can't enjoy *anything* together any more."

He said, "Now wait a minute . . . ."

But she had already stepped into the bedroom and slammed the door. He heard the lock click.

"Hey," he said, "what am I supposed to do, sleep out here?"

He took the ensuing silence to mean that he was.

And he did.

*

The next morning, as he came into the office, Pell scowled deeply and went to his desk without saying good morning to anybody. Ciel had kept herself locked in the bedroom and he had made his own breakfast. How it was all going to end he didn't know. He had the feeling that she was working herself up to the decision to leave him. And the real hell of it was that he couldn't exactly blame her.

"Morning, partner," said a voice above him. He looked up. Way up. Steve Kronski was built along the general lines of a water buffalo. The usual battered grin was smeared across his face. "I see we got a new assignment."

"Oh—did Larkin brief you on it already?"

"Yeah. Before I could get my hat off. Funny set-up, all right. I punched for basic data before you got in. Hardly any."

"Maybe that means something in itself. Maybe somebody saw to it that the information never got into the central banks."

The C.I.B. computers could be hooked into the central banks which stored information on nearly everything and everybody. If you incorporated, filed for a patent, paid taxes, voted, or just were born, the central banks had an electronic record of it.

Kronski jerked his thumb toward the computer room. "I punched for names of Supremist members coupla minutes ago. Thought maybe we could start in that way."

Pell followed, his mind not really on the job yet. He wasn't at his best working with the computers, and yet operating them was ninety per cent of investigation. He supposed he'd get used to it sometime.

Three walls of the big computer room were lined with control racks, consisting mostly of keyboard setups. Code symbols and index cards were placed in handy positions. The C.I.B. circuits, of course, were adapted to the specialized work of investigation. In the memory banks of tubes and relays there was a master file of all names—aliases and nicknames included—with which the organization had ever been concerned. Criminals, witnesses, complaints, everyone. Code numbers linked to the names showed where data on their owner could be found. A name picked at random might show that person to have data in the suspect file, the arrest file, the psychological file, the modus operandi file, and so forth. Any of the data in these files could be checked, conversely, against the names.

Kronski walked over to where letter sized cards were flipping from a slot into a small bin. He said, "Didn't even have to dial in Central Data for these. Seems we got a lot of Supremist members right in our own little collection."

Pell picked up one of the cards and examined it idly. Vertical columns were inscribed along the card, each with a heading, and with further sub-headed columns. Under the column marked *Modus Operandi*, for instance, there were subcolumns titled *Person Attacked, Property Attacked, How Attacked, Means of Attack, Object of Attack*, and *Trademark*. Columns of digits, one to nine, were under each item. If the digits 3 and 2 were punched under *Trademark* the number 32 could be fed into the Operational Data machine and this machine would then give back the information on a printed slip that number 32 stood for the trademark of leaving cigar butts at the scene of the crime.

"Got five hundred now," said Kronski. "I'll let a few more run in case we need alternates."

"Okay," said Pell. "I'll start this batch through the analyzer."

He took the cards across the room to a machine about twenty feet long and dropped them into the feeder at one end. Channels and rollers ran along the top of this machine and under them were a series of vertical slots into which the selected cards could drop. He cleared the previous setting and ran the pointer to *Constants*. He set the qualitative dial to 85%. This meant that on the first run the punch hole combinations in the cards would be scanned and any item common to 85% of the total would be registered in a relay. Upon the second run the machine would select the cards with this constant and drop them into a slot corresponding with that heading. Further scanning, within the slot itself, would pick out the constant number.

Pell started the rollers whirring.

Kronski came over. He rubbed his battered nose. "Hope we get outside on this case. I'm gettin' sick o' the office. Haven't been out in weeks."

Pell nodded. Oh, for the life of a C.I.B. man. In teleplays they cornered desperate criminals in the dark ruins of the ancient cities topside, and fought it out with freezers. The fact was, although regulations called for them to carry freezers in their shoulder holsters, one in a thousand ever got a chance to use them.

Pell said, "Maybe you need a vacation."

"Maybe. Only I keep putting my vacation off. Got a whole month saved up now."

"Me, too." Pell sighed. Ciel would probably be pacing the floor back home now, trying to make up her mind. To break it up, or not to break it up? There would be no difficulty, really: she had been a pretty good commercial artist before they were married and she wouldn't have any trouble finding a job again somewhere in World City.

The rollers kept whirring and the cards flipping along with a whispering sound.

"Wonder what we're looking into these Supremists for?" asked Kronski. "I always thought they were some kind of harmless crackpots."

"The Chief doesn't think so. Neither does Theodor Rysland." He told Kronski more about the interview last night.

Presently the machine stopped, clicked several times and began rolling the other way.

"Well, it found something," said Kronski.

They kept watching. Oh, for the life of a C.I.B. man. Cards began to drop into one of the slots. The main heading was *Physical* and the sub-heading *Medical History*. Pell frowned and said, "Certainly didn't expect to find a constant in this department." He picked up a few of the first cards and looked at them, hoping to catch the constant by eye. He caught it. "What's 445 under this heading?"

*

Kronski said, "I'll find out," and stepped over to the Operational Data board. He worked it, took the printed slip that came out and called back: "Record of inoculation."

"That's a funny one."

"Yup. Sure is." Kronski stared at the slip and scratched his neck. "It must be just any old kind inoculation. If it was special—like typhoid or tetanus or something—it'd have another digit."

"There must be some other boil-downs, if we could think of them." Pell was frowning heavily. Some of the other men, used to the machines, could grab a boil-down out of thin air, run the cards again and get another significant constant. The machine, however, inhibited Pell. It made him feel uneasy and stupid whenever he was around it.

"How about location?" suggested Kronski.

Pell shook his head. "I checked a few by eye. All different numbers under location. Some of 'em come from World City, some from Mars Landing, some from way out in the sticks. Nothing significant there."

"Maybe what we need is a cup of coffee."

Pell grinned. "Best idea all morning. Come on."

Some minutes later they sat across from each other at a table in the big cafeteria on the seventy-third level. It was beginning to be crowded now with personnel from other departments and bureaus. The coffee urge came for nearly everybody in the government offices at about the same time. Pell was studying by eye a handful of spare data cards he'd brought along and Kronski was reading faxpaper clippings from a large manila envelope marked *Supremist Party*. Just on a vague hunch Pell had viewplated Central Public Relations and had them send the envelope down by tube.

"*Prominent Educator Addresses Supremist Rally,*" Kronski muttered. "*Three Spaceport Cargomen Arrested at Supremist Riot. Young Supremists Form Rocket Club.* Looks like anybody and everybody can be a Supremist. And his grandmother. Wonder how they do it?"

"Don't know." Pell wasn't really listening.

"And here's a whole town went over to the Supremists. On the moon."

"Uh-huh," said Pell.

Kronski sipped his coffee loudly. A few slender, graceful young men from World Commerce looked at him distastefully. "Happened just this year. New Year they all went over. Augea, in the Hercules Mountains. Big celebration."

Pell looked up and said, "Wait a minute . . . ."

"Wait for what? I'm not goin' anywhere. Not on this swivel-chair of a job, damn it."

"New Year they all become Supremists. And the last week of December everybody on the moon gets his inoculations, right?"

"Search me."

"But I know that. I found that out when I was tailing those two gamblers who had a place on the moon, remember?"

"So it may be a connection." Kronski shrugged.

"It may be the place where we can study a bunch of these cases in a batch instead of picking 'em one by one."

"You mean we oughta take a trip to the moon?"

"Might not hurt for a few days."

Kronski was grinning at him.

"What are you grinning at?"

"First you got to stay over on your vacation, so you can't go to the moon with your wife. Now all of a sudden you decide duty has got to take you to the moon, huh?"

Pell grinned back then. "What are you squawking about? You said you wanted to get out on this case."

Kronski, still grinning, got up. "I'm not complaining. I'm just demonstrating my powers of deduction, as they say in teleplays. Come on, let's go make rocket reservations."

CHAPTER III

The big tourist rocket let them down at the Endymion Crater Landing, and they went through the usual immigration and customs formalities in the underground city there. They stayed in a hotel overnight, Pell and Ciel looking very much like tourists, Kronski tagging along and looking faintly out of place. In the morning—morning according to the 24 hour earth clock, that is—they took the jitney rocket to the resort town of Augea, in the Hercules Mountains. The town was really a cliff dwelling, built into the side of a great precipice with quartz windows overlooking a tremendous, stark valley.

It was hard to say just what attraction the moon had as a vacation land, and it was a matter of unfathomable taste. You either liked it, or you didn't. If you didn't, you couldn't understand what people who liked it saw in it. They couldn't quite explain. "It's so quiet. It's so vast. It's so beautiful," they'd say, but never anything clearer than that.

Augea itself was like twenty other resorts scattered throughout both the northern and southern latitudes of the moon. Except for the military posts and scientific research stations the moon had little value other than as a vacation land. People came there to rest, to look at the bizarre landscape through quartz, or occasionally to don spacesuits and go out on guided exploration trips.

Immediately after checking into their hotel Pell and Kronski got directions to the office of the Resident Surgeon and prepared to go there. Ciel looked on quietly as Pell tightened the straps of his shoulder holster and checked the setting on his freezer.

Ciel said, "I knew it."

"Knew what, honey?" Pell went to the mirror to brush his hair. He wasn't sure it would materially improve the beauty of his long, knobby, faintly melancholy face, but he did it any way.

"The minute we get here you have to go out on business."

He turned, kissed her, then held and patted her hand. "That's just because I want to get it over with. Then I'll have time for you. Then we'll have lots of time together."

She melted into him suddenly. She put her arms around his neck and held him tightly. "If I didn't love you, you big lug, it wouldn't be so bad. But, Dick, I can't go on like this much longer. I just can't."

"Now, baby," he started to say.

There was a knock on the door then and he knew Kronski was ready. He broke away from her, threw a kiss and said, "Later. Later, baby."

She nodded and held her under lip in with her upper teeth.

He sighed and left.

*

Pell and Kronski left the hotel and started walking along the winding tunnel with the side wall of quartz. On their right the huge valley, with its stark, unearthly landshapes, stretched away. It was near the end of the daylight period and the shadows from the distant peaks, across the valley, were long and deep. Some of them, with little reflected light, seemed to be patches of nothingness. Pell fancied he could step through them into another dimension.

All about them, even here in the side of the mountain, and behind the thick quartz, there was the odd, utterly dead silence of the moon.

Their footsteps echoed sparsely in the corridor.

Pell said to Kronski, "Got the story all straight?"

"Like as if it was true."

"Remember the signal?"

"Sure. Soon as you say we're out of cigarettes. What's the matter, you think I'm a moron, I can't remember?"

Pell laughed and clapped him on the shoulder blade.

Minutes later they turned in from the corridor, went through another, shorter passageway and then came to a door marked: Resident Surgeon. They knocked and a deep voice boomed: "Come in!"

It was a medium-sized room, clearly a dispensary. There was an operating table, a sterilizer, tall glass-fronted instrument cabinets and a refrigerator. At the far end of the room a hulking, bear-like man sat behind a magnalloy desk. The nameplate on the desk said: Hal H. Wilcox, M.D.

"Howdy, gents," said Dr. Hal H. Wilcox, shattering the moon-silence with a vengeance. "What can I do for you?" he was all smiles.

That smile, decided Pell, didn't quite match the shrewdness of his eyes. Have to watch this boy, maybe. There was a big quartz window behind the man so that for the moment Pell saw him almost in silhouette. "We're from *Current* magazine," said Pell. "I'm Dick Pell and this is Steve Kronski. You got our radio, I guess."

"Oh, yes. Yes, indeed." Wilcox creaked way back in his chair. "You're the fellas want to do a story on us moon surgeons."

"That's right." Pell fumbled a little self-consciously with the gravity weights clipped to his trousers. Took a while for moon visitors to get used to them, everybody said.

"Well, I don't know exactly as how there's much of a story in what we do. We're just a bunch of sawbones stationed here, that's all."

"We're interested in the diseases peculiar to the moon," said Pell. "For instance, why do the permanent residents up here have to have an inoculation every year?"

"That's for the Venusian rash. Thought everybody knew that."

"Venusian rash?"

"Nearest thing we ever had to it on Earth was Rocky Mountain Spotted Fever. It's a rickettsia disease. Makes a fella pretty sick; sometimes kills him in two, three days. It started when they had those Venusian construction workers and tunnel men here, oh, long before the war. Under certain conditions the rickettsia stays dormant and then pops up again."

"And the inoculation's for that?"

"Standard. Once a year. You got the inoculation yourself, no doubt, before you jumped off for the moon."

"Where does the serum or whatever you call it come from?"

Pell thought he saw Wilcox's eyes flicker. The doctor said, "It's stored at the main landings. We draw it as we need it from there."

"Have any here now?"

Wilcox's eyes did move this time. He looked at the refrigerator—but only for the veriest moment. "Don't really reckon so," he said finally. He was staring blankly at Pell again.

Pell patted his pockets, turned to Kronski and said, "You know, I think we're out of cigarettes." Before Kronski could answer he moved to the big quartz window behind Wilcox's desk. He gazed at the moonscape. "Just can't get over how big and quiet it is," he said.

Wilcox turned and gazed with him.

Kronski drew his freezer. He pointed it, squeezed, and there was a soft, momentary buzzing and a twinkling of violet sparks at the muzzle of the weapon.

Wilcox sat where he was, frozen, knowing nothing.

*

Pell turned fast. "Come on, Steve. Let's get it." They both stepped to the refrigerator.

They had only seconds; Kronski's weapon had been set at a low reading. The time of paralysis varied with the individual and Doc Wilcox looked husky enough not to stay frozen very long. If Pell and Kronski returned to their original positions after he came out of it he would never know that anything had happened.

Far back on a lower shelf of the refrigerator were a dozen small bottles of the same type. Pell grabbed one, glanced at the label, nodded, and dropped it into his pocket. They took their places again.

A few moments later Wilcox moved slightly and said, "Yup. Moon's a funny place all right. You either like it or you don't."

The rest of the conversation was fairly uninspired. Pell didn't want to walk out too quickly, and had to keep up the pretense of interviewing Wilcox for a magazine story. It wasn't easy. They excused themselves finally, saying they'd be back for more information as soon as they made up some notes and got the overall picture—whatever that meant. Wilcox seemed satisfied with it.

They hurried back along the tunnel, descended to another level and found the Augea Post Office. They showed the postmaster their C.I.B. shields and identification cards and arranged for quick and special handling for the bottle of vaccine. Pell marked it *Attention, Lab,* and it was scheduled to take a quick rocket to the Endymion landing and the next unmanned mail rocket back to World City.

Pell stayed at the Post Office to make out a quick report on the incident so he wouldn't have to bore Ciel by doing it in the room, and Kronski sauntered on back to the hotel.

There was a fax receiver there and Pell, missing the hourly voice bulletins of World City Underground, checked it for news. The pages were coming out in a long tongue. He looked at the first headline:

VENUSIAN OBSERVERS ADMITTED TO WORLD CONGRESS

Well, that was a step in the right direction. Maybe one of these days they'd get around to a Solar Congress, as they ought to. The recent open war with Venus had taught both Earthmen and Venusians a lot about space travel, and it was probably possible to explore the solar system further right now. No one had yet gone beyond the asteroids. Recent observations from the telescope stations here on the moon had found what seemed to be geometrical markings on some of Jupiter's satellites. Life there? Could be. Candidates for a brotherhood of the zodiac—if both Terrans and Venusians could get the concept of brotherhood pounded through their still partially savage skulls.

Another headline:

'WE CAN LICK UNIVERSE'—WAR SEC

Not so good, that. Loose talk. Actually it was an Undersecretary of War who had said it. Pell ran over the rest of the article quickly and came to what seemed to him a significant excerpt. "*Certain patriotic groups in the world today are ready and willing to make the necessary sacrifices to get it over with. There is a fundamental difference between Earthmen and other creatures of the system, and this difference can be resolved only by the dominance of one over the other.*"

Supremist stuff. Strictly. If this Undersecretary were not actually a member he was at least a supporter of the Supremist line. And that line had an appeal for the unthinking, Pell had to admit. It was pleasant to convince yourself that you were a superior specimen, that you were chosen . . . .

VENUSIAN SPY SUSPECTS HELD ON MARS

Pell frowned deeply at that one and read the story. A couple of Venusian miners on Mars had wandered too close to one of the Earth military outposts, and had been nabbed. He doubted that they were spies; he doubted that the authorities holding them thought so. But it seemed to make a better story with a slight scare angle. He thought about how Mars was divided at an arbitrary meridian—half to Venus, half to Earth. The division solved nothing, pleased nobody. Joe Citizen, the man in the tunnels could see these things, why couldn't these so-called trained diplomats?

Pell finished his report, questioned the Postmaster a little on routine facts concerning the town, and went back to the hotel.

*

Ciel was waiting for him. She was in a smart, frontless frock of silvercloth. Her golden hair shone. Her large, dark eyes looked deep, moist, alive. She looked at him questioningly? and he read the silent question: *Now can you spare a little time?*

"Baby," he said softly, and kissed her.

"Mm," he said when he had finished kissing her.

The voice-phone rang.

He said, "Damn it."

It was Kronski, in his own room next door. "Did Wilcox leave yet?" he asked.

"Wilcox?"

"Yeah. The Doc. Is he still there?"

"I didn't know he was here at all."

Kronski said, "Huh?"

Pell said, "Maybe we better back up and start all over again."

"Wilcox, the Resident Surgeon Doc Wilcox," said Kronski, not too patiently. "He was in my room a little while ago. Said he'd drop by on his way out and see if you were in."

Pell glanced at Ciel. She was busy lighting a cigarette at the other end of the room. Or pretending to be busy. Pell said, "I just got here. Just this minute. I didn't see any Wilcox. What'd he want?"

"I don't know exactly. He was kind of vague about it. Wanted to know if he could answer any more questions for us, or anything like that."

"Sounds screwy."

"Yeah. It sure does, now that I think it over."

"Let me call you back," said Pell and hung up. He turned to Ciel. "Was Doc Wilcox here?"

"Why, yes. He stopped in." Nothing but blank innocence on her face.

"Why didn't you tell me?"

"Hm?" She raised her eyebrows. "He just stopped in to see if you were here, that was all. I told him you weren't and he went out again."

"But you didn't mention it."

"Well, why should I?"

"I don't know. I'd think you'd say something about it."

"Now, listen, Dick—I'm not some suspect you're grilling. What's the matter with you, anyway?"

"It just strikes me as funny that Wilcox should drop in here and you shouldn't say one word about it, that's all."

"Well, I like that." She folded her arms. "You're getting to be so much of a cop you're starting to be suspicious of your own wife."

"Now, you know it's not that at all."

"What else is it? Dick, I'm sick of it. I'm sick of this whole stupid business you're in. The first time we get a few minutes alone together you start giving me the third degree. I won't stand for it, that's all!"

"Now, baby," he said and took a step toward her.

The deeper tone of the viewer sounded.

*

"Agh, for Pete's sake," he said disgustedly and answered the call. The image of Chief Larkin's boyishly handsome face came into focus on the screen. Pell lifted a surprised eyebrow and said, "Oh, hello, Chief."

Larkin's eye was cold. Especially cold in the setting of that boyish face. "What in hell," he asked, "are you and Kronski doing on the moon?"

"Hm?" Now it was Pell's turn to look innocent. "Why, you know what we're doing, Chief. We're investigating that case. You know the one—I don't want to mention it over the viewer."

"Who the devil authorized you to go traipsing to the *moon* to do it?"

"Why, nobody authorized us. I thought—I mean, when you're working on a case and you have a lead, you're supposed to go after it, aren't you?"

"Yes, but not when it's a crazy wild goose chase." In the viewer Pell saw the Chief slam his desk with the palm of his hand. "I'd like to know what in blazes you think you can do on the moon that you can't do in a good healthy session at the computers?"

"Well, that's kind of hard to explain over the viewer. We have made some progress, though. I just sent you a report on it."

Larkin narrowed one eye. "Pell, who do you think you're fooling?"

"Fooling?"

"You heard me. I know damn well you wanted to take a vacation on the moon. But we have a little job for you that holds you up, and what do you do? The next best thing, eh? You see to it that the job *takes* you to the moon."

"Now, Chief, it wasn't that at all . . . ."

"The devil it wasn't. Now, listen to me, Pell. You pack your bags and get right back to World City. The next rocket you can get. You understand?"

Before he answered the question he looked at Ciel. She was staring at him quietly. Again he could read something of what was in her mind. He knew well enough that she was trying to say to him: "*Make a clean break now. Tell him No, you won't come back. Quit. Now's the time to do it—unless you want that stupid job of yours more than you want me . . . .*"

Pell sighed deeply, slowly looked into the viewer again and said, "Kronski and I'll be back on the next rocket, Chief."

CHAPTER IV

Back again in the underground offices of C.I.B., Agent Richard Pell plunged into his job. Up to his neck. It was the only way he could keep from brooding about Ciel. She was somewhere in the city at this very moment and if he really wanted to take the trouble he'd be able to find her easily enough—but he didn't want it to happen that way. She'd never really be his again unless *she* came to *him* . . . .

And so once more he found himself in the office late at night. Alone. Poring over the lab reports that had come in that afternoon, turning them over in his mind and hoping, he supposed, for a nice intuitive flash, free of charge.

As a matter of fact the analysis of the vaccine he'd lifted from Wilcox's dispensary was not without significance. There was definitely an extraneous substance. The only question was just what this substance might be. Take a little longer to find that out, the report said.

It made Pell think of the corny sign World Government officials always had on their desks, the one about doing the difficult right away and taking a little longer for the impossible. Some day, when he was a big-shot, he would have a sign on his desk saying: *Why make things difficult when with even less effort you can make them impossible?* Of course, ideas like that were probably the very reason he'd never be a big-shot . . . .

The Identifier humming. Someone coming again.

He looked up, and then had the curious feeling of being jerked back in time to several nights ago. Chief Larkin and Theodor Rysland entered.

"Hello, Dick," said Larkin, with a touch of studied democracy. He glanced at the government adviser as if to say: *See? Knew we'd find him here.*

Pell made a sour face. "Some day I'm going to stop giving all this free overtime. Some day I'm not going to show up at all."

Rysland smiled, dislodging some of the rock strata of his curiously pale face. He seemed a little weary this evening. He moved slowly and with even more than his usual dignity. He said, "I hope, Mr. Pell, that you'll wait at least until you finish this job for us. I understand you've made some progress."

Pell shrugged and gestured at the lab report. "Progress, maybe—but I don't know how far. Just a bunch of new puzzles to be perfectly frank."

Rysland sat down at the other desk and drummed on it with his fingertips. He looked at Pell gravely. "As a matter of fact, since we last talked to you the situation has become even more urgent. A Supremist congressman introduced a bill today before the world delegates which may prove very dangerous. Perhaps you know the one I refer to."

"I was too busy to follow the news today," said Pell, looking meaningfully at Larkin.

Larkin didn't seem to notice.

Rysland said, "I'll brief you then. The bill purports to prohibit material aid of any kind to a non-Terran government. That means both credit and goods. And since the only real non-Terran government we know is Venus, it's obviously directed specifically at the Venusians."

Pell thought it over. High level stuff again. He nodded to show he followed.

"On the surface," continued Rysland, "this would seem to be a sort of anti-espionage bill. Actually, it's a deliberately provocative act. I know the Venusians will take it that way. But right now certain quarters are secretly trying to negotiate a trade treaty with Venus which would be a major step toward peaceful relations. If this bill became law, such a treaty would be impossible."

"But World Congress isn't likely to pass such a bill, is it? Won't they see through it?"

Rysland frowned. "That's what we're not sure of. Messages are pouring in urging passage—all of them from Supremists, of course. The Supremists are relatively few, but they make a lot of noise. Sometimes noise like that is effective. It could swing a lot of delegates who don't see the real danger of this bill and are at the moment undecided. The Defender side, with its desire to isolate and fortify, is especially susceptible."

"That *is* bad," said Pell thoughtfully.

*

Rysland put his palm on the desk. "Now then, if we can somehow discredit the Supremists—get to the bottom of this thing quickly enough—I'm sure that bill will be killed. I came here tonight, I suppose, out of pure anxiety. In other words, Mr. Pell, just how far are you?"

Pell smiled and shook his head. "Not very, I'm afraid. This Supremist thing is the damndest I ever came across. No central headquarters, no officers, no propaganda mill—entirely word of mouth as far as I can see. No way of finding out how it started, or even how the new members are proselyted. Ask any member how he became a Supremist. He just looks kind of dreamy and mutters something about the truth suddenly dawning upon him one day."

"But don't you have any theories?"

"I've got a hunch," Pell said, picking up the lab report.

Chief Larkin snorted softly. The snort said clearly enough that an efficient investigator didn't depend on hunches these days: he went after something doggedly on the computer, or by other approved techniques.

Pell pretended not to hear the snort. "First of all we discovered that nearly all Supremists received some kind of an inoculation before they became Supremists. Then we found a whole village, one of those moon resort towns, that had gone over. There was the record of inoculation there, too. I got hold of some of the vaccine and had the lab analyze it. It's mostly vaccine all right, but there *is* a foreign substance in it. Listen." He read from the report: "*Isolated point oh six four seven grams unclassified crystal compound, apparently form of nucleotide enzyme. Further analysis necessary.*"

"You think this enzyme, or whatever it is, has something to do with it?"

"I don't know. All I have is a pretty wild theory. To begin, when our lab can't analyze something right away, it's pretty rare—possibly even unknown to chemistry in general. Now it's just possible that this substance does something to the brain that makes a man into a Supremist, and that somebody's behind the whole thing, deliberately planting the stuff so that people here and there become injected with it."

"Pell." Larkin made a pained face. "Really."

Pell shrugged. "Well, as I say, it's a hunch, that's all."

"It's a pipe dream," said Larkin. "I never heard of anything so fantastic."

"That's what folks said a couple of centuries ago when the Venusians were first trying to make contact and their ships were sighted all over the place. 'I never heard of anything so fantastic,' they all said."

Theodor Rysland still looked interested. "Granted there is some connection between the Supremist mental state and this, er, enzyme. What then, Mr. Pell?"

"Well," said Pell, stretching his legs out, "I had an idea maybe your friend Dr. Nebel could give us some help on that."

"Nebel?"

"He's interested in this thing, isn't he?"

"Definitely. Nebel's a very public spirited man."

"Well, I understand he's one of the top psychobiologists in the country today. Seems to me this new enzyme, whatever it is, would be right up his alley. Of course the lab should get to it eventually, but he might do it a lot quicker."

Larkin had been examining some statistical crime charts on the wall. He turned from them. "Pell, does Kronski know about all these wild hunches of yours?"

"I haven't talked with him about them yet. He left today before the lab report came in. Why?"

"I was just wondering," said Larkin evenly, "whether I had two maniacs in my organization or only one."

Rysland, frowning, turned to the chief. "I wouldn't be hasty, Larkin," he said. "Crazy as it sounds Pell may have something here."

Larkin snorted again, and this time along with it he shook his head sadly.

"What's your next move then?" Rysland asked Pell.

"Tomorrow morning, first thing," Pell said, "I'll take a sample of this stuff to Dr. Nebel and see what he can do with it. Of course the lab can keep on working on it in the meantime."

"Don't you think you might do better to get busy on those computers?" Larkin asked.

Pell shook his head. "This hunch is too strong, Chief."

Rysland smiled, and got up. "I'm inclined to put a little stock into this man's hunches. He's done pretty well with them so far. I'd even say he's pretty close to a solution of this thing—possibly."

Larkin shrugged and started to look at the crime charts again.

Rysland held out his hand. "Good night, Mr. Pell. You've encouraged me. Larkin and I are going topside for a little night cap before we turn in. Like to join us?"

"No, thanks," said Pell. "I'm sleepy. I want to get home and hit that sack."

"Very well. Good night again." The two men went toward the door.

Pell watched them quietly. He had lied. He wasn't sleepy at all. He just wanted to get home and sit by that viewer and hope, hope against hope, that it would ring and that Ciel's lovely image would swirl into view . . . .

*

On the way home he was just the least bit tempted to go topside, however. He thought he might like to walk the broad, quiet boulevards under the stars. His brain functioned better there. The tunnels were so clean and bright and sterile, so wonderfully functional and sensible, that they oppressed him somehow. Maybe, he sometimes thought, he wasn't fit for this age. Maybe he should have been born a couple of hundred years ago. But common sense told him that people in *that* age must have often thought exactly the same thing to themselves.

He looked at his chrono and decided he had better go home.

The apartment, when he came to it, was cold and empty without Ciel. He bathed and tried to keep up his spirits by singing in his tuneless way, but it didn't help.

He went back into the living room, selected a film from the library and slipped it into a lap projector. He sat down and tried to concentrate on the film, a historical adventure about the days of the first moon rockets. He couldn't follow it.

The viewer rang.

He bounded from the chair as though he had triggered a high speed ejection seat in a burning jet. He went to the viewer and flicked it on. The plate shimmered, and then Ciel's image came into focus.

"*Baby!*" He was certain his shout overmodulated every amp tube in the entire World City viewer system. But he felt better, wonderfully better, already.

She was smiling. "Hello, Dick."

"Hello."

And then they looked at each other in affectionate embarrassment for a moment.

"One of us," said Pell, "ought to have his script writer along."

"Dick, I don't know exactly how to say what I want to say . . . ."

"Don't. Don't say anything. Just pretend nothing ever happened. Just come on home fast as you can."

"No, Dick. Not yet. I still want to talk about—well, everything. Dick, we've got to reach some sort of compromise. There *must* be a way."

"Come on home. We'll find a way."

"Not home. Too many memories there. Besides," she smiled a little, "I don't trust us alone together. You know what would happen. We wouldn't get *any* talking done. Not any sensible talking anyway. You'd better meet me someplace."

He sighed. "Okay. Where can I meet you?"

"How about the Stardust Cafe?"

"Again? That place didn't help us much the last time."

"I know, but it's the handiest. I'm sure we can find a quiet place. Out on the terrace or something."

"Is there a terrace?"

"Yes, I think so. I'm sure there must be."

He looked at his chrono. "All right, baby. Half an hour?"

"Half an hour."

When she clicked off he felt his heart pounding. He felt dizzy. He felt as though he had just taken a quart of meth at one jolt—intravenously. He sang, more loudly and more off-key than ever. He went into the bedroom and started to get dressed again.

It wasn't until he was finishing the knot in his tie that the hunch hit him.

*

It was funny about that hunch. He would have said it came out of nowhere, and yet it must have broken from the bottom of his mind through some kind of restraining layer into the conscious levels. He didn't remember thinking anything that might have brought it on—his mind was strictly on Ciel. Maybe that was how it came through, with the attention of his conscious mind directed elsewhere.

With the hunch he heard Ciel's voice again, heard it very clearly, saying: "*I'm sure we can find a quiet place. Out on the terrace or something.*" And with that other things started to fall into place.

As he thought, and as the possibilities of his hunch fanned out to embrace other possibilities he became suddenly cold and sick inside. He fought the feeling. "Got to go through with it," he muttered to himself. "Got to."

As soon as he was dressed he took the tunnel cars to Station D-90, changing twice. People were aboard at this hour, returning from the evening. Lots of men and women in uniform: the green of the landfighters, the white of the seamen, the blue of the flyers, the silver and black of the space force. Young people. Kids mostly: kids who had never seen war, smelled death, heard the wounded scream. He hoped they never would. But if his hunch was correct they might be dangerously near to it right now.

If only he had time to call Kronski. He'd feel a lot safer . . . .

He shook himself. Have to stop thinking about it. Proceed cautiously now, and take each thing as it came. That was the only thing to do.

He went topside and stepped from the elevator kiosk into the night air. Ahead he saw the bright globular sign of the Stardust Cafe. But he didn't go toward it right away. He turned in the other direction, walked swiftly, and kept a sharp eye on the shadows. He turned off on a side street, circled a small park, and then crossed a sloping lawn toward the back of the night club. He headed for the light of the service entrance.

A half-credit bill got him inside through the back entrance. He found the door with the temporary sign saying: Marco the Mentalist. He knocked.

Marco the Mentalist opened the door. He didn't look quite as tall face-to-face as he did out on the floor, nor quite as impressive. His face was still dark and faintly saturnine, but the jowls seemed a little puffier now, there was a faint network of capillaries around his nostrils and his eyes looked just the least bit weary and tired. In a pleasant enough voice he said, "Yes?"

Pell showed his C.I.B. identification.

Marco raised his eyebrows a little and said, "Come inside, please." Inside he found a chair for Pell. He sat across from him at his dressing table, half-turned toward the room. "I must get ready for my show in a little while. You understand that, of course."

Pell nodded. "What's on my mind won't take long. First of all, I want to ask a few questions about hypnotism. They may seem silly to you, or maybe a little elementary, but I'd like you to answer 'em just the same."

Marco's eyebrows went a little bit higher and he said, "Proceed."

"Okay. Question number one: can anybody be hypnotized against his will?"

"Some can, some can't." Marco smiled. "The average person, under average circumstances—no. I appear in my act to hypnotize people against their wills. Actually, subconsciously, they *wish* to be hypnotized, which is why they volunteer to let me try in the first place."

"Okay, number two. Is there any drug that can hypnotize a person?"

Marco frowned. "Pentothal and several things *appear* to do that. You could argue it either way, whether the subject is actually hypnotized or not. I believe post-hypnotic commands have been given to subjects under sodium pentothol and carried out, even back in the dark ages of psychiatry several hundred years ago."

"I've got one more really important question," Pell said then. "I'd understood that somebody under hypnosis won't do anything against his moral or ethical sense. An honest man, for instance, can't be forced to steal. Is that true?"

Marco laughed and gestured with his graceful fingers. "I don't think it is true. It was once believed to be, because hypnotic technique was not strong enough. That is, the subject's hypnosis was not strong enough to overcome a strong moral sense, which is actually a surface veneer on a deeper, more brutal nature. But I think with deep enough hypnosis, and the right kind of command, you can get a person to do most anything in post-hypnotic behavior—and of course not know why he *must* do it, even knowing it's wrong. Do you follow me?"

"I hope I do." Then Pell leaned forward. "And now I have a very great favor to ask of you."

"Yes?"

"I want you to put on a little special private performance for me, right here and now."

"I'm afraid I don't understand."

"You will, in about sixty seconds. Just listen carefully . . . ."

CHAPTER V

He was late for his date with Ciel, of course. He glanced at his chrono as he entered the Stardust Cafe by the front door and saw that he was twenty minutes late. However, this time he was certain Ciel wouldn't complain too vigorously.

Again the askarins were playing, and once more the green-skinned Venusian girls were doing their writhing, spasmodic, aphrodisiacal dance. It was remarkable how they could achieve such an effect of utter abandon and yet keep their faces blank and frozen. He looked around the rest of the room swiftly. Not so crowded tonight, and people were generally quieter. There were no oversexed spacemen clawing after the dancers on the floor.

Ciel was again in a rear booth, in the same corner of the room she had chosen before. She had spotted him now; she was looking his way. She lifted a white-gloved hand and waved.

He smiled and headed for her. He forced his smile, and made himself forget the prickling of his wrists and the feeling of bristling fur along his spine. And he held his smile all the way across the room. *Why, hello, darling, fancy seeing you here; no, nothing's wrong, nothing at all, why on earth would you think anything was wrong?*

"Hi, baby," was all he actually said.

"I'm—I'm glad you're here, Dick." Her eyes didn't show much. They roved over his face a little too much perhaps, but otherwise they seemed simply as large and dark as ever. He noticed that the meth glass in front of her was empty.

Grinning, he sat down. "This is a big moment. This is almost too much for me to handle. Maybe that's what I need—a good slug of meth."

"No."

"No?"

"Let's not waste time. Let's go out on the terrace. I want you to kiss me."

"Best offer I've had all evening." He rose again. "Where's the terrace?"

"Through that door. There's a dining room there that's closed at night. You go through the dining room and out to the terrace."

"Okay."

He took her arm and led her in and out of tables, across the room. They moved swiftly through the quiet, nearly dark dining room, and after that through a pair of window-doors. They were on the terrace then, a flagstoned space with a low wall. It overlooked the scattered lights of World City's topside area and some distance beyond they could see the river, a blue-silver ribbon in the moonlight.

They stopped at the wall. She turned toward him. He looked down at her, at her pale face and deep, dark eyes. He smelled her perfume and he felt her live warmth near him and coming nearer. He saw her eyes close, her lips part just slightly, and each lip glistening, faintly moist . . . .

He was wondering when it would happen. He was wondering when he would be struck.

As he wondered that he suddenly discovered he wasn't on the terrace any more.

*

He looked about him in some surprise. It was nearly dark. He was in a room; he could sense the walls about him. He heard a curious, high-pitched metallic voice—and recognized it.

"Pell? Are you awake now?"

It had happened then, just as he had expected. Someone had thrown a freezer on him there in the patio, and during his complete unconsciousness he'd been taken here, wherever this was. He sighed. The least they could have done would have been to let him finish kissing Ciel.

As calmly as he could he said to the four blank walls, "I'm awake."

Soft glowlights came on gradually and he saw that the room about him was fairly small—twenty by fifteen, roughly—and very plain. It contained a bed and a few odd pieces of furniture, all apparently of good quality. There was a door in one wall. He tried the door. Locked. He went back to the middle of the room.

"Chief," he said to the blank walls, "what's this all about? Is it some kind of a joke?"

The metallic voice chuckled. It belonged to Eustace J. Larkin, Chief, Central Investigation Bureau, and even filtered like this it was somewhat prim and precise. "No, Dick, it's not a joke, I'm afraid. I'm surprised you haven't guessed what it's all about. Or at least had one of your brilliant hunches." There was sarcasm in this last.

"Where's Ciel?" Pell asked.

"Right here with me. In the next room. Here—listen."

Ciel's voice said, "Don't worry, darling, we'll explain everything. And when it's all over it will be for the best. You'll see that it will."

"All right, everybody," said Pell, half-belligerently, "what's the big idea?"

"Big idea is right," Larkin's voice came back. "The biggest that ever hit the human race. And as Ciel says we'll explain it all in a moment. But first I'd like your word that you won't be foolish and make any kind of a struggle. If you'll promise that you can come in the other room here and we can all talk face to face."

Pell frowned. "I don't know—I'm not so sure I can honestly promise that."

"Suit yourself, then. A few minutes from now it won't make any difference anyway."

"Will you stop being so damned mysterious and tell me what it's all about?"

Larkin's voice laughed. "Very well. I haven't had much chance to tell about it, frankly. And I think you'll agree we've rather neatly kept our parts under cover—until you got dangerously close to the answer, anyway."

"Until I got close?"

"Certainly. Doc Wilcox's office on the moon was perhaps our one weakness in the whole set-up. How you managed to stumble on to that, I'll never know—your luck must have been with you."

"It wasn't luck, Larkin, it was a hunch."

"Still believe in hunches, eh? Well, we won't argue the point. At any rate you wouldn't have found the enzyme any place else but there."

"Oh, so the enzyme does have something to do with it."

"Everything. Here—suppose I let Doctor Nebel explain it to you. He developed it, after all."

Pell lifted his eyebrows in surprise and Dr. Walter Nebel's sibilant voice came through the hidden speakers. "I think you should know how it works, Mr. Pell. You may know that a certain part of the brain called Rossi's area is, to put it figuratively, the hypnotic center. The cut-off of the adrenal cortex, so to speak. In ordinary hypnosis the function of that area is dulled by overexercising the motor senses. By that method the intensity of hypnosis is widely variable and never really one hundred per cent effective. My compound, however, brings about complete and absolute cut-off. Any post-hypnotic suggestion given under those circumstances takes permanently and deeply. It can only be removed by further post-hypnosis under the same treatment, negating the original command."

Pell stared at the blank walls. "Go on," he said in a soft, tense voice. "What's the rest?"

Larkin spoke again. "Suppose we briefly examine a little history as a kind of introduction to this matter. The human race, since the beginning of recorded time, has failed to achieve real peace and stability, right? Every time there has been a chance for cooperative effort—for total agreement—certain selfish interests have spoiled it. There have been times, however, when certain groups—states or combinations of states—came close to permanent peace and prosperity. The Napoleonic era was one. Hitler two hundred years ago almost brought it about. The only reason they failed was that they didn't achieve their goal—*complete* conquest."

Did Pell hear correctly? Was there a faint simmering of madness in that metallic voice now? In the words there was madness, surely . . . .

*

It went on: "The fact is, Pell, people simply don't know what's good for them. Look at the blunderers and even downright crooks who are elected to World Government. Never the best brains, never the best talents. When a really able man gets into a position of leadership it's an accident—a fluke."

"I still don't see what all this has got to do with it," said Pell.

There was a shrug in the metallic voice. "For once the ablest men are going to take over. There are a number of us. You know already about myself and Doctor Nebel. Rysland will be with us, too, as soon as we can get him conditioned."

"By conditioned, you mean this enzyme of yours?"

"Exactly. We started out in a small way, using force or trickery where necessary, and managed to condition a number of doctors and nurses. Conditioning simply means injecting Nebel's compound and then giving the post-hypnotic command to be unquestioningly loyal to the Supremists. We created the Supremists, of course. In order for us to take over it will be necessary to have another war, and to conquer Venus. That can be done if Earth strikes quickly. Within the next few days I think there'll be enough Supremist influence to get this war started."

Pell stared back, open-mouthed. To hear it coldly and calmly like this was shock, cold-water shock. "Let me get this straight now. Your group made Supremists of doctors and nurses and they in turn made new members by installing this hypnosis stuff whenever anybody came for a hypodermic injection of any kind, is that it?"

"That's it."

"But how does this stuff work? Does it knock you out, or what?"

"You'll be finding that out at first hand very shortly."

Pell stiffened, made fists and unconsciously lifted them and looked around him, warily.

Larkin laughed. "It won't do you much good to put up a fight. I'm sending a couple of my assistants in there. They specialize in people who want to make a struggle. And there's no reason to feel unhappy about it, Pell: once you're conditioned you'll simply be unable to do anything against the Supremist cause. You'll be happier, in fact, having such a cause. Ask your wife if that isn't so."

Pell trembled with anger. "How did you get to her? How did you make her do what she did?"

"You mean luring you into our little trap on the terrace, so to speak? You mustn't blame Ciel for that. She couldn't help herself; she had to obey, after all. You see she was conditioned in Augea on the moon by Dr. Wilcox, one of our very loyal men. He simply dropped in when you were at the Post Office, pretended that Ciel needed a routine injection and she, not at all suspicious, allowed him to do it. He gave her the command of loyalty, and also cautioned her not to say anything about it. So you see, Ciel's been one of us for several days. It was just a little precaution of mine, in case you should become troublesome. I had to assign somebody to the investigation, of course, because Rysland and his crowd would have been too suspicious if I hadn't complied with their request."

"You're stark crazy, Larkin! You ought to be in a mental hospital!"

"You'll be over that idea in a minute or so. Meanwhile, we're wasting time. I'm sending the boys in now. You'll make it easier for yourself if you submit without giving them any trouble."

The door opened, then. Pell caught a quick glimpse of the other room and saw that it was a tastefully furnished living room. He recognized it, and knew where he was. This was a country house of Larkin's, topside, not far from the outskirts of World City. Whoever turned the freezer on him must have set the control at high intensity because it would take at least an hour to get to this place from the Stardust Cafe and he had been unconscious at least that long.

He had the momentary impulse to rush that partly opened door—and then the boys, as Larkin had called them, appeared.

*

They were specialists, little doubt of that. They regarded Pell with flat, almost disinterested looks as the door closed behind them. One held a hypodermic needle. He was the shorter of the two, but he had shoulders like ox-yokes. His face had been kneaded in the prize ring, and his bare arms were muscular and hairy but the top of his head was bald. The other had red hair, close-cropped. He was big and well-proportioned; Pell might have taken him for a professional football player.

Red did the talking. He spoke quietly, almost pleasantly. "Gonna cooperate?" he asked Pell.

Pell said, "You touch me, brother, and I'll make your face look like Baldy's."

Red glanced at Baldy and seemed to sigh. Abruptly he whirled, jumped at Pell and brought a sizzling right hand punch through the air. Pell ducked it. He saw Baldy move in as he did so, and a painful blow struck the back of his neck. His teeth rattled when it struck. Something caught him under the chin, straightened him. When he was straight a pile driver struck him in the midsection.

It was all over within a matter of seconds. Under different circumstances Pell might have found time to admire their technique.

As it was, he was now face down on the floor and Red was straddling him, holding him there. The pain in his stomach made him gasp. His face and the back of his neck ached terribly.

Red had his arm in the small of his back. Pell tried to struggle.

"I can break the arm if you move," said Red cheerfully.

And then Pell felt the bite of the needle just below his shoulder.

A misty feeling came. He felt as though he were in a red whirlpool, spinning, going down—down . . . . He fought to rise. He could still hear. He could hear footsteps and the slam of the door when somebody else came into the room. And then he seemed abruptly to be detached from his own body and floating in a huge gray void . . . .

Words hammered at his brain. Larkin's voice, at his ear now and no longer metallic. "*You will be loyal to the Supremist cause. You will do nothing against the Supremist doctrine. You will believe that Earthmen are meant to rule the Universe—*"

He felt an overpowering impulse to nod, to agree, to believe that it was right to do this. He fought this impulse, straining his mind and his very being until it seemed that something might burst with the effort.

"*You will work for the cause; you will give your life for it if necessary.*"

Yes, perhaps it was better to succumb. The words were too strong. He couldn't fight them. Larkin was right, Earthmen were supreme, and they were destined to rule . . . .

Somewhere in the depths a tiny spot of resistance still glowed. He tried desperately to evoke it. It seemed then that it became brighter. He *could* resist—he *would* . . . . He kept thinking over and over again: "*No, no, no!*"

Larkin's voice said, "Carry him in the other room. He'll come to in a moment."

*

He came to slowly, and he saw that he was lying on a couch and that several people were gathered around him smiling down at him. Something detached itself from the group, knelt by his side. He blinked. It was Ciel. Her golden hair shone and her dark eyes searched his face and she was smiling. "Hello, darling," she said.

"Hello, Ciel." He kissed her, and then sat up on the couch and looked around.

Larkin and Dr. Nebel were standing together, and Red and Baldy were a few steps behind them, still looking indifferent.

"Now you're one of us, Dick," said Larkin, flashing his professional smile, dimples and everything. Pell rose. Nebel held his hands behind his back and beamed, blinking his heavy reptilian eyelids and Larkin stepped forward and held out his hand.

"Yes," said Pell, shaking the hand, "I guess we're all working for the same thing now. What do you want me to do?"

Larkin laughed. "Nothing right away. We'll give you instructions when the time comes. I think you might as well go home with Ciel now; I have a copter and a chauffeur outside that'll take you to the station near your apartment."

"Okay, Chief, whatever you say." He smiled and took Ciel's arm. He started toward the door. Then he stopped, patted his chest and said, "Oh—my freezer. I guess the boys took it away . . . ."

Larkin turned to Baldy. "Give him his weapon."

Baldy took the freezer from his pocket and casually tossed it to Pell.

A sudden change came over Pell, then. His smile disappeared. He stepped quickly away from Ciel, whirled and faced all of them. He pointed the freezer. "All right, everybody stay perfectly still—you, too, Ciel. This is where we break up your little Supremist nightmare."

Larkin stared in utter amazement. Nebel's turtle lids opened wide. Ciel brought her hand to her throat.

Red's hand blurred suddenly, going for his own weapon. Pell squeezed the trigger, the violet sparks danced for an instant, and then Red stood frozen with his hand almost to his chest.

"I'd advise nobody else to try that," said Pell, and then in an ironical tone to Larkin: "C.I.B. agents are trained to be pretty quick with a freezer, right, Chief?"

Larkin seemed to find his voice now. "But—how—what happened? You were injected. How can you . . . ."

"I just took a little precaution, that's all," said Pell. "There'll be plenty of time to explain it all later. You'll probably hear the whole thing in court, Larkin, when I testify at your trial for treason. Meanwhile, all of you just stay nice and calm while I use the viewer."

He stepped to the viewer and dialed with his free hand. The plate glowed, shimmered and a moment later the pale, grave face of Theodor Rysland came into view. His eyebrows rose as he saw the weapon in Pell's hand and glimpsed the people beyond Pell. "Hello—what's this all about?"

"Haven't time to explain fully now," said Pell, "but I want you to get to Larkin's country house as soon as you can. I'll call agent Kronski in a moment and have him bring some others, and together we'll take Larkin and Nebel into custody. They're behind the Supremist movement—a deliberate attempt to take over the government. They did it with a drug; that's how Supremist's are made."

"What's this? A drug?"

"Think about it later," said Pell. "Just grab the facts right now. The drug makes a person subject to post-hypnotic commands—that's why your Supremists are blindly, unthinkingly loyal. However, the command can be erased by a second treatment. That'll be tough and take a lot of ferreting out, but it won't be impossible." He glanced at Ciel, and saw that she was staring at him with horror—with enmity. It sickened him, but he steadied himself with the realization that Ciel would be one of the first to be re-treated.

*

Several minutes later he had completed his calls. Rysland, Kronski and the others were on the way. He kept the freezer pointed, and watched his captives carefully. Ciel had gone over to the couch and was sitting there, her face in her hands, weeping softly.

"I don't know how you did it," said Larkin. "I don't understand it. The injection should have worked. It always did before."

"Well, it almost worked," said Pell. "I must admit I had quite a time fighting off your commands. But, you see, I knew you'd gotten to Ciel somehow when she called me up to make the date this evening. She spoke of going out to the terrace at the Stardust Cafe. It was a little odd that she should speak of the terrace like that, out of a clear sky—and I wondered why it should be on her mind. Then it struck me that neither of us had ever noticed a terrace there, and Ciel must have some special reason for knowing about it.

"She did, of course—she'd been instructed to get me out there where your boys could slap a freezer on me. So I started guessing with that hunch to work on. Everything more or less fell into place after that. It was pretty certain that they'd try to make a loyal Supremist out of me, too, and that's when I took that little precaution I mentioned to you."

"What precaution?"

Pell smiled. "I had Marco the mentalist hypnotize me and give me a rather special post-hypnotic command. He ordered me not to believe any *subsequent* post-hypnotic commands. That's why your conditioning didn't work on me."

Larkin could find no words; he just stared.

"Think about it, Larkin," said Pell. "Think hard. Maybe you'd convinced yourself you were doing good, but your purpose was still tyranny. And like any tyranny it contained the means of its own destruction. It always works out that way, Larkin—maybe it's a law, or something."

It had been a long speech for Pell, practically an oration. He was, after all, a cop, not a philosopher. Just a guy trying to get along. Just an ordinary citizen whose name was legion, looking at his wife now and waiting with what patience he could find for the time when she would be cleared of the poisonous doctrine that any one race or group or even species was supreme.

He was thinking, too, that the trial would keep him busy as the very devil and that they *still* wouldn't get to that vacation and second honeymoon for a long time . . . .

That, considering everything, was not too much to put up with.

LOVE STORY

by Irving E. Cox, Jr.

Everything was aimed at satisfying the whims of women. The popular cliches, the pretty romances, the catchwords of advertising became realities; and the compound kept the men enslaved. George knew what he had to do . . . .

The duty bell rang and obediently George clattered down the steps from his confinement cubicle over the garage. His mother's chartreuse-colored Cadillac convertible purred to a stop in the drive.

"It's so sweet of you to come, Georgie," his mother said when George opened the door for her.

"Whenever you need me, Mummy." It was no effort at all to keep the sneer out of his voice. Deception had become a part of his character.

His mother squeezed his arm. "I can always count on my little boy to do the right thing."

"Yes, Mummy." They were mouthing a formula of words. They were both very much aware that if George hadn't snapped to attention as soon as the duty bell rang, he risked being sentenced, at least temporarily, to the national hero's corps.

Still in the customary, martyr's whisper, George's mother said, "This has been such a tiring day. A man can never understand what a woman has to endure, Georgie; my life is such an ordeal." Her tone turned at once coldly practical. "I've two packages in the trunk; carry them to the house for me."

George picked up the cardboard boxes and followed her along the brick walk in the direction of the white, Colonial mansion where his mother and her two daughters and her current husband lived. George, being a boy, was allowed in the house only when his mother invited him, or when he was being shown off to a prospective bride. George was nineteen, the most acceptable marriage age; because he had a magnificent build and the reputation for being a good boy, his mother was rumored to be asking twenty thousand shares for him.

As they passed the rose arbor, his mother dropped on the wooden seat and drew George down beside her. "I've a surprise for you, George—a new bidder. Mrs. Harper is thinking about you for her daughter."

"Jenny Harper?" Suddenly his throat was dust dry with excitement.

"You'd like that, wouldn't you, Georgie?"

"Whatever arrangement you make, Mummy." Jenny Harper was one of the few outsiders George had occasionally seen as he grew up. She was approximately his age, a stunning, dark-eyed brunette.

"Jenny and her mother are coming to dinner to talk over a marriage settlement." Speculatively she ran her hand over the tanned, muscle-hard curve of his upper arm. "You're anxious to have your own woman, aren't you, George?"

"So I can begin to work for her, Mummy." That, at least, was the correct answer, if not an honest one.

"And begin taking the compound every day." His mother smiled. "Oh, I know you wicked boys! Put on your dress trunks tonight. We want Jenny to see you at your best."

320

She got up and strode toward the house again. George followed respectfully two paces behind her. As they passed beyond the garden hedge, she saw the old business coupe parked in the delivery court. Her body stiffened in anger. "Why is your father home so early, may I ask?" It was an accusation, rather than a question.

"I don't know, Mother. I heard my sisters talking in the yard; I think he was taken sick at work."

"Sick! Some men never stop pampering themselves."

"They said it was a heart attack or—"

"Ridiculous; he isn't dead, is he? Georgie, this is the last straw. I intend to trade your father in today on a younger man." She snatched the two packages from him and stormed into the house.

Since his mother hadn't asked him in, George returned to his confinement cubicle in the garage. He felt sorry, in an impersonal way, for the husband his mother was about to dispose of, but otherwise the fate of the old man was quite normal. He had outlived his economic usefulness; George had seen it happen before. His real father had died a natural death—from strain and overwork—when George was four. His mother had since then bought four other husbands; but, because boys were brought up in rigid isolation, George had known none of them well. For the same reason, he had no personal friends.

He climbed the narrow stairway to his cubicle. It was already late afternoon, almost time for dinner. He showered and oiled his body carefully, before he put on his dress trunks, briefs made of black silk studded with seed pearls and small diamonds. He was permitted to wear the jewels because his mother's stockholdings were large enough to make her an Associate Director. His family status gave George a high marriage value and his Adonis physique kicked the asking price still higher. At nineteen he stood more than six feet tall, even without his formal, high-heeled boots. He weighed one hundred and eighty-five, not an ounce of it superfluous fat. His skin was deeply bronzed by the sunlamps in the gym; his eyes were sapphire blue; his crewcut was a platinum blond—thanks to the peroxide wash his mother made him use.

Observing himself critically in the full-length mirror, George knew his mother was justified in asking twenty thousand shares for him. Marriage was an essential part of his own plans; without it revenge was out of his reach. He desperately hoped the deal would be made with Jenny Harper. A young woman would be far less difficult for him to handle.

When the oil on his skin was dry, he lay down on his bunk to catch up on his required viewing until the duty bell called him to the house. The automatic circuit snapped on the television screen above his bunk; wearily George fixed his eyes on the unreeling love story.

For as long as he could remember, television had been a fundamental part of his education. A federal law required every male to watch the TV romances three hours a day. Failure to do so—and that was determined by monthly form tests mailed out by the Directorate—meant a three month sentence to the national hero's corps. If the statistics periodically published by the Directorate were true, George was a relatively rare case, having survived adolescence without serving a single tour of duty as a national hero. For that he indirectly thanked his immunity to the compound. Fear and guilt kept him so much on his toes, he grew up an amazingly well-disciplined child.

George was aware that the television romances were designed to shape his attitudes and his emotional reactions. The stories endlessly repeated his mother's philosophy. All men were pictured as beasts crudely dominated by lust. Women, on the other hand, were always sensitive, delicate, modest, and intelligent; their martyrdom to the men in their lives was called love. To pay for their animal lusts, men were expected to slave away their lives earning things—kitchen gadgets, household appliances, fancy cars, luxuries and stockholdings—for their patient, long-suffering wives.

And it's all a fake! George thought. He had seen his Mother drive two men to their graves and trade off two others because they hadn't produced luxuries as fast as she demanded. His mother and his pinch-faced sisters were pampered, selfish, rock-hard Amazons; by no conceivable twist of imagination could they be called martyrs to anything.

That seemed self-evident, but George had no way of knowing if any other man had ever reasoned out the same conclusion. Maybe he was unique because of his immunity to the compound. He was sure that very few men—possibly none—had reached marriage age with their immunity still undiscovered.

*

George was lucky, in a way: he knew the truth about himself when he was seven, and he had time to adjust to it—to plan the role he had been acting for the past twelve years. His early childhood had been a livid nightmare, primarily because of the precocious cruelty of his two sisters. Shortly before his seventh birthday they forced him to take part in a game they called cocktail party. The game involved only one activity: the two little girls filled a glass with an unidentified liquid, and ordered George to drink. Afterward, dancing up and down in girlish glee, they said they had given him the compound.

George had seen the love stories on television; he knew how he was expected to act. He gave a good performance—better than his sisters realized, for inside his mind George was in turmoil. They had given him the compound (true, years before he should have taken it), and nothing had happened. He had felt absolutely nothing; he was immune! If anyone had ever found out, George would have been given a life sentence to the national hero's corps; or, more probably, the Morals Squad would have disposed of him altogether.

From that day on, George lived with guilt and fear. As the years passed, he several times stole capsules of the compound from his mother's love-cabinet and gulped them down. Sometimes he felt a little giddy, and once he was sick. But he experienced no reaction which could possibly be defined as love. Not that he had any idea what that reaction should have been, but he knew he was supposed to feel very wicked and he never did.

Each failure increased the agony of guilt; George drove himself to be far better behaved than he was required to be. He dreaded making one mistake. If his mother or a Director examined it too closely, they might find out his real secret.

George's basic education began when he was assigned to his confinement room above the garage after his tenth birthday. Thereafter his time was thoroughly regulated by law. Three hours a day he watched television; three hours he spent in his gym, building a magnificent—and salable—body; for four hours he listened to the educational tapes. Arithmetic, economics, salesmanship, business techniques, accounting, mechanics, practical science: the things he had to know in order to earn a satisfactory living for the woman who bought him in marriage.

He learned nothing else and as he grew older he became very conscious of the gaps in his education. For instance, what of the past? Had the world always been this sham he lived in? That question he had the good sense not to ask.

But George had learned enough from his lessons in practical science to guess what the compound really was, what it had to be: a mixture of aphrodisiacs and a habit-forming drug. The compound was calculated to stir up a man's desire to the point where he would give up anything in order to satisfy it. Boys were given increased doses during their adolescence; by the time they married, they were addicts, unable to leave the compound alone.

George couldn't prove his conclusion. He had no idea how many other men had followed the same line of reasoning and come up with the same answer. But why was George immune? There was only one way he could figure it: it must have happened because his sisters gave him the first draft when he was seven. But logically that didn't make much sense.

Bachelors were another sort of enemy: men who shirked their duty and deserted their wives. It seemed unreasonable to believe a man could desert his wife, when first he had to break himself of addiction to the compound. George had always supposed that bachelor was a boogy word contrived to frighten growing children.

As a consequence, he was very surprised when the house next door was raided. Through the window of his confinement cubicle, he actually saw the five gray-haired men who were rounded up by the Morals Squad. The Squad—heavily armed, six-foot Amazons—tried to question their captives. They used injections of a truth serum. Two of the old men died at once. The others went berserk, frothing at the mouth and screaming animal profanity until the Squad captain ordered them shot.

George overheard one of the women say, "It's always like this. They take something so our serum can't be effective."

Later that afternoon George found a scrap of paper in his mother's garden. It had blown out of the bonfire which the Morals Squad made of the papers they took out of the house next door. The burned page had apparently been part of an informational bulletin, compiled by the bachelors for distribution among themselves.

" . . . data compiled from old publications," the fragment began, "and interpreted by our most reliable authorities." At that point a part of the page was burned away. " . . . and perhaps less than ninety years ago men and women lived in equality. The evidence on that point is entirely conclusive. The present matriarchy evolved by accident, not design. Ninety years ago entertainment and advertising were exclusively directed at satisfying a woman's whim. No product was sold without some sort of tie-in with women. Fiction, drama, television, motion pictures—all glorified a romantic thing called love. In that same period business was in the process of taking over government from statesmen and politicians. Women, of course, were the stockholders who owned big business, although the directors and managers at that time were still men—operating under the illusion that they were the executives who represented ownership. In effect, however, women owned the country and women governed it; suddenly the matriarchy existed. There is no evidence that it was imposed; there is no suggestion of civil strife or . . . ." More words burned away. "However, the women were not unwilling to consolidate their gains. Consequently the popular cliches, the pretty romances, and the catchwords of advertising became a substitute for reality. As for the compound . . . ."

There the fragment ended. Much of it George did not understand. But it gave him a great deal of courage simply to know the bachelors actually existed. He began to plan his own escape to a bachelor hideout. He would have no opportunity, no freedom of any sort, until he married. Every boy was rigidly isolated in his confinement cubicle, under the watchful eye of his mother's spy-cameras, until he was bought in his first marriage.

Then, as he thought more about it, George realized there was a better way for him to use his immunity. He couldn't be sure of finding a bachelor hideout before the Morals Squad tracked him down. But George could force his bride to tell him where the compound was made, since he was not an addict and she could not use the compound to enslave him. Once he knew the location of the factory, he would destroy it. How, he wasn't sure; he didn't plan that far ahead. If the supply of the drug could be interrupted, many hundreds of men might be goaded into making a break for the hills.

*

The duty bell rang. George snapped to attention on the edge of his bunk. He saw his mother waving from the back door of her house.

"I'll be down right away, Mummy."

His mother was waiting for him in the pantry. Under the glaring overhead light he stopped for her last minute inspection. She used a pocket-stick to touch up a spot on his chest where the oil gleam had faded a little. And she gave him a glass of the compound to drink.

"Jenny really wants to marry you, George," she confided. "I know the symptoms; half our battle's won for us. And my former husband won't be around to worry us with his aches and pains. I made the trade this afternoon."

He followed her into the dining room where the cocktails were being served. Aside from the Harpers, George's mother had rented two handsome, muscular escorts for his sisters. In the confusion, George saw Jenny Harper's mother stealthily lace his water glass with a dose of the compound. He suppressed a grin. Apparently she was anxious to complete the deal, too.

George found it almost impossible to hold back hilarious laughter when Jenny herself shyly pressed a capsule of the compound into his hand and asked him to use it. Three full-size slugs of the drug! George wondered what would have happened if he hadn't been immune. Fortunately, he knew how to act the lusty, eager, drooling male which each of the women expected.

The negotiations moved along without a hitch. George's mother held out for twenty-eight thousand shares, and got it. The only problem left was the date for the wedding, and Jenny settled that very quickly. "I want my man, Mom," she said, "and I want him now."

Jenny always got what she wanted.

When she and her mother left that evening, she held George's hand in hers and whispered earnestly, "So they were married and lived happily ever after. That's the way it's going to be with us, isn't it, George?"

"It's up to you, Jenny; for as long as you want me."

That was the conventional answer which he was expected to make, but he saw unmasked disappointment in her face. She wanted something more genuine, with more of himself in it. He felt suddenly sorry for her, for the way he was going to use her. She was a pretty girl, even sweet and innocent—if those words still had any real meaning left after what his mother's world had done to them. Under other circumstances, George would have looked forward with keen pleasure to marrying Jenny. As it was, Jenny Harper was first a symbol of the fakery he intended to destroy, and after that a woman.

*

Five days later they were married. In spite of the short engagement, Mrs. Harper and George's mother managed to put on a splendid show in the church. George received a business sedan from his mother, the traditional gift given every bridegroom; and from Mrs. Harper he received a good job in a company where she was the majority stockholder. And so, in the customary pageantry and ceremony, George became Mr. Harper.

"Think of it—Mr. Harper," Jenny sighed, clinging to his arm. "Now you're really mine, George."

On the church steps the newlyweds posed for photographs—George in the plain, white trunks which symbolized a first marriage; Jenny in a dazzling cloud of fluff, suggestively nearly transparent. Then Mrs. Harper drew Jenny aside and whispered in her daughter's ear: the traditional telling of the secret. Now Jenny knew where the compound was manufactured; and for George revenge was within his grasp.

George's mother had arranged for their honeymoon at Memory Lodge, a resort not far from the Directorate capital in Hollywood. It was the national capital as well, though everyone conscientiously maintained the pretense that Washington, with an all-male Congress, still governed the country. George considered himself lucky that his mother had chosen Memory Lodge. He had already planned to desert Jenny in the mountains.

George knew how to drive; his mother had wanted him to do a great deal of chauffeuring for her. But he had never driven beyond town, and he had never driven anywhere alone. His mother gave him a map on which his route to the lodge was indicated in bright red. In the foothills George left the marked highway on a paved side road.

He gambled that Jenny wouldn't immediately realize what he had done, and the gamble paid off. Still wearing her nearly transparent wedding gown, she pressed close to him and ran her hands constantly over his naked chest, thoroughly satisfied with the man she had bought. In the church George had been given a tall glass of the compound; he acted the part Jenny expected.

But it was far less a role he played than George wanted to admit. His body sang with excitement. He found it very difficult to hold the excitement in check. If he had been addicted to the compound, it would have been out of the question. More than ever before he sympathized with the men who were enslaved by love. In spite of his own immunity, he nearly yielded to the sensuous appeal of her caress. He held the wheel so hard his knuckles went white; he clenched his teeth until his jaw ached.

All afternoon George drove aimless mountain roads, moving deeper into the uninhabited canyons. Carefully judging his distances with an eye on the map, he saw to it that he remained relatively close to the city; after he forced Jenny to give him the information he wanted, he wanted to be able to get out fast.

By dusk the roads he drove were no longer paved. Ruts carved deep by spring rains suggested long disuse. The swaying of the car and the constant grinding of gears eventually jolted Jenny out of her romantic dreams. She moved away from George and sat looking at the pines which met above the road.

"We're lost, aren't we?" she asked.

"What's that?" he shouted to be heard above the roar of the motor.

"Lost!"

For a minute or two longer he continued to drive until he saw an open space under the trees. He pulled the car into the clearing and snapped off the ignition. Then he looked Jenny full in the face and answered her. "No, Jenny, we aren't lost; I know exactly what I'm doing."

"Oh." He was sure she had understood him, but she said, "We can spend the night here and find the lodge in the morning. It's a pity we didn't bring something to eat." She smiled ingenuously. "But I brought the compound; and we have each other."

They got out of the car. Jenny looked up at the sunset, dull red above the trees, and shivered; she asked George to build a fire. He tucked the ignition key into the band of his white trunks and began to gather dry boughs and pine needles from the floor of the forest. He found several large branches and carried them back to the clearing. There was enough wood to last until morning—whether he stayed that long or not. Jenny had lugged the seats and a blanket out of the car and improvised a lean-to close to the fire.

He piled on two of the larger branches and the bright glow of flame lit their faces. She beckoned to him and gave him a bottle of the compound, watching bright-eyed as he emptied it.

With her lips parted, she waited. He did nothing. Slowly the light died in her eyes. Like a savage she flung herself into his arms. He steeled himself to show absolutely no reaction and finally she drew away. Trembling and with tears in her eyes, she whispered, "The compound doesn't—" The look of pain in her eyes turned to terror. "You're immune!"

"Now you know."

"But who told you—" She searched his face, shaking her head. "You don't know, do you—not really?"

"Know what?"

Instead of replying, she asked, "You brought me here deliberately, didn't you?"

"So we wouldn't be interrupted. You see, Jenny, you're going to tell me where the compound's made."

"It wouldn't do you any good. Don't you see—" He closed his hands on her wrists and jerked her rudely to her feet. He saw her face go white. And no wonder: that magnificent, granite hard body, which she had bought in good faith for her own pleasure, was suddenly out of her control. He grinned. He crushed her mouth against his and kissed her. Limp in his arms, she clung to him and said in a choked, husky whisper, "I love you, George."

"And you'll make any sacrifice for love," he replied, mocking the dialogue of the television love stories.

"Yes, anything!"

"Then tell me where the compound's manufactured."

"Hold me close, George; never let me go."

How many times had he heard that particular line! It sickened him, hearing it now from Jenny; he had expected something better of her. He pushed her from him. By accident his fist raked her face. She fell back blood trickling from her mouth. In her eyes he saw shock and a vague sense of pain; but both were overridden by adoration. She was like a whipped puppy, ready to lick his hand.

"I'll tell you, George," she whispered. "But don't leave me." She pulled herself to her feet and stood beside him, reaching for his hand. "We make it in Hollywood, in the Directorate Building, the part that used to be a sound stage."

"Thanks, Jenny." He picked up one of the car seats and walked back to the sedan. She stood motionless watching him. He fitted the seat in place and put the key in the lock. The starter ground away, but the motor did not turn over.

He glanced back at Jenny. She was smiling inscrutably, "You see, George, you have to stay with me."

He got out of the car and moved toward her.

"I was afraid you were planning to desert me," she went on, "so I took out the distributor cap while you were getting the firewood."

He stood in front of her. Coldly he demanded, "Where did you put it, Jenny?"

She tilted her lips toward his. "Kiss and tell—maybe."

"I haven't time for games. Where is it?"

His fist shot out. Jenny sprawled on the ground at his feet. Again he saw the pain and the adoration in her face. But that couldn't be right. She would hate him by this time.

He yanked her to her feet. Her lips were still bleeding and blood came now from a wound in her cheek. Yet she managed to smile again.

"I don't want to hurt you, Jenny," he told her. "But I have to have—"

"I love you, George. I never thought I'd want to give myself to a man. All the buying doesn't make any difference, does it? Not really. And I never knew that before!"

With an unconscious movement, she kicked her train aside and he saw the distributor cap lying beneath it. He picked it up. She flung herself at him screaming. He felt the hammer beat of her heart; her fingers dug into his back like cat claws. Now it didn't matter. He had the secret; he could go whenever he wanted to. Nonetheless he pushed her away—tenderly, and with regret. To surrender like this was no better than a capitulation to the compound. It was instinctively important to make her understand that. He knew that much, but his emotions were churned too close to fever pitch for him to reason out what else that implied.

He clipped her neatly on the jaw and put her unconscious body on the ground by the fire. He left the map with her so she could find her way out in the morning; he knew it was really a very short hike to a highway, where she would be picked up by a passing car or truck.

*

He drove out the way he had come in—at least he tried to remember. Four times he took a wrong turn and had to backtrack. It was, therefore, dawn before he reached the outskirts of Hollywood. In any other city he would not have been conspicuous—simply a man on his way to work; only women slept late. However, Hollywood was off-limits to every male. The city was not only the seat of the Directorate, but the manufacturing center for the cosmetics industry. And since that gave women her charm, it was a business no man worked at.

George had to have a disguise. He stopped on a residential street, where the people were still likely to be in their beds. He read names on mail boxes until he found a house where an unmarried woman lived. He had no way of knowing if she had a husband on approval with her, but the box was marked "Miss." With any luck he might have got what he wanted without disturbing her, but the woman was a light sleeper and she caught him as he was putting on the dress. He was sorry he had to slug her, but she gave him no resistance. A spark of hope, a spark of long-forgotten youth glowed in her eyes; before she slid into unconsciousness.

Wearing the stolen dress, which fit him like a tent, and an enormous hat to hide his face, George parked his sedan near the Directorate and entered the building when it opened at eight. In room after room automatons demonstrated how to dress correctly; robot faces displayed the uses of cosmetics. There were displays of kitchen gadgets, appliances, and other heavy machinery for the home; recorded lectures on stock management and market control. Here women came from every part of the country for advice, help and guidance. Here the Top Directors met to plan business policy, to govern the nation, and to supervise the production of the compound. For only the Top Directors—less than a dozen women—actually knew the formula. Like their stockholdings, the secret was hereditary, passed from mother to daughter.

George searched every floor of the building, but found nothing except exhibit rooms. Time passed, and still he did not find what he had come for. More and more women crowded in to see the exhibits. Several times he found new-comers examining him oddly; he found he had to avoid the crowds.

Eventually he went down steps into the basement, though a door marked "Keep Out." The door was neither locked nor guarded, but there was a remote chance it might lead to the production center for the compound. In the basement George found a mechanical operation underway; at first he took it for another cosmetic exhibit. Conveyor belts delivered barrels of flavoring syrup, alcohol and a widely advertised liquid vitamin compound. Machines sliced open the containers, dumping the contents into huge vats, from which pipes emptied the mixture into passing rows of bottles.

The bottles: suddenly George recognized them and the truth dawned on him, sickeningly. Here was the manufacturing center for the compound—but it might just as well have been a barn in Connecticut or a store window in Manhattan. No man was enslaved by the compound, for the compound did not exist. He was imprisoned by his own sense of guilt, his own fear of being different. George remembered his own fear and guilt: he knew how much a man could be driven to make himself conform to what he thought other men were like.

His revenge was as foolish as the sham he wanted to destroy. He should have reasoned that out long ago; he should have realized it was impossible to have immunity to an addictive drug. But, no, George believed what he saw on the television programs. He was victimized as much as any man had ever been.

He turned blindly toward the stairway, and from the shadows in the hall the Morals Squad closed in around him. With a final gesture of defiance, he ripped off the stolen dress and the absurd hat, and stood waiting for the blast from their guns. An old woman, wearing the shoulder insignia of a Top Director, pushed through the squad and faced him, a revolver in her hand. She was neither angry nor disturbed. Her voice, when she spoke, was filled with pity. Pity! That was the final indignity.

"Now you know the truth," she said. "A few men always have to try it; and we usually let them see this room and find out for themselves before—before we close the case."

Tensely he demanded, "Just how much longer do you think—"

"We can get away with this? As long as men are human beings. It's easier to make yourself believe a lie if you think everyone else believes it, than to believe a truth you've found out on your own. All of us want more than anything else to be like other people. Women have created a world for you with television programs; you grow up observing nothing else; you make yourself fit into the pattern. Only a few independent-minded characters have the courage to accept their own immunity; most of them end up here, trying to do something noble for the rest of mankind. But you have one satisfaction, for what it's worth: you've been true to yourself."

True to yourself. George found a strange comfort in the words, and his fear was gone. He squared his shoulders and faced the mouth of her gun. *True to yourself*: that was something worth dying for.

He saw a flicker of emotion in the old woman's eyes. Admiration? He couldn't be sure. For at the moment a shot rang out from the end of the corridor; and the Top Director fell back, nursing a hand suddenly bright with blood.

"Let him go." It was Jenny's voice. She was sheltered by a partly open door at the foot of the stairway.

"Don't be a fool," the old woman replied. "He's seen too much."

"It doesn't matter. Who would believe him?"

"You're upset. You don't realize—"

"He's mine and I want him."

"The Directorate will give you a refund of the purchase price."

"You didn't understand me. I don't want one of your pretty automatons; anybody can buy them for a few shares of stock. I want a man—a real man; I want to belong to him."

"He belongs to you; you bought him."

"And that's what's wrong. We really belong to each other."

The old woman glanced at George and he saw the same flicker of feeling in her eyes. And tears, tears of regret. Why? "We have you outnumbered," the old woman said quietly to Jenny.

"I don't care. I have a gun; I'll use it as long as I'm able."

The Morals Squad raised their weapons. The Director shook her head imperiously and they snapped to attention again. "If you take him from us," she called out to Jenny, "you'll be outlawed. We'll hunt you down, if we can."

"I want him," Jenny persisted. "I don't care about the rest of it."

The old woman nodded to George. He couldn't believe that she meant it. The Director was on her home ground, in her headquarters building, backed by an armed squad of stone-faced Amazons. She had no reason to let him go.

She walked beside him as he moved down the hall. When they were twenty feet from the guard, she closed her thin hand on his arm; her eyes swam with tears and she whispered, "There truly is a love potion. Not this nonsense we bottle here, but something real and very worthwhile. You and this girl have found it. I know that, from the way she talks. She doesn't say anything about ownership, and that's as it should be. As it has to be, for any of us to be happy. Hold tight to that all the rest of your life. Don't ever believe in words; don't fall for any more love stories; believe what you feel deep inside—what you know yourself to be true.

"You men who learn how to break away are our only hope, too. Most of us don't see that yet. I do; I know what it used to be like. Someday there may be enough men with the stamina to take back the place of dominance that we stole from them. We thought we wanted it; for decades before we had been screaming about women's rights." Her thin lips twisted in a sneer and she spat her disgust. "Finally we took what we wanted, and it turned to ashes in our hands. We made our men playthings; we made them slaves. And after that they weren't men any more. But what we stole isn't the sort of thing you can hand back on a silver platter; you men have to get enough courage to take it away from us."

Her grip tightened on his arm. "There's a fire door at the end of the hall; if you push the emergency button, you'll close it. That will give you a five or ten minute start. I can't help you any more . . . ."

They were abreast of Jenny. She seized Jenny's hand and thrust it into his. "Beat it, kids; there's a bachelor camp on the north ridge. You can make it.

"And from here on in, what he says goes," the old woman added. "Don't forget that."

"She won't," George answered, supremely self-assured.

He took Jenny's arm and, turning abruptly, they made their break for freedom. The Director managed to remain standing in the middle of the corridor, making a dangerous target of herself so that none of the Morals Squad could risk a shot at the fugitives. As the fire door clanged shut George looked back. He saw the old woman's lips moving in silent prayer.

NAVY DAY

by Harry Harrison

*The Army had a new theme song: "Anything you can do, we can do better!" And they meant*anything, *including up-to-date hornpipes!*

GENERAL WINGROVE looked at the rows of faces without seeing them. His vision went beyond the Congress of the United States, past the balmy June day to another day that was coming. A day when the Army would have its destined place of authority.

He drew a deep breath and delivered what was perhaps the shortest speech ever heard in the hallowed halls of Congress:

"The General Staff of the U.S. Army requests Congress to abolish the archaic branch of the armed forces known as the U.S. Navy."

The aging Senator from Georgia checked his hearing aid to see if it was in operating order, while the press box emptied itself in one concerted rush and a clatter of running feet that died off in the direction of the telephone room. A buzz of excited comment ran through the giant chamber. One by one the heads turned to face the Naval section where rows of blue figures stirred and buzzed like smoked-out bees. The knot of men around a paunchy figure heavy with gold braid broke up and Admiral Fitzjames climbed slowly to his feet.

Lesser men have quailed before that piercing stare, but General Wingrove was never the lesser man. The admiral tossed his head with disgust, every line of his body denoting outraged dignity. He turned to his audience, a small pulse beating in his forehead.

"I cannot comprehend the general's attitude, nor can I understand why he has attacked the Navy in this unwarranted fashion. The Navy has existed and will always exist as the first barrier of American defense. I ask you, gentlemen, to ignore this request as you would ignore the statements of any person . . . er, slightly demented. I should like to offer a recommendation that the general's sanity be investigated, and an inquiry be made as to the mental health of anyone else connected with this preposterous proposal!"

The general smiled calmly. "I understand, Admiral, and really don't blame you for being slightly annoyed. But, please let us not bring this issue of national importance down to a shallow personal level. The Army has facts to back up this request—facts that shall be demonstrated tomorrow morning."

Turning his back on the raging admiral, General Wingrove included all the assembled solons in one sweeping gesture.

"Reserve your judgment until that time, gentlemen, make no hasty judgments until you have seen the force of argument with which we back up our request. It is the end of an era. In the morning the Navy joins its fellow fossils, the dodo and the brontosaurus."

The admiral's blood pressure mounted to a new record and the gentle thud of his unconscious body striking the floor was the only sound to break the shocked silence of the giant hall.

*

THE EARLY morning sun warmed the white marble of the Jefferson Memorial and glinted from the soldiers' helmets and the roofs of the packed cars that crowded forward in a slow-moving stream. All the gentlemen of Congress were there, the passage of their cars cleared by the screaming sirens of motorcycle policemen. Around and under the wheels of the official cars pressed a solid wave of government workers and common citizens of the capital city. The trucks of the radio and television services pressed close, microphones and cameras extended.

The stage was set for a great day. Neat rows of olive drab vehicles curved along the water's edge. Jeeps and half-tracks shouldered close by weapons carriers and six-bys, all of them shrinking to insignificance beside the looming Patton tanks. A speakers' platform was set up in the center of the line, near the audience.

At precisely 10 a.m., General Wingrove stepped forward and scowled at the crowd until they settled into an uncomfortable silence. His speech was short and consisted of nothing more than amplifications of his opening statement that actions speak louder than words. He pointed to the first truck in line, a 2½-ton filled with an infantry squad sitting stiffly at attention.

The driver caught the signal and kicked the engine into life; with a grind of gears it moved forward toward the river's edge. There was an indrawn gasp from the crowd as the front wheels ground over the marble parapet—then the truck was plunging down toward the muddy waters of the Potomac.

The wheels touched the water and the surface seemed to sink while taking on a strange glassy character. The truck roared into high gear and rode forward on the surface of the water surrounded by a saucer-shaped depression. It parked two hundred yards off shore and the soldiers, goaded by the sergeant's bark, leapt out and lined up with a showy *present arms*.

The general returned the salute and waved to the remaining vehicles. They moved forward in a series of maneuvers that indicated a great number of rehearsal hours on some hidden pond. The tanks rumbled slowly over the water while the jeeps cut back and forth through their lines in intricate patterns. The trucks backed and turned like puffing ballerinas.

The audience was rooted in a hushed silence, their eyeballs bulging. They continued to watch the amazing display as General Wingrove spoke again:

"You see before you a typical example of Army ingenuity, developed in Army laboratories. These motor units are supported on the surface of the water by an intensifying of the surface tension in their immediate area. Their weight is evenly distributed over the surface, causing the shallow depressions you see around them.

"This remarkable feat has been accomplished by the use of the *Dornifier*. A remarkable invention that is named after that brilliant scientist, Colonel Robert A. Dorn, Commander of the Brooke Point Experimental Laboratory. It was there that one of the civilian employees discovered the Dorn effect—under the Colonel's constant guidance, of course.

"Utilizing this invention the Army now becomes master of the sea as well as the land. Army convoys of trucks and tanks can blanket the world. The surface of the water is our highway, our motor park, our battleground—the airfield and runway for our planes."

Mechanics were pushing a Shooting Star onto the water. They stepped clear as flame gushed from the tail pipe; with the familiar whooshing rumble it sped down the Potomac and hurled itself into the air.

"When this cheap and simple method of crossing oceans is adopted, it will of course mean the end of that fantastic medieval anachronism, the Navy. No need for billion-dollar aircraft carriers, battleships, drydocks and all the other cumbersome junk that keeps those boats and things afloat. Give the taxpayer back his hard-earned dollar!"

Teeth grated in the Naval section as carriers and battleships were called "boats" and the rest of America's sea might lumped under the casual heading of "things." Lips were curled at the transparent appeal to the taxpayer's pocketbook. But with leaden hearts they knew that all this justified wrath and contempt would avail them nothing. This was Army Day with a vengeance, and the doom of the Navy seemed inescapable.

The Army had made elaborate plans for what they called "Operation Sinker." Even as the general spoke the publicity mills ground into high gear. From coast to coast the citizens absorbed the news with their morning nourishment.

" . . . Agnes, you hear what the radio said! The Army's gonna give a trip around the world in a B-36 as first prize in this limerick contest. All you have to do is fill in the last line, and mail one copy to the Pentagon and the other to the Navy . . ."

The Naval mail room had standing orders to burn all the limericks when they came in, but some of the newer men seemed to think the entire thing was a big joke. Commander Bullman found one in the mess hall:

The Army will always be there,On the land, on the sea, in the air.So why should the NavyTake all of the gravy . . .

to which a seagoing scribe had added:

And not give us ensigns our share?

The newspapers were filled daily with photographs of mighty B-36's landing on Lake Erie, and grinning soldiers making mock beachhead attacks on Coney Island. Each man wore a buzzing black box at his waist and walked on the bosom of the now quiet Atlantic like a biblical prophet.

Radio and television also carried the thousands of news releases that poured in an unending flow from the Pentagon Building. Cards, letters, telegrams and packages descended on Washington in an overwhelming torrent. The Navy Department was the unhappy recipient of deprecatory letters and a vast quantity of little cardboard battleships.

The people spoke and their representatives listened closely. This was an election year. There didn't seem to be much doubt as to the decision, particularly when the reduction in the budget was considered.

It took Congress only two months to make up its collective mind. The people were all pro-Army. The novelty of the idea had fired their imaginations.

They were about to take the final vote in the lower house. If the amendment passed it would go to the states for ratification, and their votes were certain to follow that of Congress. The Navy had fought a last-ditch battle to no avail. The balloting was going to be pretty much of a sure thing—the wet water Navy would soon become ancient history.

For some reason the admirals didn't look as unhappy as they should.

*

THE NAVAL Department had requested one last opportunity to address the Congress. Congress had patronizingly granted permission, for even the doomed man is allowed one last speech. Admiral Fitzjames, who had recovered from his choleric attack, was the appointed speaker.

"Gentlemen of the Congress of the United States. We in the Navy have a fighting tradition. We 'damn the torpedoes' and sail straight ahead into the enemy's fire if that is necessary. We have been stabbed in the back—we have suffered a second Pearl Harbor sneak attack! The Army relinquished its rights to fair treatment with this attack. Therefore we are *counter-attacking*!" Worn out by his attacking and mixed metaphors, the Admiral mopped his brow.

"Our laboratories have been working night and day on the perfection of a device we hoped we would never be forced to use. It is now in operation, having passed the final trials a few days ago.

"The significance of this device *cannot* be underestimated. We are so positive of its importance that—we are *demanding* that the *Army* be abolished!"

He waved his hand toward the window and bellowed one word.

"LOOK!"

Everyone looked. They blinked and looked again. They rubbed their eyes and kept looking.

Sailing majestically up the middle of Constitution Avenue was the battleship Missouri.

The Admiral's voice rang through the room like a trumpet of victory.

"The Mark-1 Debinder, as you see, temporarily lessens the binding energies that hold molecules of solid matter together. Solids become liquids, and a ship equipped with this device can sail anywhere in the world—on sea *or* land. Take your vote, gentlemen; the world awaits your decision."

THE ANGLERS OF ARZ

by Roger Dee

In order to make Izaak Walton's sport complete, there must be an angler, a fish, and some bait. All three existed on Arz but there was a question as to which was which.

The third night of the *Marco Four's* landfall on the moonless Altarian planet was a repetition of the two before it, a nine-hour intermission of drowsy, pastoral peace. Navigator Arthur Farrell—it was his turn to stand watch—was sitting at an open-side port with a magnoscanner ready; but in spite of his vigilance he had not exposed a film when the inevitable pre-dawn rainbow began to shimmer over the eastern ocean.

Sunrise brought him alert with a jerk, frowning at sight of two pinkish, bipedal Arzian fishermen posted on the tiny coral islet a quarter-mile offshore, their blank triangular faces turned stolidly toward the beach.

"They're at it again," Farrell called, and dropped to the mossy turf outside. "Roll out on the double! I'm going to magnofilm this!"

Stryker and Gibson came out of their sleeping cubicles reluctantly, belting on the loose shorts which all three wore in the balmy Arzian climate. Stryker blinked and yawned as he let himself through the port, his fringe of white hair tousled and his naked paunch sweating. He looked, Farrell thought for the thousandth time, more like a retired cook than like the veteran commander of a Terran Colonies expedition.

Gibson followed, stretching his powerfully-muscled body like a wrestler to throw off the effects of sleep. Gibson was linguist-ethnologist of the crew, a blocky man in his early thirties with thick black hair and heavy brows that shaded a square, humorless face.

"Any sign of the squids yet?" he asked.

"They won't show up until the dragons come," Farrell said. He adjusted the light filter of the magnoscanner and scowled at Stryker. "Lee, I wish you'd let me break up the show this time with a dis-beam. This butchery gets on my nerves."

Stryker shielded his eyes with his hands against the glare of sun on water. "You know I can't do that, Arthur. These Arzians may turn out to be Fifth Order beings or higher, and under Terran Regulations our tampering with what may be a basic culture-pattern would amount to armed invasion. We'll have to crack that cackle-and-grunt language of theirs and learn something of their mores before we can interfere."

Farrell turned an irritable stare on the incurious group of Arzians gathering, nets and fishing spears in hand, at the edge of the sheltering bramble forest.

"What stumps me is their motivation," he said. "Why do the fools go out to that islet every night, when they must know damned well what will happen next morning?"

Gibson answered him with an older problem, his square face puzzled. "For that matter, what became of the city I saw when we came in through the stratosphere? It must be a tremendous thing, yet we've searched the entire globe in the scouter and found nothing but water and a scattering of little islands like this one, all covered with bramble. It wasn't a city these pink fishers could have built, either. The architecture was beyond them by a million years."

*

Stryker and Farrell traded baffled looks. The city had become something of a fixation with Gibson, and his dogged insistence—coupled with an irritating habit of being right—had worn their patience thin.

"There never was a city here, Gib," Stryker said. "You dozed off while we were making planetfall, that's all."

Gibson stiffened resentfully, but Farrell's voice cut his protest short. "Get set! Here they come!"

Out of the morning rainbow dropped a swarm of winged lizards, twenty feet in length and a glistening chlorophyll green in the early light. They stooped like hawks upon the islet offshore, burying the two Arzian fishers instantly under their snapping, threshing bodies. Then around the outcrop the sea boiled whitely, churned to foam by a sudden uprushing of black, octopoid shapes.

"The squids," Stryker grunted. "Right on schedule. Two seconds too late, as usual, to stop the slaughter."

A barrage of barbed tentacles lashed out of the foam and drove into the melee of winged lizards. The lizards took the air at once, leaving behind three of their number who disappeared under the surface like harpooned seals. No trace remained of the two Arzian natives.

"A neat example of dog eat dog," Farrell said, snapping off the magnoscanner. "Do any of those beauties look like city-builders, Gib?"

Chattering pink natives straggled past from the shelter of the thorn forest, ignoring the Earthmen, and lined the casting ledges along the beach to begin their day's fishing.

"Nothing we've seen yet could have built that city," Gibson said stubbornly. "But it's here somewhere, and I'm going to find it. Will either of you be using the scouter today?"

Stryker threw up his hands. "I've a mountain of data to collate, and Arthur is off duty after standing watch last night. Help yourself, but you won't find anything."

*

The scouter was a speeding dot on the horizon when Farrell crawled into his sleeping cubicle a short time later, leaving Stryker to mutter over his litter of notes. Sleep did not come to him at once; a vague sense of something overlooked prodded irritatingly at the back of his consciousness, but it was not until drowsiness had finally overtaken him that the discrepancy assumed definite form.

He recalled then that on the first day of the *Marco's* planetfall one of the pink fishers had fallen from a casting ledge into the water, and had all but drowned before his fellows pulled him out with extended spear-shafts. Which meant that the fishers could not swim, else some would surely have gone in after him.

And the Marco's crew had explored Arz exhaustively without finding any slightest trace of boats or of boat landings. The train of association completed itself with automatic logic, almost rousing Farrell out of his doze.

"I'll be damned," he muttered. "No boats, and they don't swim. *Then how the devil do they get out to that islet?*"

He fell asleep with the paradox unresolved.

*

Stryker was still humped over his records when Farrell came out of his cubicle and broke a packaged meal from the food locker. The visicom over the control board hummed softly, its screen blank on open channel.

"Gibson found his lost city yet?" Farrell asked, and grinned when Stryker snorted.

"He's scouring the daylight side now," Stryker said. "Arthur, I'm going to ground Gib tomorrow, much as I dislike giving him a direct order. He's got that phantom city on the brain, and he lacks the imagination to understand how dangerous to our assignment an obsession of that sort can be."

Farrell shrugged. "I'd agree with you offhand if it weren't for Gib's bullheaded habit of being right. I hope he finds it soon, if it's here. I'll probably be standing his watch until he's satisfied."

Stryker looked relieved. "Would you mind taking it tonight? I'm completely bushed after today's logging."

Farrell waved a hand and took up his magnoscanner. It was dark outside already, the close, soft night of a moonless tropical world whose moist atmosphere absorbed even starlight. He dragged a chair to the open port and packed his pipe, settling himself comfortably while Stryker mixed a nightcap before turning in.

Later he remembered that Stryker dissolved a tablet in his glass, but at the moment it meant nothing. In a matter of minutes the older man's snoring drifted to him, a sound faintly irritating against the velvety hush outside.

Farrell lit his pipe and turned to the inconsistencies he had uncovered. The Arzians did not swim, and without boats . . . .

It occurred to him then that there had been two of the pink fishers on the islet each morning, and the coincidence made him sit up suddenly, startled. Why two? Why not three or four, or only one?

He stepped out through the open lock and paced restlessly up and down on the springy turf, feeling the ocean breeze soft on his face. Three days of dull routine logwork had built up a need for physical action that chafed his temper; he was intrigued and at the same time annoyed by the enigmatic relation that linked the Arzian fishers to the dragons and squids, and his desire to understand that relation was aggravated by the knowledge that Arz could be a perfect world for Terran colonization. That is, he thought wryly, if Terran colonists could stomach the weird custom pursued by its natives of committing suicide in pairs.

He went over again the improbable drama of the past three mornings, and found it not too unnatural until he came to the motivation and the means of transportation that placed the Arzians in pairs on the islet, when his whole fabric of speculation fell into a tangled snarl of inconsistencies. He gave it up finally; how could any Earthman rationalize the outlandish compulsions that actuated so alien a race?

He went inside again, and the sound of Stryker's muffled snoring fanned his restlessness. He made his decision abruptly, laying aside the magnoscanner for a hand-flash and a pocket-sized audicom unit which he clipped to the belt of his shorts.

He did not choose a weapon because he saw no need for one. The torch would show him how the natives reached the outcrop, and if he should need help the audicom would summon

Stryker. Investigating without Stryker's sanction was, strictly speaking, a breach of Terran Regulations, but—

"Damn Terran Regulations," he muttered. "I've got to *know*."

Farrell snapped on the torch at the edge of the thorn forest and entered briskly, eager for action now that he had begun. Just inside the edge of the bramble he came upon a pair of Arzians curled up together on the mossy ground, sleeping soundly, their triangular faces wholly blank and unrevealing.

He worked deeper into the underbrush and found other sleeping couples, but nothing else. There were no humming insects, no twittering night-birds or scurrying rodents. He had worked his way close to the center of the island without further discovery and was on the point of turning back, disgusted, when something bulky and powerful seized him from behind.

A sharp sting burned his shoulder, wasp-like, and a sudden overwhelming lassitude swept him into a darkness deeper than the Arzian night. His last conscious thought was not of his own danger, but of Stryker—asleep and unprotected behind the *Marco's* open port . . . .

*

He was standing erect when he woke, his back to the open sea and a prismatic glimmer of early-dawn rainbow shining on the water before him. For a moment he was totally disoriented; then from the corner of an eye he caught the pinkish blur of an Arzian fisher standing beside him, and cried out hoarsely in sudden panic when he tried to turn his head and could not.

He was on the coral outcropping offshore, and except for the involuntary muscles of balance and respiration his body was paralyzed.

The first red glow of sunrise blurred the reflected rainbow at his feet, but for some seconds his shuttling mind was too busy to consider the danger of predicament. *Whatever brought me here anesthetized me first*, he thought. *That sting in my shoulder was like a hypo needle.*

Panic seized him again when he remembered the green flying-lizards; more seconds passed before he gained control of himself, sweating with the effort. He had to get help. If he could switch on the audicom at his belt and call Stryker . . . .

He bent every ounce of his will toward raising his right hand, and failed.

His arm was like a limb of lead, its inertia too great to budge. He relaxed the effort with a groan, sweating again when he saw a fiery half-disk of sun on the water, edges blurred and distorted by tiny surface ripples.

On shore he could see the *Marco Four* resting between thorn forest and beach, its silvered sides glistening with dew. The port was still open, and the empty carrier rack in the bow told him that Gibson had not yet returned with the scouter.

He grew aware then that sensation was returning to him slowly, that the cold surface of the audicom unit at his hip—unfelt before—was pressing against the inner curve of his elbow. He bent his will again toward motion; this time the arm tensed a little, enough to send hope flaring through him. If he could put pressure enough against the stud . . . .

The tiny click of its engaging sent him faint with relief.

"Stryker!" he yelled. "Lee, roll out—*Stryker!*"

The audicom hummed gently, without answer.

He gathered himself for another shout, and recalled with a chill of horror the tablet Stryker had mixed into his nightcap the night before. Worn out by his work, Stryker had made certain that he would not be easily disturbed.

The flattened sun-disk on the water brightened and grew rounder. Above its reflected glare he caught a flicker of movement, a restless suggestion of flapping wings.

*

He tried again. "Stryker, help me! I'm on the islet!"

The audicom crackled. The voice that answered was not Stryker's, but Gibson's.

"Farrell! What the devil are you doing on that butcher's block?"

Farrell fought down an insane desire to laugh. "Never mind that—get here fast, Gib! The flying-lizards—"

He broke off, seeing for the first time the octopods that ringed the outcrop just under the surface of the water, waiting with barbed tentacles spread and yellow eyes studying him glassily. He heard the unmistakable flapping of wings behind and above him then, and thought with shock-born lucidity: *I wanted a backstage look at this show, and now I'm one of the cast.*

The scouter roared in from the west across the thorn forest, flashing so close above his head that he felt the wind of its passage. Almost instantly he heard the shrilling blast of its emergency bow jets as Gibson met the lizard swarm head on.

Gibson's voice came tinnily from the audicom. "Scattered them for the moment, Arthur—blinded the whole crew with the exhaust, I think. Stand fast, now. I'm going to pick you up."

The scouter settled on the outcrop beside Farrell, so close that the hot wash of its exhaust gases scorched his bare legs. Gibson put out thick brown arms and hauled him inside like a straw man, ignoring the native. The scouter darted for shore with Farrell lying across Gibson's knees in the cockpit, his head hanging half overside.

Farrell had a last dizzy glimpse of the islet against the rush of green water below, and felt his shaky laugh of relief stick in his throat. Two of the octopods were swimming strongly for shore, holding the rigid Arzian native carefully above water between them.

"Gib," Farrell croaked. "Gib, can you risk a look back? I think I've gone mad."

The scouter swerved briefly as Gibson looked back. "You're all right, Arthur. Just hang on tight. I'll explain everything when we get you safe in the *Marco*."

Farrell forced himself to relax, more relieved than alarmed by the painful pricking of returning sensation. "I might have known it, damn you," he said. "You found your lost city, didn't you?"

Gibson sounded a little disgusted, as if he were still angry with himself over some private stupidity. "I'd have found it sooner if I'd had any brains. It was under water, of course."

*

In the *Marco Four*, Gibson routed Stryker out of his cubicle and mixed drinks around, leaving Farrell comfortably relaxed in the padded control chair. The paralysis was still wearing off slowly, easing Farrell's fear of being permanently disabled.

"We never saw the city from the scouter because we didn't go high enough," Gibson said. "I realized that finally, remembering how they used high-altitude blimps during the First Wars to spot submarines, and when I took the scouter up far enough there it was, at the ocean bottom—a city to compare with anything men ever built."

Stryker stared. "A marine city? What use would sea-creatures have for buildings?"

"None," Gibson said. "I think the city must have been built ages ago—by men or by a manlike race, judging from the architecture—and was submerged later by a sinking of land masses that killed off the original builders and left Arz nothing but an oversized archipelago. The squids took over then, and from all appearances they've developed a culture of their own."

"I don't see it," Stryker complained, shaking his head. "The pink fishers—"

"Are cattle, or less," Gibson finished. "The octopods are the dominant race, and they're so far above Fifth Order that we're completely out of bounds here. Under Terran Regulations we can't colonize Arz. It would be armed invasion."

"Invasion of a squid world?" Farrell protested, baffled. "Why should surface colonization conflict with an undersea culture, Gib? Why couldn't we share the planet?"

"Because the octopods own the islands too, and keep them policed," Gibson said patiently. "They even own the pink fishers. It was one of the squid-people, making a dry-land canvass of his preserve here to pick a couple of victims for this morning's show, that carried you off last night."

"Behold a familiar pattern shaping up," Stryker said. He laughed suddenly, a great irrepressible bellow of sound. "Arz is a squid's world, Arthur, don't you see? And like most civilized peoples, they're sportsmen. The flying-lizards are the game they hunt, and they raise the pink fishers for—"

Farrell swore in astonishment. "Then those poor devils are put out there deliberately, like worms on a hook—angling in reverse! No wonder I couldn't spot their motivation!"

Gibson got up and sealed the port, shutting out the soft morning breeze. "Colonization being out of the question, we may as well move on before the octopods get curious enough about us to make trouble. Do you feel up to the acceleration, Arthur?"

Farrell and Stryker looked at each other, grinning. Farrell said: "You don't think I want to stick here and be used for bait again, do you?"

He and Stryker were still grinning over it when Gibson, unamused, blasted the *Marco Four* free of Arz.

SINISTER PARADISE

by Robert Moore Williams

It was like a mirage in reverse, this strange island off the California coast—it couldn't always be seen, but it was there—in Time.

"There's the island, Parker!" Retch called.

Bill Parker shifted the controls of the 'copter and the big craft swung in the direction Retch was pointing. Squinting his eyes against the sun glare rising from the Pacific, Parker clearly saw the island. It was miles away as yet but it swam like a mirage suspended just above the surface of the sea.

The island was not large—Parker guessed it as probably being less than two miles in circumference—but he could make out a fringe of trees along the shore and a central peak rising like a cliff in the center.

"I've found it again!" Retch spoke with fierce satisfaction—clenched fists. Parker heard the indrawn hiss of breath following the words; a hiss that seemed to hold a promise for the future. Revenge, vengeance, triumph, or something else? Parker could not determine what emotional overtone had found expression in Retch's words. But the emotional overtone was there. Out of the corner of his eyes, Parker glanced at the man sitting in the seat next to him. What he saw did not please him.

Retch was big. He had the muscular build of a prize fighter. The scar over his left cheekbone did not add to the attractiveness of his appearance. He did not, in Parker's opinion, look like the scientist he had claimed to be.

Parker shrugged such thoughts aside. What difference did it make what Retch was, or the nature of his business here? He had paid charter charges on the big helicopter.

"There it is, Parker!" Retch almost screamed the words. As he pointed again toward the island in the far distance, Parker caught a glimpse of a pistol in a shoulder holster under the man's arm.

The sight of the gun caused a split second of alarm in the big pilot. He had not known that Retch was armed. Then the alarm subsided. Parker pressed his left arm down against his body, assuring himself that his own gun was where it belonged.

The woman, Mercedes Valdar, seemed to catch some of Retch's excitement. She leaned forward across Retch's shoulder to stare at the island. Parker caught another whiff of the musky perfume that she used. He noticed again what he had realized the first time he met her—that in any man's language she was a beauty. Aquiline face, smouldering black eyes, high cheek bones, a delicate brown complexion that hinted at Indian blood back several generations in the past, she looked like something out of an exotic movie. The slacks and sport coat that she wore accentuated the fact that she was a woman.

Parker was aware again of the enigma of her presence. Retch had introduced her as his secretary. Parker, accepting the man's statement, had asked no questions. Asking questions in a matter such as this was a fine way to get a bust in the snoot.

"It ees the island!" Her whisper was sharp. A glow appeared on her face. "Soon we will be reech!" She slapped Parker heartily on the shoulder. "Beel, is not that wonderful!"

"It sure is," Parker answered. He was as astonished by the statement as he was by the slap on the shoulder.

"Shut up, Mercedes!" Retch spoke. "Parker, turn some juice into this thing."

"She's cruising at about her best speed," Parker answered.

"Then get her faster than cruising speed. We've found the island." His manner indicated that finding the island was very important but that something else perhaps of equal importance remained to be done.

"What's the big rush!" Parker countered. "You don't think it will vanish before we get there, do you?"

A startled look appeared on Retch's face. "No, of course not. That is—"

A thudding jar went through the ship.

"What 'appened?" Mercedes screamed in fear.

With a snarling crash of breaking metal, one of the helicopter blades was yanked from its mounting above them.

Parker had the dazed impression that he saw the big blade jerked away through the air. Then, like a leaf suddenly caught in a violent hurricane, the helicopter began to turn flip-flops in the air.

"Do somesing!" Mercedes cried.

As the ship jumped and began to yaw, she was thrown across the cabin. Jerking, buckling, jumping, twisting, the big helicopter lurched its way toward the surface of the sea below. Cutting the power, Parker leaped from his seat. He knew what was going to happen. He intended to try and be ready for it.

*

Retch, gripping his seat with both hands, yelled. "We're falling!"

"It's not news to me," Parker answered, jerking open the door to the compartment at the rear. Inside that compartment was a mass of synthetic fabric. Tossed to the surface of the sea, inflated by the self-contained flask of gas under pressure, it would make a rubber raft.

"You've left the controls!" Retch barked. "Do something to stop us. We're going to fall." The man's face was wild with fear as he twisted his head around to see what Parker was doing.

"You damned right I've left the controls!" Parker answered. "We've lost the equivalent of a wing in an ordinary plane. If you know any way to stop a plane from falling you tell me." Working with deft, sure hands, he pulled the mass of synthetic fabric out of its compartment.

"But we've got to get to that island. We've found it. We've got to get there while—"

"If we get there, we'll have to swim," Parker answered. "Personally, I'll consider myself lucky to get there by swimming. Here we go."

The last was spoken as the helicopter began its final plunge to the surface of the blue water below them.

Parker, with the mass of fabric clutched firmly in both hands, threw himself flat on the floor.

The 'copter hit with a terrific thud. An instant later, Parker was on his feet. The life raft was under one hand. With the other hand, he was reaching for the handle that opened the cabin door.

"We've got to get out of here. This ship will go the bottom like a rock."

Behind him, Mercedes and Retch were struggling to their feet. Parker yanked on the handle that opened the cabin door.

The handle did not budge.

The heavy jolt the craft had taken when it struck the surface had twisted the whole frame.

"Get that door open!" Retch moaned. "We'll be drowned like rats."

"Hell, I'm trying!" Parker answered. He yanked upward with all his strength.

The door still did not budge.

Outside Parker could see the green water rising around the cabin.

He backed away, ducked his head, threw himself with all his strength against the door.

Under the driving impact of his body, the door was knocked open. The mass of synthetic fabric in his arms, Parker catapulted through the opening and into the sea. He hit with a terrific splash. Mercedes followed him. Parker, treading water and working with the valve that would release the gas and inflate the raft, saw that Retch was still standing in the door of the 'copter.

"What am I going to do?" Retch screamed.

"Jump."

"But I can't swim."

"Then wait until I get this goddamned raft inflated. Ugh!" Parker's voice went into silence as arms came up out of the water and closed around his neck with a grip of death.

Mercedes, in a panic that often comes to people catapulted suddenly and unexpectedly into the water, was grabbing the nearest source of potential safety.

"Let go!" Even as he spoke, Parker felt her arms close even tighter around his neck. He knew then that she was not going to let go. She was pulling him under with her.

Giving one final jerk at the valve of the gas container, Parker found himself pulled under water.

The arms around his neck seemed to grip like iron. He caught them in both hands, yanked at them. His hands slipped. He grabbed again. She was behind him, on his back, so he could not slug her. Meanwhile each passing second was sending both of them deeper into the sea. He yanked at her arms again. This time his fingers held. Her grip was broken.

Twisting, he grabbed her hair. Then he began to fight his way to the surface.

His head broke water. As he gulped air, he realized the blessed sight before his eyes.

The rubber raft! His last jerk at the valve before Mercedes dragged him under had opened it.

From the door of the sinking helicopter Retch was staring at the raft. At the same instant in final desperation, he jumped. His clutching fingers caught the edge of the rubber raft. Like a frightened river rat, he pulled himself out of the water.

*

Treading water, Parker dragged Mercedes to the edge of the raft. Retch leaned over and lifted her in. For an instant, Parker remained in the water, his fingers firm on the raft, letting it support him while he gasped air into his lungs. Behind him, with a gurgle and a rumble, the helicopter sank. He swung himself into the raft. Mercedes, her masculine garb clinging to her, was sitting up.

"I am sorry, Beel," she said. "I get the scare up and I grab at you. I not know for sure what I am doing. You will forgive me, no?"

"Think nothing of it," Parker answered. "Anybody can get scared under these circumstances."

"That I know," she answered. "But you saved my life. And that I will remember."

"Forget it," Parker said. "I did what had to be done, nothing more."

"But I will remember it," she calmly repeated.

Parker was silent. Under her hardness for the first time he glimpsed something deeper, finer. She was the type who meant what she said. She was a woman who paid her debts. Under other circumstances . . . . Parker put the thought out of his mind.

Now he set about doing what had to be done—paddling to the island. He turned his eyes toward it.

The island was gone. Calm, serene, the level face of the sea stretched away to the horizon.

Fear, dark, sudden, and overwhelming, arose in Bill Parker. The fear did not come up just because the face of the sea was level and calm, the island not visible, but because of something else, something that he had forgotten, something that he had put out of his mind and out of his life. Could it be possible that—

He caught himself. In that direction lay madness. Words exploded out of him. "Hey, what the hell? Am I nuts? What became of that island? I saw it!"

"I told you we had to hurry to get there when we saw it." Retch was hesitant. "It's—it's not always there."

"But it's got to be there! I saw it!"

"There is a trick about that island," Retch said. "I—it—I—you don't always see it. Something funny."

Parker was across the shaking, unsteady raft. His impulse was to take Retch by the throat, to shake words out of him. "What do you mean?" He was restraining himself with difficulty.

Retch spread his hands. "I'm sorry, I can't explain. That's all I know. Believe me."

Retch was telling the truth Parker decided. The big pilot swung his gaze in every direction, searching for land. Somewhere in the far distance was the peninsula of Lower California. But it was beyond range of his eyes. As far as he could see, was barren water.

Setting his course by the small compass that was included as part of the standard equipment on the life raft, Parker paddled toward the south. The clumsy raft made little progress. Parker hardly noticed, hardly cared. Deep in his mind was a lurking thought he was trying to keep below his consciousness.

In the front of the raft, Retch sat with his back to Parker. From Retch's motions, Parker knew the man was cleaning his gun. Parker made no comment. When Retch had finished and had turned back to him, Parker spoke. "I want to know a little more about that island. How does it happen we can't see it?"

"I'm not certain," Retch answered. "I think it's a lot like the mirages you see on the desert. This island is something like that, only in reverse. In a mirage, you see something that doesn't exist. In the case of this island, you *don't* see something that *does* exist."

"Um," Parker said, then was silent. The explanation sounded reasonable enough, as far as it went. The trouble was it didn't go far enough, not nearly far enough to quiet the thought lurking deep in the big pilot's mind. He worked with the paddle. "When you hired me to fly you down here, you told me that you knew where this island was located but you didn't tell me it had a bad habit of vanishing."

"I didn't believe it myself," Retch answered. "So far as I was concerned, it was just a wild rumor."

"Um," Parker said again. As he spoke, part of the thought that he had been keeping buried in his mind came blasting to the surface. "She said it was a mirage too!" he blurted out the words. "And that goddamned Dr. Yammer—" He caught himself. Into his mind had come a vision of a woman he had once known, and a psychiatrist called Dr. Yammer. Pain crossed his face.

"What?" Retch asked. "Who are you talking about?"

"Nobody," Parker answered. "Just a woman I once knew."

Her name had been Effra. Effra of the Green Eyes, he had called her. Rigidly he forced the thought of her from his mind, forced himself to think of what Retch had said. But it was no good. His mind kept going back to Effra and Yammer.

"She is caught, trapped in a net of delusion and hallucination that is as solid as a block of steel," Dr. Yammer had once said, his voice precise with authoritarian certainty. "I cannot get her out of this steel block unless I hospitalize her, perhaps operate. There is no other choice, no other decision that can be made. Putting it bluntly—she is insane. A delicate thing, insanity. We still work in the dark with things of the mind."

*

At the memory of Yammer's words, Parker twisted uncomfortably. He used the paddle much more vigorously than was necessary. It was as if Yammer's face showed in the water into which he thrust the paddle.

Mercedes was studying Parker. "About this woman—"

"She was just a woman I once knew."

"You loved her, yes?"

"Well—" Parker was silent.

"Tell me what 'appened."

"Nothing," Parker said. "Oh, hell—all right. Up in LA three years ago I knew Effra. She was a pilot too, and we got to running around together. She liked to fly out over the Pacific all by herself. I don't know why; she just liked to flirt with danger, maybe. One time she came in a couple of hours over-due. Figuring she was down in the drink, I was about to rouse out the Navy to hunt for her when she came in." He paused.

Mercedes was silent. In the front of the raft, Retch said nothing. His eyes were still searching the skyline.

"She was wildly excited," Parker went on. "She said she had made a forced landing on an island somewhere off the coast of Southern Cal. She also said there were a lot of strange people living on the island." He shook his head. There was a feeling in him he did not like.

His eyes came to focus on a ripple in the water. A shark. It made him think of Dr. Yammer.

"What 'appened then?" Mercedes asked softly.

"I helped her look for the island," Parker said. "We spent months looking in our spare time. We flew over more ocean than I ever knew existed. But we didn't find it."

"No?"

"That island was awfully important to her. She thought something wonderful was there, what it was, she could not tell me, just that it was there. When we could not find it, she began to doubt herself, to think perhaps she had not seen it, that she had not landed there. She reached the conclusion then—well, she went to see one of these fancy mental specialists who know everything about nothing and nothing about anything."

Under the water, he could see the eyes of the shark. They reminded him of the expression in Dr. Yammer's eyes, except that the shark's eyes looked more honest.

"And then?" Mercedes said, very softly.

"She—vanished," Parker said. "Yammer was going to stick her into a hospital, use something that he called 'shock' on her, maybe operate. She ran away."

"Did you try to find her, Beel?"

"For asking that question, Mercedes, I ought to choke you!" Parker said hotly. "I hunted high and low. All we knew for certain was that her plane was missing. I think she decided she would simply fly out to the sea she loved, and never come back." Again his voice sank to a whisper as he visualized Effra of the Green Eyes flying out over this wilderness of waters.

"I am sorry, Beel," Mercedes said gently. "Will you remember one thing, Beel?"

"Sure. What is it?"

"You saved my life back there. I will not forget it. If the time ever comes, I will pay my debt."

"Thank you," Parker said. "But there is no debt."

"You think this island we are hunting might be the same island your girl claimed she found?" Retch spoke from the front end of the boat.

"And if it is the same island?" Mercedes said.

Anger came boiling up in Parker. "If it is that island, and if I ever get back to Los Angeles, I am going to hunt up a psychiatrist by the name of Yammer and take care of him!" Parker dug the water savagely. Gradually, his anger subsided. "Where did you run into the rumor about this island?"

Retch shrugged. "It was just one of those things you hear." He studied the landscape. "We should spot a boat soon."

"We are not exactly on the well-traveled ocean lanes," Parker pointed out. "Does it happen that there are any other little things about this island that you forgot to tell me when you chartered my ship to fly you down here?"

Retch flushed. "Such as—"

"Such as how it happened that my 'copter threw a vane just after we sighted the place?"

Retch did not answer.

"Seemed as though somebody shot at us."

"Oh hell no! The loss of the vane was accidental."

"Accidents like that can happen but they usually don't. I checked the ship before we took off." Parker turned silent. There was no proof that the wrecking of the 'copter had been anything but an accident. "What do you expect to find on this island?"

"I told you—"

"Just before the 'copter started down, Miss Valdar was yakking about how we were all going to be rich," Parker interrupted.

The glance Retch gave Mercedes had no love in it. "Sometimes she's got her mouth open when she ought to have it shut."

*

Mercedes was silent. "I see," Parker said. "When you chartered my ship, you told me you were a scientist and that you wanted to investigate certain phenomena on this island. You said your investigation would take only a few hours. I was to fly you here and wait for you. You said you might want me to fly you back to the mainland, or might not, depending on what you found here. Is this correct?"

"Certainly," Retch answered. "I'm sorry you lost your ship but the insurance will take care of it."

"Insurance will take care of the 'copter but not of my neck. *Are* you a scientist?"

"Of course. Didn't I tell you—"

"What kind of a scientist are you?"

"I—ah—What do you mean?"

"What's your specialty? Are you a biologist, a physicist, or what?"

"I—"

"I don't believe you are a scientist at all. You don't talk like one."

"Damn it, I told you what I am and that's what I am!" Retch's face showed sullen and his hand moved toward the gun. Parker tensed. Retch stopped the movement of his hand. He glared at the big pilot.

"Okay," Parker said. "It doesn't make any difference anyhow." He resumed paddling.

The sun slid down the western sky. Retch and Mercedes huddled in the front end of the raft and whispered to each other. From time to time, the woman glanced at Parker. He paid no attention to her.

The sea was calm. In the distance, a school of flying fish skittered over the surface. A dozen gulls played near the surface. A high-riding fin cut the water. Shark, sensing food.

The sun reached the horizon and wallowed in the sea like a fat, round shining pig on fire.

Mercedes screamed, pointed, jerked a terror-stricken face toward Parker. "Beel! Beel!" She scuttled across the raft, threw herself into his arms. "Look, Beel, look!"

Terror and panic almost beyond understanding were in her words.

Parker looked where she was pointing. His heart climbed up into his mouth and threatened to choke him. He had thought he was shock-proof, that nothing could jar him. But here was something that made his mind reel.

Walking across the water toward the raft were three men.

Clad in knee-length breeches, wearing cloaks, the three men looked as if they had just stepped out of the 17th century. Two wore big, broad-brimmed hats, the third had a handkerchief wrapped around his head. He also had a wooden leg and he stalked across the surface of the sea with all the sureness he might have had with concrete under him. He carried a curved cutlass in one hand. The other two men were armed with swords, in scabbards. In addition, heavy, clumsy-looking pistols were thrust into sashes at their belts.

They looked like men out of a nightmare—or like pirates out of the olden days; swash-buckling buccaneers who had somehow managed to survive their proper period in history and to live into the 20th century.

"Ghosts!" Mercedes screamed. "Devils! They've come up out of hell because of our sins!" She wrapped her arms around Parker's neck. "Save me, Beel, save me!"

Parker caught her wrists, jerked her arms loose from his neck, and rose quickly to his feet. He hoped fervidly that his eyes had been deceiving him and that standing up would cause this mirage to disappear.

His eyes continued to deceive him. The three men did not disappear. They continued to walk across the water toward the raft. They moved with the sureness of men who know where they are going.

Behind them, suddenly outlined against the fat sun that was wallowing in the sea, rocky, grim, and forbidding, the mysterious island was now visible. It had reappeared. They had found it.

Three men coming from it had found them.

The shark found the three men.

Parker saw the triangular fin cut through the water toward them. Like a speed boat taking off on a race, the fin gathered momentum.

The three men saw it coming.

"Ho!" one yelled.

"A shark!" the second said.

"Have at him, boys!" the third shouted.

*

The shark charged them. Drawing their swords, the three men executed a nimble dance on the surface of the sea. They thrust downward—their swords entering the water with no difficulty whatsoever although their feet did not enter it—drew them back dripping red. They skipped lightly out of the way of the wounded and infuriated monster.

"Zounds!"

"Chop the sea pig down!"

"Carve his heart out!"

Old battle cries rang in the air as they fought the shark. Blood colored the surface of the sea.

The wounded shark suddenly took its death blow. It dived, was gone from sight, then broke the surface a hundred yards away. It beat the water into foam, threshing out its life.

With pleased interest, the three men watched the shark die. Dipping their blades into the sea to clean the blood from them, they wiped them dry on their pants legs.

Again they moved toward the raft.

Parker's hand went to the pistol inside his leather jacket. He loosed it in its holster but did not draw it.

Mercedes moaned and covered her eyes. At the other end of the boat, Retch had risen to his feet.

Bracing himself, Bill Parker waited for—whatever was to happen. Out of the corner of his eye, he saw Retch slowly drawing his gun.

"Damn it, Retch, put that gun away!" Parker shouted. "Don't shoot until you know what the hell is going on."

Retch turned, the gun visible in his hand. "What the hell—" Retch didn't put the gun away. He lifted it. Parker found himself staring into the muzzle.

"Get your hands up!" Retch snarled the words. "Mercedes, get that gun out of his holster. Get your goddamned hands up or I'll blow your blasted head off!"

The last was spoken to Parker as the dazed pilot tried to understand what had happened. He could hardly believe his own eyes. Automatically he lifted his hands. Mercedes slid past him, got behind him, taking no chances on getting between him and Retch's gun. He felt her fingers go inside his jacket. Expertly she lifted the gun from its holster.

"Toss me the gun!" Retch said. He caught the weapon the woman tossed toward him, glanced at Parker. "You thought I was going to start shooting at *them*?" He gestured toward the three approaching men. "You made a slight mistake." The grin on his face was wolfish.

"What the hell have I got into?"

"You'll find out, if you live long enough," Retch said. "Just behave yourself and do as you're told and maybe you'll stay alive." Again the wolfish grin showed on his face but under the grin, the words were harsh with meaning.

"Ho, Johnny!" the three men were drawing near the raft. "Ho, Johnny Retch! What kind of a flying ship is this that you have brought back with you?"

Retch turned to the three men. "Gotch! Peg-leg! Masterville!" Retch greeted them as old friends. The one he had called Gotch had spoken. All three of them stared at the raft and its occupants. Mercedes drew bold, appreciative stares. Parker got blank looks. Standing lightly and easily on the water, the three men surveyed the raft with doubtful contempt.

"Does this thing fly through the air like the Jez—" Gotch caught himself. "It looks to me as if it were more fit for sailing on a mill pond back in Devon."

"This is not the ship that flies through the air, that ship was wrecked. This is a rubber boat that it carried."

"Wrecked?" Gotch spoke. "But where does that leave us?"

"Everything has been taken care of," Retch spoke quickly. "You can always trust Johnny Retch to have two strings for his bow."

"Hmmmm. And who is this?" Gotch gestured toward Parker.

"The pilot of the flying ship that was wrecked," Retch answered.

"Ummmm. And what are we going to do with him?" Gotch glanced around toward the still floundering and dying shark as if he regretted their haste in disposing of what might have been a handy scavenger. "Um." He moved around the raft and stood close to Parker, staring at him. The sword in his hands still showed faint traces of red from the blood of the shark.

"We do not need any more men on the island!" Lifting his blade, Gotch glared at Parker.

"Do you, per'aps, need women?" Mercedes spoke quickly. Gotch turned his eyes on her. As he looked, some of the anger seemed to go out of him.

"Perhaps what you need on the island are more women," Mercedes said. She smiled boldly.

*

Gotch broke into a grin. "But definitely, we need more women, if they are like you."

"Hey, lay off of her, she belongs to me!" Retch spoke violently.

"Come, let us pull the boat to the island," Peg-leg spoke quickly. "We have too many things to do to stand waiting here."

Grumbling, Gotch allowed himself to be persuaded to get in front of the raft and join the other men in pulling it.

Not until then did Parker dare to breathe. "Thanks," he spoke to Mercedes.

"It was nothing, Beel. Anyone could have done it."

"Thanks, anyhow," Parker said. "But what have we got ourselves into here?"

"I do not know for sure, Beel. Johnny, he like me, and he ask me to come along. He say we will both get reech—"

"Shut up!" Retch spoke.

Parker, sitting in the raft, watched the three men tow it toward the shore. He watched their feet. Where they stepped, the water seemed to grow firm. Pirates, cut-throats, killers, they certainly were. But added to that was the equally obvious fact that they could walk on water. In all history, Parker had only heard of one man who could do that, and he hadn't been a man, but a God.

Ahead of them, the island loomed in the sunset; a long strip of white, sandy beach; behind it a thick growth of trees; behind the trees the rocky central mass of the island rising up into the sky. Off to the right, Parker caught a glimpse of a wreck that lay against rocks jutting from the shore. He stared at it. Unless his eyes were deceiving him, it was the wreck of a Spanish galleon, a ship that belonged to the days when Spain had been draining the gold and silver and jewels of the new world into her coffers.

The men stopped, stared uneasily at the shore. Parker could make out two men barely visible between the beach and the grove of trees.

"Rozeno and Ulnar!" Gotch spoke. "Watching us." His lips curled and his hand went automatically to the hilt of the sword he was wearing. "Some day I will slit the throats of that priest and that Indian." Gotch spat into the sea.

"They're not causing any trouble," Peg-leg spoke.

"They're witches, by Gad!" Gotch answered. "They're warlocks, wizards."

"Father Rozeno is a very devout and holy man," Peg-leg said.

"He pretends to be a priest but he is more of a warlock than he is a holy man. As for that Indian, if he ever gives me the chance—" Gotch glared at the figures at the edge of the grove.

"Come on," Peg-leg said.

Mercedes contrived to move closer to Parker. "Beel, what are theese theengs here? I do not understand them. I do not like them."

"Nor do I," Parker said.

A shiver passed over her.

"What's the matter, baby, you cold?" Retch grinned at her. "Don't worry about it. We'll get you warmed up on the island."

Imperceptibly she again moved closer to Parker. "Beel, it ees not good."

"You got into this of your own free will."

"Yes, but I did not know that theengs like theese were going to 'appen. I just thought—"

"Mercedes, if you open your mouth again, I'll knock your teeth down your throat!" Retch said.

Mercedes was silent.

As they came in to the shore, the two men who had been visible on the beach disappeared. Off to the left something else came into view. It was a small cabin plane, wrecked there in what had apparently been an attempt at a forced landing.

Before they reached the shore, the fat sun had wallowed itself out of sight into the sea. In the dusk, the island looked like a vast, rocky pinnacle thrust up out of the Pacific Ocean, or out of the ocean of time—Parker couldn't tell which. Mysterious, silent, it waited in the darkness like a vast sleeping monster on the surface of the sea, a monster on which Spanish galleons and planes had been wrecked. Parker, his nerves jumpy, halfway expected it to vanish beneath the surface before they reached it.

But it didn't vanish. It remained fixed, solid, firm. When they stepped from the raft, the sand under their feet was solid, the crunch of it reassuring.

*

A breeze whispered through the trees. The island was quiet, too quiet. It seemed to brood in the darkness. In the vast stillness that hung like a pall over the place, the only sound was that of a bird, chittering sleepily in the dark woods.

It was the most out-of-place sound Bill Parker had ever heard.

It seemed to affect the others. At the bird-sound they were suddenly quiet, listening.

"To hell with it, it's nothing," Gotch said. "Come on."

Following a well defined path, they moved inland, toward the base of the cliff. Through the trees, Parker glimpsed fires. As he moved closer, he saw the source of the lights, the cooking fires of a village set against the base of the cliff.

"Ho!" Peg-leg called, announcing their arrival.

As they entered the village, the inhabitants came rushing out to them. They were the queerest lot of human beings Parker had ever seen. Spaniards, bearded grandees in tattered and mended bits of ancient finery, Indians, squat, stalwart, Englishmen, tall and blond, a motley crew.

They looked like the relics of half a dozen different nations, drawn from the fringes of time. Their garments did not belong in the 20th century. Their weapons were knives, swords, bell-mouthed pistols. Their language was a mixture of Spanish, English, Portuguese, and Indian dialects.

"What kind of a mad-house is this?" Parker muttered. "Get away, you!" The last was spoken to a slender Spaniard who was trying to jerk Parker's leather jacket from his back.

The man snarled at him, drew back.

"Get out of our way!" Retch yelled. The crowd made way for him. Calling greetings, snarling, Retch seemed very much at home here.

Mercedes looked hopelessly confused and at a loss. She stared around her as if she was appalled at what she saw. Parker drew the obvious inference. Mercedes had never been here before. All this was as new to her as it was to him. But Retch had been here.

Off in the woodland behind them somewhere a bird chirped, the same sleepy quiet sound that Parker had heard as they landed. Now it was louder, nearer, and even more out of place than it had been before.

The people around Parker also heard the sound. Startled faces turned toward the dark forest.

The sound came again, louder now. Parker was certain it was the call of a bird.

But if it was the chirp of a bird, it was frightening these people. Why should a bird-sound in the night frighten grown men? Utter silence fell. Even Gotch was still. Parker saw that the man's face had turned gray, that all the bristling bravado had passed out of him.

Even Retch, showing signs of strain and growing temper, was silent.

"The Jezbro!" someone whispered.

At the words, the strain and temper coming up in Retch burst the surface. "There is no such thing as the Jezbro!" His voice was almost a scream. "It's only superstitious nonsense—" His shouting voice went into silence as the sound came again.

The chirp was louder now. It was no longer one bird chirping in the dark night, it was a dozen. And it wasn't quite the sound of a bird any longer, it was a musical tinkle, an airborne throbbing somewhat similar to the sound of a harp, a softly ringing chime. Parker could easily imagine that somewhere among those dark trees was a harper, moving closer.

The harpist did not seem to be upon the ground. He—or she—seemed to be up in the air, somewhere near the tree tops, moving in the dark night.

As the sound came louder, a man in the village suddenly went down on his knees, then another and another, until the whole group, including Gotch, were kneeling. Even Mercedes went to her knees in response to deep internal, superstitious pressures. Only Retch and Parker stood erect as two men strong enough to face the sound coming from the night.

"Get down, you fools!" Peg-leg's voice had real anguish in it.

"Get down, hell!" Retch answered. He had a gun in each hand, his own and the one he had taken from Parker.

"Beel! Beel!" Mercedes was jerking at Parker's leg. "What is 'appening?"

"Something," Parker answered. "I don't know what." There was fear in him. He could feel it in his heart, sense it in his bones, taste in his mouth. He rose above it.

The sound swept through the air. It came out over the trees above them. On the ground, the kneelers moaned in response.

The harping sound leaped up, became a melody of weird notes filling the night air. Mingled with the eerie music were the moans from the prostrate humans.

Looking upward, Parker caught a glimpse of something moving through the sky. It blotted out the light of the stars and it looked a lot like a bird but like no bird he had ever seen before. It was too big to be any bird that had ever flown through Earth's air, but yet it flew. As it flew, it made the sound of a gigantic harp.

*

The bird passed over the village, moving along the cliff. As it slid into the distance, the harp music faded slowly away, became again the sound of a sleepy bird.

Around the village, the prostrate humans moaned, stirred, began to rise.

"What the hell was that thing?" Parker gasped.

"The damned fools call it the Jezbro!" Retch snarled. "The yellow cowards are afraid of it. I don't know what it is."

Parker was silent. To him, Retch sounded like a man scared right down to the soles of his shoes but desperately trying to pretend he wasn't.

"It was a warning sent by them," Peg-leg whispered, gesturing up toward the cliff in the darkness. "A warning to us to mend our ways."

"It was no such thing!" Retch shouted.

Peg-leg did not argue. He got slowly and silently to his feet. The group was silent, perturbed, and afraid. Even Gotch was silent. Whatever had passed overhead, had cast a pall of fear over them.

"You bilious, yellow-livered cowards!" Retch raged at them.

They made no response. The fear the Jezbro had inspired in them seemed to have made even his anger unimportant.

"But what is the Jezbro?" Parker questioned again. "I mean—"

"I told you it's nothing and that's enough of an answer. Hey!" The guns that Retch held came up sharply as another figure came soundlessly out of the forest and moved toward them. An old, bent, wrinkled Indian who hobbled along with the aid of a staff.

"Oh, it's you, Pedro!" Retch said. "What the hell do you want?"

For all the sign he gave, the Indian, Pedro, did not hear Retch's question. He hobbled straight to Parker.

"*En la manana Padre Rozeno huit nole el hombre e la mujer.* Father Rozeno will see the man and the woman in the morning." The voice was broken with age.

"I don't get it," Parker said. The Indian was already turning. He had delivered his message, his errand was finished.

"That damned Rozeno is not going to see anybody in the morning!" Retch yelled.

The Indian staffed his way into the forest. He still seemed not to hear Retch.

"Tell him they won't be there!" Retch screamed.

Pedro's back went out of the firelight as he moved into the trees.

Retch seemed almost to go mad. His face turned purple. Both guns came to focus on the spot where the Indian had disappeared.

"Why shoot him?" Parker said. "He was just a messenger."

"Damn it!" Slowly, while the group watched impassively, Retch got himself under control. Suddenly he began to laugh. Strangely his laughter in this moment was more horrible than his anger had been.

"He sent for you, and the woman. All right, he'll get you. But I'll go with you. If he wants you, I'll take you to him." Again the laughter sounded.

"Who is Rozeno?" Parker asked.

"He is, or he was once, a Spanish priest. He and Ulnar think they rule this island. They are the two men we saw watching us from the shore. You'll see them in the morning."

That was the last word Retch said on the subject. He took Gotch apart, to talk to him. Peg-leg found food for Parker, but refused to talk. "Na, na, my son, when the Jezbro passes over us as a great bird—when it goes through the woods at night as a great howling beast—we do not talk about it."

Parker pressed for more information, but the old man turned stubbornly silent. Later he found Parker a place to sleep in his own hut. Parker had the impression that, all during the night Peg-leg, sat on guard at the entrance.

But nothing came in the night. In the morning Retch was there, saying, with grim bitterness, that now it was time to go up the cliff to see Rozeno and Ulnar. Mercedes, looking wan and bedraggled, with hate in her hot black eyes, was with him. So was Gotch. Gotch did not look in the least happy.

"What's biting you?" Parker said to Retch.

"Nothing."

"I get the impression something around here is just about scaring the pants off of you."

"You're crazy!" Retch's voice was a snarl. "I'm not afraid of anything around here—you—or anybody else." As he spoke, the man's face was a mask and his eyes were wild.

"Sure, okay, I get it," the pilot answered.

They moved along the cliff until they came to a ledge that sloped upward.

"We go up here," Gotch grunted.

*

As they went upward, they rose above the tops of the trees. Sparkling thinly in the morning sunlight, the sea came into sight. Circling the shoreline at a distance of about a mile, a curtain of mist was visible. It seemed to close in above them too, shielding the island like a thin, shining dome.

"That's a strange fog," Parker said.

"It's not a fog," Retch answered. "I don't know exactly what it is, but when it is there, the island is invisible. If you are on the other side of it, you see nothing at all."

"Um," Parker said. They continued upward. The ledge twisted, curved, went around the rising cliff. Slowly Parker became aware that the rising ledge was not a natural formation, it was a pathway cut into the face of the cliff.

At the realization, the pilot felt a touch of awe rise in him. This ledge was old. It must have been cut into this cliff long before Columbus had sailed westward.

Off in the distance beyond the curtain of mist was the coast of California, the beaches bright with bathers, the cities wrapped in warm sunshine, the roads alive with traffic. Over there in the distance were orange groves and millions of people.

Here on this island, behind this mist, unknown to millions of people so close to it, was something that did not belong in the 20th century, or in any other century Parker could imagine.

His back felt cold. In him, somewhere, was gnawing anger. This island, this place, was real. Back in his past a horrible wrong had been done, a wrong that now could never be corrected. He put the thought out of his mind.

The ledge turned into the cliff and became a tunnel that had been carved into solid stone. The walls of the tunnel were as smooth as polished marble. What tools could men have used in the old days to cut a tunnel with walls so smooth that they looked like glass? Modern equipment could not have done the job so well.

Niches in the wall of the tunnel admitted light and gave them glimpses of the island.

"Where the hell will we find—Oh, Pedro!" Retch spoke. The Indian messenger of the night before had appeared in the tunnel. He beckoned to them. They followed him into a large room cut out of solid stone.

It was one of the cleanest and most simply furnished rooms Parker had ever seen. It contained hand-made chairs along the wall and a big table, also hand-made. Light from a wall slit flowed into the room.

Seated behind the table, illumined by the light flowing in from the wall slit behind them, were Rozeno and Ulnar. Rozeno had a thin nose, the narrow face of the typical high bred Spaniard. Ulnar was short and squat, his cheeks were flat, his nose hooked. Both had black eyes that were utterly fathomless.

The faces were old, wrinkled, and kind. Parker took one look at this priest, and instantly liked him. As he glanced at Rozeno, saw the kindness on that face, he also saw, out of the corners of his eyes, Retch drawing a gun.

In that split second he knew why Retch had laughed so violently the night before, when Retch had said that he would go with them to see Rozeno and Ulnar.

Retch intended to kill both of them; to shoot them as they sat there at that table, unarmed and defenseless; shoot them like dogs!

The gun was already in Retch's hand. Parker's fist went out, up, connected with Retch's jaw, a blow that had all the pilot's strength behind it.

Retch's head was twisted to one side. He reeled away from Parker's blow. The snarl that came from his lips was the snarl of a wild animal. Metal thudded as the gun hit the floor. The room echoed with sound—Mercedes screaming. Parker followed Retch, followed him as a dog follows a rat. He caught a wild man.

Retch stumbled against the wall, caught himself on one of the hand-made chairs, jerked himself up, and drove at Parker. The pilot met the charge head on. They went down locked together.

Retch was a tornado erupting with violent fury. He threw Parker away from him, leaped to his feet. Parker pulled himself to one knee. The fallen pistol lay in front of him. He snatched it up.

Retch was coming toward him. He saw the gun in Parker's hand, hesitated.

"I'll kill you," the pilot said.

*

Retch caught himself. For an instant he seemed to hang in the air before Parker, yellow glaring in his eyes as he tried to make up his mind whether or not to buck the gun.

"Get your hands up," Parker said.

Slowly the yellow went out of Retch's eyes.

"Get your hands up!" Parker repeated.

This time Retch obeyed him. Parker backed him against the wall, took the second pistol from his pocket, his own gun.

"Damn you!" Retch snarled. Parker saw that the man was not speaking to him but to Gotch, he saw also that during all this Gotch had not moved. The man stood transfixed; afraid to move.

Parker turned to the two men behind the table. They had not moved either, though Ulnar looked as if he was about to come to his feet. Rozeno sat very still. There was sadness on his face.

"Go away," he gestured toward Retch. "And you, too, Gotch, go away."

"You mean we can go after—" Gotch faltered.

"I don't want to see either of you again," Rozeno said. There was actual living pain in his voice. "Go!"

"Wait a minute," Parker spoke quickly.

"Yes, my son?" Rozeno's face lost its sadness when he looked at Parker, it came alive with sudden animation.

"You don't mean to tell me you are going to let these two go?" the pilot protested.

"Of course."

"But Retch tried to kill you."

"I know—"

"And he'll try it again. There's something here that's driving him crazy. I don't know what it is but he knows. If you turn him loose—I would just as soon turn loose a rattlesnake, Johnny Retch."

Parker's words were hard, blunt, forceful. But for all the effect they had on the old priest, he might as well not have spoken them. Rozeno smiled. "I do not think Retch or Gotch will ever harm us. They have no means to harm us." He made a gesture with his hands, spoke a single word, "Go!"

Retch and Gotch went quickly from the room, like men who were very glad to go.

"I hope you know what you are doing," Parker said, saw that Rozeno was not looking at him. The old priest was watching Mercedes.

"You may stay here, with us," Rozeno added.

Mercedes' face mirrored gratitude. "Thank you."

Rozeno turned his attention to Parker. "You are new to our island, are you not, my son?"

"Yes."

"How did you arrive here? Was your ship wrecked?"

"Yes. Actually, however, we were looking for this island." Swiftly Parker explained what had happened.

"Retch went away, he hired you to bring him back in a ship that flies?" Rozeno seemed a little perturbed.

For the first time, Ulnar spoke, a single grunted sound. Rozeno answered with a swift flow of gutturals that Parker did not understand. Ulnar grunted again, a hot light appeared in his eyes. "Kill him!" His fist came down upon the table.

Again Rozeno looked pained. "I have worked so long and so hard with him, trying to show him the Way, trying to explain to him that killing is not a part of the Way. But the old savagery is still in his heart. Sometimes I despair of him." He shook his head very gently. The light flowing in from behind him made a halo of his long white hair. His eyes searched Parker. They were the kindest and at the same time the keenest eyes the pilot had ever met. They looked at him and through him; they probed deep down inside of him; they seemed to search down to the bottom of his soul. Parker had the feeling he was being weighed, measured, probed.

"It is not often that I offer a choice to those who come here," Rozeno spoke. "Usually they prefer to live in the village at the base of the cliff. You may live here with us, if you wish." The smile on Rozeno's face was a living thing.

Deep down inside of him, Parker felt his soul come to sudden life. "I'll stay here, Father, if I may."

The smile on Rozeno's face became even brighter. "Good, my son. You have made a very wise choice."

Parker was silent, perturbed, suddenly uneasy. Here in this place two old men lived in rooms near the top of a cliff. Down below was a village where brawling men lived, men who could walk on water. In the night, in this place something called a Jezbro went on the wings of a harp. There was magic here, mysteries that went beyond his understanding. What else was here?

"Tell me about this place, Father?"

Rozeno nodded. "Gladly, my son, gladly. I will show you and tell you as I show you. There are things here that even I do not understand." For a second, the old priest frowned as if he was contemplating mysteries that lay afar. Then his smile came back and he was rising to his feet. "Come with me, my son."

*

As they moved from the big room, Ulnar grunted hastily and gestured toward the wall slit. Looking through it, Parker saw a speedy craft moving inside the veil—a PT boat. His heart jumped at the thought that the Navy had finally penetrated the secret of this strange island. His heart sank when he saw that even if this was a PT boat, it was not a Navy ship. The craft was dirty, unkempt, it was not the smart, spick and span vessel that the Navy would operate.

As he watched, the boat veered abruptly, slowed, almost came to a halt as if its occupants had suddenly discovered the presence of the island.

Ulnar shook his fist at the boat. "*Vondel me sego!*" he said.

"No, no, Ulnar," Rozeno spoke hastily. "You must not *vondel* them. They are just some people who have stumbled through the veil and now are bewildered."

"Me make 'em more frightened," the Indian spoke. He brought one fist down into the other fist, a smacking sound.

"What is *vondel?*" Parker spoke.

Rozeno seemed not to hear him. The priest was already moving from the room.

"We do not know who cut these passages here," Rozeno said. "We do not know who cut these rooms into the rock. Some race that lived a long, long time ago—perhaps the legendary Murians, perhaps some other race—had this island as an outpost. I think, also, they used it as a scientific laboratory; a dangerous laboratory that they put far away from their homeland. A place where their wise men—their philosophers—could seek out the mysteries of nature."

"Um," Parker said. There was cold in him. He tried to force it away, discovered it would not go.

"There is something else that is very strange about this island," the priest continued. "Time is different here."

357

"How is time different?"

"In this way," Rozeno answered. "I came to the New World with Cortez."

"I see," Parker said.

"You take it very calmly."

"I do not doubt my own eyes nor do I doubt you."

The old priest glowed. "Good. Good. Tell me, my son, are there many men like you in the world of today? I have a dream, a secret private dream, that the scientists from your world might come here and study the strange things on this island."

"They would come here in droves if they knew about it. And so would everybody else. You would be over-run by hordes of the curious."

"Yes, we know that. That isn't quite what I meant. It was my hope that perhaps we could make this island what it was in the olden days—secret place where the wise men could come to study." The priest's face glowed again. "There is so much here to be learned and here, also, is the time in which to learn. Here great discoveries might be made. Here could possibly be discovered not only the secrets of nature but the secrets of the minds and the hearts of men. From this place, as the centuries passed, there might be fed out, little by little, knowledge that would change the world; knowledge that would change the hearts and the minds of men; knowledge that would eliminate poverty, stop wars, knowledge that would help the human race become what it must one day be."

The glow on Rozeno's face was bright. The dream he dreamed was suddenly, in Parker's mind, a living, breathing vital hope, the hope of all honest men everywhere, that tomorrow might be better!

"Would you, my son, help me achieve that dream? Will you go back through the veil and explain to some of your greatest scientists what we have here?"

"I would like nothing better," the big pilot answered. In a way, this was his dream too, though up until now it had always been a secret, hidden, impossible-to-accomplish thing. His hand went out to Rozeno. Deep inside of him, the glow grew to greater heights. Only one other thing was needed to make this glow a really perfect feeling, Effra, who had found this island and had tried to tell him about it. But Effra was gone.

They moved on to a big room where some of the scientific equipment of the vanished race still functioned. Set in a sunken pool ten feet in diameter in the center of the room was a circle of what looked like mercury. Leading up from it were heavy bus bars of some unknown metal. The bus bars came together and marched across the room to a control panel, one of the strangest control panels Parker had ever seen. The meters were graduated in colors. In front of the chair where the operator sat was a keyboard like that of a vast pipe organ. How much training would an operator need to operate this keyboard? Directly in front of the operator's seat was a square panel that looked like a television screen.

*

Set in niches where the right hand of the operator could reach them easily were statuettes of birds, animals, reptiles. Made of some metal, they were perfect representations. Parker saw a condor, a bald-headed eagle, a humming-bird, a cougar, a jaguar, an alligator. His eyes went back to the pool in the center of the room.

"It is generating power," Rozeno said. "As it turns, it creates some force, some energy. I do not understand this energy. No one now alive understands it. Understanding is one of the things I hope your scientists may achieve—come away, Ulnar." The last was spoken as the Indian strayed near the operator's seat.

Ulnar grunted impatiently. There was something about that seat that lured him. But he came away. They went into another room, leaving behind them the pool of mercury that turned slowly, like a miniature earth on some axis of its own. Parker took one look at the contents of this room, and gasped.

The crown jewels of England were no greater than these! Here were crowns of pounded yellow gold; here were gargoyle masks made of the same yellow metal; masks that sparkled with gems. Here, lying on the rock shelves, were ingots of what looked to be solid gold, each one heavy enough to be a full load for a grown man.

Ulnar was examining a gargoyle mask. He touched a gold bar, his old withered fingers seeming to savor the feel of it.

Rozeno smiled gently. "Ulnar treasures these things, they were put in his charge a very long time ago. He has been faithful to his trust."

"But—" Parker whispered.

"This is a part of Montezuma's treasure, a part that Cortez did not get. There is as much of it here as 400 men could carry away. Ulnar was one of Montezuma's most trusted sub-chiefs. He brought the treasure here, to keep it for his Chieftan."

Ulnar's wrinkled face broke into a grin. "Me take good care," he said simply. "Me clean, me polish, me save for my Chief."

"Tell me one thing?" he said.

"Gladly, my son."

"Does Johnny Retch know this is here?"

"I suppose so. All who live on our island know about it."

Muscles knotted at the corners of Parker's jaws. He pressed his arms down against his jacket so that he could feel the guns in the pockets. The guns felt good.

"Father Rozeno!" a voice called from a corridor outside the treasure room. "Father Rozeno? Where are you?"

"Here I am, my dear," the priest answered.

At the sound of that voice, Bill Parker forgot all about the guns in his pockets, Johnny Retch, Montezuma's treasure, and everything else that was on this island. He stood stock still, paralyzed.

A girl came through the opening into the treasure room. She wore a dark dress; sandals; her hands were gloved; she had apparently been working at some task. She smiled at Ulnar, glanced at Parker, nodded, looked at Rozeno, smiled, then glanced back quickly at Parker as if he reminded her of someone she had once known, then turned again to the priest. "Father, I have been cleaning all morning—"

So far she got. Bill Parker broke his paralysis and swept her into his arms.

"Effra—Effra—Effra—" His voice was a choked whisper, almost inaudible in the treasure chamber of Montezuma. As she had come through the door, his mind had given him a flashing picture of the plane wrecked on the shore. Effra, fleeing from Dr. Yammer, had taken one last desperate chance on finding her island; one last lonely flight out over the Pacific. No wonder he had been unable to find her. She had found her island. She had come here. She *was* here, in his arms.

There was wonder and awe and bewilderment in the big pilot. Here was a miracle almost past the understanding. "I've found you—Effra—"

For an instant, she lay in his arms like a frightened child who dared not move. "Please—" she whispered. He did not hear her. His lips sought hers, found them. She did not draw away, but neither did she respond. "Effra—" Parker looked up. Rozeno and Ulnar were regarding him with mild astonishment. In his arms, Effra stirred again. "Please—let me go."

This time the big pilot heard her. Setting her back on her feet was one of the hastiest movements he had ever made in his life. "Effra—I did not mean to startle you—but darling—"

She stood irresolute, staring at him. "Please—You have no right—"

He saw that her eyes, fixed on him, regarded him as an utter and complete stranger.

"Don't you know me, Effra?" There was almost a sob in his voice.

"I never saw you before in my life."

*

Parker turned, moved to a window slot, stood looking out. The trees below him, the island, the sea, the PT boat lying at anchor off shore, he saw all of these things, but yet he did not see them.

He had found Effra and she did not remember him, did not know him. Inside of him was agony, such pain as he had never known. He felt a touch on his arm. Rozeno stood there, his face troubled. "Do you know our Effra, my son?"

"Yes."

"Do you, perhaps, love her?"

"Yes."

"And you are very unhappy because she does not respond?"

"Yes."

The old priest's face grew a little more sad. "When she landed here, the last time, she made an awkward landing. She was thrown forward and she hit her head. She does not remember anything that happened before that." Rozeno's finger bit deeply into Parker's arm. "Come now, and I will introduce you to her, as a stranger."

Bill Parker found himself being introduced to the woman he loved. "I'm sorry about my actions of a minute ago," he said. "I thought you were someone else."

The smile she gave him was forgiving but it was also cool and distant. "That's all right, Mr. Parker. I understand." Her voice went into silence as another sound came into the room. The sound of rapid gunfire.

Parker had thought he had in his pocket the only two modern weapons on the island, but somewhere in the growth of trees far below the window slot, someone was firing a submachine gun.

Parker raced to the slot. Below him the island lay quiet. He turned. Mercedes, her face working, was staring at him.

"Beel—Beel—I have not told you everything! That Johnny Retch, he hire you to fly him here in 'copter, to find thees island. He also have men in boat coming. Your job, which you did not know, was to find island, then lead men in boat to it. Johnny means to take all thees." The gesture of her hand included all the treasure of Montezuma. "He have men in boat to help him take it. He does not mean to let anything stop him. Not anything!"

Parker saw what he had not seen before, that Johnny Retch was a man who would always have two strings for his bow. Too late, he saw that the boat lying at anchor was not an accident.

"I should have killed that dog when I had the chance!" he snarled.

Shambling feet sounded in the corridor outside. Pedro burst into the room. He grunted words at Ulnar.

"Pedro says men come up the ledge," Rozeno said. "They must be from the boat. We must go to meet them. It will be a great pleasure to them. Come, Ulnar. Come, Bill." He moved toward the door.

Parker was across the room in quick strides, catching Rozeno's arm. "You can't do it, Father Rozeno. Those men who are coming up the ledge mean to kill."

"My son!" Hurt showed on the priest's face. "Surely you do not know what you are talking about!"

"But I do know!" Parker almost shouted the words. Quickly, desperately he tried to explain the situation to Rozeno. To his growing horror, he saw no comprehension in the old priest's eyes. Slowly Parker began to realize that this old man was so gentle and so kind himself that he could not comprehend even the thought of anyone else being—evil!

"You may stay here, if you wish, my son, but Ulnar and I will go speak to these people who are coming up the ledge. Come, Ulnar."

His face glowing at the thought of meeting new people, the priest moved from the room. Ulnar grunted once, a hot, savage sound, then followed Rozeno like a dog following its master.

Effra started to follow them.

Parker caught her arm. "Please, at least you stay here. Understand me now if you never understood me before. Is there a window slot from which the ledge can be seen?"

"Yes."

"Then take me to it. Quickly!"

*

From the slot, Parker could see a section of the ledge. Two men were crawling along it, advancing as cautiously as scouts trying to surprise an outpost. Parker had never seen either of them before but their faces confirmed everything Mercedes had said—they were thugs, killers. Thrusting the pistol through the slot, the pilot took careful aim, pulled the trigger.

The thunder of the gun rang through the room, echoed across the island. The bullet knocked rock chips into the face of the lead man. He recoiled as if he had been stung. The Tommy-gun in his hand spouted lead blindly at the face of the cliff. The second man spun around—began shooting blindly.

Parker moved away from the slot, listened to the rattle of the guns outside. He could distinguish the heavy thud of the Tommy-gun, the sharper crack of the carbine, but other weapons were also firing. "They've got men with high-powered rifles posted in the tree down below."

He glanced from the slot. The men had disappeared from the ledge. As he moved back, a slug whined into the room. Mercedes cowered against the wall. Effra remained cool and poised. She was looking at Parker. "Haven't I met you somewhere before?" She seemed completely unaware of the rifle bullet that had just screamed through the slot.

"I—" Parker caught himself. There was agony in him. What good would it do if she did, finally, remember who he was, who she was? What they had once been to each other? He had three old men, and two women, and himself, with which to defend Montezuma's treasure against Johnny Retch, who had a small army of trained killers at his back.

What chance did they have? Johnny Retch, even if given Montezuma's gold, would not leave anyone alive except possibly Mercedes and Effra.

"Do—do you know anything we can do to stop those men?" Parker said.

Light seemed to come into Effra's eyes.

"We might—we might use the Jezbro!"

From the shelter of the trees, Johnny Retch operated like a general in charge of a force of Commandos engaged in attacking a miniature Gibralter. He was a very deliberate general. When the first shot from a slot in the cliff had driven the two men downward, he met them at the bottom of the ledge, a cigarette dangling from his lips, a sub-machine gun in his hands. "Okay, boys, go back on up."

"There's a guy in there with a gun," one of the two protested. "He's inside and we're outside. We're sittin' ducks for him."

"We're covering the slots with rifles in the trees."

"But—" Neither of the men wanted to go up that ledge again. They might be hardened killers but they did not like the idea of facing a gun they could not see.

"Go on back up, boys," Retch said. He lifted the muzzle of the gun he held.

"But—"

"Either go back up or you'll stay down here a long time!"

They went back up the ledge. Retch retired to the shelter of the trees and watched.

No shots came until they reached the mouth of the tunnel leading into the cliff. There, one of the men was killed. He fell backward from the ledge, screaming as he turned over and over.

The falling man broke his way through the top of a tree and sprawled thudding on the ground. He did not move after he hit. Retch did not waste a second glance on him.

Muffled but clearly audible, the blasting roar of the machine gun came from the tunnel.

"He got in," Retch said. "Okay. Two more of you go up."

Two more men went up the ledge.

The entire population of the village had gathered to watch this storming of the cliff. They regarded Retch with wonder and with awe. Some of these men had been pirates in their day, they had known how to loot a tall ship, to kill its crew, to take over any wealth and any women it happened to carry.

Watching Retch, they discovered they had been amateurs in the fine art of attacking and killing. They had needed a man from the modern world to show them how the job ought to be done. They were greatly impressed, Gotch most of all.

Waving his sword, Gotch explained what he would do to that black priest, Rozeno, and to that cowardly Indian, Ulnar. Of all the listening group, only Peg-leg protested.

"Yeah, you'll get them all right—if the Jezbro don't get you first!" Peg-leg said.

Retch overheard the words. "Come here, Peg-leg, I want to talk to you."

The old sailor stumped his way to where Retch stood.

"Aye, Cap'n." He saluted. A look of surprise appeared on the old sailor's face as the first heavy slug hit him. As the second, third, and fourth slugs hit him, the expression of surprise became one of agony. He fell without a sound.

*

Retch stood looking down at him.

The group was silent. Gotch hastily lowered his sword.

"I don't want to hear any more superstitious talk," Retch said. "There are a lot of funny things here on this island but there is nothing to be afraid of—except *this*!" He patted the stock of the stumpy little gun he held. "And there's enough stuff up there to make all of us rich; we'll have everything we can ever want." A glow crept into Retch's eyes as he spoke. They glowed with a yellow color and the yellow seemed to come out of his eyes and spread over his face. He glanced down at Peg-leg.

"Dump him into the sea," he said, walking away.

The two men climbing the ledge reached the opening. They stopped there and apparently held a conference with the man who was already inside. They went inside. A few minutes later, one appeared at the opening.

"You can come on up now," he yelled, waving his gun. "All secure here."

"Gotch!"

"Yes, Cap'n."

"Come on."

Gotch went up the ledge with Retch. He went in shivering fear which he tried desperately to conceal.

"What the hell are you scared of?" Retch snarled at him.

"Nuthin', nuthin', Cap'n. Nuthin'."

"You yellow-livered—" Retch stopped in midsentence. A sound was in the air, the cheeping of a sleepy bird. It was a tiny sound, fragile, distant, far-away, almost too weak to register on the ears. Hearing it, Retch jerked his eyes to the sky, seeking the source.

Gotch threw himself flat on the ledge.

"The Jezbro!" Gotch gasped. "God—God—"

Looking at the sky, Retch caught a glimpse of something moving there. It looked like a bird, but it was like no bird he had ever seen in his life. It was more like shadow—a darkness that had a darting elusive silver color about it.

Like a swooping hawk, it was diving toward the ground, aiming at the group clustered in the trees at the spot where the ledge began to rise up the face of the cliff. As it dived, the cheeping sound of a sleeping bird was becoming a flooding blast of wild harp notes.

"The Jezbro!" Gotch wailed.

The Jezbro dived at the men on the ground. They heard it, saw it; they scattered through the trees like frightened chickens fleeing from a hawk.

The Jezbro selected a victim. Retch caught a glimpse of long, cruel talons extended; saw the man grasped in them. The man screamed as the talons touched him, tried to throw himself flat, tried to jerk away from them. Huge wings fluttered, beating the air. The man did not escape. The talons held. The beating wings lifted him.

Wild notes flooded outward. There was triumph in the music now. Huge wings beat the air. The Jezbro climbed up above the trees. Held firmly in the extended talons was a fully grown man.

Watching, Johnny Retch felt panic tumble through him, panic that was like a sudden touch of an ice cold hand. They had warned him about the Jezbro. Old Peg-leg had tried to tell him. Gotch had trembled in fear. They had all insisted that there was *something* here that did not belong in the world as he knew it.

He had laughed at them, he had called them superstitious fools. To him, there was nothing that was not of this world.

Nor was there now, when the moment of wild panic had passed. As the Jezbro swept upward through the air, rising along the face of the cliff, Retch jerked up the Tommy gun.

Smoke and lead blasted from the muzzle. The Jezbro was unharmed. Taking careful aim this time, Retch fired again, a furious blast of rattling sound.

The Jezbro swerved, the harp notes missed a beat.

From the suddenly loosened talons a figure plummeted downward, screamed as it fell, stopped screaming as it crunched against the ground.

The Jezbro circled in the air. It rose upward, swooped. Huge wings flapped, a tail structure was extended. From the gaping, extended mouth, a scream arose. The Jezbro seemed to leap toward the summit of the sky.

A flash of light as brilliant as the explosion of a miniature atom bomb flared for a brief second. Thunder clapped, rolled around the horizon; echoed back. In the distance the veil that circled the island shimmered and twisted as if it was about to collapse. It righted itself.

Except for a puff of swiftly dissipating white vapor, the air was clear. Where wild harp notes had once flooded now was silence. Where a creature that had once looked like a giant bird had flapped through the air now there was nothing.

*

On the ledge, Johnny Retch wiped sweat from his face. From his pockets, he methodically refilled the almost empty clip of the gun. He looked down at Gotch, who was sitting up.

"You killed the Jezbro!" Gotch was whispering. His eyes were searching the sky as if he still did not believe what he had seen happen.

"Sure," Retch answered. "I don't know what the hell it was, but it could be killed. Anything can be killed, Gotch. Remember that." The sting of acid crept into his voice. "Get up. We're going on up the ledge."

"By God, Johnny, you can do anything!" Gotch spoke. He rose with suddenly renewed confidence. "Wait'll we get to them—" He looked up the ledge toward the mouth of the tunnel.

Effra was seated in the operator's chair in front of the complex control panel that resembled the key board of a strange organ. She had been watching an image move in the screen directly in front of her eyes.

This image—it had been that of a great bird—had suddenly vanished.

"The Jezbro was destroyed!" she whispered. "The core of it was struck. When that happens, the complete projection is torn to pieces!" Her face was white with strain.

Parker took his eyes off the screen where he had been watching something that he did not pretend to understand.

"Sometimes they are very difficult to control," Effra continued, her voice a whisper. "Once set in motion, they seem almost to achieve life of their own. I did not send the Jezbro against the men on the ground, I sent it against the man on the ledge, against this Retch. But—" her voice faltered.

"I saw it get away," Parker said. There was turmoil in his mind, confusion. He was in a place where miracles came to life. The secret of the ability to walk on the water lay here in this room. Effra, in swift sentences had explained to him that the men who walked on the water carried little pieces of metal in their pockets; pieces of metal which increased tremendously the surface tension of the water where they stepped on it. She had also told him that Ulnar, working this equipment, had *vondeled* his helicopter, had sent out a tiny Jezbro that had struck at the ship, wrecking it. The Jezbro, the secret of the men walking on the water, had come from this room. The striking of the Jezbro was to Ulnar the act of *vondel*. Even the veil that surrounded the island was generated here; in the power being generated in the slowly circling pool of mercury; power that was changed and modified by the other equipment.

Here was the heart and the secret of the magic of this island; here even time was set aside.

Ulnar poked at Effra, grunted harshly. "I know," the girl said quickly. "In just a minute."

Ulnar grunted again. He hovered over her like some massive brooding spirit. He was eager to get his hands on the control board but his old fingers were no longer sufficiently flexible to play on that key board the tune that had to be played.

"*Pater noster*—Our Father—" In the silence came Rozeno's voice as he knelt in prayer. Bewildered and hurt and horrified, Rozeno and Ulnar had come back into the room to find Parker and Effra and Mercedes already there. Mercedes knelt beside him.

Pedro thrust his head through the opening behind them. "Him two more men, him man that kill Jezbro, him still coming up ledge."

"That's Johnny Retch," Parker said. "He's still coming. And there are probably others already inside here, looking for us in the rooms and corridors. We've got to move, Effra."

"I know, Bill." Her fingers started toward the control board, drew back. "I called you Bill. Is that your name?"

"Yes."

"It's a nice name."

"But now we must hurry," Parker said. As he spoke, Ulnar grunted a single sound that set the girl into motion.

Her fingers went to one of the little statuettes, an eagle, a perfect thing in its way, a marvelous representation of the bird of prey. Effra had told Parker, in hasty sentences, how these images were made, deep down in the mountain, of a particular kind of metal that was almost weightless. He watched her slip the eagle into a slot, held his breath as her fingers darted across the key board.

A soft hum sounded—currents moving—a glow sprang into existence surrounding the little image. Slowly, the statuette began to glow with a silver light. The glow played over it, it shifted, changed, was one thing this instant, was something else the next instant. It looked like a moth emerging from a cocoon and becoming a butterfly. The tiny wings came free, the head moved.

The cheeping of a sleepy bird was in the room.

At the sound, a wave of cold from the deepest depths of space seemed to sweep over Parker. Here was magic beyond the comprehension of the mind. Only it wasn't magic, it was a scientific achievement of the highest caliber.

*

At the cheeping sound, Effra's fingers moved swiftly on the control board, playing a symphony that only she understood. The little eagle moved out of the slot, it spread its wings, they fluttered, it moved upward into the air of the room.

With each circling of the room, it grew larger. The cheeping sound became louder, there was a touch of harp music in it now. Effra's fingers moved like lightning over the control panel. The growing eagle seemed to pick up its controls, it swirled, circled, went through the open slot, went out of the room, and into the air outside. It was now the Jezbro.

Its image appeared on the screen. It shot high into the air, still growing. The scene on the screen revealed in miniature the whole island, the sea lapping its shores, the boat lying at anchor. Effra's fingers moved frantically over the controls. "This is one of the hardest things to do. They seem to be attracted to the sun, when first released. They struggle desperately to escape into space—There! I've got it under control."

The scene changed, became a group of men climbing the ledge. Parker saw these men suddenly jerk their heads toward the sky as they became aware of the Jezbro. He could imagine the fear that was shooting through them. They had seen Johnny Retch destroy the Jezbro, only here the Jezbro was again.

From their viewpoint, it had miraculously come back to life and was diving again upon them from the sky. Guns were fired upward. But these men did not have the cool, hard nerves of Johnny Retch, did not have his shooting eye. They missed. The Jezbro dived among them.

They scattered, screaming. Two went off the ledge, three raced down it. One mounted to the sky to the triumphant harping of the Jezbro.

Parker felt a wave of relief flow through him. Here in the Jezbro was actually a most potent weapon, the means of stopping an attack. "Girl! You've done it!"

A second later he caught himself. "But Johnny Retch wasn't in that bunch. He must already be inside the cliff."

A gun roared three times inside the mountain. Footsteps faltered in the corridor outside. Pedro stumbled into the room. His face was a bloody mask.

"Him men inside." As he coughed out the words, he coughed out blood—and his life. He stumbled, caught himself, stumbled again, went down the way a dead man goes down, never to rise again.

"*Qui est in Coelis*—who are in Heaven—" Rozeno's voice whispered through the room. The only sound.

Ulnar moved slowly, stood beside Pedro. They had been master and servant but in the old days they had come up out of Mexico together, guarding a treasure. Ulnar moved to the wall, took down a heavy battle axe that hung there. "Time come for me," he said. "Me go meet men as my chief went to meet Cortez!" His eyes glinted.

"Wait!" Rozeno called. The priest was on his feet. "I have resolved the conflict in my soul. There comes a time when men, even good men, must fight against the forces of evil." From the wall he took a spear.

"I'll go with you two," Parker said. "In just a moment." From his jacket, he took one of the two pistols. Silently he passed it to Effra. "As a last resort, use it."

"But, Bill, there is still time—"

Parker didn't hear her. He was moving with Rozeno and Ulnar through another opening. "At least," Rozeno was saying. "We have this advantage. We know our way around here."

They moved silently, by side passages, through the rooms. "Find Retch," Parker whispered over and over again. "He's the heart and the core of this business. With him out of the way, we can handle the others."

"Do you see anybody, Pfluger?" Retch's voice came from somewhere.

"Naw. I think I got the old gink but he ducked out of sight somewhere."

"Retch is on the other side of the corridor," Rozeno whispered. "The man who spoke last is in the next room."

They slipped to the opening, peering into the next room. A man in there was crouching against the wall and watching the opening into the corridor. At the sight of the man, Ulnar went berserk. This was the man who had killed Pedro.

A shrill battle cry pealing from his lips, massive axe uplifted, Ulnar charged through the door.

The crouching man whirled. Smoke and thunder rolled from the gun in his hand. Ulnar had taken death wounds before he was halfway across the room. But death wounds or not, he kept going.

The heavy axe came down on the head of the man who was desperately trying to fend it off. The man went down. For an instant, Ulnar's battle cry of triumph, wild and savage and fierce, roared through the honeycomb of passages, then went into silence with Ulnar, forever.

"Hey, Pfluger, what the hell happened?" Retch's startled voice came.

"We've got to cross the corridor to get at him," Parker whispered. "And there are other men in here somewhere."

"Listen!" Rozeno whispered.

Voices, a babble of sound, were coming from behind them.

"The men from the village," Rozeno whispered. "When they ceased fearing the Jezbro, they found the courage to come up here."

*

The babble grew stronger. Running feet moved along the corridor. Retch shouted somewhere, but the words were lost.

Rising above the other sounds was the cry of a woman—Effra.

Parker cursed beneath his breath as he ran. At the side entrance to the big room where the pool of mercury turned, he stopped, appalled.

The room seemed full of men. Some of them he recognized as coming from the village, others he had never seen before. From their appearance he judged they had come in the boat. Retch was coming through the door that led into the main corridor. The gun in his hands was centered on Effra, who crouched at the key board of the vast machine. There was a smile on Retch's face.

"Parker!" Retch's voice lifted in a yell. "Parker! I've got your girl. Come on out and give yourself up or I'll let her have it."

This was his moment of triumph, this was the moment when he won his victory. Parker, peering around the edge of the doorway, knew now that he had no way to go. If he moved into the room, and tried to shoot Retch, the man would certainly kill Effra in one wild burst of slugs as he turned the gun on the pilot.

"Parker!" Retch yelled again. A smile on his face, he waited for an answer.

Effra's fingers moved on the control panel. Mercedes got slowly to her feet. The men in the room were silent, waiting for an answer to Retch's command. Parker stood just outside the door, hesitant. No matter what he did, it seemed to him that there was only one answer.

Behind Retch, coming from the corridor, something moved. At the sight of it, Parker felt a flood of biting cold surge through him.

It was a puma—a gigantic puma. In its jaws, as it swung its head from side to side, dangled the body of a man it had killed in the corridor.

It was a Jezbro puma.

Once it had been a little image in a niche beside the machine from the old time. Then life had flowed into it, its own kind of life, now it walked as a huge ravening beast through the room where once it had been a tiny image.

The first man who saw it went dead white and slumped downward in a faint. The others saw it in almost the same instant. Pandemonium swept through the room. No man's nerves were proof against such a sight as this. Screaming men were suddenly trying to fight their way out of a place that had suddenly become haunted.

The puma flowed into the room. Like Retch, it had yellow eyes. They glared now, with a burning light. There was a vague mistiness about this puma but there was also about it the appearance of solid reality.

Retch spun to face the menace coming from behind him. The gun in his hands spat flame and fury.

He had destroyed the Jezbro hawk. He would also destroy this Jezbro puma.

The puma dropped the man from its jaws. It crouched. It leaped straight at the gun spouting lead. Retch slid to one side. The puma missed. It hit the floor, slid, tried to turn as a frantic girl moved buttons on the key board.

The floor was slick, the padded feet did not grip. The tail of the sliding puma touched the pool of mercury. The tail smoked as if it was suddenly on fire.

The puma screamed. It seemed to be drawn into the pool. It was as if something in the pool caught the puma, held it, pulled it into the mercury.

It went out of sight, vanished. No puff of flame followed. The life that had animated it had come from this pool. Now the life had returned to its source.

The dazed Retch lowered his smoking gun.

Parker moved silently forward.

"Lay down the gun, Johnny Retch!" he said.

Retch seemed to stiffen. His back was to Parker. He did not attempt to turn.

"You called for me," Parker said. "Here I am. Drop the gun!"

Retch snarled, spun, dropping flat as he turned. His eyes were narrowed. They glared at Parker like twin flames of yellow hate. He tried to bring up the gun.

Something came through the air, something that he did not see. It grabbed his arms, clutched them with a fierce grip, screamed at him. Mercedes!

Retch, with one savage thrust, flung her aside. Again the two yellow eyes glared at Parker as Retch brought up the weapon that he held.

"You haven't licked me yet!" Retch screamed.

The gun in Parker's hand exploded.

Suddenly Retch had three eyes. One of them was in the middle of his forehead. It was round and blue.

He stood for a second, transfixed. Something had happened to him. He did not know exactly what it was. He had come here seeking Montezuma's treasure. He had it in the reach of his hand. But something had happened to him. What it was he did not quite know. Something—

He tried to lift the gun he held. His hands would not obey him. Or perhaps the gun had suddenly grown too heavy for him to lift. He could not raise it.

The yellow light in his eyes did not change. But suddenly he collapsed, went down, did not move.

*

Even after he was on the floor, his eyes remained fixed on Parker, glaring, yellow. Then, little by little, the yellow flames began to go out.

In the silence were two sounds. The first, Mercedes, whispering. "'Ave I paid my debt, Beel? I tried."

"You have paid it," Parker said.

The other sound was that of the old priest beginning the prayers for the dying. He had laid aside his spear. Now he was kneeling again, his voice lifting as he prayed even for those who had mis-used him.

Then there was another sound, voices shouting in the distance. The men who had run from this room were trying to regain their courage, trying to find the will to come back again.

Parker moved to the girl who sat at the key board.

"Effra, my dear, if you would—"

Catching his idea, she nodded. Her fingers lifted the image of an alligator from its niche.

Parker saw the 'gator waddle from this room of mystery and of magic, from this room of lost science, from this forgotten laboratory of a vanished race.

After the alligator, went a jungle cat, full of spit and scratch and the sounds of fury. After the cat went a jaguar, black, fanged, also with yellow eyes.

In the corridors the screaming stopped. Parker, listening, shuddered. He was glad he was not out in one of those corridors; one of the men who had tried to steal the treasure of Montezuma, one of the men who had followed Johnny Retch. Hell was walking through those

369

tunnels—hell in the form of an alligator; hell in the form of a jungle cat; hell in the form of a jaguar with yellow eyes.

From the window slot, Parker watched men swarm out of the cliff. Some found the small boats, pushed out in them to the PT boat. Others swam. A jaguar went along the shoreline screeching at them. A jungle cat spat at them from the edge of the water.

On the boat, the anchors were hastily cast off. Powerful motors growled. Gathering speed, leaving a growing wake behind it, the boat drove itself into the veil, went out of sight.

Parker went back to the girl at the key board.

Her eyes came up to him. "Hello, Bill," she said.

"Effra?" he whispered.

"As I was sitting here, I remembered who you were—and who I am—Bill—Bill—" She came into his arms.

Hours later, on a balcony in front of one of the window slots, they still stood very close together. Rozeno and Mercedes were with them. Rozeno was speaking.

"Do you think, my son, that you can go out into the world, and contact the great men of this time, and bring them here one by one, so that we may build in this secure spot a group from which the lines of progress can flow out to all men in all the corners of the earth?"

"I can, Father," Parker answered.

"Unto all men—" Rozeno's lips moved in prayer. "Unto all men—"

ASSASSIN

by J. F. Bone

The aliens wooed Earth with gifts, love, patience and peace. Who could resist them? After all, no one shoots Santa Claus!

The rifle lay comfortably in his hands, a gleaming precision instrument that exuded a faint odor of gun oil and powder solvent. It was a perfect specimen of the gunsmith's art, a semi-automatic rifle with a telescopic sight—a precisely engineered tool that could hurl death with pinpoint accuracy for better than half a mile.

Daniel Matson eyed the weapon with bleak gray eyes, the eyes of a hunter framed in the passionless face of an executioner. His blunt hands were steady as they lifted the gun and tried a dry shot at an imaginary target. He nodded to himself. He was ready. Carefully he laid the rifle down on the mattress which covered the floor of his firing point, and looked out through the hole in the brickwork to the narrow canyon of the street below.

The crowd had thickened. It had been gathering since early morning, and the growing press of spectators had now become solid walls of people lining the street, packed tightly together on the sidewalks. Yet despite the fact that there were virtually no police, the crowd did not overflow into the streets, nor was there any of the pushing crowding impatience that once attended an assemblage of this sort. Instead there was a placid tolerance, a spirit of friendly good will, an ingenuous complaisance that grated on Matson's nerves like the screeching rasp of a file drawn across the edge of thin metal. He shivered uncontrollably. It was hard to be a free man in a world of slaves.

It was a measure of the Aztlan's triumph that only a bare half-dozen police 'copters patrolled the empty skies above the parade route. The aliens had done this—had conquered the world without firing a shot or speaking a word in anger. They had wooed Earth with understanding patience and superlative guile—and Earth had fallen into their hands like a lovesick virgin! There never had been any real opposition, and what there was had been completely ineffective. Most of those who had opposed the aliens were out of circulation, imprisoned in correctional institutions, undergoing rehabilitation. Rehabilitation! a six bit word for dehumanizing. When those poor devils finished their treatment with Aztlan brain-washing techniques, they would be just like these sheep below, with the difference that they would never be able to be anything else. But these other stupid fools crowding the sidewalks, waiting to hail their destruction—these were the ones who must be saved. They not the martyrs of the underground, were the important part of humanity.

A police 'copter windmilled slowly down the avenue toward his hiding place, the rotating vanes and insect body of the craft starkly outlined against the jagged backdrop of the city's skyline. He laughed soundlessly as the susurrating flutter of the rotor blades beat overhead and died whispering in the distance down the long canyon of the street. His position had been chosen with care, and was invisible from air and ground alike. He had selected it months ago, and had taken considerable pains to conceal its true purpose. But after today concealment wouldn't matter. If things went as he hoped, the place might someday become a shrine. The idea amused him.

Strange, he mused, how events conspire to change a man's career. Seven years ago he had been a respected and important member of that far different sort of crowd which had welcomed the visitors from space. That was a human crowd—half afraid, wholly curious, jostling, noisy, pushing—a teeming swarm that clustered in a thick disorderly ring around the silver disc that lay in the center of the International Airport overlooking Puget Sound. Then—he could have predicted his career. And none of the predictions would have been true—for none included a man with a rifle waiting in a blind for the game to approach within range . . . .

The Aztlan ship had landed early that July morning, dropping silently through the overcast covering International Airport. It settled gently to rest precisely in the center of the junction of the three main runways of the field, effectively tying up the transcontinental and transoceanic traffic. Fully five hundred feet in diameter, the giant ship squatted massively on the runway junction, cracking and buckling the thick concrete runways under its enormous weight.

By noon, after the first skepticism had died, and the unbelievable TV pictures had been flashed to their waiting audience, the crowd began to gather. All through that hot July morning they came, increasing by the minute as farther outlying districts poured their curious into the Airport. By early afternoon, literally hundreds of millions of eyes were watching the great ship over a world-wide network of television stations which cancelled their regular programs to give their viewers an uninterrupted view of the enigmatic craft.

By mid-morning the sun had burned off the overcast and was shining with brassy brilliance upon the squads of sweating soldiers from Fort Lewis, and more sweating squads of blue-clad police from the metropolitan area of Seattle-Tacoma. The police and soldiery quickly formed a ring around the ship and cleared a narrow lane around the periphery, and this they maintained despite the increasing pressure of the crowd.

The hours passed and nothing happened. The faint creaking and snapping sounds as the seamless hull of the vessel warmed its space-chilled metal in the warmth of the summer sun were lost in the growing impatience of the crowd. They wanted something to happen. Shouts and catcalls filled the air as more nervous individuals clamored to relieve the tension. Off to one side a small group began to clap their hands rhythmically. The little claque gained recruits, and within moments the air was riven by the thunder of thousands of palms meeting in unison. Frightened the crowd might be, but greater than fear was the desire to see what sort of creatures were inside.

Matson stood in the cleared area surrounding the ship, a position of privilege he shared with a few city and state officials and the high brass from McChord Field, Fort Lewis, and Bremerton Navy Yard. He was one of the bright young men who had chosen Government Service as a career, and who, in these days of science-consciousness had risen rapidly through ability and merit promotions to become the Director of the Office of Scientific Research while still in his early thirties. A dedicated man, trained in the bitter school of ideological survival, he understood what the alien science could mean to this world. Their knowledge would secure peace in whatever terms the possessors cared to name, and Matson intended to make sure that his nation was the one which possessed that knowledge.

He stood beside a tall scholarly looking man named Roger Thornton, who was his friend and incidentally the Commissioner of Police for the Twin City metropolitan area. To a casual eye, their positions should be reversed, for the lean ascetic Thornton looked far more like the accepted idea of a scientist than burly, thick shouldered, square faced Matson, whose every movement shouted Cop.

Matson glanced quizzically at the taller man. "Well, Roger, I wonder how long those birds inside are going to keep us waiting before we get a look at them?"

"You'd be surprised if they really were birds, wouldn't you?" Thornton asked with a faint smile. "But seriously, I hope it isn't too much longer. This mob is giving the boys a bad time." He looked anxiously at the strained line of police and soldiery. "I guess I should have ordered out the night shift and reserves instead of just the riot squad. From the looks of things they'll be needed if this crowd gets any more unruly."

Matson chuckled. "You're an alarmist," he said mildly. "As far as I can see they're doing all right. I'm not worried about them—or the crowd, for that matter. The thing that's bothering me is my feet. I've been standing on 'em for six hours and they're killing me!"

"Mine too," Thornton sighed. "Tell you what I'll do. When this is all over I'll split a bucket of hot water and a pint of arnica with you."

"It's a deal," Matson said.

As he spoke a deep musical hum came from inside the ship, and a section of the rim beside him separated along invisible lines of juncture, swinging downward to form a broad ramp leading upward to a square orifice in the rim of the ship. A bright shadowless light that seemed to come from the metal walls of the opening framed the shape of the star traveller who stood there, rigidly erect, looking over the heads of the section of the crowd before him.

A concerted gasp of awe and admiration rose from the crowd—a gasp that was echoed throughout the entire ring that surrounded the ship. There must be other openings like this one, Matson thought dully as he stared at the being from space. Behind him an Army tank rumbled noisily on its treads as it drove through the crowd toward the ship, the long gun in its turret lifting like an alert finger to point at the figure of the alien.

The stranger didn't move from his unnaturally stiff position. His oddly luminous eyes never wavered from their fixed stare at a point far beyond the outermost fringes of the crowd. Seven feet tall, obviously masculine, he differed from mankind only in minor details. His long slender hands lacked the little finger, and his waist was abnormally small. Other than that, he was human in external appearance. A wide sleeved tunic of metallic fabric covered his upper body, gathered in at his narrow waist by a broad metal belt studded with tiny bosses. The tunic ended halfway between hip and knee, revealing powerfully muscled legs encased in silvery hose. Bright yellow hair hung to his shoulders, clipped short in a square bang across his forehead. His face was long, clean featured and extraordinarily calm—almost godlike in its repose. Matson stared, fascinated. He had the curious impression that the visitor had stepped bodily out of the Middle Ages. His dress and haircut were almost identical with that of a medieval courtier.

The starman raised his hand—his strangely luminous steel gray eyes scanned the crowd—and into Matson's mind came a wave of peaceful calm, a warm feeling of goodwill and brotherhood, an indescribable feeling of soothing relaxation. With an odd sense of shock

Matson realized that he was not the only one to experience this. As far back as the farthest hangers-on near the airport gates the tenseness of the waiting crowd relaxed. The effect was amazing! Troops lowered their weapons with shamefaced smiles on their faces. Police relaxed their sweating vigilance. The crowd stirred, moving backward to give its members room. The emotion-charged atmosphere vanished as though it had never been. And a cold chill played icy fingers up the spine of Daniel Matson. He had felt the full impact of the alien's projection, and he was more frightened than he had ever been in his life!

*

They had been clever—damnably clever! That initial greeting with its disarming undertones of empathy and innocence had accomplished its purpose. It had emasculated Mankind's natural suspicion of strangers. And their subsequent actions—so beautifully timed—so careful to avoid the slightest hint of evil, had completed what their magnificently staged appearance had begun.

The feeling of trust had persisted. It lasted through quarantine, clearance, the public receptions, and the private meetings with scientists and the heads of government. It had persisted unabated through the entire two months they remained in the Twin City area. The aliens remained as they had been in the beginning—completely unspoiled by the interest shown in them. They remained simple, unaffected, and friendly, displaying an ingenuous innocence that demanded a corresponding faith in return.

Most of their time was spent at the University of Washington, where at their own request they were studied by curious scholars, and in return were given courses in human history and behavior. They were quite frank about their reasons for following such a course of action—according to their spokesman Ixtl they wanted to learn human ways in order to make a better impression when they visited the rest of Mankind. Matson read that blurb in an official press release and laughed cynically. Better impression, hah! They couldn't have done any better if they had an entire corps of public relations specialists assisting them! They struck exactly the right note—and how could they improve on perfection?

From the beginning they left their great ship open and unguarded while they commuted back and forth from the airport to the campus. And naturally the government quickly rectified the second error and took instant advantage of the first. A guard was posted around the ship to keep it clear of the unofficially curious, while the officially curious combed the vessel's interior with a fine tooth comb. Teams of scientists and technicians under Matson's direction swarmed through the ship, searching with the most advanced methods of human science for the secrets of the aliens.

They quickly discovered that while the star travellers might be trusting, they were not exactly fools. There was nothing about the impenetrably shielded mechanisms that gave the slightest clue as to their purpose or to the principles upon which they operated—nor were there any visible controls. The ship was as blankly uncommunicative as a brick wall.

Matson was annoyed. He had expected more than this, and his frustration drove him to watch the aliens closely. He followed them, sat in on their sessions with the scholars at the University, watched them at their frequent public appearances, and came to know them well enough to recognize the microscopic differences that made them individuals. To the casual eye they were as alike as peas in a pod, but Matson could separate Farn from Quicha, and Laz from Acana—and Ixtl—well he would have stood out from the others in any circumstances. But Matson never intruded. He was content to sit in the background and observe.

And what he saw bothered him. They gave him no reason for their appearance on Earth, and whenever the question came up Ixtl parried it adroitly. They were obviously not explorers for they displayed a startling familiarity with Earth's geography and ecology. They were possibly ambassadors, although they behaved like no ambassadors he had ever seen. They might be traders, although what they would trade only God and the aliens knew—and neither party was in a talking mood. Mysteries bothered Matson. He didn't like them. But they could keep their mystery if he could only have the technical knowledge that was concealed beneath their beautifully shaped skulls.

At that, he had to admit that their appearance had come at precisely the right time. No one better than he knew how close Mankind had been to the final war, when the last two major antagonists on Earth were girding their human and industrial power for a final showdown. But the aliens had become a diversion. The impending war was forgotten while men waited to see what was coming next. It was obvious that the starmen had a reason for being here, and until they chose to reveal it, humanity would forget its deadly problems in anticipation of the answer to this delightful puzzle that had come to them from outer space. Matson was thankful for the breathing space, all too well aware that it might be the last that Mankind might have, but the enigma of the aliens still bothered him.

*

He was walking down the main corridor of the Physics Building on the University campus, wondering as he constantly did about how he could extract some useful knowledge from the aliens when a quiet voice speaking accentless English sounded behind him.

"What precisely do you wish to know, Dr. Matson?" the voice said.

Matson whirled to face the questioner, and looked into the face of Ixtl. The alien was smiling, apparently pleased at having startled him. "What gave you the idea that I wanted to know anything?" he asked.

"You did," Ixtl said. "We all have been conscious of your thoughts for many days. Forgive me for intruding, but I must. Your speculations radiate on such a broad band that we cannot help being aware of them. It has been quite difficult for us to study your customs and history with this high level background noise. We are aware of your interest, but your thoughts are so confused that we have never found questions we could answer. If you would be more specific we would be happy to give you the information which you seek."

"Oh yeah!" Matson thought.

"Of course. It would be to our advantage to have your disturbing speculations satisfied and your fears set at rest. We could accomplish more in a calmer environment. It is too bad that you do not receive as strongly as you transmit. If you did, direct mental contact would convince you that our reasons for satisfying you are good. But you need not fear us, Earthman. We intend you no harm. Indeed, we plan to help you once we learn enough to formulate a proper program."

"I do not fear you," Matson said—knowing that he lied.

"Perhaps not consciously," Ixtl said graciously, "but nevertheless fear is in you. It is too bad—and besides," he continued with a faint smile "it is very uncomfortable. Your glandular emotions are quite primitive, and very disturbing."

"I'll try to keep them under control," Matson said dryly.

"Physical control is not enough. With you there would have to be mental control as well. Unfortunately you radiate much more strongly than your fellow men, and we are unable to shut you out without exerting considerable effort that could better be employed elsewhere." The alien eyed Matson speculatively. "There you go again," he said. "Now you're angry."

Matson tried to force his mind to utter blankness, and the alien smiled at him. "It does some good—but not much," he said. "Conscious control is never perfect."

"Well then, what can I do?"

"Go away. Your range fortunately is short."

Matson looked at the alien. "Not yet," he said coldly. "I'm still looking for something."

"Our technology," Ixtl nodded. "I know. However I can assure you it will be of no help to you. You simply do not have the necessary background. Our science is based upon a completely different philosophy from yours."

To Matson the terms were contradictory.

"Not as much as you think," Ixtl continued imperturbably. "As you will find out, I was speaking quite precisely." He paused and eyed Matson thoughtfully. "It seems as though the only way to remove your disturbing presence is to show you that our technology is of no help to you. I will make a bargain with you. We shall show you our machines, and in return you will stop harassing us. We will do all in our power to make you understand; but whether you do or do not, you will promise to leave and allow us to continue our studies in peace. Is that agreeable?"

Matson swallowed the lump in his throat. Here it was—handed to him on a silver platter—and suddenly he wasn't sure that he wanted it!

"It is," he said. After all, it was all he could expect.

They met that night at the spaceship. The aliens, tall, calm and cool; Matson stocky, heavy-set and sweating. The contrast was infernally sharp, Matson thought. It was as if a primitive savage were meeting a group of nuclear physicists at Los Alamos. For some unknown reason he felt ashamed that he had forced these people to his wishes. But the aliens were pleasant about it. They took the imposition in their usual friendly way.

"Now," Ixtl said. "Exactly what do you want to see—to know?"

"First of all, what is the principle of your space drive?"

"There are two," the alien said. "The drive that moves this ship in normal space time is derived from Lurgil's Fourth Order equations concerning the release of subatomic energy in a restricted space time continuum. Now don't protest! I know you know nothing of Lurgil, nor of Fourth Order equations. And while I can show you the mathematics, I'm afraid they will be of little help. You see, our Fourth Order is based upon a process which you would call Psychomathematics and that is something I am sure you have not yet achieved."

Matson shook his head. "I never heard of it," he admitted.

"The second drive operates in warped space time," Ixtl continued, "hyperspace in your language, and its theory is much more difficult than that of our normal drive, although its application is quite simple, merely involving apposition of congruent surfaces of hyper and normal space at stress points in the ether where high gravitational fields balance. Navigation in hyperspace is done by electronic computer—somewhat more advanced models than yours. However, I can't give you the basis behind the hyperspace drive." Ixtl smiled depreciatingly. "You see, I don't know them myself. Only a few of the most advanced minds of Aztlan can understand. We merely operate the machines."

Matson shrugged. He had expected something like this. Now they would stall him off about the machines after handing him a fast line of double-talk.

"As I said," Ixtl went on, "there is no basis for understanding. Still, if it will satisfy you, we will show you our machines—and the mathematics that created them although I doubt that you will learn anything more from them than you have from our explanation."

"I could try," Matson said grimly.

"Very well," Ixtl replied.

He led the way into the center of the ship where the seamless housings stood, the housings that had baffled some of the better minds of Earth. Matson watched while the star men proceeded to be helpful. The housings fell apart at invisible lines of juncture, revealing mechanisms of baffling simplicity, and some things that didn't look like machines at all. The aliens stripped the strange devices and Ixtl attempted to explain. They had anti-gravity, forcefields, faster than light drive, and advanced design computers that could be packed in a suitcase. There were weird devices whose components seemed to run out of sight at crazily impossible angles, other things that rotated frictionlessly, suspended in fields of pure force, and still others which his mind could not envisage even after his eyes had seen them. All about him lay the evidence of a science so advanced and alien that his brain shrank from the sight, refusing to believe such things existed. And their math was worse! It began where Einstein left off and went off at an incomprehensible tangent that involved psychology and ESP. Matson was lost after the first five seconds!

Stunned, uncomprehending and deflated, he left the ship. An impression that he was standing with his toe barely inside the door of knowledge became a conscious certainty as he walked slowly to his car. The wry thought crossed his mind that if the aliens were trying to convince him of his abysmal ignorance, they had succeeded far beyond their fondest dreams!

They certainly had! Matson thought grimly as he selected five cartridges from the box lying beside him. In fact they had succeeded too well. They had turned his deflation into antagonism, his ignorance into distrust. Like a savage, he suspected what he could not understand. But unlike the true primitive, the emotional distrust didn't interfere with his ability to reason or to draw logical inferences from the data which he accumulated. In attempting to convince, Ixtl had oversold his case.

*

It was shortly after he had returned to Washington, that the aliens gave the waiting world the reasons for their appearance on Earth. They were, they said, members of a very ancient highly evolved culture called Aztlan. And the Aztlans, long past the need for conquest and expansion, had turned their mighty science to the help of other, less fortunate, races in the galaxy. The aliens were, in a sense, missionaries—one of hundreds of teams travelling the star

377

lanes to bring the benefits of Aztlan culture to less favored worlds. They were, they unblushingly admitted, altruists—interested only in helping others.

It was pure corn, Matson reflected cynically, but the world lapped it up and howled for more. After decades of cold war, lukewarm war, and sporadic outbreaks of violence, that were inevitably building to atomic destruction, men were willing to try anything that would ease the continual burden of strain and worry. To Mankind, the Aztlans' words were as refreshing as a cool breeze of hope in a desert of despair.

And the world got what it wanted.

Quite suddenly the aliens left the Northwest, and accompanied by protective squads of FBI and Secret Service began to cross the nation. Taking widely separated paths they visited cities, towns, and farms, exhibiting the greatest curiosity about the workings of human civilization. And, in turn, they were examined by hordes of hopeful humans. Everywhere they went, they spread their message of good will and hope backed by the incredibly convincing power of their telepathic minds. Behind them, they left peace and hopeful calm; before them, anticipation mounted. It rose to a crescendo in New York where the paths of the star men met.

The Aztlans invaded the United Nations. They spoke to the General Assembly and the Security Council, were interviewed by the secretariat and reporters from a hundred foreign lands. They told their story with such conviction that even the Communist bloc failed to raise an objection, which was as amazing to the majority of the delegates as the fact of the star men themselves. Altruism, it seemed, had no conflict with dialectic materialism. The aliens offered a watered-down variety of their technology to the peoples of Earth with no strings attached, and the governments of Earth accepted with open hands, much as a small boy accepts a cookie from his mother. It was impossible for men to resist the lure of something for nothing, particularly when it was offered by such people as the Aztlans. After all, Matson reflected bitterly, nobody shoots Santa Claus!

From every nation in the world came invitations to the aliens to visit their lands. The star men cheerfully accepted. They moved across Europe, Asia, and Africa—visited South America, Central America, the Middle East and Oceania. No country escaped them. They absorbed languages, learned customs, and spread good will. Everywhere they went relaxation followed in their footsteps, and throughout the world arose a realization of the essential brotherhood of man.

It took nearly three years of continual travelling before the aliens again assembled at UN headquarters to begin the second part of their promised plan—to give their science to Earth. And men waited with calm expectation for the dawn of Golden Age.

*

Matson's lips twisted. Fools! Blind, stupid fools! Selling their birthright for a mess of pottage! He shifted the rifle across his knees and began filling the magazine with cartridges. He felt an empty loneliness as he closed the action over the filled magazine and turned the safety to "on". There was no comforting knowledge of support and sympathy to sustain him in what he was about to do. There was no real hope that there ever would be. His was a voice crying in the wilderness, a voice that was ignored—as it had been when he visited the President of the United States . . . .

*

Matson entered the White House, presented his appointment card, and was ushered past ice-eyed Secret Service men into the presidential office. It was as close as he had ever been to the Chief Executive, and he stared with polite curiosity across the width of desk which separated them.

"I wanted to see you about the Aztlan business," the President began without preamble. "You were there when their ship landed, and you are also one of the few men in the country who has seen them alone. In addition, your office will probably be handling the bulk of our requests in regard to the offer they made yesterday in the UN. You're in a favorable spot." The President smiled and shrugged. "I wanted to talk with you sooner, but business and routine play the devil with one's desires in this office.

"Now tell me," he continued, "your impression of these people."

"They're an enigma," Matson said flatly. "To tell the truth, I can't figure them out." He ran his fingers through his hair with a worried gesture. "I'm supposed to be a pretty fair physicist, and I've had quite a bit of training in the social sciences, but both the mechanisms and the psychology of these Aztlans are beyond my comprehension. All I can say for sure is that they're as far beyond us as we are beyond the cavemen. In fact, we have so little in common that I can't think of a single reason why they would want to stay here, and the fact that they do only adds to my confusion."

"But you must have learned something," the President said.

"Oh we've managed to collect data," Matson replied. "But there's a lot of difference between data and knowledge."

"I can appreciate that, but I'd still like to know what you think. Your opinion could have some weight."

Matson doubted it. His opinions were contrary to those of the majority. Still, the Chief asked for it—and he might possibly have an open mind. It was a chance worth taking.

"Well, Sir, I suppose you've heard of the so-called "wild talents" some of our own people occasionally possess?"

The President nodded.

"It is my belief," Matson continued, "that the Aztlans possess these to a far greater degree than we do, and that their science is based upon them. They have something which they call psychomathematics, which by definition is the mathematics of the mind, and this seems to be the basis of their physical science. I saw their machines, and I must confess that their purpose baffled me until I realized that they must be mechanisms for amplifying their own natural equipment. We know little or nothing about psi phenomena, so it is no wonder I couldn't figure them out. As a matter of fact we've always treated psi as something that shouldn't be mentioned in polite scientific conversation."

The President grinned. "I always thought you boys had your blind spots."

"We do—but when we're confronted with a fact, we try to find out something about it—that is if the fact hits us hard enough, often enough."

"Well, you've been hit hard and often," the President chuckled, "What did you find out?"

379

"Facts," Matson said grimly, "just facts. Things that could be determined by observation and measurement. We know that the aliens are telepathic. We also know that they have a form of ESP—or perhaps a recognition of danger would be a better term—and we know its range is somewhat over a third of a mile. We know that they're telekinetic. The lack of visible controls in their ship would tell us that, even if we hadn't seen them move small objects at a distance. We know that they have eidetic memories, and that they can reason on an extremely high level. Other than that we know nothing. We don't even know their physical structure. We've tried X-ray but they're radio-opaque. We've tried using some human sensitives from the Rhine Institute, but they're unable to get anywhere. They just turn empathic in the aliens' presence, and when we get them back, they do nothing but babble about the beauty of the Aztlan soul."

"Considering the difficulties, you haven't done too badly," the President said. "I take it then, that you're convinced that they are an advanced life form. But do you think they're sincere in their attitude toward us?"

"Oh, they're sincere enough," Matson said. "The only trouble is that we don't know just what they're sincere about. You see, sir, we are in the position of a savage to whom a trader brings the luxuries of civilization. To the savage, the trader may represent purest altruism, giving away such valuable things as glass beads and machine made cloth for useless pieces of yellow rock and the skins of some native pest. The savage hasn't the slightest inkling that he's being exploited. By the time he realizes he's been had, and the yellow rock is gold and the skins are mink, he has become so dependent upon the goods for which the trader has whetted his appetite that he inevitably becomes an economic slave.

"Of course you can argue that the cloth and beads are far more valuable to the savage than the gold or mink. But in the last analysis, value is determined by the higher culture, and by that standard, the savage gets taken. And ultimately civilization moves in and the superior culture of the trader's race determines how the savage will act.

"Still, the savage has a basis for his acts. He is giving something for something—making a trade. But we're not even in that position. The aliens apparently want nothing from us. They have asked for nothing except our good will, and that isn't a tradable item."

"But they're altruists!" the President protested.

"Sir, do you think that they're insane?" Matson asked curiously. "Do they appear like fanatics to you?"

"But we can't apply our standards to them. You yourself have said that their civilization is more advanced than ours."

"Whose standards can we apply?" Matson asked. "If not ours, then whose? The only standards that we can possibly apply are our own, and in the entire history of human experience there has never been a single culture that has had a basis of pure altruism. Such a culture could not possibly exist. It would be overrun and gobbled up by its practical neighbors before it drew its first breath.

"We must assume that the culture from which these aliens come has had a practical basis in its evolutionary history. It could not have risen full blown and altruistic like Minerva from the brain of Jove. And if the culture had a practical basis in the past, it logically follows that it has a practical basis in the present. Such a survival trait as practicality would probably never be lost no matter how far the Aztlan race has evolved. Therefore, we must concede that they are practical people—people who do not give away something for nothing. But the question still remains—what do they want?

"Whatever it is, I don't think it is anything from which we will profit. No matter how good it looks, I am convinced that cooperation with these aliens will not ultimately be to our advantage. Despite the reports of every investigative agency in this government, I cannot believe that any such thing as pure altruism exists in a sane mind. And whatever I may believe about the Aztlans, I do not think they're insane."

The President sighed. "You are a suspicious man, Matson, and perhaps you are right; but it doesn't matter what you believe—or what I believe for that matter. This government has decided to accept the help the Aztlans are so graciously offering. And until the reverse is proven, we must accept the fact that the star men *are* altruists, and work with them on that basis. You will organize your office along those lines, and extract every gram of information that you can. Even you must admit that they have knowledge that will improve our American way of life."

Matson shook his head doggedly. "I'm afraid, Sir, if you expect Aztlan science to improve the American way of life, you are going to be disappointed. It might promote an Aztlan way of life, but the reverse is hardly possible."

"It's not my decision," the President said. "My hands are tied. Congress voted for the deal by acclamation early this morning. I couldn't veto it even if I wanted to."

"I cannot cooperate in what I believe is our destruction." Matson said in a flat voice.

"Then you have only one course," the President said. "I will be forced to accept your resignation." He sighed wearily.

"Personally, I think you're making a mistake. Think it over before you decide. You're a good man, and Lord knows the government can use good men. There are far too many fools in politics." He shrugged and stood up. The interview was over.

Matson returned to his offices, filled with cold frustration. Even the President believed he could do nothing, and these shortsighted politicians who could see nothing more than the immediate gains—there was a special hell reserved for them. There were too many fools in politics. However, he would do what he could. His sense of duty was stronger than his resentment. He would stay on and try to cushion some of the damage which the Aztlans would inevitably cause, no matter how innocent their motives. And perhaps the President was right—perhaps the alien science would bring more good than harm.

*

For the next two years Matson watched the spread of Aztlan ideas throughout the world. He saw Aztlan devices bring health, food and shelter to millions in underprivileged countries, and improve the lot of those in more favored nations. He watched tyrannies and authoritarian governments fall under the passive resistance of their peoples. He saw militarism crumble to impotence as the Aztlan influence spread through every facet of society, first as a trickle, then as a steady stream, and finally as a rushing torrent. He saw Mankind on the brink of a Golden Age—and he was unsatisfied.

Reason said that the star men were exactly what they claimed to be. Their every action proved it. Their consistency was perfect, their motives unimpeachable, and the results of their efforts were astounding. Life on Earth was becoming pleasant for millions who never knew the meaning of the word. Living standards improved, and everywhere men were conscious of a feeling of warmth and brotherhood. There was no question that the aliens were doing exactly what they promised.

But reason also told him that the aliens were subtly and methodically destroying everything that man had created, turning him from an individual into a satisfied puppet operated by Aztlan strings. For man is essentially lazy—always searching for the easier way. Why should he struggle to find an answer when the Aztlans had discovered it millennia ago and were perfectly willing to share their knowledge? Why should he use inept human devices when those of the aliens performed similar operations with infinitely more ease and efficiency? Why should he work when all he had to do was ask? There was plan behind their acts.

But at that point reason dissolved into pure speculation. Why were they doing this? Was it merely mistaken kindliness or was there a deeper more subtle motive? Matson didn't know, and in that lack of knowledge lay the hell in which he struggled.

*

For two years he stayed on with the OSR, watching humanity rush down an unmarked road to an uncertain future. Then he ran away. He could take no more of this blind dependence upon alien wisdom. And with the change in administration that had occurred in the fall elections he no longer had the sense of personal loyalty to the President which had kept him working at a job he despised. He wanted no part of this brave new world the aliens were creating. He wanted to be alone. Like a hermit of ancient times who abandoned society to seek his soul, Matson fled to the desert country of the South-west—as far as possible from the Aztlans and their works.

The grimly beautiful land toughened his muscles, blackened his skin, and brought him a measure of peace. Humanity retreated to remoteness except for Seth Winters, a leathery old-timer he had met on his first trip into the desert. The acquaintance had ripened to friendship. Seth furnished a knowledge of the desert country which Matson lacked, and Matson's money provided the occasional grubstake they needed. For weeks at a time they never saw another human—and Matson was satisfied. The world could go its own way. He would go his.

Running away was the smartest thing he could have done. Others more brave perhaps, or perhaps less rational—had tried to fight, to form an underground movement to oppose these altruists from space; but they were a tiny minority so divided in motives and purpose that they could not act as a unit. They were never more than a nuisance, and without popular support they never had a chance. After the failure of a complicated plot to assassinate the aliens, they were quickly rounded up and confined. And the aliens continued their work.

*

Matson shrugged. It was funny how little things could mark mileposts in a man's life. If he had known of the underground he probably would have joined it and suffered the same penalty for failure. If he hadn't fled, if he hadn't met Seth Winters, if he hadn't taken that last trip into the desert, if any one of a hundred little things had happened differently he would not be here. That last trip into the desert—he remembered it as though it were yesterday . . . .

The yellow flare of a greasewood fire cast flickering spears of light into the encircling darkness. Above, in the purplish black vault of the moonless sky the stars shone down with icy splendor. The air was quiet, the evening breeze had died, and the stillness of the desert night pressed softly upon the earth. Far away, muted by distance, came the ululating wail of a coyote.

Seth Winters laid another stick of quick-burning greasewood on the fire and squinted across the smoke at Matson who was lying on his back, arms crossed behind his head, eyeing the night sky with the fascination of a dreamer.

"It's certainly peaceful out here," Matson murmured as he rose to his feet, stretched, and sat down again looking into the tiny fire.

"'Tain't nothin' unusual, Dan'l. Not out here it ain't. It's been plumb peaceful on this here desert nigh onto a million years. An' why's it peaceful? Mainly 'cuz there ain't too many humans messin' around in it."

"Possibly you're right, Seth."

"Shore I'm right. It jest ain't nacheral fer a bunch of Homo saps to get together without an argyment startin' somewhere. 'Tain't the nature of the critter to be peaceable. An' y'know, thet's the part of this here sweetness an' light between nations that bothers me. Last time I was in Prescott, I set down an' read six months of newspapers—an' everything's jest too damn good to be true. Seems like everybody's gettin' to love everybody else." He shook his head. "The hull world's as sticky-sweet as molasses candy. It jest ain't nacheral!"

"The star men are keeping their word. They said that they would bring us peace. Isn't that what they're doing?"

"Shucks Dan'l—that don't give 'em no call to make the world a blasted honey-pot with everybody bubblin' over with brotherly love. There ain't no real excitement left. Even the Commies ain't raisin' hell like they useta. People are gettin' more like a bunch of damn woolies every day."

"I'll admit that Mankind had herd instincts," Matson replied lazily, "but I've never thought of them as particularly sheeplike. More like a wolf pack, I'd say."

"Wal, there's nothin' wolflike about 'em right now. Look, Dan'l, yuh know what a wolf pack's like. They're smart, tough, and mean—an' the old boss wolf is the smartest, toughest, and meanest critter in the hull pack. The others respect him 'cuz he's proved his ability to lead. But take a sheep flock now—the bellwether is jest a nice gentle old castrate thet'll do jest whut the sheepherder wants. He's got no originality. He's jest a noise thet the rest foller."

"Could be."

"It shore is! Jes f'r instance, an' speakin' of bellwethers, have yuh ever heard of a character called Throckmorton Bixbee?"

"Can't say I have. He sounds like a nance."

"Whutever a nance is—he's it! But yuh're talkin' about our next President, unless all the prophets are wrong. He's jest as bad as his name. Of all the gutless wonders I've ever heard of that pilgrim takes the prize. He even looks like a rabbit!"

"I can see where I had better catch up on some contemporary history," Matson said. "I've been out in the sticks too long."

"If yuh know what's good fer yuh, yuh'll stay here. The rest of the country's goin' t'hell. Brother Bixbee's jest a sample. About the only thing that'd recommend him is that he's hot fer peace—an' he's got those furriners' blessing. Seems like those freaks swing a lotta weight nowadays, an' they ain't shy about tellin' folks who an' what they favor. They've got bold as brass this past year."

Matson nodded idly—then stiffened—turning a wide eyed stare on Seth. A blinding light exploded in his brain as the words sank in. With crystal clarity he knew the answer! He laughed harshly.

Winters stared at him with mild surprise. "What's bit yuh, Dan'l?"

But Matson was completely oblivious, busily buttressing the flash of inspiration. Sure—that was the only thing it could be! Those aliens were working on a program—one that was grimly recognizable once his attention was focussed on it. There must have been considerable pressure to make them move so fast that a short-lived human could see what they were planning—but Matson had a good idea of what was driving them, an atomic war that could decimate the world would be all the spur they'd need!

They weren't playing for penny ante stakes. They didn't want to exploit Mankind. They didn't give a damn about Mankind! To them humanity was merely an unavoidable nuisance—something to be pushed aside, to be made harmless and dependent, and ultimately to be quietly and bloodlessly eliminated. Man's civilization held nothing that the star men wanted, but man's planet—that was a different story! Truly the aliens were right when they considered man a savage. Like the savage, man didn't realize his most valuable possession was his land!

The peaceful penetration was what had fooled him. Mankind, faced with a similar situation, and working from a position of overwhelming strength would have reacted differently. Humanity would have invaded and conquered. But the aliens had not even considered this obvious step.

Why?

The answer was simple and logical. They couldn't! Even though their technology was advanced enough to exterminate man with little or no loss to themselves, combat and slaughter must be repulsive to them. It had to be. With their telepathic minds they would necessarily have a pathologic horror of suffering. They were so highly evolved that they simply couldn't fight—at least not with the weapons of humanity. But they could use the subtler weapon of altruism!

And even more important—uncontrolled emotions were poison to them. In fact Ixtl had admitted it back in Seattle. The primitive psi waves of humanity's hates, lusts, fears, and exultations must be unbearable torture to a race long past such animal outbursts. That was—must be—why they were moving so fast. For their own safety, emotion had to be damped out of the human race.

Matson had a faint conception of what the aliens must have suffered when they first surveyed that crowd at International Airport. No wonder they looked so strangely immobile at that first contact! The raw emotion must have nearly killed them! He felt a reluctant stir of admiration for their courage, for the dedicated bravery needed to face that crowd and establish a beachhead of tranquility. Those first few minutes must have had compressed in them the agonies of a lifetime!

Matson grinned coldly. The aliens were not invulnerable. If Mankind could be taught to fear and hate them, and if that emotion could be focussed, they never again would try to take this world. It would be sheer suicide. As long as Mankind kept its emotions it would be safe from this sort of invasion. But the problem was to teach Mankind to fear and hate. Shock would do it, but how could that shock be applied?

The thought led inevitably to the only possible conclusion. The aliens would have to be killed, and in such a manner as to make humanity fear retaliation from the stars. Fear would unite men against a possible invasion, and fear would force men to reach for the stars to forestall retribution.

Matson grinned thinly. Human nature couldn't have changed much these past years. Even with master psychologists like the Aztlans operating upon it, changes in emotional pattern would require generations. He sighed, looked into the anxious face of Seth Winters, and returned to the reality of the desert night. His course was set. He knew what he had to do.

*

He laid the rifle across his knees and opened the little leather box sewn to the side of the guncase. With precise, careful movements he removed the silencer and fitted it to the threaded muzzle of the gun. The bulky, blue excrescence changed the rifle from a thing of beauty to one of murder. He looked at it distastefully, then shrugged and stretched out on the mattress, easing the ugly muzzle through the hole in the brickwork. It wouldn't be long now . . . .

He glanced upward through the window above him at the Weather Bureau instruments atop a nearby building. The metal cups of the anemometer hung motionless against the metallic blue of the sky. No wind stirred in the deep canyons of the city streets as the sun climbed in blazing splendor above the towering buildings. He moved a trifle, shifting the muzzle of the gun until it bore upon the sidewalks. The telescopic sight picked out faces from the waiting crowd with a crystal clarity. Everywhere was the same sheeplike placidity. He shuddered, the sights jumping crazily from one face to another,—wondering if he had misjudged his race, if he had really come too late, if he had underestimated the powers of the Aztlans.

Far down the avenue, an excited hum came to his ears, and the watching crowd stirred. Faces lighted and Matson sighed. He was not wrong. Emotion was only suppressed, not vanished. There was still time!

The aliens were coming. Coming to cap the climax of their pioneer work, to drive the first nail in humanity's coffin! For the first time in history man's dream of the brotherhood of man was close to reality.

And he was about to destroy it! The irony bit into Matson's soul, and for a moment he hesitated, feeling the wave of tolerance and good will rising from the street below. Did he have the right to destroy man's dream? Did he dare tamper with the will of the world? Had he the right to play God?

The parade came slowly down the happy street, a kaleidoscope of color and movement that approached and went past in successive waves and masses. This was a gala day, this eve of world union! The insigne of the UN was everywhere. The aliens had used the organization to further their plans and it was now all-powerful. A solid bank of UN flags led the van of delegates, smiling and swathed in formal dress, sitting erect in their black official cars draped with the flags of native lands that would soon be furled forever if the aliens had their way.

And behind them came the Aztlans!

*

They rode together, standing on a pure white float, a bar of dazzling white in a sea of color. All equal, their inhumanly beautiful faces calm and remote, the Aztlans rode through the joyful crowd. There was something inspiring about the sight and for a moment, Matson felt a wave of revulsion sweep through him.

He sighed and thumbed the safety to "off", pulled the cocking lever and slid the first cartridge into the breech. He settled himself drawing a breath of air into his lungs, letting a little dribble out through slack lips, catching the remainder of the exhalation with closed glottis. The sights wavered and steadied upon the head of the center alien, framing the pale noble face with its aureole of golden hair. The luminous eyes were dull and introspective as the alien tried to withdraw from the emotions of the crowd. There was no awareness of danger on the alien's face. At 600 yards he was beyond their esper range and he was further covered by the feelings of the crowd. The sights lowered to the broad chest and centered there as Matson's spatulate fingers took up the slack in the trigger and squeezed softly and steadily.

A coruscating glow bathed the bodies of three of the aliens as their tall forms jerked to the smashing impact of the bullets! Their metallic tunics melted and sloughed as inner fires ate away the fragile garments that covered them! Flexible synthetic skin cracked and curled in the infernal heat, revealing padding, wirelike tendons, rope-like cords of flexible tubing and a metallic skeleton that melted and dripped in white hot drops in the heat of atomic flame—

"Robots!" Matson gasped with sudden blinding realization. "I should have known! No wonder they seemed inhuman. Their builders would never dare expose themselves to the furies and conflicts of our emotionally uncontrolled world!"

One of the aliens crouched on the float, his four-fingered hands pressed against a smoking hole in his metal tunic. The smoke thickened and a yellowish ichor poured out bursting into flame on contact with the air. The fifth alien, Ixtl, was untouched, standing with hands widestretched in a gesture that at once held command and appeal.

Matson reloaded quickly, but held his fire. The swarming crowd surrounding the alien was too thick for a clear shot and Matson, with sudden revulsion, was unwilling to risk further murder in a cause already won. The tall, silver figure of the alien winced and shuddered, his huge body shaking like a leaf in a storm! His builders had never designed him to withstand the barrage of focussed emotion that was sweeping from the crowd. Terror, shock, sympathy, hate, loathing, grief, and disillusionment—the incredible gamut of human feelings wrenched and tore at the Aztlan, shorting delicate circuits, ripping the poised balance of his being as the violent discordant blasts lanced through him with destroying energy! Ixtl's classic features twisted in a spasm of inconceivable agony, a thin curl of smoke drifted from his distorted tragic mask of a mouth as he crumpled, a pitiful deflated figure against the whiteness of the float.

The cries of fear and horror changed their note as the aliens' true nature dawned upon the crowd. Pride of flesh recoiled as the swarming humans realized the facts. Revulsion at being led by machines swelled into raw red rage. The mob madness spread as an ominous growl began rising from the streets.

A panicky policeman triggered it, firing his Aztlan-built shock tube into the forefront of the mob. A dozen men fell, to be trampled by their neighbors as a swarm of men and women poured over the struggling officer and buried him from sight. Like wildfire, pent-up emotions blazed out in a flame of fury. The parade vanished, sucked into the maelstrom and torn apart. Fists flew, flesh tore, men and women screamed in high bitter agony as the mob clawed and trampled in a surging press of writhing forms that filled the street from one line of buildings to the other.

Half-mad with triumph, drunk with victory, shocked at the terrible form that death had taken in coming to Ixtl, Matson raised his clenched hands to the sky and screamed in a raw inhuman voice, a cry in which all of man's violence and pride were blended! The spasm passed as quickly as it came, and with its passing came exhaustion. The job was done. The aliens were destroyed. Tomorrow would bring reaction and with it would come fear.

Tomorrow or the next day man would hammer out a true world union, spurred by the thought of a retribution that would never come. Yet all that didn't matter. The important thing—the only important thing—was preserved. Mankind would have to unite for survival—or so men would think—and he would never disillusion them. For this was man's world, and men were again free to work out their own destiny for better or for worse, without interference, and without help. The golden dream was over. Man might fail, but if he did he would fail on his own terms. And if he succeeded—Matson looked up grimly at the shining sky . . . .

Slowly he rose to his feet and descended to the raging street below.

PROBABILITY

by Louis Trimble

If you ever get to drinking beer in your favorite saloon and meet a scared little guy who wants to buy you the joint, supply you with fur coats and dolls and run you for Congress—listen well! That is, if you really want the joint, the fur coats, the dolls and a seat in Congress. Just ask Mike Murphy . . . .

The first time this little guy comes in I'm new on the job. He looks around as if he's scared a prohibition agent will pop out of the walls and bite him. Then he gets up his nerve and sidles to the bar. His voice is as thin as the rest of him.

"Glass of beer."

I draw. He drinks and pays and goes out.

That keeps on, Monday through Friday at five-ten p.m., year in and year out. He slips in, peers around, has his beer, and pops out. Even in '33, when we become legitimate, he acts the same way—scared of his shadow. Except he isn't big enough to have a shadow.

During the war, when we're rationed, I save him his daily glass. He never fails to come in except for two weeks every summer when he's on vacation. From 1922 to 1953 he drinks one daily beer.

In thirty-one years, he and I grow older together, and after the first ten he talks a little so that over a period of time I manage to learn something about him. That first day he'd come in, he was on his first job out of college. Well, so was I, only I went to bartending school to learn how to mix prohibition liquor. But even so, it gave us something in common, and when he learned we had started life together—as he put it—he talked a little more.

His name is Pettis. Six months after I learn that, I get his first name. It's Rabelais, and I could see why he doesn't like it. But when he breaks down and tells me, he gets real bold and says:

"And what's yours, my male Hebe?"

"Mike Murphy."

"Naturally," he said. He laughs. It is the only time I hear him laugh in thirty-one years. I can't see anything funny.

He is a draftsman for those old skinflints Cartner and Dillson. When they die, their sons take over and are even worse. In the depression, Pettis gets a little shabby but he always has the price of a glass of beer. In '53 he's at the same desk and doing the same job he started on in '22.

In '35 he gets married. He tells me so. Tasting his beer, he says, "I'll be married this time tomorrow." I often wonder what his wife looks like but I never see her. Not even when it gets decent for ladies to come in, she never shows. Marriage doesn't seem to change him; he never looks happier or less shabby or less browbeat.

In '42 I heard his first complaint. By then we're both getting into our forties and, what with his lack of size and caved-in chest and my insides all busted up from pre-World War I football, the army doesn't want us. So he never misses a day except on his vacation.

He says, "I can't get raw materials." About three months later, I understand what he means when he says, "My hobby is inventing."

In '45 I ask him, "What do you invent?"

It takes him two years to decide to tell me. By now we are pretty good pals. He never tells anyone else that I know of. He says, "I invent machines. Super machines."

In '48 he says, "But they don't work. Someday . . . ."

*

And in '53, on the day of our thirty-first anniversary, you might say, he comes in and things are different. All different. I can feel it when he opens the door and comes in at five-o-nine instead of five-ten. There is plenty more different, too. He walks up to the bar like it's his and roars:

"Two beers, Mike!"

I drop a glass I'm so surprised, but I give him two beers like he wants. He gulps them both down, puts a foot on the rail and looks me straight in the eye. His eyes are a sort of washed blue. I've never noticed them before.

"Beer for the house!" he yells at me.

"Take it easy, Mr. Pettis," I says.

"Easy, hell!" he shouts and slaps a roll as big as his hand on the bar. "And call me Rabelais, Mike. We're pals, aren't we?"

"You bet," I assures him. And I mean it. Not because of the dough. That makes me sweat. I can't figure where this little guy gets such a wad. And good money, too.

He sets them up three times. By now he's feeling fine. I suggest he get going before he misses the last train home.

"I already missed it," he says proudly. "And I'm not going home. Let the old battle-axe really have something to complain about. Beer, Mike!"

In a way I hate to see it, but then I figure a man has a right to let off a little steam once every thirty-one years. Even so, I get a little worried when he asks for the phone and calls up his wife.

He says, "Myrtle, this Rabelais. Rabelais, your husband, you old sow." He takes a breath and says, "You're damned right I'm drunk. And I'm staying that way. Go home to your mother . . . . Oh yes, you are. You're leaving on the 12:05 tomorrow and you'll eat chicken a la king on the train and fall asleep at Holt's Corner and snore all the way home. And your mother will be mad because her left fender will get dented on the way to the station." Bang! He hangs up.

"Beer, Mike."

"Now look, Mr.—Rabelais—"

He ignores me. "Mike, who owns this place?"

I don't, but I'd like to. I tell him who my boss is and he hunts him up in the phone book and calls him. He says, "This is Rabelais Pettis. I want to buy your Fifth Avenue Tavern. How much? . . . Sold!"

And so help me, the boss comes down and Rabelais hauls bills from every pocket and lays it on the bar in a great big pile. Then he has the boss sign the place over to me. Me, Mike Murphy. I figure tomorrow when he wakes up broke I'll have to give it back. But tonight I own it. I'm real proud.

But I don't get to enjoy it. He says, "Mike, let's do the town." Can you refuse a guy who just gives you a thirty thousand dollar property? We do the town. We do the girl shows, and he yells at all the dames and tries to date the usherettes until we finally get pitched out. We get pitched out of five before I steer him to a hash house.

"Phooey," he says. "We'll go to the Buster for a steak." That's our fanciest place where the food starts at ten dollars. We have two of the biggest steaks I ever saw with champagne and stuff, and so help me, when Rabelais tries to date the floor show girls, instead of getting pitched out, we walk out with two of the cutest kids I ever hope to see. Only they're young enough to be our daughters or maybe grand-daughters even.

Rabelais is big hearted if not big in any other way. He says to his kid, a redhead a foot taller than he, "Do you have a fur coat?"

"No, Rabelais." She learns fast that he likes the name now.

"Ha," he says. "Then we'll get some."

"In the summer?" I asks.

"We'll make it winter," Rabelais says. "I'm tired of summer. Besides in '56 there's a new bar in town and it's a pip."

Now the three of us are halfway sober and we just look at each other and shrug. But Rabelais acts and talks normal enough. He calls a cab and has us hauled to an old cottage in the suburbs. He waves the cabby off with a twenty dollar bill. When we go inside, he points across the way. "I live there. This is my secret laboratory."

We think he is kidding us some more because there isn't anything but dust and cobwebs in the place. But he takes us to the basement and there is a whole mess of junk lying around. There are bars and gears and wires and some stuff that doesn't make any sense at all. It has cobwebs and dust on it too.

"My super machines," he says. "They don't work."

The redhead looks a little as if she thinks he's nuts. But what can she do? Already he's given her a hundred dollar bill just for fun.

"But," he says, leading us into another room, "this one does work."

There isn't anything in the room but a big metal plate on the floor with a wooden bench on it and levers and rods in front of the bench. "Climb on," Rabelais says.

We sit on the bench to humor him and he pulls one lever as far left as he can, then another a little ways, then another, and a fourth. Then he twists a rod to the right. The lights go out and a cold draft of air comes in through a window. When the lights come on the air is still cold. The girls are shivering.

"Three p.m., January 12, 1956," says Rabelais. "Let's go get fur coats."

So we go out the way we came in and it's daylight. And there's snow on the ground. The cottage is the same but the street is a highway now. Rabalais hails the fanciest looking cab I ever see and we get driven to town where he buys all of us fur coats in a store I never heard of. Then we go to a dinner club that makes the Buster look like a greasy spoon. None of us can say a word.

After he pays the check, Rabelais says, "I'm short of cash. Let's go to the bank."

"Banks ain't open," I remind him.

"Mine is," he says and makes a phone call. Pretty soon a big fancy limousine with a chauffeur drives up and we all pile in. I manage to balk long enough to buy a newspaper. Sure enough, the date is January 12, 1956.

We go to the financial section and right past my tavern. It's all lighted up and fancy looking and there's a big sign saying, "MIKE'S" outside.

Rabelais says, "You're making a mint, Mike."

"I see," I agrees, dazed. Rabelais flicks the paper with a silly grin and tells me to look on page four. I do and there's an editorial beside a cartoon of me, pot belly and all, and it says, "Mayor Mike Murphy agrees to run for Congress . . . ."

"Me?"

"You," says Rabelais. "You make it, too, Mike."

Before I can answer, we stop at a building lighted up. Over the door it says, "Pettis." That's all. It's his, the whole building. And it's full of offices. He shows me one where his former bosses are slaving over drafting boards. The bank part is closed but some slavies are working late as people in banks always do and we go in and Rabelais gets a wad of money and we leave.

It goes on like that. I'm ashamed to say we get sort of looped and the next thing we know we're in Paris and having a fine time. Then we take another flier on his machine and it's summer. We enjoy that for a while and then try another season. It goes on that way for a couple weeks. Once we accept the fact that we're traveling in time, it's easy.

But Rabelais, even when he's looped, won't take us into the past or far into the future. He just says, "We have to watch probability, Mike."

I don't get the idea but it doesn't seem to matter much. We're having too good a time kicking around in the near future. Finally when we all feel ready for a Keeley cure, Rabelais takes us home. We land in the basement at the very moment we left it but with our fur coats and fancy luggage and souvenirs. Rabelais looks over all the gadgets we have and those that are too much ahead of our time, he throws away.

In a taxi heading for town, I smoke my dollar cigar. I'm happy. The girls are quiet, a little sad.

"It was fun," the redhead sighs. "Kicking won't seem the same."

"Quit that kind of work," Rabelais says. "Go to college or something." And he hands each of them a big wad of money.

Downtown we split up, each of us going off somewhere to get the rest we need. I sleep around the clock and a little more. When I wake up I'm the owner of a tavern still, so I figure I'm to be mayor in '54 and congressman in '56. It's a wonderful life for a while. The only thing is that I miss Rabelais coming in at five-ten for his beer.

In '54 I get elected Mayor like he said. My business gets remodelled and all is swell.

*

Then one night I go to sleep in my new house and I wake up in the middle of the night feeling a cold draft. When I turn over I roll onto a lump in the mattress and I know it was all a dream and I'm Mike Murphy, bartender, again.

The next a.m. I pick up the paper and it's the summer of '53, the day of Rabelais and my thirty-first anniversary and I'm back at the old stand. It was a fine dream, I says, and go to work.

At five-o-nine, though, I can't help looking at the clock. And sure enough, Rabelais comes in, walks up to the bar like he owns it and roars at me, "Two beers, Mike!"

I can't help saying, "Look, haven't we done this before?"

He grins at me. "And we may have to do it again a few times," he says.

By now I know him pretty well, I think—or maybe I dreamed I know him; I'm not sure. Anyway, I give him the two beers and wait for him to get around to telling me whatever is on his mind.

He goes through the same act as before—only I can't be sure he did go through the act or I dreamed he did. "Beer for the house," he yells.

"Take it easy," I cautions. "Take it easy, Rabelais."

"You never called me by my first name before, did you, Mike?"

I open my mouth to remind him that he told me to back in 1953 and then I remember it is 1953. That confuses me because I remember, too, that in 1954 I was—or maybe it's that I'm going to be—mayor. I just close my mouth and wait.

Rabelais takes his time. When the early rush clears out, he gets me off to one end of the bar and says, "Sorry to keep you waiting, Mike, but we have to do it all over again."

"Then it wasn't a dream?"

"No dream," he says.

"But everything was going fine."

"Up to a point," he says. "Up to the sixties."

Then he explains the way his machine works. But all I get out of what he says is that there's a law of probability so he can't go back and shoot his grandfather when the old man is a boy or juggle stocks in '47 to pay off and make him rich in '53 and things like that. That is why he wouldn't let us go back into the past. He was afraid we would do something to change history and—bingo.

And he wouldn't let us go into the future very far because up a way the atom bomb gets loose and it is awfully sad to see and dangerous besides.

"That was in the sixties," he says. "Or will be in the sixties. Only I got it figured out so it won't be, Mike."

It's over my head; I just keep on waiting.

He explains that he made a pile of dough in the near future by betting on horse races and cleaning out a few bookies and investing his winnings in stocks he knew were going up (and in fact they wouldn't have gone up if he hadn't looked into the future and known they would so he could go back and buy them) and anyway, he figured the exact day it would be safe to start and so he did.

"Only," he says, "we made a mistake by making you mayor and then congressman. I have it figured out for you to be congressman right from the start—in fifty-four. That gives you two extra years of seniority on Congress and so when the chips are down you have a little more pull."

"Fine," I says and start to take off my apron.

"The thing is," he explains, "there are a couple of lunkheads in Congress that get super-patriotic and they're the ones who cause the trouble with the bomb getting loose." He leans over the bar and looks real serious at me. "And you," he goes on, "are the one who stops them before they get started."

"Me? Me, Mike Murphy?"

"You," he says. "We just go on a different time track from the one we tried before. And this one ought to work." He gives me his grin. "You should see the history books about the year 2000. You're a real national hero, Mike."

I throw my apron into a corner and roll down my sleeves. I'm ready.

And it goes just like Rabelais says. I pass up the mayor's job and go straight to Congress. In my third term I get a chance to cool those two excitable characters—cool them politically, that is, and I do.

The only thing wrong is that Rabelais never lets me go into the future to read the history books that tell what a great guy I was and the things I did. So I'm never sure I'm doing the right thing. Like I tell him, how can I be sure what to do if he won't let me read about what I did?

SJAMBAK

by Jack Vance

Wilbur Murphy sought romance, excitement, and an impossible Horseman of Space. With polite smiles, the planet frustrated him at every turn—until he found them all the hard way!

HOWARD FRAYBERG, Production Director of *Know Your Universe!*, was a man of sudden unpredictable moods; and Sam Catlin, the show's Continuity Editor, had learned to expect the worst.

"Sam," said Frayberg, "regarding the show last night . . . ." He paused to seek the proper words, and Catlin relaxed. Frayberg's frame of mind was merely critical. "Sam, we're in a rut. What's worse, the show's dull!"

Sam Catlin shrugged, not committing himself.

"*Seaweed Processors of Alphard IX*—who cares about seaweed?"

"It's factual stuff," said Sam, defensive but not wanting to go too far out on a limb. "We bring 'em everything—color, fact, romance, sight, sound, smell . . . . Next week, it's the Ball Expedition to the Mixtup Mountains on Gropus."

Frayberg leaned forward. "Sam, we're working the wrong slant on this stuff . . . . We've got to loosen up, sock 'em! Shift our ground! Give 'em the old human angle—glamor, mystery, thrills!"

Sam Catlin curled his lips. "I got just what you want."

"Yeah? Show me."

Catlin reached into his waste basket. "I filed this just ten minutes ago . . . ." He smoothed out the pages. "'Sequence idea, by Wilbur Murphy. Investigate "Horseman of Space," the man who rides up to meet incoming space-ships.'"

Frayberg tilted his head to the side. "Rides up on a *horse?*"

"That's what Wilbur Murphy says."

"How far up?"

"Does it make any difference?"

"No—I guess not."

"Well, for your information, it's up ten thousand, twenty thousand miles. He waves to the pilot, takes off his hat to the passengers, then rides back down."

"And where does all this take place?"

"On—on—" Catlin frowned. "I can write it, but I can't pronounce it." He printed on his scratch-screen: CIRGAMESÇ.

"Sirgamesk," read Frayberg.

Catlin shook his head. "That's what it looks like—but those consonants are all aspirated gutturals. It's more like 'Hrrghameshgrrh'."

"Where did Murphy get this tip?"

"I didn't bother to ask."

"Well," mused Frayberg, "we could always do a show on strange superstitions. Is Murphy around?"

"He's explaining his expense account to Shifkin."

"Get him in here; let's talk to him."

394

*

WILBUR MURPHY had a blond crew-cut, a broad freckled nose, and a serious sidelong squint. He looked from his crumpled sequence idea to Catlin and Frayberg. "Didn't like it, eh?"

"We thought the emphasis should be a little different," explained Catlin. "Instead of 'The Space Horseman,' we'd give it the working title, 'Odd Superstitions of Hrrghameshgrrh'."

"Oh, hell!" said Frayberg. "Call it Sirgamesk."

"Anyway," said Catlin, "that's the angle."

"But it's not superstition," said Murphy.

"Oh, come, Wilbur . . ."

"I got this for sheer sober-sided fact. A man rides a horse up to meet the incoming ships!"

"Where did you get this wild fable?"

"My brother-in-law is purser on the *Celestial Traveller*. At Riker's Planet they make connection with the feeder line out of Cirgamesç."

"Wait a minute," said Catlin. "How did you pronounce that?"

"Cirgamesç. The steward on the shuttle-ship gave out this story, and my brother-in-law passed it along to me."

"Somebody's pulling somebody's leg."

"My brother-in-law wasn't, and the steward was cold sober."

"They've been eating *bhang*. Sirgamesk is a Javanese planet, isn't it?"

"Javanese, Arab, Malay."

"Then they took a *bhang* supply with them, and *hashish*, *chat*, and a few other sociable herbs."

"Well, this horseman isn't any drug-dream."

"No? What is it?"

"So far as I know it's a man on a horse."

"Ten thousand miles up? In a vacuum?"

"Exactly."

"No space-suit?"

"That's the story."

Catlin and Frayberg looked at each other.

"Well, Wilbur," Catlin began.

Frayberg interrupted. "What we can use, Wilbur, is a sequence on Sirgamesk superstition. Emphasis on voodoo or witchcraft—naked girls dancing—stuff with roots in Earth, but now typically Sirgamesk. Lots of color. Secret rite stuff . . . ."

"Not much room on Cirgamesç for secret rites."

"It's a big planet, isn't it?"

"Not quite as big as Mars. There's no atmosphere. The settlers live in mountain valleys, with air-tight lids over 'em."

Catlin flipped the pages of *Thumbnail Sketches of the Inhabited Worlds*. "Says here there's ancient ruins millions of years old. When the atmosphere went, the population went with it."

Frayberg became animated. "There's lots of material out there! Go get it, Wilbur! Life! Sex! Excitement! Mystery!"

"Okay," said Wilbur Murphy.

"But lay off this horseman-in-space. There *is* a limit to public credulity, and don't you let anyone tell you different."

*

CIRGAMESÇ hung outside the port, twenty thousand miles ahead. The steward leaned over Wilbur Murphy's shoulder and pointed a long brown finger. "It was right out there, sir. He came riding up—"

"What kind of a man was it? Strange-looking?"

"No. He was Cirgameski."

"Oh. You saw him with your own eyes, eh?"

The steward bowed, and his loose white mantle fell forward. "Exactly, sir."

"No helmet, no space-suit?"

"He wore a short Singhalût vest and pantaloons and a yellow Hadrasi hat. No more."

"And the horse?"

"Ah, the horse! There's a different matter."

"Different how?"

"I can't describe the horse. I was intent on the man."

"Did you recognize him?"

"By the brow of Lord Allah, it's well not to look too closely when such matters occur."

"Then—you *did* recognize him!"

"I must be at my task, sir."

Murphy frowned in vexation at the steward's retreating back, then bent over his camera to check the tape-feed. If anything appeared now, and his eyes could see it, the two-hundred million audience of *Know Your Universe!* could see it with him.

When he looked up, Murphy made a frantic grab for the stanchion, then relaxed. Cirgamesç had taken the Great Twitch. It was an illusion, a psychological quirk. One instant the planet lay ahead; then a man winked or turned away, and when he looked back, "ahead" had become "below"; the planet had swung an astonishing ninety degrees across the sky, and they were *falling!*

Murphy leaned against the stanchion. "'The Great Twitch'," he muttered to himself, "I'd like to get *that* on two hundred million screens!"

Several hours passed. Cirgamesç grew. The Sampan Range rose up like a dark scab; the valley sultanates of Singhalût, Hadra, New Batavia, and Boeng-Bohôt showed like glistening chicken-tracks; the Great Rift Colony of Sundaman stretched down through the foothills like the trail of a slug.

A loudspeaker voice rattled the ship. "Attention passengers for Singhalût and other points on Cirgamesç! Kindly prepare your luggage for disembarkation. Customs at Singhalût are extremely thorough. Passengers are warned to take no weapons, drugs or explosives ashore. This is important!"

*

THE WARNING turned out to be an understatement. Murphy was plied with questions. He suffered search of an intimate nature. He was three-dimensionally X-rayed with a range

396

of frequencies calculated to excite fluorescence in whatever object he might have secreted in his stomach, in a hollow bone, or under a layer of flesh.

His luggage was explored with similar minute attention, and Murphy rescued his cameras with difficulty. "What're you so damn anxious about? I don't have drugs; I don't have contraband . . ."

"It's guns, your excellency. Guns, weapons, explosives . . ."

"I don't have any guns."

"But these objects here?"

"They're cameras. They record pictures and sounds and smells."

The inspector seized the cases with a glittering smile of triumph. "They resemble no cameras of my experience; I fear I shall have to impound . . ."

A young man in loose white pantaloons, a pink vest, pale green cravat and a complex black turban strolled up. The inspector made a swift obeisance, with arms spread wide. "Excellency."

The young man raised two fingers. "You may find it possible to spare Mr. Murphy any unnecessary formality."

"As your Excellency recommends . . . ." The inspector nimbly repacked Murphy's belongings, while the young man looked on benignly.

Murphy covertly inspected his face. The skin was smooth, the color of the rising moon; the eyes were narrow, dark, superficially placid. The effect was of silken punctilio with hot ruby blood close beneath.

Satisfied with the inspector's zeal, he turned to Murphy. "Allow me to introduce myself, Tuan Murphy. I am Ali-Tomás, of the House of Singhalût, and my father the Sultan begs you to accept our poor hospitality."

"Why, thank you," said Murphy. "This is a very pleasant surprise."

"If you will allow me to conduct you . . . ." He turned to the inspector. "Mr. Murphy's luggage to the palace."

*

MURPHY accompanied Ali-Tomás into the outside light, fitting his own quick step to the prince's feline saunter. This is coming it pretty soft, he said to himself. I'll have a magnificent suite, with bowls of fruit and gin pahits, not to mention two or three silken girls with skin like rich cream bringing me towels in the shower . . . . Well, well, well, it's not so bad working for *Know Your Universe!* after all! I suppose I ought to unlimber my camera . . . .

Prince Ali-Tomás watched him with interest. "And what is the audience of *Know Your Universe!?*"

"We call 'em 'participants'."

"Expressive. And how many participants do you serve?"

"Oh, the Bowdler Index rises and falls. We've got about two hundred million screens, with five hundred million participants."

"Fascinating! And tell me—how do you record smells?"

Murphy displayed the odor recorder on the side of the camera, with its gelatinous track which fixed the molecular design.

"And the odors recreated—they are like the originals?"

"Pretty close. Never exact, but none of the participants knows the difference. Sometimes the synthetic odor is an improvement."

"Astounding!" murmured the prince.

"And sometimes . . . Well, Carson Tenlake went out to get the myrrh-blossoms on Venus. It was a hot day—as days usually are on Venus—and a long climb. When the show was run off, there was more smell of Carson than of flowers."

Prince Ali-Tomás laughed politely. "We turn through here."

They came out into a compound paved with red, green and white tiles. Beneath the valley roof was a sinuous trough, full of haze and warmth and golden light. As far in either direction as the eye could reach, the hillsides were terraced, barred in various shades of green. Spattering the valley floor were tall canvas pavilions, tents, booths, shelters.

"Naturally," said Prince Ali-Tomás, "we hope that you and your participants will enjoy Singhalût. It is a truism that, in order to import, we must export; we wish to encourage a pleasurable response to the 'Made in Singhalût' tag on our *batiks*, carvings, lacquers."

They rolled quietly across the square in a surface-car displaying the House emblem. Murphy rested against deep, cool cushions. "Your inspectors are pretty careful about weapons."

Ali-Tomás smiled complacently. "Our existence is ordered and peaceful. You may be familiar with the concept of *adak*?"

"I don't think so."

"A word, an idea from old Earth. Every living act is ordered by ritual. But our heritage is passionate—and when unyielding *adak* stands in the way of an irresistible emotion, there is turbulence, sometimes even killing."

"An *amok*."

"Exactly. It is as well that the *amok* has no weapons other than his knife. Otherwise he would kill twenty where now he kills one."

The car rolled along a narrow avenue, scattering pedestrians to either side like the bow of a boat spreading foam. The men wore loose white pantaloons and a short open vest; the women wore only the pantaloons.

"Handsome set of people," remarked Murphy.

Ali-Tomás again smiled complacently. "I'm sure Singhalût will present an inspiring and beautiful spectacle for your program."

Murphy remembered the keynote to Howard Frayberg's instructions: "*Excitement! Sex! Mystery!*" Frayberg cared little for inspiration or beauty. "I imagine," he said casually, "that you celebrate a number of interesting festivals? Colorful dancing? Unique customs?"

Ali-Tomás shook his head. "To the contrary. We left our superstitions and ancestor-worship back on Earth. We are quiet Mohammedans and indulge in very little festivity. Perhaps here is the reason for *amoks* and sjambaks."

"Sjambaks?"

"We are not proud of them. You will hear sly rumor, and it is better that I arm you beforehand with truth."

"What is a sjambak?"

"They are bandits, flouters of authority. I will show you one presently."

"I heard," said Murphy, "of a man riding a horse up to meet the space-ships. What would account for a story like that?"

"It can have no possible basis," said Prince Ali-Tomás. "We have no horses on Cirgamesç. None whatever."

"But . . ."

"The veriest idle talk. Such nonsense will have no interest for your intelligent participants."

The car rolled into a square a hundred yards on a side, lined with luxuriant banana palms. Opposite was an enormous pavilion of gold and violet silk, with a dozen peaked gables casting various changing sheens. In the center of the square a twenty-foot pole supported a cage about two feet wide, three feet long, and four feet high.

Inside this cage crouched a naked man.

The car rolled past. Prince Ali-Tomás waved an idle hand. The caged man glared down from bloodshot eyes. "That," said Ali-Tomás, "is a sjambak. As you see," a faint note of apology entered his voice, "we attempt to discourage them."

"What's that metal object on his chest?"

"The mark of his trade. By that you may know all sjambak. In these unsettled times only we of the House may cover our chests—all others must show themselves and declare themselves true Singhalûsi."

Murphy said tentatively, "I must come back here and photograph that cage."

Ali-Tomás smilingly shook his head. "I will show you our farms, our vines and orchards. Your participants will enjoy these; they have no interest in the dolor of an ignoble sjambak."

"Well," said Murphy, "our aim is a well-rounded production. We want to show the farmers at work, the members of the great House at their responsibilities, as well as the deserved fate of wrongdoers."

"Exactly. For every sjambak there are ten thousand industrious Singhalûsi. It follows then that only one ten-thousandth part of your film should be devoted to this infamous minority."

"About three-tenths of a second, eh?"

"No more than they deserve."

"You don't know my Production Director. His name is Howard Frayberg, and . . ."

*

HOWARD FRAYBERG was deep in conference with Sam Catlin, under the influence of what Catlin called his philosophic kick. It was the phase which Catlin feared most.

"Sam," said Frayberg, "do you know the danger of this business?"

"Ulcers," Catlin replied promptly.

Frayberg shook his head. "We've got an occupational disease to fight—progressive mental myopia."

"Speak for yourself," said Catlin.

"Consider. We sit in this office. We think we know what kind of show we want. We send out our staff to get it. We're signing the checks, so back it comes the way we asked for it. We look at it, hear it, smell it—and pretty soon we believe it: our version of the universe, full-blown from our brains like Minerva stepping out of Zeus. You see what I mean?"

"I understand the words."

"We've got our own picture of what's going on. We ask for it, we get it. It builds up and up—and finally we're like mice in a trap built of our own ideas. We cannibalize our own brains."

"Nobody'll ever accuse you of being stingy with a metaphor."

"Sam, let's have the truth. How many times have you been off Earth?"

"I went to Mars once. And I spent a couple of weeks at Aristillus Resort on the Moon."

Frayberg leaned back in his chair as if shocked. "And we're supposed to be a couple of learned planetologists!"

Catlin made grumbling noise in his throat. "I haven't been around the zodiac, so what? You sneezed a few minutes ago and I said *gesundheit*, but I don't have any doctor's degree."

"There comes a time in a man's life," said Frayberg, "when he wants to take stock, get a new perspective."

"Relax, Howard, relax."

"In our case it means taking out our preconceived ideas, looking at them, checking our illusions against reality."

"Are you serious about this?"

"Another thing," said Frayberg, "I want to check up a little. Shifkin says the expense accounts are frightful. But he can't fight it. When Keeler says he paid ten munits for a loaf of bread on Nekkar IV, who's gonna call him on it?"

"Hell, let him eat bread! That's cheaper than making a safari around the cluster, spot-checking the super-markets."

Frayberg paid no heed. He touched a button; a three-foot sphere full of glistening motes appeared. Earth was at the center, with thin red lines, the scheduled space-ship routes, radiating out in all directions.

"Let's see what kind of circle we can make," said Frayberg. "Gower's here at Canopus, Keeler's over here at Blue Moon, Wilbur Murphy's at Sirgamesk . . ."

"Don't forget," muttered Catlin, "we got a show to put on."

"We've got material for a year," scoffed Frayberg. "Get hold of Space-Lines. We'll start with Sirgamesk, and see what Wilbur Murphy's up to."

*

WILBUR MURPHY was being presented to the Sultan of Singhalût by the Prince Ali-Tomás. The Sultan, a small mild man of seventy, sat crosslegged on an enormous pink and green air-cushion. "Be at your ease, Mr. Murphy. We dispense with as much protocol here as practicable." The Sultan had a dry clipped voice and the air of a rather harassed corporation executive. "I understand you represent Earth-Central Home Screen Network?"

"I'm a staff photographer for the *Know Your Universe!* show."

"We export a great deal to Earth," mused the Sultan, "but not as much as we'd like. We're very pleased with your interest in us, and naturally we want to help you in every way possible. Tomorrow the Keeper of the Archives will present a series of charts analyzing our economy. Ali-Tomás shall personally conduct you through the fish-hatcheries. We want you to know we're doing a great job out here on Singhalût."

"I'm sure you are," said Murphy uncomfortably. "However, that isn't quite the stuff I want."

400

"No? Just where do your desires lie?"

Ali-Tomás said delicately. "Mr. Murphy took a rather profound interest in the sjambak displayed in the square."

"Oh. And you explained that these renegades could hold no interest for serious students of our planet?"

Murphy started to explain that clustered around two hundred million screens tuned to *Know Your Universe!* were four or five hundred million participants, the greater part of them neither serious nor students. The Sultan cut in decisively. "I will now impart something truly interesting. We Singhalûsi are making preparations to reclaim four more valleys, with an added area of six hundred thousand acres! I shall put my physiographic models at your disposal; you may use them to the fullest extent!"

"I'll be pleased for the opportunity," declared Murphy. "But tomorrow I'd like to prowl around the valley, meet your people, observe their customs, religious rites, courtships, funerals . . ."

The Sultan pulled a sour face. "We are ditch-water dull. Festivals are celebrated quietly in the home; there is small religious fervor; courtships are consummated by family contract. I fear you will find little sensational material here in Singhalût."

"You have no temple dances?" asked Murphy. "No fire-walkers, snake-charmers—voodoo?"

The Sultan smiled patronizingly. "We came out here to Cirgamesç to escape the ancient superstitions. Our lives are calm, orderly. Even the *amoks* have practically disappeared."

"But the sjambaks—"

"Negligible."

"Well," said Murphy, "I'd like to visit some of these ancient cities."

"I advise against it," declared the Sultan. "They are shards, weathered stone. There are no inscriptions, no art. There is no stimulation in dead stone. Now. Tomorrow I will hear a report on hybrid soybean plantings in the Upper Kam District. You will want to be present."

*

MURPHY'S SUITE matched or even excelled his expectation. He had four rooms and a private garden enclosed by a thicket of bamboo. His bathroom walls were slabs of glossy actinolite, inlaid with cinnabar, jade, galena, pyrite and blue malachite, in representations of fantastic birds. His bedroom was a tent thirty feet high. Two walls were dark green fabric; a third was golden rust; the fourth opened upon the private garden.

Murphy's bed was a pink and yellow creation ten feet square, soft as cobweb, smelling of rose sandalwood. Carved black lacquer tubs held fruit; two dozen wines, liquors, syrups, essences flowed at a touch from as many ebony spigots.

The garden centered on a pool of cool water, very pleasant in the hothouse climate of Singhalût. The only shortcoming was the lack of the lovely young servitors Murphy had envisioned. He took it upon himself to repair this lack, and in a shady wine-house behind the palace, called the Barangipan, he made the acquaintance of a girl-musician named Soek Panjoebang. He found her enticing tones of quavering sweetness from the *gamelan*, an instrument well-loved in Old Bali. Soek Panjoebang had the delicate features and transparent skin of Sumatra, the supple long limbs of Arabia and in a pair of wide and golden eyes a heritage from somewhere in Celtic Europe. Murphy bought her a goblet of frozen shavings, each a different perfume, while he himself drank white rice-beer. Soek Panjoebang displayed an intense interest in the ways of Earth, and Murphy found it hard to guide the conversation. "Weelbrrr," she said. "Such a funny name, Weelbrrr. Do you think I could play the *gamelan* in the great cities, the great palaces of Earth?"

"Sure. There's no law against *gamelans*."

"You talk so funny, Weelbrrr. I like to hear you talk."

"I suppose you get kinda bored here in Singhalût?"

She shrugged. "Life is pleasant, but it concerns with little things. We have no great adventures. We grow flowers, we play the *gamelan*." She eyed him archly sidelong. "We love . . . . We sleep . . . ."

Murphy grinned. "You run *amok*."

"No, no, no. That is no more."

"Not since the sjambaks, eh?"

"The sjambaks are bad. But better than *amok*. When a man feels the knot forming around his chest, he no longer takes his kris and runs down the street—he becomes sjambak."

This was getting interesting. "Where does he go? What does he do?"

"He robs."

"Who does he rob? What does he do with his loot?"

She leaned toward him. "It is not well to talk of them."

"Why not?"

"The Sultan does not wish it. Everywhere are listeners. When one talks sjambak, the Sultan's ears rise, like the points on a cat."

"Suppose they do—what's the difference? I've got a legitimate interest. I saw one of them in that cage out there. That's torture. I want to know about it."

"He is very bad. He opened the monorail car and the air rushed out. Forty-two Singhalûsi and Hadrasi bloated and blew up."

"And what happened to the sjambak?"

"He took all the gold and money and jewels and ran away."

"Ran where?"

"Out across Great Pharasang Plain. But he was a fool. He came back to Singhalût for his wife; he was caught and set up for all people to look at, so they might tell each other, 'thus it is for sjambaks.'"

"Where do the sjambaks hide out?"

"Oh," she looked vaguely around the room, "out on the plains. In the mountains."

"They must have some shelter—an air-dome."

"No. The Sultan would send out his patrol-boat and destroy them. They roam quietly. They hide among the rocks and tend their oxygen stills. Sometimes they visit the old cities."

"I wonder," said Murphy, staring into his beer, "could it be sjambaks who ride horses up to meet the space-ship?"

Soek Panjoebang knit her black eyebrows, as if preoccupied.

"That's what brought me out here," Murphy went on. "This story of a man riding a horse out in space."

"Ridiculous; we have no horses in Cirgamesç."

"All right, the steward won't swear to the horse. Suppose the man was up there on foot or riding a bicycle. But the steward recognized the man."

"Who was this man, pray?"

"The steward clammed up . . . . The name would have been just noise to me, anyway."

"I might recognize the name . . . ."

"Ask him yourself. The ship's still out at the field."

She shook her head slowly, holding her golden eyes on his face. "I do not care to attract the attention of either steward, sjambak—or Sultan."

Murphy said impatiently. "In any event, it's not who—but *how*. How does the man breathe? Vacuum sucks a man's lungs up out of his mouth, bursts his stomach, his ears . . . ."

"We have excellent doctors," said Soek Panjoebang shuddering, "but alas! I am not one of them."

*

MURPHY LOOKED at her sharply. Her voice held the plangent sweetness of her instrument, with additional overtones of mockery. "There must be some kind of invisible dome around him, holding in air," said Murphy.

"And what if there is?"

"It's something new, and if it is, I want to find out about it."

Soek smiled languidly. "You are so typical an old-lander—worried, frowning, dynamic. You should relax, cultivate *napaû*, enjoy life as we do here in Singhalût."

"What's *napaû*?"

"It's our philosophy, where we find meaning and life and beauty in every aspect of the world."

"That sjambak in the cage could do with a little less *napaû* right now."

"No doubt he is unhappy," she agreed.

"Unhappy! He's being tortured!"

"He broke the Sultan's law. His life is no longer his own. It belongs to Singhalût. If the Sultan wishes to use it to warn other wrongdoers, the fact that the man suffers is of small interest."

"If they all wear that metal ornament, how can they hope to hide out?" He glanced at her own bare bosom.

"They appear by night—slip through the streets like ghosts . . . ." She looked in turn at Murphy's loose shirt. "You will notice persons brushing up against you, feeling you," she laid her hand along his breast, "and when this happens you will know they are agents of the Sultan, because only strangers and the House may wear shirts. But now, let me sing to you—a song from the Old Land, old Java. You will not understand the tongue, but no other words so join the voice of the *gamelan*."

*

"THIS IS the gravy-train," said Murphy. "Instead of a garden suite with a private pool, I usually sleep in a bubble-tent, with nothing to eat but condensed food."

Soek Panjoebang flung the water out of her sleek black hair. "Perhaps, Weelbrrr, you will regret leaving Cirgamesç?"

403

"Well," he looked up to the transparent roof, barely visible where the sunlight collected and refracted, "I don't particularly like being shut up like a bird in an aviary . . . . Mildly claustrophobic, I guess."

After breakfast, drinking thick coffee from tiny silver cups, Murphy looked long and reflectively at Soek Panjoebang.

"What are you thinking, Weelbrrr?"

Murphy drained his coffee. "I'm thinking that I'd better be getting to work."

"And what do you do?"

"First I'm going to shoot the palace, and you sitting here in the garden playing your *gamelan*."

"But Weelbrrr—not *me*!"

"You're a part of the universe, rather an interesting part. Then I'll take the square . . . ."

"And the sjambak?"

A quiet voice spoke from behind. "A visitor, Tuan Murphy."

Murphy turned his head. "Bring him in." He looked back to Soek Panjoebang. She was on her feet.

"It is necessary that I go."

"When will I see you?"

"Tonight—at the Barangipan."

*

THE QUIET VOICE said, "Mr. Rube Trimmer, Tuan."

Trimmer was small and middle-aged, with thin shoulders and a paunch. He carried himself with a hell-raising swagger, left over from a time twenty years gone. His skin had the waxy look of lost floridity, his tuft of white hair was coarse and thin, his eyelids hung in the off-side droop that amateur physiognomists like to associate with guile.

"I'm Resident Director of the Import-Export Bank," said Trimmer. "Heard you were here and thought I'd pay my respects."

"I suppose you don't see many strangers."

"Not too many—there's nothing much to bring 'em. Cirgamesç isn't a comfortable tourist planet. Too confined, shut in. A man with a sensitive psyche goes nuts pretty easy here."

"Yeah," said Murphy. "I was thinking the same thing this morning. That dome begins to give a man the willies. How do the natives stand it? Or do they?"

Trimmer pulled out a cigar case. Murphy refused the offer.

"Local tobacco," said Trimmer. "Very good." He lit up thoughtfully. "Well, you might say that the Cirgameski are schizophrenic. They've got the docile Javanese blood, plus the Arabian élan. The Javanese part is on top, but every once in a while you see a flash of arrogance . . . . You never know. I've been out here nine years and I'm still a stranger." He puffed on his cigar, studied Murphy with his careful eyes. "You work for *Know Your Universe!*, I hear."

"Yeah. I'm one of the leg men."

"Must be a great job."

"A man sees a lot of the galaxy, and he runs into queer tales, like this sjambak stuff."

Trimmer nodded without surprise. "My advice to you, Murphy, is lay off the sjambaks. They're not healthy around here."

Murphy was startled by the bluntness. "What's the big mystery about these sjambaks?"

Trimmer looked around the room. "This place is bugged."

"I found two pick-ups and plugged 'em," said Murphy.

Trimmer laughed. "Those were just plants. They hide 'em where a man might just barely spot 'em. You can't catch the real ones. They're woven into the cloth—pressure-sensitive wires."

Murphy looked critically at the cloth walls.

"Don't let it worry you," said Trimmer. "They listen more out of habit than anything else. If you're fussy we'll go for a walk."

The road led past the palace into the country. Murphy and Trimmer sauntered along a placid river, overgrown with lily pads, swarming with large white ducks.

"This sjambak business," said Murphy. "Everybody talks around it. You can't pin anybody down."

"Including me," said Trimmer. "I'm more or less privileged around here. The Sultan finances his reclamation through the bank, on the basis of my reports. But there's more to Singhalût than the Sultan."

"Namely?"

Trimmer waved his cigar waggishly. "Now we're getting in where I don't like to talk. I'll give you a hint. Prince Ali thinks roofing-in more valleys is a waste of money, when there's Hadra and New Batavia and Sundaman so close."

"You mean—armed conquest?"

Trimmer laughed. "You said it, not me."

"They can't carry on much of a war—unless the soldiers commute by monorail."

"Maybe Prince Ali thinks he's got the answer."

"Sjambaks?"

"I didn't say it," said Trimmer blandly.

Murphy grinned. After a moment he said. "I picked up with a girl named Soek Panjoebang who plays the *gamelan*. I suppose she's working for either the Sultan or Prince Ali. Do you know which?"

Trimmer's eyes sparkled. He shook his head. "Might be either one. There's a way to find out."

"Yeah?"

"Get her off where you're sure there's no spy-cells. Tell her two things—one for Ali, the other for the Sultan. Whichever one reacts you know you've got her tagged."

"For instance?"

"Well, for instance she learns that you can rig up a hypnotic ray from a flashlight battery, a piece of bamboo, and a few lengths of wire. That'll get Ali in an awful sweat. He can't get weapons. None at all. And for the Sultan," Trimmer was warming up to his intrigue, chewing on his cigar with gusto, "tell her you're on to a catalyst that turns clay into aluminum and oxygen in the presence of sunlight. The Sultan would sell his right leg for something like that. He tries hard for Singhalût and Cirgamesç."

"And Ali?"

Trimmer hesitated. "I never said what I'm gonna say. Don't forget—I never said it."

"Okay, you never said it."

"Ever hear of a *jehad*?"

"Mohammedan holy wars."

"Believe it or not, Ali wants a *jehad*."

"Sounds kinda fantastic."

"Sure it's fantastic. Don't forget, I never said anything about it. But suppose someone—strictly unofficial, of course—let the idea percolate around the Peace Office back home."

"Ah," said Murphy. "That's why you came to see me."

*

TRIMMER TURNED a look of injured innocence. "Now, Murphy, you're a little unfair. I'm a friendly guy. Of course I don't like to see the bank lose what we've got tied up in the Sultan."

"Why don't you send in a report yourself?"

"I have! But when they hear the same thing from you, a *Know Your Universe!* man, they might make a move."

Murphy nodded.

"Well, we understand each other," said Trimmer heartily, "and everything's clear."

"Not entirely. How's Ali going to launch a *jehad* when he doesn't have any weapons, no warships, no supplies?"

"Now," said Trimmer, "we're getting into the realm of supposition." He paused, looked behind him. A farmer pushing a rotary tiller, bowed politely, trundled ahead. Behind was a young man in a black turban, gold earrings, a black and red vest, white pantaloons, black curl-toed slippers. He bowed, started past. Trimmer held up his hand. "Don't waste your time up there; we're going back in a few minutes."

"Thank you, Tuan."

"Who are you reporting to? The Sultan or Prince Ali?"

"The Tuan is sure to pierce the veil of my evasions. I shall not dissemble. I am the Sultan's man."

Trimmer nodded. "Now, if you'll kindly remove to about a hundred yards, where your whisper pick-up won't work."

"By your leave, I go." He retreated without haste.

"He's almost certainly working for Ali," said Trimmer.

"Not a very subtle lie."

"Oh, yes—third level. He figured I'd take it second level."

"How's that again?"

"Naturally I wouldn't believe him. He knew I knew that he knew it. So when he said 'Sultan', I'd think he wouldn't lie simply, but that he'd lie double—that he actually was working for the Sultan."

Murphy laughed. "Suppose he told you a fourth-level lie?"

"It starts to be a toss-up pretty soon," Trimmer admitted. "I don't think he gives me credit for that much subtlety . . . . What are you doing the rest of the day?"

"Taking footage. Do you know where I can find some picturesque rites? Mystical dances, human sacrifice? I've got to work up some glamor and exotic lore."

"There's this sjambak in the cage. That's about as close to the medieval as you'll find anywhere in Earth Commonwealth."

"Speaking of sjambaks . . ."

"No time," said Trimmer. "Got to get back. Drop in at my office—right down the square from the palace."

*

MURPHY RETURNED to his suite. The shadowy figure of his room servant said, "His Highness the Sultan desires the Tuan's attendance in the Cascade Garden."

"Thank you," said Murphy. "As soon as I load my camera."

The Cascade Room was an open patio in front of an artificial waterfall. The Sultan was pacing back and forth, wearing dusty khaki puttees, brown plastic boots, a yellow polo shirt. He carried a twig which he used as a riding crop, slapping his boots as he walked. He turned his head as Murphy appeared, pointed his twig at a wicker bench.

"I pray you sit down, Mr. Murphy." He paced once up and back. "How is your suite? You find it to your liking?"

"Very much so."

"Excellent," said the Sultan. "You do me honor with your presence."

Murphy waited patiently.

"I understand that you had a visitor this morning," said the Sultan.

"Yes. Mr. Trimmer."

"May I inquire the nature of the conversation?"

"It was of a personal nature," said Murphy, rather more shortly than he meant.

The Sultan nodded wistfully. "A Singhalûsi would have wasted an hour telling me half-truths—distorted enough to confuse, but not sufficiently inaccurate to anger me if I had a spy-cell on him all the time."

Murphy grinned. "A Singhalûsi has to live here the rest of his life."

A servant wheeled a frosted cabinet before them, placed goblets under two spigots, withdrew. The Sultan cleared his throat. "Trimmer is an excellent fellow, but unbelievably loquacious."

Murphy drew himself two inches of chilled rosy-pale liquor. The Sultan slapped his boots with the twig. "Undoubtedly he confided all my private business to you, or at least as much as I have allowed him to learn."

"Well—he spoke of your hope to increase the compass of Singhalût."

"That, my friend, is no hope; it's absolute necessity. Our population density is fifteen hundred to the square mile. We must expand or smother. There'll be too little food to eat, too little oxygen to breathe."

Murphy suddenly came to life. "I could make that idea the theme of my feature! Singhalût Dilemma: Expand or Perish!"

"No, that would be inadvisable, inapplicable."

407

Murphy was not convinced. "It sounds like a natural."

The Sultan smiled. "I'll impart an item of confidential information—although Trimmer no doubt has preceded me with it." He gave his boots an irritated whack. "To expand I need funds. Funds are best secured in an atmosphere of calm and confidence. The implication of emergency would be disastrous to my aims."

"Well," said Murphy, "I see your position."

The Sultan glanced at Murphy sidelong. "Anticipating your cooperation, my Minister of Propaganda has arranged an hour's program, stressing our progressive social attitude, our prosperity and financial prospects . . ."

"But, Sultan . . ."

"Well?"

"I can't allow your Minister of Propaganda to use me and *Know Your Universe!* as a kind of investment brochure."

The Sultan nodded wearily. "I expected you to take that attitude . . . . Well—what do you yourself have in mind?"

"I've been looking for something to tie to," said Murphy. "I think it's going to be the dramatic contrast between the ruined cities and the new domed valleys. How the Earth settlers succeeded where the ancient people failed to meet the challenge of the dissipating atmosphere."

"Well," the Sultan said grudgingly, "that's not too bad."

"Today I want to take some shots of the palace, the dome, the city, the paddies, groves, orchards, farms. Tomorrow I'm taking a trip out to one of the ruins."

"I see," said the Sultan. "Then you won't need my charts and statistics?"

"Well, Sultan, I could film the stuff your Propaganda Minister cooked up, and I could take it back to Earth. Howard Frayberg or Sam Catlin would tear into it, rip it apart, lard in some head-hunting, a little cannibalism and temple prostitution, and you'd never know you were watching Singhalût. You'd scream with horror, and I'd be fired."

"In that case," said the Sultan, "I will leave you to the dictates of your conscience."

*

HOWARD FRAYBERG looked around the gray landscape of Riker's Planet, gazed out over the roaring black Mogador Ocean. "Sam, I think there's a story out there."

Sam Catlin shivered inside his electrically heated glass overcoat. "Out on that ocean? It's full of man-eating plesiosaurs—horrible things forty feet long."

"Suppose we worked something out on the line of Moby Dick? *The White Monster of the Mogador Ocean.* We'd set sail in a catamaran—"

"Us?"

"No," said Frayberg impatiently. "Of course not us. Two or three of the staff. They'd sail out there, look over these gray and red monsters, maybe fake a fight or two, but all the time they're after the legendary white one. How's it sound?"

"I don't think we pay our men enough money."

"Wilbur Murphy might do it. He's willing to look for a man riding a horse up to meet his space-ships."

"He might draw the line at a white plesiosaur riding up to meet his catamaran."

Frayberg turned away. "Somebody's got to have ideas around here . . . ."

"We'd better head back to the space-port," said Catlin. "We got two hours to make the Sirgamesk shuttle."

*

WILBUR MURPHY sat in the Barangipan, watching marionettes performing to xylophone, castanet, gong and *gamelan*. The drama had its roots in proto-historic Mohenjō-Darō. It had filtered down through ancient India, medieval Burma, Malaya, across the Straits of Malacca to Sumatra and Java; from modern Java across space to Cirgamesç, five thousand years of time, two hundred light-years of space. Somewhere along the route it had met and assimilated modern technology. Magnetic beams controlled arms, legs and bodies, guided the poses and posturings. The manipulator's face, by agency of clip, wire, radio control and minuscule selsyn, projected his scowl, smile, sneer or grimace to the peaked little face he controlled. The language was that of Old Java, which perhaps a third of the spectators understood. This portion did not include Murphy, and when the performance ended he was no wiser than at the start.

Soek Panjoebang slipped into the seat beside Murphy. She wore musician's garb: a sarong of brown, blue, and black *batik*, and a fantastic headdress of tiny silver bells. She greeted him with enthusiasm.

"Weelbrrr! I saw you watching . . . ."

"It was very interesting."

"Ah, yes." She sighed. "Weelbrrr, you take me with you back to Earth? You make me a great picturama star, please, Weelbrrr?"

"Well, I don't know about that."

"I behave very well, Weelbrrr." She nuzzled his shoulder, looked soulfully up with her shiny yellow-hazel eyes. Murphy nearly forgot the experiment he intended to perform.

"What did you do today, Weelbrrr? You look at all the pretty girls?"

"Nope. I ran footage. Got the palace, climbed the ridge up to the condensation vanes. I never knew there was so much water in the air till I saw the stream pouring off those vanes! And *hot*!"

"We have much sunlight; it makes the rice grow."

"The Sultan ought to put some of that excess light to work. There's a secret process . . . . Well, I'd better not say."

"Oh come, Weelbrrr! Tell me your secrets!"

"It's not much of a secret. Just a catalyst that separates clay into aluminum and oxygen when sunlight shines on it."

Soek's eyebrows rose, poised in place like a seagull riding the wind. "Weelbrrr! I did not know you for a man of learning!"

"Oh, you thought I was just a bum, eh? Good enough to make picturama stars out of *gamelan* players, but no special genius . . . ."

"No, no, Weelbrrr."

"I know lots of tricks. I can take a flashlight battery, a piece of copper foil, a few transistors and bamboo tube and turn out a paralyzer gun that'll stop a man cold in his tracks. And you know how much it costs?"

"No, Weelbrrr. How much?"

"Ten cents. It wears out after two or three months, but what's the difference? I make 'em as a hobby—turn out two or three an hour."

"Weelbrrr! You're a man of marvels! Hello! We will drink!"

And Murphy settled back in the wicker chair, sipping his rice beer.

*

"TODAY," said Murphy, "I get into a space-suit, and ride out to the ruins in the plain. Ghatamipol, I think they're called. Like to come?"

"No, Weelbrrr." Soek Panjoebang looked off into the garden, her hands busy tucking a flower into her hair. A few minutes later she said, "Why must you waste your time among the rocks? There are better things to do and see. And it might well be—dangerous." She murmured the last word off-handedly.

"Danger? From the sjambaks?"

"Yes, perhaps."

"The Sultan's giving me a guard. Twenty men with crossbows."

"The sjambaks carry shields."

"Why should they risk their lives attacking me?"

Soek Panjoebang shrugged. After a moment she rose to her feet. "Goodbye, Weelbrrr."

"Goodbye? Isn't this rather abrupt? Won't I see you tonight?"

"If so be Allah's will."

Murphy looked after the lithe swaying figure. She paused, plucked a yellow flower, looked over her shoulder. Her eyes, yellow as the flower, lucent as water-jewels, held his. Her face was utterly expressionless. She turned, tossed away the flower with a jaunty gesture, and continued, her shoulders swinging.

Murphy breathed deeply. She might have made picturama at that . . . .

One hour later he met his escort at the valley gate. They were dressed in space-suits for the plains, twenty men with sullen faces. The trip to Ghatamipol clearly was not to their liking. Murphy climbed into his own suit, checked the oxygen pressure gauge, the seal at his collar. "All ready, boys?"

No one spoke. The silence drew out. The gatekeeper, on hand to let the party out, snickered. "They're all ready, Tuan."

"Well," said Murphy, "let's go then."

Outside the gate Murphy made a second check of his equipment. No leaks in his suit. Inside pressure: 14.6. Outside pressure: zero. His twenty guards morosely inspected their crossbows and slim swords.

The white ruins of Ghatamipol lay five miles across Pharasang Plain. The horizon was clear, the sun was high, the sky was black.

Murphy's radio hummed. Someone said sharply, "Look! There it goes!" He wheeled around; his guards had halted, and were pointing. He saw a fleet something vanishing into the distance.

"Let's go," said Murphy. "There's nothing out there."

"Sjambak."

"Well, there's only one of them."

410

"Where one walks, others follow."

"That's why the twenty of you are here."

"It is madness! Challenging the sjambaks!"

"What is gained?" another argued.

"I'll be the judge of that," said Murphy, and set off along the plain. The warriors reluctantly followed, muttering to each other over their radio intercoms.

*

THE ERODED city walls rose above them, occupied more and more of the sky. The platoon leader said in an angry voice, "We have gone far enough."

"You're under my orders," said Murphy. "We're going through the gate." He punched the button on his camera and passed under the monstrous portal.

The city was frailer stuff than the wall, and had succumbed to the thin storms which had raged a million years after the passing of life. Murphy marvelled at the scope of the ruins. Virgin archaeological territory! No telling what a few weeks digging might turn up. Murphy considered his expense account. Shifkin was the obstacle.

There'd be tremendous prestige and publicity for *Know Your Universe!* if Murphy uncovered a tomb, a library, works of art. The Sultan would gladly provide diggers. They were a sturdy enough people; they could make quite a showing in a week, if they were able to put aside their superstitions, fears and dreads.

Murphy sized one of them up from the corner of his eye. He sat on a sunny slab of rock, and if he felt uneasy he concealed it quite successfully. In fact, thought Murphy, he appeared completely relaxed. Maybe the problem of securing diggers was a minor one after all . . . .

And here was an odd sidelight on the Singhalûsi character. Once clear of the valley the man openly wore his shirt, a fine loose garment of electric blue, in defiance of the Sultan's edict. Of course out here he might be cold . . . .

Murphy felt his own skin crawling. How could he be cold? How could he be alive? Where was his space-suit? He lounged on the rock, grinning sardonically at Murphy. He wore heavy sandals, a black turban, loose breeches, the blue shirt. Nothing more.

Where were the others?

Murphy turned a feverish glance over his shoulder. A good three miles distant, bounding and leaping toward Singhalût, were twenty desperate figures. They all wore space-suits. This man here . . . A sjambak? A wizard? A hallucination?

⚔

THE CREATURE rose to his feet, strode springily toward Murphy. He carried a crossbow and a sword, like those of Murphy's fleet-footed guards. But he wore no space-suit. Could there be breathable traces of an atmosphere? Murphy glanced at his gauge. Outside pressure: zero.

Two other men appeared, moving with long elastic steps. Their eyes were bright, their faces flushed. They came up to Murphy, took his arm. They were solid, corporeal. They had no invisible force fields around their heads.

Murphy jerked his arm free. "Let go of me, damn it!" But they certainly couldn't hear him through the vacuum.

He glanced over his shoulder. The first man held his naked blade a foot or two behind Murphy's bulging space-suit. Murphy made no further resistance. He punched the button on his camera to automatic. It would now run for several hours, recording one hundred pictures per second, a thousand to the inch.

The sjambaks led Murphy two hundred yards to a metal door. They opened it, pushed Murphy inside, banged it shut. Murphy felt the vibration through his shoes, heard a gradually waxing hum. His gauge showed an outside pressure of 5, 10, 12, 14, 14.5. An inner door opened. Hands pulled Murphy in, unclamped his dome.

"Just what's going on here?" demanded Murphy angrily.

Prince Ali-Tomás pointed to a table. Murphy saw a flashlight battery, aluminum foil, wire, a transistor kit, metal tubing, tools, a few other odds and ends.

"There it is," said Prince Ali-Tomás. "Get to work. Let's see one of these paralysis weapons you boast of."

"Just like that, eh?"

"Just like that."

"What do you want 'em for?"

"Does it matter?"

"I'd like to know." Murphy was conscious of his camera, recording sight, sound, odor.

"I lead an army," said Ali-Tomás, "but they march without weapons. Give me weapons! I will carry the word to Hadra, to New Batavia, to Sundaman, to Boeng-Bohôt!"

"How? Why?"

"It is enough that I will it. Again, I beg of you . . ." He indicated the table.

Murphy laughed. "I've got myself in a fine mess. Suppose I don't make this weapon for you?"

"You'll remain until you do, under increasingly difficult conditions."

"I'll be here a long time."

"If such is the case," said Ali-Tomás, "we must make our arrangements for your care on a long-term basis."

Ali made a gesture. Hands seized Murphy's shoulders. A respirator was held to his nostrils. He thought of his camera, and he could have laughed. Mystery! Excitement! Thrills! Dramatic sequence for*Know Your Universe!* Staff-man murdered by fanatics! The crime recorded on his own camera! See the blood, hear his death-rattle, smell the poison!

The vapor choked him. *What a break! What a sequence!*

*

"SIRGAMESK," said Howard Frayberg, "bigger and brighter every minute."

"It must've been just about in here," said Catlin, "that Wilbur's horseback rider appeared."

"That's right! Steward!"

"Yes, sir?"

"We're about twenty thousand miles out, aren't we?"

"About fifteen thousand, sir."

"Sidereal Cavalry! What an idea! I wonder how Wilbur's making out on his superstition angle?"

Sam Catlin, watching out the window, said in a tight voice, "Why not ask him yourself?"

412

"Eh?"

"Ask him for yourself! There he is—outside, riding some kind of critter . . . ."

"It's a ghost," whispered Frayberg. "A man without a space-suit . . . . There's no such thing!"

"He sees us . . . . Look . . . ."

Murphy was staring at them, and his surprise seemed equal to their own. He waved his hand. Catlin gingerly waved back.

Said Frayberg, "That's not a horse he's riding. It's a combination ram-jet and kiddie car with stirrups!"

"He's coming aboard the ship," said Catlin. "That's the entrance port down there . . . ."

*

WILBUR MURPHY sat in the captain's stateroom, taking careful breaths of air.

"How are you now?" asked Frayberg.

"Fine. A little sore in the lungs."

"I shouldn't wonder," the ship's doctor growled. "I never saw anything like it."

"How does it feel out there, Wilbur?" Catlin asked.

"It feels awful lonesome and empty. And the breath seeping up out of your lungs, never going in—that's a funny feeling. And you miss the air blowing on your skin. I never realized it before. Air feels like—like silk, like whipped cream—it's got texture . . . ."

"But aren't you cold? Space is supposed to be absolute zero!"

"Space is nothing. It's not hot and it's not cold. When you're in the sunlight you get warm. It's better in the shade. You don't lose any heat by air convection, but radiation and sweat evaporation keep you comfortably cool."

"I still can't understand it," said Frayberg. "This Prince Ali, he's a kind of a rebel, eh?"

"I don't blame him in a way. A normal man living under those domes has to let off steam somehow. Prince Ali decided to go out crusading. I think he would have made it too—at least on Cirgamesç."

"Certainly there are many more men inside the domes . . . ."

"When it comes to fighting," said Murphy, "a sjambak can lick twenty men in space-suits. A little nick doesn't hurt him, but a little nick bursts open a space-suit, and the man inside comes apart."

"Well," said the Captain. "I imagine the Peace Office will send out a team to put things in order now."

Catlin asked, "What happened when you woke up from the chloroform?"

"Well, nothing very much. I felt this attachment on my chest, but didn't think much about it. Still kinda woozy. I was halfway through decompression. They keep a man there eight hours, drop pressure on him two pounds an hour, nice and slow so he don't get the bends."

"Was this the same place they took you, when you met Ali?"

"Yeah, that was their decompression chamber. They had to make a sjambak out of me; there wasn't anywhere else they could keep me. Well, pretty soon my head cleared, and I saw this apparatus stuck to my chest." He poked at the mechanism on the table. "I saw the oxygen tank, I saw the blood running through the plastic pipes—blue from me to that carburetor arrangement, red on the way back in—and I figured out the whole arrangement.

413

Carbon dioxide still exhales up through your lungs, but the vein back to the left auricle is routed through the carburetor and supercharged with oxygen. A man doesn't need to breathe. The carburetor flushes his blood with oxygen, the decompression tank adjusts him to the lack of air-pressure. There's only one thing to look out for; that's not to touch anything with your naked flesh. If it's in the sunshine it's blazing hot; if it's in the shade it's cold enough to cut. Otherwise you're free as a bird."

"But—how did you get away?"

"I saw those little rocket-bikes, and began figuring. I couldn't go back to Singhalût; I'd be lynched on sight as a sjambak. I couldn't fly to another planet—the bikes don't carry enough fuel.

"I knew when the ship would be coming in, so I figured I'd fly up to meet it. I told the guard I was going outside a minute, and I got on one of the rocket-bikes. There was nothing much to it."

"Well," said Frayberg, "it's a great feature, Wilbur—a great film! Maybe we can stretch it into two hours."

"There's one thing bothering me," said Catlin. "Who did the steward see up here the first time?"

Murphy shrugged. "It might have been somebody up here skylarking. A little too much oxygen and you start cutting all kinds of capers. Or it might have been someone who decided he had enough crusading.

"There's a sjambak in a cage, right in the middle of Singhalût. Prince Ali walks past; they look at each other eye to eye. Ali smiles a little and walks on. Suppose this sjambak tried to escape to the ship. He's taken aboard, turned over to the Sultan and the Sultan makes an example of him . . . ."

"What'll the Sultan do to Ali?"

Murphy shook his head. "If I were Ali I'd disappear."

A loudspeaker turned on. "Attention all passengers. We have just passed through quarantine. Passengers may now disembark. Important: no weapons or explosives allowed on Singhalût!"

"This is where I came in," said Murphy.

DEADLY CITY

by Ivar Jorgenson

You're all alone in a deserted city. You walk down an empty street, yearning for the sight of one living face—one moving figure. Then you see a man on a corner and you know your terror has only begun.

He awoke slowly, like a man plodding knee-deep through the thick stuff of nightmares. There was no definite line between the dream-state and wakefulness. Only a dawning knowledge that he was finally conscious and would have to do something about it.

He opened his eyes, but this made no difference. The blackness remained. The pain in his head brightened and he reached up and found the big lump they'd evidently put on his head for good measure—a margin of safety.

They must have been prudent people, because the bang on the head had hardly been necessary. The spiked drink which they had given him would have felled an ox. He remembered going down into the darkness after drinking it, and of knowing what it was. He remembered the helpless feeling.

It did not worry him now. He was a philosophical person, and the fact he was still alive cancelled out the drink and its result. He thought, with savor, of the chestnut-haired girl who had watched him take the drink. She had worn a very low bodice, and that was where his eyes had been at the last moment—on the beautiful, tanned breasts—until they'd wavered and puddled into a blur and then into nothing.

The chestnut-haired girl had been nice, but now she was gone and there were more pressing problems.

He sat up, his hands behind him at the ends of stiff arms clawing into long-undisturbed dust and filth. His movement stirred the dust and it rose into his nostrils.

He straightened and banged his head against a low ceiling. The pain made him sick for a minute and he sat down to regain his senses. He cursed the ceiling, as a matter of course, in an agonized whisper.

Ready to move again, he got onto his hands and knees and crawled cautiously forward, exploring as he went. His hand pushed through cobwebs and found a rough, cement wall. He went around and around. It was all cement—all solid.

Hell! They hadn't sealed him up in this place! There had been a way in so there had to be a way out. He went around again.

Then he tried the ceiling and found the opening—a wooden trap covering a four-by-four hole—covering it snugly. He pushed the trap away and daylight streamed in. He raised himself up until he was eye-level with a discarded shaving cream jar lying on the bricks of an alley. He could read the trade mark on the jar, and the slogan: "For the Meticulous Man".

He pulled himself up into the alley. As a result of an orderly childhood, he replaced the wooden trap and kicked the shaving cream jar against a garbage can. He rubbed his chin and looked up and down the alley.

It was high noon. An uncovered sun blazed down to tell him this.

And there was no one in sight.

*

He started walking toward the nearer mouth of the alley. He had been in that hole a long time, he decided. This conviction came from his hunger and the heavy growth of beard he'd sprouted. Twenty-four hours—maybe longer. That mickey must have been a lulu.

He walked out into the cross street. It was empty. No people—no cars parked at the curbs—only a cat washing its dirty face on a tenement stoop across the street. He looked up at the tenement windows. They stared back. There was an empty, deserted look about them.

The cat flowed down the front steps of the tenement and away toward the rear and he was truly alone. He rubbed his harsh chin. Must be Sunday, he thought. Then he knew it could not be Sunday. He'd gone into the tavern on a Tuesday night. That would make it five days. Too long.

He had been walking and now he was at an intersection where he could look up and down a new street. There were no cars—no people. Not even a cat.

A sign overhanging the sidewalk said: Restaurant. He went in under the sign and tried the door. It was locked. There were no lights inside. He turned away—grinning to reassure himself. Everything was all right. Just some kind of a holiday. In a big city like Chicago the people go away on hot summer holidays. They go to the beaches and the parks and sometimes you can't see a living soul on the streets. And of course you can't find any cars because the people use them to drive to the beaches and the parks and out into the country. He breathed a little easier and started walking again.

Sure—that was it. Now what the hell holiday was it? He tried to remember. He couldn't think of what holiday it could be. Maybe they'd dreamed up a new one. He grinned at that, but the grin was a little tight and he had to force it. He forced it carefully until his teeth showed white.

Pretty soon he would come to a section where everybody hadn't gone to the beaches and the parks and a restaurant would be open and he'd get a good meal.

A meal? He fumbled toward his pockets. He dug into them and found a handkerchief and a button from his cuff. He remembered that the button had hung loose so he'd pulled it off to keep from losing it. He hadn't lost the button, but everything else was gone. He scowled. The least they could have done was to leave a man eating money.

He turned another corner—into another street—and it was like the one before. No cars—no people—not even any cats.

Panic welled up. He stopped and whirled around to look behind him. No one was there. He walked in a tight circle, looking in all directions. Windows stared back at him—eyes that didn't care where everybody had gone or when they would come back. The windows could wait. The windows were not hungry. Their heads didn't ache. They weren't scared.

He began walking and his path veered outward from the sidewalk until he was in the exact center of the silent street. He walked down the worn white line. When he got to the next corner he noticed that the traffic signals were not working. Black, empty eyes.

His pace quickened. He walked faster—ever faster until he was trotting on the brittle pavement, his sharp steps echoing against the buildings. Faster. Another corner. And he was running, filled with panic, down the empty street.

*

The girl opened her eyes and stared at the ceiling. The ceiling was a blur but it began to clear as her mind cleared. The ceiling became a surface of dirty, cracked plaster and there was a feeling of dirt and squalor in her mind.

It was always like that at these times of awakening, but doubly bitter now, because she had never expected to awaken again. She reached down and pulled the wadded sheet from beneath her legs and spread it over them. She looked at the bottle on the shabby bed-table. There were three sleeping pills left in it. The girl's eyes clouded with resentment. You'd think seven pills would have done it. She reached down and took the sheet in both hands and drew it taut over her stomach. This was a gesture of frustration. Seven hadn't been enough, and here she was again—awake in the world she'd wanted to leave. Awake with the necessary edge of determination gone.

She pulled the sheet into a wad and threw it at the wall. She got up and walked to the window and looked out. Bright daylight. She wondered how long she had slept. A long time, no doubt.

Her naked thigh pressed against the windowsill and her bare stomach touched the dirty pane. Naked in the window, but it didn't matter, because it gave onto an airshaft and other windows so caked with grime as to be of no value as windows.

But even aside from that, it didn't matter. It didn't matter in the least.

She went to the washstand, her bare feet making no sound on the worn rug. She turned on the faucets, but no water came. No water, and she had a terrible thirst. She went to the door and had thrown the bolt before she remembered again that she was naked. She turned back and saw the half-empty Pepsi-Cola bottle on the floor beside the bed table. Someone else had left it there—how many nights ago?—but she drank it anyhow, and even though it was flat and warm it soothed her throat.

She bent over to pick up garments from the floor and dizziness came, forcing her to the edge of the bed. After a while it passed and she got her legs into one of the garments and pulled it on.

Taking cosmetics from her bag, she went again to the washstand and tried the taps. Still no water. She combed her hair, jerking the comb through the mats and gnarls with a satisfying viciousness. When the hair fell into its natural, blond curls, she applied powder and lip-stick. She went back to the bed, picked up her brassiere and began putting it on as she walked to the cracked, full-length mirror in the closet door. With the brassiere in place, she stood looking at her slim image. She assayed herself with complete impersonality.

She shouldn't look as good as she did—not after the beating she'd taken. Not after the long nights and the days and the years, even though the years did not add up to very many.

I could be someone's wife, she thought, with wry humor. I could be sending kids to school and going out to argue with the grocer about the tomatoes being too soft. I don't look bad at all.

She raised her eyes until they were staring into their own images in the glass and she spoke aloud in a low, wondering voice. She said, "Who the hell am I, anyway? Who am I? A body named Linda—that's who I am. No—that's *what* I am. A body's not a *who*—it's a *what*. One hundred and fourteen pounds of well-built blond body called Linda—model 1931—no fender dents—nice paint job. Come in and drive me away. Price tag—"

She bit into the lower lip she'd just finished reddening and turned quickly to walk to the bed and wriggle into her dress—a gray and green cotton—the only one she had. She picked up her bag and went to the door. There she stopped to turn and thumb her nose at the three sleeping pills in the bottle before she went out and closed the door after herself.

The desk clerk was away from the cubbyhole from which he presided over the lobby, and there were no loungers to undress her as she walked toward the door.

Nor was there anyone out in the street. The girl looked north and south. No cars in sight either. No buses waddling up to the curb to spew out passengers.

The girl went five doors north and tried to enter a place called Tim's Hamburger House. As the lock held and the door refused to open, she saw that there were no lights on inside—no one behind the counter. The place was closed.

She walked on down the street followed only by the lonesome sound of her own clicking heels. All the stores were closed. All the lights were out.

All the people were gone.

*

He was a huge man, and the place of concealment of the Chicago Avenue police station was very small—merely an indentation low in the cement wall behind two steam pipes. The big man had lain in this niche for forty-eight hours. He had slugged a man over the turn of a card in a poolroom pinochle game, had been arrested in due course, and was awaiting the disposal of his case.

He was sorry he had slugged the man. He had not had any deep hatred for him, but rather a rage of the moment that demanded violence as its outlet. Although he did not consider it a matter of any great importance, he did not look forward to the six month's jail sentence he would doubtless be given.

His opportunity to hide in the niche had come as accidentally and as suddenly as his opportunity to slug his card partner. It had come after the prisoners had been advised of the crisis and were being herded into vans for transportation elsewhere. He had snatched the opportunity without giving any consideration whatever to the crisis. Probably because he did not have enough imagination to fear anything—however terrible—which might occur in the future. And because he treasured his freedom above all else. Freedom for today, tomorrow could take care of itself.

Now, after forty-eight hours, he writhed and twisted his huge body out of the niche and onto the floor of the furnace room. His legs were numb and he found that he could not stand. He managed to sit up and was able to bend his back enough so his great hands could reach his legs and begin to massage life back into them.

So elementally brutal was this man that he pounded his legs until they were black and blue, before feeling returned to them. In a few minutes he was walking out of the furnace room through a jail house which should now be utterly deserted. But was it? He went slowly, gliding along close to the walls to reach the front door unchallenged.

He walked out into the street. It was daylight and the street was completely deserted. The man took a deep breath and grinned. "I'll be damned," he muttered. "I'll be double and triple damned. They're all gone. Every damn one of them run off like rats and I'm the only one left. I'll be damned!"

A tremendous sense of exultation seized him. He clenched his fists and laughed loud, his laugh echoing up the street. He was happier than he had ever been in his quick, violent life. And his joy was that of a child locked in a pantry with a huge chocolate cake.

He rubbed a hand across his mouth, looked up the street, began walking. "I wonder if they took all the whisky with them," he said. Then he grinned; he was sure they had not.

He began walking in long strides toward Clark Street. In toward the still heart of the empty city.

*

He was a slim, pale-skinned little man, and very dangerous. He was also very clever. Eventually they would have found out, but he had been clever enough to deceive them and now they would never know. There was great wealth in his family, and with the rest of them occupied with leaving the city and taking what valuables they could on such short notice, he had been put in charge of one of the chauffeurs.

The chauffeur had been given the responsibility of getting the pale-skinned young man out of the city. But the young man had caused several delays until all the rest were gone. Then, meekly enough, he had accompanied the chauffeur to the garage. The chauffeur got behind the wheel of the last remaining car—a Cadillac sedan—and the young man had gotten into the rear seat.

But before the chauffeur could start the motor, the young man hit him on the head with a tire bar he had taken from a shelf as they had entered the garage.

The bar went deep into the chauffeur's skull with a solid sound, and thus the chauffeur found the death he was in the very act of fleeing.

The young man pulled the dead chauffeur from the car and laid him on the cement floor. He laid him down very carefully, so that he was in the exact center of a large square of outlined cement with his feet pointing straight north and his outstretched arms pointing south.

The young man placed the chauffeur's cap very carefully upon his chest, because neatness pleased him. Then he got into the car, started it, and headed east toward Lake Michigan and the downtown section.

After traveling three or four miles, he turned the car off the road and drove it into a telephone post. Then he walked until he came to some high weeds. He lay down in the weeds and waited.

He knew there would probably be a last vanguard of militia hunting for stragglers. If they saw a moving car they would investigate. They would take him into custody and force him to leave the city.

This, he felt, they had no right to do. All his life he had been ordered about—told to do this and that and the other thing. Stupid orders from stupid people. Idiots who went so far as to claim the whole city would be destroyed, just to make people do as they said. God! The ends to which stupid people would go in order to assert their wills over brilliant people.

The young man lay in the weeds and dozed off, his mind occupied with the pleasant memory of the tire iron settling into the skull of the chauffeur.

After a while he awoke and heard the cars of the last vanguard passing down the road. They stopped, inspected the Cadillac and found it serviceable. They took it with them, but they did not search the weeds along the road.

When they had disappeared toward the west, the young man came back to the road and began walking east, in toward the city.

Complete destruction in two days?

Preposterous.

The young man smiled.

*

The girl was afraid. For hours she had walked the streets of the empty city and the fear, strengthened by weariness, was now mounting toward terror. "One face," she whispered. "Just one person coming out of a house or walking across the street. That's all I ask. Somebody to tell me what this is all about. If I can find one person, I won't be afraid any more."

And the irony of it struck her. A few hours previously she had attempted suicide. Sick of herself and of all people, she had tried to end her own life. Therefore, by acknowledging death as the answer, she should now have no fear whatever of anything. Reconciled to crossing the bridge into death, no facet of life should have held terror for her.

But the empty city did hold terror. One face—one moving form was all she asked for.

Then, a second irony. When she saw the man at the corner of Washington and Wells, her terror increased. They saw each other at almost the same moment. Both stopped and stared. Fingers of panic ran up the girl's spine. The man raised a hand and the spell was broken. The girl turned and ran, and there was more terror in her than there had been before.

She knew how absurd this was, but still she ran blindly. What had she to fear? She knew all about men; all the things men could do they had already done to her. Murder was the ultimate, but she was fresh from a suicide attempt. Death should hold no terrors for her.

She thought of these things as the man's footsteps sounded behind her and she turned into a narrow alley seeking a hiding place. She found none and the man turned in after her.

She found a passageway, entered with the same blindness which had brought her into the alley. There was a steel door at the end and a brick lying by the sill. The door was locked. She picked up the brick and turned. The man skidded on the filthy alley surface as he turned into the areaway.

The girl raised the brick over her head. "Keep away! Stay away from me!"

"Wait a minute! Take it easy. I'm not going to hurt you!"

"Get away!"

Her arm moved downward. The man rushed in and caught her wrist. The brick went over his shoulder and the nails of her other hand raked his face. He seized her without regard for niceties and they went to the ground. She fought with everything she had and he methodically neutralized all her weapons—her hands, her legs, her teeth—until she could not move.

"Leave me alone. Please!"

"What's wrong with you? I'm not going to hurt you. But I'm not going to let you hit me with a brick, either!"

"What do you want? Why did you chase me?"

"Look—I'm a peaceful guy, but I'm not going to let you get away. I spent all afternoon looking for somebody. I found you and you ran away. I came after you."

"I haven't done anything to you."

"That's silly talk. Come on—grow up! I said I'm not going to hurt you."

"Let me up."

"So you can run away again? Not for a while. I want to talk to you."

"I—I won't run. I was scared. I don't know why. You're hurting me."

He got up—gingerly—and lifted her to her feet. He smiled, still holding both her hands. "I'm sorry. I guess it's natural for you to be scared. My name's Frank Brooks. I just want to find out what the hell happened to this town."

He let her withdraw her hands, but he still blocked her escape. She moved a pace backward and straightened her clothing. "I don't know what happened. I was looking for someone too."

He smiled again. "And then you ran."

"I don't know why. I guess—"

"What's your name."

"Nora—Nora Spade."

"You slept through it too?"

"Yes . . . yes. I slept through it and came out and they were all gone."

"Let's get out of this alley." He preceded her out, but he waited for her when there was room for them to walk side by side, and she did not try to run away. That phase was evidently over.

"I got slipped a mickey in a tavern," Frank Brooks said. "Then they slugged me and put me in a hole."

His eyes questioned. She felt their demand and said, "I was—asleep in my hotel room."

"They overlooked you?"

"I guess so."

"Then you don't know anything about it?"

"Nothing. Something terrible must have happened."

"Let's go down this way," Frank said, and they moved toward Madison Street. He had taken her arm and she did not pull away. Rather, she walked invitingly close to him.

She said, "It's so spooky. So . . . empty. I guess that's what scared me."

"It would scare anybody. There must have been an evacuation of some kind."

"Maybe the Russians are going to drop a bomb."

Frank shook his head. "That wouldn't explain it. I mean, the Russians wouldn't let us know ahead of time. Besides, the army would be here. Everybody wouldn't be gone."

"There's been a lot of talk about germ warfare. Do you suppose the water, maybe, has been poisoned?"

He shook his head. "The same thing holds true. Even if they moved the people out, the army would be here."

"I don't know. It just doesn't make sense."

"It happened, so it has to make sense. It was something that came up all of a sudden. They didn't have much more than twenty-four hours." He stopped suddenly and looked at her. "We've got to get out of here!"

Nora Spade smiled for the first time, but without humor. "How? I haven't seen one car. The buses aren't running."

His mind was elsewhere. They had started walking again. "Funny I didn't think of that before."

"Think of what?"

"That anybody left in this town is a dead pigeon. The only reason they'd clear out a city would be to get away from certain death. That would mean death is here for anybody that stays. Funny. I was so busy looking for somebody to talk to that I never thought of that."

"I did."

"Is that what you were scared of?"

"Not particularly. I'm not afraid to die. It was something else that scared me. The aloneness, I guess."

"We'd better start walking west—out of the city. Maybe we'll find a car or something."

"I don't think we'll find any cars."

He drew her to a halt and looked into her face. "You aren't afraid at all, are you?"

She thought for a moment. "No, I guess I'm not. Not of dying, that is. Dying is a normal thing. But I was afraid of the empty streets—nobody around. That was weird."

"It isn't weird now?"

"Not—not as much."

"I wonder how much time we've got?"

Nora shrugged. "I don't know, but I'm hungry."

"We can fix that. I broke into a restaurant a few blocks back and got myself a sandwich. I think there's still food around. They couldn't take it all with them."

They were on Madison Street and they turned east on the south side of the street. Nora said, "I wonder if there are any other people still here—like us?"

"I think there must be. Not very many, but a few. They would have had to clean four million people out overnight. It stands to reason they must have missed a few. Did you ever try to empty a sack of sugar? Really empty it? It's impossible. Some of the grains always stick to the sack."

A few minutes later the wisdom of this observation was proven when they came to a restaurant with the front window broken out and saw a man and a woman sitting at one of the tables.

*

He was a huge man with a shock of black hair and a mouth slightly open showing a set of incredibly white teeth. He waved an arm and shouted, "Come on in! Come on in for crissake and sit down! We got beer and roast beef and the beer's still cold. Come on in and meet Minna."

This was different, Nora thought. Not eerie. Not weird, like seeing a man standing on a deserted street corner with no one else around. This seemed normal, natural, and even the smashed window didn't detract too much from the naturalness.

They went inside. There were chairs at the table and they sat down. The big man did not get up. He waved a hand toward his companion and said, "This is Minna. Ain't she something? I found her sitting at an empty bar scared to death. We came to an understanding and I brought her along." He grinned at the woman and winked. "We came to a real understanding, didn't we, Minna?"

Minna was a completely colorless woman of perhaps thirty-five. Her skin was smooth and pale and she wore no makeup of any kind. Her hair was drawn straight back into a bun. The hair had no predominating color. It was somewhere between light brown and blond.

She smiled a little sadly, but the laugh did not cover her worn, tired look. It seemed more like a gesture of obedience than anything else. "Yes. We came to an understanding."

"I'm Jim Wilson," the big man boomed. "I was in the Chicago Avenue jug for slugging a guy in a card game. They kind of overlooked me when they cleaned the joint out." He winked again. "I kind of helped them overlook me. Then I found Minna." There was tremendous relish in his words.

Frank started introductions which Nora Spade cut in on. "Maybe you know what happened?" she asked.

Wilson shook his head. "I was in the jug and they didn't tell us. They just started cleaning out the joint. There was talk in the bullpen—invasion or something. Nobody knew for sure. Have some beer and meat."

Nora turned to the quiet Minna. "Did you hear anything?"

"Naw," Wilson said with a kind of affectionate contempt. "She don't know anything about it. She lived in some attic dump and was down with a sore throat. She took some pills or something and when she woke up they were gone."

"I went to work and—" Minna began, but Wilson cut her off.

"She swabs out some joints on Chicago Avenue for a living and that was how she happened to be sitting in that tavern. It's payday, and Minna was waiting for her dough!" He exploded into laughter and slapped the table with a huge hand. "Can you beat that? Waiting for her pay at a time like this."

Frank Brooks set down his beer bottle. The beer was cold and it tasted good. "Have you met anybody else? There must be some other people around."

"Uh-uh. Haven't met anybody but Minna." He turned his eyes on the woman again, then got to his feet. "Come on, Minna. You and I got to have a little conference. We got things to talk about." Grinning, he walked toward the rear of the restaurant. Minna got up more slowly. She followed him behind the counter and into the rear of the place.

Alone with Nora, Frank said, "You aren't eating. Want me to look for something else?"

"No—I'm not very hungry. I was just wondering—"

"Wondering about what?"

"When it will happen. When whatever is going to happen—you know what I mean."

"I'd rather know *what's* going to happen. I hate puzzles. It's hell to have to get killed and not know what killed you."

"We aren't being very sensible, are we?"

"How do you mean?"

"We should at least act normal."

"I don't get it."

Nora frowned in slight annoyance. "Normal people would be trying to reach safety. They wouldn't be sitting in a restaurant drinking beer. We should be trying to get away. Even if it does mean walking. Normal people would be trying to get away."

Frank stared at his bottle for a moment. "We should be scared stiff, shouldn't we?"

It was Nora's turn to ponder. "I'm not sure. Maybe not. I know I'm not fighting anything inside—fear, I mean. I just don't seem to care one way or another."

"I care," Frank replied. "I care. I don't want to die. But we're faced with a situation, and either way it's a gamble. We might be dead before I finish this bottle of beer. If that's true, why not sit here and be comfortable? Or we might have time to walk far enough to get out of range of whatever it is that chased everybody."

"Which way do you think it is?"

"I don't think we have time to get out of town. They cleaned it out too fast. We'd need at least four or five hours to get away. If we had that much time the army, or whoever did it, would still be around."

"Maybe they didn't know themselves when it's going to happen."

He made an impatient gesture. "What difference does it make? We're in a situation we didn't ask to get in. Our luck put us here and I'm damned if I'm going to kick a hole in the ceiling and yell for help."

Nora was going to reply, but at that moment Jim Wilson came striding out front. He wore his big grin and he carried another half-dozen bottles of beer. "Minna'll be out in a minute," he said. "Women are always slower than hell."

He dropped into a chair and snapped the cap off a beer bottle with his thumb. He held the bottle up and squinted through it, sighing gustily. "Man! I ain't never had it so good." He tilted the bottle in salute, and drank.

*

The sun was lowering in the west now, and when Minna reappeared it seemed that she materialized from the shadows, so quietly did she move. Jim Wilson opened another bottle and put it before her. "Here—have a drink, baby."

Obediently, she tilted the bottle and drank.

"What do you plan to do?" Frank asked.

"It'll be dark soon," Wilson said. "We ought to go out and try to scrounge some flashlights. I bet the power plants are dead. Probably aren't any flashlights either."

"Are you going to stay here?" Nora asked. "Here in the Loop?"

He seemed surprised. "Why not? A man'd be a fool to walk out on all this. All he wants to eat and drink. No goddam cops around. The life of Reilly and I should walk out?"

"Aren't you afraid of what's going to happen?"

"I don't give a good goddam what's going to happen. What the hell! Something's always going to happen."

"They didn't evacuate the city for nothing," Frank said.

"You mean we can all get killed?" Jim Wilson laughed. "Sure we can. We could have got killed last week too. We could of got batted in the can by a truck anytime we crossed the street." He emptied his bottle, threw it accurately at a mirror over the cash register. The crash was thunderous. "Trouble with you people, you're worry warts," he said with an expansive grin. "Let's go get us some flashlights so we can find our way to bed in one of those fancy hotels."

He got to his feet and Minna arose also, a little tired, a little apprehensive, but entirely submissive. Jim Wilson said, "Come on, baby. I sure won't want to lose *you*." He grinned at the others. "You guys coming?"

Frank's eyes met Nora's. He shrugged. "Why not?" he said. "Unless you want to start walking."

"I'm too tired," Nora said.

As they stepped out through the smashed window, both Nora and Frank half-expected to see other forms moving up and down Madison Street. But there was no one. Only the unreal desolation of the lonely pavement and the dark-windowed buildings.

"The biggest ghost town on earth," Frank muttered.

Nora's hand had slipped into Frank's. He squeezed it and neither of them seemed conscious of the contact.

"I wonder," Nora said. "Maybe this is only one of them. Maybe all the other big cities are evacuated too."

Jim Wilson and Minna were walking ahead. He turned. "If you two can't sleep without finding out what's up, it's plenty easy to do."

"You think we could find a battery radio in some store?" Frank asked.

"Hell no! They'll all be gone. But all you'd have to do is snoop around in some newspaper office. If you can read you can find out what happened."

It seemed strange to Frank that he had not thought of this. Then he realized he hadn't tried very hard to think of anything at all. He was surprised, also, at his lack of fear. He's gone through life pretty much taking things as they came—as big a sucker as the next man—making more than his quota of mistakes and blunders. Finding himself completely alone in a deserted city for the first time in his life, he had naturally fallen prey to sudden fright. But that had gradually passed, and now he was able to accept the new reality fairly passively. He wondered if that wasn't pretty much the way of all people. New situations brought a surge of whatever emotion fitted the picture. Then the emotion subsided and the new thing became the ordinary.

This, he decided, was the manner in which humanity survived. Humanity took things as they came. Pile on enough of anything and it becomes the ordinary.

Jim Wilson had picked up a garbage box and hurled it through the window of an electric shop. The glass came down with a crash that shuddered up the empty darkening street and grumbled off into silence. Jim Wilson went inside. "I'll see what I can find. You stay out here and watch for cops." His laughter echoed out as he disappeared.

Minna stood waiting silently, unmoving, and somehow she reminded Frank of a dumb animal; an unreasoning creature with no mind of her own, waiting for a signal from her master. Strangely, he resented this, but at the same time could find no reason for his resentment, except the feeling that no one should appear as much a slave as Minna.

Jim Wilson reappeared in the window. He motioned to Minna. "Come on in, baby. You and me's got to have a little conference." His exaggerated wink was barely perceptible in the gloom as Minna stepped over the low sill into the store. "Won't be long, folks," Wilson said in high good humor, and the two of them vanished into the darkness beyond.

Frank Brooks glanced at Nora, but her face was turned away. He cursed softy under his breath. He said, "Wait a minute," and went into the store through the huge, jagged opening.

Inside, he could barely make out the counters. The place was larger than it had appeared from the outside. Wilson and Minna were nowhere about.

Frank found the counter he was looking for and pawed out several flashlights. They were only empty tubes, but he found a case of batteries in a panel compartment against the wall.

"Who's there?"

"Me. I came in for some flashlights."

"Couldn't you wait?"

"It's getting dark."

"You don't have to be so damn impatient." Jim Wilson's voice was hostile and surly.

Frank stifled his quick anger. "We'll be outside," he said. He found Nora waiting where he'd left her. He loaded batteries into four flashlights before Jim Wilson and Minna reappeared.

Wilson's good humor was back. "How about the Morrison or the Sherman," he said. "Or do you want to get real ritzy and walk up to the Drake?"

"My feet hurt," Minna said. The woman spoke so rarely, Frank Brooks was startled by her words.

"Morrison's the closest," Jim Wilson said. "Let's go." He took Minna by the arm and swung off up the street. Frank and Nora fell in behind.

Nora shivered. Frank, holding her arm, asked, "Cold?"

"No. It's just all—unreal again."

"I see what you mean."

"I never expected to see the Loop dark. I can't get used to it."

A vagrant, whispering wind picked up a scrap of paper and whirled it along the street. It caught against Nora's ankle. She jerked perceptibly and kicked the scrap away. The wind caught it again and spiralled it away into the darkness.

"I want to tell you something," she said.

"Tell away."

"I told you before that I slept through the—the evacuation, or whatever it was. That wasn't exactly true. I did sleep through it, but it was my fault. I put myself to sleep."

"I don't get it."

"I tried to kill myself. Sleeping tablets. Seven of them. They weren't enough."

Frank said nothing while they paced off ten steps through the dark canyon that was Madison Street. Nora wondered if he had heard.

"I tried to commit suicide."

"Why?"

"I was tired of life, I guess."

"What do you want—sympathy?"

The sudden harshness in his voice brought her eyes around, but his face was a white blur.

"No—no, I don't think so."

"Well, you won't get it from me. Suicide is silly. You can have troubles and all that—everybody has them—but suicide—why did you try it?"

A high, thin whine—a wordless vibration of eloquence—needled out of the darkness into their ears. The shock was like a sudden shower of ice water dashed over their bodies. Nora's fingers dug into Frank's arm, but he did not feel the cutting nails. "We're—there's someone out there in the street!"

*

Twenty-five feet ahead of where Frank and Nora stood frozen there burst the booming voice of Jim Wilson. "What the hell was that?" And the shock was dispelled. The white circle from Wilson's flash bit out across the blackness to outline movement on the far side of the street. Then Frank Brook's light, and Nora's, went exploring.

"There's somebody over there," Wilson bellowed. "Hey, you! Show your face! Quit sneaking around!"

Frank's light swept an arc that clearly outlined the buildings across the street and then weakened as it swung westward. There was something or someone back there, but obscured by the dimness. He was swept by a sense of unreality again.

"Did you see them?"

Nora's light beam had dropped to her feet as though she feared to point it out into the darkness. "I thought I saw something."

Jim Wilson was swearing industriously. "There was a guy over there. He ducked around the corner. Some damn fool out scrounging. Wish I had a gun."

Frank and Nora moved ahead and the four stood in a group. "Put out your lights," Wilson said. "They make good targets if the jerk's got any weapons."

They stood in the darkness, Nora holding tightly to Frank's arm. Frank said, "That was the damndest noise I ever heard."

"Like a siren?" Frank thought Jim Wilson spoke hopefully, as though wanting somebody to agree with him.

"Not like any I ever heard. Not like a whistle, either. More of a moan."

"Let's get into that goddam hotel and—"

Jim Wilson's words were cut off by a new welling-up of the melancholy howling. It had a new pattern this time. It sounded from many places; not nearer, Frank thought, than Lake Street on the north, but spreading outward and backward and growing fainter until it died on the wind.

Nora was shivering, clinging to Frank without reserve.

Jim Wilson said, "I'll be damned if it doesn't sound like a signal of some kind."

"Maybe it's a language—a way of communication."

"But who the hell's communicating?"

"How would I know?"

"We best get to that hotel and bar a few doors. A man can't fight in the dark—and nothing to fight with."

They hurried up the street, but it was all different now. Gone was the illusion of being alone; gone the sense of solitude. Around them the ghost town had come suddenly alive. Sinister forces more frightening than the previous solitude had now to be reckoned with.

"Something's happened—something in the last few minutes," Nora whispered.

Frank leaned close as they crossed the street to the dark silent pile that was the Morrison hotel. "I think I know what you mean."

"It's as though there was no one around and then, suddenly, they came."

"I think they came and went away again."

"Did you actually *see* anyone when you flashed your light?"

"No—I can't say positively that I did. But I got the impression there were figures out there—at least dozens of them—and that they moved back away from the light. Always just on the edge of it."

"I'm scared, Frank."

"So am I."

"Do you think it could all be imagination?"

"Those moans? Maybe the first one—I've heard of people imagining sounds. But not the last ones. And besides, we all heard them."

Jim Wilson, utterly oblivious of any subtle emanations in the air, boomed out in satisfaction: "We don't have to bust the joint open. The revolving door works."

"Then maybe we ought to be careful," Frank said. "Maybe somebody else is around here."

"Could be. We'll find out."

"Why are we afraid?" Nora whispered.

"It's natural, isn't it?" Frank melted the beam of his light with that of Jim Wilson. The white finger pierced the darkness inside. Nothing moved.

"I don't see why it should be. If there are people in there they must be as scared as we are." Nora was very close to him as they entered.

The lobby seemed deserted. The flashlight beams scanned the empty chairs and couches. The glass of the deserted cages threw back reflections.

"The keys are in there," Frank said. He vaulted the desk and scanned the numbers under the pigeon holes.

"We'd better stay down low," Jim Wilson said. "Damned if I'm going to climb to the penthouse."

"How about the fourth floor?"

"That's plenty high enough."

Frank came out with a handful of keys. "Odd numbers," he said. "Four in a row."

"Well I'll be damned," Jim Wilson muttered. But he said no more and they climbed the stairs in silence. They passed the quiet dining rooms and banquet halls, and by the time they reached the fourth floor the doors giving off the corridors had assumed a uniformity.

"Here they are." He handed a key to Wilson. "That's the end one." He said nothing as he gave Minna her key, but Wilson grunted, "For crissake!" in a disgusted voice, took Minna's key and threw it on the floor.

Frank and Nora watched as Wilson unlocked his door. Wilson turned. "Well, goodnight all. If you get goosed by any spooks, just yell."

Minna followed him without a word and the door closed.

Frank handed Nora her key. "Lock your door and you'll be safe. I'll check the room first." He unlocked the door and flashed his light inside. Nora was close behind him as he entered. He checked the bathroom. "Everything clear. Lock your door and you'll be safe."

"Frank."

"Yes?"

"I'm afraid to stay alone."

"You mean you want me to—"

"There are two beds here."

His reply was slow in coming. Nora didn't wait for it. Her voice rose to the edge of hysteria. "Quit being so damned righteous. Things have changed! Can't you realize that? What does it matter how or where we sleep? Does the world care? Will it make a damn bit of difference to the world whether I strip stark naked in front of you?" A sob choked in her throat. "Or would that outrage your morality."

He moved toward her, stopped six inches away. "It isn't that. For God's sake! I'm no saint. It's just that I thought you—"

"I'm plain scared, and I don't want to be alone. To me that's all that's important."

Her face was against his chest and his arms went around her. But her own hands were fists held together against him until he could feel her knuckles, hard, against his chest. She was crying.

"Sure," Frank said. "I'll stay with you. Now take it easy. Everything's going to be all right."

Nora sniffled without bothering to reach for her handkerchief. "Stop lying. You know it isn't going to be all right."

Frank was at somewhat of a loss. This flareup of Nora's was entirely unexpected. He eased toward the place the flashlight had shown the bed to be. Her legs hit its edge and she sat down.

"You—you want me to sleep in the other one?" he asked.

"Of course," Nora replied with marked bitterness. "I'm afraid you wouldn't be very comfortable in with me."

There was a time of silence. Frank took off his jacket, shirt and trousers. It was funny, he thought. He'd spent his money, been drugged, beaten and robbed as a result of one objective—to get into a room alone with a girl. And a girl not nearly as nice as Nora at that. Now, here he was alone with a real dream, and he was tongue-tied. It didn't make sense. He shrugged. Life was crazy sometimes.

He heard the rustle of garments and wondered how much Nora was taking off. Then he dropped his trousers, forgotten, to the floor. "Did you hear that?"

"Yes. It's that—"

Frank went to the window, raised the sash. The moaning sound came in louder, but it was from far distance. "I think that's out around Evanston."

Frank felt a warmth on his cheek and he realized Nora was by his side, leaning forward. He put an arm around her and they stood unmoving in complete silence. Although their ears were straining for the sound coming down from the north, Frank could not be oblivious of the warm flesh under his hand.

Nora's breathing was soft against his cheek. She said, "Listen to how it rises and falls. It's almost as though they were using it to talk with. The inflection changes."

"I think that's what it is. It's coming from a lot of different places. It stops in some places and starts in others."

"It's so—weird."

"Spooky," Frank said, "but in a way it makes me feel better."

"I don't see how it could." Nora pressed closer to him.

"It does though, because of what I was afraid of. I had it figured out that the city was going to blow up—that a bomb had been planted that they couldn't find, or something like that. Now, I'm pretty sure it's something else. I'm willing to bet we'll be alive in the morning."

Nora thought that over in silence. "If that's the way it is—if some kind of invaders are coming down from the north—isn't it stupid to stay here? Even if we are tired we ought to be trying to get away from them."

"I was thinking the same thing. I'll go and talk to Wilson."

They crossed the room together and he left her by the bed and went on to the door. Then he remembered he was in his shorts and went back and got his trousers. After he'd put them on, he wondered why he'd bothered. He opened the door.

Something warned him—some instinct—or possibly his natural fear and caution coincided with the presence of danger. He heard the footsteps on the carpeting down the hall—soft, but unmistakably footsteps. He called, "Wilson—Wilson—that you?"

The creature outside threw caution to the winds, Frank sensed rather than heard a body hurtling toward the door. A shrill, mad laughter raked his ears and the weight of a body hit the door.

Frank drew strength from pure panic as he threw his weight against the panel, but perhaps an inch or two from the latch the door wavered from opposing strength. Through the narrow opening he could feel the hoarse breath of exertion in his face. Insane giggles and curses sounded through the black stillness.

Frank had the wild conviction he was losing the battle, and added strength came from somewhere. He heaved and there was a scream and he knew he had at least one finger caught between the door and the jamb. He threw his weight against the door with frenzied effort and heard the squash of the finger. The voice kited up to a shriek of agony, like that of a wounded animal.

Even with his life at stake, and the life of Nora, Frank could not deliberately slice the man's fingers off. Even as he fought the urge, and called himself a fool, he allowed the door to give slightly inward. The hand was jerked to safety.

At that moment another door opened close by and Jim Wilson's voice boomed: "What the hell's going on out here?"

Simultaneous with this, racing footsteps receded down the hall and from the well of the stairway came a whining cry of pain.

"Jumping jees!" Wilson bellowed. "We got company. We ain't alone!"

"He tried to get into my room."

"You shouldn't have opened the door. Nora okay?"

"Yeah. She's all right."

"Tell her to stay in her room. And you do the same. We'd be crazy to go after that coot in the dark. He'll keep 'til morning."

Frank closed the door, double-locked it and went back to Nora's bed. He could hear a soft sobbing. He reached down and pulled back the covers and the sobbing came louder. Then he was down on the bed and she was in his arms.

She cried until the panic subsided, while he held her and said nothing. After a while she got control of herself. "Don't leave me, Frank," she begged. "Please don't leave me."

He stroked her shoulder. "I won't," he whispered.

They lay for a long time in utter silence, each seeking strength in the other's closeness. The silence was finally broken by Nora.

"Frank?"

"Yes."

"Do you want me?"

He did not answer.

"If you want me you can have me, Frank."

Frank said nothing.

"I told you today that I tried to commit suicide. Remember?"

"I remember."

"That was the truth. I did it because I was tired of everything. Because I've made a terrible mess of things. I didn't want to go on living."

He remained silent, holding her.

As she spoke again, her voice sharpened. "Can't you understand what I'm telling you? I'm no good! I'm just a bum! Other men have had me! Why shouldn't you? Why should you be cheated out of what other men have had?"

He remained silent. After a few moments, Nora said, "For God's sake, talk! Say something!"

"How do you feel about it now? Will you try again to kill yourself the next chance you get?"

"No—no, I don't think I'll ever try it again."

"Then things must look better."

"I don't know anything about that. I just don't want to do it now."

She did not urge him this time and he was slow in speaking. "It's kind of funny. It really is. Don't get the idea I've got morals. I haven't. I've had my share of women. I was working on one the night they slipped me the mickey—the night before I woke up to this tomb of a city. But now—tonight—it's kind of different. I feel like I want to protect you. Is that strange?"

"No," she said quietly. "I guess not."

They lay there silently, their thoughts going off into the blackness of the sepulchral night. After a long while, Nora's even breathing told him she was asleep. He got up quietly, covered her, and went to the other bed.

But before he slept, the weird wailings from out Evanston way came again—rose and fell in that strange conversational cadence—then died away into nothing.

*

431

Frank awoke to the first fingers of daylight. Nora still slept. He dressed and stood for some moments with his hand on the door knob. Then he threw the bolt and cautiously opened the door.

The hallway was deserted. At this point it came to him forcibly that he was not a brave man. All his life, he realized, he had avoided physical danger and had refused to recognize the true reason for so doing. He had classified himself as a man who dodged trouble through good sense; that the truly civilized person went out of his way to keep the peace.

He realized now that that attitude was merely salve for his ego. He faced the empty corridor and did not wish to proceed further. But stripped of the life-long alibi, he forced himself to walk through the doorway, close the door softly, and move toward the stairs.

He paused in front of the door behind which Jim Wilson and Minna were no doubt sleeping. He stared at it wistfully. It certainly would not be a mark of cowardice to get Jim Wilson up under circumstances such as these. In fact, he would be a fool not to do so.

Stubbornness forbade such a move, however. He walked softly toward the place where the hallway dead-ended and became a cross-corridor. He made the turn carefully, pressed against one wall. There was no one in sight. He got to the stairway and started down.

His muscles and nerves tightened with each step. When he reached the lobby he was ready to jump sky-high at the drop of a pin.

But no one dropped any pins, and he reached the modernistic glass doorway to the drugstore with only silence screaming in his ears. The door was unlocked. One hinge squeaked slightly as he pushed the door inward.

It was in the drugstore that Frank found signs of the fourth-floor intruder. An inside counter near the prescription department was red with blood. Bandages and first-aid supplies had been unboxed and thrown around with abandon. Here the man had no doubt administered to his smashed hand.

But where had he gone? Asleep, probably, in one of the rooms upstairs. Frank wished fervently for a weapon. Beyond doubt there was not a gun left in the Loop.

A gun was not the only weapon ever created, though, and Frank searched the store and found a line of pocket knives still in neat boxes near the perfume counter.

He picked four of the largest and found, also, a wooden-handled, lead-tipped bludgeon, used evidently for cracking ice.

Thus armed, he went out through the revolving door. He walked through streets that were like death under the climbing sun. Through streets and canyons of dead buildings upon which the new daylight had failed to shed life or diminish the terror of the night past.

At Dearborn he found the door to the Tribune Public Service Building locked. He used the ice breaker to smash a glass door panel. The crash of the glass on the cement was an explosion in the screaming silence. He went inside. Here the sense of desolation was complete; brought sharply to focus, probably, by the pigeon holes filled with letters behind the want-ad counter. Answers to a thousand and one queries, waiting patiently for someone to come after them.

Before going to the basement and the back files of the Chicago Tribune, Frank climbed to the second floor and found what he thought might be there—a row of teletype machines with a file-board hooked to the side of each machine.

Swiftly, he stripped the copy sheets off each board, made a bundle of them and went back downstairs. He covered the block back to the hotel at a dog-trot, filled with a sudden urge to get back to the fourth floor as soon as possible.

He stopped in the drugstore and filled his pockets with soap, a razor, shaving cream and face lotion. As an afterthought, he picked up a lavish cosmetic kit that retailed, according to the price tag, for thirty-eight dollars plus tax.

He let himself back into the room and closed the door softly. Nora rolled over, exposing a shoulder and one breast. The breast held his gaze for a full minute. Then a feeling of guilt swept him and he went into the bathroom and closed the door.

Luckily, a supply tank on the roof still contained water and Frank was able to shower and shave. Dressed again, he felt like a new man. But he regretted not hunting up a haberdashery shop and getting himself a clean shirt.

Nora had still not awakened when he came out of the bathroom. He went to the bed and stood looking down at her for some time. Then he touched her shoulder.

"Wake up. It's morning."

Nora stirred. Her eyes opened, but Frank got the impression she did not really awaken for several seconds. Her eyes went to his face, to the window, back to his face.

"What time is it?"

"I don't know. I think it's around eight o'clock."

Nora stretched both arms luxuriously. As she sat up, her slip fell back into place and Frank got the impression she hadn't even been aware of her partial nudity.

She stared up at him, clarity dawning in her eyes, "You're all cleaned up."

"I went downstairs and got some things."

"You went out—alone?"

"Why not. We can't stay in here all day. We've got to hit the road and get out of here. We've overshot our luck already."

"But that—that man in the hall last night! You shouldn't have taken a chance."

"I didn't bump into him. I found the place he fixed his hand, down in the drugstore."

Frank went to the table and came back with the cosmetic set. He put it in Nora's lap. "I brought this up for you."

Surprise and true pleasure were mixed in her expression. "That was very nice. I think I'd better get dressed."

Frank turned toward the window where he had left the bundle of teletype clips. "I've got a little reading to do."

As he sat down, he saw, from the corner of his eye, a flash of slim brown legs moving toward the bathroom. Just inside the door, Nora turned. "Are Jim Wilson and Minna up yet?"

"I don't think so."

Nora's eyes remained on him. "I think you were very brave to go downstairs alone. But it was a foolish thing to do. You should have waited for Jim Wilson."

"You're right about it being foolish. But I had to go."

"Why?"

"Because I'm not brave at all. Maybe that was the reason."

Nora left the bathroom door open about six inches and Frank heard the sound of the shower. He sat with the papers in his hand wondering about the water. When he had gone to the bathroom the thought had never occurred to him. It was natural that it should. Now he wondered about it. Why was it still running? After a while he considered the possibility of the supply tank on the roof.

Then he wondered about Nora. It was strange how he could think about her personally and impersonally at the same time. He remembered her words of the previous night. They made her—he shied from the term. What was the old cliche? A woman of easy virtue.

What made a woman of that type, he wondered. Was it something inherent in their makeup? That partially opened door was symbolic somehow. He was sure that many wives closed the bathroom door upon their husbands; did it without thinking, instinctively. He was sure Nora had left it partially open without thinking. Could a behavior pattern be traced from such an insignificant thing?

He wondered about his own attitude toward Nora. He had drawn away from what she'd offered him during the night. And yet from no sense of disgust. There was certainly far more about Nora to attract than to repel.

Morals, he realized dimly, were imposed—or at least functioned—for the protection of society. With society gone—vanished overnight—did the moral code still hold?

If and when they got back among masses of people, would his feelings toward Nora change? He thought not. He would marry her, he told himself firmly, as quick as he'd marry any other girl. He would not hold what she was against her. I guess I'm just fundamentally unmoral myself, he thought, and began reading the news clips.

*

There was a knock on the door accompanied by the booming voice of Jim Wilson. "You in there! Ready for breakfast?"

Frank got up and walked toward the door. As he did so, the door to the bathroom closed.

Jim Wilson wore a two-day growth of beard and it didn't seem to bother him at all. As he entered the room he rubbed his hands together in great gusto. "Well, where'll we eat, folks? Let's pick the classiest restaurant in town. Nothing but the best for Minna here."

He winked broadly as Minna, expressionless and silent, followed him in exactly as a shadow would have followed him and sat primly down in a straight-backed chair by the wall.

"We'd better start moving south," Frank said, "and not bother about breakfast."

"Getting scared?" Jim Wilson asked.

"You're damn right I'm scared—now. We're right in the middle of a big no-man's-land."

"I don't get you."

At that moment the bathroom door opened and Nora came out. Jim Wilson forgot about the question he'd asked. He let forth a loud whistle of appreciation. Then he turned his eyes on Frank and his thought was crystal clear. He was envying Frank the night just passed.

A sudden irritation welled up in Frank Brooks, a distinct feeling of disgust. "Let's start worrying about important things—our lives. Or don't you consider your life very important?"

Jim Wilson seemed puzzled. "What the hell's got into you? Didn't you sleep good?"

"I went down the block this morning and found some teletype machines. I've just been reading the reports."

"What about that guy that tried to get into your room last night?"

"I didn't see him. I didn't see anybody. But I know why the city's been cleaned out." Frank went back to the window and picked up the sheaf on clips he had gone through. Jim Wilson sat down on the edge of the bed, frowning. Nora followed Frank and perched on the edge of the chair he dropped into.

"The city going to blow up?" Wilson asked.

"No. We've been invaded by some form of alien life."

"Is that what the papers said?"

"It was the biggest and fastest mass evacuation ever attempted. I pieced the reports together. There was hell popping around here during the two days we—we waited it out."

"Where did they all go?" Nora asked.

"South. They've evacuated a forty-mile strip from the lake west. The first Terran defense line is set up in northern Indiana."

"What do you mean—Terra."

"It's a word that means Earth—this planet. The invaders came from some other planet, they think—at least from no place on Earth."

"That's the silliest damn thing I ever heard of," Wilson said.

"A lot of people probably thought the same thing," Frank replied. "Flying saucers were pretty common. Nobody thought they were anything and nobody paid much attention. Then they hit—three days ago—and wiped out every living soul in three little southern Michigan towns. From there they began spreading out. They—"

Each of them heard the sound at the same time. A faint rumble, increasing swiftly into high thunder. They moved as one to the window and saw four jet planes, in formation, moving across the sky from the south.

"There they come," Frank said. "The fight's started. Up to now the army has been trying to get set, I suppose."

Nora said, "Is there any way we can hail them? Let them know—"

Her words were cut off by the horror of what happened. As they watched, the plane skimmed low across the Loop. At a point, approximately over Lake Street, Frank estimated, the planes were annihilated. There was a flash of blue fire coming in like jagged lightning to form four balls of fire around the planes. The fire balls turned, almost instantly, into globes of white smoke that drifted lazily away.

And that was all. But the planes vanished completely.

"What happened?" Wilson muttered. "Where'd they go?"

"It was as if they hit a wall," Nora said, her voice hushed with awe.

"I think that *was* what happened," Frank said. "The invaders have some kind of a weapon that holds us helpless. Otherwise the army wouldn't have established this no-man's-land and pulled out. The reports said we have them surrounded on all sides with the help of the lake. We're trying to keep them isolated."

Jim Wilson snorted. "It looks like we've got them right where they want us."

"Anyhow, we're damn fools to stick around here. We'd better head south."

Wilson looked wistfully about the room. "I guess so, but it's a shame—walking away from all this."

Nora was staring out the window, a small frown on her face. "I wonder who they are and where they came from?"

"The teletype releases were pretty vague on that."

She turned quickly. "There's something peculiar about them. Something really strange."

"What do you mean?"

"Last night when we were walking up the street. It must have been these invaders we heard. They must have been across the street. But they didn't act like invaders. They seemed—well, scared. I got the feeling they ran from us in panic. And they haven't been back."

Wilson said, "They may not have been there at all. Probably our imaginations."

"I don't think so," Frank cut in. "They were there and then they were gone. I'm sure of it."

"Those wailing noises. They were certainly signalling to each other. Do you suppose that's the only language they have?" Nora walked over and offered the silent Minna a cigarette. Minna refused with a shake of her head.

"I wish we knew what they looked like," Frank said. "But let's not sit here talking. Let's get going."

Jim Wilson was scowling. There was a marked sullenness in his manner. "Not Minna and me. I've changed my mind. I'm sticking here."

Frank blinked in surprise. "Are you crazy? We've run our luck out already. Did you see what happened to those planes?"

"The hell with the planes. We've got it good here. This I like. I like it a lot. We'll stay."

"Okay," Frank replied hotly, "but talk for yourself. You're not making Minna stay!"

Wilson's eyes narrowed. "I'm not? Look, buster—how about minding your own goddam business?"

The vague feelings of disgust Frank had had now crystallized into words. "I won't let you get away with it! You think I'm blind? Hauling her into the back room every ten minutes! Don't you think I know why? You're nothing but a damn sex maniac! You've got her terrorized until she's afraid to open her mouth. She goes with us!"

Jim Wilson was on his feet. His face blazed with rage. The urge to kill was written in the crouch of his body and the twist of his mouth. "You goddam nosey little squirt. I'll—"

Wilson charged across the short, intervening distance. His arms went out in a clutching motion.

But Frank Brooks wasn't full of knockout drops this time, and with a clear head he was no pushover. Blinded with rage, Jim Wilson *was* a pushover. Frank stepped in between his outstretched arms and slugged him squarely on top of the head with the telephone. Wilson went down like a felled steer.

The scream came from Minna as she sprang across the room. She had turned from a colorless rag doll into a tigress. She hit Frank square in the belly with small fists at the end of stiff, outstretched arms. The full force of her charge was behind the fists, and Frank went backward over the bed.

Minna did not follow up her attack. She dropped to the floor beside Jim Wilson and took his huge head in her lap. "You killed him," she sobbed. "You—you murderer! You killed him! You had no right!"

Frank sat wide-eyed. "Minna! For God's sake! I was helping you. I did it for you!"

"Why don't you mind your business? I didn't ask you to protect me? I don't need any protection—not from Jim."

"You mean you didn't mind the way he's treated you—"

"You've killed him—killed him—" Minna raised her head slowly. She looked at Frank as though she saw him for the first time. "You're a fool" she said dully. "A big fool. What right have you got to meddle with other people's affairs? Are you God or something, to run people's lives?"

"Minna—I—"

It was as though he hadn't spoken. "Do you know what it's like to have nobody? All your life to go on and grow older without anybody? I didn't have no one and then Jim came along and wanted me."

Frank walked close to her and bent down. She reacted like a tiger. "Leave him alone! Leave him alone! You've done enough!"

Nonplused, Frank backed away.

"People with big noses—always sticking them in. That's you. Was that any of your business what he wanted of me? Did I complain?"

"I'm sorry, Minna. I didn't know."

"I'd rather go into back rooms with him than stay in front rooms without nobody."

She began to cry now. Wordlessly—soundlessly, rocking back and forth with the huge man's bloody head in her lap. "Anytime," she crooned. "Anytime I would—"

The body in her arms stirred. She looked down through her tears and saw the small black eyes open. They were slightly crossed, unfocused as they were by the force of the blow. They straightened and Jim mumbled, "What the hell—what the hell—"

Minna's time for talking seemed over. She smiled—a smile hardly perceptible, as though it was for herself alone. "You're all right," she said. "That's good. You're all right."

Jim pushed her roughly away and staggered to his feet. He stood swaying for a moment, his head turning; for all the world like a bull blinded and tormented. Then his eyes focused on Frank.

"You hit me with the goddam phone."

"Yeah—I hit you."

"I'm gonna kill you."

"Look—I made a mistake." Frank picked up the phone and backed against the wall. "I hit you, but you were coming at me. I made a mistake and I'm sorry."

"I'll smash your goddam skull."

"Maybe you will," Frank said grimly. "But you'll work for it. It won't come easy."

A new voice bit across the room. "Cut it out. I'll do the killing. That's what I like best. Everybody quiet down."

They turned and saw a slim, pale-skinned young man in the open doorway. The door had opened quietly and no one had heard it. Now the pale young man was standing in the room with a small, nickle-plated revolver in his right hand.

The left hand was close down at his side. It was swathed generously in white bandage.

The young man chuckled. "The last four people in the world were in a room," he said, "and there was a knock on the door."

His chuckle deepened to one of pure merriment. "Only there wasn't a knock. A man just walked in with a gun that made him boss."

No one moved. No one spoke. The man waited, then went on: "My name is Leroy Davis. I lived out west and I always had a keeper because they said I wasn't quite right. They wanted me to pull out with the rest of them, but I slugged my keeper and here I am."

"Put down the gun and we'll talk it over," Frank said. "We're all in this together."

"No, we aren't. I've got a gun, so that makes me top man. You're all in it together, but I'm not. I'm the boss, and which one of you tried to cut my hand off last night."

"You tried to break in here yelling and screaming like a madman. I held the door. What else could I do?"

"It's all right. I'm not mad. My type—we may be nuts, but we never hold a grudge. I can't remember much about last night. I found some whisky in a place down the street and whisky drives me nuts. I don't know what I'm doing when I drink whisky. They say once about five years ago I got drunk and killed a little kid, but I don't remember."

Nobody spoke.

"I got out of it. They got me out some way. High priced lawyers got me out. Cost my dad a pile."

Hysteria had been piling up inside of Nora. She had held it back, but now a little of it spurted out from between her set teeth. "Do something, somebody. *Isn't anybody going to do anything?*"

Leroy Davis blinked at her. "There's nothing they can do, honey," he said in a kindly voice. "I've got the gun. They'd be crazy to try anything."

Nora's laugh was like the rattle of dry peas. She sat down on the bed and looked up at the ceiling and laughed. "It's crazy. It's all so crazy! We're sitting here in a doomed city with some kind of alien invaders all around us and we don't know what they look like. They haven't hurt us at all. We don't even know what they look like. We don't worry a bit about them because we're too busy trying to kill each other."

Frank Brooks took Nora by the arm. "Stop it! Quit laughing like that!"

Nora shook him off. "Maybe we need someone to take us over. It's all pretty crazy!"

"Stop it."

Nora's eyes dulled down as she looked at Frank. She dropped her head and seemed a little ashamed of herself. "I'm sorry. I'll be quiet."

Jim Wilson had been standing by the wall looking first at the newcomer, then back at Frank Brooks. Wilson seemed confused as to who his true enemy really was. Finally he took a step toward Leroy Davis.

Frank Brooks stopped him with a motion, but kept his eyes on Davis. "Have you seen anybody else?"

Davis regarded Frank with long, careful consideration. His eyes were bright and birdlike. They reminded Frank of a squirrel's eyes. Davis said, "I bumped into an old man out on Halstead Street. He wanted to know where everybody had gone. He asked me, but I didn't know."

"What happened to the old man?" Nora asked. She asked the question as though dreading to do it; but as though some compulsion forced her to speak.

"I shot him," Davis said cheerfully. "It was a favor, really. Here was this old man staggering down the street with nothing but a lot of wasted years to show for his efforts. He was no good alive, and he didn't have the courage to die." Davis stopped and cocked his head brightly. "You know—I think that's what's been wrong with the world. Too many people without the guts to die, and a law against killing them."

It had now dawned upon Jim Wilson that they were faced by a maniac. His eyes met those of Frank Brooks and they were—on this point at least—in complete agreement. A working procedure sprang up, unworded, between them. Jim Wilson took a slow, casual step toward the homicidal maniac.

"You didn't see anyone else?" Frank asked.

Davis ignored the question. "Look at it this way," he said. "In the old days they had Texas long horns. Thin stringy cattle that gave up meat as tough as leather. Do we have cattle like that today? No. Because we bred out the weak line."

Frank said, "There are some cigarettes on that table if you want one."

Jim Wilson took another slow step toward Davis.

Davis said, "We bred with intelligence, with a thought to what a steer was for and we produced a walking chunk of meat as wide as it is long."

"Uh-huh," Frank said.

"Get the point? See what I'm driving at? Humans are more important than cattle, but can we make them breed intelligently? Oh, no! That interferes with damn silly human liberties. You can't tell a man he can only have two kids. It's his God-given right to have twelve when the damn moron can't support three. Get what I mean?"

"Sure—sure, I get it."

"You better think it over, mister—and tell that fat bastard to quit sneaking up on me or I'll blow his brains all over the carpet!"

If the situation hadn't been so grim it would have appeared ludicrous. Jim Wilson, feeling success almost in his grasp, was balanced on tiptoe for a lunge. He teetered, almost lost his balance and fell back against the wall.

"Take it easy," Frank said.

"I'll take it easy," Davis replied. "I'll kill every goddam one of you—" he pointed the gun at Jim Wilson "—starting with him."

"Now wait a minute," Frank said. "You're unreasonable. What right have you got to do that? What about the law of survival? You're standing there with a gun on us. You're going to kill us. Isn't it natural to try anything we can to save our own lives?"

A look of admiration brightened Davis' eyes. "Say! I like you. You're all right. You're logical. A man can talk to you. If there's anything I like it's talking to a logical man."

"Thanks."

"Too bad I'm going to have to kill you. We could sit down and have some nice long talks together."

"Why do you want to kill us?" Minna asked. She had not spoken before. In fact, she had spoken so seldom during the entire time they'd been together that her voice was a novelty to Frank. He was inclined to discount her tirade on the floor with Wilson's head in her lap. She had been a different person then. Now she had lapsed back into her old shell.

Davis regarded thoughtfully. "Must you have a reason?"

"You should have a reason to kill people."

Davis said, "All right, if it will make you any happier. I told you about killing my keeper when they tried to make me leave town. He got in the car, behind the wheel. I got into the back seat and split his skull with a tire iron."

"What's that got to do with us?"

"Just this. Tommy was a better person than anyone of you or all of you put together. If he had to die, what right have you got to live? Is that enough of a reason for you?"

"This is all too damn crazy," Jim Wilson roared. He was on the point of leaping at Davis and his gun.

At that moment, from the north, came a sudden crescendo of the weird invader wailings. It was louder than it had previously been but did not seem nearer.

The group froze, all ears trained upon the sound. "They're talking again," Nora whispered.

"Uh-huh," Frank replied. "But it's different this time. As if—"

"—as if they were getting ready for something," Nora said. "Do you suppose they're going to move south?"

Davis said, "I'm not going to kill you here. We're going down stairs."

The pivotal moment, hinged in Jim Wilson's mind, that could have changed the situation, had come and gone. The fine edge of additional madness that would make a man hurl himself at a loaded gun, was dulled. Leroy Davis motioned pre-emptorily toward Minna.

"You first—then the other babe. You walk side by side down the hall with the men behind you. Straight down to the lobby."

They complied without resistance. There was only Jim Wilson's scowl, Frank Brooks' clouded eyes, and the white, taut look of Nora.

Nora's mind was not on the gun. It was filled with thoughts of the pale maniac who held it. He was in command. Instinctively, she felt that maniacs in command have one of but two motivations—sex and murder. Her reaction to possible murder was secondary. But what if this man insisted upon laying his hands upon her. What if he forced her into the age old thing she had done so often? Nora shuddered. But it was also in her mind to question, and be surprised at the reason for her revulsion. She visualized the hands upon her body—the old familiar things, and the taste in her mouth was one of horror.

She had never experienced such shrinkings before. Why now. Had she herself changed? Had something happened during the night that made the past a time of shame? Or was it the madman himself? She did not know.

Nora returned from her musings to find herself standing in the empty lobby. Leroy Davis, speaking to Frank, was saying, "You look kind of tricky to me. Put your hands on your head. Lock your fingers together over your head and keep your hands there."

Jim Wilson was standing close to the mute Minna. She had followed all the orders without any show of anger, with no outward expression. Always she had kept her eyes on Jim Wilson. Obviously, whatever Jim ordered, she would have done without question.

Wilson leaned his head down toward her. He said, "Listen, baby, there's something I keep meaning to ask but I always forget it. What's your last name?"

"Trumble—Minna Trumble. I thought I told you."

"Maybe you did. Maybe I didn't get it."

Nora felt the hysteria welling again. "How long are you going to keep doing this?" she asked.

Leroy Davis cocked his head as he looked at her. "Doing what?"

"Play cat and mouse like this. Holding us on a pin like flies in an exhibit."

Leroy Davis smiled brightly. "Like a butterfly in your case, honey. A big, beautiful butterfly."

"What are you going to do," Frank Brooks snapped. "Whatever it is, let's get it over with?"

"Can't you see what I'm doing?" Davis asked with genuine wonder. "Are you that stupid? I'm being the boss. I'm in command and I like it. I hold life and death over four people and I'm savoring the thrill of it. You're pretty stupid, mister, and if you use that 'can't get away with it' line, I'll put a bullet into your left ear and watch it come out your right one."

Jim Wilson's fists were doubled. He was again approaching the reckless point. And again it was dulled by the gradually increasing sound of a motor—not in the air, but from the street level to the south.

It was a sane, cheerful sound and was resented instantly by the insane mind of Leroy Davis.

He tightened even to the point that his face grew more pale from the tension. He backed to a window, looked out quickly, and turned back. "It's a jeep," he said. "They're going by the hotel. If anybody makes a move, or yells, they'll find four bodies in here and me gone. That's what I'm telling you and you know I'll do it."

They knew he *would* do it and they stood silent, trying to dredge up the nerve to make a move. The jeep's motor backfired a couple of times as it approached Madison Street. Each time, Leroy Davis' nerves reacted sharply and the four people kept their eyes trained on the gun in his hand.

The jeep came to the intersection and slowed down. There was a conference between its two occupants—helmeted soldiers in dark brown battle dress. Then the jeep moved on up Clark Street toward Lake.

A choked sigh escaped from Nora's throat. Frank Brooks turned toward her. "Take it easy," he said. "We're not dead yet. I don't think he wants to kill us."

The reply came from Minna. She spoke quietly. "I don't care. I can't stand any more of this. After all, we aren't animals. We're human beings and we have a right to live and die as we please."

Minna walked toward Leroy Davis. "I'm not afraid of your gun any more. All you can do with it is kill me. Go ahead and do it."

Minna walked up to Leroy Davis. He gaped at her and said, "You're crazy! Get back there. You're a crazy dame!"

He fired the gun twice and Minna died appreciating the incongruity of his words. She went out on a note of laughter and as she fell, Jim Wilson, with an echoing animal roar, lunged at Leroy Davis. His great hand closed completely over that of Davis, hiding the gun. There was a muffled explosion and the bullet cut unnoticed through Wilson's palm. Wilson jerked the gun from Davis' weak grasp and hurled it away. Then he killed Davis.

He did it slowly, a surprising thing for Wilson. He lifted Davis by his neck and held him with his feet off the floor. He squeezed Davis' neck, seeming to do it with great leisure as Davis made horrible noises and kicked his legs.

Nora turned her eyes away, buried them in Frank Brooks' shoulder, but she could not keep the sounds from reaching her ears. Frank held her close. "Take it easy," he said. "Take it easy." And he was probably not conscious of saying it.

"Tell him to hurry," Nora whispered. "Tell him to get it over with. It's like killing—killing an animal."

"That's what he is—an animal."

Frank Brooks stared in fascination at Leroy Davis' distorted, darkening face. It was beyond semblance of anything human now. The eyes bulged and the tongue came from his mouth as though frantically seeking relief.

The animal sounds quieted and died away. Nora heard the sound of the body falling to the floor—a limp, soft sound of finality. She turned and saw Jim Wilson with his hands still extended and cupped. The terrible hands from which the stench of a terrible life was drifting away into empty air.

Wilson looked down at his handiwork. "He's dead," Wilson said slowly. He turned to face Frank and Nora. There was a great disappointment in his face. "That's all there is to it," he said, dully. "He's just—dead." Without knowing it for what it was, Jim Wilson was full of the futile aftertaste of revenge.

He bent down to pick up Minna's body. There was a small blue hole in the right cheek and another one over the left eye. With a glance at Frank and Nora, Jim Wilson covered the wounds with his hand as though they were not decent. He picked her up in his arms and walked across the lobby and up the stairs with the slow, quiet tread of a weary man.

The sound of the jeep welled up again, but it was further away now. Frank Brooks took Nora's hand and they hurried out into the street. As they crossed the sidewalk, the sound of the jeep was drowned by a sudden swelling of the wailings to the northward.

On still a new note, they rose and fell on the still air. A note of panic, of new knowledge, it seemed, but Frank and Nora were not paying close attention. The sounds of the jeep motor had come from the west and they got within sight of the Madison-Well intersection in time to see the jeep hurtle southward at its maximum speed.

Frank yelled and waved his arms, but he knew he had been neither seen nor heard. They were given little time for disappointment however, because a new center of interest appeared to the northward. From around the corner of Washington Street, into Clark, moved three strange figures.

There was a mixture of belligerence and distress in their actions. They carried odd looking weapons and seemed interested in using them upon something or someone, but they apparently lacked the energy to raise them although they appeared to be rather light.

The creatures themselves were humanoid, Frank thought. He tightened his grip on Nora's hand. "They've seen us."

"Let's not run," Nora said. "I'm tired of running. All it's gotten us is trouble. Let's just stand here."

"Don't be foolish."

"I'm not running. You can if you want to."

Frank turned his attention back to the three strange creatures. He allowed natural curiosity full reign. Thoughts of flight vanished from his mind.

"They're so thin—so fragile," Nora said.

"But their weapons aren't."

"It's hard to believe, even seeing them, that they're from another planet."

"How so? They certainly don't look much like us."

"I mean with the talk, for so long, about flying saucers and space flight and things like that. Here they are, but it doesn't seem possible."

"There's something wrong with them."

This was true. Two of the strange beings had fallen to the sidewalk. The third came doggedly on, dragging one foot after the other until he went to his hands and knees. He remained motionless for a long time, his head hanging limply. Then he too, sank to the cement and lay still.

The wailings from the north now took on a tone of intense agony—great desperation. After that came a yawning silence.

*

"They defeated themselves," the military man said. "Or rather, natural forces defeated them. We certainly had little to do with it."

Nora, Frank, and Jim Wilson stood at the curb beside a motorcycle. The man on the cycle supported it with a leg propped against the curb as he talked.

"We saw three of them die up the street," Frank said.

"Our scouting party saw the same thing happen. That's why we moved in. It's about over now. We'll know a lot more about them and where they came from in twenty-four hours."

They had nothing further to say. The military man regarded them thoughtfully. "I don't know about you three. If you ignored the evacuation through no fault of your own and can prove it—"

"There were four of us," Jim Wilson said. "Then we met another man. He's inside on the floor. I killed him."

"Murder?" the military man said sharply.

"He killed a woman who was with us," Frank said. "He was a maniac. When he's identified I'm pretty sure he'll have a past record."

"Where is the woman's body?"

"On a bed upstairs," Wilson said.

"I'll have to hold all of you. Martial law exists in this area. You're in the hands of the army."

*

The streets were full of people now, going about their business, pushing and jostling, eating in the restaurants, making electricity for the lights, generating power for the telephones.

Nora, Frank, and Jim Wilson sat in a restaurant on Clark Street. "We're all different people now," Nora said. "No one could go through what we've been through and be the same."

Jim Wilson took her statement listlessly. "Did they find out what it was about our atmosphere that killed them?"

"They're still working on that, I think." Frank Brooks stirred his coffee, raised a spoonful and let it drip back into the cup.

"I'm going up to the Chicago Avenue police station," Wilson said.

Frank and Nora looked up in surprise. Frank asked, "Why? The military court missed it—the fact you escaped from jail."

"They didn't miss it I don't think. I don't think they cared much. I'm going back anyway."

"It won't be much of a rap."

"No, a pretty small one. I want to get it over with."

He got up from his chair. "So long. Maybe I'll see you around."

"So long."

"Goodbye."

Frank said, "I think I'll beat it too. I've got a job in a factory up north. Maybe they're operating again." He got to his feet and stood awkwardly by the table. "Besides—I've got some pay coming."

Nora didn't say anything.

Frank said, "Well—so long. Maybe I'll see you around."

"Maybe. Goodbye."

*

Frank Brooks walked north on Clark Street. He was glad to get away from the restaurant. Nora was a good kid but hell—you didn't take up with a hooker. A guy played around, but you didn't stick with them.

But it made a guy think. He was past the kid stage. It was time for him to find a girl and settle down. A guy didn't want to knock around all his life.

*

Nora walked west on Madison Street. Then she remembered the Halstead Street slums were in that direction and turned south on Wells. She had nine dollars in her bag and that worried her. You couldn't get along on nine dollars in Chicago very long.

There was a tavern on Jackson near Wells. Nora went inside. The barkeep didn't frown at her. That was good. She went to the bar and ordered a beer and was served.

After a while a man came in. A middle aged man who might have just come into Chicago—whose bags might still be at the LaSalle Street Station down the block. The man looked at Nora, then away. After a while looked at her again.

Nora smiled.

THE MIGHTIEST MAN

by Patrick Fahy

He had betrayed mankind, but he was not afraid of the consequences—ever!

THEY caught up with him in Belgrade.

The aliens had gone by then, only a few shining metal huts in the Siberian tundra giving mute evidence that they had been anything other than a nightmare.

It had seemed exactly like that. A nightmare in which all of Earth stood helpless, unable to resist or flee, while the obscene shapes slithered and flopped over all her green fields and fair cities. And the awakening had not brought the reassurance that it had all been a bad dream. That if it had happened in reality, the people of Earth would have been capable of dealing with the terrible menace. It had been real. And they had been no more capable of resisting the giant intelligences than a child of killing the ogre in his favorite fairy story.

It was an ironic parallel, because that was what finally saved Earth for its own people. A fairy story.

The old fable of the lion and the mouse. When the lion had exhausted his atomic armor and proud science against the invincible and immortal invaders of Earth—for they could not be killed by any means—the mouse attacked and vanquished them.

The mouse, the lowest form of life: the fungoids, the air of Earth swarming with millions of their spores, attacked the monstrous bodies, grew and entwined within the gray convolutions that were their brain centers. And as the tiny thread-roots probed and tightened, the aliens screamed soundlessly. The intelligences toppled and fell, and at last that few among them who retained sanity gathered their lunatic brethren and fled as they had come.

If he had known the effect the fungoids would have on them, he would have told them that too. He had told them everything else, when he had been snatched from a busy city street, a random specimen of humanity to be probed and investigated.

They had chosen well. For the payment they offered him he was willing to barter the whole human race. As far as it lay in his power he did just that.

He was not an educated man, though he was intelligent. It was child's play to them to strip his mind bare; but they had to know the intangibles too, the determined will of humanity to survive, the probabilities of the pattern of human behavior in a situation which humanity had never before faced. He told them all he could, gladly and willingly. He would have descended to any treachery for the vast glittering reward they tempted him with.

It wasn't easy for the Yugoslavs to guard him and, anyway, their hearts weren't in the task. His treachery, the ultimate treason, the betrayal of the whole human race, was commonly known.

Inevitably the mob got him and killed three policemen in the process. When they had sated their anger a little and the traitor had lost most of his clothes and the thumb of his right hand, they dragged him to the junction where the Danube meets the Sava and held him under the gray waters with long poles, as if he was some poisonous reptile.

He lay supinely on the bed of the river and smiled evilly while a hundred thousand people writhed in neural agony.

TWENTY-FOUR hours later the neural plague had spread to Zagreb and into Albania as far as Tirana. When it crossed to Leghorn in Italy the Balkans held twenty million lunatics and the Danube was an artificial lake a hundred miles wide.

They had used a "clean" bomb. So they were able to bring a loudspeaker van to its edge and boom at him to come out. He allowed them to do that for some inscrutable reason; perhaps to demonstrate that his powers were selective. Then it seemed he got tired of the farce, and cruel fingers twined themselves into the nerve centers of the President of Italy and the Prime Minister of the government of United Europe. He made them dance a horribly twisted *pas de deux* on the banks of the Danube for his perverted amusement.

Then he released them, and released the millions of gibbering, twitching idiots that inhabited Southern Europe, and he came out of the river bed in which he had lain for forty-eight hours.

He walked alone through the deserted streets of Belgrade until he came to the United Nations building. There he told a very brave lieutenant that he was willing to stand trial any place in the world they wished.

For three days nobody came to arrest him. He sat alone with the lieutenant in the peopleless city of Belgrade and waited for his captors. They came then, timidly reassured by his non-violence. While he talked to them pleasantly the citizens of London and Paris suddenly began to dance jerky and grotesque jigs on the pavements of their cities. In the same moment the Chief Justice of the Court of the Nations, at a cocktail party in Washington, writhed in the exquisite pain of total muscle cramp, his august features twisted into a mask of abject fear.

The trial itself was a legal farce. The prisoner promptly pleaded guilty to the charge of betraying mankind to an alien race, but he didn't allow them to question him. When one lawyer persisted in face of his pleasant refusals, he died suddenly in a cramped ball of screaming agony.

The gray-faced Chief Justice inquired whether he wished to be sentenced and he answered yes, but not to death. They couldn't kill him, he explained. That was part of the reward the aliens had given him. The other part was that he could kill or immobilize anybody in the world—or everybody—from any distance. He sat back and smiled at the stricken courtroom. Then he lost his composure and his mouth twitched. He laughed uproariously and slapped his knees in ecstasy.

It was plain that he was fond of a joke.

An anonymous lawyer stood up and waited patiently for his merriment to subside.

If this was true, he asked, why had not the aliens used this power? Why had they not simply killed off the inhabitants and taken over the vacant planet? The traitor gazed kindly at him; and a court stenographer who had cautiously picked up a pencil returned agonizingly to her foetal position and, that way, died.

The traitor looked at his fingers and shrugged. The thumb that had been snapped off in the mob's frenzy was more than half grown again.

"They needed slaves," he said simply.

"And at the end, while some of them were still sane?"

446

The traitor raised his eyebrows, giving him his full courteous attention. The lawyer sat down abruptly, his question unfinished. The creature who had betrayed his own race smiled at him and permitted him to live.

He even completed his question for him, and answered it. "Why did they not kill then? They had something else on their minds—fungoids!" He laughed uproariously at his macabre joke. "And in their minds too!"

The lawyer's blue eyes gazed at him steadily and he stopped laughing. In the bated hush of the courtroom he said softly, "What a pity I'm not an alien too. You could have the fungoids destroy me!"

He laughed again helplessly, the tears running down his cheeks.

THE Chief Justice adjourned the Court then and the prisoner sauntered to his comfortable quarters in front of his frightened guards.

That night, in his own living room, the Chief Justice danced an agonized fandango in front of his horror-stricken wife and the anonymous lawyer sat in his apartment, staring at the blank wall. He was glad the aliens had not made the traitor telepathic too.

He had found the chink in his armor.

The neural paralysis, the murders by remote control, were acts of a conscious will. He had himself admitted that if his mind was destroyed his powers would be destroyed with it. The aliens had not sought revenge because their minds were totally occupied with saving themselves. The stricken ones had simply lost the power.

The knowledge was useless to him. There was no way they could attack his mind without his knowing it.

Possibly they could steal away his consciousness by drugging or bludgeoning, but it would be racial suicide to attempt it. In the split moment of realization he would kill every human being on Earth. There would be nobody left to operate on his brain, to make him a mindless, powerless idiot for the rest of time. For any period of time, he corrected himself. His brain would heal again.

It was useless to think about it. There was nothing they could use against his invincibility. The only hope was to attack him unawares . . . and if that hope was a fraction less than a certainty it could only mean final and absolute catastrophe.

The lawyer looked at his watch. It was four in the morning.

He went into the kitchenette and then shrugged himself into his coat. He walked through the silent streets, past the city hospital where the Chief Justice lay in agony while the motor impulses from his nerve centers wrenched and twisted his body. He entered the foyer of the luxury hotel where the race betrayer was held prisoner and took the elevator to the sixth floor.

Two sleepy guards jerked erect outside the unlocked door. He put his finger to his lips, enjoining them to silence. Then he entered the room and stood for a moment over the man who was invincible and immortal—and human. Human, and subject to the involuntary unconsciousness which nature demands from all men. He slept.

The eyelids fluttered. The lawyer took the steel meat skewer from his pocket. He thrust it through a half-opened eye and rotated it, methodically reducing the soft brain to formless mush.

After that the trial proceeded normally.

The prisoner stared vacantly in front of him and all his movements had to be directed. But he was alive and his thumb was full grown again.

It was the lawyer that noticed this and pointed out the implications. The thumb had grown to full size in less than six weeks. They must regard that as their maximum period of immunity.

They ruminated over it for another four days. The question was a tricky one, for malignant immortality was beyond human solution. It was not just a matter of dealing out punishment. The problem now was the protection of the race from sudden annihilation. An insolvable problem, but one that must be solved. They could only do their best.

He was sentenced to life imprisonment, with a special feature.

It was decided he should be guillotined once a month as long as he lived.

MUTINEER

by Robert J. Shea

For every weapon there was a defense, but not against the deadliest weapon—man himself!

RAGING, Trooper Lane hovered three thousand feet above Tammany Square.

The cool cybrain surgically implanted in him was working on the problem. But Lane had no more patience. They'd sweat, he thought, hating the chill air-currents that threw his hovering body this way and that. He glared down at the three towers bordering on the Square. He spat, and watched the little white speck fall, fall. *Lock me up in barracks. All I wanted was a little time off. Did I fight in Chi for them? Damn right I did. Just a little time off, so I shouldn't blow my top. Now the lid's gone.*

He was going over all their heads. He'd bowled those city cops over like paper dolls, back at the Armory. The black dog was on Lane's back. Old Mayor himself was going to hear about it.

Why not? Ain't old Mayor the CinC of the Newyork Troopers?

The humming paragrav-paks embedded beneath his shoulder blades held him motionless above Newyork's three administrative towers. Tammany Hall. Mayor's Palace. Court House. Lane cursed his stupidity. He hadn't found out which one was which ahead of time. *They keep Troopers in the Armory and teach them how to fight. They don't teach them about their own city, that they'll be fighting for. There's no time. From seven years old up, Troopers have too much to learn about fighting.*

The Mayor was behind one of those thousands of windows.

Old cybrain, a gift from the Trooper surgeons, compliments of the city, would have to figure out which one. Blood churned in his veins, nerves shrieked with impatience. Lane waited for the electronic brain to come up with the answer.

Then his head jerked up, to a distant buzz. There were cops coming. Two black paragrav-boats whirred along the translucent underside of Newyork's anti-missile force-shield, the Shell.

Old cybrain better be fast. Damn fast!

The cybrain jolted an impulse through his spine. Lane somersaulted. Cybrain had taken charge of his motor nerves. Lane's own mind was just along for the ride.

*

HIS body snapped into a stiff dive position. He began to plummet down, picking up speed. His mailed hands glittered like arrowheads out in front. They pointed to a particular window in one of the towers. A predatory excitement rippled through him as he sailed down through the air. It was like going into battle again. A little red-white-and-green flag fluttered on a staff below the window. Whose flag? The city flag was orange and blue. He shrugged away the problem. Cybrain knew what it was doing.

The little finger of his right hand vibrated in its metal sheath. A pale vibray leaped from the lensed fingertip. Breakthrough! The glasstic pane dissolved. Lane streamed through the window.

The paragrav-paks cut off. Lane dropped lightly to the floor, inside the room, in battle-crouch. A 3V set was yammering. A girl screamed. Lane's hand shot out automatically. A

449

finger vibrated. Out of the corner of his eye, Lane saw the girl fold to the floor. There was no one else in the room. Lane, still in a crouch, chewed his lip.

The Mayor?

His head swung around and he peered at the 3V set. He saw his own face.

"Lashing police with his vibray," said the announcer, "Lane broke through the cordon surrounding Manhattan Armory. Two policemen were killed, four others seriously injured. Tammany Hall has warned that this man is extremely dangerous. Citizens are cautioned to keep clear of him. Lane is an insane killer. He is armed with the latest military weapons. A built-in electronic brain controls his reflexes—"

"At ease with that jazz," said Lane, and a sheathed finger snapped out. There was a loud bang. The 3V screen dissolved into a puddle of glasstic.

The Mayor.

Lane strode to the window. The two police boats were hovering above the towers. Lane's mailed hand snapped open a pouch at his belt. He flipped a fist-sized cube to the floor.

The force-bomb "exploded"—swelled or inflated, really, but with the speed of a blast. Lane glanced out the window. A section of the energy globe bellied out from above. It shaded the view from his window and re-entered the tower wall just below.

Now the girl.

He turned back to the room. "Wake up, outa-towner." He gave the blonde girl a light dose of the vibray to slap her awake.

"Who are you?" she said, shakily.

Lane grinned. "Trooper Lane, of the Newyork Special Troops, is all." He threw her a mock salute. "You from outa-town, girlie. I ain't seen a Newyork girl with yellow hair in years. Orange or green is the action. Whatcha doing in the Mayor's room?"

*

THE girl pushed herself to her feet. Built, Lane saw. She was pretty and clean-looking, very out-of-town. She held herself straight and her blue-violet eyes snapped at him.

"What the devil do you think you're doing, soldier? I am a diplomat of the Grassroots Republic of Mars. This is an embassy, if you know what that means."

"I don't," said Lane, unconcerned.

"Well, you should have had brains enough to honor the flag outside this window. That's the Martian flag, soldier. If you've never heard of diplomatic immunity, you'll suffer for your ignorance." Her large, dark eyes narrowed. "Who sent you?"

"My cybrain sent me."

She went openmouthed. "You're *Lane*."

"I'm the guy they told you about on the 3V. Where's the Mayor? Ain't this his place?"

"No. No, you're in the wrong room. The wrong building. That's the Mayor's suite over there." She pointed. "See where the balcony is? This is the Embassy suite. If you want the Mayor you'll have to go over there."

"Whaddaya know," said Lane. "Cybrain didn't know, no more than me."

The girl noticed the dark swell of the force-globe. "What's that out there?"

"Force-screen. Nothing gets past, except maybe a full-size blaster-beam. Keeps cops out. Keeps you in. You anybody important?"

"I told you, I'm an ambassador. From Mars. I'm on a diplomatic mission."

"Yeah? Mars a big city?"

She stared at him, violet eyes wide. "The *planet* Mars."

"Planet? Oh, *that* Mars. Sure, I've heard of it—you gotta go by spaceship. What's your name?"

"Gerri Kin. Look, Lane, holding me is no good. It'll just get you in worse trouble. What are you trying to do?"

"I wanna see the Mayor. Me and my buddies, we just come back from fighting in Chi, Gerri. We won. They got a new Mayor out there in Chi. He takes orders from Newyork."

Gerri Kin said, "That's what the force-domes did. The perfect defense. But also the road to the return to city-states. Anarchy."

Lane said, "Yeah? Well, we done what they wanted us to do. We did the fighting for them. So we come back home to Newyork and they lock us up in the Armory. Won't pay us. Won't let us go nowhere. They had cops guarding us. City cops." Lane sneered. "I busted out. I wanna see the Mayor and find out why we can't have time off. I don't play games, Gerri. I go right to the top."

Lane broke off. There was a hum outside the window. He whirled and stared out. The rounded black hulls of the two police paragrav-boats were nosing toward the force-screen. Lane could read the white numbers painted on their bows.

A loudspeaker shouted into the room: "Come out of there, Lane, or we'll blast you out."

"You can't," Lane called. "This girl from Mars is here."

"I repeat, Lane—come out or we'll blast you out."

Lane turned to the girl. "I thought you were important."

*

SHE stood there with her hands together, calmly looking at him. "I am. But you are too, to them. Mars is millions of miles away, and you're right across the Square from the Mayor's suite."

"Yeah, but—" Lane shook his head and turned back to the window. "All right, look! Move them boats away and I'll let this girl out!"

"No deal, Lane. We're coming in." The police boats backed away slowly, then shot straight up, out of the line of vision.

Lane looked down at the Square. Far below, the long, gleaming barrel of a blaster cannon caught the dim light filtering down through Newyork's Shell. The cannon trundled into the Square on its olive-drab, box-shaped caterpillar mounting and took up a position equidistant from the bases of the three towers.

Now a rumble of many voices rose from below. Lane stared down to see a large crowd gathering in Tammany Square. Sound trucks were rolling to a stop around the edges of the crowd. The people were all looking up.

Lane looked across the Square. The windows of the tower opposite, the ones he could see clearly, were crowded with faces. There were white dot faces on the balcony that Gerri Kin had pointed out as the Mayor's suite.

The voice of a 3V newscaster rolled up from the Square, reechoing against the tower walls.

"Lane is holding the Martian Ambassador, Gerri Kin, hostage. You can see the Martian tricolor behind his force-globe. Police are bringing up blaster cannon. Lane's defense is a globe of energy similar to the one which protects Newyork from aerial attack."

Lane grinned back at Gerri Kin. "Whole town's down there." Then his grin faded. Nice-looking, nice-talking girl like this probably cared a lot more about dying than he did. Why the hell didn't they give him a chance to let her out? Maybe he could do it now.

Cybrain said no. It said the second he dropped his force-screen, they'd blast this room to hell. Poor girl from Mars, she didn't have a chance.

Gerri Kin put her hand to her forehead. "Why did you have to pick my room? Why did they send me to this crazy city? Private soldiers. Twenty million people living under a Shell like worms in a corpse. Earth is sick and it's going to kill me. What's going to happen?"

Lane looked sadly at her. Only two kinds of girls ever went near a Trooper—the crazy ones and the ones the city paid. Why did he have to be so near getting killed when he met one he liked? Now that she was showing a little less fear and anger, she was talking straight to him. She was good, but she wasn't acting as if she was too good for him.

"They'll start shooting pretty quick," said Lane. "I'm sorry about you."

"I wish I could write a letter to my parents," she said.

"What?"

"Didn't you understand what I said?"

"What's a letter?"

"You don't know where Mars is. You don't know what a letter is. You probably can't even read and write!"

*

LANE shrugged. He carried on the conversation disinterestedly, professionally relaxed before battle. "What's these things I can't do? They important?"

"Yes. The more I see of this city and its people, the more important I realize they are. You know how to fight, don't you? I'll bet you're perfect with those weapons."

"Listen. They been training me to fight since I was a little kid. Why shouldn't I be a great little fighter?"

"Specialization," said the girl from Mars.

"What?"

"Specialization. Everyone I've met in this city is a specialist. SocioSpecs run the government. TechnoSpecs run the machinery. Troopers fight the wars. And ninety per cent of the people don't work at all because they're not trained to do anything."

"The Fans," said Lane. "They got it soft. That's them down there, come to watch the fight."

"You know why you were kept in the Armory, Lane? I heard them talking about it, at the dinner I went to last night."

"Why?"

"Because they're afraid of the Troopers. You men did too good a job out in Chi. You are the deadliest weapon that has ever been made. You. Single airborne infantrymen!"

Lane said, "They told us in Trooper Academy that it's the men that win the wars."

"Yes, but people had forgotten it until the SocioSpecs of Newyork came up with the Troopers. Before the Troopers, governments concentrated on the big weapons, the missiles, the bombs. And the cities, with the Shells, were safe from bombs. They learned to be self-sufficient under the Shells. They were so safe, so isolated, that national governments collapsed. But you Troopers wiped out that feeling of security, when you infiltrated Chi and conquered it."

"We scared them, huh?"

Gerri said, "You scared them so much that they were afraid to let you have a furlough in the city when you came back. Afraid you Troopers would realize that you could easily take over the city if you wanted to. You scared them so much that they'll let me be killed. They'll actually risk trouble with Mars just to kill you."

"I'm sorry about you. I mean it, I like—"

At that moment a titanic, ear-splitting explosion hurled him to the carpet, deafened and blinded him.

He recovered and saw Gerri a few feet away, dazed, groping on hands and knees.

Lane jumped to the window, looked quickly, sprang back. Cybrain pumped orders to his nervous system.

"Blaster cannon," he said. "But just one. Gotcha, cybrain. I can beat that."

He picked up the black box that generated his protective screen. Snapping it open with thumb-pressure, he turned a small dial. Then he waited.

Again an enormous, brain-shattering concussion.

Again Lane and Gerri were thrown to the floor. But this time there was a second explosion and a blinding flash from below.

Lane laughed boyishly and ran to the window.

"Look!" he called to Gerri.

*

THERE was a huge gap in the crowd below. The pavement was blackened and shattered to rubble. In and around the open space sprawled dozens of tiny black figures, not moving.

"Backfire," said Lane. "I set the screen to throw their blaster beam right back at them."

"And they knew you might—and yet they let a crowd congregate!"

Gerri reeled away from the window, sick.

Lane said, "I can do that a couple times more, but it burns out the force-globe. Then I'm dead."

He heard the 3V newscaster's amplified voice: "—approximately fifty killed. But Lane is through now. He has been able to outthink police with the help of his cybrain. Now police are feeding the problem to their giant analogue computer in the sub-basement of the Court House. The police analogue computer will be able to outthink Lane's cybrain, will predict Lane's moves in advance. Four more blaster cannon are coming down Broadway—"

"Why don't they clear those people out of the Square?" Gerri cried.

"What? Oh, the Fans—nobody clears them out." He paused. "I got one more chance to try." He raised a mailed glove to his mouth and pressed a small stud in the wrist. He said, "Trooper HQ, this is Lane."

A voice spoke in his helmet. "Lane, this is Trooper HQ. We figured you'd call."

453

"Get me Colonel Klett."

Thirty seconds passed. Lane could hear the clank of caterpillar treads as the mobile blaster cannon rolled into Tammany Square.

The voice of the commanding officer of the Troopers rasped into Lane's ear: "Meat-head! You broke out against my orders! *Now* look at you!"

"I knew you didn't mean them orders, sir."

"If you get out of there alive, I'll hang you for disobeying them!"

"Yes, sir. Sir, there's a girl here—somebody important—from Mars. You know, the planet. Sir, she told me we could take over the city if we got loose. That right, sir?"

There was a pause. "Your girl from Mars is right, Lane. But it's too late now. If we had moved first, captured the city government, we might have done it. But they're ready for us. They'd chop us down with blaster cannon."

"Sir, I'm asking for help. I know you're on my side."

"I am, Lane." The voice of Colonel Klett was lower. "I'd never admit it if you had a chance of getting out of there alive. You've had it, son. I'd only lose more men trying to rescue you. When they feed the data into that analogue computer, you're finished."

"Yes, sir."

"I'm sorry, Lane."

"Yes, sir. Over and out."

Lane pressed the stud on his gauntlet again. He turned to Gerri.

"You're okay. I wish I could let you out. Old cybrain says I can't. Says if I drop the force-globe for a second, they'll fire into the room, and then we'll both be dead."

*

GERRI stood with folded arms and looked at him. "Do what you have to do. As far as I can see, you're the only person in this city that has even a little bit of right on his side."

Lane laughed. "Any of them purple-haired broads I know would be crazy scared. You're different."

"When my grandparents landed on Mars, they found out that selfishness was a luxury. Martians can't afford it."

Lane frowned with the effort of thinking. "You said I had a little right on my side. That's a good feeling. Nobody ever told me to feel that way about myself before. It'll be better to die knowing that."

"I know," she said.

The amplified voice from below said, "The police analogue computer is now hooked directly to the controls of the blaster cannon battery. It will outguess Lane's cybrain and check his moves ahead of time."

Lane looked at Gerri. "How about giving me a kiss before they get us? Be nice if I kissed a girl like you just once in my life."

She smiled and walked forward. "You deserve it, Lane."

He kissed her and it filled him with longings for things he couldn't name. Then he stepped back and shook his head. "It ain't right you should get killed. If I take a dive out that window, they shoot at me, not in here."

"And kill you all the sooner."

"Better than getting burned up in this lousy little room. You also got right on your side. There's too many damn Troopers and not enough good persons like you. Old cybrain says stay here, but I don't guess I will. I'm gonna pay you back for that kiss."

"But you're safe in here!"

"Worry about yourself, not about me." Lane picked up the force-bomb and handed it to her. "When I say now, press this. Then take your hand off, real fast. It'll shut off the screen for a second."

He stepped up on to the window ledge. Automatically, the cybrain cut in his paragrav-paks. "So long, outa-towner. *Now!*"

He jumped. He was hurtling across the Square when the blaster cannons opened up. They weren't aimed at the window where the little red-white-and-green tricolor was flying. But they weren't aimed at Lane, either. They were shooting wild.

Which way now? Looks like I got a chance. Old cybrain says fly right for the cannons.

He saw the Mayor's balcony ahead. *Go to hell, old cybrain. I'm doing all right by myself. I come to see the Mayor, and I'm gonna see him.*

Lane plunged forward. He heard the shouts of frightened men.

He swooped over the balcony railing. A man was pointing a blaster pistol at him. There were five men on the balcony—emergency! Years of training and cybrain took over. Lane's hand shot out, fingers vibrating. As he dropped to the balcony floor in battle-crouch, the men slumped around him.

He had seen the man with the blaster pistol before. It was the Mayor of Newyork.

Lane stood for a moment in the midst of the sprawled men, the shrieks of the crowd floating up to him. Then he raised his glove to his lips. He made contact with Manhattan Armory.

"Colonel Klett, sir. You said if we captured the city government we might have a chance. Well, I captured the city government. What do we do with it now?"

*

LANE was uncomfortable in his dress uniform. First there had been a ceremony in Tammany Square inaugurating Newyork's new Military Protectorate, and honoring Trooper Lane. Now there was a formal dinner. Colonel Klett and Gerri Kin sat on either side of Lane.

Klett said, "Call me an opportunist if you like, Miss Kin, my government will be stable, and Mars can negotiate with it." He was a lean, sharp-featured man with deep grooves in his face, and gray hair.

Gerri shook her head. "Recognition for a new government takes time. I'm going back to Mars, and I think they'll send another ambassador next time. Nothing personal—I just don't like it here."

Lane said, "I'm going to Mars, too."

"Did she ask you to?" demanded Klett.

Lane shook his head. "She's got too much class for me. But I like what she told me about Mars. It's healthy, like."

Klett frowned. "If I thought there was a gram of talent involved in your capture of the Mayor, Lane, I'd never release you from duty. But I know better. You beat that analogue computer by sheer stupidity—by disregarding your cybrain."

455

Lane said, "It wasn't so stupid if it worked."

"That's what bothers me. It calls for a revision in our tactics. We've got a way of beating those big computers now, should anyone use them against us."

"I just didn't want her to be hurt."

"Exactly. The computer could outguess a machine, like your cybrain. But you introduced a totally unpredictable factor—human emotion. Which proves what I, as a military man, have always maintained—that the deadliest weapon in man's arsenal is still, and will always be, the individual soldier."

"What you just said there, sir," said Lane. "That's why I'm leaving Newyork."

"What do you mean?" asked Colonel Klett.

"I'm tired of being a weapon, sir. I want to be a human being."

Work is the elimination of the traces of work.—Michelangelo

AND THAT'S HOW IT WAS, OFFICER

by Ralph Sholto

When Uncle Peter decided to clean out the underworld, it was a fine thing for the town, but it was tough on the folks in Tibet.

DAVID NIXON,
Chief of Police,
Morton City.
Dear Chief Nixon:

No doubt, by this time, you and your boys are a pretty bewildered lot. You have all probably lost weight wondering what has been going on in Morton City; where all the gangsters went, and why the underworld has vanished like a bucket of soap bubbles.

Not being acquainted with my uncle, Peter Nicholas, with Bag Ears Mulligan, with the gorgeous Joy Nicholas, my bride of scarcely twenty-four hours, or with me, Homer Nicholas, you have of course been out of touch with a series of swiftly moving events just culminated.

You, above all others, are entitled to know what has been happening in our fair city. Hence this letter. When you receive it, Joy and I will be on the way to Europe in pursuit of a most elusive honeymoon. Uncle Peter will be headed for Tibet in order to interview certain very important people you and your department never heard of. Bag Ears will probably be off somewhere searching for his bells, and I suggest you let him keep right on searching, because Bag Ears isn't one to answer questions with very much intelligence.

So, because of the fact that a great deal of good has been done at no cost whatever to the taxpayers, I suggest you read this letter and then forget about the whole thing.

It all started when Joy and I finally got an audience with Uncle Peter in his laboratory yesterday morning. Possibly you will think it strange that I should have difficulty in contacting my own close relative. But you don't know Uncle Peter.

He is a strange mixture of the doer and the dreamer—the genius and the child. Parts of his brain never passed third grade while other parts could sit down and tie Einstein in knots during a discussion of nuclear physics, advanced mathematics or what have you. He lives in a small bungalow at the edge of town, in the basement of which is his laboratory. A steel door bars the public from this laboratory and it was upon this door that Joy and I pounded futilely for three days. Finally the door opened and Uncle Peter greeted us.

"Homer—my dear boy! Have you been knocking long?"

"Quite a while, Uncle Peter—off and on that is. I have some news for you. I am going to get married."

My uncle became visibly disturbed. "My boy! That's wonderful—truly wonderful. But I'm certainly surprised at you. Tsk-tsk-tsk!"

"What do you mean by tsk-tsk-tsk?"

"Your moral training has been badly neglected. You plan marriage even while traveling about in the company of this woman you have with you."

457

Joy is a lady of the finest breeding, but she can be caught off-guard at times. This was one of the times. She said, "Listen here, you bald-headed jerk. Nobody calls me a woman—"

Uncle Peter was mildly interested. "Then if you aren't a woman, what—?"

I hastened to intervene. "You didn't let Joy finish, Uncle Peter. She no doubt would have added—'in that tone of voice.' And I think her attitude is entirely justified. Joy is a fine girl and my intended bride."

"Oh, why didn't you say so?"

"I supposed you would assume as much."

"My boy, I am a scientist. A scientist assumes nothing. But I wish to apologize to the young lady and I hope you two will be very happy."

"That's better," Joy said, with only a shade of truculence.

"And now," Uncle Peter went on. "It would be very thoughtful of you to leave. I am working on a serum which will have a great deal to do with changing the course of civilization. In fact it is already perfected and must be tested. It is a matter of utmost urgency to me that I be left alone to arrange the tests."

"I am afraid," I said, "that you will have to delay your work a few hours. It is not every day that your nephew gets married and in all decency you must attend the wedding and the reception. I don't wish you to be inconvenienced too greatly, but—"

Uncle Peter's mind had gone off on another track. He stopped me with a wave of his hand and said, "Homer, are you still running around with those bums from the wrong side of town?"

*

THESE words from anyone but Uncle Peter would have been insulting. But Uncle Peter is the most impersonal man I have known. He never bothers insulting people for any personal satisfaction. When he asks a question, he always has a reason for so doing.

By way of explaining Uncle Peter's question, let me say that I am a firm believer in democracy and I demonstrate this belief in my daily life. More than once I have had to apologize for the definitely unsocial attitude of my family. They have a tendency to look down on those less fortunate in environment and financial stability than we Nicholases.

I, however, do not approve of this snobbishness. I cannot forget that a great-uncle, Phinias Nicholas, laid the foundations of our fortune by stealing cattle in the days of the Early West and selling them at an amazing profit.

I personally am a believer in the precept that all men are created equal. I'll admit they don't remain equal very long, but that is beside the point.

In defense of my convictions, I have always sought friends among the underprivileged brotherhood sometimes scathingly referred to as bums, tramps, screwballs, and I've found them, on the whole, to be pretty swell people.

But to get back—I answered Uncle Peter rather stiffly. "My friends are my own affair and are not to be discussed."

"No offense. My question had to do with an idea I got rather suddenly. Will any of these—ah, friends, be present at the reception?"

"It is entirely possible."

"Then I could easily infiltrate—"

"You could what?"

"Never mind, my boy. It is not important. I'll be indeed honored to attend your wedding."

At that moment there was a muffled commotion from beyond a closed door to our left; the sound of heels kicking on the panel and an irate female voice:

"They gone yet? There's cobwebs in this damn closet—and it's dark!"

Uncle Peter had the grace to blush. In fact he could do little else as the closet door opened and a young lady stepped forth.

In the vulgar parlance of the day, this girl could be described only as a dream-boat. This beyond all doubt, because the trim hull, from stem to stern, was bared to the gaze of all who cared to observe and admire. She was a blonde dream-boat—and most of her present apparel had come from lying under a sun lamp.

Uncle Peter gasped. "Cora! In the name of all decency—"

Joy, with admirable aplomb, laughed gayly. "Why, Uncle Peter! So it's that kind of research! And no wonder it's top-secret!"

Uncle Peter's frantic attention was upon the girl. "I was never so mortified—"

She raised her hair-line eyebrows. "Why the beef, Winky? Aren't we among friends?"

"Never mind! Never mind!" Uncle Peter fell back upon his dignity—having nothing else to fall back on—and said, "Homer—Joy—this is Cora, my ah—assistant. She was ah—in the process of taking a shower, and—"

Joy reached forth and pinched Uncle Peter's flaming cheek. "It's all right, uncle dear. Perfectly all right. And I'll bet this chick can give a terrific assist, too."

I felt the scene should be broken up at the earliest possible moment. I steered Joy toward the door. I said, "We'll see you later, then, Uncle Peter."

"And you too, Miss Courtney," Joy cut in. "Make Winky bring you and don't bother to dress. The reception is informal."

I got Joy out the door but I couldn't suppress her laughter. "Winky," she gasped. "Oh, my orange and purple garter-belt!"

*

WE WILL proceed now, to the reception, which was given by my Aunt Gretchen in the big house on Shore Drive. We were married at City Hall and—after a delicious interlude while the cab was carrying us cross-town—we arrived there, a happy bride and groom.

I am indeed fortunate to have wooed and won such a talented and beautiful girl as Joy. A graduate of Vassar, she is an accomplished pianist, a brilliant conversationalist, and is supercharged with a vitality and effervescence which—while they sometimes manifest in disturbing ways—are wonderful to behold. But more of that later.

The reception began smoothly enough. The press was satisfactorily represented, much to Aunt Gretchen's gratification. Joy and I stood at the door for a time, receiving. Then, tiring of handshakes and congratulations, we retired to the conservatory to be alone for a few minutes.

Or so we thought.

Almost immediately, Aunt Gretchen ferreted us out. Aunt Gretchen has long-since lost the smooth silhouette for which the Nicholas women are noted. She has broadened in all departments and she came waddling along between banks of yellow roses in a manner suggesting an outraged circus tent.

"Homer," she called. "Homer!"

I reluctantly took my hands away and answered her.

"Oh, there you are! Homer—I want an explanation."

"An explanation of what?"

"There is a person at the door who calls himself Bag Ears Mulligan. He has the audacity to claim you invited him to—to this *brawl* as he terms it."

I must here explain—with sorrow—that my Aunt Gretchen is a snob. There is no other term for it. It has gotten to be such a habit with her that any friend of mine is automatically a person to be looked down on.

And Bag Ears Mulligan is one of my dearest friends. Of course I had invited him to my wedding, and felt honored by his attendance. Bag Ears is a habitue of one of the less glittering places I frequent in search of lasting fellowship—Red Nose Tessie's Bar, to be exact. A place of dirty beer glasses but of warm hearts and sincere people.

"I'll see this man, Aunt Gretchen," I said with calm dignity. "He is to be an honored guest. While somewhat rugged in appearance, Bag Ears has a sensitive nature and must be treated with understanding."

Aunt Gretchen's lips quivered. "Homer—I'm through—absolutely and finally through! You can get someone else to handle your next wedding reception. Hold it in a barn or a stable. Never again in my house."

After this tactless outburst, Aunt Gretchen came about and sailed out of the conservatory. Joy and I followed wordlessly.

Upon arriving at the front door, we found Aunt Gretchen had spoken the truth. Bag Ears was waiting there. He had been herded into a corner by Johnson, Aunt Gretchen's stuffed shirt of a butler, who was standing guard over him.

Bag Ears grinned happily when he caught sight of me and I smiled reassuringly. While Bag Ears is not too richly endowed with good looks, he has a great heart and at one time was possessed of a lightning-fast brain. However, he took a great deal of punishment during his unsuccessful climb toward the lightweight title, and his brain has been slowed down to the point where it sometimes comes to a complete halt. His features reflect the fury of a hundred battles in the squared ring. They are in a sad state, his ears particularly. They hang wearily downward like the leaves of a dying cabbage plant.

Also, Bag Ears has fallen into the misfortune of hearing bells at various times—bells that exist only in his poor, bewildered mind. But he is cheerful and warm-hearted nonetheless.

He said, "Homer, this character says I should o' brung along my invite. But I don't remember you givin' me one. You just ast me to come."

"That is true," I returned, "and you are most welcome. You may go, Johnson." I gave the butler a cold look and he stalked away.

*

I THEN introduced Bag Ears to my new bride. "This is Joy. I am certainly a lucky man, Bag Ears. Isn't she the most beautiful thing you ever saw?"

Bag Ears was of course impressed. "Golly, what gams!" he breathed. His eyes traveled upward and he said, "Golly, what—what things and stuff." He came finally to her face. "Baby, you got it!"

Joy was rocked back on her heels. Caught unawares by the open admiration in his eyes, she whispered, "Oh, my ancient step-ins!"

But she rallied like a thoroughbred and gave Bag Ears a dazzling smile. "I'm delighted, Mr. Mulligan. Homer's friends are my friends—I think—and I'm sure everything will turn out all right."

Bag Ears said, "Lady—leave us not be formal. Just call me Bag Ears."

"Of course—Bag Ears—leave us be chummy."

He now turned his remarks to me and evinced even more intense admiration for my bride. "She reminds me of a fast lightweight—the most beautiful sight in the world."

"Let us repair to the conservatory," I said, "where we can have a quiet chat." I said this because I felt that some of the other guests might not be as tactful as Joy and might make Bag Ears feel uncomfortable. Aunt Gretchen had rudely vanished without waiting for an introduction and the actions of the hostess often set the pattern for those of the guests.

As we moved toward the rear of the house, Joy took my arm and said, "Speaking of being stripped down for action—what do you suppose happened to Uncle Peter? I haven't seen him around anywhere."

"He gave his word, so I'm sure he'll come."

"That's what I'm afraid of."

"I don't understand."

"I don't quite understand myself, but I feel uneasy. I remember the calculating look in his eye when he suddenly agreed to honor us with his presence. There was something too eager about that look. And his asking whether any of your friends would be here."

"Uncle Peter is basically a good follow. I think he envies me my wide contacts."

"Maybe."

"If he seemed a trifle peculiar, you must remember that he is a scientist. Even now he is engaged in some important project—some experiment—"

"I know—we met her."

"Joy! Please!"

"—but I wouldn't think he'd have to experiment at his age. I'd think—"

I put my hand firmly over her mouth. "Darling—we have a guest—Bag Ears—"

"Oh, of course."

Safely hidden behind a bank of tropical grass, I took Joy in my arms and kissed her. Bag Ears obligingly looked in the other direction. But Joy didn't quite get her heart into it. She seemed preoccupied—I might almost say, bewildered.

"Bag Ears," she whispered to no one in particular, "and what did you say the lady's name was? Oh— I remember—Red Nose Tessie." She pondered for a moment and then smiled up at me dreamily. "Darling—I never realized what a versatile person you are—"

Bag Ears perked up. "Verseetile? You ain't just a hootin', babe. And *tough*. You should see his right."

I strove to quiet him down. "Never mind, Bag Ears—"

But Joy evinced great interest. "Tell me—"

"Babe—the kid could be the next heavyweight champ in a breeze. I mind me one night a monkey comes into the tavern rodded—"

Joy held up a hand. "Just a moment. I don't like to appear stupid, but—"

"A moke wid a heater—a goon wid a gat."

"Oh—you mean a man with a gun."

"Sure—that's what I said. Anyhow, this droolie makes a crack about Tessie's beak—"

"An insult relative to her nose?"

"Sure—sure. And Tessie's hot to kiss him wid a bottle when he pulls the iron."

"Imagine that," Joy said, and I felt a slight shiver go through her body.

"Then Homer here, gets off his stool and says very polite-like, 'That remark, sir, was in bad taste and entirely uncalled-for. I believe an apology is in order.' And the monkey standing there with the gat in his mitt. What Homer meant was the jerk'd cracked out o' turn and to eat his words fast."

"I gathered that was what he meant."

"But the screwball raises the hardware and—wham—Homer hits him. What a sock! The goon back-pedals across the room and into a cardboard wall next to the door marked 'ladies'. He busts right through the wall and lands in a frail's lap inside who's—"

"Powdering her nose?"

"That's right! What a sock!"

*

JOY'S eyes were upon mine.

"Darling! I didn't have the least idea. Why, it's going to be wonderful! Never a dull moment!"

I kissed my bride, after which she said, "I think I could do with a drink, sweetheart."

"Your wish is my command."

I got up and started toward the liquor supply inside the house. Joy's soft call stopped me.

"What is it, angel?" I inquired.

"Not just a drink, sweet. Bring the bottle."

I went into the kitchen and got a bottle of brandy. But upon returning, I discovered I'd neglected to bring glasses.

But Joy took the bottle from me in a rather dazed manner, knocked off the neck against a leg of the bench and tipped the bottle to her beautiful lips. She took a pull of brandy large enough to ward off the worst case of pneumonia and then passed the bottle to Bag Ears.

"Drink hearty, pal," she murmured, and sort of sank down into herself.

I never got my turn at the bottle because, just at that moment, Aunt Gretchen came sailing like a pink cloud along the conservatory walk. She was no longer the old familiar Aunt Gretchen. Her eyes were glazed and her face was drawn and weary.

Bag Ears looked up politely and asked, "Who's the fat sack?"

I was hoping Aunt Gretchen hadn't heard the question because she would fail to understand that while his words were uncouth, he had a heart of gold and meant well. And I don't think she *did* hear him. She didn't even hear Joy, who replied,

"That's the dame that owns the joint."

Aunt Gretchen fixed her accusing eyes upon me to the exclusion of everyone else. Her button of a chin quivered. "Please understand, Homer—I'm not criticizing. Things have gotten past that stage. I've merely come to report that the house is filling up with an astounding assortment of characters. Johnson resigned a half-hour ago. But before he left, he suggested a man who could handle the situation far better than he himself. A man named Frank Buck."

"But, my dear aunt," I protested. "There must be some mistake. I did not invite any unusual people to this reception. I issued only three invitations. I invited Willie Shank, who could not come because of a dispute with the police over the ownership of a car he was driving yesterday; John Smith, who could not come because this is the day he reports to the parole board, and my good friend Bag Ears Mulligan."

"How did you happen to overlook Red Nose Tessie?" Joy asked.

"The poor woman is emotional. She does not enjoy wedding receptions. She weeps."

"So does Aunt Gretchen," Joy observed.

Aunt Gretchen was indeed weeping—quietly, under the blanket of reserve with which the Nicholases cover their emotions. I was about to comfort her when she turned and fled. I started to run after her but decided against it and returned to Joy.

"Perhaps," I said, "we had better investigate this strange turn of events. Possibly our reception has been crashed by some undesirable persons."

"Impossible," Joy replied. "But it might be fun to look them over. Shall we have a quick one first—just to stiffen the old spine a bit?"

It sounded like a good suggestion so we stiffened our spines with what was left in the bottle, and quitted the conservatory.

*

BACK in the house, one thing became swiftly apparent. We had guests who were utter strangers to me. But it was Bag Ears who summed up the situation with the briefest possible statement. "Jees!" he ejaculated. "It's a crooks' convention!"

"You can identify some of these intruders?"

"If you mean do I know 'em, the answer is without a doubt, pal. Somehow, the whole Cement Mixer Zinsky mob has infiltered into the joint."

"Cement Mixer Zinsky," Joy murmured. "Another of those odd names."

"It's on account of he invented something. Zinsky was the first gee to think up a very novel way of getting rid of people that crowd you. He got the idea to mix up a tub of cement—place the unwanted character's feet in same and then throw the whole thing into the lake. Result—no more crowding by that guy."

"He was the first one who thought of it? A sort of trail blazer."

"Of course Cement Mixer is a big shot now and his boys take care of things like that. But sometimes he goes along to mix the cement—just to keep his hand in you might say."

"A sentimentalist no doubt."

"No doubt," Bag Ears agreed.

I patted Joy's hand and said, "Don't be alarmed, darling. I will take care of everything."

The situation was definitely obnoxious to me. Tolerance of one's fellow men is one thing, but this was something entirely different. These people had come uninvited to our festive board and were of the criminal element, pure and unadulterated by any instincts of honesty or decency. And it made me angry to see them wading into Aunt Gretchen's liquor supply as though the stuff came out of a pump.

They were easy to count, these hoodlums, segregated as they were. The more respectable of the guests who had not already left, were clustered together in one corner of the living room, possibly as a gesture toward self-protection. None of these elite were making any effort to approach the buffet or the portable bar at the other side of the room. And in thus refraining, they showed a superior brand of intelligence. Under present circumstances any attempt to reach the refreshments would have been as dangerous as crossing the Hialeah race track on crutches.

In fact, as I surveyed the scene, one brave lady made a half-hearted attempt to cross over and spear a sandwich off the corner of the buffet. She was promptly shoved out of range by a lean, hungry-looking customer in a pink shirt, who snarled, "Scram, Three Chins! You're overfed now."

Unhooking Joy's dear fingers from my arm, I said, "You will pardon me, but it is time for action. Bag Ears will see that you are not harmed."

I started toward the buffet, or rather toward the crowd of male and female hoodlums who completely blocked it from my sight. But Bag Ears snatched me by the sleeve and whispered,

"For cri-yi, Homer! Don't be a fool! This mob is loaded wid hardware. They don't horse around none. Start slugging and they'll dress you in red polka dots. Better call in some law."

I shook my head firmly and pulled Bag Ears' hand from my sleeve. But, his attention now turned in another direction, he held on even harder and muttered,

"Jeeps! I'm seeing things!"

I glanced around and saw him staring wide-eyed at the entrance hall, his battered mouth ajar. I followed his eyes but could see nothing unusual. Only the hall itself, through an arched doorway, and the lower section of the staircase that gave access to the second floor of the house. It appeared to be the least-troubled spot in view. I frowned at Bag Ears.

"Maybe I've gone nuts," he said, "but I'll swear I just saw a face peeking down around them stairs."

"Whose face?"

"Hands McCaffery's face! That's whose!"

"And who is Hands McCaffery?"

Bag Ears looked at me with stark unbelief. "You mean you don't know? Maybe your mom didn't give you the facts of life! Chum, they's two really tough monkeys in this town. One of them is Cement Mixer Zinsky and the other is Hands McCaffery. At the moment they're slugging it out to see which one gets to levy a head tax on the juke boxes in this section. It's a sweet take and neither boy will be satisfied with less than all. Seeing them both in one place is like seeing Truman and that music critic sit down at the piano together. And I know damn well that Hands is up on them stairs!"

"You are obviously overwrought. If I have this type of person sized up correctly, none of them would be dallying on the stairs. If this Hands person were here, he'd be at the buffet fighting for a helping of pickled beets and a gin wash. Pardon me—I have work to do."

But there was another interruption. I froze in sudden alarm when I realized Joy was no longer at my side. Just as I made this discovery, there was an upsurge of commotion at the bar; a commotion that went head and shoulders over the minor ones going on constantly. A short angry scream came to my ears, then a bull-voiced roar of agony.

*

THE crowd at the buffet surged back and I saw a bucktoothed hooligan bent double, both hands gripping his ankle. Thick moans came from his lips.

And standing close to him was my Joy. But a new Joy. A different Joy than I had ever seen. A glorious Joy, with her head thrown back, her teeth showing, and the light of battle in her eyes. She was holding a plate of jello in one hand and a bottle of beer in the other and was shouting in outraged dignity.

"Watch who you're shoving, you jug-headed gorilla! And keep your mitts out of the herring! Eat like a man or go back to the zoo!"

With that she placed an accurate kick against the offending character's other shine-bone and aimed the beer bottle at his skull.

Joy turned and smiled gayly. "He pushed me," she said. "It's the most wonderful wedding reception I ever attended. Have a pickle."

But surprise was piling upon surprise. Again I froze as a new phase of this horrible affair presented itself.

Uncle Peter.

Clad in apron and cap, he was behind the bar serving out drinks. This shook me to the core. It was a little like seeing Barney Baruch hit a three-bagger in Yankee Stadium and slide into third base.

But there he was, taking orders and dishing out drinks with an attitude as solemn and impersonal as an owl on a tree branch.

Also, he had an assistant—his blonde bombshell. She was fully dressed now and I was struck by the peculiar manner in which this peculiar team functioned.

Uncle Peter would mix a drink, glance at his wrist watch as he served it, then turn and whisper some sort of information to the girl. She noted it down in a small book and the routine was repeated.

At this exact moment, I felt a sharp dig in the ribs. This brought my attention back to Joy, who had done the digging.

"I'm still here, husband mine. Your bride—remember? Or are you waiting for that blonde hussy to start stripping?"

"Darling, I'm afraid you're not paying close attention to things of importance. Don't you see Uncle Peter there—serving drinks?"

"Of course I see him. What of it? If the old roue feels like dishing out a little alcohol to the boys, what—"

"It's absolutely beyond all conception. Uncle Peter never does anything without a good reason. And *this*—"

My reply was cut short by a cold, brutal voice that knifed through the room and put a chill on all present. "Hold it, everybody! Stand still and don't move a finger!"

Not a finger in the room moved. But all eyes turned toward the arched doorway leading to the entrance hall. In its exact center, there stood a man—a short man of slight stature. He stood spread-legged, wearing a colored kerchief over the lower part of his face. Only his eyes were visible—icy, black, narrowed. Those eyes seemed to be smiling a grim smile. Possibly his hidden teeth were bared in a snarl. But no one cared about that. Everyone was far more interested in the black Thompson sub-machine gun he held cradled over one arm.

He toyed with the trigger, knifing the room with quick side glances. He said, "Okay. Start sorting yourselves out. You, pretty boy, and the frail with the beer bottle— out of the line of fire." He motioned with the gun barrel and I drew Joy toward the wall.

"Now you, Cora—and old puddle-puss. Out of the way. And not a peep out of anybody."

No one was inclined to peep, and now the stage was set in a manner which seemed to satisfy the masked gunman. The Cement Mixer Zinsky crowd was clustered, cowering, around the buffet, staring at the machine gun as though it possessed the hypnotic eyes of a snake.

The situation was entirely plain. The masked man fully intended to break the law by committing murder in Aunt Gretchen's living room. The only moot point seemed to be whether he intended to slay the whole mob or be selective and cut down only important members. His trigger finger turned white at the knuckle.

Then Uncle Peter stepped forward to hold up a protesting hand. "You mustn't fire that weapon, my good fellow. Indeed you must not."

His matter-of-fact attitude, rather than his words, was what gave the gunman pause. He had hardly expected the display of completely impersonal bravery that Uncle Peter put on. The gunman asked, "Are you nuts, fiddlefoot?"

"Far from it. But you must not, under any circumstances, fire that gun. It will upset one of the most important experiments in the history of science. That experiment is now in progress."

"Look, brother. I came here to mow down Zinsky and his mob. And I'm mowing. The St. Valentine's deal in Chi'll look like a Sunday school binge after this one."

"Possibly it will not be necessary to use your weapon."

*

UNCLE Peter's words, it seemed, were prophetic. At that exact moment, Cement Mixer Zinsky exploded. Not violently, or with any peril to those standing close by. Yet no other term can describe it. There was a soft pop—as though a large, poorly inflated balloon had been pricked with a pin. Zinsky seemed to go in all directions—fragments of him that is. Yet, as each fragment flew away from the main body, it shriveled up so that there was no blood, and no bystander suffered the inconvenience of messed-up clothing. Just the *pop* and Zinsky expanded like a human bomb and then turned into dust.

As this phenomenon occurred I saw Uncle Peter nod with great satisfaction and consult a passage in the book presided over by his blonde assistant. He made a check mark in the book.

Then a second member of the buffet group went *pop*. The masked man stared in slack-jawed wonder. In fact his jaw went so slack the kerchief dropped away revealing his entire visage. He lowered his head and looked down at the gun in his hands; the gun that had not been fired.

Two more members of Zinsky's party followed him into whatever oblivion was achieved by going *pop* and dissolving into dust. Uncle Peter evinced bright interest and made two more check marks in the book.

The balance of the mob moved as one, but in many directions. They paid no attention to their own weapons as they headed for cover. One of their number exploded as he was halfway through the French doors. Uncle Peter checked him off and Bag Ears said, "Jeeps! tomorrow every juke box in town can play 'Nearer my God to Thee.'" Then he added, "Leave us blow this joint. Goofy things is happening here. I don't like it."

I was perspiring. I mopped my forehead. "A most amazing occurrence," I observed.

Joy was digging the fingers on one hand into my arm. I had been watching Hands McCaffery back crestfallen out of the living room and toward the front door, terrific slaughter having been accomplished without the firing of a shot. I turned my eyes now to follow the direction in which Joy pointed with her other hand and saw the blonde assistant hauling Uncle Peter through one of the French windows. He did not seem to be enthusiastic about leaving. In fact he appeared to argue quite strenuously against it, but her will prevailed and they disappeared out onto the lawn.

Now, with all the danger past, people began fainting in wholesale lots. Aunt Gretchen was resting comfortably with her head braced against the brass rail of the portable bar. Those who didn't faint contributed variously intonated screams to the general unrest. And over all this brooded the dank clouds of acrid dust that had so lately been Cement Mixer Zinsky and certain members of his mob. Indeed, the scene took on a startling semblance to one of Dore's etchings in an old edition of Dante's Inferno.

"I repeat," Bag Ears bleated plaintively. "Leave us blow this joint. It ain't healthy here."

"He's right," Joy said. "A lot of explanation is wanting. There are some people we've got to catch up with. Let's go."

With that, she drew Bag Ears and me toward the French doors through which had recently passed some of the fastest moving objects in this or any other world. We made the flag-stone terrace above the drive where Bag Ears cordially grasped my hand and said,

"Well, it was a nice party, folks, and if I ever get spliced I'll sure give you a invite and I sure had a swell time and remember me to your aunt when she wakes up and—"

He was backing down the steps when Joy cut in with, "Bag Ears. Don't be so rude. You're in no hurry."

Bag Ears slowed down and allowed us to catch up with him. He gave us a sickly smile. "That's where you're wrong, babe."

"Bag Ears," Joy went on. "I heard you whisper to Homer that you know who that blonde is."

"What blonde? Me? I don't know nothing about no blonde no-how."

"Don't hedge. I mean the girl who was assisting Uncle Peter behind the bar. Who is she, really?"

"Oh—her. Everybody knows her. She's Hands McCaffery's moll. He likes 'em blonde and—"

Bag Ears was on the move again, striding in the direction of the gate. We hurried to catch up. "That babe's poison," he told us. "Any skirt that'd flock with Hands McCaffery is poison. I'll tell you kids what I'd do. If she drives south—I'd drive north. Goodbye now."

Just at that moment a big blue sports roadster pushed a bright chromium nose around the corner of the house. I took a firm grip on Bag Ears' collar, grabbed Joy by the arm, and the three of us leaped behind a bush. The car rolled past us. We saw the blonde behind the wheel and Uncle Peter seated beside her, evidently still protesting the hasty exodus.

*

BUT the girl looked very sharp and businesslike; the way a girl would look who knew where she was going and why. The car picked up speed and swung north.

"I wonder," Joy murmured, "how Uncle Peter happened to select Hands McCaffery's girl friend as his assistant."

"She was a burlycue queen last time I heard of her," Bag Ears said. "Still is, I guess."

"That could explain it," I told Joy. "You see, Uncle Peter has—ah, facets to his personality. A tendency to admire women. Ah—"

"Women—period; isn't that what you mean?"

"Well, it would be perfectly logical for Uncle Peter to select an assistant from the stage of a burlesque theater."

"Enough of this," Joy snapped. "We're wasting time. Go get—oh, never mind! Wait here."

Joy was off in the direction of the garage and in no time at all she was back in my Cadillac convertible. As she sailed by I managed to hook a finger around the door handle and get a foot inside.

This was no mean feat, as I was also occupied in hauling Bag Ears along by the collar. I managed to deposit him in the seat beside Joy and squeeze in beside him.

"A burlycue queen, eh?" Joy was muttering. "Well, she's not so much! If she couldn't get her clothes off she'd starve to death."

"Darling," I said, "I don't think this is the sort of thing you should be doing. It's far too dangerous for a girl."

"Or anybody else," Bag Ears moaned. There was a bleak look on his face. "I don't like playing around with a guy like Hands McCaffery or friends of a guy like him. It's a good way to collect your insurance."

"She's heading for Higgins Drive," Joy observed.

Which was entirely true. The roadster had made a turn on two wheels and was going west.

"But our honeymoon," I said, plaintively.

"Yeah," Bag Ears repeated, "what about our—your honeymoon?"

Joy's eyes were sparkling. She turned them on me. The car lurched. She returned her eyes to the road. "Yes, darling. Our honeymoon! Isn't it wonderful?"

"But this isn't it! This isn't what people do on their honeymoons."

"Oh, you mean—but don't worry about that, darling. We'll have plenty of time for—"

"Lemme out o' here," Bag Ears moaned. "I got a date to take Red Nose Tessie to the movies."

Joy apparently did not hear him. "I wish we had all the parts to this puzzle. It looks as though somebody put somebody on the spot for a rubout. But it would seem that somebody else got the same idea but didn't know that somebody else was going to achieve the same result in a more spectacular way and—"

"I think you've figured it out most accurately."

"Some of it fits together. Uncle Peter was no doubt responsible for the Zinsky boys coming to our reception. We'll get the dope on that when we catch up with him. But the blonde must not have known what was going to happen, so she tipped Hands off that he could find the whole Zinsky mob at the reception. He decided it would be a good place to settle certain matters of his own."

"But why did Uncle Peter want them there?"

Joy glanced at me with love in her eyes. "Darling, we're going to be wonderful companions through life, but most of the fun will be strictly physical. Mental exercises aren't your forte."

"When Red Nose Tessie makes a date with a guy," Bag Ears said, "she expects the guy to keep it."

"The blonde Cora is no doubt heading for a rendezvous with Hands McCaffery," Joy went on. "And she's taking our dear uncle with her."

"Okay," Bag Ears replied. "So we mind our business and keep our noses clean and live a long time."

Joy was weaving through traffic, trying to keep the roadster in sight. "Turn on the radio," she told me. "There might be some news."

I snapped the switch and we discovered there was news indeed; an evening commentator regaling the public with the latest:

"—an amazing mass phenomena which leading scientific minds have pronounced to be basically similar to the flying-saucer craze. Relative to that—you will remember—otherwise reliable citizens swore they saw space ships from other planets hovering over our cities spying on us.

"This phase of the hysteria takes an entirely different turn. It seems now that these otherwise entirely reliable citizens are seeing other citizens explode and vanish into thin air. The police and the newspapers have been deluged with frantic telephone calls. In the public interest, we have several persons here in the studio who claim to have seen this phenomena. Your commentator will now interview them over the air. You—you, sir—what is your name?"

"Sam—Sam Glutz."

"Thank you, Mr. Glutz. And will you tell the radio audience what you saw?"

"It wasn't nothing—nothing at all. That is—this guy was running down the street like maybe the cops was after him—I don't know. Then—there wasn't nothing."

"You mean the man disappeared?"

"He went pop, kind of—like a firecracker only not so loud—and then pieces of him flew all over and they disappeared and there wasn't nothing—nothing at all."

"Thank you, Mr. Glutz. And now this lady—"

"Turn it off," Joy snapped. "The blonde's pulling up."

*

THIS was evident to all three of us. "And by a cop yet," Bag Ears marveled. "Looks like they're going to give theirselves up."

It was Uncle Peter who got out of the car and approached the traffic officer standing at the intersection.

"What'll we do?" Joy asked. "Do you want to try and keep the old goat out of jail or shall we let him go to the chair as he deserves?"

The possibility stunned me to a point where it was hard to think clearly. "Good Lord, Joy! Think of the scandal! I don't care about myself, but Aunt Gretchen would never live it down! She'd be black-balled at all her clubs and—"

"Then," Joy replied sweetly, "I'd suggest you get out and slug that cop quick and grab Uncle Peter before he makes a confession."

I had come to the cross-roads, so to speak. The necessity of a weighty decision lay upon my shoulders. Was blood thicker than water? Was I justified in breaking the law—assaulting an officer in order to keep my uncle from becoming a blot on the family name?

I decided, grimly, that one owed all to one's relatives and I was halfway out of the car. Then I paused. Uncle Peter did not seem to be making a confession at all. He chatted easily with the officer and indicated my Cadillac with a movement of his thumb. Something passed from his hand to the hand of the policeman and the latter looked toward us and scowled.

"Uncle Peter is pulling a fast one," Joy said. "The cop's coming after *us!*"

I was uncertain as how to proceed now. I watched the scowling policeman approach our car while Uncle Peter got back in with the blonde Cora and drove away.

"Are you going to hang one on him, sweetheart?" Joy asked.

"What—what do you recommend?"

"I've got a hunch that if you don't, we go to the pokey and Uncle Peter will be left free to blow up everybody in town."

I don't believe the officer meant to arrest us but at the moment my mind wasn't too clear and I accepted Joy's point of view.

I doubled my fist as the officer approached. He wasted no time in getting acquainted. He said, "How come you guys are tailing those guys? You figuring a stickup or something?"

It was now or never. I hunched my right shoulder and aimed a stiff knockout jolt at the officer's jaw. It wasn't too good a target because he had a lantern jaw and it was bobbing up and down as he munched on a wad of chewing gum.

But I did not connect. As my fist completed but half its lethal orbit, the officer blew up in my face! He went *pop*, just as so many others had gone *pop* at our wedding reception; his entire anatomy flying in all directions, to turn into a cloud of sooty smoke and mix with the elements.

I was frozen with consternation. But not Joy. Instantly she dragged me back into the car. "Don't you get it? Uncle Peter gave him that stick of gum!"

"You're damn right!" Bag Ears stated. "The old monkey's gone clear off his trolley. Maybe he plans to clean out the whole town!"

Joy, her eyes slitted, was weaving in and out of traffic so as not to lose track of the blue roadster. "It's as plain as your nose! He's hand in glove with McCaffery and that blonde is bird-dogging him around town and pointing out McCaffery's enemies. Uncle Peter is knocking them off like clay pigeons."

I was amazed at this revelation, but was also thunderstruck by the underworld jargon flowing so easily from Joy's luscious lips. "Angel," I gasped. "Where did you learn to talk like that? Those underworld terms!"

"I read all the true detective magazines I can get my hands on," she said. "They're good fun, but that's beside the point. We've got to nail Uncle Peter and nail him quick, or Aunt Gretchen will ring up a nice big zero in the social world."

"How about nailing him without me?" Bag Ears suggested. "It's nine o'clock and Red Nose Tessie never likes to miss none of the show."

"I'm sure, Bag Ears," Joy said, "that Tessie would sympathize with our efforts to keep Uncle Peter out of the electric chair."

"I doubt it," he replied dubiously. "Tessie's brother got burned in Frisco for knocking over a bank clerk and Tessie never even attended. Let him fry in his own grease was what she said about it."

"Nevertheless," Joy said, "I have no time to stop and let you out."

A fast, fifteen-block chase followed. Once we lost the blue roadster completely, but, by sheer luck, picked it up three blocks further on as it came wheeling out of a side street.

We were in a quiet residential section now, so there was no one to interfere as Joy skillfully forced the roadster to the curb. I jumped out and leaped swiftly toward the driver's door.

*

THE blonde sat behind the wheel with a sullen look on her face. "What is this?" she asked. "A stickup?"

"Don't be vulgar," I replied. "We are here to take charge of my uncle. This weird slaughter must cease!"

Joy was by my side now, but Bag Ears hung back as though somewhat worried about the possible consequences of our act.

I heard him muttering: "What if he can just shoot the stuff in your eye maybe? What if a guy doesn't have to swallow it—?"

Joy's gayety was again coming to the surface. Her eyes were bright and I was struck by the fact that she seemed to thrive on this sort of thing. "Hello, Blondy," she said. "Get out from behind—"

The blonde's eyes threw sparks. "Who you think you're talking to, you lard—"

"Not Truman," Joy said. "Now get—"

I seized Joy's wrist. "Angel! He's gone! Uncle Peter isn't here!" I stared at Joy in horror. "Do you suppose he inadvertently chewed some of his own gum?"

Joy did not reply. She shouldered me aside, opened the car door and surprised me by getting a very scientific grip on Cora.

"Okay—where is he? What did you do with him?"

"He's not here!"

"Any fool can see that. Did he blow up?"

"Of course not. He went to keep a date."

The blonde jerked herself loose from Joy's hold and was sullenly straightening her clothing. "I don't see why you and Pretty Boy have to stick your big noses into this. It's none of your business."

"We're making it our business."

"You don't seem to realize," I said stiffly, "that Uncle Peter is very dear to me. He has performed some horrible deeds, and as his loving nephew—"

The blonde seemed puzzled. "You're off your crock! Pete's okay. He just entered into a little private deal to help out Hands McCaffery. I don't see where it's anybody's business, either. If he wanted your help he'd ask for it!"

It made my blood run cold to hear this girl refer so casually to the wholesale slaughter that had been going on around us. I strove to find words to shame her, but Joy cut in. And apparently my dear wife was more interested, at the moment, in the details of the affair rather than the morals involved.

"McCaffery and Uncle Peter haven't got any deal," she said to the blonde. "You lie as easily as you undress. If they had an arrangement to knock off all those parties at our wedding reception, how come McCaffery brought a machine gun along?"

The blonde had an answer. "Hands was a little doubtful. He didn't think Pete could do it—blow people into thin air just from something they et. He was willing to go along with the gag but he wasn't going to pass up an opportunity to rub out the Zinsky gang—or as many as he could hit—if the gimmick didn't click. That's why he brought the Tommy—just in case."

Joy turned to me. "It fits," she said. "I've been trying to give Uncle Pete the benefit of every doubt, but it looks as though you've got a mad dog sniffing at the trunk of your family tree."

*

CORA frowned. "You've got him all wrong. He's not—"

I continued with the questioning. "You are denying that Uncle Peter had anything to do with this deadly serum that disintegrates people before one's eyes?"

"I'm *not* denying it."

"Then it follows that your moral sense is so badly corroded you no longer consider murder to be a crime—"

"Now listen here!"

"In law," I went on, "the victim's standing in society is not taken into consideration where murder is involved. It is just as wrong in the eyes of the law to murder Cement Mixer Zinsky as the pastor of the First Congregational Church."

The blonde looked wonderingly at Joy. "Is this guy for real?"

Joy reestablished her hold upon the blonde's anatomy. "Never mind that. All we want from you is answers. Where did Uncle Peter go? Tell me!"

"Nuts to you!" Cora replied. "He doesn't want you bothering him."

Joy applied pressure. Cora squealed but remained mute. I stepped forward. "Darling," I said grimly. "This sort of thing is not in your line. I realize this woman must be made to talk so I will take over. It will be distasteful to me, but duty is duty."

I got a withering look from my dear wife. "Distasteful? In a pig's eye! You'd like nothing better than to get your hands on her—by way of duty of course."

"Joy!"

"Don't Joy me." And with an expert twist, she flipped the struggling Cora out of the roadster, goose-stepped her across and into the back seat of the Cadillac.

"You and Bag Ears get in and start driving—slow. I'll have some answers in a minute or two."

We did as we were told and I eased the car away from the curb. I had to watch the road, of course, so could not turn to witness what was going on rearward. In the mirror I saw flashes of up-ended legs and, from time to time, other and sundry anatomical parts that flew up in range only to vanish again as the grim struggle went on.

Bag Ears, however, turned to witness the bringing forth of the answers. His first comment was, "Oh boy!"

Joy was breathing heavily. She said, "Okay, babe. Talk, or I'll put real pressure on this scissors!"

Bag Ears said, "Man oh man!"

Joy said, "Quit gaping, you moron! I'm back here too."

I gave Bag Ears a stern admonition to keep his eyes front.

"Give," Joy gritted.

"Ouch! No!"

"Give!"

Cora gave forth an agonized wail. Then an indignant gasp. "Cut it out! You fight dirty! That ain't fair!"

"Give!"

"All right! All right. Pete's meeting Hands at—ouch—Joe's—ouch—Tavern on Clark Street. Ouch! Cut it out, will you?"

And it was here that I detected a trace of sadism in my lovely wife. "All right," she said regretfully. "Sit up. Gee, but you talk easy."

"Just where is this tavern?" I asked. "And what is the purpose of the meeting?"

Cora's resistance was entirely gone. "In the 2800 block. Pete went there to get some money from Hands to skip town with."

Joy now spoke with relish. "Lying again. I'll have to—"

"I ain't lying!"

"Don't give us that! Uncle Peter is wealthy. He doesn't need Hands' money. Come here, baby."

"Wait, Joy," I cut in hastily. "The young lady may be telling the truth. Uncle Peter is always short of funds. You see, Aunt Gretchen holds the purse strings in our family and Uncle Peter is always overdrawn on his allowance."

"Then let's get to that tavern and find out what's going on."

It took ten minutes to reach the tavern; a standard gin mill with a red neon sign proclaiming its presence. We quitted the car and I entered first, Joy bringing Cora along with a certain amount of force, and Bag Ears bringing up the rear.

And I was just in time to prevent another murder.

As I came through the door, I saw Hands and Uncle Peter leaning casually against the bar. There was no one else in the place. The barkeep was facing his two customers and there were three glasses set before them. The barkeep held one in his hand.

Uncle Peter had just finished spiking the barkeep's drink with a clear fluid from a small vial. Uncle Peter said, "It's something new I invented. Pure dynamite. You haven't lived until you've tasted my elixir."

*

HANDS said, "Go ahead. Drink it. I want to make sure I wasn't seeing things back at that dame's house."

The barkeep said, "Pure dynamite, huh?"

"Your not fooling, chum."

He raised the glass and grinned. "Salud."

I got to the bar just in time to knock the glass out of his hairy paw. He grunted, "What the hell—oh, a wise guy, huh?" and started over the bar.

I yelled, "It's murder. They're trying to poison you!"

"Oh, a crackpot!"

He came toward me, shaking off Uncle Peter's restraining hand. I took a step backward, thankful he was coming in wide open because I had seen few tougher-looking characters in my lifetime.

I set myself and sent a short knockout punch against his chin. It was a good punch. Everything was in it. It sounded like a sledge hammer hitting a barn door.

The barkeep shook his head and came on in. I stepped back and slugged him again. No result.

Then Joy slipped into the narrow space between us. She was smiling and, with her upturned waiting lips, she was temptation personified. The barkeep dropped his hands, paralyzed by her intoxicating nearness.

She said, "Hello, Iron Head. How about you and I taking a little vacation together somewhere."

He grinned and reached for her. This, it developed, was a mistake, because Joy reached for him at the same time. She lifted his two-hundred-odd pounds as though he were a baby and he went flying across the room like a projectile. He hit a radiator head-on and lay still.

Again I was stupefied. It seemed I knew nothing at all about this girl I'd married. She smiled at me and said, "Don't be alarmed, angel. There's an explanation. You see, my mother gave me money for piano lessons and I invested most of it in a course of ju-jitsu. I thought an occasion like this might arise sometime. Do you want to take McCaffery, or shall I do it? I doubt if he'll come to the station peaceably."

But Hands McCaffery was not to be caught flatfooted. Without his machine gun he was just an ordinary little man who didn't want to go with us. He took one look at the prone barkeep, muttered, "Geez!" and headed for the back door.

"Get him," Joy yelled. "Maybe we can make a deal with the cops to fry Hands in place of Uncle Peter!"

I started after Hands and as I went through the back door I heard Uncle Peter protesting feebly. "I say now. This is all uncalled-for—"

"Don't let him get away!" Joy called. "He's got the serum!"

That cleared things up somewhat and made me even more resolute. Evidently we had interrupted Uncle Peter and Hands in the process of doing away with all the latter's enemies.

With that bottle in his possession, he was a menace to the entire population of the city. A man of his type would certainly have far more enemies than friends.

Outside in the dark alley, I was guided only by footsteps. The sound of Hands' retreat told me he was moving up the smelly passageway toward Division Street. I went after him.

I am no mean sprinter, having won laurels in college for my fleetness in the two-twenty and the four-forty, and I had no trouble in overtaking the little assassin. We were fast approaching the alley entrance where I would have had the aid of street lights and could have swiftly collared McCaffery whose heavy breathing I could now hear—when disaster struck in the form of a painful obstacle. It was heavy and it caught me just below the knees.

I tripped and fell headlong, plowing along a couple of yards of slippery brick pavement on my face. I got groggily to my feet and shook my head to clear my brain. From the deposits of old eggs, rejected tomatoes and other such refuse in my face and ears, I gathered that I had tripped over a garbage can.

This delayed me for some moments. When I finally staggered out into Division Street, a strange sight met my eyes. Hands McCaffery had been apprehended. It seemed that the police had orders to pick him up because two uniformed patrolmen had him backed against the wall and were approaching him with caution. They had him covered and were taking no chances of his pulling a belly gun on them.

But he did not draw a gun. Instead, while I stared wide-eyed, he raised Uncle Peter's vial to his lips and drank the contents.

I will not bore you with details of his going *pop*. If you have read this letter carefully, the details are not necessary.

I turned and retraced my steps, realizing Hands McCaffery had been vicious and defiant to the last. Rather than submit to arrest, he had taken the wild animal's way out.

I arrived back in Joe's Tavern to find the barkeep had been revived and bore none of us any ill-will. This no doubt because of Joy's persuasive abilities. Cora was sulking in a booth and Uncle Peter was patching the gash on the barkeep's head.

*

I ENTERED with a heavy heart, realizing, as a good citizen, I must turn my own uncle over to the police. But there was an interlude before I would be forced into this unpleasant task. This interlude was furnished by Bag Ears. After I acquainted the group with the news of how Hands had taken the easy way out, Bag Ears' face took on a rapt, silent look of happiness. He was staring at Joy. He said, "Pretty—very pretty!"

Joy said, "Thank you."

Bag Ears said, "Pretty—pretty—pretty."

Joy looked at me. "What's eating *him*?"

There was a bottle on the bar together with some glasses. I stepped over and poured myself a drink. I certainly needed it. "Bag Ears isn't referring to you, dear. He's alluding to his bells. He's hearing them again."

"Oh, my sky-blue panties! Pour me a drink."

I complied. "You see, Bag Ears is somewhat punch-drunk from his years in the prize ring. I've seen this happen before."

We sipped our brandy and watched Bag Ears move toward the door.

"That's the way it always is. When he hears the bells, he feels a terrific urge to go forth and search for them. But he always ends up at Red Nose Tessie's and she takes him home. It's no use trying to stop him. He'll hang one on you."

As Bag Ears disappeared into the street, there were tears in Joy's eyes. "He's dreaming of his bells," she murmured. "I think that's beautiful." She held up her glass. "May he find his bells. Pour me another drink."

I poured two and we drank to that.

"May we all someday find our bells," Joy said with emotion, and I was delighted to find my wife a girl of such deep sentiment. "Pour me another."

I did. "Your quotation was wrong, sweetheart," I said. "Don't you mean, 'May we all find our Shangri-La?'"

"Of course. Let's drink to it."

We drank to it and were rudely interrupted by the barkeep who said, "I hope you got some dough. That stuff ain't water."

I gave him a ten-dollar bill and—with a heavy heart—turned to Uncle Peter. "Come, Uncle," I said gently. "We might as well get it over with."

"Get what over with?"

"Our trip to the police station. You must give yourself up of course."

"What for?"

I shook my head sadly. Uncle Peter would never fry. His mind was obviously out of joint. "For murder."

He looked at Joy. He said, "Oh, my broken test tube! There is no need of—"

"I know it will be hard for them to convict you without *corpus delicti*, but you must confess."

"Let's all go over to my laboratory."

"If you wish. You may have one last visit there."

"Excellent—one last visit." He smiled and I wondered if I saw a certain craftiness behind it.

Cora voiced no objections, seemingly anxious to stay near Uncle Peter. When we got to his laboratory, he went on through into his living quarters and took a suit case from the closet.

"What are you going to do?"

"Pack my things."

"Oh, of course. You'll need some things in jail."

"Who said anything about jail? I'm going to Tibet."

"*Tibet!* Uncle Peter! I won't allow it. You must stay here and face the music."

"The music is in Tibet, Homer. That's one of the reasons I'm going there. To a monastery high in Himalayas. There are some wonderful men there I've always wanted to meet—yogis who have such control over natural laws that they can walk on water and move straight through solid walls."

"But, Uncle Peter! If you want to go to Tibet, you should have thought of it before. It's too late now. You've committed murder."

"Bosh! I haven't killed anyone. The serum I discovered is one of transition, not murder. It causes the stepping-up of the human physical structure into an infinitely higher rate of vibration. Two controls are distilled into it. One is a timer that sets off the catalysis, and the other is a directive element based upon higher mathematics which allows the creator of the serum to direct the higher vibratory residue of the physical form to be put down at any prearranged point on the globe before the reforming element takes effect."

Joy said, "Oh, my painted G-string!"

I strove to absorb all this. "You mean those people weren't destroyed?"

Joy was quicker on the reaction. "Of course. I couldn't picture Uncle Peter as a killer somehow. He merely picked them up here and set them down in Tibet. Can't you understand? He just explained it to you."

Of course I didn't want to admit my mental haziness to Joy, so I skipped hastily over it and pointed an accusing finger at Uncle Peter. "But why couldn't you have conducted your experiments on a higher plane. Why did you have to consort with law-breakers?"

*

JOY had apparently lost interest. She planted a wifely kiss on my cheek and started toward the door. "I'm going back to Joe's Tavern," she said. "It's more fun there. When you get all this straightened out, come on over."

I moved to protest but she waved me down. "Never mind. I'll take a cab." She smiled at me sweetly. "And don't stay too long, darling. I'm sure Cora is anxious to get her clothes off."

Cora distinctly pronounced an unprintable name but Joy did not hear it. She was already gone.

I turned to Uncle Peter. "You did not answer my question."

"It's very simple. Even one of your limited brain power should be able to understand it. You see, with finishing my experiments I was not averse to doing the city a favor. Why not, I asked myself, perform them upon persons undesirable to our law-abiding populace? Cora was acquainted with Hands McCaffery and it was through him that I learned who the really undesirable people were."

"But why did you invite them to my wedding reception? I'd think you could find a more appropriate place to carry out your—"

"It was an ideal place to get the Zinsky mob together. Like your Aunt Gretchen, Mr. Zinsky has social ambitions, and he anticipated no danger at the reception."

"I can see your point."

"Also, I wanted to get back at your Aunt Gretchen. She's been very niggardly with funds lately and I wanted to highlight my displeasure in a way she would remember."

I had a fairly clear picture of things now. But I still felt Uncle Peter should be upbraided on a last point. "Uncle Peter, I think it was shameful of you to inflict those hoodlums on the monks in that monastery in Tibet. They'll be in panic."

"No. I was careful to send along two policemen to keep them in hand."

"So you're leaving for Tibet?"

"Of course. I've got to follow up and check on the success of my serum, though there is really no doubt as to its potency. Also I'll be able to achieve a life-long ambition—that of meeting the yogis from whom I should learn a great deal."

I glanced at Cora. "Are you taking her with you?"

477

"Of course."

"But yogis are above things of the flesh."

Uncle Peter looked me straight in the eye. "Maybe the yogis are, but I'm not."

There seemed nothing else to discuss, so I left Uncle Peter's chambers and went back to Joe's Tavern. My mind, now at ease, was filled again with thought of the honeymoon to come. I would pick up Joy and we would be off to pink-tinted lands.

But there was a slight hitch. When I arrived at Joe's Tavern, Joy was gone.

I inquired of the barkeep and he brought me up to date. "That screwy dame that can throw a guy around? Sure, she was here. She had a few drinks and then left again. She said something about having to help a friend find some bells he lost. I don't know what kind of bells they was but that dame can locate them if anybody can."

As I was about to leave the tavern, it occurred to me you would want to know the truth of what's been going on, so I'm now in the backroom writing this report which I will drop into the nearest mailbox. Then I will go out and find my bride and start upon a well-earned honeymoon. If you have any questions, they'll have to wait until I get back.

Yours truly,
Homer Nicholas.

NO SHIELD FROM THE DEAD

by Gordon R. Dickson

No conceivable force could penetrate Terri's shield. Yet he was defenseless.

It was a nice little party, but a bit obvious. Terri Mac saw through it before he had taken half a dozen steps into the apartment. A light flush staining his high cheek-bones. "This is ridiculous," he said.

The light chatter ceased. Cocktail glasses were set down on various handy tables and ledges; and all faces in the room turned toward a man in his late fifties who sat propped up invalid-wise on pillows in a chair in a corner of the room.

"The Comptroller is perspicacious," said the old man, agreeably, waving one hand in a casual manner. "On your way, children."

And the people present smiled and nodded. Quite as if it were an ordinary leave-taking, they pushed past Terri Mac and filed out the door. Even the blonde, Terri had picked up at the embassy ball and who had brought him here, strolled off casually, but in a decidedly less drunken fashion than she had exhibited earlier in the evening.

"Sit down," said the old man. Terri Mac did so, gazing searchingly at the skinny frame and white eyebrows in an unsuccessful effort to connect him with something in memory. "This is ridiculous," he repeated.

"Really?" The old man smiled benignly. "And why so?"

"Why—" the situation was so obvious that Terri fumbled—a little at a loss for words. "Obviously you intend some form of coercion, or else you would have come to me along recognized channels. And any thought of coercion is obviously—well, ridiculous."

"Why?"

"Why? You senile old fool, don't you know that I'm shielded? Don't you know all government officials from the fifth class up wear complete personal shields that are not only crack-proof but contain all the necessary elements to support life independently within the shield for more than twenty hours? Don't you know that I'll be missed in two hours at the most and tracked down in less than sixty minutes more? Are you crazy?"

The old man chuckled, rubbing dry hands together. He said, "I'm shielded too. You can't get at me. And now the room's shielded. You can't get out of it."

Terri stared at him. The initial shock was passing. His own statements anent the completeness of his protection had brought back confidence, and his natural coolness was returning. "What do you want?" he asked, eyeing the other narrowly.

"Pleasure of your company," said the old man. "There are some very strong connections between us. Yes, very strong. We must get to know each other personally."

*

It occurred to Terri that he had misinterpreted the situation. Relief came, mixed with a certain amount of chagrin at the way in which he allowed himself to show alarm. He had looked ridiculous. He leaned back in the chair and allowed a note of official hauteur and annoyance to creep into his voice. "I see," he said. "You want something?"

The old man nodded energetically.

"I do. Indeed I do."

479

"And you think you have some kind of a bargaining tool that is useful but might not be so if it became known to official channels."

"Well—" said the old man cautiously.

"Don't waste my time," interrupted Terri, harshly. "I'm not an ordinary politician. No man who works his way up to the fifth level of the government is. I didn't get to where I am today by pussy-footing around and I haven't the leisure to spend on people who do. Now *what* do you want?"

The other cackled. "Now, what do you think?" he said, putting one finger to his nose cunningly.

"You are old," Terri said. "And therefore cautious. Consequently you would not risk trying to force something from me, but are almost certainly trying to sell me something. Now what do I want? Not the usual things, certainly. Within my position I have all the material things a man could want; and within my shield I enjoy complete immunity. No one but the Central Bureau, itself, can crack this shield. And no one but they can prevent the conditioned reflex that stops my heart if for some reason the shield should be broached. I have a hold on every man beneath me that prevents him from knifing me in the back. There could be only one thing that I want that you could give me—" he leaned forward, staring into the deep-pouched eyes—"and that is a means of getting at the man above me. Am I right?"

"No," said the old man.

Terri stiffened.

"No?" he echoed in angry incredulity.

Their eyes locked. For a long time they held, and at last Terri looked away.

The old man sighed—sipped noisily from a drink on the table beside his chair.

"Wait!" said Terri. To his own surprise, his voice was eager, even a little timorous in its hopefulness. "Wait. I've got it. There will be a test. There always is a test every time a man moves up. His superiors watch him when he doesn't suspect it. It will be that way for me when I am ready for the fourth level. And you have some kind of advance information. You know what the test will be. Maybe you know the man who will administer it. You want to sell me this information."

The other said nothing.

"Well," Terri spread his hands openly. "I am interested. I'll buy. What do you want. Money? A favor? Protection?"

"No."

"No?" Terri shouted, starting up from his chair. "What do you mean by no? Can't you say anything but 'no'?" A rage possessed him. He flung himself forward two furious steps to stand threateningly over the aged figure. "You doddering idiot! Say what you want, and quickly! My two hours are nearly up. I'll be missed. They'll be here in a few minutes—the Bureau Guards. They'll crack the room shield. They'll rescue me. And they'll take you into custody. To be questioned. To be executed. At my order. Do you understand? Your life depends on me."

After a little, the old man chuckled again. "Yes," he muttered, in a high-pitched old voice. "That's the way it'll be."

Terri stared at him. "You don't seem to understand. You're going to die."

"Oh yes," said the old man, nodding his head indulgently. "I'll die. But I'm an old man. I'd die anyway in a year or so—maybe in a day or so. But for you—for a young man like you—the up and coming young governmental with everything to lose—" he leered slyly at Terri. "Your death won't be so easy for you to take."

"I die?" echoed Terri, stupefied. "But I'm not going to die. They're coming to *rescue* me."

"Oh, are they?" said the old man, ironically.

"Of course!" said Terri. "Of course, why shouldn't they?"

The old man winked one faded eye portentously.

"Fine young man," he said. "Up and coming young man. Brilliant. Never a thought for the people he trampled on the way up the ladder. Dear me, no."

"What do you mean?" said Terri.

The old eyes, looking up suddenly, pierced him.

"Do you remember Kilaren?"

"K-Kilaren?"

"Kilaren," recited the old man as if quoting from a newspaper. "The beautiful young secretary of a provincial governor whose lecherous and unnatural pursuit drove her to suicide. So that one day to escape the governor, she jumped or fell from a high window. And the people of the province, who had for a long time heard ugly stories and rumors, finally mobbed the office and lynched the governor, hanging him from the same window from which the girl had jumped. They said that even the fall had not spoiled her beauty, but that was probably false." The old man's words dwindled away into silence.

"If so what of it?" said Terri. "What's that to do with me?"

"Why, you were there. You were the governor's aide, and when the mob had gone home and feeling had slackened off, you stepped into the gap and seized up the reins of government, handling matters so skillfully that you were immediately promoted to an under-post at Government City."

"What of it?"

"Why it was all your doing," replied the other, in a mildly reproving voice, "the rumors, the stories, the mob, even the suicide. Poor Kilaren—a pitiful pawn in your ruthless game to eliminate the governor in your mad dash up the ladder."

"I never touched her!" cried Terri, his voice cracking. "I swear it."

"Who said you did? The type of mind that stoops to murder would never have gotten you this far. But you were the one who hired her, knowing the governor's tendencies. You were the one that gave her work that kept her, night after night, alone with the man. You preyed upon her fear of losing her job. You threw the sin in her face after she had committed it. You told her what she might have been, and what she was, and what she would be. You broke her, day after day. In the sterile privacy of the office you reviled her, scorned her, brought her to believe that she was what she was not, a creature of filth and dishonor. You blocked off all avenues of escape but the one that led through one high window. *You killed her!*"

"No!"

"Yes!"

*

Terri brought his quivering hands together and clenched them in his lap. He stared at the old man. "Who are you?"

"I was a friend of hers. We lived in the same hotel-apartment. She had no family. I believe you knew that when you hired her."

"I see," said Terri. He drew a long, deep, shuddering breath, and leaned back in the chair. "So that's the story," he said, his voice strengthening, "I might have known it. Blackmail. There are always fools that want to try blackmail."

"No," said the old man. "Not Blackmail, Comptroller. I want your life."

Terri laughed shortly, contemptuously. "No knowledge that you have can threaten my life."

"They will come," said the old man, leaning wearily back against his cushions. "As you said, the Bureau Guards will come; and I think I shall kill myself when I hear them starting to crack the shield around this room. They will come in and find you with a dead man. What will you tell them, Terri?"

"Tell them? Anything I choose. They won't question *me*."

"No. The guards won't. But the Bureau will. How can they raise a man to the fourth level when there is a two-hour mystery in his background? They will want to know what you were doing here."

"I was kidnapped," said Terri.

"By whom? Can you prove it? And why?"

"I've been held a prisoner here."

"By a dead man? No, no, Terri. The circumstances are suspicious. You walk away from the embassy under your own power. You disappear and are found in a shielded room with a man who has committed suicide. This must be explained, and in the end you will have to tell them the truth."

"And what if I do?" said Terri, truculently.

"But the truth is so fantastic, Terri. So uncheckable. I am dead, and I am the only one who could have supported your story. These people who were here when you came in are common actors. They have no idea why I wanted you decoyed here. These are my rooms. And there is no obvious connection between me and the dead Kilaren. And perhaps I will decide to live just long enough to denounce you as a traitor when they enter."

Ashen-faced, Terri stared.

"The Bureau will have to question you. They will clamp a block on your mind so that you can't operate the reflex that stops your heart. And they will question you over and over again, because the Bureau cannot afford to take chances. You will go into a private hell of your own, Terri Mac. You will tell the story of your own evil to that girl over and over again, pleading to be believed. And they will not believe you. And in the end they will kill you, just to be on the safe side. Because, you see, you *might* have been doing something traitorous in these two shielded hours."

Terri's head bobbed limply, like a drunken man's. He made one last effort. "Why?" he said. "Why do you do this? Your life. For a girl who was no connection to you?"

The old man folded his hands.

"I was a little like your governor," he said. "We all have our sins. I loved Kilaren and the shock of her death wrecked my health." He cocked his head suddenly on one side. "Listen," he said.

From beyond the closed door of the room, a high-pitched humming was barely audible. It grew in volume, going up the scale. Terri leaped to his feet; and for the space of a couple of seconds, he lunged first this way then that, like a wild animal beating against its trap. Then, as if all will had at last gone out of him, he stopped in the middle of the room and closed his eyes. For a fraction of a moment he stood there, before a faint convulsion seized him and he fell.

With a faint smile on his face, the old man reached out to a hidden switch and cut the shield about the room. Uniformed guards tumbled through the door, to pull up in dismay at the sight of the body on the floor.

"I'm sorry," said the old man, "I must have turned the shield on by mistake. I was trying to signal someone. The Comptroller seems to have had a heart attack."

SEVEN-DAY TERROR

by R.A. Lafferty

"Is there anything you want to make disappear?" Clarence Willoughby asked his mother.

"A sink full of dishes is all I can think of. How will you do it?"

"I just built a disappearer. All you do is cut the other end out of a beer can. Then you take two pieces of red cardboard with peepholes in the middle and fit them in the ends. You look through the peepholes and blink. Whatever you look at will disappear."

"Oh."

"But I don't know if I can make them come back. We'd better try it on something else. Dishes cost money."

As always, Myra Willoughby had to admire the wisdom of her nine-year-old son. She would not have had such foresight herself. He always did. "You can try it on Blanche Manners' cat outside there. Nobody will care if it disappears except Blanche Manners."

"All right."

He put the disappearer to his eye and blinked. The cat disappeared from the sidewalk outside.

His mother was interested. "I wonder how it works. Do you know how it works?"

"Yes. You take a beer can with both ends cut out and put in two pieces of cardboard. Then you blink."

"Never mind. Take it outside and play with it. You hadn't better make anything disappear in here till I think about this."

But when he had gone his mother was oddly disturbed.

"I wonder if I have a precocious child. Why, there's lots of grown people who wouldn't know how to make a disappearer that would work. I wonder if Blanche Manners will miss her cat very much?"

Clarence went down to the Plugged Nickel, a pot house on the corner.

"Do you have anything you want to make disappear, Nokomis?"

"Only my paunch."

"If I make it disappear it'll leave a hole in you and you'll bleed to death."

"That's right, I would. Why don't you try it on the fireplug outside?"

This in a way was one of the happiest afternoons ever in the neighborhood. The children came from blocks around to play in the flooded streets and gutters, and if some of them drowned (and we don't say that they did drown) in the flood (and brother! it was a flood), why you have to expect things like that. The fire engines (whoever heard of calling fire engines to put out a flood?) were apparatus-deep in water. The policemen and ambulance men wandered around wet and bewildered.

"Resuscitator, resuscitator, anybody wanna resuscitator," chanted Clarissa Willoughby.

"Oh, shut up," said the ambulance attendants.

Nokomis, the bar man in the Plugged Nickel, called Clarence inside.

"I don't believe, just for the moment, I'd tell anyone what happened to that fireplug."

"I won't tell if you won't tell," said Clarence.

484

Officer Comstock was suspicious. "There's only seven possible explanations: one of the seven Willoughby kids did it. I dunno how. It'd take a bulldozer to do it, and then there'd be something left of the plug. But however they did it, one of them did it."

Officer Comstock had a talent for getting near the truth of dark matters. This is why he was walking a beat out here in the boondocks instead of sitting in a chair downtown.

"Clarissa!" said Officer Comstock in a voice like thunder.

"Resuscitator, resuscitator, anybody wanna resuscitator?" chanted Clarissa.

"Do you know what happened to that fireplug?" asked Officer C.

"I have an uncanny suspicion. As yet it is no more than that. When I am better informed I will advise you."

Clarissa was eight years old and much given to uncanny suspicions.

"Clementine, Harold, Corinne, Jimmy, Cyril," he asked the five younger Willoughby children. "Do you know what happened to that fireplug?"

"There was a man around yesterday. I bet he took it," said Clementine.

"I don't even remember a fireplug there. I think you're making a fuss about nothing," said Harold.

"City hall's going to hear about this," said Corinne.

"Pretty dommed sure," said Jimmy, "but I won't tell."

"Cyril!" cried Officer Comstock in a terrible voice. Not a terrifying voice, a terrible voice. He felt terrible now.

"Great green bananas," said Cyril, "I'm only three years old. I don't see how it's even my responsibility."

"Clarence," said Officer Comstock.

Clarence gulped.

"Do you know where the fireplug went?"

Clarence brightened. "No, sir. I don't know where it went."

A bunch of smart alecs from the water department came out and shut off the water for a few blocks around and put some kind of cap on in place of the fireplug. "This sure is going to be a funny-sounding report," said one of them.

Officer Comstock walked away discouraged. "Don't bother me, Miss Manners," he said. "I don't know where to look for your cat. I don't even know where to look for a fireplug."

"I have an idea," said Clarissa, "that when you find the cat you will find the fireplug in the same place. As yet it's only an idea."

Ozzie Murphy wore a little hat on top of his head. Clarence pointed his weapon and winked. The hat was no longer there, but a little trickle of blood was running down the pate.

"I don't believe I'd play with that any more," said Nokomis.

"Who's playing?" said Clarence. "This is for real."

This was the beginning of the seven-day terror in the heretofore obscure neighborhood. Trees disappeared from the parks; lamp posts were as though they had never been; Wally Waldorf drove home, got out, slammed the door of his car, and there was no car. As George Mullendorf came up the walk to his house his dog Pete ran to meet him and took a flying leap to his arms. The dog left the sidewalk but something happened; the dog was gone and only a bark lingered for a moment in the puzzled air.

But the worst were the fireplugs. The second plug was installed the morning after the disappearance of the first. In eight minutes it was gone and the flood waters returned. Another one was in by twelve o'clock. Within three minutes it had vanished. The next morning fireplug number four was installed.

The water commissioner was there, the city engineer was there, the chief of police was there with a riot squad, the president of the Parent-Teachers Association was there, the president of the university was there, the mayor was there, three gentlemen of the FBI, a newsreel photographer, eminent scientists and a crowd of honest citizens.

"Let's see it disappear now," said the city engineer.

"Let's see it disappear now," said the police chief.

"Let's see it disa—it did, didn't it?" said one of the eminent scientists.

And it was gone and everybody was very wet.

"At least I have the picture sequence of the year," said the photographer. But his camera and apparatus disappeared from the midst of them.

"Shut off the water and cap it," said the commissioner. "And don't put in another plug yet. That was the last plug in the warehouse."

"This is too big for me," said the mayor. "I wonder that Tass doesn't have it yet."

"Tass has it," said a little round man. "I am Tass."

"If all of you gentlemen will come into the Plugged Nickel," said Nokomis, "and try one of our new Fire Hydrant Highballs you will all be happier. These are made of good corn whiskey, brown sugar, and hydrant water from this very gutter. You can be the first to drink them."

Business was phenomenal at the Plugged Nickel, for it was in front of its very doors that the fireplugs disappeared in floods of gushing water.

"I know a way we can get rich," said Clarissa several days later to her father, Tom Willoughby. "Everybody says there going to sell their houses for nothing and move out of the neighborhood. Go get a lot of money and buy them all. Then you can sell them again and get rich."

"I wouldn't buy them for a dollar each. Three of them have disappeared already, and all the families but us have their furniture moved out in their front yards. There might be nothing but vacant lots in the morning."

"Good, then buy the vacant lots. And you can be ready when the houses come back."

"Come back? Are the houses going to come back? Do you know anything about this, young lady?"

"I have a suspicion verging on a certainty. As of now I can say no more."

*

Three eminent scientists were gathered in an untidy suite that looked as though it belonged to a drunken sultan.

"This transcends the metaphysical. It impinges on the quantum continuum. In some way it obsoletes Boff," said Dr. Velikof Vonk.

"The contingence of the intransigence is the most mystifying aspect," said Arpad Arkbaranan.

"Yes," said Willy McGilly. "Who would have thought that you could do it with a beer can and two pieces of cardboard? When I was a boy I used an oatmeal box and red crayola."

"I do not always follow you," said Dr. Vonk. "I wish you would speak plainer."

So far no human had been injured or disappeared—except for a little blood on the pate of Ozzie Murphy, on the lobes of Conchita when her gaudy earrings disappeared from her very ears, a clipped flinger or so when a house vanished as the front doorknob was touched, a lost toe when a neighborhood boy kicked a can and the can was not; probably not more than a pint of blood and three or four ounces of flesh all together.

Now, however, Mr. Buckle the grocery man disappeared before witnesses. This was serious.

Some mean-looking investigators from downtown came out to the Willoughbys. The meanest-looking one was the mayor. In happier days he had not been a mean man, but the terror had now reigned for seven days.

"There have been ugly rumors," said one of the mean investigators, "that link certain events to this household. Do any of you know anything about them?"

"I started most of them," said Clarissa. "But I didn't consider them ugly. Cryptic, rather. But if you want to get to the bottom of this just ask me a question."

"Did you make those things disappear?" asked the investigator.

"That isn't the question," said Clarissa.

"Do you know where they have gone?" asked the investigator.

"That isn't the question either," said Clarissa.

"Can you make them come back?"

"Why, of course I can. Anybody can. Can't you?"

"I cannot. If you can, please do so at once."

"I need some stuff. Get me a gold watch and a hammer. Then go down to the drug store and get me this list of chemicals. And I need a yard of black velvet and a pound of rock candy."

"Shall we?" asked one of the investigators.

"Yes," said the mayor. "It's our only hope. Get her anything she wants."

And it was all assembled.

"Why does she get all the attention?" asked Clarence. "I was the one who made all the things disappear. How does she know how to get them back?"

"I knew it!" cried Clarissa with hate. "I knew he was the one that did it. He read in my diary how to make a disappearer. If I was his mother I'd whip him for reading his little sister's diary. That's what happens when things like that fall into irresponsible hands."

She poised the hammer over the mayor's gold watch, now on the floor.

"I have to wait a few seconds. This can't be hurried. It'll only be a little while."

The second hand swept around to the point that was preordained for it before the world began. Clarissa suddenly brought down the hammer with all her force on the beautiful gold watch.

"That's all," she said. "Your troubles are over. See, there is Blanche Manners' cat on the sidewalk just where she was seven days ago."

And the cat was back.

"Now let's go down to the Plugged Nickel and watch the fireplugs come back."

They had only a few minutes to wait. It came from nowhere and clanged into the street like a sign and a witness.

"Now I predict," said Clarissa, "that every single object will return exactly seven days from the time of its disappearance."

The seven-day terror had ended. The objects began to reappear.

"How," asked the mayor, "did you know they would come back in seven days?"

"Because it was a seven-day disappearer that Clarence made. I also know how to make a nine-day, a thirteen-day, a twenty-seven day, and an eleven-year disappearer. I was going to make a thirteen-year one, but for that you have to color the ends with the blood from a little boy's heart, and Cyril cried every time I tried to make a good cut."

"You really know how to make all of these?"

"Yes. But I shudder if the knowledge should ever come into unauthorized hands."

"I shudder, too, Clarissa. But tell me, why did you want the chemicals?

"For my chemistry set."

"And the black velvet?"

"For doll dresses."

"And the pound of rock candy?"

"How did you ever get to be mayor of this town if you have to ask questions like that? What do you think I wanted the rock candy for?"

"One last question," said the mayor. "Why did you smash my gold watch with the hammer?"

"Oh," said Clarissa, "that was for dramatic effect."

I'LL KILL YOU TOMORROW

by Helen Huber

The entities were utterly, ambitiously evil; their line of defense, apparently, was absolutely impregnable.

IT WAS NOT a sinister silence. No silence is sinister until it acquires a background of understandable menace. Here there was only the night quiet of Maternity, the silence of noiseless rubber heels on the hospital corridor floor, the faint brush of starched white skirts brushing through doorways into darkened and semi-darkened rooms.

But there was something wrong with the silence in the "basket room" of Maternity, the glass-walled room containing row on row, the tiny hopes of tomorrow. The curtain was drawn across the window through which, during visiting hours, peered the proud fathers who did the hoping. The night-light was dim.

The silence should not have been there.

Lorry Kane, standing in the doorway, looked out over the rows of silent baskets and felt her blonde hair tighten at the roots. The tightening came from instinct, even before her brain had a chance to function, from the instincts and training of a registered nurse.

Thirty-odd babies grouped in one room and—*complete silence.*

Not a single whimper. Not one tiny cry of protest against the annoying phenomenon of birth.

Thirty babies—*dead?* That was the thought that flashed, unbidden, into Lorry's pretty head. The absurdity of it followed swiftly, and Lorry moved on rubber soles between a line of baskets. She bent down and explored with practiced fingers.

A warm, living bundle in a white basket.

The feeling of relief was genuine. Relief, even from an absurdity, is a welcome thing. Lorry smiled and bent closer.

Staring up at Lorry from the basket were two clear blue eyes. Two eyes, steady and fixed in a round baby face. An immobile, pink baby face housing two blue eyes that stared up into Lorry's with a quiet concentration that was chilling.

Lorry said, "What's the matter with you?" She spoke in a whisper and was addressing herself. She'd gone short on sleep lately—the only way, really, to get a few hours with Pete. Pete was an interne at General Hospital, and the kind of a homely grinning carrot-top a girl like Lorry could put into dreams as the center of a satisfactory future.

But all this didn't justify a case of jitters in the "basket room."

Lorry said. "Hi, short stuff," and lifted Baby Newcomb—Male, out of his crib for a cuddling.

Baby Newcomb didn't object. The blue eyes came closer. The week-old eyes with the hundred-year-old look. Lorry laid the bundle over her shoulder and smiled into the dimness.

"You want to be president, Shorty?" Lorry felt the warmth of a new life, felt the little body wriggle in snug contentment. "I wouldn't advise it. Tough job." Baby Newcomb twisted in his blanket. Lorry stiffened.

Snug contentment?

Lorry felt two tiny hands clutch and dig into her throat. Not just pawing baby hands. Little fingers that reached and explored for the windpipe.

489

She uncuddled the soft bundle, held it out. There were the eyes. She chilled. No imagination here. No spectre from lack of sleep.

Ancient murder-hatred glowing in new-born eyes.

*

"CAREFUL, you fool! You'll drop this body." A thin piping voice. A shrill symphony in malevolence.

Fear weakened Lorry. She found a chair and sat down. She held the boy baby in her hands. Training would not allow her to drop Baby Newcomb. Even if she had fainted, she would not have let go.

*

THE shrill voice: "It was stupid of me. Very stupid."

Lorry was cold, sick, mute.

"Very stupid. These hands are too fragile. There are no muscles in the arms. I couldn't have killed you."

"Please—I . . ."

"Dreaming? No. I'm surprised at—well, at your surprise. You have a trained mind. You should have learned, long ago, to trust your senses."

"I don't understand."

"Don't look at the doorway. Nobody's coming in. Look at me. Give me a little attention and I'll explain."

"Explain?" Lorry pulled her eyes down to the cherubic little face as she parroted dully.

"I'll begin by reminding you that there are more things in existence than your obscene medical books tell you about."

"Who are you? What are you?"

"One of those things."

"You're not a baby!"

"Of course not. I'm . . ." The beastly, brittle voice drifted into silence as though halted by an intruding thought. Then the thought voiced—voiced with a yearning at once pathetic and terrible: "It would be nice to kill you. Someday I will. Someday I'll kill you if I can find you."

"Why? Why?" Insane words in an insane world. But life had not stopped even though madness had taken over. "Why?"

The voice was matter-of-fact again. No more time for pleasant daydreams. "I'm something your books didn't tell you about. Naturally you're bewildered. Did you ever hear of a bodyless entity?"

Lorry shuddered in silence.

"You've heard of bodyless entities, of course—but you denied their existence in your smug world of precise tidy detail. I'm a bodyless entity. I'm one of a swarm. We come from a dimension your mind wouldn't accept even if I explained it, so I'll save words. We of the swarm seek unfoldment—fulfillment—even as you in your stupid, blind world. Do you want to hear more?"

"I . . ."

"You're a fool, but I enjoy practicing with these new vocal chords, just as I enjoyed flexing the fingers and muscles. That's why I revealed myself. We are, basically of course, parasites. In the dimension where we exist in profusion, evolution has provided for us. There, we seek out and move into a dimensional entity far more intelligent than yourself. We destroy it in a way you wouldn't understand, and it is not important that you should. In fact, I can't see what importance there is in your existing at all."

"You plan to—kill all these babies?"

"Let me congratulate you. You've finally managed to voice an intelligent question. The answer is, no. We aren't strong enough to kill them. We dwelt in a far more delicate dimension than this one and all was in proportion. That was our difficulty when we came here. We could find no entities weak enough to take possession of until we came upon this roomful of infants."

"Then, if you're helpless . . ."

"What do we plan to do? That's quite simple. These material entities will grow. We will remain attached—ingrained, so to speak. When the bodies enlarge sufficiently . . ."

"*Thirty potential assassins . . . .*" Lorry spoke again to herself, then hurled the words back into her own mind as her sickness deepened.

The shrill chirping: "What do you mean, potential? The word expresses a doubt. Here there is none." The entity's chuckle sounded like a baby, content over a full bottle. "Thirty certain assassins."

"But why must you kill?"

Lorry was sure the tiny shoulders shrugged. "Why? I don't know. I never thought to wonder. Why must you join with a man and propagate some day? Why do you feel sorry for what you term an unfortunate? Explain your instincts and I'll explain mine."

Lorry felt herself rising. Stiffly, she put Baby Newcomb back into his basket. As she did so, a ripple of shrill, jerky laughter crackled through the room. Lorry put her hands to her ears. "You know I can't say anything. You'd keep quiet. They'd call me mad."

"Precisely."

Malicious laughter, like driven sleet, cut into her ears as she fled from the room.

*

PETER LARCHMONT, M.D., was smoking a quick cigarette by an open fire-escape door on the third floor. He turned as Lorry came down the corridor, flipped his cigarette down into the alley and grinned. "Women shouldn't float on rubber heels," he said. "A man should have warning."

Lorry came close. "Kiss me. Kiss me—hard."

Pete kissed her, then held her away. "You're trembling. Anticipation, pet?" He looked into her face and the grin faded. "Lorry, what is it?"

"Pete—Pete. I'm crazy. I've gone mad. Hold me."

He could have laughed, but he had looked closely into her eyes and he was a doctor. He didn't laugh. "Tell me. Just stand here. I'll hang onto you and you tell me."

"The babies—they've gone mad." She clung to him. "Not exactly that. Something's taken them over. Something terrible. Oh, Pete! Nobody would believe me."

"I believe the end result," he said, quietly. "That's what I'm for, angel. When you shake like this I'll always believe. But I'll have to know more. And I'll hunt for an answer."

"There isn't any answer, Pete. I *know*."

"We'll still look. Tell me more, first."

"There isn't any more." Her eyes widened as she stared into his with the shock of a new thought. "Oh, Lord! One of them talked to me, but maybe he—or it—won't talk to you. Then you'll never know for sure! You'll think I'm . . ."

"Stop it. Quit predicting what I'll do. Let's go to the nursery."

They went to the nursery and stayed there for three-quarters of an hour. They left with the tinny laughter filling their minds—and the last words of the monstrous entity.

"We'll say no more, of course. Perhaps even this incident has been indiscreet. But it's in the form of a celebration. Never before has a whole swarm gotten through. Only a single entity on rare occasions."

Pete leaned against the corridor wall and wiped his face with the sleeve of his jacket. "We're the only ones who know," he said.

"Or ever will know." Lorry pushed back a lock of his curly hair. She wanted to kiss him, but this didn't seem to be the place or the time.

"We can never tell anyone."

"We'd look foolish."

"We've got a horror on our hands and we can't pass it on."

"What are we going to do?" Lorry asked.

"I don't know. Let's recap a little. Got a cigarette?"

They went to the fire door and dragged long and deep on two from Lorry's pack. "They'll be quiet from now on. No more talking—just baby squalls."

"And thirty little assassins will go into thirty homes," Lorry said. "All dressed in soft pink and blue, all filled with hatred. Waiting, biding their time, growing more clever." She shuddered.

"The electric chair will get them all, eventually."

"But how many will they get in the meantime?"

Pete put his arms around her and drew her close and whispered into her ear. "There's nothing we can do—nothing."

"We've got to do something." Lorry heard again the thin, brittle laughter following her, taunting her.

"It was a bad dream. It didn't happen. We'll just have to sleep it off."

She put her cheek against his. The rising stubble of his beard scratched her face. She was grateful for the rough touch of solid reality.

Pete said, "The shock will wear out of our minds. Time will pass. After a while, we won't believe it ourselves."

"That's what I'm afraid of."

"It's got to be that way."

"We've got to do something."

Pete lowered his arm wearily. "Yeah—we've got to do something. Where there's nothing that can be done. What are we—miracle workers?"

"We've got to do something."

"Sure—finish out the watch and then get some sleep."

*

LORRY AWOKE with the lowering sun in her window. It was a blood red sun. She picked up the phone by her bedside. "Room 307 Resident's extension."

Pete answered drowsily. Lorry said, "Tell me—did I dream, or did it really happen."

"I was going to ask you the same thing. I guess it happened. What are you doing?"

"Lying in bed."

"So am I. But two different beds. Things are done all wrong."

"Want to take a chance and sneak over? I've got an illegal coffee pot."

"Leave the door unlocked."

Lorry put on the coffee. She showered and got into her slip. She was brushing her hair when Pete came in. He looked at her and extended beckoning, clutching fingers. "The hell with phantoms. Come here."

After a couple of minutes, Lorry pulled away and poured the coffee. She reached for her uniform. Pete said, "Don't put it on yet."

"Too dangerous—leaving it off."

He eyed her dreamily. "I'll dredge up will power. I'll also get scads of fat rich clients. Then we'll get married so I can assault you legally."

Lorry studied him. "You're not even listening to yourself. What is it, Pete? What have you dreamed up?"

"Okay. I've got an idea. You said something would have to be done."

"What?"

"A drastic cure for a drastic case. With maybe disaster as the end product."

"Tell me."

"I'll tell you a little, but not too much."

"Why not all?"

"Because if we ever land in court. I want you to be able to say under oath, 'He didn't tell me what he planned to do.'"

"I don't like that."

"I don't care if you like it or not. Tell me, what's the one basic thing that stands out in your mind about these—entities?"

"That they're . . ."

"Fragile?"

"Yes—fragile."

"Give me some more coffee."

*

LORRY demanded to know what was in Pete's mind. All she got was kissed, and she did not see Pete again until eleven o'clock that night. He found her in the corridor in Maternity and motioned her toward the nursery. He carried a tray under a white towel. He said, "You watch the door. I'm going inside. I'll be about a half an hour."

"What are you going to do?"

"You stay out here and mind your business. Your business will be to steer any nosey party away. If you can't, make noise coming in."

Doc Pete turned away and entered the nursery. Lorry stood at the doorway, in the silence, under the brooding night-light, and prayed.

Twenty-five minutes later, Pete came out. His face was white and drawn. He looked like a man who had lately had a preview of Hell's inverted pleasures. His hands trembled. The towel still covered the tray. He said, "Watch them close. Don't move ten steps from here." He started away—turned back. "All hell is scheduled to break loose in this hospital shortly. Let's hope God remains in charge."

Lorry saw the sick dread of his heart underneath his words.

*

IT COULD have been a major scandal. An epidemic of measles on the maternity floor of a modern hospital indicates the unforgivable medical sin—carelessness. It was hushed up as much as possible, pending the time when the top people could shake off the shock and recover their wits. The ultimate recovery of thirty babies was a tribute to everyone concerned.

Wan, done-in, Doc Pete drank coffee in Lorry's room. Lorry gave him three lumps of sugar and said, "But are you sure the sickness killed the entities?"

"Quite sure. Somehow they *knew* when I made the injections. They screamed. They knew they were done for."

"It took courage. Tell me: why are you so strong, so brave? Why are you so wonderful?"

"Cut it out. I was scared stiff. If *one* baby had died, I'd have gone through life weighing the cure against the end. It isn't easy to risk doing murder—however urgent the need."

She leaned across and kissed him. "And you were all alone. You wouldn't let me help. Was that fair?"

He grinned, then sobered. "But I can't help remembering what that—that invisible monster said: '*Never before has a whole swarm gotten through. Only a single entity on rare occasions.*'

"I can't help wondering what happens to those single entities. I think of the newspaper headlines I've seen: Child Kills Parents in Sleep. Youth Slays Father. I'll probably always wonder—and I'll always remember . . . ."

Lorry got up and crossed to him and put her arms around him. "Not always," she whispered. "There will be times when I'll make you forget. For a little while, anyhow."

SECURITY RISK

by Ed M. Clinton, Jr.

At moments like this, General David Walker always thought fleetingly of the good old days when he had hated the army. As usual, he smashed the thought out of his mind with a distinct sense of remorse.

He looked up again at the seamed face of the Chief of Staff, General Marcus Meriwether. "This could be serious," he said slowly, with a sick sense of the statement's inadequacy. An old tic suddenly returned, tugging at the left corner of his mouth.

The deadly, unsmiling expression on Meriwether's face did not change as he slid more tightly into his chair. "You know as well as I that it means the Interplanetary Confederation is ready to go to war with us."

Walker stared at the typed statement on his desk. It was a decoded intelligence message from United Terra's prime agent in the Interplanetary Confederation, and it was very brief: the Confederation had developed a long-range neural weapon effectively cancelling out every armament development achieved by United Terra in fifteen years of a cold war that of late had become bitter cold. The all-but-autonomous colonies of Mars and Venus, united now for twenty years in an economic league, had been itching for independence for a quarter of a century. The itch had developed into a mighty burning.

"You are fully aware," Meriwether continued, his face still set, "of our feeling that the Confederation has been eager to take on Terra. They've clearly been waiting for some positive advantage to offset our pure strength-in-numbers."

Walker forced his eyes upward and stared at his superior. "Your tone says that such a war might be—"

"Unwelcome at this time. Unwelcome at this time." Meriwether shifted around in his chair, and scratched at its leather arms with the manicured tips of his gnarled fingers. "Walker, I don't have to tell you that this weapon, if it is what our agent infers—and there is no reason to believe otherwise—that this weapon makes it impossible for us to go to war with the Confederation—unless, as Chief of Weapons Development, you can tell me that we have something in our arsenal to combat it."

Walker rubbed at the tic. "Nothing," he said quietly.

Meriwether leaned forward, his hands crooked backward against the chair arms like catapult springs. "That answer is unacceptable. There are other questions you must answer, Walker, questions in some ways even more important than that basic one. Why haven't we developed this weapon ourselves? Why haven't we been aware of its potential existence? Where are the defensive devices which would naturally develop from such cognizance? These things are all your department, Walker." His voice pitched upward an hysterical fraction. "It just doesn't make sense, you know. We've a hundred times the personnel, ten times the facilities, unlimited funds—but they've beaten us to it." He stood up and pushed his chair back, eyes squinting out of a reddening face that seemed on the point of bursting. "Why, Walker?"

Once again Walker thought about how he had hated the army when he was a bright young physics student. That was a long time ago—So much had happened. The doors had closed around him, one at a time, doors closing on the scientific mind. And so now, instead of a

495

research scientist in white smock with textbook, he was a military administrator in smart greys with glittering stars of military rank.

"I'll say this, Walker," Meriwether shouted, his voice breaking again. "We'd better catch up quick. Mighty quick. Let's put it this way. It might mean your rank and your job, Walker. But you won't give a damn. Because we'll have lost the war. We'll have lost the colonies. And you know what that would mean, Walker?" He bent forward across the desk, his face exploding into Walker's eyes. "Only a fool believes that United Terra can survive in an economy without tri-planetary hegemony.

"Walker, you've all the authority within my power to grant. You'll have no trouble getting money. But—get the answer. *Quick.*"

Walker blinked after him as he strode to the door. "I'll try to hold off a federal investigation as long as I can," Meriwether added, turning from the half-opened door. "But I can't guarantee a thing."

*

Walker sat alone in a cubicle of light in the darkened city and gulped down his twentieth cup of coffee. It had grown cold in the cup and with a grimace he pushed it aside.

There was no doubt about it. He thumbed through the sheaf of scribbled notes he had transcribed from stacks of documents and racks of spools from Security files. Clearly, he had the answer to Meriwether's questions. But, having it, he did not quite know what to do with it.

There was, however, no doubt at all: United Terra had been on the track of the neural weapon—ten years earlier. Could have had it—and had lost the chance.

He rubbed his thumbs hard against his tired eyes and tried to remember back that ten years: at that time he had been Chief of Weapons Development for perhaps three years. His own name, though, had appeared in none of the files he had examined, so apparently he had not been directly involved in the security hearings. But he *should*remember.

Dr. Otto Millet. *Otto Millet.* He let the name roll around his brain, until shortly an image began to form—an image of a smiling man, greying at the temples, wearing a flamboyant sports shirt and affecting a very close haircut. A man perhaps forty. In the image, he was a laughing man.

He remembered now. Dr. Otto Millet: into government service on the inertia of a fantastic reputation as a research physicist specializing in magnetic field studies. A man he had instantly disliked.

He bent forward and reread what he had scrawled in his last notes, a verbatim extract from the report of the security committee.

"It is clear that Dr. Millet's conversations and letters with Professor Greyman, together with his unrepentant attitude, render him a security risk. His various security clearances are therefore revoked, and he is hereafter prohibited access to all classified files and to any government research and development laboratory."

Since virtually all laboratories were government supported, that was to all intents and purposes the end of Millet's career as an experimental physicist.

Where had Millet gone? What had he done since? Walker scraped a cigarette out of the half-empty pack in his pocket. More important: what was he doing now?

He inhaled deeply and sent clouds of smoke skewing across the room. Had the man really been a traitor? Walker tried to place himself in the time of Millet's hearing. He'd been not too many years out of school then, with the bitterness of his frustrated ambition to be a research physicist still rankling him; perhaps this had colored his view of Millet. He stared at his desk, almost shocked that this thought should have occurred to him. It shook him, for it told him something about himself which he did not particularly care to know.

Nowhere had he been able to find any evidence as to what had happened to Millet since. Banished, the government seemed to forget him. But one thing was clear to Walker, and he pondered it deeply as he sucked on the last quarter-inch of his cigarette and poured himself another cup of cold black coffee. One big thing: Millet had been directing development along lines that would have led to the neural weapon; he had even signed a report, early in his project effort, which had referred to the possibility of "a neural device."

Had he gone over to the Confederation? It would account for their possession of the weapon now. But surely—*surely*, this fact would have been observed and reported by Terran intelligence agents.

Walker, infinitely tired, forgot his coffee and began to tidy up the desk, filing everything he wanted to keep in an electronically locked cabinet, shoving everything else into the destruction of the vibrator. He pondered for a moment the powdered secrets that were heaped like black dust in the bottom of the canister: a symbol of safety to a terrified world.

Step one: find Millet. *Find Millet.*

*

It took the Secret Service exactly twenty-nine hours to locate Dr. Otto Millet. Thirty minutes later, Walker was climbing out of a government helicopter and staring at Millet's small house through squinted eyes which he shielded with both hands against the blazing desert sun. The house was fronted by a neat lawn and a white fence entwined with red roses; there appeared to be a rather large garden in the rear. The style of the house bothered him a little: it had passed out of popularity thirty years before. Its lack of a conventional roofport had forced them to land the 'copter on the desert itself.

He straightened and pushed through the creaking gate. Flagstone steps curved toward the porch, and he minced along them, uncertain, now that he had arrived, of what he would say to Millet. The damned house, he thought—so different from what he had expected; it had thrown his whole thinking out of order.

He hated himself for feeling uneasy.

There was neither vodor nor contact system of any kind at the door, and he brushed his hand against his forehead in a gesture of frustration. He stared at his palm—it had come away wet with sweat, and he wondered if it were all because of the desert sun.

Tentatively, he banged on the door with his fist. There was no answer.

Damn Millet, he thought, wiping his forehead again. Why couldn't the man have a videophone like any normal person so you could find out if he were home without taking a trip halfway across the country?

He turned, stamping angrily as he did so, and was startled to see a man, wearing work clothes and holding a pair of heavy soiled gloves in his left hand, standing on the ground by the end of the porch. He was nearly bald, intensely bronzed, and he was smiling.

"Wondered when you'd see me." He nodded toward the gate. "I was standing right there when you came up. You just breezed right past." His smile broadened. "You were so interested in being surprised that you couldn't see what you came for."

"It must have been that damned glare," muttered Walker, shaking his head. Then, impolitely, "Are you Millet?"

"Otto Millet," the other replied, inclining his head slightly. "You're from the government. I can tell because of the uniform, you see." Walker flushed. "The government hasn't thought about me in a number of years," the scientist added. He came up onto the porch and peered at the symbol on the left lapel of Walker's jacket. "Ah! Alma mater. Weapons Development." He squinted at Walker. "David Walker, I presume?" He chuckled loudly but Walker failed to see the humor. "I remember you, you see; what a shame you can't return the compliment."

"It's hot out here," complained Walker, in growing discomfort.

Millet opened the door. "Won't you come in? It's better inside."

There it was again, thought Walker; the insolence, the imperturbable smile. He grunted and went in; it was, mercifully, considerably cooler.

He looked around. It was a very cluttered living room, not messy but tossed about with the artifacts that the man obviously liked to have around him. There was an ancient painting by Bonestell hanging on one wall, a startlingly accurate twentieth-century concept of the appearance of Mars; several long pipe racks, filled to overflowing, in various spots around the room; a typewriter on a table in a corner, and piles of paper; books lining the walls, and stacked on the floor in heaps and on the table beside the typewriter; a map of the earth on the wall above the typewriter, a three-dimensional Waterson projection. The furniture was clean but—not old; *lived with.*

Walker went over to the wall map and peered closely.

"One of Waterson's first," remarked Millet, closing the door. "Sit down, Walker, and tell me all about Weapons Development. How is the mass murder department doing these days?"

Walker felt his ears redden and he was arrested in the very act of sitting down. "Really," he said, "it's not something we *like* to think about, you know."

"Suppose not." Millet fiddled with several pipes in a rack beside his chair, selected one, and began filling it with rough-cut tobacco from a battered canister. "To business, then. Why the visit?"

Walker cleared his throat and tried to remember the little prefatory weasel words he had painfully assembled during the flight from Omaha. "First of all, Dr. Millet, I find myself a little embarrassed. After all, your parting from government service was not of the happiest nature for you—"

"Don't be foolish. Happiest day of my life, Walker."

Walker had a sudden sense of being impaled, and the rest of the little speech was dissipated in the wave of shock which swept over him. He forced his mouth shut, and gasped, "You're not serious!"

Millet shook out his second match and puffed until the pipe bowl glowed warmly, edge to edge. "Of course I'm serious." He jabbed his pipe at Walker. "You like your job?"

"It's a job that has to be done."

Millet smiled and shrugged. "You haven't really answered my question."

Walker, sensing that he had already lost control of the conversation, waved his hands in dismissal. "Well, that is not really important. The fact remains, you did leave Weapons Development at the . . . ah . . . request of the government."

"Talk on, talk on—you'll get to the point eventually. When you're through, I'd like to show you around the place. I'm very proud of my gardens. You're sort of responsible for them, you know."

Walker set his jaw and bored ahead. "However, at the time you left government service, you were pursuing certain lines of research—"

Millet leaned back and began laughing, his eyes squinted shut. "Walker, don't tell me they want me *back*!"

It seemed his chance to dominate the discussion again. "I don't think you'd be allowed back."

"Good," said Millet, looking up, his laughter fading into a smile. "I was a bit concerned for a moment."

There was silence in the room. Walker began to wish that he were somewhere else: Millet simply baffled him. He obviously did not care about his disgrace. Walker felt a resurgence of the old resentment.

Millet's face suddenly became very kindly. "Perhaps, as a fellow scientist"—Walker almost winced, and knew, furiously, that his response had shown—"you would be interested in knowing what I've been doing since my unhappy marriage with bureaucracy ended."

It was a welcome gambit, and Walker accepted it eagerly. "I certainly would. One of the reasons I came here, as a matter of fact."

Millet waved his pipe. "Good. Afterwards, you can stop beating around the bush, eh?"

"Yes, of course," mumbled Walker.

"You know," said Millet as he got up and went to a bookcase, "a man's got to earn a living. Do much reading?"

"Not these days. Used to." He scratched a cigarette on the sole of his shoe and inhaled hugely. "Not enough time these days for reading."

Millet reached into the bookcase and came out with a stack of magazines. "Well, that's how I make my living." He handed the stack to Walker. "Writing. Use a pen name of course." He chuckled. "Write everything—always happiest doing science fiction, though."

Walker flipped through the magazines; he looked up. "Obviously, you're doing rather well at it."

"Have been for the last seven or eight years. Lot of fun."

"And this has been your life since you left us?" Walker set the stack of magazines aside. "Seems a waste of genius, somehow."

"As a matter of fact, this is not my life's work. As I said, a man's got to earn a living. This is just a lucrative hobby that pays the way. You see, I've been involved in an expensive research program."

"Ah." Walker sat forward and smashed out his cigarette. "This may be important."

"Oh, it is, it is. But not, I am afraid, in the way you mean."

"You can never tell. What have you been doing?"

"Completing a unified theory of life. Why a crystal grows but isn't alive, why an organism that dies isn't like a crystal. What is the process we call life? What is its relationship to the space-time continuum—"

He said it so casually that Walker was caught off his guard completely. "Are you serious, Millet?" he said.

"Certainly. I expect to publish in about two years."

"Is this an independent effort?"

"Not entirely. Others have contributed. Some pioneers long dead, some among the living." His eyes twinkled. "You see, important things beside the development of weapons of destruction do continue in the scientific world. Did you think that was the end of everything for me, ten years ago?" He shook his head in mock gravity. "It was just the beginning. I *wanted* out, you see."

"You wanted out?" Walker leaned forward, unwilling to believe what he had heard. "Are you trying to tell me that you *arranged* your discharge?"

Millet shrugged. "Why, of course. Nobody ever has bothered to ask me about that up to now, but I certainly did arrange it. It wasn't hard, you know. All I had to do was set up some sort of relationship with a so-called security risk, and I was on my way out."

"Why . . . that's damned near treason."

"Don't be silly. I had other important things to do. In order to do them—to continue work on the unified life theory—it was necessary for me to contact scientists with whom professional relationships were made illegal by security regulations. The choice was simple; besides, I didn't enjoy the idea of spending my life developing ways of destroying the very thing I wanted most to understand."

"This is fantastic, Millet, utterly fantastic."

"But true nonetheless. Walker, you look like you could use a drink."

"By all means." He stared emptily into the air, thinking about the good old days.

"Walker, a toast," said Millet, holding a tall glass out to him. "To scientific freedom."

Walker blinked. "By all means," he repeated hoarsely, and there was a blurriness to his vision. "To scientific freedom."

They drank, and Walker said: "I feel a bit freer to say what I have come for."

"Shoot," nodded Millet, sipping his drink.

"For security reasons, I'll talk in generalities. But the basic fact is, United Terra is faced with a serious situation. It is most desirable that the research you were conducting when you left us, be continued."

"There are a lot of other capable physicists, both eager to be a part of such activity and blessed with security clearances."

"You know very well, Millet, that this was an unique, almost independent line of development that comes to a stop in your brain. Besides," and suddenly he felt silly, "the lines of communication for research which might enable us to pick up where you left off, in time—too much time—are somewhat entangled in security." He glared. "Don't laugh, Millet; it's a fact of life which must be faced."

Millet finished his drink and set the glass on an end table. "What you're doing is asking me to come back if you can arrange it."

Walker spread his hands. "Dr. Millet, you have put it in a nutshell."

Millet shook his head, and for the first time since their conversation had started he frowned. "Walker, you know how I feel about developing weapons. I'm just plain opposed to it."

"The soldier is opposed to losing his life, but many have to do just that in the interests of civilization."

"That serious, eh?"

Walker crumpled under the weight of his fear. "That serious," he said wearily.

Millet thoughtfully relit his pipe. "Of course, I'm not at all sure that United Terra is very right in this thing."

"In times like these, that kind of thought is out of bounds," snapped Walker. "Whether you like it or not, you are a part of this culture. You might disapprove of many things in it, but you don't want to see it fall."

Millet puffed gently. "No, I suppose not." Again the frown flickered across his face. "I've been very happy. I don't want my work interrupted. It's too important, Walker."

"Undoubtedly this would more than interrupt your work. It would replace it."

Millet's eyes drifted affectionately about the room. "Most unpleasant." A smile curled his lips. "Frankly, though, I don't think you can clear me again."

"My problem."

"Indeed." A weary resignation seemed to settle over Millet, and Walker suddenly felt very miserable. "I suppose I'll have to accept," Millet said, pulling his pipe out of his mouth and staring unhappily at its trail of smoke.

*

Walker put his hands flat on his desk and sighed deeply. Some of the pressure, at least, was off; he had managed to cancel part of the Confederation's advantage. Terran industrial strength and technological supremacy, coupled with Millet's genius, might yet equate, or at least circumvent, the frightful weapon the Confederation held.

However, he still had to get Millet back into the government. Though, on the basis of the information he had gained regarding the scientist's motivations, and considering the critical nature of the situation, it shouldn't be too difficult.

He clicked on his video and dialed a secret line into Security Data. Gyrating colors danced across the screen before it went black. He scowled, depressed the cancel button, and dialed again; this time, the black was finally replaced by a recorded image, which said, sweetly out of pouting red lips,

"This line is not cleared for the Security Information you seek. The problem you are handling should be routed through an individual permitted access to this information." The image faded into blackness, the sound track into static.

Walker stared, stupefied. No line, no contact, no source of information had been denied to him in over twelve years.

His door swung open; he came to his feet abruptly, furious that someone should enter unannounced.

He felt sickness strike him like a fist in the stomach: Meriwether, flanked by two security guards, pushed through the door. His voice slashed across the office like a broadsword.

"Walker, I'm shocked. Shocked. And at a time like this . . . ."

Walker pounded his desk. "What the hell is going on? I can't get Security Data, you come marching in here with security men . . . what gives?"

Meriwether gestured to the guards, and they came forward and each took one of Walker's arms. "You're out of a job, Walker," snarled General Marcus Meriwether.

"In the name of God, *why?*"

"You know very well. Take him to security detention, Sergeant."

And suddenly he knew. Meriwether stared indignantly when he started laughing. It was a hell of a thing to laugh at, but it was also the most hilarious tragedy he ever hoped to encounter.

Millet. *Security risk.* Untouchable.

Millet would finish his great unified theory, and go down in history as neither Walker nor Meriwether nor the genius who invented the Confederation's neural weapon would. Millet was as safe as he could possibly want to be.

And so was the Interplanetary Confederation.

CONFIDENCE GAME

by James Mckimmey, Jr.

Cutter demanded more and more and more efficiency—and got it! But, as in anything, enough is enough, and too much is ...

GEORGE H. CUTTER wheeled his big convertible into his reserved space in the Company parking lot with a flourish. A bright California sun drove its early brightness down on him as he strode toward the square, four-story brick building which said *Cutter Products, Inc.* over its front door. A two-ton truck was grinding backward, toward the loading doors, the thick-shouldered driver craning his neck. Cutter moved briskly forward, a thick-shouldered man himself, though not very tall. A glint of light appeared in his eyes, as he saw Kurt, the truck driver, fitting the truck's rear end into the tight opening.

"Get that junk out of the way!" he yelled, and his voice roared over the noise of the truck's engine.

Kurt snapped his head around, his blue eyes thinning, then recognition spread humor crinkles around his eyes and mouth. "All right, sir," he said. "Just a second while I jump out, and I'll lift it out of your way."

"With bare hands?" Cutter said.

"With bare hands," Kurt said.

Cutter's laugh boomed, and as he rounded the front of the truck, he struck the right front fender with his fist. Kurt roared back from the cab with his own laughter.

He liked joking harshly with Kurt and with the rest of the truck drivers. They were simple, and they didn't have his mental strength. But they had another kind of strength. They had muscle and energy, and most important, they had guts. Twenty years before Cutter had driven a truck himself. The drivers knew that, and there was a bond between them, the drivers and himself, that seldom existed between employer and employee.

The guard at the door came to a reflex attention, and Cutter bobbed his head curtly. Then, instead of taking the stairway that led up the front to the second floor and his office, he strode down the hallway to the left, angling through the shop on the first floor. He always walked through the shop. He liked the heavy driving sound of the machines in his ears, and the muscled look of the men, in their coarse work shirts and heavy-soled shoes. Here again was strength, in the machines and in the men.

And here again too, the bond between Cutter and his employees was a thing as real as the whir and grind and thump of the machines, as real as the spray of metal dust, spitting away from a spinning saw blade. He was able to drive himself through to them, through the hard wall of unions and prejudices against business suits and white collars and soft clean hands, because they knew that at one time he had also been a machinist and then tool and die operator and then a shop foreman. He got through to them, and they respected him. They were even inspired by him, Cutter knew, by his energy and alertness and steel confidence. It was one good reason why their production continually skimmed along near the top level of efficiency.

Cutter turned abruptly and started up the metal-lipped concrete steps to the second floor. He went up quickly, his square, almost chunky figure moving smoothly, and there was not the faintest shortening in his breath when he reached the level of his own office.

Coming up the back steps required him to cross the entire administration office which contained the combined personnel of Production Control, Procurement, and Purchasing. And here, the sharp edge of elation, whetted by the walk past the loading dock and the truck drivers and the machine shop and the machinists, was dulled slightly.

On either side of him as he paced rapidly across the room, were the rows of light-oak desks which contained the kind of men he did not like: fragile men, whether thin or fat, fragile just the same, in the eyes and mouth, and pale with their fragility. They affected steel postures behind those desks, but Cutter knew that the steel was synthetic, that there was nothing in that mimicked look of alertness and virility but posing. They were a breed he did not understand, because he had never been a part of them, and so this time, the invisible but very real quality of employer-employee relationship turned coldly brittle, like frozen cellophane.

The sounds now, the clicking of typewriters, the sliding of file drawers, the squeak of adjusted swivel chairs—all of it—irritated him, rather than giving him inspiration, and so he hurried his way, especially when he passed that one fellow with the sad, frightened eyes, who touched his slim hands at the papers on his desk, like a cautious fawn testing the soundness of the earth in front of him. What was his name? Linden? God, Cutter thought, the epitome of the breed, this man: sallow and slow and so hesitant that he appeared to be about to leap from his chair at the slightest alarm.

Cutter broke his aloofness long enough to glare at the man, and Linden turned his frightened eyes quickly to his desk and began shuffling his papers nervously. Some day, Cutter promised himself, he was going to stop in front of the man and shout, "Booo!" and scare the poor devil to hell and back.

He pushed the glass doors that led to his own offices, and moving into Lucile's ante-room restored his humor. Lucile, matronly yet quick and youthfully spirited, smiled at him and met his eyes directly. Here was some strength again, and he felt the full energy of his early-morning drive returning fully. Lucile, behind her desk in this plain but expensive reception room, reminded him of fast, hard efficiency, the quality of accomplishment that he had dedicated himself to.

"Goddamned sweet morning, eh, Lucy?" he called.

"Beautiful, George," she said. She had called him by his first name for years. He didn't mind, from her. Not many could do it, but those who could, successfully, he respected.

"What's up first?" he asked, and she followed him into his own office. It was a high-ceilinged room, with walls bare except for a picture of Alexander Hamilton on one wall, and an award plaque from the State Chamber of Commerce on the opposite side of the room. He spun his leather-cushioned swivel chair toward him and sat down and placed his thick hands against the surface of the desk. Lucile took the only other chair in the office, to the side of the desk, and flipped open her appointment pad.

"Quay wants to see you right away. Says it's important."

Cutter nodded slightly and closed his eyes. Lucile went on, calling his appointments for the day with clicking precision. He stored the information, leaning back in his chair, adjusting his mind to each, so that there would be no energy wasted during the hard, swift day.

"That's it," Lucile said. "Do you want to see Quay?"

"Send him in," Cutter said, and he was already leaning into his desk, signing his name to the first of a dozen letters which he had dictated into the machine during the last ten minutes of the preceding day.

Lucile disappeared, and three minutes later Robert Quay took her place in the chair beside Cutter's desk. He was a taller man than Cutter, and thinner. Still, there was an athletic grace about him, a sureness of step and facial expression, that made it obvious that he was physically fit. He was single and only thirty-five, twelve years younger than Cutter, but he had been with Cutter Products, Inc. for thirteen years. In college he had been a Phi Beta Kappa and lettered three years on the varsity as a quarterback. He was the kind of rare combination that Cutter liked, and Cutter had offered him more than the Chicago Cardinals to get him at graduation.

Cutter felt Quay's presence, without looking up at him. "Goddamned sweet morning, eh, Bob?"

"It really is, George," Quay said.

"What's up?" Cutter stopped signing, having finished the entire job, and he stared directly into Quay's eyes. Quay met the stare unflinchingly.

"I've got a report from Sid Perry at Adacam Research."

"Your under-cover agent again, eh?"

Quay grinned. Adacam Research conducted industrial experimentation which included government work. The only way to find out what really went on there, Cutter had found out, was to find a key man who didn't mind talking for a certain amount of compensation, regardless of sworn oaths and signatures to government statements. You could always get somebody, Cutter knew, and Quay had been able to get a young chemist, Sidney Perry.

"Okay," Cutter said. "What are they doing over there?"

"There's a fellow who's offered Adacam his project for testing. They're highly interested, but they're not going to handle it."

"Why not?"

Quay shrugged. "Too touchy. It's a device that's based on electronics—"

"What the hell is touchy about electronics?"

"This deals with the human personality," Quay said, as though that were explanation enough.

Cutter understood. He snorted. "Christ, anything that deals with the human personality scares them over there, doesn't it?"

Quay spread his hands.

"All right," Cutter said. "What's this device supposed to do?"

"The theory behind it is to produce energy units which reach a plane of intensity great enough to affect the function of the human ego."

"Will it?" Cutter never wasted time on surprise or curiosity or theory. His mind acted directly. Would it or wouldn't it? Performance versus non-performance. Efficiency versus inefficiency. Would it improve production of Cutter Products, Inc., or would it not?

"Sid swears they're convinced it will. The factors, on paper, check out. But there's been no experimentation, because it involves the human personality. This thing, when used, is supposed to perform a definite personality change on the individual subjected."

"How?"

"You know the theory of psychiatric therapy—the theory of shock treatment. The effect is some what similar, but a thousand times more effective."

"What *is* the effect?"

"A gradual dissolving of inferiority influences, or inhibitions, from the personality. A clear mind resulting. A healthy ego."

"And?"

"Confidence."

Cutter stared at Quay's eyes, assimilating the information. "That's all very damned nice. Now where does it fit in with Cutter Products?"

Quay drew a notebook from his coat pocket swiftly. "You remember that efficiency check we had made two months ago—the rating of individual departments on comparable work produced?"

Cutter nodded.

Quay looked at his notebook. "All administrative personnel departments showed an average of—"

"Thirty-six point eight less efficiency than the skilled and unskilled labor departments," Cutter finished.

Quay smiled slightly. He snapped the notebook shut. "Right. So that's our personnel efficiency bug."

"Christ, I've known that for twenty years," Cutter snapped.

"Okay," Quay said quickly, alerting himself back to the serious effort. "Now then, you'll remember we submitted this efficiency report to Babcock and Steele for analysis, and their report offered no answer, because their experience showed that you *always* get that kind of ratio, because of personality differences. The administrative personnel show more inferiority influences per man, thus less confidence, thus less efficiency."

"I remember all that," Cutter said.

"Their report also pointed out that this inevitable loss of efficiency is leveled out, by proportionately smaller wage compensation. The administrative personnel gets approximately twenty-five percent less compensation than the skilled labor personnel, and the remaining eleven point eight percent loss of efficiency is made up by the more highly efficient unskilled labor receiving approximately the same compensation as the administrative personnel."

"I remember all that nonsense, too," Cutter reddened faintly with a sudden anger. He did not believe the statistics were nonsense, only that you should expect to write off a thirty-six point eight efficiency loss on the basis of adjusted compensation. A thirty-six point eight efficiency loss was a comparable loss in profits. You never compensated a loss in profits, except by erasing that loss. "And so this is supposed to fix it?"

Quay's head bobbed. "It's worth a try, it seems to me. I've talked to Sid about it extensively, and he tells me that Bolen, who's developed this thing, would be willing to install enough units to cover the entire administrative force, from the department-head level down."

"How?"

Quay motioned a hand. "It's no larger than a slightly thick saucer. It could be put inside the chairs." Quay smiled faintly. "They sit on it, you see, and—"

Cutter was not amused. "How much?"

"Nothing," Quay said quickly. "Absolutely nothing. Bolen wants actual tests badly, and the Institute wouldn't do it. Snap your fingers, and give him a hundred and fifty people to work on, and it's yours to use for nothing. He'll do the installing, and he *wants* to keep it secret. It's essential, he says, to get an accurate reaction from the subjects affected. For him it's perfect, because we're running a continuous efficiency check, and if this thing does the job like it's supposed to do it, we'll have gained the entire benefits for nothing. How can we lose?"

Cutter stared at Quay for a moment, his mind working swiftly. "Call Horner in on this, but nobody else. Absolutely nobody else. Tell Horner to write up a contract for this fellow to sign. Get a clause in there to the effect that this fellow, Bolen, assumes all responsibility for any effects not designated in the defining part of the contract. Fix it up so that he's entirely liable, then get it signed, and let's see what happens."

Quay smiled fully and stood up. "Right, sir." He had done a good job, he knew. This was the sort of thing that would keep him solidly entrenched in Cutter's favor. "Right, George," he said, remembering that he didn't need to call Cutter sir anymore, but he knew he wouldn't hear any more from Cutter, because Cutter was already looking over a blueprint, eyes thin and careful, mind completely adjusted to a new problem.

*

EDWARD BOLEN called the saucer-sized disk, the Confidet. He was a thin, short, smiling man with fine brown hair which looked as though it had just been ruffled by a high wind, and he moved, Cutter noticed, with quick, but certain motions. The installing was done two nights after Cutter's lawyer, Horner, had written up the contract and gotten it signed by Bolen. Only Quay, Bolen, and Cutter were present.

Bolen fitted the disks into the base of the plastic chair cushions, and he explained, as he inserted one, then another:

"The energy is inside each one, you see. The life of it is indefinite, and the amount of energy used is proportionate to the demand created."

"What the hell do you mean by energy?" Cutter demanded, watching the small man work.

Bolen laughed contentedly, and Quay flushed with embarrassment over anyone laughing at a question out of Cutter's lips. But Cutter did not react, only looked at Bolen, as though he could see somehow, beneath that smallness and quietness, a certain strength. Quay had seen that look on Cutter's face before, and it meant simply that Cutter would wait, analyzing expertly in the meantime, until he found his advantage. Quay wondered, if this gadget worked, how long Bolen would own the rights to it.

Cutter drove the Cadillac into Hallery Boulevard, as though the automobile were an English Austin, and just beyond the boundaries of the city, cut off into the hills, sliding into the night and the relative darkness of the exclusive, sparsely populated Green Oaks section.

Ten minutes later, his house, a massive stone structure which looked as though it had been shifted intact from the center of some medieval moat, loomed up, gray and stony, and Capra, his handyman, took over the car and drove it into the garage, while Cutter strode up the wide steps to the door.

Niels took his hat, and Mary was waiting for him in the library.

She was a rather large woman, although not fat, and when she wore high heels—which she was not prone to do, because although Cutter would not have cared, she kept trying to project into other people's minds and trying, as she said, "Not to do anything to them, that I wouldn't want them to do to me."—she rose a good inch above Cutter. She was pleasant humored, and cooperative, and the one great irritant about her that annoyed Cutter, was the fact that she was not capable of meeting life wholeheartedly and with strength.

She steadily worried about other people's feelings and thoughts, so that Cutter wondered if she were capable of the slightest personal conviction. Yet that weakness was an advantage at the same time, to him, because she worked constantly toward making him happy. The house was run to his minutest liking, and the servants liked her, so that while she did not use a strong enough hand, they somehow got things done for her, and Cutter had no real complaint. Someday, he knew, he would be able to develop her into the full potential he knew she was capable of achieving, and then there wouldn't be even that one annoyance about her.

He sat down in the large, worn, leather chair, and she handed him a Scotch and water, and kissed his cheek, and then sat down opposite him in a smaller striped-satin chair.

"Did you have a nice day, dear?" she asked.

She was always pleasant and she always smiled at him, and she was indeed a handsome woman. They had been married but five years, and she was almost fifteen years younger than he, but they had a solid understanding. She respected his work, and she was careful with the money he allowed her, and she never forgot the Scotch and water. "The day was all right," he said.

"My goodness," she said, "you worked late. Do you want dinner right away?"

"I had some sandwiches at the office," he said, drinking slowly.

"That isn't enough," she said reproachfully, and he enjoyed her concern over him. "You'd better have some nice roast beef that Andre did just perfectly. And there's some wonderful dressing that I made myself, for just a small salad."

He smiled finally. "All right," he said. "All right."

She got up and kissed him again, and he relaxed in the large chair, sipping contentedly at his drink, listening to her footsteps hurrying away, the sound another indication that she was doing something for him. He felt tired and easy. He let his mind relax with his body. The gadget, the Confidet; that was going to work, he knew. It would erase the last important bug in his operational efficiency, and then he might even expand, the way he had wanted to all along. He closed his eyes for a moment, tasting of his contentment, and then he heard the sound of his dinner being placed on the dining room table, and he stood up briskly and walked out of the library. He really was hungry, he realized. Not only hungry but, he thought, he might make love to Mary that evening.

*

THE FIRST indication that the Confidet might be working, came three weeks later, when Quay handed Cutter the report showing an efficiency increase of 3.7 percent. "I think that should tell the story," Quay said elatedly.

"Doesn't mean anything," Cutter said. "Could be a thousand other factors besides that damned gimmick."

"But we've never been able to show more than one point five variance on the administrative checks."

"The trouble with you, Quay," Cutter said brusquely, "is you keep looking for miracles. You think the way to get things in this world is to hope real hard. Nothing comes easy, and I've got half a notion to get those damned silly things jerked out." He bent over his work, obviously finished with Quay, and Quay, deflated, paced out of the office.

Cutter smiled inside the empty office. He liked to see Quay's enthusiasm broken now and then. It took that, to mold a really good man, because that way he assumed real strength after a while. If he got knocked down and got up enough, he didn't fall apart when he hit a really tough obstacle. Cutter was not unhappy about the efficiency figures at all, and he knew as well as Quay that they were decisive.

Give it another two weeks, he thought, and if the increase was comparable, then they might have a real improvement on their hands. Those limp, jumpy creatures on the desks out there might actually start earning their keep. He was thinking about that, what it would mean to the total profit, when Lucile opened his door and he caught a glimpse of the office outside, including the clerk with the sad, frightened eyes. Even you, Linden, Cutter thought, we might even improve you.

The increase *was* comparable after another two weeks. In fact, the efficiency figure jumped to 8.9. Quay was too excited to be knocked down this time, and Cutter was unable to suppress his own pleasure.

"This is really it this time, George," Quay said. "It really is. And here." He handed Cutter a set of figures. "Here's what accounting estimates the profit to be on this eight-nine figure."

Cutter nodded, his eyes thinning the slightest bit. "We won't see that for a while."

"No," Quay said, "but we'll see it! We'll sure as hell see it! And if it goes much higher, we'll absolutely balance out!"

"What does Bolen figure the top to be?"

"Ten percent."

"Why not thirty-six point eight?" Cutter said, his eyes bright and narrow.

Quay whistled. "Even at ten, at the wage we're paying—"

"Never settle for quarters or thirds," Cutter said. "Get the whole thing. Send for Bolen. I want to talk to him. And in the meantime, Bob, this is such a goddamned sweet morning, what do you say we go to lunch early?"

Quay blinked only once, which proved his adaptability. Cutter had just asked him to lunch, as though it were their habit to lunch together regularly, when in reality, Quay had never once gone to lunch with Cutter before. Quay was quite nonchalant, however, and he said, "Why, fine, George. I think that's a good idea."

*

BOLEN appeared in Cutter's office the next morning, smiling, his eyes darting quickly about Cutter's desk and walls, so that Cutter felt, for a moment, that showing Bolen anything as personal as his office, was a little like letting the man look into his brain.

"Quay tells me you've set ten percent as the top efficiency increase we can count on, Bolen." Cutter said it directly, to the point.

Bolen smiled, examining Cutter's hands and suit and eyes. "That's right, Mr. Cutter."

"Why?"

Bolen placed his small hands on his lap, looked at the tapered fingers, then up again at Cutter. He kept smiling. "It's a matter of saturation."

"How in hell could ten percent more efficiency turn into saturation?"

"Not ten percent more efficiency," Bolen said quietly. "Ten percent *effect* on the individual who *creates* the efficiency. Ten percent effect of that which *causes* him to be ten percent more efficient."

Cutter snorted. "Whatever the hell that damned gimmick does, it creates confidence, drive, strength, doesn't it? Isn't that what you said?"

"Yes," Bolen said politely. "Approximately."

"Can you explain to me then, how ten percent more confidence in a man is saturation?"

Bolen studied what he was going to say carefully, smiling all the while. "Some men," he said very slowly, "are different than others, Mr. Cutter. Some men will react to personality changes as abrupt as this in different ways than others. You aren't too concerned, are you, with what those changes might already have done to any of the individuals affected?"

"Hell, no," Cutter said loudly. "Why should I be? All I'm interested in is efficiency. Tell me about efficiency, and I'll know what you're talking about."

"All right," Bolen said. "We have no way of knowing right now which men have been affected more than others. All we have is an average. The average right now is eight and nine-tenths percent. But perhaps you have some workers who do not react, because they really do not suffer the lacks or compulsions or inhibitions that the Confidet is concerned with. Perhaps they are working at top efficiency right now, and no amount of further subjection to the Confidet will change them."

"All right then," Cutter said quickly, "we'll ferret that kind of deadwood out, and replace them!"

"How will you know which are deadwood?" Bolen asked pleasantly.

"Individual checks, of course!"

Bolen shook his head, looking back at his tapering fingers. "It won't necessarily work. You see, the work that these men are concerned with is not particularly demanding work, is it? And that means you want to strike a balance between capability and demand. It's the unbalance of these things that creates trouble, and in your case, the demand outweighed the capability. Now, if you get a total ten-percent increase, then you're balanced. If you go over that, you'll break the balance all over again, except that you'll have, in certain cases, capability outweighing the demand of the work."

510

"Good," Cutter said. "Any man whose capability outweighs the work he's doing will simply keep increasing his efficiency."

Bolen shook his head. "No. He'll react quite the other way. He'll lose interest, because the work will no longer be a challenge, and then the efficiency will drop."

Cutter's jaw hardened. "All right then. I'll move that man up, and fill his place with someone else."

Bolen looked at Cutter's eyes, examined them curiously. "Some men have a great deal of latent talent, Mr. Cutter. This talent released—"

Cutter frowned, studying Bolen carefully. Then he laughed suddenly. "You think I might not be able to handle it?"

"Well, let's say that you've got a stable of gentle, quiet mares, and you turn them suddenly into thoroughbreds. You have to make allowances for that, Mr. Cutter. The same stalls, the same railings, the same stable boys might not be able to do the job anymore."

"Yes," Cutter said, smiling without humor, "but the *owner* has nothing to do with stalls and railings and stable boys, only in the sense that they are subsidiary. The owner is the owner, and if he has to make a few subsidiary changes, all right. But nothing really affects the owner, no matter whether you've got gentle mares or thoroughbreds."

Bolen nodded, as though he had expected that exact answer. "You are a very certain man, aren't you, Mr. Cutter?"

"Would I be here, in this office, heading this company, if I weren't, Bolen?"

Bolen smiled.

Cutter straightened in his chair. "All right, do we go on? Do we shoot for the limit?"

Bolen chose his words carefully. "I am interested in testing my Confidet, Mr. Cutter. This is the most important thing in the world to me. I don't recommend what you want to do. But, as long as you'll give me accurate reports on the effects of the Confidet, I'll go along with you. Providing you grant me one concession."

Cutter frowned.

"I want our written contract dissolved."

Cutter reddened faintly. Nobody ever demanded anything of him and got it easily, but his mind turned over rapidly, judging the increase in efficiency, the increase in profits. He would not necessarily have to stop with administrative personnel. There were other departments, too, that could stand a little sharpening. Finally he nodded, reluctantly. "All right, Bolen."

Bolen smiled and left quickly, and Cutter stared at his desk for a moment, tense. Then, he relaxed and the hard sternness of his face softened a bit. He put his finger on his desk calendar, and looked at a date Lucile had circled for him. He grinned, and picked up the telephone, and dialed.

"This is George H. Cutter," he said to the man who answered. "My wife's birthday is next Saturday. Do you remember that antique desk I bought her last year? Good. Well, the truth is, she uses it all the time, so this year I'd like a good chair to match it. She's just using an occasional chair right now, and ..."

*

LIKE EVERYTHING he gave her, Mary liked his gift extremely well, and night after night, after the birthday, he came home to find her at the desk, using the chair, captaining her house and her servant staff. And the improvement was noticeable in her, almost from the first day. Within a month, he could detect a remarkable change, and for the first time, since they had been married, Mary gave a dinner for thirty people without crying just before it started.

There were other changes.

Quay brought in efficiency report after efficiency report, and by the end of three months, they had hit eighteen and seven-tenths percent increase. The administrative office was no longer the dull, listless place it had been; now it thrived and hummed like the shop below. Cutter could see the difference with his own eyes, and he could particularly see the differences in certain individuals.

Brown and Kennedy showed remarkable improvement, but it was really Harry Linden who astonished Cutter. An individual check showed a sixty-percent increase by Linden, and there was a definite change in the man's looks. He walked differently, with a quick, virile step, and the look of his face and eyes had become strong and alive. He began appearing early in the morning, ahead of the starting hour, and working late, and the only time he missed any work hours, was one afternoon, during which, Lucile informed Cutter, he had appeared in court for his divorce trial.

Within a month, Cutter had fired Stole and Lackter and Grant, as department heads, and replaced them with Brown, Kennedy, and Linden. He had formulated plans for installation of the Confidets in the drafting department and the supply department, and already the profits of increased efficiency were beginning to show in the records. Cutter was full of new enthusiasm and ambition, and there was only one thorn in the entire development.

Quay had resigned.

Cutter had been startled and extremely angry, but Quay had been unperturbed and stubborn. "I've enjoyed working with you immensely, George, but my mind is made up. No hard feelings?"

Cutter had not even shaken his hand.

It had bothered him for days, and he checked every industrial company in the area, to see where Quay had found a better position. He was highly surprised, when he learned, finally, that Quay had purchased a small boat and was earning his living by carrying fishermen out onto the Bay. Quay had also married, four days after his resignation, and Cutter pushed the entire thing out of his mind, checking it off to partial insanity.

By February of the next year, he had promoted Harry Linden to Quay's old job, gotten rid of the deadwood that showed up so plainly on the individual checks, and the total efficiency average had reached thirty-three percent. His and Mary's anniversary was on the fourth of March, and when that day arrived, he was certain that he had reached that point where he could expand to another plant.

He was about to order her a mink stole in celebration, but it was also that day that he was informed that she was suing him for divorce. He rushed home, furious, but she was gone. She had taken her clothes and jewelry and the second Cadillac. In fact, all that she had left of her personal possessions were the antique desk and chair. When the trial was over, months later, she had won enough support to take her to France, where, he learned, she purchased a chateau at Cannes.

He tried to lose himself in his work, but for the first time in his life, he had begun to get faintly worried. It was only a sliver of worry, but it kept him from going on with the expansion. Stocks in the company had turned over at an amazingly rapid rate, and while it was still nothing more than intuition on his part, he began to tighten up, readying himself to meet anything.

The explosion came in July.

Drindor Products had picked up forty-nine percent of the stock on the market, by using secondary buyers. There had been a leak somewhere, Cutter realized, that had told his competitor, Drindor, the kind of profit he was making. He knew who it had been instantly, but before he could fire Harry Linden, all of his walls crashed down. Four months before, to put more *esprit de corps* into Linden, he had allowed Linden eight shares of his own stock, intending to pick it up later from the market. Linden had coerced with Drindor. Cutter lost control.

A board of directors was elected by Drindor, and Drindor assumed the presidency by proxy. Harry Linden took over Cutter's office, as Vice President In Charge.

Cutter had wildly ordered Edward Bolen to remove the Confidets one week before, but even then he had known that it was too late, and the smiling, knowing look on Bolen's face had infuriated him to a screaming rage. Bolen remained undisturbed, and quietly carried the disks away. Cutter, when he left his office that final day, moved slowly, very slowly.

*

HE BROODED for many long days after that, searching his mind for a way to counterattack. He still had enough stock to keep him comfortable if he lived another hundred years. But he no longer had the power, and he thirsted for that. He turned it around and around in his brain, trying to figure out how he could do it, and the one thing he finally knew, the one certain thing, was that if he used enough drive, enough strength, then he would regain control of the company he had built with his own hands and mind.

He paced the library and the long living room and the dining room, and his eyes were lost, until he saw, through the doorway of the sewing room, that desk and that chair, and he remembered he hadn't done anything about that.

He paused only briefly, because he had not lost an ounce of his ability to make a sudden decision, and then he removed that disk and carried it to the library and fitted it under the cushion of the large, worn, leather chair.

By fall, he had done nothing to regain control, and he was less certain of how he should act than he had been months before. He kept driving by the plant and looking at it, but he did so carefully, so that no one would see him, and he was surprised to find that, above all, he didn't want to face Harry Linden. The memory of the man's firm look, the sharp, bold eyes, frightened him, and the knowledge of his fright crushed him inside. He wished desperately that Mary were back with him, and he even wrote her letters, pleading letters, but they came back, unopened.

Finally he went to see Robert Quay, because Quay was the only man in his memory whom he somehow didn't fear talking to. He found Quay in a small cottage near the beach. There was a six-day old infant in a crib in the bedroom, and Quay's wife was a sparkling-eyed girl with a smile that made Cutter feel relatively at ease for the first time in weeks.

She politely left them alone, and Cutter sat there, embarrassed faintly, but glad to be in Quay's home and presence. They talked of how it had been, when Quay was with the company, and finally Cutter pushed himself into asking about it:

"I've often wondered, Bob, why you left?"

Quay blushed slightly, then grinned. "I might as well admit it. I got one of those things from Bolen, and had it installed in my own chair."

Cutter thought about it, surprised. He cleared his throat. "And then you quit?"

"Sure," Quay said. "All my life, I'd wanted to do just what I'm doing. But things just came easy to me, and the opportunities were always there, and I just never had the guts to pass anything by. Finally I did."

Quay smiled at him, and Cutter shifted in his chair. "The Confidet did that."

Cutter nodded.

It came to him suddenly, something he'd never suspected until that moment. There was something very definitely wrong with what had happened to him. The Confidet had affected everyone but him; there must have been something wrong with the one he had been using. It had worked with Mary, but hadn't Bolen said something about the energy being used in proportion to the demand? Mary had certainly created a demand. Bolen said the life of it was indefinite, but couldn't the energy have been used up?

"Ah," he said carefully, smiling, to Quay. "You wouldn't have it around, would you? That Confidet of yours?"

"Oh, hell, no," Quay said. "I gave it to Bolen a long time ago. He came around for it, in fact. Said he had to keep track of all of them."

Cutter left hurriedly, with Quay and his wife following him to his car. He drove straight to Bolen's house.

Fury built inside of him. All this time, Bolen had kept track of his Confidet, the one that Mary had used, and all this time, he had known Cutter still had it. Cutter was furious over the realization that Bolen had been using him for experimentation, and also because the Confidet that he had tried to use had turned worthless.

All his hatred, all his anger churned inside of him like the heat from shaken coals, but when he walked up the path to Bolen's small house, he did so quietly, with extreme care.

When he saw Bolen's face in the doorway, he wanted to strike the man, but he kept his hands quietly at his sides; and though he hated himself for it, he even smiled a little at the man.

"Come in," Bolen smiled, and he spoke softly, and at the same time he examined Cutter with quick, penetrating eyes. "Come in, Mr. Cutter."

Cutter wanted to stand there and demand another Confidet, a good one, and not walk inside, politely, like he did. And he wished that his voice would come out, quickly, with the power and hate in it that he had once been capable of. But for some reason, he couldn't say a word.

Bolen was extremely polite. "You've been using that Confidet, haven't you?" He spoke gently, almost as though he were speaking to a frightened child.

"Yes," Cutter managed to say.

"And what you expected to happen, didn't. That's what you want to tell me, isn't it?"

Cutter's insides quivered with rage, but he was able only to nod.

"Would you like to know why?" Bolen said.

Cutter rubbed his damp palms over his knees. He nodded.

Bolen smiled, his eyes sparkling. "Very simple really. It wasn't the fault of the Confidet so much, Mr. Cutter, as you. You see, you are a rare exception. What you are, or possibly I should say, what you were, was a complete super ego. There are very few of those, Mr. Cutter, in this world, but you happened to be one of them. A really absolute, complete super ego, and the Confidet's effect was simply the reverse of what it would have been with anyone else." Bolen shook his head, sympathetically, but he didn't stop smiling, and his eyes didn't stop their infuriating exploration of Cutter's face and eyes and hands. "It's really a shame, because I was almost certain you were a super ego, Mr. Cutter. And when you didn't return that last Confidet, I somehow felt that you might use it, after all that nasty business at the company and all.

"But while I was fairly certain of the effects, Mr. Cutter, I wasn't absolutely *sure*, you see, and so like the rest of the experiments, I had to forget my conscience. I'm really very sorry."

The anger was a wild thing inside Cutter now, and it made his hands tremble and sweat, and his mouth quiver, and he hated the man in front of him, the man who was responsible for what had happened to him, the smiling man with the soft voice and exploring eyes. But he didn't say anything, not a word. He didn't show his anger or his frustration or his resentment. He didn't indicate to Bolen a particle of his inner wildness.

He didn't have the nerve.

Printed in Great Britain
by Amazon

31041481R00289